# REVOLUTIONARIES AND REBELS

## 1775-1865

### A HISTORICAL NOVEL

#### JERRY R. BARKSDALE

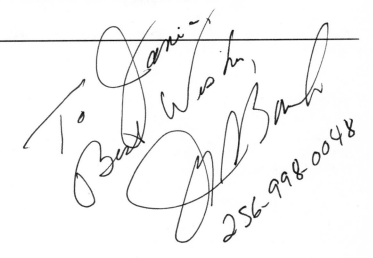

ISBN
(Print): 978-0-615-89388-4
(Ebook): 978-0-615-90992-9

Additional copies may be ordered from:

Jerry R. Barksdale
18351 Dement Road
Athens, AL  35611

E-mail: jbarks1248@aol.com
Website: www.jerrybarksdale.com
www.facebook.com/JerryRBarksdale

**About the cover**: The cover painting and design was created by Athens artist, Lisa Norris Milby.  It depicts, from top down: Micajah McElroy during the American Revolution; his son, Archibald McElroy, II at the Battle of New Orleans; his son-in-law, Daniel Barksdale and grandson, William Coleman Barksdale, 50th Alabama Regiment, CSA.

**Also by Jerry R. Barksdale**

**Fiction**

*The Fuhrer Document*

**Non Fiction**

*When Duty Called*

*Cornbread Chronicles*

*Duty*

*Dedicated to my generation of kinsmen*

*so that they may know the sacrifice*

*of our ancestors upon whose*

*shoulders we stand.*

# CONTENTS

James Daniel Barksdale's old home place on AL Highway 251 in Athens, Ala.

# AUTHOR'S NOTE

I suppose that Grandpa Edgar Eugene Barksdale, who was born to William Coleman and Eliza Barksdale two months following General Lee's surrender, is partly to blame for my interest in history. When I was 11 years old and still riding a broomstick horse, Grandpa visited us in Birmingham. We sat on the front porch where he puffed his homemade pipe carved from a blackberry root and told me about going to Texas as a young man to visit his older brother, Emmit. They worked as drovers on a cattle drive until Grandpa grew tired of dust, cactus and rattlesnakes and longed to return to Athens and see Miss Ada, the narrow-waisted granddaughter of Emanuel Isom.

"I'm head'n back to Alabama," he said to Emmit.

"You can't draw your wages 'til we reach the railhead."

"Tell you what," said Grandpa. "Give me your fiddle and you can have my wages when you get there." He headed back to Alabama with his fiddle and in 1896 married Ada Isom.

I soon forgot about cowboys and my attention eventually turned to a willowy brunette in the 11th grade at Athens High School. We married in 1961, moved to Tuscaloosa and after I graduated from the University of Alabama Law School, we returned to Athens.

In 1972, we moved into our new home three miles east of town. On the way to the office each morning I passed an old house with a chimney at each end, a log structure that had been fabricated with siding. My father remarked that it once belonged to my great-great-grandfather, James Daniel Barksdale. I was curious. I began scratching around in dusty old records and what I discovered intrigued me. I suppose that's the way every amateur genealogist becomes hooked.

Over the next 37 years, I researched my family tree until I accumulated two large boxes of documents. I sat down to write their story. After writing 200 footnoted pages, I decided it read like a legal brief. Dull. I put it aside and fretted. A story that isn't working is a writer's greatest frustration.

It occurred to me that I could still tell the story and hopefully make it interesting to readers. Thus, the historical novel. I have dropped the footnotes, given voice to actual characters and attempted to stick to the facts as they happened. All of the characters existed except for a slim few whose names have been changed. I've endeavored to tell their story as it really happened. It's a story of war and peace, hardship, struggle, love, hope and survival by my family who lived it. It's a story of early America in the South. I enjoyed writing it. I hope you enjoy reading it.

Jerry R. Barksdale
18351 Dement Road
Athens, AL 35611
Christmas, 2012

**Micajah McElroy's old home place on Hamwood Road in Fayetteville, Tenn.**

# ACKNOWLEDGEMENT

This historical novel would not have been possible without the assistance of many individuals who have helped add flesh to the bones of the story. Early research on the Barksdale family was done by Mary Clark Barksdale, Athens, decades ago. I picked up the torch in earnest in early 1990's while living in Huntsville. As information was collected I poked it into a folder and filed it in a large storage box. Soon I had two bulging boxes stuffed with information. My cousin, Joe Williams, Athens entrusted me with the leather-bound Bible that James Daniel Barksdale purchased. He also gave me numerous old photographs of my family. Thanks, Joe.

A special thanks to Dr. and Mrs. Farish Beasley, Fayetteville, Tennessee, who own a portion of the old Micajah McElroy Plantation and gave generously of their time and permitted me to visit and photograph the McElroy log house that still exists on Hamwood Road. Ms. Sherrie Thomason, Archivist of Lincoln County, Tennessee, answered my early request for information, and without her assistance the Lincoln County portion of the book couldn't have been written. I'm grateful to Ms. Tammy Moore, Lincoln County Assessor of Property, Deputy Assessor Connie Quick and Field Appraiser/Mapper Billy W. Crabtree, whose assistance was invaluable in helping me locate the Micajah McElroy and Daniel Barksdale tracts. A special thanks to Billy Crabtree, an avid coon hunter who gave me useful information on that arcane subject.

I am indebted to cousin, Danny Barksdale, who began researching the Barksdale family years ago and whose assistance and advice has been invaluable; the same for Pam Ezell, Albert Dudley Barksdale and wife Sarah, all of Athens. Local Historian, James Croley Smith, Athens, who knew the answers to all my questions; Phillip Reyer, Sandra Birdwell, Rebekah Davis and April Davis of the Limestone County Archives were also eager to assist me; good friend, Bert Wilson, Athens, brick mason par excellence and all around great human being supplied technical information regarding masonry; Wayne Kuykendall, Athens, a preservationist of renown who knows everything from splitting shingles to building a cabin – and more. Milton Looney, Athens, who owns the James Daniel Barksdale log house at the intersection of Lindsay Lane and Highway 251, permitted me to visit and also gave me old photographs of the house. To all of the above, I am greatly indebted.

Chris Paysinger, Athens, school teacher and history hound who provided valuable information regarding the 1860 Presidential election in Limestone County, as well as copies of claims made following the Civil War. My good friend, Richard Martin, Athens, lover of history and preservationist, lent me numerous books which were essential research tools. Mrs. Connie Ruth (Laxson) Yarbrough, Athens, Isom researcher who supplied invaluable information regarding my great-great grandfather, Emanuel Isom and the Church he founded. Regretfully, Annie Ruth died February, 2012. She is sorely missed.

Many thanks to Robert Parham of Parham's Civil War Relics and memorabilia, 726 Bank Street, N.E., of Decatur, Alabama for permission to use *The Court Martial of Colonel John B. Turchin; The Sack of Athens, Alabama, May 12, 1862.* A copy of the transcript details the horrible war crimes inflicted against Athenians and can be purchased at the Limestone County Archives in Athens.

I owe a special debt of gratitude to my good friend and historian of renown, Ronald Pettus, Athens, for his assistance and advice regarding the 35th Alabama Infantry Regiment.

A great big thanks to Mr. and Mrs. John Braxton, Graham, South Carolina, experts on the Battle of Lindley's Mill who shared an afternoon with me inside their lovely old home and directed me to the battle site only a stone's throw away. Mrs. Diane L. Richards, Professional Researcher of Durham, North Carolina provided me with copies of Micajah McElroy's deed and map along Crabtree Creek; Ms. Frances Fox, researcher of Elkton, Kentucky, supplied information regarding the Barksdales of Kentucky.

*The Sword of "Bushwhacker" Johnston,* edited and annotated by Charles S. Rice, Huntsville, Alabama, was valuable to my story about Robert Beasley Barksdale as I relied on it heavily. I strongly recommend this book to anyone interested in the Civil War in North Alabama.

A big thanks to Lisa Milby, Athens artist, who painted and designed the cover.

I especially thank a wonderful friend and sometimes red-head, Pat Goodin, who traveled with me to each site; patiently walked over the ground, whether battle field or mountain pass, and prepared sumptuous meals for me while I closeted myself and wrote.

My able and faithful secretary, Tami Peek, typed and retyped the manuscript countless times; without her help the book would not be possible. A huge thanks to my friend, Rebekah Davis, Athens, journalist and writer whose professional eye perfected the manuscript.

Most of all, I thank my kinsmen who opened up their hearts and memories with wonderful stories about our family.

Lastly, I take full responsibility for any errors that may come to light.

# THE McELROY & BARKSDALE FAMILIES

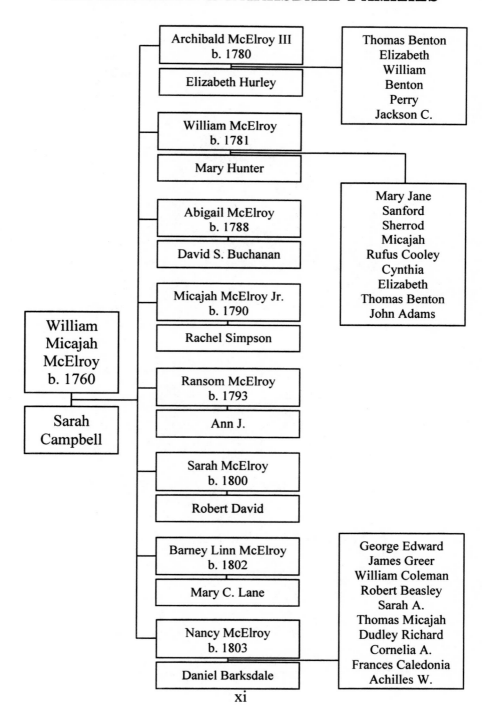

Archibald McElroy III
b. 1780

Elizabeth Hurley

Thomas Benton
Elizabeth
William
Benton
Perry
Jackson C.

William McElroy
b. 1781

Mary Hunter

Mary Jane
Sanford
Sherrod
Micajah
Rufus Cooley
Cynthia
Elizabeth
Thomas Benton
John Adams

Abigail McElroy
b. 1788

David S. Buchanan

Micajah McElroy Jr.
b. 1790

Rachel Simpson

William
Micajah
McElroy
b. 1760

Sarah
Campbell

Ransom McElroy
b. 1793

Ann J.

Sarah McElroy
b. 1800

Robert David

Barney Linn McElroy
b. 1802

Mary C. Lane

George Edward
James Greer
William Coleman
Robert Beasley
Sarah A.
Thomas Micajah
Dudley Richard
Cornelia A.
Frances Caledonia
Achilles W.

Nancy McElroy
b. 1803

Daniel Barksdale

# FAMILY PORTRAITS

**James Martin Newby and Sarah "Sallie" Barksdale Newby**

**Frances Caledonia "Cal" Barksdale**
Spinster daughter of Daniel and Nancy Barksdale

**Thomas Micajah Barksdale**
Bachelor son of Daniel and
Nancy Barksdale

**Robert Beasley Barksdale**
Son of Daniel and Nancy
Barksdale

**James Greer "Jim"
Barksdale**
Son of Daniel and Nancy
Barksdale

**Emanuel Isom**

# Part I

# 1 | WAR IS COMING

Wake County, North Carolina.

Early April, 1775.

Abington McElroy's Scotch-Irish was showing this morning.

"Aye lad, mark my word. War is coming and the sooner the better!"

Like all of the McElroys of Wake County, Abington was a peaceable man, but only to a point. And it appeared to his young nephew Micajah that the point had been reached. His Uncle had grumbled about the Crown for as long as Micajah could remember, but now he was talking rebellion.

"Tis a sad day when free Englishmen have to bear the indignities of the Crown and be treated like bastard children," Abington added, his blues eyes blazing and red rising up his neck. "Years of talking have gained us nothing. One day we will speak - and with powder and ball."

"Against the Crown!" exclaimed young Micajah, aghast.

"Aye."

"But Uncle that… that's treason," Micajah whispered.

"Some will call it treason; others will call it our struggle for liberty to secure our birthright as freeborn Englishmen."

For Micajah it was frightening talk. "Uncle, you could be hanged for saying that."

"Lad, before this matter is finished many men will die. It will be the price of liberty."

Micajah and Cook had been at the barn feeding the oxen corn and fodder when Abington had ridden up on his big bay horse to visit a spell before riding to Bloomsbury for monthly militia drills. Abington, who operated a gristmill on Polk's Branch, was Micajah's favorite Uncle. Of medium stature and muscular, with black hair in a ponytail beneath a tricorn hat, his face was ruddy and chin strong. Everyone said that he looked like Micajah's deceased father with one exception - Uncle Abington had a missing ear.

"Lad, you'll be turning sixteen soon and it's time to think of enlisting in the militia," Abington said.

"Yes sir, I'll think about that," replied Micajah, noncommittal.

When Abington entered the residence to visit his elderly mother, Micajah and Cook yoked the oxen and prepared to break ground.

---

It was Micajah's favorite spot on the entire plantation. He strolled through the strands of tall white oaks, chestnut and poplar, enjoying the coolness of the damp moss on the soles of his bare feet. Ranging in front of him, nose in the air, was his Redbone coonhound, Luther, and following several yards behind was a middle-aged Negro man whose grizzled hair had turned white above his ears. When they reached Crabtree Creek the boy walked through a thicket of cane that grew along the bank and sat down on a flat rock that protruded over the water. He unrolled a fishing line that he always carried in his pocket while the Negro man cut a cane pole and dug a worm beneath a rotted log.

A hush fell over the countryside at this time of the afternoon. After plowing all day with cantankerous oxen preparing the earth for spring planting, the creek was a welcome respite. He watched the rippling current shoot around rocks and listened to the gurgle of pristine water for a moment before threading a worm on his hook and dropping it into the water. He turned and spoke to the Negro man who sat on his haunches watching the cork.

"Cook, ever since I can remember you've always been with me."

"Yessuh massa, yo' grandpappy Massa Archibald gimme to ya when he passed. Yo daddy, Massa Archibald, Jr. be already dead."

"I've never seen the document since mother says I'm too young to see it, but I've heard that grandfather willed me this 181-acre plantation."

"Yassuh, that's what I heahs too. De center of de creek be the boundary line."

"I'm almost sixteen, but Mother will still be my guardian for five more years," said Micajah, frowning. "She still treats me like a child and tells me I'm too young to run my own affairs. When I'm sixteen I'm eligible to join the militia and fight, and I'm strong enough to plow all day. Yet, I can't run my own plantation. It isn't right. No sir!" He pushed the end of the pole into the soft earth and stood. "Cook, I'm going to stand up just like this, flat-footed, eyeball-to-eyeball, and tell Mother in no uncertain terms that it's time I run my plantation."

"De fur be fly'n when you say all dat, massa."

"And if Mr. Heartsfield interferes, I'll speak candid with him too," said Micajah. "Ever since mother married him he backs her up."

"More fur be fly'n, massa."

Micajah exhaled loudly. "Yeah, you're right, but that's what I'd like to say." He looked around and remarked, "Sure is peaceful here."

"Yassuh massa shore is."

"Uncle Abington said we'd be at war with England before the end of the year," said Micajah.

"Massa Abington oughta know. He be a smart man."

"I won't tell Uncle Abington, but I'm not interested in getting involved in some old war that I know nothing about," Micajah said. "No one is bothering me and I don't intend to bother them."

"Sometimes trouble be com'n anyhow."

Before Micajah could respond, a bell rang in the distance.

"It's the supper bell. If I'm late Mother will be madder than a wet hen. Come on Cook, let's go!"

Micajah forgot his fishing line and tore out through the woods and across the plowed ground toward home, the hound barking and Cook huffing trying to catch up.

Home was Grandmother Catherine McElroy's house, which was located adjacent to Micajah's plantation. When his grandfather died in 1760 she was given the land and house for her lifetime. Since Micajah's father, Archibald, Jr. was already dead, he and his mother, Sarah, moved in with his grandmother until his mother remarried a neighbor, Jacob Heartsfield. Micajah loved the old two-story clapboard sided house, with its wooden shingles and a fireplace in the center. In the front yard was a garden, enclosed by a stick fence. Nearby was the kitchen, a square log building with a fireplace, and on beyond a log smokehouse. Behind the house were several small log cabins, each with a chimney at one end, where the Negroes lived. The well was behind the residence and on the opposite end was a privy and on beyond that a log barn enclosed by a rail fence that also encompassed a pasture where milk cows, cattle and horses grazed. Hogs ranged wild, living on acorns they rooted up in the surrounding forest. It was the only home that Micajah had known. He ran through a flock of geese making their last scratches in the front yard before retiring to roost.

"Shoo ... shoo." They scattered squawking.

He skied up to the front door; paused, caught his breath and entered the house.

His grandmother was seated by the window in her favorite rocker creaking back and forth, watching a crimson western sky, a white cap fitted snuggly around her wrinkled head.

"Hello Grandmother. Am I late?"

The old woman looked over and smiled at her grandson, one of many. Her six children had given her a passel of grandchildren, and she loved them all, but Micajah had lived with her since his birth. He had a special place in her heart.

"No, I had the bell sounded early so you wouldn't be late. Been down to the creek again?" she asked, looking at mud between his toes.

"Yes, Grandmother." He walked over and kissed her on the cheek. She gripped his arm and squeezed it tightly. "You are growing more handsome by the day," she said. "I've seen the way young girls look at you, especially that young Sarah Campbell."

Micajah blushed.

Jane, one of the Negro servants, stopped operating the spinning wheel, lit a candle, covered the table board with a linen broad cloth and set out napkins, pewter plates and spoons. In the center of the table she placed a salt shaker. Doll, the other Negro woman, shuttled food in from the outside kitchen. His mother, Sarah Heartsfield, who was visiting, entered the room, her long-sleeved, ankle-length black dress swishing across the top of her barely visible shoes. She also wore a white cap. About the only visible parts of her body were her face and hands.

"Been to the creek again?" she asked.

"Yes Mother. It's peaceful. I like to go there and just think about things."

"Yes, peace is a wonderful thing. Remember that 'Reading makes a man full – meditation a profound man.'"

When they were seated at the table, Doll ladled pork stew from a blackened cast iron pot onto Micajah's plate and poured hot tea. Wheat bread sat in the center of the table.

Micajah ate his stew in silence for several moments, thinking about his grandfather and the inheritance he had passed on – and yes, he thought of his father also. He realized how little he knew about them.

"Grandmother, tell me about Grandfather and Father," he said.

The old woman laid her spoon down and wiped her mouth with a linen napkin. "Well your grandfather, Archibald, was born in Hartford, Connecticut, on February 14, 1719. I heard him say that his father John was born sometime before 1700 in Sligo, Ireland. The McElroys are originally from Scotland, but way back yonder they migrated from Ulster in Northern Ireland. Your grandfather and I married – I was a Simpson – and we had six children; Salley, Abington, Frankey, John and Andrew. And, of course, your father, Archibald, Jr. who died in December, 1760, right before your grandfather passed away at age forty-one. Both came down with ague fever and died only a few weeks apart."

"What was grandfather's trade?" he asked.

"Mostly a gunsmith. After the family moved to Johnston County – now Wake County – sometime before 1743, he and his brothers, William and John, purchased land

4

on Crabtree Creek and also some over in Craven County. He bought and sold land, raised tobacco, corn and such."

"And Father?" Micajah asked.

"A fine son, he was; died in his early twenties, way before his time. You're his only child and he would've been proud of you."

"He served as Quartermaster in Johnston's Regiment," interjected Micajah's mother. "He always believed in doing his duty."

"Uncle Abington wants me to join the militia when I'm sixteen," said Micajah. "But I haven't made up my mind."

"Young man, you're going to learn a trade," his mother said with firmness. "I've already talked to Silas Willingham."

"I don't want to be a carpenter, especially if I have to be indentured to him," said Micajah. "I'd rather work with Uncle Abington at his gristmill and learn to be a miller."

"We'll see," she replied.

"After I learn the mill trade from Uncle Abington," Micajah said, "I'm going to build my own mill on my own land on Crabtree Creek."

"You are still a minor," his mother shot back. "Your father is dead so I have the responsibility to see that your inheritance is protected and that you learn a trade."

"Mother, I'm old enough to manage my estate. I don't need a guardian."

"The law says when you reach twenty-one years you are an adult, but not until then. The law is the law–"

"But Mother–"

"Please don't argue," she said, giving him a hard stare.

Micajah wilted, dropped his head and spooned out stew.

After they finished eating, Doll and Jane cleared the table and his grandmother returned to her creaking rocker.

"Micajah, your birthday is September twentieth," said his grandmother, sensing that the subject needed to be changed. "That's about five months away. I've planned to give you a special gift on your birthday, but I may not live that long. I'm going to give it to you now so there won't be any arguing about it when I die." She looked over at Doll. "Go up to my room and look under my bed and bring what you find down here. Now hurry along."

"Yessum."

Micajah instantly perked up. He knew what was there. He had sneaked a peek under the bed numerous times over the years.

Doll came down carrying a long barrel rifle.

"Your grandfather made this rifle and I know he'd want you to have it," said his grandmother. "I don't know much about rifles, but I know that he prized it highly."

Micajah knew exactly what it was, as any young boy of his age would know – a Pennsylvania-style long rifle. He took the rifle and ran his hand over the polished curly maple stock, then across the crescent-shaped metal butt plate. It was a flintlock and fired a 50 caliber ball; the barrel was 46 inches long and more importantly, it was rifled. In steady hands, it could blow a turkey's head off at 200 yards. Not only was it beautiful, it was also a valuable possession. "I'll take good care of it. I promise," he said, beaming.

That night he tossed and turned on his shuck mattress, too excited to sleep. A cool breeze blew through an open window and somewhere in the distance he heard the mating call of a hoot owl which was quickly answered. Momentarily, he forgot about the rifle and building a gristmill and his thoughts turned to pretty Sarah Campbell. Finally he drifted off into a peaceful sleep.

---

The following afternoon when his grandmother was away visiting his Aunt Frankey, Micajah noticed that the lid on the trunk that sat at the foot of her bed was ajar. He had never looked inside, but suspected that it contained important papers. He sneaked a peek and saw a rolled parchment tied with a red ribbon. It appeared to be a legal document. It was none of his business, but he was curious. He untied the ribbon and unrolled the document. It was his grandfather Archibald McElroy, Sr.'s last will and testament. It had apparently been copied by the court schrivner after probate and returned to his grandmother. Not seeing or hearing anyone nearby, he read the document.

> Will of ARCHIBALD McELROY, Sr.
> IN THE NAME OF GOD, I, ARCH MACKLEROY, of the County of Johnston, in the province of North Carolina, gunsmith of sound mine & body & knowing that it is appointed for all man once to die. I hereby make & ordain this my will & testament following, that today 1$^{st}$ & principally, I give & bequeath my soul into the hands of Almighty God that gave it to me, nothing doubting but that I shall receive the same again from the hands of my blessed Redeemer at the Day of General Resurrection & my body to the earth from whence it came to be buried after a Christian decent manner at the discretion of my executors whom I shall hereafter appoint, & as for what worldly goods it hath been pleased God to bestow on me. After my just debts & funeral expenses are paid I give & bequeath as followeth Viz:
> IMPRIMIS:  I give & bequeath to my beloved wife CATHARINE MACKLEROY 3 negroes named Cesar, Jane, & Doll, & 1 stallion called Bull, & the plantation whereon I now live during her life.
>> ITEM: I give & bequeath to my beloved grandson MICAJAH MACKLEROY, the plantation & tract of land on Crabtree Creek whereon James Childres formerly dwelt & 1 Negro boy named Cook to him & his heirs forever.
>> ITEM: I give & bequeath to my beloved son AVONTON MACKLEROY, my mill & all the land adjoining to it as low as Polk's branch, & 1 negro boy named Buck, to him & his heirs forever.
>> ITEM: I give & bequeath unto my beloved son, JOHN MACKLEROY, the plantation & part of the tract of land I now live on after the decease of my wife Catharine, & 1 negro boy named Peter, to him & his heirs forever.
>> ITEM: I give & bequeath to my beloved son, ANDREW MACKLEROY, 100 acres of land taken out of the tract I now live on lying on Marsh Creek & not coming nearer the plantation than the red hill, & 1 negro boy named Will, to him

6

& his heirs forever.

ITEM: I give & bequeath to my beloved daughter, Salley, 100 acres of land out of the tract I now live on adjoining the land left to my son Andrew, at the lower end of his land, & 1 negro girl named Cloe, to her & her heirs forever, & also, 1 mare called Poll.

ITEM: I give & bequeath to my beloved daughter, Frankey the upper end of the North Creek land called the hog farm, & a negro boy named Dick, to her & her heirs forever.

ITEM: My will & desire is that if it should please God any of my children abovementioned or my grandchild, MICAJAH, should die before they come to age, the boys 21 & the girls 16, or married, that then his or her part to be equally divided among the survivors.

ITEM: My will & desire is that all the remainder of my estate, both real & personal, may be equally divided between my wife & children at the discretion of my executors for my desire is that my estate may be inventoried but not appraised.

I do hereby appoint my beloved wife, CATHARINE MACKLEROY, executrix, & my brother William & my friend, Andrew Heartsfield, executors of this my last will & testament, revoking all the wills formerly by me made. Allowing this & no other to be my last will & testament, Thos. Hunter & Nathaniel Jones to assist in dividing the estate. In witness whereof I do hereunto set my hand & seal this 9th day of December of 1760.

Signed & sealed in                                HIS
Presence of Joseph Chatwin ARCH MACKLEROY
John Polk    Fran Chatwin              MARK

There it was in the will. He did in fact own the plantation, just like he had heard.

He carefully rolled up the document and retied it with the ribbon and placed it back in the trunk where he had found it.

# 2 | REBELLION

Lexington, Massachusetts.

April 18, 1775.

Seven hundred miles north of peaceful Wake County, at Lexington, Massachusetts, war was looming. A rabble of 4,000 disorganized Colonials had confronted 1,800 British regulars and gave them a good licking.

The alarm went out and militiamen from Massachusetts, New Hampshire, Rhode Island and Connecticut began pouring into the outlying villages near Boston.

The gauntlet had been thrown at the feet of King George III. The American Revolution had begun.

---

News of the Battle of Lexington spread like wildfire throughout the thirteen colonies. It reached Chowan County, North Carolina by a courier on horseback on May 3rd. A courier of the Committee of Safety immediately carried the news to the adjoining counties until all had been alerted by May 9th.

It was early morning and Micajah and Cook were at the barn yoking the oxen and preparing to plant corn when they heard approaching hoof beats. Uncle Abington rode up fast on his big bay mare and reined abruptly. The mare was panting and dripping with white lather. It was unusual for his uncle to appear at this time of the day. He looked serious. His three-cornered hat was pulled down firmly, almost covering the nub of his left ear. Micajah suspected that something bad had happened. Someone was either dead or about to die.

"Good morning Uncle, won't you get down?"

"No time lad. If you haven't already heard, there was a bloody battle at Lexington in the Massachusetts colony in mid-April. The militia killed and wounded nearly 250 British regulars and have laid siege to Boston. Aye, the die is cast!"

Micajah's jaw dropped. He didn't know anything about politics, but he knew that sane people didn't attack the King's soldiers.

What does that mean Uncle?"

"In due time war will come."

"To Wake County?" asked Micajah, surprised.

"Aye, the greatest danger to us will come from the Tories. Those scoundrels will fight for George the Third. Keep your eyes and ears open for any suspicious activity and report to me immediately. Tell Mother and Sarah the news. The militia is assembling. I must ride on and spread the word." He kicked the horse's flanks and the big mare bolted forward at a gallop.

Uncle Abington had been an outspoken critic of the British for as long as Micajah could remember. A member of the militia, he called himself a Patriot.

Micajah's knowledge of the turmoil and violence that had been slowly building over the preceding years between Patriots and Loyalists, or Tories as they were called in North Carolina, was sketchy. At family gatherings, he had listened quietly while Uncles Abington, John and Andrew had discussed pitched battles, house burnings and confiscation of property that each side had inflicted on the other. He knew that Governor Josiah Martin was a Tory – the biggest one of all. Many folks had already chosen sides, but there seemed to be an equal number standing in the middle.

8

Several days later, Abington stopped by to visit his mother, Catherine, whose health was failing. Micajah entered the room.

"Aye lad, how does your corn grow?"

"It's sprouting."

"A word of warning," he said. "When you are in the field plowing, always have your rifle nearby, primed and ready. Those devilish Tories comb the countryside committing despicable acts against Patriots."

Micajah's life thus far had been spent traipsing through the woods with Cook, target practicing, fishing in Crabtree Creek, hunting and plowing oxen. He had never been outside of Wake County and knew nothing about events occurring elsewhere. His news came from Uncle Abington. He didn't understand why so many people were against the Crown. Now that he was sixteen years old and almost a man, it was time that he knew such things.

"Uncle Abington, why are citizens fighting one another?"

"For liberty, lad!"

"But we have liberty."

"Aye, do we have a young Tory in the making? A McElroy siding with the Tories? Never!" exclaimed Abington. "The McElroys are proud Scotch-Irish and we are not easily beholden to anyone. Some of our kilt and kin are Loyalists, but never a McElroy." He gestured toward an empty chair. "Sit lad, it's time you heard the truth."

Micajah sat down and watched his uncle fill his long-stem clay pipe and light it.

"Lad, 'tis a long tale but worth the telling. Englishmen sailed to these shores more than a hundred years ago and established colonies up and down the seacoast. They turned a wilderness into productive crop land, built great cities and engaged in lucrative commerce. And they pretty much ruled themselves without interference from London. No English king has ever visited our shores. Over the years new generations of Americans grew more independent and less dependent on the Crown. Today, the majority of the colonists have never visited the Motherland." Abington took a deep pull on his pipe and exhaled. "Do you ever think about visiting England?"

"No sir."

"It proves my point lad."

"But I still don't understand why citizens are fighting."

"Patience." Abington relit his pipe. "The growing independence on our part has frightened the Crown. They began to feel they were losing control and to re-establish their power they levied intolerable taxes against us. We had no voice in the debate. It is taxation without representation!" His voice rose. "Corpulent men wearing powdered wigs sit in London, sip Claret and discuss how they will tax us further—"

"But—"

"When George the Third and his men tax us without our consent it is equivalent to a masked highwayman stopping you on the King's road, and at point of sword or pistol demanding your money; money that you earned by the sweat of your brow. The more taxes that we send to England the more power the Crown has over our lives. The Tories are determined to drive us into damnation.

"The Royal Navy has blockaded Boston Harbor; a standing Army has been kept among us during a time of peace and without our consent; homes have been entered without proper writ. Lad, a man's home is his castle and the King himself shall not enter uninvited. Free Englishmen will not sit idly by and suffer such intolerable abuses."

9

"But Uncle, his Majesty rules by divine right, doesn't he?"

"Bah." Abington waved off the comment. "He is a man who derives his power from the people. We are still Englishmen and entitled to be treated as such, protected by the same laws that protect those in England. But that is not the case. The Crown has imposed punitive laws on us and treated us like bastard children."

Micajah thought about what his uncle had said. Most of the Tories that he knew were rich and arrogant and he didn't particularly like them. If he had to fight them, he would, but on the other hand, if they didn't bother him and his family he wouldn't bother them. A war with England was hard to imagine. There might be fighting in Boston and in the northern colonies but peaceful Wake County was far removed from the violence. In the meantime, he couldn't worry about Tories, no matter what Uncle Abington said. He had to put seed in the ground. And then there was that matter of learning a trade.

---

It was just after 5 a.m. when Micajah arrived at Silas Willingham's shop, located three miles down a dirt road beneath the shade of an ancient oak tree. A candle glowed through an open shutter. Barking dogs, some growling, ran from the residence toward Micajah.

"MISTER WILLINGHAM! IT'S ME – MICAJAH."

"Don't just stand there like a knot on a log lad," answered a high-pitched voice from inside the building. "Come in."

With the dogs at his heels, Micajah ran into the shop and slammed the door behind him. "Will they bite?" he asked, gesturing toward the pack of hounds.

"Some will – some won't."

Silas Willingham was not only tall and spare of build, he was also spare with words. Between Willingham's remarkably squeaky voice and his mumbling, Micajah had a hard time understanding what little the man said.

"You're late," Willingham said. "The sleeping fox catch no poultry."

"Yes sir."

He tossed Micajah a soiled leather apron to put on. "Rules are to be obeyed," said Willingham. "Arrive on time, listen to what I say and do what I tell you to do. Questions?"

"No sir."

Willingham handed Micajah a board. "Plane this."

Micajah set to work pushing the planer, catching furtive glances at his new taskmaster. Willingham's back was slightly humped from a lifetime of bending over while sawing and planing boards. Pulling a saw had made his arms and shoulders stout. His scarred hands were thick as hams. Uncombed hair, streaked with gray, fell harum-scarum past his shoulders. Most of his foreteeth were missing and his face was pockmarked. He wore dirty breeches and equally dirty fluffy shirt and leather apron. He and his emaciated wife were childless, all of their three children having died of smallpox.

Silas Willingham was known throughout Wake County as a master carpenter. Micajah's mother had indentured him to Willingham for a period of four years which represented a fourth of his life to date. The thought depressed Micajah. Instead of farming and lazing on Crabtree Creek with Cook, he was now virtually imprisoned.

It was night when Willingham finally closed the shop and sent Micajah home with tired and aching arms. The only words that Willingham had spoken to Micajah after

the initial meeting was, "He that has a trade has an office of profit $ $
again Micajah wasn't sure if he was talking to him or himself. *I'll nev*
Micajah thought as he stumbled home in the darkness.

Micajah lived in constant fear that he would be late for work
counting the clock chimes.    Days were all the same. He planed w
carved pegs and swept up wood shavings and sawdust.    "When w
carpenter?" he reluctantly asked Willingham.

"Half-wits talk much but say little," mumbled Willingham.

Days turned to weeks.    Micajah learned nothing about calculations, sawing
angles or actually constructing a building.  A rider on a black gelding frequently appeared
outside the shop and Willingham would put down his tools and go outside to confer with
him. The conversations were always brief, and then the horseman would gallop off.
Willingham never mentioned the visits.    In fact, he never said anything that wasn't
absolutely necessary.  Micajah couldn't help but wonder about the rider.

---

Wake County.
May, 1775.

David Fanning had no doubt about where his loyalty lay.  He knew exactly
which side he was on and was ready to fight.  Born in 1754 in what was then called
Johnston County (later Wake County) and orphaned at 8 years old when his father died,
he was apprenticed at a young age to be taught the art of farming and to read and write.
Because of harsh treatment he ran away at age 16.    Under his ever-present silk cap,
Fanning's head was nearly bare from "scald head" caused by ringworm.

As Abington McElroy was spreading the news about the Battle of Lexington,
that May, Fanning and his militia company were also taking action. The company was
given the opportunity to sign an oath declaring whether they would be loyal to the King
or in favor of rebellion. The two groups clashed.   Thomas Brown chose the Tories and
sided with the King.  The Patriots burned his feet, cut his hair and tarred and feathered
him.   Fanning also chose the King, moved to Chatham County and volunteered for
service in a Tory militia company.  He began a life of tumult and turmoil.  In January,
1776, he was captured, refused to take a loyalty oath and was stripped of his property
before being released on parole.  Later he was recaptured and jailed, but he later escaped
and returned home. He was tried for treason and acquitted, but ordered to pay 300 pounds
sterling for fees and expense of confinement.

As sure as George III was the King in England and God was in his heaven,
Fanning promised himself, the Patriots wouldn't forget his name.

---

Wake County.
June, 1776.

Micajah had other concerns that were more immediate than worrying about
Tories.  Grandmother Catherine died.  Her children, Abington, John, Andrew, Frankey
and Salley and their passel of children, all clad in black, gathered beneath a threatening
sky around an open grave.  Parson Smith, wearing a big black flat brim hat and black
waistcoat, read from the scriptures with the solemnity of Moses delivering the Ten
Commandments.  "'Let not your heart be troubled: ye believe in God, believe also in me.

father's house are many mansions: if it were not so, I would have told you. I go to prepare a place for you. And if I go and prepare a place for you, I will come again, and receive you unto myself; that where I am, there ye may be also.'"

Having finished reading, he removed his big hat and placed it over his heart and prayed long and hard that God would accept this Godly woman into his eternal bosom. Micajah sneaked a peek at young Sarah Campbell, who stood with her family across the open grave. She was doing the same. Their eyes met for an instant and for that brief moment, Micajah forgot about his grandmother. Sarah's blue eyes were enchanting. A tuft of blonde hair poked from beneath the black cap tied under her chin. He wondered what she looked like without her cap.

Micajah was still watching when Sarah cut her eyes toward Angus McDonald, who was standing near the open grave with his family. He gave her a slight smile, or did he? Angus was about Micajah's age, a short, stocky, blue-eyed redhead with a ruddy complexion. Micajah felt a surge of jealousy rise in his belly. He watched Angus as the Reverend droned on and thought he saw McDonald wink at Sarah. *The impudent knave!* Winking at his grandmother's burial.

"Amen," said Parson Smith.

"Amen – Amen," echoed the mourners.

Micajah's thoughts snapped back to his grandmother's death. She was the only grandmother he knew and had been a strong and long influence in his life. After the crowd faded away, he stood over her open grave, stared at the wooden coffin resting at the bottom of the hole, and wept. Bending over, he grasped a handful of dirt and sprinkled it on her coffin.

"Goodbye Grandmother. I love you."

Micajah stepped back, and Cook and the other Negroes shoveled dirt into the grave, the clods thumping on the wooden coffin like drumbeats.

At his grandmother's residence, now owned by Uncle John, Cook and the Negroes had roasted several pigs over an open pit for the family and mourners. Fresh bread had been baked and there was pork stew, pudding, pie and cakes. True to the tradition of Wake County, a feast followed the funeral. Tears and sadness were soon replaced by good food, good friends and laughter. Uncle John brought out a keg of beer and someone sawed a tune on the fiddle. It was seldom that people had a chance to socialize and a funeral provided that opportunity. Micajah caught Sarah Campbell stealing a glance at him. He gnawed on his hunk of roasted pig and pretended to ignore her, which proved impossible. If only he could gather the courage to speak to her.

Just as he was summoning the courage to approach her, Angus McDonald did so. Micajah couldn't hear what they were saying but Sarah was smiling. That same bad feeling he had experienced at the graveyard welled up inside him again. He decided then and there he didn't like Angus McDonald, nor any of his clan.

Micajah was still brooding when Sarah walked near Micajah as if he wasn't present and dropped her handkerchief on the ground.

"Oh – oh – you dropped something," he said, tongue tied.

"A true gentleman would pick it up."

"Uh, I'm... I'm sorry." He picked up the handkerchief and handed it to her. Their hands touched briefly and he thought he felt a shiver go over his body. Then she walked off, chin up, and never thanked him.

"Why, that little wench," he muttered under his breath.

Micajah's heart was heavy with sorrow. His first memory was living in his grandmother's house where she had loved and cared for him. After his mother had married Jacob Heartsfield, he lived with them part time, but spent more time with his grandmother. Her death was a big loss. His comfortable world was falling apart.

Each day brought fresh news of Tory atrocities and depredations against Patriots and subsequent reprisals by Patriots. It seemed that all of North Carolina had erupted in killing, stealing and hangings. Now that Grandmother Catherine had died, he felt more alone and more vulnerable than ever.

Uncle Abington was appointed Administrator of her estate and filed his written inventory of personal property. Micajah saw a copy on the table and read it.

WAKE COUNTY, N. C.
Inventory of the estate of CATHERINE MACKLEROY, dec'd: to wit: 1 negro fellow named Season, 1 negro woman named Jane, 22 head of cattle, 8 head of mares & horses, 2 feather beds, 3 sheets, 1 blanket & 1 bag of feathers, 4 dishes, 4 basins, 12 plates, 6 spoons, 1 pint pot, 1 small mugg, some knives & forks, 5 iron potts, 3 pr pott hooks, rings & boxes for pr cast wheels, 10 old hoes, 1 iron wedge, 1 box iron & heaters, 1 hackel (?) and plough hoe, 4 axis, 1 grubing hoe, 1 mallock, 1 frying pan, 1 cotton wheel, 2 flax wheels, 1 real hook, 1 real, 1 large chest, 2 boxes, 1 trunk with papers, 1 pr shears & chearner, 1 tub, 1 pail, 2 piggins, 2 meal sifters, parcel of old casks, 1 side saddle & bridle, 3 old chairs, 4 hides, parcel of cotton, 1 small cooking vessel, 2 geese, 4 ducks, 2 pr of old cards, 1 bofat , 1030 Wt. pork, 4 old books, 1 pr flesh forks, 1 pr spoon molders, 1 stack of flax, some oates & some wheat & hogshead, 5 or 6 bushels flaxseed, a debt due from Mr. John Shaw of 100 lbs. Virginia money, a parcel of corn, 1 meal bag, 2 ewes, some fallow, 1 old rug, 1 gallon jug, 1 basket, 1 meal bag, 2 bread trays, 29 head of hogs, 1 old table, 1 butter pott, 1 inch auger, some soap, a piece of a side of leather & some salt.

This was the within inventory of the estate of CATHERINE MACKLEROY, dec'd, in Open Court duly proved by the Oath of Abington Mackleroy, and ordered to be recorded.

Her interest in the plantation was extinguished and, pursuant to his grandfather's Last Will and Testament, it passed to Uncle John McElroy. It appeared that Micajah would have to live with his mother and stepfather, but Uncle Abington, who had previously inherited a plantation and grist mill on Polk's Branch and a negro boy named Buck, took him in. He strongly recommended that Micajah apply himself as an apprentice under Silas Willingham. Micajah could read, write and cipher; hit a bulls eye with his long rifle, but he had no interest in carpentry. Cook continued to farm the plantation raising corn, tobacco and such, but the returns were meager.

While Micajah mourned the loss of his grandmother, another event far away was destined to alter his life. Uncle Abington returned home one evening after stopping at the crossroads tavern and having several mugs of "Kill-Devil" rum made from molasses. He was glassy-eyed, red-faced and grinning.

"Great news lad! The Second Continental Congress sitting in Philadelphia has declared our independence."

"Sir?" Micajah didn't understand.

"We have thrown off the yoke of George the Third, lad. Don't you understand? We will no longer be beholden to the Crown. We'll bow to no one except God. This is a great day. We are Americans! We are free," he paused, "That is, provided that we can keep our freedom."

Micajah listened in silence.

"But it may prove costly," Abington added.

The word was spread throughout Wake County by courier on horseback and notices were posted in taverns and on the town square. Citizens were urged to gather at the county seat at Bloomsbury August 21st through August 28th to hear the reading of the Declaration of Independence.

On Saturday morning, August 24, Cook hitched up a team of horses to Uncle Abington's wagon and drove to the front of his house. It was seldom that Micajah got to visit the county seat, and since apprenticing to Silas Willingham, he hadn't been at all. Today he was wearing his finest clothes – black round hat with one side turned up and fastened with a feather dangling down; black waist coat, fluffy white shirt, knee breeches, stockings and black buckle shoes. Uncle Abington, who always wore his finest clothes, climbed in the wagon and nodded to Cook.

"Git up hosses." Cook slapped the leather lines against the horse's backs and the wagon creaked forward.

"This is a momentous day in our lives lad," said Uncle Abington. "You'll remember it until the day you die and will tell your children and grandchildren about it. When our representatives gathered in Congress in Philadelphia, penned the document and signed their names to it, they not only pledged their lives and fortunes, but ours also. The die has been cast and there is no turning back. We will either live free or we will die trying."

The impact of what had been done in Philadelphia didn't register with Micajah. All his life the King of England had been master and sovereign. He couldn't imagine a world being otherwise.

A large crowd, mostly men, had already gathered on the public square when they arrived.

"Cook, remain with the wagon," commanded Uncle Abington.

"Yassuh."

There was much milling about, loud talking, dogs barking and chasing each other, horses neighing, stamping their feet and swishing their tails at flies. It was a festive occasion. Micajah had never seen so many people nor heard so much noise. It was exciting. The Town Crier, a tall, skinny man wearing a tricorn hat, knee breeches and carrying a scroll mounted a platform and rang a bell.

"HEAR YE, HEAR YE!"

People gathered closer, pushing and shoving so they could hear what was about to be read. Micajah craned to see the Crier and then realized it was more important to listen.

The Crier cleared the nervousness from his throat and unrolled the scroll. A hush fell over the crowd. "The Second Continental Congress assembled in Philadelphia," he began in high voice, "did on the second day of July in the year of our Lord, One Thousand Seven Hundred and Seventy-Six adopt the following declaration which was proclaimed on July fourth and urged it be read to all the citizens of the Thirteen Colonies. Silence please.

"When in the course of human events," read the Crier, "it becomes necessary for one people to dissolve the political bands which have connected them with another, and to assume among the powers of the earth, the separate and equal station to which the laws of nature and of nature's God entitles them, a descent respect to the opinions of mankind requires that they should declare the causes which impel them to the separation."

The crowd was deathly quiet.

"We hold these truths to be self-evident, that all men are created equal, that they are endowed by their Creator with certain unalienable rights, that among these are life, liberty and the pursuit of happiness...."

The Crier droned on and named all the wrongs that the Crown had inflicted against the Colonies, including sending swarms of officers to harass the people, and eat out their substance, by importing large armies of foreign mercenaries, by imposing taxes on the people without their consent and a host of other abuses. Some of the wrongs Uncle Abington had already told Micajah, but much he didn't understand. It was difficult to hear everything that was read, but he did hear the conclusion.

"And for the support of this declaration, with a firm reliance on the protection of divine providence we mutually pledge to each other our lives, our fortunes and our sacred honor.

"So concludes the reading of the Declaration of Independence," said the Crier. "There were 56 signers representing all thirteen colonies."

The crowd stood silent, seemingly stunned by what they had heard. Then someone shouted. "HURRAH FOR AMERICA!" The crowd erupted in unison, yelling, cheering and hurrahing. When they had finally quieted down someone exclaimed, "GOD BLESS AMERICA!" More cheering. Then someone yelled, "DOWN WITH THE KING!" The crowd erupted with even louder cheering. "DOWN WITH THE KING - DOWN WITH THE KING - DOWN WITH THE KING," they chanted.

Micajah noticed several well-dressed gentlemen standing far back from the crowd, scowls on their faces. Tories!

It was approaching twilight when Cook shouted "Git up hosses!" and cracked his whip. They moved down the dirt road where shadows were growing longer. Uncle Abington, who had been unusually quiet, turned to Micajah. "Lad, you heard the reading of a document unlike any other in the history of mankind."

"How is that Uncle?"

"There has never been anything like it in the history of the world," Uncle Abington said. 'Kings and families have always ruled the people. The Declaration envisions that we will rule ourselves."

"What will his Majesty do?"

"I've heard that General Gage has already sent British troops in search of the signers to arrest them as traitors. When they signed their names to the document, they may have been signing their death warrant." He paused. "Lad, you have witnessed the beginning of a revolution. I pray to a merciful God that we may be successful." He took a deep breath. "And may he have mercy on us and our families if we fail."

Micajah swallowed hard.

When they reached the tavern at the crossroads, Abington viewed the many horses tethered outside and then commanded Cook to stop. "Come lad, it's time that you become a man." Micajah had ridden past the two-story tavern in the past but had never peeked inside. It was an "ordinary" where up to six men slept in the same bed. They entered to loud talking and laughing. It was dimly lit with candles, and a cloud of tobacco smoke hung near the ceiling. When his eyes had adjusted, Micajah saw a sign meant for overnight bed guests. "No Boots or Spurs, Please."

Someone hailed Abington and they sat down at a table where Micajah was introduced to the men around him. They were all drinking and smoking their pipes and all were Patriots. A bosomy young girl with a beautiful décolletage that Micajah couldn't help noticing came over to the table.

"Lassie, a pint of rum for me and a gill for my nephew," Abington said.

"Aye McElroy," said one of the men, "you are the only man in Wake County that has a court order explaining why the top of your ear is missing."

"You are jealous my friend, because you don't have an order explaining why you are so ugly," said Abington.

The men roared with laughter.

"Did you see the man bite your ear off?"

"No, but I saw him spit it out," replied Abington. More raucous laughter.

"Aye lad," said one of the men to Micajah. "After your Uncle's ear was bitten off in a fight, he hired counsel and sued in equity, obtaining an order that he 'lost his ear when it was bitten off by an opponent in battle.'"

"I willingly spent the money," said Abington. "I did not want to be branded like a distant relative whose ear was cut off by a hangman in prison before being deported to America."

Conversation turned to the Declaration of Independence and many rounds of drinks were ordered. It was late when Abington half-carried Micajah to the wagon.

"Uncle, I'm sick."

"Aye lad, he that drinks fast, pays slow."

Micajah barely managed to get undressed and put on his night shirt before collapsing into bed. Then it began spinning, making him sick. When he planted a foot on the floor to get up and puke, the spinning stopped. He decided that he had learned much that day – a lot about politics but more about the effects of alcohol. He didn't like how he felt. With one foot on the floor, his thoughts turned to girls and particularly Sarah Campbell.

Several days later, when Micajah and Cook were yoking the oxens, Cook asked, "Massa, I heard de man read de paper and he say dat all men are created free. Do dat mean I be free too?"

Micajah didn't expect that question. Cook had been like a brother – nay – like a father to him all of his life. He had no memory of life without Cook. "No, it doesn't apply to slaves," he said sadly.

"I'se won't be free?"

"No."

---

Sunday afternoon.

It was late September when Micajah and his hound Luther set out by "shanks mare," walking toward the Campbell Plantation located several miles away. He had dressed in his finest black waist coat, knee breeches, stockings and buckle shoes. The feather on his black felt hat had been replaced with a racoon's tail. He plodded down the dirt road enjoying the surrounding landscape, while Luther chased butterflies. The tree tops were turning a rust color and the weeds were in full and glorious bloom. He was almost 17 years old and as far as he was concerned he was now a man. Seldom a day passed that he didn't think of Sarah Campbell.

When he neared the Campbell place, doubt crept in. What if Sarah didn't want to see him? Or worse still, what if Mr. Campbell didn't want him to come calling? He had walked for over two hours and it was too late to turn back. Anyway, big anvil-shaped thunder heads were building in the west and he might get caught in lightning if he started back now.

When he reached the Campbell house, a pack of hounds ran out barking and growling. Luther barked, but stayed close to Micajah. He was a hunting dog, not a fighting dog. He stood in the road and waited until someone came out to check on the commotion. A middle-aged Negro woman opened the door and scolded the dogs. "Hesh up dogs! Who is you?" she asked.

"Micajah McElroy. I've come to see Miss Sarah."

"Just a minute, I'll fetch her."

This was the worst part. Micajah stood halfway between the house and the road, still not fully trusting what the hounds might do. The door opened and Sarah came out. She was beautiful – blond hair and sparkling blue eyes.

"Well, if it isn't Micajah McElroy," she said coyly. "Did thee come to see Father?"

"Well, uh- uh- no," he stammered, "I just happen to be nearby and thought I'd stop by and say hello."

"My, my, and all dressed up like thee going to worship." she said.

"Yes, Sarah, I mean ma'am," he stammered, "but I'm not going to church."

"And wearing a coon's tail too? How awful!"

"I shot the coon with my long rifle at 200 yards–"

"Poor raccoon," moaned Sarah.

*Why couldn't she stop making him feel like a fool? He couldn't speak properly in her presence.*

"Since thee happen to be in the neighborhood," she said, emphasizing "happen," "thee might as well come in."

Mrs. Campbell greeted him courteously and offered tea. Mr. Campbell, a tall, lanky man with a sunken chest, arrived as Micajah was taking the first nervous sip.

"Well Micajah, what brings thee here?" he asked.

"He just happened to be in the neighborhood and stopped by, Father," Sarah interjected.

"Is that so?" said Mr. Campbell. "Sarah, why don't you escort Micajah to the parlor so he can enjoy his tea?"

"Yes Father."

They sat down. Micajah tugged at his collar, which suddenly seemed too tight.

17

"M I C A J A H," she said, letting the name slowly roll off her tongue. "Thee do have a nice name. Father says it's Biblical and means 'Who is like God.'"

Micajah swelled with pride, and then looked down modestly. "Well, it's only a name. I'm… I'm not anything like God."

She laughed. "That's what I told Father, silly boy."

Micajah twisted in his chair, feeling like a fool. *Why does she enjoy torturing me?*

"Micajah McElroy, has thee come courting?" asked Sarah.

"Well… maybe."

"The man I marry will be somebody," she said, "all thee knows how to do is plow oxen and say, 'gee' and 'haw.'"

"Huh," harrumphed Micajah. "Angus McDonald couldn't plow a straight row in his life depended on it. Anyway, I can read and write and cipher too."

"Angus can too plow," she snapped.

"And he's probably a Tory too… Many of the McDonalds are."

"I don't care about that," she said.

"You will be when they burn you out."

"Are you a Patriot?"

"I ain't a Tory."

Sarah shifted the subject. "Thee doesn't even know a trade."

"I'm learning one."

"Doing what?"

"Carpentry."

"Well," she said, somewhat pleased.

Thunder was rolling in the distance and moving closer. The sky grew dark and a young Negro woman brought a candle into the room and placed it on a table. The flickering light danced up and down the wall casting a soft light across Sarah's face. Her nose was nondescript, but her blue eyes and well-shaped lips were enchanting. She seemed to grow more beautiful each time he saw her. She sipped her tea and looked at him over the rim of her cup. "Well….. I guess being a carpenter is better than plowing old oxen."

"Just you wait and see."

A deafening pop of lightning startled both of them and Micajah spilled his tea on the table. "Uh, uh, I'm sorry, I'll clean it up."

"No, that's all right, but I must admit thee do have good manners."

Micajah had a bellyful of this little wench's insolence.

"How did you acquire so much knowledge about things in only thirteen years?" he asked.

"I don't know a lot about things," she said, taken aback, "but I can read and write…. well… I almost can."

Hail pounded the wooden shingle roof and through the rain-splattered window Micajah could see large ice balls dancing in the front yard. The rain came in torrents. It roared on the roof and splattered against the window. After a while it settled down to a steady downpour. Sarah's two younger sisters raced through the house, setting out crock jars to catch the water that leaked through the shingle roof. Then Mrs. Campbell came in to announce supper and invited Micajah to join them.

Around a long table made from wide pine boards, Mr. Campbell, who wheezed

18

and coughed a lot and didn't say much, took his seat at the head of the table. Mrs. Campbell sat at the opposite end and Micajah and Sarah sat next to each other across from her two sisters.

After Mr. Campbell returned thanks for the food, a Negro servant girl passed around roasted pork and boiled pudding and poured hot tea. It was a fine meal.

"Father," said Sarah, "Micajah is going to be a carpenter."

"Excellent trade," he said and returned to eating pudding and coughing.

"I'm indentured to Silas Willingham," Micajah said. "And he's the best carpenter in Wake County."

"Do thee like carpentry?" asked Mrs. Campbell.

"Well, I'd rather be a miller –"

"A miller!" exclaimed Sarah.

"What's wrong with that?" Micajah asked, irritated by her tone.

"Daughter, be courteous to thy guest," said Mrs. Campbell.

Micajah felt something against his leg and realized it was Sarah's knee. He glanced at her, but she didn't respond nor did she move her leg. Through her long black dress he felt the warmth of her body. And it felt good. He was blushing – he knew he was. He didn't understand females. First, she made fun of him, now she was touching his leg.

After supper Micajah wiped his mouth with a napkin and pushed back from the table. "The meal was very good," he said addressing Mrs. Campbell. "May I be excused? I must be going home."

"Thee can't get out in this rain," she said. "Thee'll catch cold and die."

"You stay here tonight lad," said Mr. Campbell.

The wind was still howling when Mrs. Campbell, holding a candle, escorted Micajah and Sarah to an upstairs bedroom where there were two beds – one for the younger sisters. A bundling board had been inserted in the center of the bed where Sarah and Micajah were to sleep. Mr. Campbell came up and inspected the board and found it to be secure.

"There is the chamber pot," said Mrs. Campbell pointing to a crock pot at the foot of the bed.

Micajah unbuckled his shoes and climbed into his side of the bed fully clothed. Sarah did likewise. The mattress was stuffed with shucks, and every time he breathed, the shucks rattled. He scooted close to the bundling board and heard Sarah breathing. Was she thinking of him? He thought about her leg against his at the supper table and couldn't stop his mind running wild with thoughts about her. She was only inches away, but the bundling board made it impossible to touch her. The sisters in the other bed were sound asleep.

"Pssst. Sarah," he whispered. "Are you asleep?"

"No."

"I'm not either. I can't sleep."

"Nor can I."

"Do you really like Angus McDonald?" he whispered.

Silence.

Micajah finally drifted off to sleep near midnight but he rolled and turned until dawn thinking about Sarah, so close but yet so far away.

---

A half moon shone when Micajah pulled on his coat and made ready to depart Silas Willingham's shop for home.

"It's awfully late," he said to Willingham, who looked tired. "Maybe you should get some rest." Over the past two years, Micajah had taken a slight liking to his taskmaster.

"I'm fine lad. Tomorrow at 5 a.m."

"Yes sir, at five," replied Micajah.

Micajah departed for home, moon beams filtering through the trees that bordered the narrow road. He was thinking of pretty Sarah Campbell when he thought he heard a noise. He stopped and cocked an ear. Horses. Many of them! He quickly stepped off the road and into the dark shadows just as a dozen or more horsemen thundered past. Sabers and muskets reflected in the moonlight. When the dust settled, he stepped onto the road and watched as the riders reined up in front of Willingham's shop, where candlelight glowed through the open shutter. The night was still and quiet, tree frogs and night sounds having been scared silent by the thundering hooves.

"SILAS WILLINGHAM!" a horseman called out.

Micajah saw Willingham step out the front door.

"Who disturbs my peace?" Willingham asked.

"The King's men," replied a rider.

"Rotten Tories!"

"Bind him!" ordered another man.

"Fanning, you murdering Devil!" exclaimed Willingham and ran toward the shop door. Two men slid from their saddles and grabbed Willingham and bound his arms behind his back.

"You'll pay for this Fanning," said Willingham. "As God as my witness, you'll pay."

"Shut up you fool," said Fanning and slapped Willingham across the face.

Micajah crept closer so that he could hear and see better. The one called Fanning wore a silk cap.

"No, you are the one that will pay," replied Fanning. "And with your life. You and your so-called Patriots will answer for your crimes against the Crown. Take him to the tree!"

The men dragged Willingham beneath a low-hanging limb of the big oak next to the shop and tossed a rope over it; dropped a hangman's noose over his neck and lifted him into the saddle. "I'm a religious man," said Fanning. "Would you like to confess your crimes against the Crown?"

"Yeah," Willingham mumbled.

"What did you say?" asked Fanning and moved near Willingham.

"Yeah, I have something to say."

"Then say it."

"I'll see you in hell you murdering Devil!" said Willingham and spat in Fanning's face.

Fanning wiped spittle away with his hand and said, "I'm going to enjoy this."

He slapped the horse and it ran from beneath Willingham, leaving him gasping and kicking, trying to find solid ground. His body twitched a few times and grew still. One of the men threw a torch under the shop and it was quickly enveloped in flames.

20

Micajah was frozen by fear for several seconds, unable to move, and then panic overtook him. He tore out across a corn field, riding down stalks, scared, gasping for air and making strange animal-like sounds.

"I hear someone over there!" he heard one of the men yell.

Micajah ran pell-mell through the corn, ears striking him on the face and head, afraid to look back. If the Tories caught him they would kill him too. Horses were coming. If he could reach the copse of woods to his front, he knew he would be safe. The forest was thick with vines, bushes and briers. He sprang from the corn patch and darted into the dark undergrowth. He stopped behind a large tree and listened. The horsemen were talking and searching for him. "We need to find him," said the one called Fanning. "He saw what happened."

Micajah could feel his heart thumping against his chest. He held his breath and dared not move. Finally, the men gave up and rode away. But Micajah didn't move for a long time. It could be a trick, he thought. After remaining motionless for a half an hour or more, he quietly exited the forest and followed the tree line toward home. Everyone was in bed when he arrived. He told no one, not even Uncle Abington what he had witnessed. He went to bed, but couldn't sleep. Had the Tories seen him well enough in the moonlight to recognize him? He worried. If they learned his identity he knew they would come for him. He must be careful. From henceforth, he would go nowhere without his rifle.

Then he thought about the end of his carpentry training. With Silas Willingham dead, had he learned enough that he could carry on the trade? Willingham had been a hard taskmaster, but Micajah had to admit he had learned much from the man.

---

The following day, a rider – the same one that had frequently visited Silas Willingham outside his shop – rode up fast and reined abruptly in front of Micajah at Abington McElroy's gristmill on Polk's Branch. The horse was lathered and breathing hard. "Lad, where is your uncle?" the rider demanded.

"Inside."

"Fetch him and be quick about it!"

"Yes sir," replied Micajah and ran inside for Abington, who came out brushing flour and corn dust from his shirt. When Abington saw the rider, his face grew serious. Micajah hung back as they conferred with animation. He thought of the story he had told his uncle, that Willingham wasn't feeling well and had given him the day off. In moments, the rider departed in a cloud of dust. Abington turned to Micajah, his jaw set and blue eyes blazing.

"Lad, you knew. Why didn't you tell me?"

Micajah's hands trembled as he wiped his mouth. He had buried the horrible scene so deep inside him he couldn't summon the words. "I... I... I–"

"Tell me lad. Tell me now!"

"I was scared." Tears welled in his eyes. "It was horrible... Uncle Abington..."

Abington faced Micajah and gripped his shoulder. "No one is going to harm you lad. Now tell me what you know."

Micajah slowly related the awful scene he had witnessed. Abington's face turned hard as stone and red shot up his neck.

21

"Did they see you?" he asked.

"They chased me across the corn field, but I lost 'em in the woods."

"Do you think they recognized you?" Abington asked.

"I don't know Uncle, that's what I'm worried about."

"One day that devil Fanning will answer for his crimes!" exclaimed Abington and slammed his fist against the wall.

"I hope so," said Micajah, his voice barely audible.

# 3 | REDCOATS AND TORIES

Late September, 1779.

The tall large white oaks bordering Crabtree Creek had turned bright orange and yellow, the sky was deep blue, and the air was crisp. Fall was galloping into Wake County. Micajah cradled his Pennsylvania long rifle in the crook of his arm, keeping a sharp look out as he approached his favorite spot on the creek. Nowadays, he never went outside the house without his rifle. Luther, his red-boned coon hound that Uncle Abington had given him, though older and somewhat slower, still had his sense of smell, and he seemed to sense danger. He walked ahead, sniffing, listening and looking. If anyone came within a mile upwind he would set off the alarm with a long, lonesome howl.

Micajah propped his rifle against a tree, sat on the limestone rock that hung over the creek and let his feet dangle near the rippling water. Whenever thoughts weighed on his mind, he came here. Blades of sunlight pierced the tall trees and sparkled on the water as it raced headlong toward the river and eventually to its ultimate destination, the sea. Where rocks obstructed the current, it went around or over them. That's how life is, Micajah thought. One has to move forward in life just like the current moves toward the sea. He was twenty years old, in good health, owned a plantation and had a trade as a carpenter, yet he felt stuck. Something was missing from his life. He knew exactly what it was – a woman. And not just any woman, but a special one – Sarah Campbell. He had been seeing her occasionally since he was 16 years old at socials and had courted her at home, but he had never broached marriage. He had wanted to, but he couldn't muster the courage. Now, it might be too late. He had recently learned that she was courting Angus McDonald and that didn't sit well with him at all.

He knew that he loved Sarah and could support her, but it wasn't the best time to be making plans for the future. The war had been dragging on for four years. Fortunately, the fighting had little effect on faraway Wake County except that the Tories continued their reign of terror against Patriots, killing, stealing and burning houses. And Patriots retaliated. He was fairly certain that Uncle Abington was participating, but the subject was never mentioned. No one was safe in their home. He didn't know which side would win the war or whether he would be killed or burned out by the Tories. There was great uncertainty. Yet, life, like the water current, had to move on. The thought of having Sarah as his wife made his insides tingle. But the thought of asking her father for her hand made his stomach churn.

A few days later he sat down with Uncle Abington in front of the fireplace. "Aye, tis a fine evening, lad," Abington said puffing on his pipe.

"Yes sir, it is," agreed Micajah.

"Something on your mind lad?"

"Well, yes sir."

"Let's have it."

"I'm thinking of asking for Sarah's hand in marriage."

Abington didn't respond immediately. "Aye, a house without a woman and firelight, is like a body without soul." He drew on his long stem pipe and blew smoke, then added, "But he that takes a wife must take care."

He had expected his Uncle to heartily endorse his plan. Why did he hesitate? "I've known Sarah all my life and feel I know her well," said Micajah. "And I can support her."

"I'm sure she is a fine woman," Abington said. "But one cannot pluck roses without the fear of thorns, nor enjoy a fair wife without danger of horns."

Uncle Abington had a saying about every subject. Micajah gathered his brow. "What are you saying Uncle?"

Abington removed his pipe from his mouth and looked at Micajah, "Truthfully lad, I don't know which side the Campbells stand with, the Patriots or the Tories."

"Maybe they prefer to keep out of the war–"

"And let someone else fight for their freedom? It's the Quaker in them. Nay, the time will come when everyone will have to choose sides."

Now it was time for Micajah to grow quiet. He felt that Uncle Abington was speaking directly to him. After all, he hadn't enlisted in the militia to fight Tories. As long as they didn't bother him, he didn't feel compelled to bother them. Yet, he couldn't forget what they did to Silas Willingham. Finally, Abington said, "These are trying times. Perhaps it would be wise to wait awhile to marry."

"If I wait too long, she may marry Angus McDonald."

"Rotten Tories, the McDonalds!" exclaimed Uncle Abington and spat in the fire.

---

Micajah lay on his back in bed, fully awake staring at the moonlit ceiling. In the back of his mind, he had always planned to marry Sarah Campbell. Had Angus McDonald stolen her heart? Expecting to receive Uncle Abington's approval had been a foregone conclusion. Now? Not only that, Abington had gently informed him that other men were fighting for his liberty. He rolled and twisted.

The following morning, Micajah saddled his gray gelding, cradled his rifle in his arm and galloped off to the Campbell plantation. Mr. Campbell was at the barn brushing down his horse when he rode up.

"Mornin' sir," said Micajah.

"Aye, what brings thee here so early in the day?" Mr. Campbell asked before setting off with a round of coughing. Micajah slid out of the saddle all the while trying to think how to frame what he wanted to say. When the old man stopped coughing and spitting up phlegm, he looked him straight in the eye.

"I want to marry Sarah."

Campbell stared at him and doubled over coughing again. When he straightened up he said, "Aye, so you do?"

"Yes sir."

"Tis a bad time for matrimony," Campbell said tossing cold water on his proposal. "Have you discussed it with Sarah?"

"No sir. I wanted to get your permission first."

Campbell continued to brush his horse and between coughing seizures, said, "You're a fine man, Micajah McElroy."

While riding home Micajah thought about Mr. Campbell's response. Certainly, he didn't give his permission, but neither did he say no. Micajah decided his plan wasn't working. Perhaps he should forget about Sarah. Yet…

Micajah mulled over the matter for several days. On Sunday afternoon, he dressed in his best clothes and asked Cook to saddle his gray gelding.

"Massah be goin' a court'n," Cook said smiling.

"Wish me luck," Micajah said, climbing into the saddle.

The gelding was clipping down the dirt road at a good pace and Micajah was feeling confident when he came in sight of the Campbell plantation. Tied to the hitching post was a gray horse he recognized. Angus McDonald's. "Whoa," Micajah reined. He sat in the middle of the road disappointed and despondent. After several minutes he turned and rode back home.

The following Saturday afternoon Micajah mustered up the courage to again ride to Sarah's house. The damnable pack of hounds ran out spooking his gelding, almost launching him out of the saddle. Hattie, the Negro woman called them off.

"Why it's Massa Micajah," she said. "Git down, dey won't bite."

"I've come calling on Miss Sarah," Micajah said, unsaddling and tethering his horse. Hattie showed him to the parlor.

Shortly, Sarah came down the stairs. Micajah stood, hat in his hand. He met her in the center of the room; cleared his throat and straightened.

"Sarah, I have something to say to you. Now you just hear me out. I've loved you since I was a boy and I'm not giving you up for Angus McDonald or anyone else and I can support you and I'm going to marry you no matter what Uncle Abington says or your father says and I mean I'm not taking no for an answer–"

"Slow down," Sarah interrupted.

Micajah dropped to one knee. "Sarah Campbell will you marry me?"

Sarah was stunned for a moment, then burst into a big smile. "Yes – yes, now get thee off the floor and kiss me."

"You will?"

––––––––––––

1780.

The wedding took place on New Year's Day at the Campbell plantation. It was a cold, miserable afternoon with patches of lingering snow on the ground. In spite of the weather – and the war - family and neighbors had come out in droves. Most of Micajah's uncles and aunts were there together with their children. His mother Sarah and her husband, Jacob Heartsfield, arrived by carriage. Wagons, carriages and saddle horses were tethered to trees and hitching posts.

The house was packed with guests. Men were backed up to the large fireplace warming their back sides and smoking their pipes. Uncle Abington and Uncle John stayed far away from Angus McDonald and his family. At exactly 2 p.m. Reverend Elijah Smith, a Presbyterian minister, took his place in the center of the parlor, an open Bible in his hand. Micajah and his best man, Uncle Abington stood on the Reverend's left side. Micajah tugged at the sleeves of his long black waistcoat, nervous as a cat. He could feel a cold draft coming up through the plank floor, then across his feet, but still he was sweating.

Finally, he heard creaking on the stairway and looked up and saw Sarah descending the steps one at a time. She was wearing a long white dress that came to her ankles and her blonde hair was barely visible tucked beneath a white cap. She was beautiful.

Reverend Smith read from the scriptures with great solemnity, and then performed the vows. Micajah's mind was racing. Finally, he heard Reverend Smith say, "What God hath joined together, let not man put asunder. I now pronounce you man and wife."

Clapping hands brought Micajah back to reality. He was married!

Uncle Abington shook his hand firmly. "Aye lad, you have done well," he said. "Remember the old adage, 'keep your eyes wide open before marriage, half shut afterwards.'"

Then the fun began. The young single men raced to a jug of whiskey that sat on a stump. The winner had the right to kiss the bride first. Several of the boys were tripped by competitors. There was much pushing and shoving and tugging at the jug. Finally, Angus McDonald wrestled the jug from the hands of another young swain and took a long pull on the whiskey. He passed the jug, wiped his mouth and asked, "Where's the bride?"

The young men lined up behind McDonald and kissed Sarah who was thoroughly enjoying the attention, much to Micajah's chagrin.

After much feasting, the couple was finally "bedded."

"Micajah!" Someone yelled. "How many children will you have?"

"Fifteen."

"Then you better start now," someone else yelled.

There were other ribald and joking comments made as Micajah cradled Sarah in his arms and carried her, as she blushed, upstairs to bed, while guests beat on pots and pans and made great noise and merriment. This time there was no bundling board between Micajah and Sarah.

---

Wake County.
Late Spring, 1780.

Micajah stood in the doorway looking out into the morning enjoying warm sunlight on his face. The sky was clear and blue as Sarah's eyes and the air warm and fresh. Inside the house he heard floor boards gently creaking as Sarah moved about performing her duties. It was a comforting sound.

They had been married less than five months and she had filled the large hole in his soul. And just recently, she had whispered to him that a baby grew in her stomach.

He closed his eyes and inhaled deeply. "Ahhh." In spite of war, life held so much hope. The corn and wheat crop looked promising, he was earning a few schillings doing carpentry work and moreover he had plans to build a small house on Crabtree Creek. Then a dark thought crossed his mind. Many women died during childbirth. He quickly pushed the thought aside and told himself that the matter was in the Lord's hands. Today, he and Cook would plow the tender corn stalks and enjoy the gorgeous spring day that was in the making.

The sound of approaching hoof beats coming down the road drew his attention. Tories! No, they always came in packs. Luther and Uncle Abington's pack of hounds ran out barking at a lone rider on a black horse. He rode up fast and reined in the front yard. The horse was dripping sweat and breathing hard. It spelled trouble.

"I'm looking for Micajah McElroy," said the rider.

"I'm Micajah."

The man reached inside a leather courier bag that hung around his shoulder and lifted out a document which he unfolded and read aloud.

"To whom these presence shall come – greetings; The hereinafter named male citizens of Wake County, which includes Micajah McElroy," he eyes glancing at Micajah, "are hereby drafted into military service for a period of three months. You are ordered to report to Captain Mark Bryant in Bloomsbury immediately. By Order of Thomas Burke, Governor of North Carolina and Commanding General, State Militia."

Micajah had a sinking feeling and grabbed the door facing. "When do I report?" he asked, his voice unsteady.

"Immediately," replied the courier, folding the document and replacing it in the leather bag. "And may the Almighty bless our forces," he added; kicked his horse and departed at a gallop, the dogs barking and giving chase. Micajah felt like he had been slammed by a falling tree.

"Who was that?" asked Sarah who had heard the commotion and appeared as the rider departed.

"A courier," replied Micajah. "I've been drafted into the militia for three months."

"Oh no!" she blurted. "When do thee have to leave?"

"Immediately." Micajah pulled her against his chest, aware that her breasts were beginning to fill with milk. Her body trembled. This was the worst time for him to depart home. Sarah could miscarry the baby; there were crops to be tended and wheat to be gathered and threshed.

Sarah wiped her eyes and looked up at Micajah. "I – I'll be just fine," she said. "When thee return it won't be long afterwards that I will give thee a son."

"I shouldn't leave you," he said. "I had hoped it wouldn't come to this."

Sarah knew it was no time for her to show weakness. "I'll be in good care with Uncle Abington and Aunt Sarah and Mother is also nearby. Now thee don't worry about me for a minute."

Micajah, wearing a long linsey hunting shirt belted at the waist, climbed into the saddle. A powder horn and leather shot bag hung criss-cross over his shoulders, the Pennsylvania long rifle cradled in his arm.

When Micajah arrived at Bloomsbury he located the militia camped at the edge of town, near a spring. He reported to Captain Mark Bryant, who was standing outside a white tent. A tall, slender man wearing a tricorn hat, officer's coat and a sword slung at his side, he stood very erect with his hands clasped behind his back. A stern look was on his pock marked face. Micajah approached him and said, "I'm Micajah McElroy, I was told to report to you."

The Captain looked Micajah over and then glanced down at a roster he held, "Are you related to John McElroy?" he asked, looking up.

"Yes sir, he's my uncle; Uncle Abington's brother."

"Are you Archibald's son?"

"Yes sir."

The stern look disappeared. "I served with your father years ago. He was Quarter Master in Johnson's Regiment," Bryant said. "A good man he was." He pointed toward a row of tents on the edge of the woods. "I'm assigning you to John McElroy's mess. You'll find him over there."

Micajah was welcomed by his Uncle John and introduced to the men in his mess.  Except for a severely pocked marked face caused by smallpox, Uncle John favored his brother Abington in every way.

Micajah took an immediate liking to Seth McDavis, younger than himself, who had also been drafted.  Recently married and with an expecting wife, Seth lived on Upper Crabtree Creek.

After all the draftees had reported the company marched to Hillsborough, and then thirty more miles to Salisbury in the Tory hotbed of Rowan County.

Drumbeats woke Micajah each morning before daybreak.  After falling in formation, they breakfasted, usually on cornmeal porridge, and then spent the remainder of the day drilling.  The campsite was akin to a pig sty, ankle-deep in mud when it rained and a dust bowl during dry season.

At night, Micajah slept on hard, damp earth, swatted mosquitoes and scratched welt bites on his face.  Worse were the chiggers that bit his groins until he clawed himself bloody.  He thought about Sarah and their unborn baby.  Was she all right?  He hadn't received a post.  Uncle John said "no news was good news."  Hopefully so.  And he worried about the crops in the field.  Had Cook gathered and threshed the wheat and weeded the corn?  Soon his thoughts inevitably turned to the war.  When they met the Tories in battle would he have the courage to stand in place and fire while men around him were falling?  What if he was killed?  Who would care for Sarah and their baby?  The unknown was the scariest.  At this point he would silently pray that God would protect Sarah and his baby, and then he would fall asleep.

Just when he was gaining confidence in Captain Bryant, the latter fell ill with fever and was discharged home.  The company, being a large one, was divided into two companies.  Lieutenant Screws and Peoples were elevated to Captain.  Many men fell ill with fever and flux.  His friend Seth McDavis turned yellow and began vomiting black bile and was removed to the hospital tent.

"Lad, it's the 'black vomit,'" Uncle John said.  "Some call it yellow fever."

Micajah visited Seth until his health improved enough to be sent home.

The Tory threat subsided.  Micajah's enlistment ended and he was discharged.  All of the worry and endless sleepless nights had been for naught.

Tories had slunk quietly away. One never knew who they were, where they were located or when they would appear.  Micajah rode the 130 miles back home in the company of well-armed Patriots.

Sarah, who wasn't expecting his arrival, was draping her wash over the rail fence beside the house when Micajah rode up.  She almost fainted.  He slid from the saddle before his horse stopped and ran into her open arms.

"Thee are home!  Thank God," she cried out.

That night, as he lay cuddled against her warm body in bed, she moved his head over her protruding stomach and said, "Listen to the heartbeat."

"I hear it. It's strong –"

"Like a boy," she said.  "Just think, you'll be home when he's born."

---

Bad news travels fast. In late August, word came that General Horatio Gates, Commander of Revolutionary Forces in the south had been defeated at Camden, South Carolina by General Cornwallis on August 16th.  Many North Carolinians were wounded and killed, including 500 prisoners taken along with  vast amounts of supplies and wagons.   Cornwallis marched his Redcoats toward Charlotte where the remnants of Gates' Army had fallen back. North Carolina was practically defenseless.

Tories were jubilant and called for Loyalists to join their ranks and once and for all defeat the Patriots. This meant burning their homes, confiscating their personal property, taking their land and killing them. Micajah knew the threat was serious and didn't wait to be drafted. A few weeks following Gates' defeat, he volunteered for service and marched to Salisbury where General Bofetter commanded the militia. Cornwallis occupied Charlotte which was approximately 40 miles south of Salisbury.

Major Pat Ferguson of the Tory 71st Regiment, in an attempt to cause a rising sent out the following written appeal to North Carolinians:

DENARD'S FORD, BROAD RIVER

LYON COUNTY, OCTOBER 1, 1780

GENTLEMEN: Unless you wish to be lost in an inundation of barbarians who have begun by murdering an unarmed son before the aged father, and afterwards lopped off his arms, and who by their shocking cruelties and irregularities, give the best proof of their cowardice and want of discipline: I say if you wish to be pinioned, robbed, murdered and see your wives and daughters in four days abused by the dregs of mankind, in short if you wish or deserve to live, and have the name of men, grasp your arms in a moment and run to camp.

The Back Water men have crossed the mountains; McDowell, Hamilton, Shelby, and Cleveland are at their head, so that you know what you have to depend on. If you chose to be degraded forever and ever by a set of mongrels say so at once and let your women turn their back on you, and look out for real men to protect them.

PAT FERGUSON, Major 71st Regiment

Emotions ran high among the citizens. Families were divided and brother fought brother.  None of the Tories were more feared and despised by the Patriots than former Sergeant David Fanning, now a Colonel in the Tory Militia.  Among Patriots, his name was synonymous with cruelty and murder.

It was mid-November and a recent freeze had turned the sucking mud in the camp to hardpan, making drilling easier. After evening mess, Micajah was standing near the fire warming himself when Seth McDavis appeared.  Micajah couldn't believe his eyes.

"Aye, the dead arises," Uncle John McElroy said.  "It is surely the end of time."

"It's me in the flesh and I am truly alive," said Seth.

"No one survives the black vomit," said one of the men.

"God above saved my life," said Seth, smiling.

Micajah shook his hand.  "I'm glad you are back.  I too assumed that you had died."

That evening, when the other men had fallen asleep around the fire, Micajah and Seth talked. They had much in common. Both were young, recently married and had pregnant wives. Micajah confided in Seth. "I never intended to get caught up in this war," he said. "All that I wanted to do was tend to my own affairs and be left alone. My Uncle Abington urged me to join the Militia but I resisted. Even after that devil Fanning was robbing and hanging Patriots, I still didn't enlist. I guess I thought if I left them alone they would leave me alone."

"Same here," said Seth. "Now, I have a wife and will soon have a child that I must defend."

"We have no choice," said Micajah. "It's kill or be killed."

"I pray that my child can grow up in a better country," said Seth.

"That's worth fighting for," replied Micajah.

At the campsite, news trickled back from the front: How Lt. Col. Lee, leading a group of Patriots, slaughtered over 90 of Fanning's Tories and didn't lose a single man, and how General Washington had replaced Gates with Nathaniel Green.

Micajah's enlistment was near its end the day he saw General Green, the "Fighting Quaker" from Rhode Island, arrive in Salisbury. Tall, handsome and resplendent in his continental blue coat and white britches, he gave the Patriots new hope. Then one day before the end of Micajah's enlistment, he received word that Sarah had given birth. He couldn't wait to be home.

It was a cold December morning, a week before Christmas, when Micajah, along with Uncle John McElroy and Seth McDavis and a dozen or more well-armed men, mounted their horses and departed for Wake County. It would be a dangerous journey through Tory country where hatred for Patriots was rife. Guards would have to be posted at night. The horses weren't in good condition, some worse than others. If they didn't push them hard, they could easily cover 25 miles a day and be home in five days.

When the men reached Bloomsbury, they split up. Micajah grasped Seth's hand.

"I hope the next time we meet it will be over a cup of rum and not around a soldier's fire," he said. "God be with you."

"And you too my friend," replied Seth.

Micajah and Uncle John rode toward Crabtree Creek and home. An exhilarating feeling of joy surged through him. He would be home before dark, hugging Sarah and his yet unnamed child.

"Ahh, I've never seen a happier face," Uncle John said.

"God has richly blessed me," Micajah replied. "I'm alive and I'm a father."

"What are you gonna name him?"

"I have a name in mind, but I must first talk to Sarah."

The landscape grew more familiar. Home wasn't far away. When the sun set the temperature dropped and within minutes his feet and hands were numb. He kicked his horse, clucked and took off in a full gallop, leaving Uncle John behind. When he neared Uncle Abington's house the pack of hounds ran out, barking and howling, but soon realized it was Micajah and began whining and jumping with joy.

"Massa Micajah!" he heard Cook exclaim when he ran out from the quarters and took his horse.

"How's Sarah and the baby?" Micajah asked.

"Dey fit as a fiddle massa," Cook said, smiling. "You jest'n time fer supper."

Micajah bounded into the house, tossed his hat into the corner and rushed to the dining room where the family was seated around a board table in front of a warm fire. Sarah was instantly on her feet and in his arms. He squeezed her tightly, feeling her swollen breasts against his chest. Uncle Abington was smiling.

"Aye, our Patriot has returned to home and hearth. Welcome lad."

Sarah lifted the wrapped baby from the cradle and handed the tiny bundle to Micajah. He parted the blanket, looked at the child who was sleeping and smiled. "He favors me, don't you think Uncle?"

"Aye, 'tis true."

Micajah was soon warm and gorging himself on fresh milk, butter and pudding.

Uncle Abington wiped his mouth and pushed back from the table, eyes twinkling, as he said, "Aye, this fine-looking boy will no doubt bear my name."

Sarah shot a disappointed look at Micajah.

"Uncle only teases," he said, "although it is a fine name."

"Thee should choose," said Sarah. "He is our first boy and–"

"Are you sure?"

"Yes."

"Alright then, I'll name him Archibald in honor of my father and grandfather."

That night he snuggled close to Sarah, feeling the warmth of her soft body. He hadn't slept warm since leaving home. He pondered the future. Now, he had a son to think about and more the reason to defeat the English and the murderous Tories. With God's blessings, Arch wouldn't be English – he would be American. It was the best Christmas ever, he thought, just before falling into a deep sleep.

---

Micajah enjoyed the winter of 1780-81, did carpentry work, readied the ground for spring planting and laid out a foundation for a new house. Little Arch was healthy and Sarah was again pregnant and expecting to deliver in the fall. Elsewhere, however, the battle still raged. Cornwallis marched his Redcoats across North Carolina and into Virginia, 230 miles from his supply base, where he decided to retrace his steps and fall back to Hillsborough, where he was certain that local Tories would rally to his banner. He was right. Colonel David Fanning had raised 300 Tories and they were eager to join Cornwallis. Then they struck. In mid-summer, Fanning and his band marched through the countryside killing, burning and stealing horses, meeting little opposition. On September 6th he was so confident that he circulated a broadside:

> "This is to let all persons know, that do not make ready and repair immediately to camp, they should be sent to Wilmington as prisoners, and there remaining, as such in the provost; and be considered as rebels, also, if any rebel is willing to surrender and come in he shall reap the benefits of a subject.
>
> David Fanning
> Camp Cox's Mill, 6th September, 13 H, Col's Com'g Loyal Militia."

When Colonel Hardy Sanders raised a regiment of Patriots to suppress the Tories, Micajah volunteered for two months in a Light Horse Company commanded by

Captain Matthew Collier of Wake County, where Fanning and Blalock had stolen stores, supplies and many horses.

Micajah was with one of Captain Collier's squads, looking for Fanning's gang of Tories, when a pillar of smoke guided the squad to what had once been a cabin and homestead. A man and woman and a dozen or more children were standing in the road in front of a blackened chimney and a heap of smoldering coals, clinging to a few personal items, when the Patriots rode up.

"Who did this?" asked Uncle John McElroy, who was in charge.

"Fanning and Blalock," said the man. "And they stole two of my horses; a bay mare and a chestnut gelding with a left back sock."

"How long ago?"

"An hour or less; they headed north," the man said and pointed up the dusty road.

"How many?"

"Fifty, I'd guess."

Uncle John turned to Micajah and said, "Ride fast to Captain Collier and tell him we're on Fanning's trail and to come quickly."

"Yes sir," said Micajah. He spurred his big gelding and rode like the wind to deliver the message to Captain Collier. Within minutes the Light Horse Company was on its way to link up with Uncle John's squad. Captain Collier sent flankers ahead to locate the Tories and set up an ambush.

The Light Horse Company was proceeding at a trot when suddenly a rider shot from the pine woods at a fast run. A Tory Scout! Captain Collier drew his sword and held it high. "RIDE THEM DOWN. CHARGE!"

Micajah's heart jumped through his throat. He had thought about this moment many times. Now it had arrived. Momentarily he was seized with fear. Uncle John looked at him and said, "Remember our families. Let's go!"

Micajah spurred his horse and the men thundered down the road. He saw Tories scrambling to mount their horses and flee. Dark puffs of smoke appeared on each side of the encampment, fired by the flankers; some balls finding their marks and dropping Tories to the ground. Many surrendered, arms held high. The remainder fled up the road leaving a cloud of dust. A rider fell behind, his horse apparently hit with a ball in the melee. He darted off into the pine woods.

"Look!" exclaimed Uncle John. "It's a chestnut with a left-hind sock. Follow me." Micajah spurred his mount and they rode into the woods chasing the Tory. They hadn't gone far until they rode him down.

"Halt or I'll cut you in two," Uncle John commanded, his sword held high and eager to do its bloody work.

The man reined his chestnut gelding and held his arms above his head.

"Blalock, you son of Satan," said Uncle John. "Your days of stealing and murdering are over. Bind him, Micajah."

Micajah bound Blalock's hands behind his back with leather and they escorted him back to the road, where Captain Collier had assembled a throng of prisoners.

"Where did you get that chestnut gelding?" Captain Collier asked Blalock.

"He's mine. I've owned him for a long time."

"You are not only a murderer you are also a liar," Captain Collier replied.

"Hang him!" someone cried out.

The men chanted, "Hang him, hang him, hang him."

"Not until he has a fair trial," said Captain Collier who ordered the prisoners separated, and then questioned each one outside the presence of the other. Hoping to save their own lives, they confessed that Blalock had stolen the chestnut gelding from a Patriot that very morning.

Captain Collier ordered Blalock brought forward. "You stand convicted of stealing a horse," said Collier. "And for that crime you must be hanged." Blalock dropped his head. "That is, unless you desire to denounce the Crown and take an oath of allegiance to the Revolution," added the Captain.

Blalock raised his head. "Damn you Patriots. May your souls burn in hell," he said.

Someone threw a rope over a low-hanging limb and fashioned a noose. Blalock was sitting in the saddle and the noose dropped over his head and pulled tight.

"You have anything to say?" asked Captain Collier.

"Damn you all to hell!" exclaimed Blalock and spat.

Captain Collier nodded and a Patriot slapped the horse's flank. The animal bolted from beneath Blalock, leaving him kicking at thin air.

Micajah thought he would relish the moment, after witnessing what Fanning had done to Silas Willingham, but he didn't. Blalock's neck was stretched thin, his eyes bulging like a frog and his face was twisted and ghastly. A wet spot appeared in the crotch of his britches and urine dripped out onto the ground.

"Look! He needed a good piss," a Patriot shouted. Laughter. Micajah turned his head and looked away.

# 4 | BATTLE AT LINDLEY'S MILL

Hillsborough, North Carolina.
September 12, 1781.

The roll of drums at Alamance Creek woke Micajah before daybreak. It could mean only one thing – trouble. He scrambled to assemble in time to hear Colonel Robert Mebane inform the Patriots that Fanning had kidnapped Governor Thomas Burke, along with more than 200 soldiers at Hillsborough. They would move out immediately to intercept Fanning and rescue the prisoners.

Gen. John Butler, guessing that Fanning would travel the road that angled southwest from Hillsborough and crossed Cane Creek at Lindley's Mill, hastened to reach there first.

He arrived in time to scout the area and locate an ideal ambush position. A large, wooded plateau rose some fifteen feet above the creek bottom, and then abruptly angled down to the narrow winding road that was squeezed between the bottom of the hill and Cane Creek. It was an ideal place to spring an attack. Just before the road made a sharp turn around the base of the hill, Stafford Branch flowed across the road and entered the larger Cane Creek. The Tories would be slowed by having to ford both Stafford Branch and Cane Creek.

After hiding their horses on the wooded plateau, well behind the ambush site, the Patriots took up positions on the hill overlooking the road and the two creeks. Colonel Mebane, who commanded Micajah's regiment, walked down the line giving instructions.

"When the front of the Tory column reaches the ford on Cane Creek, their rear should be a mile or so back up the road near the Quaker Spring Meeting House. When they begin fording Cane Creek, you will fire on signal. It will be a turkey shoot." He paused to add emphasis. "And remember what they have done to our families. Make every shot count."

Micajah kneeled on one knee near the brow of the hill overlooking the narrow road. Seth McDavis was several yards to his left and Uncle John McElroy was on his right. He straightened the leather strap on his powder horn, and then checked his shot bag. When the firing began, he wanted nothing to hinder reloading. The weather was dry and scorching hot. He suddenly wanted a drink of water. His mouth was dry as dust. He nervously glanced at Seth, who looked as scared as he was.

"Have you been in battle?" Micajah asked Seth.

He shook his head, licked his lips. "No, have you?"

"No, but I got to think we'll be okay," Micajah said.

"Yeah, we'll kill those Devils," Seth said with bravado. No one moved. It was deathly quiet along the line when Seth whispered. "Micajah."

"Yeah."

"If something should happen to me check on my wife and baby."

Micajah nodded. "Same here."

Micajah's leg had gone to sleep. He shifted positions. Still no Tories. Maybe they had taken a different road to Wilmington. Or maybe they had learned of the planned ambush and were sneaking up behind the Patriots this very moment. The thought scared Micajah. He twisted around and looked behind just to make sure it was only a thought.

"I hear them coming," someone whispered.

Micajah's heart leapt to his throat and pounded hard. He gripped his Pennsylvania long rifle tighter and realized that his hands were sweating. Then he heard the Tories: neighing horses, clopping hooves, squeaking saddles and the rattle of equipment and men talking. Fear ran deep and doubt crept into his mind. He had never fired at any man in anger, much less killed someone. The Biblical injunction, "Thou shalt not kill" rang loudly in his head. But this was war and self-defense. He thought about Sarah at home with Arch and his unborn baby. Tories would kill and burn them out if given the chance. Then he remembered Silas Willingham hanging by his neck, his skinny legs kicking at thin air. He would look for a man wearing a silk scarf on his head. He quickly glanced to his right where Uncle John appeared calm. Micajah had expected to see scouts well ahead of the main Tory column. There were none. The Tories were flush with victory at Hillsborough and confident. Poor them. No, damn the rascals!

Then he saw them! Several horsemen wearing hunting shirts, slumping lazily in the saddle, slowly forded Stafford's Branch, followed by an unending line of men on foot. They continued, seemingly in no hurry down the narrow road between the brow of the hill and Cane Creek located several yards to the south. They neared the ford on Cane Creek where Lindley's Mill stood. Still no order to fire. *When will we fire?* he asked himself.

The advance guards were slowly guiding their horses down into Cane Creek and others behind them were fording Stafford Branch when an officer shouted: "POISE YOUR FIRELOCKS."

Micajah raised his Pennsylvania long rifle.

"COCK YOUR FIRELOCKS!"

Micajah cocked the hammer. Tories stared up the hill, surprise and fear on their faces.

"PRESENT!"

Micajah leveled his rifle and found the chest of a man on horseback.

"FIREEE!"

The long rifle spoke and a Tory fell from the saddle.

Bushes and trees overlooking the road erupted in a cloud of black smoke as the volley of muskets sent a hail of lead into Tory ranks. Men crumpled to the ground. Micajah didn't need a command to reload. He was pouring powder and ramrodding a ball. The stench of black powder burned his nostrils. Men cried out in pain, some screaming. The Tory rank recoiled. An officer on horseback yelled, "RETREAT!"

The Tories began to escape the hail of lead. Another officer rode up and ordered a countermarch. Several balls ripped into the first officer and he fell dead from the saddle. Tories took cover behind the shallow bank of Stafford Creek and returned fire, but the creek already ran red with their blood.

Meanwhile, at the rear of the Tory column, Patriots, on hearing the opening shots, launched an attack in an attempt to free Governor Burke and the prisoners. The Tory officer herded the prisoners inside the Spring Meeting House, shouting that he would execute them if further attempts were made to free them.

From the brow of the hill, Micajah saw an officer on horseback wearing a British uniform order a retreat. A scarf was wrapped around his head. Fanning! Micajah swung his long rifle around to draw a bead. Trees blocked his view. Then firing erupted behind Micajah's position on the hill. The Tories had swung around and launched a

35

counter attack from the rear. Now, the tables were turned. The Patriots were desperately fighting for their lives. The battle raged for hours. Powder was running low. Colonel Mebane walked the line, passing powder in his hat. "Take just what you need," he said. Thirst and fear sealed Micajah's mouth.

"Here they come again!" Seth McDavis yelled.

Micajah was pouring powder and reloading when he saw a Tory scrambling up the hill toward him. The Tory stopped and leveled his musket directly at Micajah. Micajah ramrodded the ball, all the while watching the Tory. He saw the Tory finger the trigger, and then hesitate. The Tory looked familiar. Angus McDonald! McDonald swung his barrel slightly and a puff of black smoke erupted from the muzzle. Micajah looked to his left and saw Seth McDavis crumble forward.

"SETH!"

"I'm killed, Micajah."

Micajah turned back to see the Tories retreating back down the hill. But he knew they would return.

In the distance, 200 yards or more, Micajah saw Fanning on horseback shouting encouragement to his men. Micajah swung the barrel of the long rifle around and drew a bead, took a deep breath, held it and squeezed the trigger. Fanning bucked in the saddle and grabbed his left arm.

After four hours of firing, both sides gradually pulled back, exhausted. The attempt to rescue the prisoners had failed. The Tories proceeded to Wilmington.

That evening, Patriots sat quietly around their campfires, exhausted by the day's fight. It had been vicious. Micajah didn't know who had won the battle, only that many men were dead and wounded. Darkness brought chill. He scooted closer to the fire and felt its warmth on his aching muscles. The tension in his body caused by fear was slowly melting away, replaced by hunger. Finally bread arrived and was passed around, giving the men much-needed energy. He chewed on stale bread and thought about Sarah. Had she birthed the baby? Was it healthy? Was she? *Ohh, to hold her in my arms.* Uncle John McElroy walked up, interrupting Micajah's thoughts. He reported that between 200 and 300 Patriots and Tories had been killed and many men were wounded. Micajah dropped his head and silently thanked God that he wasn't one of them.

"Aye, but the good news is that Colonel Fanning received a ball," said Uncle John.

"In his evil head, I pray," a Patriot replied.

"Nay, his left arm was shattered in several places and he suffered much loss of blood," said Uncle John. "A captured Tory who was present said that Fanning relinquished his command and hid in the woods." The men's spirits lifted.

"Tis good news," said one.

"The Patriot who sent that bullet flying did a good day's work," added Uncle John. Micajah wondered if he was that Patriot.

Later, Micajah, too exhausted to make his bed, fell back on the ground. His last thoughts were of home, and Sarah.

---

The Battle at Lindley's Mill on September 13th mostly ended the war in North Carolina. One month later, Cornwallis surrendered his Army to General Washington at Yorktown, Virginia, and the revolution ended. But the reign of terror in North Carolina didn't stop. Many of the Tories were anxious for peace, but until terms could be reached, hangings and burnings continued.

It was mid-November and the weather had turned cold when Micajah's two-month enlistment ended and he was discharged for home. He rode hard for two days, arriving on Crabtree Creek after dark. In the distance he saw a candlelight glowing in the front window of the cabin. Luther and the hounds under the house bounded out to greet him. He slid from the saddle and ran toward the open front door.

"Sarrrraaaaah!"

Sarah was holding a candle in her hand, baby Arch cradled in her free arm.

"Ohhhh my God, thee are home!"

"Yes, I'm home – home at last."

Cook appeared, smiling. "Massa be home. Thank de Lord," he said and took the horse away.

"Are you okay?" Micajah asked Sarah, looking at her flattened belly and swollen breasts, then pulled her into his arms.

"Yes, I'm fine."

"What about–"

"Baby is fine too."

Inside, Sarah lifted a tiny bundle from a cradle, pulled open the blanket and said, "I present thee with another fine son."

Micajah took the child into his arms and, looking down at him sleeping peacefully, said. "Thanks to a merciful God, the Revolution is won and my children will live free and in peace." They named the child William.

---

Colonel Fanning left the state in May, 1782, and went to Halifax, Nova Scotia. The Treaty of Paris was signed on September 3, 1783, granting America its independence. Finally, peace reigned and, true to his word, Micajah checked on Seth McDavis's widow and children from time to time and saw to their needs.

# 5 | PEACE AND PROSPERITY

Peace brought both prosperity and contentment to Micajah. He completed building his home, a modest but well-constructed one on Crabtree Creek. On October 7, 1783, he had prospered enough to purchase 100 acres on the north bank of Crabtree Creek from Godfrey Heartsfield, a relative of his stepfather, Jacob Heartsfield. Three weeks later he purchased another 200-acre tract on the creek from Heartsfield.

Spring of 1786 brought sadness. Uncle Abington and Aunt Sarah and their nine children sold out in Wake County and moved to Oglethorpe County, Georgia, where he was granted 900 acres along the Broad River. Micajah dreaded the farewell, which might well be his last. Emotions flooded his being until he thought his chest would explode.

"Aye, I will miss you lad," said Abington. After all these years he still called him lad, but it was a term of endearment and Micajah didn't mind. "Goodbye lad and may God always bless you and Sarah and the children."

"It isn't forever, Uncle," said Micajah choking up. "Perhaps we'll see each other again. I hope so." He shook his hand, and then grabbed him in a tight hug, but he knew it was goodbye and he'd never see him again.

---

Great joy came to the household in the fall of 1788. Their first daughter, Abigail, was born. Arch, who was almost 8 years old, and William, age 7, were happy to have a little sister, but also somewhat jealous of the little blue-eyed girl who was now the center of attention.

There was also sadness. Cook, who had been his faithful servant and companion since he had a memory, died with fever. At last, he was a free man. Micajah built a coffin in his shop, constructed of cedar befitting the wealthiest Tory in North Carolina. The Negroes dug a grave beneath a large white oak tree located not too far from Crabtree Creek where Cook had spent most of his life. The family gathered around the open grave on a windy Sunday afternoon and watched as the Negroes lowered the casket down into the grave with ropes. Micajah removed his hat and looked down at the grave, then read from the Twenty-Third Psalm. Afterwards, he said a few words. "Cook was bequeathed to me by Grandfather Archibald. I've known him since my first memory and he was a good and faithful servant. He'll be missed. Like all of us, he has returned to the earth from whence all of us came. Rest in peace, Cook."

Micajah directed the Negroes to fill the grave and shape the top. Arch and William had picked wild flowers which they placed on the fresh earth. One day, he promised himself, he would construct a tombstone and place it over Cook's grave.

---

The McElroy family was experiencing great change and so was the new country. On June 21, 1788, the Continental Congress in Philadelphia adopted a Constitution of the United States which was ratified on September 17, 1789.

Arch and William were learning to read and write, and on cold winter nights when the wind moaned through the tops of the nearby pine trees the family gathered around a warm fire blazing in the fireplace.

"Father, tell us about fighting the Tories," said Arch.

"It's more important to know the consequences of the war than how it was

38

fought," said Micajah.

"What do you mean?" asked William.

"Because of what we did both of you will live in peace," Micajah said. "We are no longer thirteen separate colonies beholden to a King. We are now a nation called the United States. We are Americans. Be proud of that."

"Tell us about when you shot the evil Tory, Colonel Fanning," said Arch.

"Yes," chimed William.

"Aye lads, I've never claimed that I shot Fanning."

"I overheard some men say that you did," said Arch.

"The truth is, no one knows for sure who shot the devil," said Micajah. "I aimed at a man who resembled him, but I'm sure other Patriots did the same."

---

Wake County, which was carved out of Johnston County, was growing and prospering. In 1790, it had a population of 10,192, a quarter of which were slaves. Micajah continued to prosper as his family grew. In 1790, Micajah, Jr. (called Mike) was born, giving him 3 fine sons and a beautiful daughter.

The happy times were interrupted with the death of his dear mother, Sarah. She died in Wake County in 1797 and was buried near his grandmother, Catherine McElroy, in the family plot. She was the only person who kept Micajah anchored to Wake County. He had a passel of aunts and uncles and cousins, but it was his mother who kept his wanderlust in check.

Two big events occurred in 1799. A fourth son, Ransom, was born and Micajah was low bidder on a contract with the local governing body to build a market house for 298 pounds sterling. It was to be of "octagon form, 30 feet in diameter with a cupola on top for a bell; to be set upon eight posts; to have four gates, banister all around 3 feet high, floor laid with brick and the whole to be neatly painted."

Micajah had plenty of assistance building the market house. Arch, who was 19 years old at the time, and William, age 18, were becoming skilled carpenters and masons in their own right. They could measure, cut and fabricate about as well as their father, to say nothing of their masonry skills. The job was completed in early May, 1800, just before a second daughter, Sarah, was born. They fondly nicknamed her Sallie.

On cold winter nights when the oak logs popped and hissed in the fireplace, Micajah often stared at the leaping flames and pondered the future. He was doing well financially, owned land, his little family was healthy and growing, and he had every reason to be content.

But something gnawed at his guts. Since turning 40 years of age, a thirst welled up inside him that he couldn't quench. In a word, it was discontent. He had an urge to move, explore, take on new challenges and acquire land. His mother had called it wanderlust. "You'll find nothing out there," she had said, pointing west toward the mountains, "that you don't already have here. The only thing that will change is experiencing more hardship and uncertainty."

"Maybe it's uncertainty that appeals to me," he had said.

"Be content, stay where you are and forget such nonsense," she'd replied.

"Mother, I'm sure you are right." But in his heart he wondered what lay across the great mountain range to the west.

One evening he stopped at the tavern at the crossroads to have a pint of grog and overheard a man talking about his recent journey to the Southwest Territory, called Tennessee.

"The Elk is small, but she's about the prettiest little river I've ever seen," he said. "Fed by creeks clear as spring water running from surrounding hills. Why, a gristmill could be built about anywhere a man points his finger. There's plenty of game and a man won't starve. And, if he likes to fish, well, the river is full of 'em. The creek and river bottoms are rich and will grow anything. I've never seen such big chestnuts, white oaks and poplar trees. Land is cheap and there's plenty of it. I tell you, it's a land of milk 'n honey. I'm selling out next spring and head'n to Tennessee."

Micajah tried to dismiss what the man said, but his words kept ringing in his head, especially on cold winter nights when there was nothing else to do but warm in front of the fireplace, and think. But, thinking about it was all that he did.

In 1802, Sarah gave birth to another son, Barney Linn. The following year, Nancy was born. Time was fleeting.

---

Tavern at the Crossroads.

August, 1805.

It was early evening and Micajah was tired after a day's ride to the courthouse in Bloomsbury. He reined up at the tavern where numerous horses were tethered outside. A pint of grog would soothe his aching muscles and lift his spirits. Inside, he was greeted by loud talking, laughter and tobacco smoke. Several old friends whom he had served with in the militia were at a nearby table. He walked over and took a seat.

William Smith looked up. "Aye, 'tis Micajah McElroy, master builder."

"I've no doubt he could he could build the pyramid if the Pharaoh hired him," said another man.

A pint of grog was placed before Micajah and he took a sip.

"Who taught you your craft?" asked Smith.

"Silas Willingham," replied Micajah.

"Aye, poor Silas," said Smith. "A true Patriot he was."

The men fell silent and raised their cups.

"To Silas," said one and they drank.

"I haven't seen you in months," Micajah said to Smith.

"Aye, 'tis because I've been to Tennessee to see my land and make preparations to move there," he replied. "Tis a place of beauty, I tell you, where creeks flow through fertile bottom land and corn stalks are so tall that a man can't reach the tassles."

Micajah listened with rapt attention. "Is it so?" he asked.

"Better than the tongue can describe," said Smith, reaching inside his coat and pulling out a document. "This is Land Warrant No. 117 for 1,000 acres lying on both sides of Cane Creek."

"A lucky man you are," said one of the men. And they all agreed.

When Micajah told Sarah about the fertile lands west of the mountains where creeks ran cold and clear and the corn was so tall that a man couldn't reach the tassles, she said, "Micajah, we have good land; the land of our ancestors. Thee cannot be satisfied."

---

After William Smith died unexpectedly, his executor visited Micajah at his workshop one afternoon. He got right to the point. "I understand that you and the deceased once discussed the 1,000 acres he held a warrant to in Tennessee."

"Aye," replied Micajah.

"His heirs have asked me to ascertain if you would be interested in purchasing the warrant."

Micajah was caught off guard. "Well...uh..."

"If you are, the heirs will assign their interest to you."

"Let me think about it," said Micajah.

Micajah did consider the proposition. If he purchased the warrant, it would have to be surveyed and carried through the legal process and grant obtained and signed by the Governor of Tennessee. Currently, no one came to mind to do the work. He put the matter aside and tried to forget about it. Yet...

# 6 | UPHEAVAL

Wake County, North Carolina.
1809.

Spring came like a thief in the night. It seemed to Micajah that when he had gone to bed on Saturday night it was winter and when he woke on Sunday morning it was spring. Redbuds had blossomed and trees were budding. Sunday mornings were unusually beautiful. His mother used to say it was because God gave folks good weather so they could attend worship. Sap was rising and the earth was waking. Micajah's sap was rising too. A restlessness grew inside him that he couldn't quell. He may have looked all of his 49 years, but he sure didn't feel it.

He strolled through the tall white oaks bordering Crabtree Creek, hands clasped behind his back. It seemed to him he always did his best thinking when he was near the creek. Glancing around, he looked for the flat limestone rock where he used to come as a child and hang his feet over the edge. He realized he hadn't sat on the rock in years. He clucked to the brown coonhound that trailed behind him, "Com'n Luther help me find the rock." This was old Luther's grandpup, a dead ringer for his ancestor, who had died years earlier of old age. He found the flat rock and climbed down on it, his knee and hip bones creaking as he did so. Morning sunlight spilled through the treetops, warming his face. He listened to rushing water and tried to remember the first time he had come here. It seemed only yesterday, he was a mere lad. Cook was with him – and yes, old Luther too. As the scriptures say, life is like a vapor; here one moment and gone the next. If he ever intended to go beyond the Western mountains, he had to act now. Time wouldn't stop for him to think about it another year.

There were great opportunities on the frontier – new people to meet and buildings to construct. Most importantly, land was cheap and plentiful. Land meant wealth and wealth meant he could better provide for Sarah and their growing brood. There would be plenty of work for his sons constructing buildings and furniture. He had already talked over the idea with Arch and William and they were chomping at the bits to move. Arch had married Elizabeth Hurley of Wake County and Elizabeth had decided, in spite of leaving her folks, she would go to Tennessee. Micajah grew excited at the thought of pulling up stakes and moving to the unknown, but that's exactly how Sarah would see it – the unknown. It would upset her comfortable world and work a great hardship on the family. The journey would be long and hazardous, fraught with great danger from sickness, accident and robbers who made their livelihood from pouncing on unwary travelers. Nevertheless, he decided to purchase the 1,000-acre land warrant from the heirs of William Smith.

He had dreaded this moment. Sarah was seated by the window operating her spinning wheel, occasionally, glancing outside at Ransom, Abigail and Mike, who were breaking ground in the kitchen garden in front of the house. Little Nancy, barely six years old, was standing on a stool nearby churning milk, her black hair swinging with each stroke of the churn handle. Micajah didn't say anything for a long time – he was trying to figure out exactly how to say it.

Sarah looked over at him. "It's written all over thy face, Micajah McElroy, so just say it."

When she was irritated at him, she always called him by both his Christian and surname.

He lit his pipe again, got a good fire going and inhaled a lung full of smoke before he spoke.

"I've been thinking a lot about Tennessee. They say it's a land of milk and honey, just like the Promised Land in the Old Testament. Land is plentiful and cheap. Why, we could be wealthy in no time."

Sarah lowered her eyes and was silent for a long time. Finally she said, "We have land and a good home right here in Wake County where our kinsmen and friends live."

"But, it's a new land with new opportunities. We have each other and our children and that's all we need. We can always make new friends."

"I'm getting old and tired, Micajah. I've birthed eight children and I'm ready to settle in my nest. Starting over scares me."

"It's a chance for a fresh start; to get away from the old hatreds that have lingered here since the war ended," he said. "There won't be any Patriots or Tories in Tennessee, just Americans. Why, they say that the river and creek bottoms grow corn so high you can't reach the tassles."

Sarah spun the wheel in silence.

"There will be buildings to construct and furniture to make. It's truly a land of opportunity," added Micajah.

"It's also a raw land," replied Sarah. "And you know what kind of people that attracts." She fell silent for a moment, then added: "I overheard Arch and William talking when they didn't know I was around. They want to go. And I know how much you want to go. I prayed about it a lot." She looked up at Micajah with trembling lips. "This is the land of our ancestors. They are buried in this soil. It makes it sacred soil. But, I love thee and will follow thee to the ends of the earth. Where thou goest, I go also."

---

Late March, 1809.

Micajah woke early, excited and unable to sleep, long before ol' Red began crowing from his perch on the barn gate post. It was still dark outside when he eased out of bed, careful not to wake Sarah who was quietly snoring. He shed his nightshirt and poked around in the dark until he found his linen shirt and trousers, and then he slipped them on and went to the kitchen. He lit a candle and glanced at the ticking clock – 3:45 a.m. – then sat down in front of the open hearth and packed his pipe with tobacco. He drew heavily on the pipe, filling his lungs with smoke that worked magic on his mind and nerves. The last few weeks had been a swirl of activities, auctioning off his land and personal property, visiting family and neighbors and making final farewells. The thought of it brought tears to his eyes. He was leaving all of his kinsmen and friends behind. Except for when he fought the Tories in the surrounding areas, his life had been spent in Wake County. And now he was leaving for the unknown where he knew no one.

Now that the time had come to depart he was filled with both doubt and anxiety. Was he doing the sensible thing? He was leaving the security of a comfortable home for an uncertain future in the wilderness. Doubt was chewing at his mind. What if...? There were so many things that could go wrong that if he considered a tenth of them, he would back out of this fool-hearted venture instantly. He must put them out of mind and focus on the reasons he initially wanted to move to Tennessee. Land – good, fertile land and plenty of it!

And he remembered Uncle Abington, who had pulled up stakes in 1786 and moved with Aunt Sarah and their nine children to Georgia. They had prospered there and he was confident he would do the same in Tennessee.

He would travel the Wilderness Road part of the way. It ran slightly southwest from Philadelphia to North Georgia, passing near western North Carolina. Instead of crossing the Cumberland Gap into Kentucky they would branch off on a road that led to Nashville, then south to Fayetteville. They would have to cross not only mountain ranges, but also several rivers. It wouldn't be easy. Micajah estimated the distance was at least 600 miles. If they averaged 15 miles a day, and barring trouble, they would arrive in Fayetteville by the middle of May. This would give him time to build shelter and plant corn and a garden before winter arrived.

And they wouldn't travel in a caravan. It would be safer to do so, but there were drawbacks – good campsites taken by others, the grass eaten and dust stirred up by their livestock and wagons. There were five men who could man a musket. Ransom was only ten years old, but he could shoot with accuracy.

Ol' Red crowing his head off from the gate post caught Micajah's attention. He looked out the window and saw a sliver of pink across the eastern horizon as dawn broke. It promised to be a fine day.

Soon, the household was up, bumping around, coughing and getting dressed. While Sarah prepared salt pork and Dutch oven biscuits, Arch, William and Mike fed fodder and corn to the horses and oxen and threw out hay to the milk cow and cattle.

Micajah walked out in the yard and was immediately accosted by six-year-old Nancy, cradling a gray speckled hen in her arms.

"Father, can I carry Mother Hen with us?"

"Nay child, we don't have any place to put her."

"But Father, we can't just leave her!"

"I don't mind the chicken coming if we had a place to keep her, but we don't," said Micajah.

"If we leave her here, the fox will eat her."

"I'm sorry, child."

Micajah entered the parlor to see Sarah was standing in the middle of the empty room, silently looking around. He walked up behind her, gently placed his hands on her shoulder and felt her body tremble.

"This has been our home for so long," she said, her voice quavering.

"I know."

"I guess I'm a little bit scared."

"So am I," said Micajah. "The unknown is always frightening, but we'll start a new life with new friends. "We'll be okay."

She had one last look, dried her eyes and turned around and faced Micajah. "I'm ready to go as I'll ever be."

Micajah had made a mental list of all the items that must be carried with them. Now, he checked them off as the Negroes, Luke and John loaded the wagons. There was gun powder, lead, flint, two cast iron kettles, cooking pots, salt, salted pork, furniture, axes, saws, farm and carpentry tools, personal property and canvas tents. Sarah's three small trunks in which she had packed their clothes and her dishes and utensils were carefully loaded inside the wagon, together with a feather bed. A barrel of molasses and a barrel of whiskey and rum were also stored inside the wagon along with a stand of pork lard, flour and corn meal. Roped to the outside was a keg of water, balanced by a keg of beer on the opposite side. Beer was sovereign for stomach ache.

After breakfast, the caravan of wagons and livestock were lined up. Ol' Luther and the hounds were excited, running around barking and howling, no doubt thinking they were going on a coon hunt. Arch was at the head of the column riding his big bay gelding. Next came a large farm wagon pulled by four oxen, driven by Micajah. Sarah was seated next to him and Nancy, the youngest child was riding in back. Behind them were two smaller wagons, the first one occupied by Barney, age 7, and driven by Abigail, who was 19 years old. Perched on top of the wagon and tied by one leg was ol' Red. Behind them was Ransom, age 10, driving, along with 9-year-old Sallie. Next was Archibald's wife, Elizabeth, driving their wagon and oxen. They were followed by several head of cattle, four oxen and a milk cow and her baby heifer calf, "Bonnie," all herded by Luke and John assisted by Shep, a black and white mongrel. William, riding his sorrel mare, was bringing up the rear of the column. Mike rode his black mare with her colt following along. The sun was well up in the morning when Arch climbed in the saddle and looked back at his father. Micajah nodded.

"LET'S MOVE OUT," hollered Arch. "WE'VE GOT 15 MILES TO COVER BEFORE SUNDOWN."

Micajah popped his whip over the oxen and yelled, "hip." They lurched against their wooden yokes and the iron rimmed wagon wheels creaked forward.

Finally, they were on their way to Tennessee.

Neighbors and relatives poured out in their yards and waved as the column of riders, wagons, and livestock rumbled past. It was a sight to behold; dogs barking, horses neighing, wooden wheels creaking, livestock bellowing, all kicking up a small cloud of dust. Even ol' Red, was crowing his head off.

"Good luck," hollered a neighbor.

"May God bless your journey," yelled his wife and waved.

"Come with us," Micajah called back.

By noon the sun was blazing down and they were well on their way to a new land.

Micajah hoped the farm wagons would make the trip. The wheels were belted with iron rims which would withstand the grind over rocks in the road and the many creeks they would have to ford. The hand brake was located on the side near the driver's seat; he could use it to slow the wagon when they descended hills. They had fashioned four hickory bows over the wagons and stretched a white canvas over them. This should keep the cargo dry. He had wanted a Conestoga wagon for the trip, but couldn't locate one. Said to have been developed by Mennonite Germans near Lancaster, Pennsylvania, they were 20 feet long, 11 feet high and 4 feet across and held 12,000 pounds of cargo. But he'd have to make do with what he had.

When they reached a small creek Arch called a halt declaring it would be a good "nooning" place to water the livestock and let them graze and rest. While they rested the women passed out salt pork and leftover biscuits. After an hour or more, they yoked the oxen, gathered in the livestock and departed.

There was at least an hour of sunlight remaining when Arch rode back to the wagon and informed Micajah that there was good grass up ahead, as well as water.

"It will be a good place to stop for the night," he said.

45

Micajah figured they had made fifteen miles that day and readily agreed.

The stock was turned loose and Shep watched them while they watered and grazed. The Negroes erected the tents, and then gathered wood.

"Watch your step everybody," said Micajah. "This is rattlesnake country."

Micajah started a fire and soon pork stew was bubbling in a cast iron pot over an open flame. Everyone received a bowl and a hunk of bread.

"Let us return thanks," said Micajah, removing his wide-brimmed black hat. "Heavenly father, like the children of Israel, of olden times, we have begun an uncertain journey across a wilderness. Guide us to our destination and protect us from Indians, robbers, murderers, wild beasts and sickness. We thank thee for the repast and pray thee will keep us strong to complete our journey and defend ourselves, if need be. Amen."

"Amen-amen," chimed the others.

That evening they gathered around dying embers, swatted mosquitoes and talked about the new land and what it would be like. But the meeting didn't last long. They were tired and ready to turn in early, but first, Micajah took his knife and cut a notch on the wagon seat. He would cut one notch every evening they traveled.

Micajah posted guards, another every-evening routine. Arch, William and Mike would be on duty two hours and off four. They drew straws and Mike went first and Arch second. That night Micajah placed the saddle bag bulging with pounds sterling between him and Sarah and kept his trusty Pennsylvania long rifle within reach. Ol' Luther slept just outside the tent flap. The last thing he remembered was hearing the incessant calls of katydids, crickets and croaking tree frogs.

The next morning they woke at the crack of dawn, watered the stock, breakfasted on leftovers and got back on the road as soon as it could be seen. They fell into a routine, nooning when the sun was directly over them and stopping before dusk to give them time to cook a large meal. Guards were always posted. The women were assigned to one side of the road for their toiletries and the men the opposite side. Bathing was done in the many creeks they crossed and always with an armed sentry nearby just in case there were lurking Indians or brigands. Their toothbrush was a sassafras twig with the end frayed. They washed their clothes with lye soap in creek water and did their daily constitution behind a bush. Rain, though bothersome, didn't stop them. They turned up their collars, pulled down their hats, trudged through mud and forded flooded creeks.

The journey was going well, averaging fifteen miles each day. Everyone was doing their job, even ol' Red, who woke everyone each morning, crowing. And no problems thus far. When the bouncing, rattling wagon seat got too tortious, Micajah got off and rode a spell and let Mike drive. So far, they had been blessed with good weather. He hoped it would continue. They had been on the road a week and he figured that they had traveled at least ninety miles, maybe more.

He knew little about his destination. Tennessee had been part of the North Carolina Colony before the Revolutionary War but, afterwards in June, 1796, was admitted to the Union. Fayetteville was on the frontier and he expected the best and the worst. There would be men like him who were seeking land and wealth, and also men who were escaping their past – ruffians and riff-raff. When Sarah expressed concerns about their daughters meeting what she called "nice young men," he had downplayed her concerns, but privately he was also troubled. He wanted them to marry well.

One evening, Micajah removed the Land Warrant from the saddle bags and looked at it in the glow of campfire. It had originally been issued to William Smith, who had died before it could be surveyed. William White, Secretary of State of North Carolina, had, on July 10, 1805, ordered William Christmas, surveyors of military land, to "lay off and survey for the heirs of William Smith --- 1,000 acres." While Micajah had pondered whether to purchase, the heirs of William Smith assigned their interest on March 4, 1806, to William Haywood; he, in turn to Lewis Haywood and then to Mathais B. Hill. Micajah had purchased from Hill on September 9, 1806. And on January 27, 1809, John Seveir, Governor of Tennessee, had signed the grant. Now, Micajah owned 1,000 acres of land he'd never laid eyes on. Previously he had struck a deal with William Polk of Wake County to survey the land and carry it to grant, which Polk had done.

There were numerous wagon tracks, mostly going in the same direction. Folks were pushing across the mountains in search of land and wealth. The road was no more than a dirt path in many places. There were no bridges across the numerous creeks and branches which they forded. As they moved west toward the distant mountains the road grew steeper and their progress slowed.

It was late afternoon when they topped a rise, giving Micajah a panoramic view to the west. And what he saw he didn't like. The sky was yellowish. For the last hour the oxen and cattle had been bellowing and acting strangely and now he knew why. He had recently noticed a black snake on a tree, leaves were showing their back and there was a ring around the moon. He knew what was coming – a storm. And it looked like a nasty one. The western sky was turning black and moving toward them. They must get off of the high ground and away from tall trees that attracted lightning. The road dipped down into a cove that was shielded by another hill on the western side.

"GO THERE!" yelled Arch riding back to the caravan. "AND HURRY!"

Micajah cracked the whip over the oxen and yelled, "Hip - Hip!" They lumbered forward, sensing the approaching danger.

When they reached the side of the hill, Micajah, yelled, "HAW" and the oxen swung left: "Whoa – whoa."

The Negroes were herding the livestock all bunched up, facing the approaching storm, bellowing and stamping their feet.

"Women and children get inside the wagons," yelled Micajah. "Everyone else crawl under them."

Strong winds slammed with fury. The canvas cover over the wagons acted as a sail catching the wind and nearly toppling them over. Then hail came, big as plums, pounding the wagon and the unfortunate animals who could only lower their heads for protection. Lightning cracked nearby and Micajah saw a ball of fire roll down the cove.

Rain fell in torrents, quickly covering the ground and running under the wagon and carts, soaking everyone beneath them to the bone. The ferocity of the rain eventually slackened to a steady downpour. It was a miserable night. There was no place to lie down in the wagon. They finally got the tents erected and crawled inside, but the ground was soaked. Little Nancy coughed and cried all night.

Micajah didn't think he'd gone to sleep, but the next morning someone woke him shaking his shoulder. He roused and saw that it was Arch.

"What's wrong?" He asked, rubbing his eyes.

"Light'n killed the milk cow," said Arch.

"What about her calf?"

"It's okay, just running around bawling and bellowing," replied Arch.

Micajah thought a moment. "The old cow's meat will be tough, but we need to

47

save what we can."

Arch and William set about butchering the cow. The meat that was too tough to eat was thrown to the dogs and the remainder was made into a stew. The livestock were turned loose to graze while the wet items were laid out to dry in the sun. All in all, the ordeal hadn't been too bad thought Micajah. There wouldn't be milk for the calf, but maybe the black mare could be coaxed to share. He was thankful. But, he was also worried about Nancy. She was coughing and running a fever.

It was past noon and the sky was a blanket of blue when Micajah cracked the whip and yelled "Hip." The caravan got back on the road and headed west. The road was muddy and the wagons were soon mired in deep ruts. They unhitched the oxen from the smaller wagons and hitched them to the large wagon and with all of the men pushing were able to move forward. But, it was slow going. After a few miles, Micajah called a halt. They would have to wait until the road dried.

After pitching camp under a large chestnut tree and turning the livestock loose to graze, Arch and William grabbed their flintlocks and rode off in search of game.

Micajah looked at Nancy lying beneath a blanket in the wagon and shaking. Sarah was kneeling beside her. He touched Nancy's forehead and it was hot.

"It's ague fever," he declared. "She needs to be purged. Get the medicine box."

Sarah located a small wooden box and opened the top and handed Micajah a bottle of Rush's Pills. Patented by America's most renowned physician, Dr. Benjamin Rush of Philadelphia, the pills were the best purgative on the market and would allegedly cure any ailment.

Sarah lifted Nancy's head. "Take this child, it will make thee well." She then gave her a swallow of beer to wash down the pill. Within minutes the purgative began working. Nancy begged to go to the woods. No sooner had she found privacy behind a tree, when her bowels exploded.

Micajah was pleased. "Rush's pills are sovereign. If she doesn't improve soon, we'll give her another dose. A being can't get well until the poisons is outta the intestines."

Late afternoon, Arch and William returned to camp, each with a deer tied across their horse. They hung the carcasses by the hind legs on a tree limb and expertly skinned them. Luther and the other hounds sat nearby on their haunches salivating as the deer were gutted. Arch sliced out the entrails and flung them among the hungry dogs, who dove into the piles of intestines and innards, snarling and fighting until each had a bloody mouthful. William then threw another mass of guts and organs to the dogs and they ate until they were sated and then went to sleep in the shade beneath the wagon.

That night the family gorged on succulent chunks of roasted venison and drank watered-down beer until they could hold no more.

The following days were uneventful. The children milked the black mare daily and gave her milk to Bonnie, the baby heifer calf. The mare didn't like her milk being stolen and neighed and stamped her feet and but never attempted to bite.

The good news was that Nancy's fever had subsided, confirming Micajah's belief that Rush's Pills were sovereign in the field of medicine.

No one went hungry. The forest was full of game and the family fattened up on wild turkey, venison and possum.

---

Micajah estimated they had traveled at least 125 miles from Wake County when they topped a ridge and he caught his first glimpse of the Blue Ridge Mountains looming ahead. Another day and a half and they would bump up against the wall of green. As the foothills gradually rose higher, movement slowed.

They stopped every few hundred feet, scotched the wagon wheels with rocks and let the oxen blow and rest, then moved forward another few hundred feet and repeated the process. Finally, they hit the wall. The road that wound through Flower's Gap was narrow and treacherous, often no more than a notch cut into the side of the mountain. One careless move by the oxen and the wagon and team would plunge into abyss. As the road grew increasingly steeper, Micajah called a halt.

"Everyone out!" he ordered. The wagons were double-teamed using spare oxen. Micajah walked alongside the wagon, his hand on the brake pole, Arch doing the same with his wagon.

Everyone else, including the women, pushed.

"Hip hip," commanded Micajah and the oxen strained forward a few yards. "Get ready to scotch!" When the oxen seemed ready to drop from exhaustion, Micajah reared back on the brake pole while someone scotched the wheels with rocks. Everyone rested, and then they repeated the process. It was slow going. As soon as they reached the top of one peak and descended, there was another one to climb.

It was late in the evening and sprinkling rain when they halted in a small cove near a gushing stream that tumbled out of the mountains, past mountain laurel, rhododendron, redbuds and dogwoods.

Micajah figured they hadn't traveled over a mile that day but he didn't care. Everyone, including the oxen, was exhausted. The Negroes had no sooner set up the tents when the sky opened up and rain fell in torrents. There would be no hot meal tonight, only leftover stale bread. Everyone went to bed hungry. He woke later that night to water running through the tent and soaking his feather bed.

Several times during the trip, doubt had crept into Micajah's mind. Tonight, it gnawed at him as never before. He was wet, miserable and exhausted and his spirits low. Mosquitoes were biting him. He couldn't sleep.

Sarah, who was also awake, spoke, "Micajah, has thee ever considered turning back?"

He didn't reply for a long time.

"I'm thinking about it now," he finally said. "What about you?"

"Yes, I have."

"Do you think we should?" he asked.

"I don't know what is best. Right now it's hard to think straight when we're both in a state of misery," she said. "Maybe we'll feel different when the sun comes up."

The next morning everyone woke wet and hungry but in better spirits. The sky was clear. Sarah had been right. She passed around the remaining stale bread while the men folk yoked the oxen.

"Let's pray that God will give us good weather until we get over the mountain," said Micajah. "Let's move out." They hadn't gone far until another problem developed. The ground was waterlogged and the wagon wheels sank into the mud, leaving deep ruts that made forward movement almost impossible. Micajah pondered the problem. They would have to triple-team the oxen with everyone pushing, move one wagon up at a time to the top of the gap and then come back and get another one.

49

It was evening and the moon was out when they finally moved the last wagon to the top of the gap. The Negroes built a big fire and soon meat was sizzling in a pot.

Dawn broke with broken clouds and Micajah and Arch climbed a rocky promontory on the spire of the Blue Ridge Mountains and looked west where undulating ridges disappeared into smoking clouds. His heart sank.

"Lord have mercy!" he exclaimed and shook his head. "How will we ever cross them?"

"I've never seen such rugged country," said Arch. "They seem to go on forever."

"Other folks have crossed them and we will too," said Micajah, without enthusiasm.

"Well, at least when we get across it should be easy going from there on," Arch said. "The worst will be behind us."

"Huh," Micajah snorted. "This is just the beginning."

Now Micajah knew in his heart there would be no turning back.

Every day was like the one before it. Shoulders to wagons, scotching the wheels with rocks, finally reaching the top of the ridge only to be confronted with more as far as the eye could see.

"Damn these mountains!" exclaimed Micajah.

As they proceeded down a steep curve, oxen pulling the wagon occupied by Ransom and Sallie were spooked by something in the nearby bushes. They bolted in the opposite direction, causing the wagon to flip over and spill the cargo into a mud hole, including a kettle of salt. Micajah ran back to inspect and found that Ransom and Sallie, as well as the oxen, were unharmed. But a wheel was broken and most all the salt was unsalvageable. The wheel would have to be repaired and he estimated it would take at least a day.

He had tools, but no lumber. He went to a wooden chest where he kept hammers, chisels, mallets, augers, planes, hatchet, axe and other tools and lifted out a saw and handed it to Arch, "You and William go 'n find a hickory tree about this big around," he said, demonstrating with his hands.

While Arch and William were absent, Mike scouted ahead and found a grassy bottom. They had already set up camp and turned the livestock loose to graze when Arch and William finally returned, dragging a small hickory log behind a horse.

"What took you so long?" asked Micajah.

"Took a while to locate the right one," said William.

Micajah chuckled. "Hickory is sovereign when it comes to making wagon spokes and axles." He sawed off a piece of the wood and shaped it into spokes. When he was satisfied that they were the proper length, he whittled the ends to fit snugly into the wheel rounds; then seasoned the wood by boiling out the sap in one of the large kettles. After it dried, he inserted the spokes into the rounds. He stepped back and admired his work. "It looks good. Mike, you 'n William sink the wheel in the creek yonder and we'll let it swell overnight." He stored the remainder of the hickory wood beneath the wagon just in case they needed it in the future.

The following morning, Mike and William removed the wheel from the creek and rolled it to the cart, greased the axle with lard and fitted on the wheel. "It's good as new," declared Arch. "Let's move out."

The delay had brought on another problem. Barney and Ransom, who had been gathering firewood, were covered with chiggers. The tiny red bugs that live on weeds, grass and bushes were ounce for ounce, more poisonous than a timber rattler. That evening when they made camp, Micajah ordered them to drop their pants. A red belt of chiggers encircled their waist and covered their testicles, not to mention the tender areas under their arms, which were also infested. They had scratched and clawed until they were bloody and miserable. He didn't have any potion in his medicine box to doctor chiggers, but he had an idea. After retrieving a saw and ax from the wagon, he hollered for Mike and William.

"Go cut a pine tree and saw it into logs about six feet in length," he said. Meanwhile, he and Arch located a sloped area and dug a trench into which they later placed the pine logs with the ends protruding. They covered the logs with kindling and dry branches and earth, and then torched the kindling. At the foot of the sloping logs, Micajah placed iron pots. "We'll have turpentine before long," he declared. When the pine logs heated, turpentine sap oozed out the ends and drained into the pots. Micajah rubbed the sticky liquid on Barney and Ransom.

"That'll be the end of chiggers," he declared. That night, he ordered that everyone, including the Negroes, apply turpentine before going to bed. "Not only is it sovereign for chiggers, it will also keep ticks at a bay," he said.

Several days later, another minor problem developed, one that Micajah had expected. While gathering firewood, the children had walked barefoot through poison oak. Mike and Ransom's feet were a red mass of itching bumps which they had scratched raw. Abigail's feet and legs were also broken out. When they stopped at noon, Micajah took action.

"Start boiling some water," he said to Sarah and walked into a nearby copse of woods, hoe in hand, in search of poke sallet. The tender leaves at the top of the stalks were fine eating when boiled and seasoned with pork lard and the purple berries made a good dye. But, he wanted the root which would dry up poison ivy. Finding a patch of poke sallet, he dug up several roots, carried them back to the camp and tossed them into the pot of boiling water. The resulting potion was a purple liquid which he applied to the inflamed skin.

"Ouch, ouch, Father this is painful, oh, oh, oh," screamed Abigail jumping and dancing up and down with pain.

"Daughter, this'll set you on fire, but it'll dry up the poison oak." He rubbed some on Mike's and Ransom's feet and they screamed and danced. "You'll be much improved by tomorrow," said Micajah. "Now stay outta poison oak!"

---

They had barely unyoked the oxen and unharnessed the horses and turned them loose to water and graze near a swift creek when Micajah heard the rumble and creaking of an approaching wagon. Ol' Luther looked up the road and barked. Micajah shaded his eyes from the setting sun and squinted up the narrow and brown dusty road. Soon a small wagon pulled by two emaciated oxen appeared, driven by a shabbily dressed man. Seated next to him was an equally shabbily dressed woman. Dirty-faced children poked their heads around the canvas wagon.

"Whoooaaa," the man commanded the oxen. "Hallo over there, mind if we share the water and grass with ya?" he asked.

"Help yourself," Micajah replied. "Where ya headed?"

51

"Back to Carolina."

Eight dirty and skinny children piled out of the wagon and stood staring at the McElroys. Wood was gathered and fire started. Sarah soon had a pork stew boiling in an iron kettle sending up mouth-watering aroma while Abigail baked bread in a Dutch oven. It was twilight when everyone lined up near the kettle and Sarah ladled stew into the bowls for her family. The dirty children watched from across the road.

"Those poor children are hungry," Sarah remarked to Micajah.

"How do you know?"

"Thee don't see them eating, do you?  They look like they are starving."

Micajah gave them a second look. "They do look poorly."

"I can't stand to see anybody go hungry, especially children," Sarah said. "We don't have much, but what we do have we can share it."

Micajah wiped his mouth with a sleeve and hollered across the road. "We have stew. There isn't much, but y'all are welcome to eat what's left."

The children looked up at their father, who nodded, then made a beeline to the stew kettle. "Don't mind if we do," he said. "I'm Joshua Hardy. What's yourn?"

"Micajah McElroy and this is my wife, Sarah and our children," Micajah said.

The Hardys ate ravenously and then sopped the kettle with bread.  The man wiped his mouth with the back of his hand.  "Where ya head'n?"

"Fayetteville, Tennessee, the Lord willing and we can get across the mountains."

The man's face hardened. "Mister, you ain't seen nothing yet. If you think it's been hard so far, just wait until you bump up against what's ahead of you.  Why them mountains are so high that they touch the sky and at every turn there is a rushing stream you have to ford. You'll be lucky if you make it. We 'bout starved to death. And two of my oxen died. That's the reason we turned back."

Micajah glanced at Sarah who was looking at him.

"Well, other folks have made the trip and we'll do it too," Micajah said.

"I wish you luck, but you'll need more than luck," said Hardy.

After the fire had died down and the children were asleep, Sarah poked Micajah who was breathing heavily. "Are thee asleep?"

"Almost."

"I've been thinking about what the strangers said.  "I can't bear to think of our children going hungry. Maybe we should consider what he said."

"And turn back?" Micajah said.

"Well, consider it."

"We've come too far to quit now," Micajah said. He laid a hand on her leg and patted.

"We'll be just fine."  But privately he had his doubts.

---

Micajah noticed that each day when they nooned, Abigail came to the back of the wagon and whispered to Nancy, then both departed together. One day as they nooned near a branch Abigail ran off. They returned shortly.

"Father - Father!" said Nancy excitedly. "Mother Hen is sett'n."

"What hen?"

Micajah knew nothing of a hen on the journey, only Ol' Red that rode the wagon with one leg tethered and crowed every morning at the crack of dawn.

"Don't you remember Father?" asked Nancy. "She always has baby chicks each spring."

"How did she get here?"

Nancy dropped her head. "I just couldn't leave her behind," she said hesitantly. "You said you didn't mind bringing her if we had space. I found space – in the small wagon."

Micajah put on a serious face, but inwardly he was pleased. "I'll overlook the matter this one time daughter, since we'll need some Wake County eggs to eat once we reach Tennessee."

"Ohhh, thank you, Father!"

"Let's go see the hen," said Micajah.

Nancy and Abigail had made a nest of leaves and grass in the back of the wagon where the hen sat. He reached to lift her up and she pecked his hand. "She's sett'n alright."

He grabbed her neck so that she couldn't peck him and lifted her up and counted seven eggs. The girls gathered more grass and leaves to make a larger nest and gave her a cup of water. Micajah shelled an ear of corn and placed kernels beside her.

"Girls, take good care of Mother Hen," he said and turned to other business.

---

"The country is much rougher up ahead," Arch said to his father following a day of scouting.

"It can't be any worse than we've crossed so far."

"I'm afraid it is. The terrain is steeper and the streams are deeper and faster."

Micajah removed his hat and finger-brushed his hair, stroking his skull. "Well, we have no choice than to keep moving forward," he said.

Arch nodded. "I knew that would be your answer."

That evening they camped beside a clear stream and after supper Micajah called his family together. "Arch says the country is rougher up ahead–" several of the children groaned.

"And that means we'll have to work harder and longer."

More groaning.

Micajah paused and studied each upturned face. The children weren't experienced enough to know that it couldn't be done, but he saw doubt on Sarah's face.

"The only way any obstacle can be overcome is by confronting it head-on and never quitting and that is what we are going to do. We'll conquer one ridge and one stream at a time. And we won't give up. Others have crossed these mountains and we'll do the same."

They were up early and ready to depart at dawn. "Tennessee is thataway!" Micajah pointed. "Let's move out."

The wagons creaked forward. Soon it became evident that Arch hadn't exaggerated. The road narrowed to a rough trail that meandered up the side of ridges and across gulleys. Afraid that the wagons would topple over, Micajah ordered everyone out. The teams were guided from the ground while someone walked beside each wagon and operated the hand brake. Micajah knew that if the load shifted, the wagon would turn over. They halted.

"We'll move one wagon over the ridge at a time," he said. The loads were repacked to prevent shifting and they inched up the hill, their backs to the wagon pushing while someone scotched the wheels with rocks. It took one whole day to get the wagons to the crest of the ridge where they rested from exhaustion. There was no water.

"We can't remain here," said Micajah. "The animals are suffering. We've got to get down to water."

They moved out at dusk, again braking and scotching wheels. Darkness fell and the uneven road became impassable. Arch walked a few yards ahead of the lead wagon, holding a lantern and directing each step. Near midnight, Micajah heard the most wonderful sound –rushing water. The animals smelled the fresh water and picked up their pace. It was all the drivers could do to restrain them.

The animals were unharnessed and made a wild dash to the rushing stream where they sucked up water until their sides bloated. It was late and everyone was exhausted and hungry, but there would be no eating tonight.

"Maybe tomorrow will be better," Micajah said to Sarah as they listened to the roaring water and fell into a deep sleep.

At early light, Micajah, Arch and William studied the stream. It was much wider, deeper and sifter than they had anticipated.

"It's the spring run-off," said William. "Maybe if we wait a few days the water will recede."

"And maybe it won't," Arch said.

Micajah was sorely disappointed – and worried. "I prayed we had seen the worst," he said. "We could rest here for several days where there is good grass for the stock and wait for the water to go down – and it eventually will. But who knows when that will be. It could be days or weeks. We can't afford to wait and see. We've got to move on."

"I'll ride up and down the stream for a mile or so and hopefully locate a better place to cross," Arch volunteered.

Micajah nodded. "Do that."

A good breakfast fire was blazing and the women were baking cornbread in the Dutch oven and frying salt pork, sending up mouth-watering aroma, when Arch returned and reported there was no better place to cross.

"If it was, the road would cross somewhere else instead of here," Micajah said, accepting that sober fact.

The stream was at least 75 feet wide and the bank had been cut low by numerous wagons, which would at least make entry and exiting easier.

They gathered rope. "We'll tie a rope to a stout tree on both sides of the stream," Micajah said and secured one end to a hickory tree. "Who wants to cross and tie off on the other side?" he asked.

"I will, Father," William answered. "I'm a pretty good swimmer." He entered the rushing stream and uncoiled the rope as he carefully made his way across. Near the middle of the stream, water rushing around his belly, he stopped and yelled: "The bottom is fairly smooth and this is the deepest place so far." William tied the rope to a tree near the bank and pulled it taut.

"Let's get the women and children across first," Micajah said.

"I believe the wagons can cross," said William, "and the more weight on them the less likely they are to wash down stream."

Micajah pondered his suggestion. "We can't take that chance. Losing a wagon

54

and our possessions is one thing, but risking someone is out of the question."

The three youngest children, Nancy, Barney and Sallie, climbed onto the backs of their older brothers, who clutched the stretched rope and inched across the rushing stream to the opposite bank. Safely across, the men returned to fetch the other women. Arch was in front. "Everyone join hands," he said. "Elizabeth you hold my hand," he commanded his wife. Next was Micajah holding Sarah's hand, then William and finally Abigail bringing up the rear. They inched across, the water coming near the necks of the women. Abigail lost her footing and water splashed in her face. She panicked. "I'M DROWNING!" She screamed and let go of the rope. William lunged for her free hand. She was thrashing in the water. "Hold my hand!" William yelled, but it was too late. The strong current swept Abigail away.

Mike, seeing his sister's predicament, ran down the stream and jumped in, catching her as she went past. Finally, he grabbed an overhanging tree limb and held on until a rope was thrown and they were pulled to safety.

"Father, I'm sorry I panicked," Abigail said, shivering in her wet clothes.

"It's alright daughter," Micajah replied and glanced at Sarah, who was drilling him with her blue eyes.

"Thee and thy hunger for land," she said and turned away.

The remainder of the day was spent getting the wagons and livestock across the stream. Ol' Red was tied at the top of a wagon and crowed all the way across. Micajah put Mother Hen and her eggs in the basket and carried them to safety.

---

A scream split the night and brought Micajah straight up on his feather bed. The hounds were barking and livestock were bellowing. The panther had finally struck! He lit a candle and grabbed his rifle and bounded out of the tent. Everyone was awake and looking in the direction of the commotion.

"Get in the wagon!" he yelled as he ran toward the livestock. Arch, William and Mike joined him, muskets in hand.

"That cat's been stalking us for days," said Micajah, short of breath. "He waited 'til the wind shifted downwind so the dogs couldn't smell 'im."

"Smart panther," said Arch. The cat screamed again. The livestock were bellowing incessantly as the hounds reached the scene. "Come on, let's hurry," said Micajah, "before he kills something."

When they reached the livestock, they were bunched together for protection. Mike yelled. "I see 'im!"

Inside the small circle of candle light, Micajah saw big yellow eyes. "He's got the calf!" exclaimed William.

The panther was black and difficult to see in the darkness, but Micajah saw him, the neck of a calf in his powerful jaws, dragging it backward into the brush. The hounds had gathered at a safe distance, barking and growling, but not quite sure they wanted to take on the big cat.

Micajah raised his rifle to fire, and was about to squeeze the trigger when the cat dropped the calf and fled into the darkness.

"Somebody check the calf," ordered Micajah. Arch walked over cautiously, carrying a candle aloft, and held it above the calf lying on the ground. "Bonnie's dead."

"Don't let the children see 'er," said Micajah. "Cut 'er up and feed the meat to the hounds."

Later, Micajah settled back on his feather bed. "Did it kill anything?" asked Sarah.

"Aye, the calf."

"Oh my! The children will be upset."

"Aye," said Micajah and blew out the candle. The cat had tasted blood and he knew it would return.

The sadness caused by the death of the calf was soon replaced with joy. "Father - Father, you must come!" It was Nancy. She was running toward the wagon where Micajah was yoking the oxen.

Micajah raised up. "What is it, daughter?"

"Mother Hen has baby chicks!"

When Micajah had finished hitching the oxen to the wagon, he walked back to the cart and looked in, counting baby chicks. The old hen clucked and pecked at his hand when he attempted to raise her to see if there were more chicks. He fed her a handful of corn kernels.

"Give 'er some water," he instructed Negro Luke. "And be sure to keep the dogs away."

"Father, I'll take good care of them and see that they are no trouble," said Nancy.

Micajah patted her on the head. "Good child, now let's move out."

The following week they made good progress, at least 15 miles a day. Everyone was in fine health and high spirits. They had been feasting on venison and wild turkey, but Arch reported that he was seeing less game. Micajah decided it was time they conducted a big hunt and stock up on meat. What they didn't eat, they could smoke for future use. They found a shady spot near a creek where there was good grass and plentiful canebrakes on the creek bank. It would be a good location to rest the livestock and give them a chance to fatten up.

"William, you and Mike stay here and watch over things," said Micajah one morning. "I'll take Arch and we'll see if we can find fresh meat."

They mounted their horses, rifles in hand, and Micajah called out to the hounds. "Heah Luther, heah!" The pack bolted from beneath the wagons, barking and yelping, anxious to hunt.

They rode up the mountain where hardwoods grew so tall that Micajah couldn't see the tops. He doubted if three men holding hands could reach around many of the trees.

"Look Father," said Arch, pointing. It was fresh bear scat. Nearby they saw draw marks on a tree and hair caught in the bark. "That's a big bear," remarked Arch. The hounds were ranging out to the front searching for scent of game. Occasionally, one would bark, but nothing more. Micajah wondered why the dogs hadn't picked up fresh bear scent, and then he heard a bark, followed by a long howl. The pack joined it.

"They're on a hot trail!" exclaimed Micajah.

"Yeah and Ol' Luther's out front," said Arch. "Just listen to 'em. It's music to my ears." Micajah had to agree. Each hound made a distinct sound and combined together they sounded like a group of musicians, all playing different instruments, but rendering a melodic tune.

"Let's go!" said Micajah. They kicked their horses in the flanks and bolted forward.

The hounds hadn't run long when Arch said, "They've treed something, probably a coon." Their sound had changed from barking to baying. When they rode up, the hounds were surrounding a tree.

Clinging to a low limb was a 600-pound bear. "It's an old bear!" exclaimed Micajah. Before Arch could raise his rifle to fire, the bear fell to the ground, either slipping or deciding to gamble on escaping.

The hounds pounced, snarling and trying to get at his flesh. The bear stood up on his hind legs and swatted the hounds like mosquitoes with his razor sharp claws. Ol' Luther went flying through the air and hit the ground, where he yelped, but didn't get up.

Arch lifted his musket and squeezed the trigger, sending a 50-caliber ball that struck the bear. The bear flinched, but didn't fall. Suddenly, the bear charged, roaring and enraged, white froth dripping from his mouth. The horses were panicking. Micajah raised his rifle and fired. A streak of fire erupted from the muzzle followed by a cloud of black smoke. Micajah didn't know if he had hit the bear or not. In an instant the smoke cleared and he saw the bear on the ground.

Arch slid out of the saddle and examined the creature. "Right through the heart," he said looking up at his father with admiration. A pitiful whining sound directed their attention to a brown heap lying on the ground. It was ol' Luther. Micajah checked him over. "It looks like had has a broken hind leg," he said. They splinted his leg, and then turned their attention toward the bear.

"He's too big to carry out," said Arch. "Let's field dress 'im here and we can pack the meat on one of the horses."

Micajah expertly skinned the animal and then gutted him, throwing entrails to the hungry hounds. Arch tied the meat across his horse and they set out for camp. Micajah rode with ol' Luther hanging across the saddle. That night while bear meat roasted over a fire, the women trimmed the fat off the remaining meat and threw it into a cast iron kettle and rendered out bear grease. The remainder of the meat, they cut into strips and smoked for future use.

---

When they reached the New River in Virginia they crossed by ferry. At Ft. Chiswell, where there was a store-tavern and other conveniences, they intersected the Great Wagon Road and stopped to rest and refurbish. Everyone was hungry for vegetables.

"Ransom, lad, you come with me," said Micajah. "I might need your help."

"Can I go too, Father?" asked seven-year-old Barney.

"Aye, I suppose so, child."

The distance to the store was short, so Micajah assisted the two boys into the saddle and lead the horses.

The tavern-store combination was run by a German with a thick accent. Micajah entered the log building and read the bill of fare: "Breakfast 20₡, dinner 25₡, supper 16 2/3₡, lodging 8 1/2₡, corn and oats per gallon 8₡, common rum per half pint 25₡, Jamaican spirit per half pint 33 1/2₡, whiskey per half pint 8₡."

"Vat for you?" asked the proprietor.

"Do you have any vegetables?"

"Nien, only turnips and turnip tops."

"What about fresh meat?"

"Just salt pork."

Micajah purchased turnips and tops.

"Zat will be three bits."

Micajah handed the German a silver dollar, which he inserted into a dollar-cutting machine and sliced the coin into eight pie-shaped bits as the McElroy children watched wide-eyed. The proprietor kept three bits and handed the remainder to Micajah.

The sack of greens and tops was draped across the saddle horn and on the return trip Micajah explained to the boys that a dollar is composed of eight bits, each one worth 12 ½₵.

"It's easy to remember," he said. "Two bits, four bits, six bits and a dollar."

He looked up at Ransom clutching the sack of greens.

"Child, if you purchased fifty cents worth of corn, how many bits would you pay?"

Ransom twisted his mouth and thought. "Four bits," he said hesitantly.

"Aye. You have learned something on this trip," Micajah said, smiling.

Sarah boiled them and added salt pork. That with fried cornbread made a sumptuous meal. "I can't wait until we have a garden and have fresh green vegetables," she said.

"If we continue to make good time we should reach our destination in time to plant a late garden," Micajah said.

"What about those mountains?" Sarah asked.

"We've been over the worst."

The Wilderness Road was wide and well-traveled and the going was easy. Large Conestoga wagons loaded with freight and pulled with six oxen moved up and down the road, churning up dust. Smaller wagons pulled by horses; ox carts and pack horses; people riding and many walking ploughed down the great road. Drovers driving bellowing cattle numbered as many as 120 head passed by, followed not long afterwards by 5,000 swine being herded to market.

Following a day of rest, the McElroys moved out down a wide valley, generally following the Holston River, the Blue Ridge Mountains in the east and the Allegehenys on the west.

They passed through Royal Oak, Seven Mile Ford, and Wolf Hills and arrived south of Saplin Grove – called Bristol by some – in the evening.

"According to local folks, we're in Tennessee," announced Micajah. "We'll camp here for the night."

"Thank thee Lord," exclaimed Sarah.

On hearing the news, the young children clapped their hands and cheered for joy.

To celebrate their arrival, Micajah went into the village and purchased milk, butter and eggs. The women baked Dutch oven biscuits and roasted wild turkey that Arch had shot that morning.

That evening, while water boiled and whistled in an iron teakettle hanging over the fire, Micajah poured a gill of rum for Arch, William and himself and stood in the dancing firelight surrounded by his family. "God above has blessed our family and our journey to a new land," he said. "Like the Israelites of Biblical times, we have braved a wilderness and finally reached the promised land. But we still have a long way to go before we reach Fayetteville and must remain strong and vigilant." He removed his wide-brimmed black hat. "Let us pray. Dear Heavenly Father, God of our forefathers, creator of the world and giver of life, thank you for guiding our little family through the mountain wilderness, for providing us with food for nourishment and making our bodies strong. Bless this fine repast and guide us onward and protect us."

No sooner had he said amen when little Nancy exclaimed, "I'll put a stop to that noise right now!" Everyone looked around just as she jammed her thumb into the whistling spout of the teakettle.

"NO CHILD!" yelled Sarah. Her warning came too late.

"AAAAAGH!" Nancy grabbed her thumb, jumped up and down with pain and ran wildly in circles. Ransom and Abigail tried to catch her to no avail.

"Child, come here!" hollered Micajah.

"Ohhh father, it hurts so much!" She alternately blew on her thumb and slung it around in the air.

"Come here and let me see," said Micajah.

Nancy reluctantly edged toward him, blowing on her thumb and groaning with pain.

"What were you thinking child?" asked Micajah.

"She wasn't thinking," interjected Barney.

"You hush!" snapped Nancy. Then to her father: "That whistling kettle was interrupting your prayer, that's why."

Micajah inspected her thumb, which was red and swollen. "You need doctoring," he said.

"Father, pleeease.... don't make me take Rush's pill.... Please."

"That wouldn't help child, lard is sovereign for burns."

Sarah dabbed lard on the thumb and blew on it. "There, that will help," she said.

"Aye, don't ever fight with a boiling teakettle again," said Micajah.

Finally they reached fairly level ground and ferried across the Holston River twice before reaching Knoxville. From there they proceeded due west; ferried over the Clinch River then encountered the Cumberland Mountains. It was rugged country where days were spent creeping up one side of the mountain, braking and scotching the wheels. When they reached the other side, they had to do the same to prevent the wagon from running over the oxen.

Rabbits prefer to feed early mornings and at twilight. In Micajah's mind, fried rabbit was sovereign when it came to good grub, especially when it was battered in flour and fried crispy brown in sizzling pork grease. The thought of it made Micajah's mouth water. There wasn't much daylight remaining when he picked up his rifle and tugged on his hat. "I'm going to bag a rabbit for supper," he said to Sarah.

"Be careful."

He whistled and called the dogs, "Heah, heah." Ol' Luther and the hounds bounded up excited, barking and howling. Shep ran up, wanting to get in on the hunt. Micajah walked off toward the creek and it wasn't long before the hounds were on a hot trail, maybe rabbit, maybe not. They loved to hunt anything. Shep didn't follow the hounds, but stayed about five steps in front of Micajah, browsing through tall grass and sniffing for rabbit, but mostly scaring grasshoppers. Micajah was listening to the hounds in the distance when he heard Shep yelp loudly then run back toward him, favoring his left back leg. Micajah saw a tiny spot of blood and immediately knew what had

59

happened. Shep had been snake bitten. Micajah crept forward and parted the tall grass. Coiled and rattling was a timber rattler, as big around as a man's arm. Micajah poked the snake with the barrel of his rifle and the snake struck, its fangs pinging against the metal. He didn't want to waste powder and lead so he found a stick and pummeled the rattler's head. When he held it high by the tail, its head touched the ground. He counted 13 rattles and a button. If Shep hadn't been in front of him he would have been bitten for sure.

Shep was whining and trying to lick his swelling leg. Micajah knew he had to get him back to camp quickly.

"Come on Shep, I'll give you a lift," he said and picked the dog up and held him under one arm.

Mike trotted up. "What's wrong, father?"

"A rattler bit 'im."

He lay Shep beneath the wagon, doctored the bite with pork and salt, and early next morning, everyone gathered, expecting to see Shep stiff and dead. Not so. Shep was on his feet, a bit wobbly, but otherwise okay. Micajah inspected the snake bite and looked up. "Like I said, pork and salt is—"

"Sovereign," interrupted Arch.

Micajah chuckled.

Days later they dropped down into a wide valley and crossed the Cumberland River by ferry before arriving in Nashville, where they turned south. The road to Lincoln County was fairly good and relatively level. Another hundred miles and they would be at their new home.

# 7 | THE PROMISED LAND

Lincoln County, Tennessee.

Late May, 1809.

The oxen huffed and blew, their tongues lolling out as they trudged up the dusty road that snaked around rolling green hills studded with hard woods and cedars. When they reached a rippling creek where water ran clear as glass, they splashed in and noisily sucked up water until their sides bloated. Micajah breathed in deeply. "Ahhh, smell that sweet honeysuckle." Above, buzzards circled lazily in the hazy blue sky searching for carrion. Nearby, a crow cawed announcing the arrival of the pilgrims. There was a noticeable excitement, especially among the laughing and chattering children. It was late May and a lovely day. They were near their destination. Even ol' Luther, whose broken leg had mended, seemed to sense the importance of the moment and moved with a livelier step. The journey was almost over. They moved on.

Micajah saw a lone rider approaching. "Whoooa." He hallooed the rider, a young fellow on a sorrel horse. "Afternoon."

The man reined his mount. "Afternoon sir," and then he looked over at Sarah and Abigail and tipped his hat. "Afternoon ladies," he added.

"McElroy's the name," said Micajah.

"Pleased to meet you. David Buchanan here. Where you folks headed?"

"Fayetteville," replied Micajah.

"It's 'bout two miles down the road, can't miss it," said the young fellow.

"We've been on the road for two months and we're plumb wore out," said Micajah. "Is there a place where we can put up for the night?"

"There's a drover stand straight ahead."

"Thanks," said Micajah.

Buchanan smiled at Abigail and again tipped his hat. "Good luck, folks." He clucked to his horse and rode off.

Micajah popped his whip. "Hip – hip."

"He likes you," said young Sallie.

Abigail smiled. "He's awfully handsome."

Shortly, they crested a rise and in front of them lay a green valley where a sparkling river snaked its way westward between low ridges. Several log buildings dotted the landscape.

"Whoa," commanded Micajah. The oxen halted and blew.

"Look!" exclaimed Micajah, pointing. "Hallelujah and praise the Lord."

The youngsters, Ransom, Nancy and Barney Linn ran up to the wagon and looked at the crude log buildings. "What is it?" asked Ransom.

"Aye child, 'tis the promised land."

The children looked at each other with dismay.

"It is?" asked Nancy, disappointed.

That evening they stopped at a drover's stand near the river, paid a fee and set up camp. Micajah cut the last notch on the wagon seat, and then counted them. There were sixty.

The livestock were put out to graze, the tents erected and firewood gathered. While Arch and the Negroes butchered a steer, Micajah rode into Fayetteville and purchased sweet milk and butter. Tonight they would feast. Sarah and the girls baked biscuits in a Dutch oven and the Negroes roasted beef over an open flame. It was late when everyone had gorged themselves on beef, butter and biscuits washed down with fresh milk. Micajah stood before the glowing embers and removed his hat.

"Tonight, my heart overflows with joy and thanksgiving," he said. "We left the home of our ancestors and traveled for two months to this new land. We've incurred foul weather, sickness, dangerous animals and hardship, but God protected and guided us with his loving hand to this promised land. To him we owe thanks. We will plant our banner in the soil of Tennessee, for it is here that we will make our stand for the future. For better or worse, we are now Tennesseans. Let us pray," he said, bowing his head. He prayed long and hard until Sarah cleared her throat several times, but he didn't care. He had a lot to thank God for.

Afterwards, he broke out rum and he, Arch and William each drank a gill.

For the first time, guards weren't posted. He crawled on his feather bed and through the open tent flaps saw a billion stars. He was thinking about what he would do tomorrow to start his new life when he fell asleep.

For the next several days they camped near the mouth of Cane Creek on property owned by James Bright. In early 1806, Bright had passed through the area with a surveying team and remained, settling on a large tract on Cane Creek. Ezekiel Norris had also arrived in the fall of 1806 and settled on 1280 acres near the mouth of Norris Creek. Perhaps the best known citizen of the county was Joseph Greer, a hero of the Battle of Kings Mountain who lived on a large estate near Petersburg. Micajah decided it would be wise to know these men.

Tennessee had been carved out of the Southwest Territory of North Carolina and as early as 1793 land grants were issued to John Hodge, Robert Walker and Jesse Comb. Later grants went to Ezekiel Norris, Matthew Buchanan and William Smith, the latter from whom Micajah derived title. In 1796, Tennessee had become the 16th State of the Union.

The bottom land along Cane Creek was fertile and thick with canebrakes. Micajah figured it would also grow good corn.

---

It was time to locate his 1,000 acres. Micajah studied the description contained in the land grant signed by Governor Sevier in 1809.

1,000 acres lying on both sides of Cane Creek a branch of Elk River, beginning at a black oak and red oak, the southwest corner of Moses and Samuel Buchanan 1800 acres survey, running thence with their line north 600 poles to two Elks on their line, thence west 160 poles to an Elm and Hackleberry on David Buchanan's 1900 acre survey and with the same South 308 poles to a hickory, Elm and horse beam his south east corner thence west 130 poles to a Hackleberry and Oak, on said Buchanan south boundary line, thence South 382 poles crossing the creek twice first at 132 poles, second at 162 poles on to a box elder and Elm, on the South banks of the creek, thence east 290 poles to the beginning.

Surveyed July 1, 1808.

62

He folded the document and placed it in his pocket. "William, saddle up our horses and come with me," said Micajah. "Arch, you stay here with the family."

He and William rode up Cane Creek in the direction of where he thought his property was located. Micajah's land description began "at a black oak and red oak tree" which was also the southwest corner of Moses and Samuel Buchanan's 1800 acre tract. Black and red oaks grew in abundance. Which ones were the beginning points?

"Buchanans are thicker'n chigger or blackberry brier," said William. "First person we met was a Buchanan, and now we are going to be adjoining neighbors. We ought to get to know them."

"We may be about to get acquainted," replied Micajah and nodded toward two approaching riders. Two men reined up.

"Howdy, y'all lost?" asked the older man.

"No sir, just searching for my land," replied Micajah.

"Well, this ain't it," said the younger fellow. "This is Buchanan land."

"Then you're who I'm looking for," said Micajah. "Maybe you can help me."

He introduced himself and William and showed them his land grant of 1,000 acres.

"Since we're gonna be neighbors we might as well get acquainted," said the elder. "I'm Moses and this is Samuel Buchanan."

After handshakes, the Buchanans led them to the black oak and red oak trees that marked Micajah's southeast corner, then rode the property line with them around the entire 1,000-acre tract. Along the creek bottom Micajah noticed that the soil was deep and fertile. The canebrakes were so thick in places that a horse couldn't pass. The higher elevation was outcropped with limestone rocks and the soil was thin, but hardwoods and cedars grew in abundance.

The oaks, chestnut and poplar would be excellent for constructing buildings and rails could be split from the cedars and chestnut. He was pleased with what he observed. And he liked his neighbors too.

"Let us know when we can help y'all get settled in," said Moses Buchanan before riding off.

Micajah moved the family onto his land and turned the livestock loose to graze on cane shoots and fat grass. There was no time to waste. The first priority was to build a temporary dwelling. Micajah selected a well-drained site on the east side of Cane Creek near a fine spring. Hamwood Road passed nearby. He and the boys quickly constructed a roomy lean-to that faced the road and roofed it with white oak shingles, which could be reused on the residence when it was completed. They dug a fire pit, and the children cleared a garden spot and planted corn, turnips, beets and such.

Transforming trees into house logs was time consuming. First, they had to be hewn. He stabilized the logs on the ground, and then made a straight line on top by using a chalk string. He scored one side of the log by making notches, and then cut several inches deep with a falling axe up to the chalk line. The remaining protrusion was chipped away and the log was smoothed with a broad axe. The other sides were flattened in the same manner until a perfectly straight log measuring twenty-plus feet was completed. Termites and ants didn't care for yellow poplar. The wood was sovereign when it came to building a house. The house was to be a "dog trot" style building with twenty-foot-square rooms on each side of an open passageway. A big fireplace would be constructed at each end of the house and a second story would run across the entire length of the building. When completed the dwelling would be large and rectangular shaped and handsome. Each log was expertly notched on the end so they would fit snugly together.

On the ground, the logs looked like a mere jumble of timber, but in Micajah's mind he saw a fine house. All that remained to be done was building foundation piers and stacking the logs. It was time to take Moses and Samuel Buchanan up on their offer of help.

Several days later on the appointed Saturday morning, Micajah rose early. Preparation had to be made. Arch had killed a deer on Cane Creek the previous day and the Negroes, Luke and John, began the slow process of roasting it over hickory coals. The fat dripping onto the simmering coals sent out an aroma that made Micajah's mouth water. Sarah made wheat bread in the Dutch oven. Everyone was excited, not only about the house, but meeting their neighbors and having fun. The Buchanans and their negroes arrived early. The men folks, under the watchful eye of Micajah, began placing large sills on limestone foundation piers, and after laying the sleepers, they began stacking logs. Meanwhile, the women prepared food and the venison slowly cooked, a breeze blowing the aroma toward the laboring men.

"Can you cook any faster?" Arch hollered to Luke, who was tending the coals. "I'm starving."

"Nah suh, massah. Meat can't be rushed."

Near 11:00 a.m. Sarah called out: "DINNERTIIIME!"

Pewter plates and forks were passed around. Abigail helped serve food. The men wasted no time lining up, elders going first, getting food and repairing to the shade of a large chestnut tree. David Buchanan paused in front of Abigail and said, "I declare, Miss Abigail, you sure do look pretty this morning."

Abigail blushed. "Why thank you, would you care for a helping of venison?"

"You already gave me a big slab," he replied.

She blushed again. "Ohhh! I did."

Buchanan smiled at her and moved forward in the line.

After the men had eaten, the women ate and finally the children. When shadows lengthened and whippoorwills called, the last log was hoisted in place. Micajah thanked each neighbor for lending a hand. "It will take quite some time to roof and shingle and lay a floor," he said, "but at least our family has shelter. I thank you mightily for coming."

He broke out a keg of whiskey he had brought from North Carolina and every man had his fill. Someone produced a fiddle, and the merriment and joy lasted until late in the evening.

White oak trees were felled and sawed into twenty-four-inch blocks. Ransom and Barney, using a froe, made shingles. Rafters were sawed and fastened with wood pegs and shingles laid. After the house was roofed, the family moved into one of the large downstairs rooms. The process of sawing and smoothing boards for the floor would require months, then there were doors and shutters to be built, fireplaces to be constructed and logs chinked.

New ground must be readied for planting. While house construction was ongoing, the Negroes went to work girding trees and clearing land.

Barney Linn, Ransom, Sallie and Nancy were assigned to mixing mud. Gray mud from the creek bank was hauled to the house, shoveled into a pit, and grass and moss

64

added.

"Children, you know what to do," said Micajah.

They jumped into the mud pit barefoot, laughing and giggling, and mixed the mud with their feet. The mud was used to chink between the logs and mortar the limestone rocks in the fireplace and chimneys. When it dried it was hard as stone.

The upstairs hadn't been completed, but by Christmas day, the family had moved into the first floor and enjoyed the warmth of a real fireplace for the first time since leaving North Carolina.

------

While Micajah was completing his home, the Tennessee Legislature passed an act carving Lincoln County out of southern Middle Tennessee, effective January 1, 1810. The act appointed five commissioners and granted them power to purchase 100 acres of land on the north bank of Elk River in the center of the county to lay out a county seat to be named Fayetteville. Two acres were to be reserved near the center for a public square where a courthouse, jail and stocks were to be built, and in the meantime, the first county court met on February 26, 1810, in Brice M. Garner's house. Sixteen Justices of the Peace were appointed, a bounty of one dollar each was allowed for wolf scalps and it was reported that 2,662 acres of land was taxable.

------

April 13, 1810.

Micajah decided he had delayed long enough. It was time to hire a lawyer. He rode to Fayetteville on a sparkling spring morning and tethered his horse to a hitching rail outside the courthouse, a crude 18-by-20-foot log building with wood shingles located in the center of a two-acre public square. A log jail, stock and whipping post was nearby. He halloed the first man he saw.

"Morn'n sir. I'm a newcomer and looking for a good lawyer."

"Then you'll wanna see Thomas Hart Benton," the man replied. "I've never had to use 'im – never had to use any lawyer, thanks to the Almighty – but folks say he's a good'un."

"Where can I find 'im?"

"I seen 'im go in the courthouse a while ago. You can usually find 'im at Garner's Tavern at dinner time."

The man pointed to a two-story log building facing High Street.

"Much obliged," Micajah said. He squinted at the sun and decided he had at least an hour and a half to kill before dinner time.

He ambled across the dusty street littered with piles of horse manure and covered with flies and walked around the square where shabby log buildings housed businesses. The courthouse sat between Market and South Streets which ran east-west and Water and High streets that ran north-south; the latter going down to Elk River where a ferry was located and rates posted. "Wagon, team and driver, 50¢; cart or 2 wheel carriage 25¢; man and horse 6 ¼ ¢; footman, 6 ¼ ¢ and horses, cattle, hogs and sheep, 2¢ a head."

The town spring was appropriately located near the corner of Spring and Mud Streets.

Before noon, Micajah stepped into the dark, smoky noise of Garner's Tavern.

He took a table in the corner near the door and studied the bill of fare posted on the wall.

"Good whiskey per half pint, 12 ½ ¢; good peach brandy per half pint, 12 ½ ¢; good west India rum 25¢; good dinner, breakfast and supper, 25¢; good lodging 6 ¼ ¢; good stabledge, hay or fodder for horses 25¢ and good corn per gallon 6 ¼ ¢"

Micajah looked around. A stairway led to the upper floor where rooms were located, and through an open back door he saw where horses were stabled. Across the room, a half dozen men or more were clustered around someone who was talking a loudly and creating much laughter and leg slapping. A man came from behind the counter and walked over.

"Howdy mister. What fer ya?" he asked.

"Aye, your whiskey is priced high," Micajah said. "A half pint cost only 8 ½ ¢ at Ft. Chiswell on the Great Wagon Road."

"Folks are flock'n in here faster than we can supply 'em."

Micajah nodded. "Aye, a half pint of the good whiskey," Micajah said, emphasizing "good," and plopped a half bit on the table.

The man returned and set a cup of whiskey before Micajah. "Hadn't seen you around here before," he said.

"Arrived here about a year ago," Micajah took a sip. "Aye, 'tis good whiskey."

"Name's Aaron Garner," the man said. "What's your'n?"

"McElroy – Micajah McElroy. Live out on Cane Creek."

"Whatche do?"

"Builder and carpenter by trade."

"I have it on good information that the county court is fix'n to build a new courthouse to replace the log one," Garner said. "Brice Garner, who owns this tavern, is also court clerk. He's my relations, you know; says bids will be put out soon."

Micajah perked up. "Aye, 'tis good to know. Thank you sir."

"What brings you to town today?"

The whiskey warmed not only Micajah's insides but also loosened his tongue. "Come to have a deed drafted. Was told that Thomas Hart Benton is a fine lawyer and could be found here."

"He's always in town on the fourth Mondays in February, May, August and November; that's when court is held. He may be away riding the Circuit."

"Somebody told me that they saw him at the courthouse," Micajah said."

"Then, he'll be here 'bout noon. He's a man to keep your eye on; good lawyer, an officer in the militia, aide-de-camp to General Jackson and on top of that a State Senator. They say he's smarter'n a whip and ambitious as Caesar himself."

"Would you point him out when he comes in?" Micajah asked.

"Sure."

Loud laughter interrupted their conversation. Micajah glanced over at the cluster of men.

"Ah, that's Davy Crockett," Garner said. "He lives up on Mulberry Creek. Comes to town occasionally to buy lead and powder. Spends most of his time hunting bear and spinning tales. Pretty good at both of 'em too."

Micajah asked Garner if he knew Joseph Greer.

"Everybody does. He's the hero of the Battle of King's Mountain. Lives up near Petersburg on Cane Creek. Owns a large tract there."

"Aye, would sure like to meet the gentleman sometimes," Micajah said.

"You'll know him when you see him coming."

Micajah lifted his eyebrows as it to ask why.

"He's the biggest man I ever saw."

The tavern began filling up with customers.

"I better git back to work," Garner said.

Just then a distinguished looking young man in his late 20's, large of stature and dressed in black pants, vest and frock coat with white shirt and black cravat entered the tavern. He had a chiseled face and long prominent nose.

"That's Benton," said Garner. "I'll introduce you." He went over and spoke to Benton and pointed toward Micajah.

Micajah rose and extended his hand.

"Senator, I'm Micajah McElroy. Please join me."

"Awfully nice to make your acquaintance," Benton said, shaking Micajah's hand.

"Aye, I was told that you are the best."

Benton gave a false laugh and asked, "How can I help you?"

Micajah got down to business. "Back in 1805, William Smith was granted a Revolutionary land warrant of 1,000 acres bordering Cane Creek. Through various assignments I ended up with it in 1806. I employed William Polk to survey the tract and obtain a grant. In return, I promised to deed him 400 acres for his work. Polk did what he promised and I'm going to do what I promised – deed him his share." Micajah pulled out the grant signed by Governor John Seveir from his coat pocket and handed it to Benton, who examined it.

"It looks in good order. When do you need it?" he asked.

"As soon as possible."

"I'll prepare it after dinner. Is that soon enough?"

"Aye, that's fast service," Micajah said.

When Micajah went to Benton's small law office on the square that evening, the latter was seated at a table on which sat ink, quill pen and law books. Benton handed Micajah the deed written in flowing script, the black ink shiny on the stiff paper. "All you need to do is go to the courthouse with William Polk and both of you sign the deed and have it acknowledged by Bruce Garner, the Clerk," Benton said. "Then record it."

Micajah paid Benton and got up to leave.

"Where do you come from?" said Benton.

"Wake County, North Carolina."

Benton smiled. "I was born at Harts Mill in Orange County near Hillsboro. It's only a rock throw from Wake County."

"Aye, I was with the patriot militia when Fanning captured Governor Burke at Hillsboro and marched off to Wilmington. We ambushed them at Lindley's Mill."

"Every North Carolinian has heard of that battle," said Benton rising to his feet. "I'm honored to know you sir."

Arriving home, the women and especially Sallie and young Nancy were eager to hear about Fayetteville.

"Father, when can we go there?" asked Sallie.

"Daughter, there are too many taverns and the prices are sky high. It isn't a fitt'n place for women and children to visit."

Micajah had worried that he had made the wrong decision by uprooting his family and moving to Tennessee; worried that they wouldn't make the long journey, and then upon arriving worried that he wouldn't complete the house before winter set in. None of those worries had materialized. Now he worried about not finding construction work.

"Thee worry too much," said Sarah one winter evening as they sat before the fireplace. "The Lord will provide for us what we need and when we need it."

Micajah busied himself finishing out the inside of the house, constructing doors and shutters. There was talk around the county about building a new courthouse and Micajah thought about that a lot. If the county commission did decide to construct a new courthouse and he could land the contract, not only would he earn money, but could demonstrate his building skills. The present courthouse was barely large enough to seat a jury of twelve, a bench for the Judge and a table for the lawyers.

William returned from Fayetteville one afternoon in early November with great news.

"Father, the county commissioners are soliciting bids to construct a new courthouse on the square," he said.

"The Lord does provide," Micajah mumbled to himself.

"Sir?"

"I said that's great news."

He and William obtained the plan and specifications and reviewed them. It was to be "40 feet square, with a stone foundation and two-story brick walls." Fireplaces were to be located in each corner of the second floor, which was accessed by stairs in the northwest corner. They agreed they could do the job and submitted a bid for $3,995.

Waiting for a reply seemed to take forever. It gave Micajah something else to worry about.

"Why don't they meet and decide?" he mumbled to Sarah.

"Thee must be patient."

"I wonder how many other bids have been submitted?" he asked mostly to himself. The uncertainty bothered Micajah. The following morning he and William rode to town and learned that the commissioners were meeting that very week. A decision would soon be made. Now, all he had to do was wait. The answer came within a few days. They were awarded the contract – provided they post a performance bond to complete the job on or before November 1, 1813.

On May 27, 1811, Micajah and William posted a performance bond, and two days later, as instructed by Thomas Hart Benton, he met William Polk at the courthouse. In the presence of Brice M. Garner, they signed the deed for 400 acres.

There was much celebration at the McElroy home. Micajah brought out the whiskey barrel and measured out a gill each for William, Arch and himself. He raised his cup. "To the finest courthouse in Tennessee," he toasted.

"Hear hear."

I've settled matters with Polk, now it's time to look to a bright future," he said.

There was no time to lose. Footings were to be dug and foundations poured, brick laid, timber cut and sawed ... the list went on.

"With winter coming on there will be many days that we can't work," said

Micajah. "And there is always the unexpected. If we fail to complete the job by November 1, 1813, we will have to pay a penalty for each day we go past the completion date. That happens, not only could we not earn a profit, we could go in the hole."

December was a bad time to do any type of masonry work. If the temperature dropped below freezing, work had to be stopped. The Negroes had dug the footing and begun pouring the foundation, but there were many days they couldn't proceed – too cold.

Finally, the Negroes began laying limestone slabs to form the foundation, followed with rows of brick on top. The masonry work was going well. Just past 8 a.m. on December 16th, while Micajah was inspecting the foundation, he felt his body sway. He pawed at the air to steady himself. He saw the Negro sway and stumble and heard bells ringing simultaneously over town, but not in a methodical manner as when pulled by a rope. It seemed that the earth was moving. He saw the rows of brick crack. William was also reeling and yelling. The Negroes began moaning, crying out and praying. The earth was moving! Micajah fell to the ground as the earth shook.

"EARTHQUAKE!" someone yelled. Scared, Micajah suddenly felt insignificant in the presence of God's power. "God spare us!" he cried out.

The quake lasted at least ten minutes, but seemed an eternity. He stood long enough to see that the foundation was cracked before an aftershock flung him back to the ground. Aftershocks lasted for days. The foundation would have to be dug out, removed and rebuilt. Time was fleeting. Weeks later Micajah heard that the earthquake was centered north of Memphis and was so strong church bells rang as far away as Richmond, Virginia and water was sloshed in Charlotte. Some folks swore that the Mississippi River had run backward.

---

On a cold and cloudy afternoon, the temperature near zero and three inches of snow on the ground, no work could be done at the courthouse, so Micajah and the boys went rabbit hunting.

Sarah sat near the warm fireplace operating her spinning wheel. Sallie and Nancy, now 13 and 10 respectively, were assisting her. Sallie fashioned wads of cotton lint into bulky ropes that were fed around the spinning wheel, and after Sarah spun them, Nancy wound the finished threads around a spindle. Later, they would weave threads into homespun clothes. Sarah and the girls enjoyed these rare moments when the men were absent. They could talk and laugh and be silly without fear of chastisement.

"Mother, tell us about when you and father courted," said Sallie.

"Yes please do!" chimed Nancy.

Sarah looked up, somewhat surprised, and continued to peddle the foot treadle on the spinning wheel. "Children, why on earth do thee want to know about that?"

"Welll….. I'll be courting pretty soon and need to know about such thing," said Sallie, blushing.

"She already knows a lot," interjected Nancy.

"No I don't!"

"You told me you knew everything there was to know about courting."

Sallie gave her younger sister the evil eye. "You hold your tongue."

"You hold yours!"

"Now girls, don't argue," said Sarah.

"Tell us, please," begged Sallie.

"My mother never talked about such things when I was a child – or even in later years," said Sarah. "Like you, I always wondered about her younger years."

Sallie and Nancy continued doing their chores, eyes on their mother, waiting for her to tell them.

"Anyway, the first time your father came courting, he was wearing a coonskin cap which I made fun of."

The girls giggled.

"How long did you court?" asked Sallie.

Sarah looked up at the ceiling as if searching for an answer. "I don't rightly remember, but we saw each other at church and wakes. Sometimes he and his coon hound, Ol' Luther would walk over to our house and we would sit in the parlor and court."

"Ol' Luther?" asked Nancy.

"Yes, every coon dog thy father owned has been named Ol' Luther."

"I should have known it wasn't our Ol' Luther - the one we have now," said Nancy.

"Nancy, will you please not get mother off the subject?" said Sallie.

"Thy father was quite handsome," continued Sarah.

"Where were you when he proposed?" asked Sallie.

"At home. I'll never forget that day as long as I live."

"Tell us!" said Sallie, clapping her hands with anticipation.

"I didn't know he was going to propose. While I was doing housework upstairs, he was downstairs talking to Father. Next thing I know, he came running up the stairs. Scared me half to death. He dropped to one knee, took my hand and started talking so fast I couldn't understand a word he said –"

"Father was on one knee!" exclaimed Sallie.

"Yes. So nervous he could hardly talk. Just babbling."

"Ohh… that's so sweet," said Sallie, smiling.

"I told him to slow down; that I didn't understand what he said. Then he said, 'will you marry me?' I was shocked."

"What did you say?"

"When I came to my senses," I said, "Micajah McElroy get thee up and kiss me.'"

"You didn't!" exclaimed Nancy, hand to her mouth.

"Sure did," said Sarah smiling.

"Ohhh, that's so sweet," said Sallie again.

They had just finished the spinning when Micajah entered the room, stamping snow from his boots and holding aloft two rabbits in each hand. "Aye, fried rabbit tonight," he exclaimed. "Ladies, get the grease hot."

Sallie jumped up and ran to him. "Father, I love you so much," she said wrapping her arms around his waist. Micajah looked puzzled at the sudden outburst of emotion. "If I'd known that killing rabbits would've brought on so much love, I'd been hunting every day."

The women looked at each other and laughed.

70

# 8 | WAR OF 1812

Fayetteville.

Late June, 1812.

The weather was warm and pleasant and courthouse grew taller each day. Barring unforeseen trouble, Micajah was confident that he and his sons could complete construction by November 1, the following year. But trouble was brewing. Far away from the pristine streams and rolling green hills of Lincoln County, politicians in Washington City were debating Great Britain's latest outrages against the United States.

The approaching war was certain to affect construction of the courthouse, but Micajah was prepared to accept the consequences. The English devils had to be defeated once and for all. In addition to boarding American ships and impressing sailors into the British Navy, the British were stirring up Indians against frontier settlers. Among the Congressional War Hawks, led by Henry Clay of Kentucky, was Felix Grundy of Tennessee, whose fiery speeches before Congress calling for a redress of grievance helped steer America to declare war on June 18, 1812.

President James Madison asked Tennessee to help defend the "Lower Country." Tennesseans responded enthusiastically and in large numbers. General Andrew Jackson, commander of the West Tennessee Militia immediately organized an expedition to Natchez, Mississippi, but after suffering great privation to get there, it was summarily recalled.

It was early September, 1813, and as was customary on Sundays – and expected by Sarah McElroy except in cases of illness – all of her eight children, sons- and daughters-in-law and grandchildren were present for dinner. Micajah sat at the head of the long board table and Sarah at the other end. In between, the adults sat elbow to elbow, talking and laughing while the children patiently waited to eat afterwards. Big Annie was jabbering to herself as she placed bowls of pork stew and corn hoecakes on the table. Outside, the hounds began barking and raising cane.

"Somebody be a com'n," Big Annie muttered.

"Aye, a visitor," said Micajah. "Put out an extra plate, Big Annie."

"Yassuh Massa," she replied and peered out the front window.

"Who is it?" Micajah asked.

"It be Mistuh Samuel Buchanan and he be in an awful big hurry."

Micajah pushed away from the table and opened the front door just as Buchanan slid from the saddle. His chestnut mare was lathered and her nostrils were flared and sucking air.

Before Micajah could invite his neighbor inside for dinner, Buchanan blurted out: "I just heard the news a while ago in town and was head'n home; thought I oughta stop and tell you –"

"What?"

"The Creeks massacred nearly 300 men, women and children at Fort Mims, north of Mobile several days ago."

Micajah was speechless for a moment.

"The militia will be called up," Buchanan added.

"Aye," Micajah said. "When the truth comes out, the British devils will be found with their hands in this crime."

Back inside, Micajah resumed his place at the head of the table and when

71

questioned about Buchanan's visit, said only, "'Tis not fitting to discuss among the women folk."

Afterwards, when the men gathered outside to smoke their pipes, Micajah revealed what Buchanan said.

"I'm going to join up and fight," said Micajah, Jr.

"We all might have to," Arch added. "Those red devils need to be killed before they reach Fayetteville."

Micajah sucked on his pipe as all eyes turned toward him. "Aye, I know how you feel. I feel the same. The Creeks must be punished severely for their crime." He paused. "But remember this: I'm depending on you boys to help me complete the courthouse. If you go away to fight, what am I do?"

The news of the massacre spread like wildfire. On August 30, approximately 750 "Redstick" Creeks had attacked Fort Mims located some 40 miles north of Mobile. They entered through an open gate and butchered 247 men, women and children. Children were seized by the legs and their brains battered out against the stockade. Women were scalped alive and those pregnant were sliced open and the fetus removed and killed. After the barbarity was completed, they torched the fort.

Tennesseans were scared, especially those living in Lincoln and the tier of counties bordering the Mississippi Territory. South of the Tennessee River was Creek country and that was only 40 miles from Fayetteville. Rumors were rampant. It was reported that Creek warriors were advancing toward the Tennessee River and could strike the Lower Country at any moment.

General Andrew Jackson called for volunteers.

"Brave Tennesseans," he exclaimed. "Your frontier is threatened with invasion by the savage foe. Already they advance towards your frontier with their scalping knives unsheathed, to butcher your wives, your children, and your helpless babe's. Time is not to be lost."

Colonel John Coffee immediately marched to Huntsville and took up a blocking position. Governor Blount ordered General Jackson to call out 2,500 militia to rendezvous at Fayetteville and the legislature authorized raising 5,000 men to serve for three months.

In early September, when it was hot and dry and leaves were caked with dust and "dog days" hadn't yet ended, volunteers began pouring into Fayetteville by the hundreds. One was David Crockett who lived east of Fayetteville on Bean's Creek with his family. Crockett had ridden to nearby Winchester and joined Captain Francis Jones' Company, 2nd Regiment of Volunteer Mounted Riflemen.

The dusty streets were clogged with hundreds of horses, and braying mules, wagon and carts hauling supplies to provision the gathering army. Taverns were filled night and day with men drinking, bragging and brawling. Volunteers swarmed to the south bank of Elk River, where several ancient white oaks near the road to Huntsville marked the rendezvous site at Camp Blount.

---

It was a hot, dry afternoon when Arch McElroy heard horses approaching from the east on Market Street. He laid down the planer he was using to smooth floor boards for the new courthouse, straightened and mopped sweat from his brow. A hundred or more armed and mounted men moved slowly down the dusty street, hooves partly muffled by the dust which rose in a brown cloud. Talking and laughing, the men, for the most part, wore brown woolen hunting shirts belted with untanned deer skin and slouch hats made from raccoon and fox skins. Their hair was long and unkempt as was their whiskers.

Folks lined up along the street and cheered as they rode past, before turning south to ford Elk River. Arch watched with admiration.

"Aye, that would be Capt'n Jones' Company from Winchester," Micajah said.

"They seem happy to be going off to war," Arch said.

One of the militiamen, a tall fellow with black hair who sat erect in the saddle, yelled to Arch. "Come with us."

"Aye, I've seen that man before," Micajah remarked. "Now I remember. It was at Garner's Tavern about three years ago. He's the bear hunter and teller of tall tales."

Arch watched in silence for a long time. He was embarrassed. Family men were going off to fight the Creeks and he, with no children, was remaining at home. Micajah sensed what he was thinking.

"'Tis not for every man to go fight."

"You left Mother to go fight Tories," Arch said. "You did your duty. How am I any different?"

"If every man enlisted and left home, who would defend the women and children?" Micajah replied. Nevertheless, Arch had a strong urge to go. Enlistment was short and he would be back home next spring in time to break ground and plant corn, tobacco and a patch of cotton.

Arch returned to planing boards, but his thoughts swirled of war.

---

That evening, after suppering on roasted venison, Arch sat outside his cabin in an effort to catch a breeze. A symphony of croaking frogs, chirping katydids, crickets and July flies filled the hot night. He packed his pipe and smoked in silence. Elizabeth walked up behind him and placed her hand on his shoulder.

"Capt'n Jones' Company from Winchester passed through town today," he said casually. "One of 'em hollered at me and said that I oughta go with 'em." He felt her fingers dig into his shoulder.

After a long silence, she asked, "What did you say?"

"Nothing."

She exhaled loudly, "Thank goodness!"

"Because I was too embarrassed," he quickly added.

"Now, Archibald McElroy, you don't have any business leaving me here and going off and getting yourself scalped and killed by savages."

"A man has to do his duty," he said. "I don't feel right about staying home when the men are off fighting my battles. If the Creeks ain't defeated, they're liable to show up here murdering and scalping women and children."

"I know that you're right, but if all the men go south to fight, who's gonna stay here and protect us?"

"That's what Father said."

"And anyway, your Father needs you to complete the courthouse," she added.

He turned around and through the dingy light could see her eyes glistening with tears. "I just don't want you to go Arch," she said haltingly. "Promise me that you won't."

"I'll think about it."

That night he lay in bed, fully awake, Elizabeth's warm body closer to him than usual, and pondered his dilemma. A strong sense of duty told him that he should enlist and take his place in the army with the other men and defend the frontier. He had never been to war and the prospect of doing so promised great adventure. He was 33 years old and had settled down to a good, but somewhat boring, life. On the other hand, he felt a strong sense of duty toward Elizabeth and her happiness. She was a good woman and a good wife.

The following morning at breakfast, he announced his decision to her.

"I've figured out a compromise," he said. "I promise I won't enlist right away. Maybe the war will be over soon and I won't have to go fight."

---

Several days later, Arch was visiting with his father when his younger sisters, Sallie and Nancy, burst into the house jabbering and pointing toward Hamwood Road.

"What is it daughters?" Micajah asked.

"Soldiers!" exclaimed Nancy.

"I'll tell Father," interrupted the older Sallie. "We went to the spring to fetch water when I looked up the road and saw soldiers coming this way."

Micajah and Arch walked to the front yard just as several men on horseback rode past. Micajah recognized the tall man with the bandaged left shoulder at the head of the long column and hollered, "Welcome, General Jackson!"

The man turned his head, looked directly at Micajah and raised his right hand and rode on.

"Aye, I use to see him when he came to Fayetteville as a Circuit Judge," Micajah remarked.

General Jackson took command of the volunteers bivouacked across the river. Between reveille each morning and retreat at night, citizens were allowed to enter Camp Blount. That's when Arch got a close look at General Jackson. Gaunt and pale as a ghost with his left arm in a sling, he was 46 years old and stood 6 feet tall. He looked sickly, Arch thought. And he was right. Jackson had been shot during a brawl in Nashville by his aide-de-camp, Thomas Hart Benton, and his brother, Jesse.

It happened shortly after Jackson returned to Nashville following his aborted march to Natchez. One could never believe second-hand information, but Arch understood that the conflict grew out of a quarrel between Major William Carroll and Jesse Benton, brother of Thomas Hart Benton. A duel ensued with Jackson acting as Carroll's second. Jesse Benton took a ball in his ass and Carroll was shot in his hand. A ball in the ass proved more embarrassing than lethal. Thomas Hart Benton was mortified at his brother's embarrassment and blamed his commander and friend, Andrew Jackson. He made derogatory statements about Jackson. The quarrel boiled over in front of the City Hotel in Nashville where Thomas Hart and Jesse Benton were standing in the entrance. Someone drew a pistol. No one disputed that Jesse Benton fired the first shot at Jackson, who caught a ball in his left shoulder. Another ball entered his left arm. When the shooting and cutting ended, Jackson lay in a puddle of blood, near death.

October 11, 1813.

The day dawned clear and chilly with the breath of fall in the air. Arch stood on the north bank of Elk River and watched Jackson's Army march south to fight the Creeks. When the last column was out of sight, he rode home. There was firewood to cut, fodder to pull and bundle and cotton to pick, none of which promised adventure. And then there was the courthouse, which was almost completed.

Late that evening, news came that the Army passed through Huntsville and crossed the Tennessee River at Ditto's Landing.

---

Micajah need not have worried. Confronted with freezing weather, rain, earthquake and war, he persevered and completed the courthouse by November 1, 1813. Dedication was scheduled for Saturday afternoon. He woke early, too excited to sleep – that and his aching bones. He walked out into the chilly morning and studied the sky. Not a cloud anywhere. A perfect day was in the making. Shortly, the family was awake and moving around. Sarah and the daughters were helping Big Annie prepare breakfast while the boys fed the livestock. Everyone was excited about going to Fayetteville, especially the girls who were discussing which bonnet to wear.

At the breakfast table, Sarah looked over at Micajah and said, "All of the hardships we endured crossing the mountains to get here were worth it. Thee has built a courthouse that will be a monument to thy skills."

"And don't forget William and the boys," Micajah quickly added. "We built it together."

"When can we leave, Father?" Sallie asked.

"Aye, after chores are done," Micajah said. "But before we go, all of you hear what I have to say." The children perked up, looking at their father.

"Fayetteville is filled with taverns, drunken men and sin. Temptation is everywhere. We'll stay together at all times. Daughters, I caution you to be ladies and don't dare leave your mother's presence. Is that understood?"

"Yes Father," they answered. The Negroes, Luke and John, who had helped build the courthouse, drove the two-horse wagons to the front of the house and waited. They were smiling from ear to ear as the horses stamped on the ground, anxious to get under way. The cool air was exhilarating. Micajah came out of the house, his family following. "Women will ride in the front wagon with me and your mother," he said. "Barney, you and Ransom and Mike ride with William and Arch."

Everyone loaded into two wagons, excited to be on the way. Luke popped his whip. "Git up hosses, we be gwine to town." The wagons creaked forward down Hamwood Road toward Fayetteville.

The rutted and dusty streets were teeming with people, dogs, horses, mules and wagons. Folks were pouring in from all over the county. The children were bug-eyed and squirming with excitement. "I've never seen this many people in my life," said 11-year-old Barney.

"Nor have I," added Nancy, who was 10.

Micajah helped his family out of the wagon and instructed Luke and John to find a hitching place and return.

"Yessuh, Massa," Luke said. "Come on John, you heard de Massa."

The new courthouse, its front draped with red, white and blue bunting, was a perfectly square, two-story, red brick structure that sat in the middle of town. It was the largest and most stately building in Lincoln County. Micajah swelled with pride when he looked upon it.

"Look, children," he said, pointing to the flag with 17 stars and 17 stripes waving over the building. "Who would have thought that America would have grown to seventeen states? Ransom, when I was your age, there was no such thing as the United States or a President. We were colonies, ruled by King George III of England. Now, we rule ourselves." Somewhere a drum and fife group was playing. Near the town spring, Negroes were barbecuing dozens of shoats over slow burning coals. Barking dogs raced past while young children pulled against their parents' hands, trying to get free to enjoy the excitement. Folks were talking and visiting with old friends and neighbors. It was a carnival atmosphere.

Someone beckoned Micajah to the front of the courthouse where a dais and chairs were located. David Buchanan walked up, removed his hat and slightly bowed. "Why Miss Abigail, what a surprise and delight to see you. You sure look pretty as a picture, if I do say so myself."

Abigail blushed. "Thank you David."

Buchanan spoke to the rest of the family. "Mister McElroy, do I have your permission to stroll with Miss Abigail?"

Micajah hesitated and glanced at Sarah, who nodded with approval.

"I guess that will be okay."

Sallie butted in. "Father, can Nancy and I go too?"

"Children, I've already told you –"

"Thee are letting Abigail go," Sarah interjected. Abigail frowned. David spoke up. "Let them come with us, they'll be no trouble at all."

Micajah hesitated and stammered. "I don't know… well... okay. But you watch them like a chicken hawk. Don't go near any taverns and be back here when the ceremony starts."

David Buchanan placed Abigail's hand on his right arm and they walked off, the two young girls following and giggling. Sarah watched them and smiled. "Ain't that sweet?" she said to Micajah. "Remember when we used to do that?"

The reverberating boom of cannon opened the dedication ceremony. Dogs jumped straight up and howled. Babies cried. Folks laughed and clapped with merriment. When the drum and fife crops struck up *Yankee Doodle*, the crowd roared its approval. After several numbers, Littleton Duty, a member of the County Court mounted the steps and raised his arms. "Citizens of Lincoln County, welcome to the dedication of the finest courthouse in Tennessee."

Loud cheering and clapping erupted. "This stately edifice, this hall of justice is a rousing symbol demonstrating that citizens of Lincoln County are not only civilized and progressive, but respecters of the rule of law as well," he said. "No man, woman or child is safe in our community and no property is secure without the rule of law."

Following his remarks, Commissioner Duty introduced members of the County Court who had authorized the construction of the courthouse, and then turned to Micajah. "Micajah McElroy and his family came here from Wake County, North Carolina, only four years ago and during that time he has shown himself to be a first-class citizen, not to

76

mention being a master builder. This edifice will be a monument of his skill for years to come. Show him your appreciation."

Loud and long applause. Micajah beamed and stepped forward and bowed.

Following several speeches, the crowd drifted toward the town spring for barbecue pork. Micajah stretched his neck searching for his daughters. "Have you seen them?" he asked Sarah.

"Thee worry too much. They are with Abigail and will be fine."

A man approached Micajah. "Good afternoon sir, I'm William McClellan. I heard them say you are from Wake County. I am recently from Rockingham County."

Micajah offered his hand. "Welcome, I think you will find Lincoln County a fine place to live."

McClellan, whose ancestor had emigrated from Northern Ireland, said that he and his wife and two-year-old son, Thomas Joyce had settled on Cane Creek.

McClellan had just stepped away when the largest man Micajah had ever beheld walked up, and extended his ham-sized hand and said, "Hello sir, I'm Joseph Greer and I offer my congratulations. You have constructed a fine courthouse that all of us can be proud of."

Micajah looked up at the giant towering over him. Greer was at least six feet seven inches tall, well-proportioned and dressed in an aristocratic style of a Virginia gentleman. Every Patriot knew of Greer. When the war was going badly in the south, Greer and approximately 910 "over the mountain men" whipped Major Patrick Ferguson's Tories at Kings Mountain, South Carolina, on October 7, 1780. Greer had ridden approximately 500 miles to Philadelphia and delivered the good news of victory to the Continental Congress.

"Sir, I'm honored to meet you," Micajah said grasping his hand. "What you and the other Patriots did at Kings Mountain was a turning point in the Revolution."

Micajah was worried about his daughters. "Ransom, go find your sisters and tell them to come. It's time to eat."

"Yes Father." Ransom and departed through the crowd, proud to be on an important mission. Shortly, he returned with Sallie and Nancy in tow.

Late afternoon, Micajah was still beaming when the family loaded into the wagons and headed home. It had been a good day – no, a great day.

He turned around and asked Sallie and Nancy, "Daughters, which part of the festivities did you enjoy most?"

Both girls froze and looked at each other. "All of it, Father," Sallie replied hesitantly.

"Nancy, what did you enjoy most?"

"What should I say?" Nancy whispered to Sallie.

Ransom piped up. "I can tell you, Father."

"Mind your own business," Sallie said giving her brother the evil eye.

"Tell me what?" asked Micajah.

"I saw them walk past Garner's Tavern –"

"Ransom, hush your mouth!" scolded Sallie.

"And they peeked inside."

Their mother gasped. "Thee didn't! Oh, I feel faint."

"Aye, the devil is a tricky one," said Micajah. "Always preying on the minds of youth."

News filtered back to Fayetteville that Jackson's Army had bloodied the Creeks at Tallusahatchee and Talladega in the Mississippi Territory. On March 27, 1814, the "Redstick" Creeks stockaded themselves at Horseshoe Bend on the Tallapoosa River, where Jackson's volunteers slaughtered 750 of them. Sam Houston, wounded and bleeding, was among the first to scale the log barricades and attack the Indians. Except for some minor skirmishes, that battle ended the Creek War, but the war against the British continued to rage.

In August, after advancing Redcoats put the American government in flight, they burned the Capitol, White House and other public buildings. The only bright news on the home front was that Mike McElroy married Rachel Simpson of neighboring Madison County in the Mississippi Territory on August 24.

Arch had lost the battle with his conscience. The courthouse was completed. It was time to act.

Fayetteville.
September 28, 1814.
Arch McElroy rode south on Hamwood Road, the big bay gelding's hooves stirring up dust. The morning chill had burned off, the sky was deep blue and the creek bottom was white with cotton where Negroes picked the "White God" and placed it into large baskets. It was the kind of day that ought to make a man feel good.

Arch was troubled. The previous day, Samuel Buchanan had reported that Captain William Martin was in town recruiting men to go south and fight the British. Elizabeth was dead set against him enlisting. He understood her feelings. No woman wanted her man to go off and risk getting killed. Yet, if every man acceded to his wife's wishes, who would protect the family and community? Her argument was that the Creeks had been defeated and no longer posed a threat. But the British were a threat. They had already put President Madison and the government in flight and burned the capital. If he didn't help defeat the British, then who would?

He topped the rise north of town and rode south down High Street toward the handsome new brick courthouse that rose above the shabby buildings that surrounded the square. He swelled with pride at seeing the magnificent structure.

Fayetteville was teeming with people, and animal hooves and wagons wheels had churned the street into a dust bowl.

Across the street where Thomas H. Benton's law office was once located, a handful of men clustered around a man seated behind a table on the front porch. A younger man holding a rifle in a military stance was standing next to him. Arch reined, tethered the bay and sauntered over.

"As I was saying," said the man seated at the table with a ledger book, ink well and quill pen, "I'm Captain William Martin and I'm filling out a company of volunteers to march south with General Coffee and help General Jackson whip the British –"

"How far south?" a man asked.

"Mobile. That's where General Jackson is currently located."

"I don't mind fight'n for Old Hickory," another fellow said. "I know he'll fight to win. But what about the officers under 'im?"

"Like I said, General Coffee will command the Volunteers," replied Martin. "Colonel Thomas Williamson will command the regiment and I'll command one of the companies. We've all had experience fighting the Creeks. I was at Tallusahatchee and Talladega where we bloodied them good."

"How much is the pay and for how long?" a young fellow asked.

"Eight dollars a month for six months."

The assembled men glanced at each other and nodded. "Ain't bad," said one. "When's it paid?"

"Partial payment when you sign the ledger. The remainder later."

"What about my horse? Will he be paid too?" someone asked, followed by laughter.

Captain Martin chuckled. "Your horse won't be paid, but you'll be paid for its use." Martin straightened. "I need good men who aren't afraid of the British; men who can ride hard and shoot straight." He stood and eyed each man." "This is our second war of Independence. Many of you have fathers who fought to gain our Independence. Now, you have to fight to keep it. If we don't defeat the British, we'll lose our country. It's that simple." He paused. "Now, who will be the first to step forward and sign the ledger?"

"I will," Arch blurted out.

"Stand aside and let the brave man pass through," said Martin.

He dipped the quill in the ink and handed it to Arch, who proudly wrote "Archibald McElroy" across the page.

---

Garner's Tavern was crowded and smoky. Arch jangled the $3.00 he had been given, stepped to the bar and forked over 12 ½ ¢ for a half pint of whiskey. He took a swig, and then screwed up his face as the liquid fire burned down his gullet. A few seconds later he began to feel warm and relaxed. He couldn't believe that he had finally volunteered. Elizabeth would cry and beg him not to go, but a man had to do what he felt. And he felt good about his decision. Just as he took another swig, he heard someone call his name. He looked toward the door and saw his younger brother Mike enter, along with his neighbors Robert and Samuel Buchanan.

"What are you doing in town today?" Mike asked. "Elizabeth run you off?"

Arch chuckled. "I oughta ask you the same question. If I'd been married for only two weeks, I'd be home with my bride."

"He's all tuckered out," deadpanned Robert Buchanan and they all laughed.

"I just volunteered to fight the British," Arch said flatly. The men looked at each other quizzically.

"You really mean it?" Mike asked.

Arch nodded. "Yep."

"If you're going off to fight, I'm going too," Mike said.

The Buchanans glanced at each other. "Me too," said Robert.

"If Robert's going, I'm going too," said Samuel.

And they had a drink of whiskey to celebrate their decision.

Elizabeth cried the remainder of the day. Finally, Arch said to her: "Elizabeth, crying and carrying on won't change a thing. Each generation has to step forward and protect our country. The country is just a bunch of families bound together and I'm doing my job as any man should do. I'm protecting you."

Finally, she wiped away her tears and straightened her shoulders. "Arch, I know in my heart you're right. I know you havta do your duty and I'm proud of you for that. It's just that a woman sometimes has to cry, but it don't mean I'm weak."

Arch pulled her into her arms and kissed her gently on the lips. "You're a mighty good woman."

Elizabeth busied herself preparing for Arch's departure. He would need food and clothes – especially a good hunting shirt that would shed water and keep him warm.

---

Mrs. McElroy threw a going-away supper attended by the entire McElroy clan. Ol' Red and the speckled hen that Nancy had stowed away on the journey from Wake County had raised their own clan of chickens, which provided plentiful eggs and meat.

Big Annie was determined to cook a supper that Arch and Mike wouldn't soon forget.

"I just about half-raised Massa Arch and Massa Mike and knows what dey likes," she said. Chicken stew bubbled in a black cast iron pot hanging over the fireplace. "I's put in an extra help'n of potatoes and onion and lots of pepper 'n salt and when it gits done, it's be fit'n for a king."

Although Big Annie liked to claim she had "half-raised" the McElroy children, it wasn't the case at all. Micajah had purchased her two years earlier when he had bought King Solomon, Blood, Moses and Sam to help build the courthouse. Big Annie was big-boned and could lift like a man and cook like a woman.

She pulled hot coals onto the hearth. "I knows how much Massa Arch loves dem hoecakes," she said as hot grease popped in a black iron skillet. She poured scalding water into a bowl of cornmeal, added salt and stirred the batter then poured it into the sizzling grease.

The rich aroma of frying cornmeal made Arch's mouth water. When the hoecakes were brown on each side, Big Annie served them with generous dollops of fresh butter.

"Un unh!" Arch said, rubbing his hands and eyeing the stack of cakes.

"Big Annie, if I'd known I'd be fed this well, I'da enlisted last year," he said. He ate chicken stew and hoecakes, washed down with sweet milk, until his stomach was about to pop.

Rachel, newly married to Mike and not fully acquainted with the entire McElroy family, ate in silence. Finally, she burst into tears. Mike put his arm around her as she shook and wept. "I'll be home before you know it," he said, trying to console her.

Mrs. McElroy pushed away from the table and went and placed a loving arm around her thin shoulders.

"I know how thee feels," she said. "Micajah was away fighting Tories when William was born. You stay here with me and I'll take care of thee like my own daughter."

"Thank you for understanding, Mrs. McElroy."

Micajah had said little during supper.

"Something wrong, Father?" asked William.

"Aye, just thinking," He looked across the table at Sallie, his 13-year-old daughter.

"I wasn't much older than you when the Declaration of Independence was adopted. I remember it well —"

"Tell us Father," said Mike. Everyone grew silent and turned toward Micajah.

"It was August 24, 1776, a Saturday afternoon in Bloomsbury," Micajah began. "Uncle Abington took me to hear it read by the Town Crier. The square was packed with folks. Uncle Abington said, 'This is a momentous day in our lives. You'll remember it until the day you die and will tell your children and grandchildren about it.'" Micajah paused. "And he was right."

No one spoke. Micajah continued. "It took us six long years to gain our independence." He eyed Arch, "I returned home following the fight at Lindley's Mill and held you and William in my arms. You was less than a year old and William had just been born. I thought we had whipped the British for good; that my fighting would ensure that my children could live in peace and not have to go off to war. Now, the devils are back." Micajah excused himself from the supper table and disappeared. In a few minutes he returned with his Pennsylvania long rifle and spoke to Arch, who had just finished his last hoecake.

"Your great-grandfather, Archibald McElroy, made this rifle," he said. "And your great-grandmother, Catherine McElroy, gave it to me when I turned sixteen. It served me well against the Tories in North Carolina and since you are the oldest and bear your grandfather's name, I want you to have it. I know that it will serve you well against the British." He looked at Mike and asked, "You understand?"

"Yes, Father."

Arch, momentarily speechless, stood and took the rifle. The maple stock was scarred and pitted in places but it was still a thing of beauty and craftsmanship.

"Thank you, Father," he said, stroking the long barrel. "I'll take good care of it. I know that it'll take good care of me."

"Aye, this is a fine rifle," said Micajah. "Neither of you should cower before the British. A lead ball will stop them as quick as it will stop any man. Aim for the chest, take a deep breath, let out halfway and hold it, then gently squeeze the trigger."

"I could never come close to what you and Patriots did at Lindley's Mill," said Arch.

"You'll do fine, son," said Micajah. But he knew that Arch and Mike would be up against British regulars, not a bunch of Tory volunteers like he had fought. And that was a big difference.

---

Clanking cookware and the aroma of brewing coffee woke Arch. Elizabeth was already in the kitchen, preparing enough food to last him for several days. He lay quietly and mentally checked off for the tenth time things that had to be done before departing home. His enlistment was for six months and he should return home by next April. He had cut plenty of firewood, jerked venison and made sure there was corn in the crib and fodder in the barn. If Elizabeth needed anything, his family was nearby and would pitch in and help her. Elizabeth was a strong woman and a good wife. He counted himself lucky to have her. He swung out of bed and dressed. In the kitchen Elizabeth was bent over the hearth shoveling hot coals onto the lid of a Dutch oven.

"Mornin'," he said.

She turned around and wiped her hands on her apron. "I'm baking enough biscuits to last you for at least three days. That 'n fried sow belly and jerked venison

81

oughta keep you fed for a while."

He walked over, took the iron shovel from her hand, set it down and wrapped his arms around her. He didn't know what the future held for him. He might not return. He had a great need to feel her warm body against him for one last time. He couldn't bring himself to tell her how much he loved her. It just didn't seem manly.

"Elizabeth, you're a fine wife," he said.

"Ohhh Arch, I'm so scared that you won't return home. Hold me." Her body trembled. "I'm sorry to be so childish, but I'm afraid that something will happen to you before we have children. Promise me that you'll be careful."

He looked into her teary eyes. "I promise. We probably won't even see a Redcoat or fire a shot."

After breakfast he slipped on the fringed woolen hunting shirt that fell below his waist and buckled on an untanned leather belt and scabbard. Into the scabbard he inserted a long butcher knife with a bone handle; slung on his shot bag and powder horn, picked up the Pennsylvania long rifle and pulled on a wide brim felt hat. He took a deep breath. He was ready to go as he would ever be.

He mounted his big bay gelding, leaned over and kissed Elizabeth on the forehead and after rendezvousing with Mike, rode to Fayetteville. The town was bustling with men on horseback and wagons, the former fording the river, the latter lining up at the ferry to cross to the south side where the 2nd Regiment, West Tennessee Volunteer Mounted Gunmen, had assembled at Camp Blount.

That night camp fires glowed up and down the river bank for a half a mile or more. Men clustered around flickering flames that pushed back an early fall chill and talked about what the future might hold for them. Many of the men, like Arch and Mike, had never been to war. Some had fought the Creeks the previous years. When a veteran spoke the others men listened.

A Third Sergeant from another camp sauntered by and one of the men who recognized him said, "Tell us about fight'n injuns."

Arch remembered seeing the man the previous year when he rode into Fayetteville. Robert Buchanan leaned over and said to Arch, "That's David Crockett. He lives up on Bean's Creek and fought the Red Sticks last year."

Crockett was broad-shouldered, lean and hard; about 6 feet tall and weighing at least 200 pounds, he stood straight as an arrow. His hair was black and his nose sharp. He wore a fringed deer skin hunting shirt with a long knife inserted in one side of a wide leather belt and a tomahawk in the opposite.

"My first fight'n was at Tallusahatchee village while the injuns slept," said Crockett, "A bunch of 'em run inside a house. I remember seeing a squaw sitt'n in the doorway with a bow and arrow. She killed one of our men which put us in a rage. We put at least 20 balls in her, then shot 'em like dogs. There was about 46 warriors inside the house when we set it on fire." Crockett spit. "The next day, some of us went back to the village searching for food to eat for we were hungry as wolves and we found a potato cellar under the burned building. The grease from them burned Indians had run down in the potatoes and they cooked like they had been stewed. I didn't want to eat 'em, but I did."

The men listened in silence.

"The two things I remember about the war was a lotta killing and being hungry."

Later that night when the dying embers were reduced to a glow, Arch looked

82

over at Mike and said, "You know something brother?"

"What?"

"I'll never eat another potato as long as I live."

The following morning the men fell in formation, their rifles at right shoulder arms. Captain Martin walked down the line inspecting muskets. A few of the men were armed with U.S. model 1803 rifles made at Harper's Ferry. They were 54 caliber with a 33" long half-round, half octagon barrel. When Captain Martin stopped in front of Arch, his eyes immediately went to the Pennsylvania long rifle that rested on his shoulder.

"Will that thing fire?" he asked.

Arch stiffened, offended. "Begging the Capt'n pardon... sir, this rifle will outshoot and outrange any guns I've seen here. It has a forty-six-inch-long barrel. It'll reach way out there."

Captain Martin smiled slightly. "Oh?"

"My great-grandfather was a gunsmith," said Arch. "He made it. My father used it during the Revolution and it served him well."

"What's the caliber?" Martin asked.

"Fifty."

"Do you have plenty of balls for it?"

"I will by the time I need 'em," Arch replied.

The volunteers were issued a black leather shot bag, wood canteen, white cloth cross belt, metal cup, spoon, wood bowl and two blankets – all regular army surplus. The company was comprised of approximately 156 men. Samuel Martin was 1st Lt. and John D. Martin was 2nd Lt. There were three Sergeant and four corporals. Henry McClure was trumpeter. Abraham Beavers was farrier and blacksmith was Thomas Fowler. Charles Read was saddler. The men divided into mess groups with Arch, Mike and the two Buchanans teaming up. Each mess was issued a cooking pot and skillet.

Early October, the brigade departed Fayetteville, passed Fort Hampton on Elk River and crossed the Tennessee River at Muscle Shoals near Melton's Bluff, then proceeded to Camp Gaines, about 30 miles from Ft. Montgomery, north of Mobile.

The march to Camp Gaines was long and arduous, the roads often no more than a pathway hacked through the wilderness. Mounted horsemen and creaking wagons pulled by grunting oxen, and some by braying mules, were strung out for miles or more sending up clouds of choking dust. When it rained, the road turned to muck. They trudged through mud holes and deep ruts wallowed out by scores of wagons and horses. The long column of mounted gunmen and rattling wagons scared off wild game. The food supply dwindled and the government contractor failed to appear with provisions. The men ate parched corn and kept marching. At first, Arch's stomach growled, and then it ached. He grew light-headed and weak. His every thought was about the fluffy biscuits that Elizabeth had baked the day he departed home and he salivated. Then one day Arch saw David Crockett again. He and his band of hunters brought in several squirrels, hawks and birds and threw them in a pile for the men to share. On another occasion he brought two turkeys, a deer and some honey. Each man received a small portion and ate ravenously.

"There ain't enough to lick off my fingers," said Mike, "but I ain't complaining."

Robert Buchanan traded powder for two potatoes with a friendly Indian he encountered along the way. That night at mess he produced them.

"Where did you get them?" Arch asked.

"From an Indian."

Arch gagged. The men quartered and ate them raw.

The nights were chilly and Arch, not yet accustomed to the change of season, shivered on the cold ground. The men were dirty and hungry most of the time and many were ill with flux and their bowels no longer held its contents.

At night he looked up at the stars and thought about Elizabeth. He missed her sorely. And he missed his folks, his mother and especially his father. Over the years he had grown to appreciate the old man more and value his wisdom and judgment. He liked to think about his folks, not only because it gave him comfort, but because it kept his mind off the present. He didn't relish confronting the British. They were the best trained, best fed and best equipped soldiers in the world. When he looked around at the rag-tag Tennesseans he wondered how they could be expected to defeat soldiers who had whipped Napoleon. Sleeping on the cold and often wet ground penetrated his body and made him stiff and achy. Going off to war wasn't nearly as romantic as he had once thought. Often in the solitude of the night when the men were snoring, he thought about his misery and what lay ahead. Would he measure up like his father had done 30 years earlier against the Tories? He wasn't so sure he could. And that bothered him too.

On the bright side, fall was creeping south, turning the tree tops rust colored and pumpkin yellow beneath cold blue sky.

Mike had been unusually quiet as they rode. The only sound was that of creaking saddles, clomping of hooves and blowing of the horses.

"Do you ever get scared thinking about what we're up against?" he asked.

Arch studied his face and eyes briefly. "Yeah, the closer we get to fighting, the more I think about it."

"When the Redcoats come marching at us with bayonets at ready," Mike continued. "Have you ever wondered if you'll stand and fight or run like a rabbit?"

"I've thought about it. I hope I don't run, but a man never knows till he sees them bayonets glinting in the sunlight. What about you?"

"I don't know what I'll do," Mike replied.

The regiment arrived at Fort Gaines about 30 miles from Fort Montgomery, weary and hungry, to join forces with General Jackson. Old Hickory had repulsed the British attack on Mobile back on September 15. Unknown to the Tennesseans, the British fleet was en route from Chesapeake to Jamaica where it would rendezvous with the Navy and additional troops arriving from England.

General Jackson strongly believed that the main British Army would attack New Orleans, either by sailing up the Mississippi River or marching over land. He had to outguess them. If they landed troops in Pensacola, which was claimed and occupied by the Spanish, he could be fighting a two-front war with insufficient troops. When he learned that General Coffee's Tennesseans had arrived at Fort Gaines, he marched out of Mobile and joined forces with him north of Pensacola on October 25. The combined Army was 4,000 strong, including several hundred Chickasaw and Choctaw allies. Using the pretense that the Spanish weren't adhering strictly to neutrality, Jackson decided to capture the port city.

Arch and the men of his company first learned of Jackson's plan when they assembled after breakfasting on salt bacon and cornbread. Captain Martin rode to the front of the company and addressed them. "Men, you have traveled far from home, gone hungry and suffered greatly in order to fight. Now that time has finally come. We are going to take Pensacola."

For a moment there was silence. Then a loud huzzah rose from their throats.

"For many of you, this will be your first time to strike a blow against our enemy. I know you will be courageous and do Tennessee proud."

Another huzzah.

That evening the men in Arch's mess were unusually quiet. None had ever fired a shot at any man in anger. Mike broke the silence. "I just want to get it done and get back home. The sooner we whip the British, the sooner we can go home."

"You're more interested in bedding your new bride than whipping Redcoats and gaining honor," Samuel Buchanan quipped.

Mike looked up and grinned. "You've been reading my mind." They all laughed and tension dissipated.

Pensacola was a tiny backwater village where about 500 Spaniards garrisoned two forts. Fort Barrancas garrisoned by British and guarding the bay presented the real threat. After demanding surrender, which the Spanish Governor refused, Jackson attacked Pensacola on November 7th. He sent about 500 men from the west to make a loud demonstration while launching his main attack from the east. Spanish resistance collapsed. Shortly, the Fort surrendered. The following morning, to everyone's surprise, the British had vacated Fort Barrancas, sailed away and didn't return. Arch and Mike never fired a shot.

"Them Redcoats showed tail," Robert Buchanan said.

"Maybe they ain't as tough as they are made out to be," said Mike.

Arch wanted to believe that, but he wasn't convinced. "They whipped Napoleon," he said.

"Napoleon is a Frenchman," Mike said. "They've never been up against Tennesseans."

"I wouldn't get too cocky little brother," Arch cautioned.

On November 9, leaving a skeleton force at Pensacola, Jackson marched west to Mobile where the men rested a few days. On November 22nd, they departed for New Orleans. The march was hard. It was low country filled with palmetto marshes and gator-filled cypress swamps where mud sucked off their shoes. When the Tennesseans arrived in New Orleans on December 1st, the men were cold, tired, hungry, dirty and ill-equipped. The locals aptly called them the "Dirty Shirts." The natural oils in his hunting shirt had long since been dissolved by sweat, sunlight and rain and Arch was in a perpetual state of misery. Cold rain fell frequently. The Tennesseans bivouacked in a swampy area near the Mississippi River. The ground in between was ankle deep in mud and horse manure. Flimsy tents turned away rain, but did nothing to neither stop water from running inside nor protect against the biting coldness. Arch massaged his numb fingers and tried to start a fire. The wood was wet. It would be another cold night and on an empty stomach. There was rancid bacon available but it couldn't be cooked. He and Mike hadn't heard from home. A word from the folks would be nice, but food and arms weren't arriving, much less mail. Mike looked out the tent flap and said, "I wish they'd show up. I want to fight and go home."

# 9 | THE BATTLE OF NEW ORLEANS

Shortly past noon.

December 23, 1814.

It was a cold and disagreeable day and Jackson's little army busied itself on the edge of New Orleans by drilling, cleaning weapons and repairing equipment. At Captain Martin's encampment, the sound of hammers striking anvil rang out as blacksmith Thomas Fowler shaped horse shoes. Company farrier Abraham Beavers, wearing a heavy leather apron, was bent over replacing a shoe that Mike's horse had thrown. Saddler Charles Read was repairing saddles, mostly belly bands that had deteriorated in the wet environment. Arch sat on his haunches by a small fire melting lead and molding 50-caliber bullets while Samuel Buchanan warmed his hands.

"Do y'all know that tomorrow is Christmas Eve?" he asked Arch nonchalantly.

"I know," Arch answered and poured hot lead into a mold.

"Reckon what our families are doing about now?" Samuel asked.

Arch looked up and squinted where the barely-visible sun tilted toward the south. "I'd say most folks just finished dinner and are sitting by the fire," he said. "It's cold back home; always is around Christmas time."

"I can just smell fresh-cut cedar and see a Christmas tree standing in the corner of the room," said Buchanan.

"Yeah," Arch said quietly. "Sure would be nice to be home."

"That's the prettiest word there is."

"What?" Arch asked.

"Home."

A loud boom interrupted their conversation. Startled, Arch jumped. "What's that?" he asked.

"The alarm gun." Drums beat incessantly. Couriers raced back and forth amid great excitement. Mike walked up, leading his horse.

"This may be the day we get to fight," Buchanan said.

"I hope so," said Mike. "I want to get it over with. This sitting around waiting and worrying, half-starved and half froze is getting to me."

Arch swallowed hard, and gathered his lead balls and dropped them into a leather pouch hanging on his side.

Trumpeter Henry McClure sounded assembly.

The men grabbed their rifles and rushed to fall in formation. Other companies did the same until the entire Second Regiment, Volunteer Mounted Gunman were standing tall.

They were a motley-looking bunch. Their brown hunting shirts were soiled and dirty; their breeches the same. Many wore homemade moccasins replacing leather shoes that had long since worn out. Their unkempt hair and whiskers only added to their disheveled appearance, but appearances are deceiving. There wasn't a man in the regiment who couldn't shoot off a turkey's head at great distance. The question always in Arch's mind was: Would they stand and fight the British regulars? Would he?

Colonel Thomas Williamson rode to the front of his regiment and addressed the men. "Tennesseans! The British have arrived." Murmuring swept through the ranks. "General Jackson has vowed they shall not sleep on our soil. I say to you, they will either leave our soil or be buried in our soil." He stood up in the saddle. "Who is ready to join me in throwing the devils off our land, dead or alive?" A loud huzzah arose.

The regiment rode south out of the city together with the remainder of General Coffee's Tennesseans. In addition, there were two regiments of the regular Army, the 44th Infantry, the 7th Infantry, a Marine attachment, artillerymen, a company of New Orleans volunteers, Major Plauche's battalion, Mississippi Dragoons, 18 Choctaws and a battalion of free blacks. In all there were about 2,100 men.

Old Hickory sat erect on his horse and returned salutes as his little army moved south to confront 1,800 Redcoats encamped on the Villere Plantation that nestled against the east bank of the Mississippi River.

It was dark when Jackson's Army arrived around 5 p.m., north of the British encampment. He had previously ordered the schooner *Carolina*, armed with 14 guns, to take a position opposite the British. The Redcoats paid no attention to the *Carolina* as they prepared supper, thinking it was a merchant ship.

Jackson quietly positioned his troops. General Coffee's 800 Tennesseans dismounted, left their horses with holders and took a position on the extreme left in a cypress swamp. They were to advance on foot attacking the enemy's flank and pushing him into the river. Jackson commanded the right where artillery was located. General Coffee walked among his Tennesseans, offering encouragement. Arch, Mike and the Buchanans were standing in cold, thigh-deep water when Coffee eased up. It was dark, but moonlight filtered through the cypress trees into the murky swamp. Arch could barely make out Coffee's features, but he instantly recognized his soft voice. "Men, the Redcoat sentries are no more than 500 yards to our front," he said in a low voice. "I know you will fight. Now is the time to prove it. Don't waste powder. Be sure of your mark before you pull the trigger."

"Yes sir," Arch whispered, then laid an arm on his younger brother's shoulder. "Mike, if I run, shoot me."

"What if I run first?"

"Then I'll shoot you," Arch said.

Mike stifled a nervous chuckle.

"Remember what father did at Lindley's Mill," Arch said. "And think what the British will do to our families if we don't stop 'em."

At 7:30 14 guns on the *Carolina* spoke, sending pandemonium into the British encampment with the grape and round shot. Fires were put out. Bugles blared. Wounded men screamed. Jackson waited as the ship continued to rain death on the enemy.

"What's he waiting for?" Robert Buchanan whispered. "My feet's freezing, I'm ready to fight."

"Maybe something went wrong?" Arch whispered. Someone whacked him on the back.

"Quiet!" It was Sergeant McNeal.

A full ten minutes passed. Finally, heavy musket fire opened up on the right. The firing was incessant. From the sound, Arch determined Jackson was advancing toward the British line. American artillery opened and shook the earth. A thick fog rolled from the river and penetrated the cypress swamp.

"FORWAARRD TENNESSEANS!" It was Captain Martin.

The Tennesseans moved forward, sloshing through the cold, murky water, some bumping into trees and cursing. Arch barely had time to be afraid or worry about Mike when they smashed into the British outpost, driving them backward. The command was given to wheel right and the Tennesseans surged toward the river in an attempt to drive the enemy into the water. They slammed into the British camp. Arch didn't hesitate nor ponder whether it was right or wrong to kill another human being. It was kill or be killed. He fired the Long rifle with effect, dropping Redcoats. Soon they were in a swarm of enemy firing at point-blank range. Some of the Tennesseans, not having time to reload, were swinging their tomahawks. Others resorted to using their long knives. It was a bloody life or death brawl. Arch lost sight of the Mike and Buchanans. Fog and smoke blotted out the moonlight and it was difficult to distinguish British from Tennesseans. They fought their way forward. Where was Mike?

Enemy fire erupted from several slave cabins on the LaCoste Plantation. The Tennesseans picked them off like shooting squirrels. Coffee's Brigade pushed forward toward the levee near the area where the *Carolina* was pitching grape shot. Coffee reported his tenuous position to Jackson and was ordered to fall back and join the main army. That's when Arch spotted Mike and the Buchanans. All were unscathed and their blood still up, anxious to kill more Redcoats. Arch joined them and slogged through the darkness. His heart was pounding, his mouth dry, and when he tried to speak no words came out. Finally, "Boys, we give 'em a good whipp'n."

Even though they spent a miserable night, cold and fireless, they felt a warmth inside. They had confronted the best troops in the world and held their own.

The Tennesseans weren't acquainted with the "proper rules of battle," and employed Indian tactics to harass the British. Small bands of men snuck up on Redcoat campfires and picked them off. Sentries were left dead, shot between the eyes, and officers on horseback were targets of opportunity.

Arch was hunkered behind a large cypress tree when Captain Martin walked up.

"McElroy, you once said that Long rifle would outrange any musket in the outfit."

"Captain, I said it and it will," Arch replied.

"Let's see if you're right or just bragging. Come with me."

The two men quietly made their way forward through the cypress swamp, studded with sharp new growth just below the water. They halted behind trees and waited in silence. In front, some 400 yards or more, Arch saw Redcoat sentries. Shortly, an officer on a black horse rode up to the outpost. Captain Martin whispered: "Take him."

Arch lifted the Long rifle to his shoulder and rested the 46-inch barrel on the side of the tree. He thought about his father and how he had knocked the bloody Tory, David Fanning from the saddle three decades earlier. In his head, he heard his voice say quietly, "Take a deep breath, exhale half, hold it and squeeze the trigger." Arch took his time and followed Micajah's instructions. He targeted the bullseye of a gorget that hung around the officer's neck; took a breath, exhaled halfway and squeezed the trigger. The Long rifle bucked as a 50-caliber ball exited the barrel and headed straight toward the officer. The Redcoat flew backward out of the saddle when the ball impacted. Arch looked at Martin. "Now, what do you say?"

"Let's get outta here."

On Christmas Eve, General Jackson pulled his Army back a couple of miles and dug in behind Rodriguez Canal, the dug-out mill race that ran into a murky cypress swamp. Near the swamp, Arch continued to mold bullets.

"I ain't never seen so many bullets," Samuel Buchanan said. "Pretty soon you won't be able to walk."

"I don't want to run out," Arch replied and kept melting lead and molding balls.

The next morning the 1,063 rag-tag men of the 2nd Regiment fell in formation. Colonel Thomas Williamson, astride a bay horse rode to their front and stood in the stirrups. "Tennesseans, we have been given the responsibility of holding the left of our line," he said. "There will be nothing to protect you from British fire other than the trees. It is imperative that we hold the line at all cost." He paused to let his words sink in. "If we fail to stand fast, the enemy will roll up our left flank and destroy our army. You are brave men. You carry the blood of your fathers who whipped the English devils a quarter century ago. Now, they are back. They have invaded our country, burned our capital and put our government in flight. It is time that we chased them from our soil once and for all. You are free men. Your ancestors purchased your liberty with their blood. Make sure they didn't die in vain.

"Remember, you are fighting for your wives, your children, your parents, your brothers and sisters and for liberty and everything dear to you.

"You are Tennesseans and Tennessee will always fight for what is just and right. In years to come when men speak of the events that occurred here, let it be said that Tennesseans did their duty."

Momentarily, the men were silent, staring at their commander, then a spontaneous shout erupted from their throats. Colonel Williamson raised his hat. "I salute you!"

———————————

On Christmas morning, the Americans hunkered behind their thin mud redoubt, cold, damp and miserable. On the extreme left of the line where the Rodriguez Canal petered out into the cypress swamp, the Tennesseans celebrated the day by frying salt bacon, eating cornbread and consuming their ration of whiskey.

"I wonder what those Redcoat devils are doing?" Mike asked, looking in the distance at the field of white tents.

"Eat'n pudding, no doubt," quipped Robert Buchanan.

"I'd give anything to be home with Elizabeth sitting in front of a crackling fire and eating one of her fat biscuits…" Arch said.

"Hush!" said Samuel Buchanan.

Mike piped up. "You know what I'd like to be doing?"

"Romancing your bride, I suspect," Robert Buchanan replied.

"Yeah, then going over to Mother and Father's house for a big Christmas dinner of ham and venison and turkey and pie and …"

Artillery salvos interrupted his sentence. Arch flinched and ducked. "Are they coming?" he asked. Loud cheering erupted from the British lines.

"Naw, they're celebrating something," Mike said.

Unknown to the Tennesseans, the British were welcoming the arrival of their new commander, Lieutenant General Sir Edward Pakenham.

"It won't be long before they come," Arch said.

"I hope so," Mike said. "I'm ready to fight and get it over with. I don't like waiting."

———————————

Days dragged by. On December 27th, the British fired hot shot into the

*Carolina,* igniting a fire that spread to the gunpowder room. The ship exploded, shaking the earth and flinging chunks of wood in every direction. That evening the British advanced forward, closer to the American lines.

The following morning, the fog burned off revealing a cool, but clear day.

"It's a good omen," Samuel Buchanan said. "At least we'll dry out."

"Yeah, but it's a better day for the Redcoats to come," Arch commented. "After sinking the *Carolina,* they are full of fight." Shortly, buglers blew and drums beat in the British camp. Mike peered out across the flat plain. "They're up to something."

Sgt. McNeal walked the line. "Be alert men – be alert."

Congreve rockets sailed across the sky toward the American lines, making a loud sputtering sound. Artillery opened up. Americans replied.

"Here they come!" someone yelled.

Arch peered over the mud barrier that had mostly melted in the swamp water and saw Redcoats marching shoulder to shoulder directly toward him. Their intent was obvious: Turn the Tennesseans flank and drive them into Jackson on the right and into the river.

At the order, Arch leveled his sight on a Redcoat chest, squeezed the trigger and saw the man crumple. Simultaneously, a blizzard of lead struck the British ranks dropping them by the scores. Arch stepped back and began reloading while Mike stepped forward and fired. "Give it to 'em for America!" someone yelled.

The Tennesseans were standing firm and firing steadily. The British line slowed, and then halted. They were in a killing field where acrid smoke filled the air. Wounded Redcoats moaned and cried out in pain.

A bugle sounded retreat. The British had had enough. A loud huzzah rose from the dry-throated Tennesseans. They had held the line against the best.

The Kentucky Militia, some 2,256 strong – arrived on January 4th in tattered clothes, two-thirds of them without weapons. They brought Jackson's Army up to a total of 6,404 men. In front of them were 14,450 Redcoats, men who had defeated Napoleon. The future of America hung in the balance.

---

Morning.

January 8, 1815.

Arch was cold, hungry and miserable. He had been standing in knee-deep water for hours. But the coldness was nothing compared to the fear that gripped his mind. He had stood and fought before, but he figured a man's luck eventually ran out. The coming fight wouldn't be a reconnaissance-in-force like the British had previously launched to probe for weakness. This one would be for real. The enemy would throw everything they had against the line. He looked up and down the rampart at the dirty, ragged Tennesseans; men not trained to fight, not even members of the militia. They were small farmers more familiar with chopping wood and plowing corn than fighting. All had volunteered to fight to save America and all understood that if America lost the war King George would be back with his boot on their necks. If Jackson's little army lost the coming battle, the British would take New Orleans and sail up the Mississippi River, slicing America in half.

"A man's gotta die sometime," he mumbled.

Mike, his face caked with dirt, looked over and asked: "What did you say?"

"Just talking to myself," Arch replied and checked his rifle to be sure it was loaded and his powder dry. Somewhere out there in the darkness were thousands of Redcoats lining up, loading their muskets and snapping on bayonets. The Tennesseans were standing behind cypress trees up to their knees in murky water. Many were coughing, swearing and cussing the coldness.

"My feet's freezing," he said to Mike.

"Mine too."

Talking took Arch's mind off his fears. "Say Mike, do you know what day it is?"

"Heard it's Sunday. You going to church?"

"Just thinking about home, wondering what Elizabeth and the family done for Christmas."

"Yeah, I bet they sat down in front of a rip roaring fire, eat pud'n and drunk hot coffee," replied Mike.

"Yeah, I'd give anything for a warm fire and a mug of coffee," said Arch.

"My teeth's chattering."

"If the Redcoats don't hurry up and kill us, the cold water will," said Arch.

"Reckon when they'll come?"

"Daylight," said Arch.

"Then it won't be long," replied Mike glancing at the eastern horizon smothered with thick fog.

"Reckon how they'll come at us?"

"Just like before, lined up, elbow to elbow and several ranks deep." Arch replied and cleared the fear from his throat. The thought of a phalanx of rifles and bayonets coming toward him sent fear scurrying into his bowels. Suddenly, he felt the need to empty them. But he couldn't. There was no time and no place. He felt inside his shot bag. Plenty of bullets. He felt the end of his powder horn to insure that the plug was firmly sealed. Powder dry. He stroked the curly maple stock of his rifle and let his hand move up to the hammer and trigger area. All in working order.

"Has your rifle ever misfired?" Robert Buchanan asked and yawned.

"No, has yours?"

"Yeah, a few times when the powder was damp." Buchanan yawned again. "I'm yawning and I ain't even sleepy," he added.

"It's fear," Mike said.

---

To the right of the Tennesseans, General Jackson, who was ill with dysentery, walked the line speaking to the men and offering encouragement. Some of the men were breakfasting on cornbread, bacon and whiskey. As daylight broke, he climbed up on the earthen ramparts and saw Congreve rockets wobble and sputter across the early morning sky. It was the British signal to attack. Redcoats, sixty men abreast, and four rows deep, marched in perfect parade order with fixed bayonets toward the Americans. When they were within five hundred yards, American artillery opened up with grapeshot, tearing arms, legs and heads apart and sending chunks of flesh sailing through the air. They closed ranks and kept coming. Jackson ordered the artillery to cease fire. "Let them get closer where they'll be easier to kill," he said. It was clear to Jackson that his Tennessee volunteers were going to take the brunt of the attack. Just before the Redcoats smashed

91

into his line, Jackson climbed down from his perch and addressed his officers.

"Gentlemen, fire when ready!"

---

Arch leaned against a cypress tree for support. He was weak from hunger. There was bacon and cornbread and whiskey available, but he had no appetite. He saw the Congreve rockets wobble across the gray sky and heard the thunder of cannon to his right. The earth shook. Then musketry rattled. He leaned forward and squinted toward the murky front where he knew the Redcoats would come. Nothing. They had to be out there – coming.

"Do you see anything?" he asked Mike, barely able to form the words inside his dry mouth.

"No – wait. I see something!"

Arch's heart jumped to his throat and pounded like a drum. "Where?"

The fog was lifting.

"Look!" exclaimed Robert Buchanan. "I see 'em coming!" Arch saw them also. There must have been at least 60 Redcoats marching elbow to elbow through the black swamp water and all lined up like they were in a parade. Behind were three more rows.

"My Gawd!" one man exclaimed.

Someone else said, "Men, we're Tennesseans. We can stop lightning."

Arch suddenly felt better. Every man was at his post.

The Redcoats came closer. *When can we fire?* "Steady men." It was Captain Martin speaking. Arch fingered the trigger of the Pennsylvania long rifle. *When?* Suddenly, his feet weren't cold anymore. Sweat dropped from his forehead and he saw the glint of bayonets in the early morning sunlight.

"Men, remember your families!" Captain Martin yelled.

Arch pulled his rifle to his shoulder.

"FIRE!"

Arch remembered what his father had said and selected a red-coated chest, took a deep breath, exhaled half, held it and squeezed the trigger. The long rifle bucked. Instantly, the Tennesseans opened up sending a blaze of fire from the muzzle of a thousand rifles and a thousand lead balls racing toward the oncoming British.

For a moment, Arch couldn't see anything because of powder smoke that hung in the damp air. He didn't need to see what was in front of him. He knew. He quickly reloaded. Smoke cleared and he saw scores of bodies strewn in the swamp. But the soldiers had closed ranks and kept coming. Tennesseans weren't fleeing. They were standing and fighting like wildcats.

Firing died out and smoke drifted to the tops of the cypress trees. Arch stared at what he saw. Hundreds of red-coated bodies sloshed in the black waters, some stacked on top of others. They looked like a row of fallen dominoes. For a moment there was silence along the line as if the men couldn't believe what they witnessed.

"We whipped 'em! We whipped 'em!" Someone shouted. Then the Tennesseans erupted with shouting and cheering.

Arch was weak. He leaned against a tree. Fear and tension drained away. He looked at Mike. "You know something?"

Mike shook his head.

92

"I could eat a whole pot full of stewed potatoes."

Mike grinned. "We whipped 'em Arch. We did it," he said.

"Yeah, we did."

---

The battle was over by 8:00 a.m. The vaunted British soldiers were beaten and their commander, Sir Edward Pakenham, lay dying. Total British casualties were 2,044 while the Americans suffered only 71.

None of the combatants knew, but a peace treaty between the belligerents had been signed at Ghent, Belgium two weeks earlier on Christmas Eve. Congress ratified the treaty on March 21st. The war was over.

The same day, with spring descending and hope abounding, the troops were assembled and General Jackson rode to their front on his white charger. Arch strained to see his fellow Tennessean who had become the hero of New Orleans citizens. He thought he looked awfully thin and mighty sickly as he sat on his horse. Jackson bade his men farewell.

"Go, full of honor wreathed with laurels whose leaves shall never wither," said Jackson in his high-pitched voice. He told them that the men who had remained home while they toiled for the country would envy them and that they would see the gratitude of a nation of free men.

Then they marched out of New Orleans and headed to Natchez, homeward bound. Arch and Mike had been gone for seven months, one month past his enlistment, but they weren't complaining. They preceded General Jackson and his entourage, who departed New Orleans in early April. At Natchez, they struck the Trace that took them to Nashville.

On the march from Nashville to Fayetteville, Arch was filled with anticipation. He hadn't heard from Elizabeth or his family since departing home the previous October. Had they wintered well? Was everyone alive and in good health? Along the way, the rolling hills of middle Tennessee were green and the rich creek bottoms were being turned and prepared for planting of corn and tobacco. He would arrive home in time to plant. Perfect timing. The Regiment followed the same route from Nashville that his family had taken when they came to Fayetteville five years earlier. He knew every hill and branch as they approached Fayetteville. When they forded Cane Creek south of Petersburg, Mike said, "We ain't far from good vittles now."

"Vittles and other things," Arch added and grinned.

Shortly, they topped a hill and in front of them lay Fayetteville, nestled against the Elk River flowing like molten silver in the bright sunlight. Captain Martin rode down the column on his dapple gray mare. "Men, I know you're tired and ready to see your folks, but straighten up and look like the soldiers you are," he said.

Arch caught sight of the two-story, red brick courthouse he had helped construct and was filled with pride. He sat tall in the saddle. High Street that lead into town was dusty and strewn with horse droppings.

"Lots of riders been through here," Mike said. "Must be trade day or something."

Horses and wagons were tethered from Washington Street all the way to the courthouse square. "Looks like the whole county is in town today," Arch said. And he was correct. Fayetteville was filled with folks who had come to welcome home the heroes of New Orleans. Arch searched through throngs of cheering people looking for Elizabeth and his folks.

"ARCH – ARCH!" someone yelled.

Arch looked and saw Elizabeth standing on her tiptoes, smiling, waving and wiping away tears of joy. Nearby were his parents, also smiling and waving.

"Mike!" It was Rachel waving. Mike beamed at her and waved back. The Regiment circled the courthouse which was bedecked with red, white and blue banners. A drum and fife corps played *Yankee Doodle*. Arch knew he had made the right decision. He was proud that he had volunteered; proud that he had helped defeat the British and now, proud to be welcomed home as a hero.

The Regiment proceeded across the river to Camp Blount where they were shortly discharged for home. Elizabeth poured a warm bath and after Arch had scrubbed himself nearly raw he enjoyed the "other things" he had mentioned to Mike. The vittles came later.

---

That evening the McElroy family gathered at their parents' home where Big Annie had cooked ham, chicken, venison, cornbread, hoe cakes, stewed potatoes, beans and laden the table with fresh butter and pitchers of sweet milk.

Younger sisters Sallie and Nancy competed to sit between Arch and Mike at the supper table.

"I'm the oldest," said Sallie.

"The youngest deserve the honor," replied Nancy.

Arch, claiming that he was full, skipped eating stewed potatoes.

There was much news to report. William, the oldest, had been appointed Constable of Lincoln County.

"Why you couldn't try a chicken thief," said Mike, teasing his elder brother.

"You say that in my Court and I'll lock you up for contempt," replied William, laughing.

Micajah poured a gill of whiskey for the men folk and stood at the head of the table. "A toast to our heroes," he said raising his cup. "My sons, you and the brave Tennesseans whipped the arrogant British and drove them from our soil. Our Republic has been saved. For as long as there are free Americans your deeds at New Orleans will be remembered."

"Here here," echoed those around the table.

# 10 | ANOTHER COURTHOUSE

Lincoln County, Tennessee.
1819.

Micajah was sinking into a financial morass. The Panic of 1819 paralyzed the nation. Some said it was caused by borrowing too heavily to finance the War of 1812. Others blamed it on overspeculation of banks. Whatever the cause, widespread foreclosures, sheriff's sales, runs on banks, bankruptcies and high unemployment resulted. The price of cotton plummeted from 32 cents a pound to 15 cents. There was no money, neither gold nor silver. Debtors' prisons quickly filled to capacity. And no end was in sight.

In Fayetteville construction came to a halt and Micajah's building enterprise dried up. He owned land and could grow a little cotton, corn and wheat and wouldn't starve to death, but money was almost non-existent. He worried.

On the other hand, he had a lot to be thankful for. The despised British had been driven from American soil and their Upper Creek allies had been practically exterminated. Peace reigned and the frontier was secure. Folks could carry on life uninterrupted by war and fear of Indians. And that's what Micajah did. He bought and sold land, as well as Negroes, but profited little. He was vexed by lawsuits, which are always plentiful during hard times. He was 59 years old and in remarkably sound health. Sarah was healthy and all the children were alive and living nearby. Sallie, who was 19 years old and Nancy, age 16, were unmarried and still living at home. Yet, there were nights he didn't sleep. He kept the faith knowing that the Lord often worked in strange ways.

The previous year, February 6, 1818, the Alabama Territorial Legislature had established the boundary of Limestone County, and subsequently the county's residents elected five commissioners with power to select a county seat. Jeremiah Tucker, Robert Pollock, Thomas Redus, Reubin Tillman and Samuel Hundley were elected, and by a margin of only two votes, Athens was chosen as county seat. A new county with a great future needed a respectable courthouse; a brick one to replace the log structure.

When the commissioners advertised for bids, Micajah wrote for plans but didn't mention it to Sarah. He promptly received a letter with the plans, no more than a crude depiction of a two-story brick building, 40-by-60 feet in dimension with a cupola on top. He was confident he could construct a fine edifice. It wasn't much different from the courthouse he had built in Fayetteville seven years earlier. He sent in his bid by post.

Several days later, he casually mentioned it to Sarah. She grew quiet. He knew what that meant.

"That's a long way from here," she finally said.

"Aye, not too far."

"How far?"

"About 40 miles."

More silence.

"I don't figure I'll get the job," he said. "They'll give it to a local fellow."

Micajah was silent. *I might be old but I still know how to build.* "You don't think I can do the job," he finally said.

"There comes a time when thee must accept we are growing old and stop wandering around," she said.

95

"Humph."

---

When he received a letter postmarked "Athens, Alabama," he didn't open it. He was afraid – afraid he didn't get the contract and on the other hand, afraid that he did. Finally, he ripped open the envelope. His bid was accepted. Work was to begin immediately.

Sarah was seated by the window operating her spinning wheel when he took off his hat and hung it on a peg by the door.

She looked up. "Big crowd in Fayetteville?"

"Most folks in the field plowing today." Hesitation. "Uh ... I went by the post office and got this." He held up an envelope. "It's from the Limestone County Court."

Sarah dropped her eyes and continued spinning.

"Don't you want to know what it says?"

"No."

"I got the job."

Her shoulders slumped. She stared straight ahead and when she finally looked at him her eyes were brimming with tears. "We'll have to move down there, won't we?"

"Aye."

"For how long?"

"About two years, I figure."

"Ohhhh Micajah!" The breath left her. "I'm old and plumb wore out. I don't think I can bear to be uprooted again. My children, grandchildren and friends are here."

"I feel the same way, but times are hard and I must go where work takes me."

"We can survive here without moving away," she said. "Thee are doing this because of pride –"

"Pride, woman!"

"Yes, pride," she said softly. "It will be another monument to thee."

"I'm doing it for us!"

"Pride cometh before the fall the scriptures say."

"Humph."

"What about Sallie and Nancy?" she asked.

"They'll have to go with us."

"Ohh, that won't set well with them," said Sarah, brows knotted. "You know how headstrong they are. Their whole world is here in Lincoln County."

"They'll soon get over it."

"I wouldn't count on it," said Sarah.

He nodded and smiled to himself. He was proud of his children. All were headstrong and independent, characteristics that were needed to survive on the frontier. But it seemed that the Lord had given his two daughters an extra helping, especially in the headstrong area.

"How about you?" he asked and walked over to where she sat. Tears welled in her eyes. She looked up and wiped her eyes with the back of her hand. "You know my answer: I go where thou goest."

---

Micajah had finished his supper, pushed back from the table and lit his pipe

96

when Sallie cleared her throat.

"Father, Nancy and I have been talking and.... well.... we don't mean to be disrespectful, but we don't want to move to Athens."

"Why not?"

"We don't know a soul there," interjected Nancy. "Our friends are in Fayetteville, not to mention our relations."

Sallie jumped back in the discussion. "If they don't have a courthouse, it can't be much of a place - at least where real gentlemen live."

"Aye daughters. Athens is growing. I'm sure you'll meet nice gentlemen there."

"We'd rather live with Arch or William or Abigail while you and mother are away," said Sallie.

"No no," said Micajah shaking his head. "What would people think? It would be scandalous! Left here you might go peeking in taverns again." He smoked and pondered for a moment. "Just give Athens a chance. Okay?"

Neither daughter responded.

---

Early morning, late July, 1819.

The sun was a large ball of orange peeking over the distant sunburnt hills when they loaded into a wagon pulled by two oxen and departed Fayetteville. Following in two ox-drawn wagons were the Negroes, King Solomon, Stubby, Blood, Luke and John. The wagons were loaded with a few personal items, but mostly construction tools including saws, sledge hammers, mallets, shovels, wedges, axes, drills, buckets and masonry tools. They crossed Elk River by ferry and traveled south fifteen miles to Hazel Green, turned west on Limestone Road and proceeded toward Athens, some 25 miles away. The road wasn't much more than a dirt path hacked through the wilderness, and the going was difficult. They splashed through Briar Fork and Beaver Dam Creeks and slowly made their way across a swamp where mosquitoes and water moccasins were plentiful. After passing through Madison Crossroads, they forded Limestone Creek, and later crossed Piney Creek. The road improved and on the third day a few miles east of Athens, they stopped at a fine spring located in a cove where they freshened up and watered the stocks.

Micajah eyed the countryside. "Aye, 'tis good water and good land," he said. "Sovereign for raising cotton. Not nearly as rocky as back home."

Rolling thunder caught his attention. He looked to the west and saw black clouds. "We better hasten on," he said. A quarter mile down the road, they were fording Swan Creek when the sky collapsed. The road quickly grew muddy and Micajah pulled off onto a knoll where cedar trees grew in abundance.

"We'll wait here 'til it slacks," he said.

This would be a pretty place to build a house," remarked Sarah. And the rain beat down on the wagon canvas.

It was late afternoon and drizzling when they reached Athens. Everyone was soaked. Micajah had never seen a bleaker day. He reined the oxen. "Whoooooaa."

"Well here it is," he announced, "The Athens of the South. It's named after Athens, Greece, you know." The town of log buildings, small shanties and two brick structures was laid out around a public square that featured a pillory and stock, just west of a large spring. The streets had turned to mud. It was a dismal sight.

"Huh," huffed Sallie shaking her head. "I say, 'Athens of the south.'"

"It looks like a pig pen to me," added Nancy.

"I'll never meet a gentleman in this God-forsaken place," Sallie said.

They drove to the home of Ezekiel Smith, who lived in a two-story log house off the square where Micajah had previously made arrangements to board.

The following morning, the sky had cleared and Micajah walked around town. The streets were ankle deep in mud and horse manure, all chopped up by horse hooves and wagon wheels and blended into a brown brew. But the town wasn't nearly as backwater as his daughters thought. There were taverns, a wagon shop, saddle shop, silversmith shop, tailor and printing shop, cotton gin and even a newspaper, *The Athenian*. Several stores were around the square along with two brick buildings. And east of town was a brickyard. That would come in handy.

He scouted the outlying area and what he observed caused him concern. In addition to the Big Spring located several hundred yards east of the square, there were others. Tan Yard Spring was located west and Allen Spring was south of downtown. Underground streams were running everywhere. The water table was high and this spelled trouble.

Limestone County, named after a creek by the same name, had been carved out of adjoining Madison County by the Legislature on February 6, 1818. There were five trustees, a tax assessor, tax collector and a constable. Robert Beaty and John D. Carroll were selling lots around the Big Spring. The invention of the cotton gin had spurred many of the county residents to plant "white wool" which was labor intensive, but rapidly becoming the main cash crop. Of the 9,871 county inhabitants, 2,949 were slaves.

---

Micajah stood in the middle of the public square near a log courthouse and studied the building site. The courthouse was to be 40-by-60 in dimension and situated in the middle of the lot. Again, he didn't like what he saw. How deep was the water table and from which direction did it flow into the nearby springs? If the foundation shifted in the slightest, the brick walls would crack. He would have preferred a different location to build, but that wasn't his choice to make. He had already made known his concerns to the county commissioners but they weren't concerned. "Build it here," they had said. He stepped off the site in several directions, made some notes on a scrap of paper and motioned to one of the Negroes.

"King Solomon, drive a stake right there," he said, placing his finger on the ground. "This will be the southeast corner of the courthouse."

"Yassuh massa."

King Solomon tied a string to the stake he had driven while Micajah measured off forty feet to what would be the southwest corner. "Stubby, drive a stake here." The young Negro drove a stake as ordered and King Solomon pulled the string taut and tied it to the stake. The process was repeated until the correct dimensions of the footing were laid out, then the Negroes went to work digging with mallets and shovels. Several days were required to dig the footing two feet wide and 20 inches deep. While the digging was in progress, Micajah busied himself searching for a source of limestone to use as foundation. He found it across a small creek approximately a mile southeast of town. He reasoned that if he used enough slabs as footing, there would be less chance of shifting.

The Negroes were good workers except for Stubby, about 16 years of age, who

Micajah had bought only recently at an estate sale in Fayetteville. He was short and stocky with black eyes so cold that Micajah wondered if ice was behind them. When ordered to perform a chore, Stubby always responded with a glare before dropping his eyes and slowly moving to action. On the other hand, King Solomon and Blood were about 35 years old and good workers, as well as being good natured. Both were accomplished stone cutters and masons and had been with Micajah for several years. Their women were currently in Fayetteville working for William and Arch. Luke and John were excellent workers whom he had brought with him from North Carolina.

Micajah figured, absent bad luck and bad weather, he could easily finish constructing the courthouse in two years, pursuant to the performance bond he had given.

When day's work was done, he occasionally walked across the street to Bill Bell's tavern on the southeast corner of the square, threw his 12 ½ cents on the table and ordered a half pint of whiskey. It was a good place to meet folks and hear news.

The price of cotton was always discussed. It was falling fast. Another topic was national politics. The Presidential election of 1820 was approaching and most folks agreed that James Monroe of Virginia would be easily reelected. A red-hot issue was slavery and whether it should be allowed in the newly-admitted territories and states. Alabama had been admitted to the Union in 1819 as a slave state, bringing equal representation in the U.S. Senate between slave and free states. Missouri Territory, its population coming mostly from the south, was expected to enter statehood as a slave state. Northerners objected, saying it would upset the balance in the Senate. Congressman James Tallmadge of New York introduced an amendment which would bar importation of slaves into Missouri and eventually free all slaves born there. This sorely upset Southern Senators.

"Why can't them damn, self-righteous Yankees who brought slaves over here in the first place mind their own business?" asked a fellow over a pint of whiskey. Everyone agreed.

On the first Monday of each month, droves of folks flocked to Athens from outlying areas to attend court, purchase supplies, transact business and just have fun. Horses, mules and oxen were tied among wagons and buggies around the square swishing their tails at flies and stamping their feet in the ever-growing mound of manure that attracted more flies. Dogs ran wild, barking and chasing each other. Bonnet-clad women, faces hardly visible, walked on the plank sidewalk while their raggedy boys chased each other in the dusty street, threw rocks and often had fist fights.

The smoke-filled taverns were packed with men drinking, swearing and talking loudly. There were always cock fights with betting on the side accompanied by yelling and swearing at the losing rooster. Dog fights were common. Fist fights were not unusual, some friendly matches with wagering and others growing out of drinking too much whiskey and rum.

On several occasions a fellow brought a bear to town and bets were taken on whether an individual could remain in the cage with it for a minute. The bear always won.

When it wasn't raining, Micajah liked to watch Nick Davis, Nat Terry, Sam Ragland and Major McLin ride their race horses around the square several times to attract attention, then proceed two blocks west to a quarter-mile track that had been measured off. Nick Davis often won. He had fine-blooded horses, and it was said on occasions he ran them against Andrew Jackson's horses.

99

Christmas Eve, 1819.

Micajah stood at the second-story window puffing his pipe and watching falling snow create a blanket of white over the rail fence and pasture beyond the house.

Below, guests were arriving, some walking, the women wrapped in shawls and the men wearing capes. Others came in buggies which the Negroes parked. It was a peaceful scene. A door creaked and Micajah turned around as Sarah entered the room. She was wearing an ankle-length black dress with a large white brocade collar.

"Well, do thee like it?" she asked.

He smiled. "Aye, you made a perfect selection."

"Such a waste of money in these hard times," she said.

"You deserve it." He walked over to the fireplace and knocked the ashes from his pipe. "Well, I'm ready to go down when you are."

She helped him slip on his old black waist coat, the same one he had worn for years, turned down the collar, and then straightened his black fluffy cravat.

"Thee can carve a bird and build a fine house, but thee can't learn to tie a simple bow."

"There's no need to learn such a thing when I have a good woman who can do it for me," he replied, smiling.

"There! Now thee are as handsome as any Mooresville planter."

"Are Sallie and Nancy dressed and ready?" asked Micajah.

"I'll go check on them and we'll be down directly."

Micajah looked in the mirror and finger brushed his gray hair and decided he looked halfway presentable. He didn't know why it mattered. The folks that were invited to the party were mostly neighbors and friends of the Smiths and he had already met them.

He walked down the creaking stairs to the buzz of many voices and laughter.

Upstairs, Sarah entered the adjoining room, where Sallie was tugging at her dress and fretting. "This dress just doesn't look good on me," she said.

"Thee didn't say that when Father bought it," replied Sarah.

"Mother, please don't say 'thee' and 'thou'! It's so old-fashioned," said Sallie.

"Young people beat all," huffed Sarah and eyed Nancy.

"Both of you are beautiful. Now hurry along or thee will be late to our own party."

---

Robert C. David arrived late. He was backed up to the fireplace, warming and about to take a sip of hot apple cider when he realized that everyone's attention had turned to the stairway. He looked up and what he saw caused him to fumble his cup. Two women were slowly descending the stairs. The one that caused him to spill cider on his clean shirt was wearing a gorgeous black dress. But, it wasn't the dress that held his attention. It was her. She was blonde, of medium height with fine features and the prettiest woman he'd ever seen, either in Athens or in his native Giles County. The oil lamps in the room didn't provide enough lights for him to determine the color of her eyes, but he could see that she had beautiful white skin. He was about to ask someone her name when the host, Ezekiel Smith, saved him the trouble. He tapped a glass with a spoon and the room fell silent.

"Ladies and Gentlemen, first permit me to say that Mrs. Smith and I are happy that you joined us on this beautiful Christmas Eve night to celebrate not only the birth of our Lord and Savior, but to meet our new friends, the McElroys. As many of you know, Mr. Micajah McElroy is constructing our new courthouse. He and his family are from Lincoln County and will be boarding with us during construction. He has with him his lovely wife, Sarah." Smith swept his arm graciously toward Micajah and Sarah, which was followed by light applause. Both took a slight bow.

"Now, you single gentlemen may be interested to know that these two lovely ladies are their daughters." Again, Smith swept his arm toward the ladies. "Sallie is wearing the beautiful black dress and Nancy the gorgeous gray one." More light applause as both women curtsied.

"Now, you single gentlemen," Smith continued, "I must ask that you not monopolize their time as I am sure all of us are looking forward to meeting them also." There was laughter. "Please meet our friends," said Smith. A receiving line quickly formed.

Robert gulped down hot cider and fell in line. The men folk lingered in front of the young women, but he couldn't blame them. He met Micajah and Sarah, then Nancy, who was warm and friendly, but his interest was in her older sister. He stepped in front of Sallie and stuck out his hand, "Good evening Madam, I'm Robert C. David. Welcome to Athens." Her hand was warm and his was cold, which happened every time he got nervous. When her blue eyes met his, his heart skipped a beat.

"I'm Sallie and I'm delighted to meet you," she said. "Poor thing, your hands are so cold, don't you own gloves?"

"Well...., yes," he stammered. He tried to think of something intelligent to say, but couldn't. "I hope to see you again."

"Thank you," said Sallie as Robert moved forward in the line.

The Negro servants were stocking the table with food. There was baked turkey, hen and ham, roasted venison, bowls of gravy and sauce, heaping piles of biscuits and cornbread, boiled eggs, pickled cucumbers and beets, pitchers of sweet milk, buttermilk and bowls of fresh butter.

Mrs. Smith announced seating arrangements and placed Robert between Anna, her 13-year-old daughter, and Sallie McElroy. Robert pulled out chairs for them.

"Ladies, won't you please be seated," Robert said.

When the women were seated, the men took their seats. Mr. Smith thanked everyone for attending and said grace. He thanked God for the food, naming most of it by dish, and everything good under the heavens, prayed that sinners might be saved, then started with President Madison and came all the way down to Governor Bibb and even Sheriff Slaughter, asking that God guide their decisions and direct their hands. By the time he got to asking God to end the economic panic, Robert was drooling after smelling the pungent aroma of the food. Mrs. Smith coughed and Mr. Smith brought the prayer to a quick conclusion.

"What a beautiful prayer," remarked one of the ladies at the table. "Yes, it was," someone else replied and everyone wagged their heads in agreement.

Robert couldn't think of anything interesting to say to Sallie. "Well, I had just said that I hoped to see you again and, here we are."

She gave a false laugh. "Yes."

"How do you like Athens?" he asked.

"I'm accustomed to Fayetteville, a much larger town," she said with an air of superiority.

"Well, we have something in common. We're both Tennesseans. I'm originally from Giles County. It adjoins Limestone on the north, you know."

"Yes, I know that."

Young Anna jumped in the conversation. "Father says that Tennesseans think they won the War of 1812 single-handedly, but they really didn't."

"Oh he did?" replied Robert.

"Yes, but he doesn't want people to know he thinks that," replied Anna. "Says it might hurt his business. You won't tell will you?"

"Absolutely not," replied Robert, grinning.

The food was passed around the table to the right. "And what do you do?" Sallie asked Robert as she lifted a biscuit from the platter.

"I'm a clerk right now," said Robert. "I work at Lane & Barnes Dry Goods on the square."

"I see."

"But I don't intend doing that for the rest of my life. I'm only 20 years old and I have plenty of time."

"Oh! What are your plans?"

"I don't know just yet."

"Good luck," said Sallie, quickly losing interest and turning right to Hudson Sims to strike up a conversation.

Robert lingered at the party until he realized that most everyone had departed. He had hoped to spend more time with Sallie, but she had been monopolized by others. He thanked the Smiths for their hospitality, bade good night to the McElroys and finally to Sallie.

"Madam, I've enjoyed meeting you," he said shaking her hand. "I do hope I get to see you again."

"The pleasure is mine," she said, rather formally.

He departed the warm house and walked out into the cold night where snow continued to fall. The cedar trees were covered with a blanket of white. There was silence except for the crunch of his shoes in the snow and a barking dog somewhere in the distance. There had been times when he had doubted his decision to move to Athens where he knew no one. Now, he was glad to be here – especially after meeting Miss Sallie McElroy.

He was one of eleven children, the son of Lewis and Anna Means David of Giles County, Tennessee. Like his great-grandfather of Wales who immigrated to Pennsylvania around 1726, he had struck out in search of new life and arrived in Athens only a couple of years ago. He was 20 years old, in good health and figured he was smart as the next fellow. He trudged up the snow-covered steps at Lane & Barnes Dry Goods and entered a small, unheated room that contained only a cot, chair and table with a wash bowl. It wasn't much, but it was free. His plan was to become a good citizen, work hard and invest in land. Since Alabama had become a state only a few months earlier, swarms of people were flocking out of Madison County looking for land, which was selling from $2.00 to $50.00 an acre. John D. Carroll and Robert Beaty had been selling town lots like hotcakes until the panic struck. There was no money and few jobs, but Robert knew that wouldn't last forever. In the meantime, he would save his money, look for good land buys and be patient. Land prices were falling. It was an opportunity to buy. He didn't have enough savings to make cash purchases outright and borrowing from a bank was next to impossible, but using a keen eye, he could purchase good properties with a small down payment and give his note for the balance. By selling a property occasionally, he could hopefully generate enough money to make his note payments. He would boot strap himself to wealth. He might be only a lowly clerk now, but one day, he promised himself, he would be someone important.

---

It was a fine Christmas Day. The McElroys joined the Smiths eating leftovers from the party. Money was scarce but wood was plentiful. After a hearty dinner they sat in front of a roaring fire while Mr. Smith regaled them with stories about his family. Born in 1787 in Virginia, the family had moved to North Carolina following the Revolution. Smith later migrated to Madison County where he had lived for a while before moving to Athens and establishing a mercantile business.

The fire was warm and the afternoon dragged on. The women huddled together, knitted and gossiped.

"What did you think of Robert David?" Mrs. Smith asked Sallie.

"He was nice enough, but not really my type."

"They say he's from a good family in Giles County," said Mrs. Smith.

"What Sallie's really saying," interjected Nancy, "Is that he isn't a wealthy gentleman."

"Don't be silly," said Sallie glaring at her younger sister.

"It's the truth."

"It may be, but you don't have to tell everyone," replied Sallie.

"He's highly regarded in Athens," said Mrs. Smith. "I'd keep my eye on him."

Mrs. Smith looked at Nancy. "Young lady, he appeared to like your company a lot."

Nancy smiled. "All for nothing, Father says I'm too young to court."

"You won't be too young for long," replied Mrs. Smith.

While the women talked and knitted, Micajah and Smith discussed the economic panic, President Madison, the price of cotton and eventually the slavery issue.

"The greatest evil ever perpetrated upon this nation is slavery," said Smith.

Micajah yawned and puffed his pipe. "I must agree and the very people who grew wealthy bringing them to this country are the ones who are hardest against it. They made their fortunes by selling Negroes to southerners and now they preach to us."

"Hypocrites, pure and simple," said Smith.

"Aye, the industrialized north doesn't need slave labor like we do in the South," said Micajah. "Cotton is our major crop and it can't be worked without slave labor. Take away slavery and our economy will collapse. But, I agree it's a sinful thing. It's like holding a tiger by the tail. If you turn loose, it's going to claw you for sure."

"Northern politicians are stirring the slavery pot," said Smith. "The issue won't go away. It'll only get worse."

"It's legal in Alabama," replied Micajah, "and I'm glad. If I didn't have slaves I couldn't build the courthouse and make a profit. I guess I'm against slavery, but I can't do without 'em." He puffed his pipe and then added. "They're nothing but trouble. I bought a boy named Stubby. He doesn't have an ounce of the love of Christ inside 'im. When I tell him something he looks at me like he could cut my throat."

"He'd probably like to," said Smith.

"I don't know why, I'm good to 'im."

---

Snow covered the ground the day after Christmas, but Micajah was back at work. There wasn't a minute to lose. If he failed to complete the job on time he would have to pay a penalty for each day he was late. He couldn't waste time. Yet, he couldn't hurry. The structure would be no stronger than the foundation on which it rested. If the foundation shifted, the walls would crack. When satisfied that the footing trench was at least two feet wide, twenty inches deep and level all around, he directed the Negroes to prepare aggregate. This was time-consuming and arduous work. Chunks of limestone rock were smashed into gravel with sledge hammers then shoveled into the trench.

Micajah examined the aggregate. None were of the same size and he worried that the larger stones would shift under the foundation. In addition there was the potential problem that an underground stream flowed beneath the structure. Satisfied that the aggregate was spread as smoothly as possible, after the weather warmed they commenced pouring concrete several inches deep on top of the aggregate. After allowing the concrete several days to dry and season, the Negroes began the laborious process of lowering thick slabs of chiseled limestone on top of the concrete. He placed a carpenter's level device on top of each stone and when satisfied they were perfectly level, additional slabs were stacked on top all the way around until stones protruded twelve inches above ground. On top of this would rest the brick walls of the courthouse. Not only would the limestone slabs support the building, they would be pleasing to the eye. Micajah intended his creation to be a lasting monument to his craftsmanship.

When the foundation was complete, Luke and John began hauling brick from Dick Hale's brickyard, a few blocks east of the square. The walls would be four bricks for a total of sixteen inches thick. Sleepers under the structure would be hewn from white oak logs and flattened on top where the floor boards would be nailed. King Solomon and Blood laid brick while Stubby mixed sand, lime and water into a mortar mix which he carried to them. Micajah kept a close eye on Stubby, who was falling behind with his work.

"Stubby, you're lazing around again," said Micajah. Stubby looked at him with coal black eyes.

"Yassuh massa, I'll try to do bett'r."

"See that you do."

---

Spring 1820 came with the usual rains slowing construction. In addition, Stubby continued to laze around until he witnessed a Negro placed in the stock for similar behavior. That temporarily improved his attitude.

By June 3rd, the red brick walls were standing and they were beginning to construct the roof. It was near dark when they knocked off for the day. Micajah backed off and eyed his creation. It was a magnificent seat of justice. Standing two stories high, it was currently the tallest building in Limestone County. He was proud of it. The question was whether he would turn a profit. He hoped to be finished and back home in

104

Fayetteville by Christmas.

He had been told that a three-story log jail was to be constructed down the hill from the southwest corner of the square. It was to be 20-by-40 in dimension, veneered with well-burnt brick one-and-a-half thick with fireplaces in each room. When finished it would be the tallest building in Athens. Debtor rooms would be located on the second floor. The way the economy was headed, they would be quickly filled. It gave him something to ponder.

---

Independence Day, 1820.

Micajah and family joined others as they walked down to the Big Spring, where a celebration was about to begin. Sallie and Nancy each carried a basket containing a dessert they had baked which would be auctioned off to the highest bidder.

"I'm sure Robert will be present," said Sarah said to Sallie.

"I don't care if he is or not."

"Storyteller," said Nancy. "You told me last night you hoped to see him."

"Will you please hush?"

"That's what you said," Nancy shot back.

"What if I did?"

"Now ladies, remember to be ladies," counseled their mother.

A large crowd had gathered near the spring. Saddle and buggy horses were tethered in the shade of large trees where they neighed, pawed the ground and swished their tails at flies. Dogs barked and chased each other while young boys ran and squealed. One boy had already fallen in the spring and was crying and looking for his mother. Metal clinked as men pitched horseshoes. However, the main interest seemed to be the several shoats that were barbecuing beneath a brush arbor. Robert Beaty and John Carroll had furnished the pork and a couple of their Negroes were brushing sauce on the meat. Fat drippings sizzled on the hot coals, sending up an aroma that made Micajah's mouth water. Tables fashioned from wide boards placed across saw horses were laden with bowls of food prepared by the women. Negro girls stood behind the tables fanning away flies with tree branches.

In the distance, a fiddler was warming up, and a pile of wood was being readied for a bonfire later. It was festive.

Mayor Samuel Tanner climbed on the back of a wagon and rang a bell. "Ladies and gentlemen, on behalf of the Town Trustees I welcome you to this Independence Day celebration," he said in his high-pitched voice. "Forty-four years ago we declared our Independence from England –"

A great hurrah went up from the crowd.

"– but declaring that we were free from the tyranny of King George did not give us freedom. We had to fight for it!"

Another loud hurrah.

"And we won!"

Loud cheering.

"Some of you present today fought in the Revolution and we honor you for your service. But, the English didn't quit easily. After we defeated them in the Revolution they returned during the War of 1812 and burned our Capital and we had to whip them again. After the licking that General Jackson gave them in New Orleans five years ago, I

105

promise you they won't be back."

More loud cheering.

"I know that all of us are anxious to taste the succulent pork and sample the repast of food the ladies have prepared, but first let us give thanks. At this time I call on one of our finest young citizens, Robert C. David, to lead us in prayer."

Sallie jerked her head around as Robert mounted the wagon and removed his black hat.

"Can you believe it?" blurted Sallie.

"Sh...shh." said Nancy.

"Don't shush me," whispered Sallie.

Sallie had spoken to Robert at church and even been on a few afternoon strolls with him, but didn't realize he was so well regarded.

Robert led a quiet, but thoughtful prayer, unencumbered by big words and colorful phrases. His language wasn't eloquent like that of the educated planter class, who were trained in elocution. It was simple and to the point.

Following the prayer, Mayor Tanner directed everyone's attention several hundred feet away where an anvil was being lifted on top of another one. Black gunpowder was placed between the two anvils.

"When the anvil shoot is over, we'll line up and eat. Now back up and watch out!"

A man touched off the powder. There was a loud explosion and an anvil shot through the black smoke and sailed into the blue sky. Horses bolted and jerked against their reins. Children screamed and babies cried. Adults laughed and clapped their hands.

Micajah and family loaded their plates with food and found the shade of a large oak tree. A gentle breeze whipped across the spring, sending cool air their way. "Aye, nothing better than a cool breeze on Independence Day," said Micajah.

Robert David was wandering around, plate in hand, looking for a shady spot when Micajah motioned to him. "Come over and join us Robert."

Robert looked up, smiled and walked over. He removed his hat. "Good afternoon everyone. Miss Sallie, how you?"

"Just fine," she said smiling.

"Won't you join us?" asked Micajah.

"Don't mind if I do." He found a level spot and plopped down.

"Thee led such a good prayer," said Sarah. "Some folks get carried away with their own voice when they pray and act like they are making an election speech."

"Mother!" Sallie was embarrassed by her mother's old-fashioned language.

"Thank you ma'am," said Robert. "The truth is, I'm a simple man and not very eloquent."

"Robert, I must say that in this day and time when many young men are wasting their time drinking, gambling, horse racing and fighting, thee are doing something that's positive," said Sarah. "I commend you."

"Thank you ma'am."

"Father loves horse racing," interjected young Nancy. "And I've seen him go into Bill Bell's Tavern."

Sallie spoke up. "Mother said, 'young men.' Father isn't young and therefore it doesn't apply to him."

Micajah chuckled and looked at Robert. "Aye, I don't know if I've been

complimented or indicted.   Living with three women is a challenge sometimes."
Everyone laughed.

Mayor Tanner mounted the wagon bed and announced that the dessert auction was about to commence.

"Now this part of the celebration will be of great interest to you single men," he said.   "The successful bidder will not only get to eat a delicious dessert, but will also enjoy the company of the young lady who prepared it.   The proceeds go to charity so reach deep in your pockets and bid like you're rich."   He picked up a dessert.   "Here is a fine-looking apple pie prepared by Miss Polly Brown.   Who'll be the lucky young man to buy this pie and enjoy the company of Miss Brown?   Who will start the bidding?"

"Twenty-five cents," yelled a man.

"Twenty-six cents," yelled another.

"We've got twenty-six cents.   Who will bid twenty-seven?"

"A half dollar," someone shouted.

The Mayor worked hard to get a higher bid before finally knocking it off at fifty cents.

The bidding for desserts went on with great gusto and frivolity.   Nancy's single-layer cake was purchased by Samuel Davis for thirty-five cents.

Sallie craned her neck searching for her double layer chocolate cake.   Mayor Tanner picked it up.   "Now here is a treat for you gentlemen.   A big chocolate cake just begging to be eaten.   Who'll start the bidding?"

"Thirty cents!"

"Well, blow me down!" exclaimed Sallie.   "My cake is worth far more than thirty cents."

"The bidding isn't over Sallie, calm down," cautioned her father.

The bidding continued.   Sallie kept watching Robert out of the corner of her eye to see if he was about to bid. He said nothing.

"I've got sixty cents," said the Mayor.   "Who'll bid sixty-five cents?"

"Sixty-one."

"Sixty-two."

"One dollar!" someone yelled.   Again Robert made no effort to bid.

"I got one dollar," said the mayor.   "Who'll raise the bid?"

No response.

"One dollar once, one dollar twice, one dollar three times.   Sold to Mister… ah sir, what's your name?"   A man wearing homespun clothes stepped up.   "Tobias Dunnavant from Pea Ridge."

Sallie turned on Robert like a chicken on a June bug.   "You didn't even bid on my chocolate cake that I spent half the night preparing so that you would buy it.   What kind of gentleman are you?   Father, I'm leaving right now!"

"Now hold your horses, daughter," said Micajah.

Dunnavant walked over and handed the basket containing the cake to Robert, who gave him a dollar piece.   "Thanks," said Robert.   "I'm indebted to you."

"What's going on?" asked Sallie.

"I purchased your cake," said Robert.   "Now let's go eat it."

Sallie was stunned.   "You mean that Dunnavant was bidding on your behalf?"

"Yes."

"I have greatly embarrassed myself," said Sallie, her face turning bright red.

107

"Please forgive me Robert."

"Forgiven." He stood and reached down and grabbed her hand. "Let's find another shady spot and we'll see what kind of cook you are." They found a level spot beneath a large oak tree near the cemetery and sat down on the ground. Robert removed a cloth from the basket, spread it on the ground and placed the cake on top of it. He sliced off a piece for each of them and placed it on a saucer. He took a mouthful and chewed it slowly, enjoying the exquisite taste of chocolate.

"Welll...?"

"Well what?" asked Robert his mouth full of cake.

"Do you like it?"

"It could use a little more chocolate," said Robert and sliced off another piece.

Sallie's brows wrinkled and her eyes narrowed. She was about to give Robert a piece of her mind and tell him how long she had labored to bake the perfect cake. Then she then realized that he was actually complimenting her in a back door way. It was so delicious he was actually saying he wanted more. She decided to turn the joke on him.

"Oh, I'm so hurt, boo hoo hoo." She dabbed fake tears from her eyes.

"Now Miss Sallie, please don't cry. I was just trying to be humorous. Don't you understand? A chocolate cake can't be more chocolate than it already is."

"Boo-hoo-hoo, I've failed."

"No... no, it's delicious. Please accept my apology."

Sallie peered between her fingers that covered her face. "Do you really mean that?"

"Yes, it's the most delicious chocolate cake ..... no, it's the most delicious of all cakes I've ever eaten in my entire life."

"Do you apologize?"

"Yes, yes, I'm sorry, I promise I'll never hurt your feelings ever again Miss Sallie."

When State Representative Nicholas Davis was introduced as guest speaker, Robert suggested to Sallie that they take a stroll. It wasn't that Robert didn't like Nick Davis, he did. Davis not only was a popular Representative, he was a framer of Alabama's Constitution and one of the wealthiest men in the county. Instead, Robert had more important things to do – entertain Miss Sallie McElroy.

The celebration ended that evening with the firing of a cannon and a huge bonfire that lit up the night sky.

---

The nation continued to slide deeper into financial ruin. Banks failed, unable to pay in specie when demanded by customers. Unemployment was running 75 percent in Philadelphia. Debtor prisons were overflowing. Micajah had never seen the economy this bad. He was concerned for himself. Huge financial outlays had been required to build the courthouse and if he turned a profit, he'd be lucky. He was having to borrow money to keep afloat. The new jail to be constructed would have a debtor's room on the second floor. No doubt it would soon be filled. He hoped that he wasn't one of the occupants.

He had hired John M. Gray, a slave from Burnett Battle, to help with construction. Battle claimed the sum of $86, which Micajah couldn't repay immediately.

Micajah wasn't surprised when he saw Sheriff Slaughter ambling toward him as he worked on the courthouse. He had an ominous feeling.

"Mornin' Sheriff. How you?"

"Tolerable, Mr. McElroy."

"Is this a social call or business?" asked Micajah.

"I'm afraid it's business," He handed Micajah a document. "Sorry."

"I was afraid of that," said Micajah as he unfolded the paper and saw that Burnett Battle had sued him for $86. "You just doing your duty Sheriff, I understand."

"Good day sir," said the Sheriff and departed.

Micajah folded the paper and stuffed it in his back pocket and returned to work. Building the courthouse had promised financial rewards, but was bringing about his financial ruin. However, there was no place to go but forward. He would complete the job and give the citizens of Limestone County a courthouse they could be proud of.

Micajah didn't appear in court to answer the suit. What was the purpose? He owed the money without question.

Several weeks later Micajah looked up and again saw Sheriff Slaughter approaching.

"Afternoon Sheriff. More papers?"

"Yes sir, I'm afraid so."

"What is it this time?"

"I've got a writ of capias signed by William T. Gamble, Clerk of the Court."

"What is that?" asked Micajah.

Sheriff Slaughter unfolded a document. "I'll read it to you. It says: 'To the Sheriff of Limestone County, greetings: You are hereby commanded to take the body of Micajah McElroy wherever he may be found in your county and him safely keep so that you have his body before the Judge of our Circuit Court to be held for the County of Limestone at the Courthouse in the Town of Athens, on the second Monday in March next, to him to answer Burnett Battle who sues for the use of John M. Gray...' so forth. He claims you owe $86 and other damages of $50."

"You mean to remain in jail until the court date?" asked Micajah.

"Yes sir, I'm afraid so. Let's go."

Micajah was embarrassed. Jailed for a debt. He didn't blame Burnett Battle. He was probably scrambling for money to stay out of debtor's prison himself.

When Robert C. David heard what had happened, he immediately paid Burnett Battle and Micajah was released from jail.

"I'll pay you back just as soon as I can raise the money," said Micajah.

"Sir, I know you will."

---

Several days later, a well-dressed stranger wearing a wide-brimmed brown hat drove up in a buggy pulled by a fine chestnut horse. He sat and watched the crew working. Finally, he got out of the buggy and walked over to where Micajah was planing boards.

"Good afternoon, sir," he said.

"And good afternoon to you," replied Micajah.

The man poked out his hand. "I'm Washington Jones from Mooresville, overseer at the Rice plantation."

"Micajah McElroy here." He took his hand.

109

"It's my pleasure sir," said Jones. "I've had my eye on that negro boy over there," he said and pointed.

"Aye, Stubby."

"He looks strong as an ox."

"That he is," said Micajah.

"I could use a strong boy on the plantation. I recently lost one of my best field hands to the fever."

"The fever don't play favorites," said Micajah. "It kills both blacks and whites."

"Is the boy healthy?"

"Aye, I take good care of him and feed 'im well."

"Would you consider selling him?"

"Everything I own is for sale if the price is right."

"What about his disposition?" asked Jones.

"Sir, I won't mislead you. He's got a streak of the devil in 'im."

"A few lashes on the back will chase the devil right out of him," said Jones.

They made a deal on the spot. Jones prepared a bill of sale, which Micajah signed in return for $900. He had money to pay his debts and at the same time was rid of a problem. Truly, the Lord works in mysterious ways.

# 11 | ROMANCE

Athens

Fall, 1821.

Robert C. David was a happy man. He stood before the mirror, head tilted back, carefully shaving his neck with a straight razor. When finished, he wiped away soap lather, and then trimmed his stubby black beard and mustache. Satisfied, he parted his black hair on the left side and combed it back where it hung to his collar. Then he dressed. He had recently purchased gray pants with matching vest, white shirt and a black waistcoat. He tied the floppy black silk cravat in a bow, slipped on his coat and stood before the mirror for one last look. He had come a long way since moving to Athens only three years earlier working as a clerk and living in an upstairs room at Lane & Barnes Dry Goods. Now he owned his own house, a modest log one, but yet comfortable; was a member of the Masonic Hall, a good Methodist and now Postmaster. The regular Postmaster, James W. Exum, was departing Athens to do surveying work in another state and just this morning he had appointed Robert to assume his duties. The job could last for months, or even years. The pay was low, but it was a positive step in Robert's plan for success.

Sometime, the hardest part of life is deciding what one wants. That was no problem for Robert. He knew what he wanted – financial success and now, Miss Sallie McElroy. With the nation sliding into economic depression, his financial successes had come in small increments, but he never gave up his dream. After all, he thought, Proverbs 23 says "as a man thinketh in his heart, so is he."

It was twilight when he departed his house just north of the square and walked south. Leaves were turning orange and yellow. Tree frogs were croaking, but the rasping mating call of the July flies had long since ceased, their hollow carcasses now clinging to tree limbs. Fall had arrived in North Alabama. He walked past the new courthouse, complete except for some finishing work to be done inside.

When he reached Ezekiel Smith's residence, he knocked, fidgeted with his coat sleeve which felt too short, and waited. Samuel, a Negro servant, opened the door.

"Good evening Mistuh David, won't you come in?"

Robert stepped inside. "Is Mr. McElroy in?"

"Yassuh," said Samuel. "He be in the parlor all by hisself smok'n his pipe and ponder'n. Come with me, suh."

"Thank you Samuel."

Robert followed Samuel into the parlor, where Micajah was staring blankly out the window and smoking his pipe. He looked up.

"Mistuh David suh," announced Samuel.

Micajah rose to his feet and offered his hand. "Aye Robert, tis good to see you. Have a seat."

"Thank you sir," Robert said and sat on the couch.

Micajah waited for Robert, who was pulling on his sleeve, to speak. He cleared his throat. "Well, uh uh... Mr. McElroy, you know how much I think of Sallie and well, I'll just tell you the truth. I'm as nervous as a cat walking on a bed of hot coals."

Micajah puffed his pipe in silence.

"To get right to the point, I've come to ask your permission to marry Miss Sallie."

111

Micajah barely nodded his head, sensing that Robert hadn't finished speaking.

"I can take good care of her and as of this morning I'm acting Postmaster. The pay isn't much, but I have income from land deals and such. She'll be comfortable in life... and I'll be good to her," he almost forgot to say. "I intend to sink my roots right here in Athens where I have many friends."

"You've made quite a splash for a young man only 23 years old," said Micajah.

"Twenty-two," Robert corrected him.

"But, do you love Sallie?"

"Oh yes sir, I do. Over the last few months we've spent lots of time together, going on buggy rides, taking long walks and having picnics. I've gotten to know her quite well. She's a mighty fine woman."

"Aye, that she is," agreed Micajah. "Now, that doesn't mean that she doesn't have a mind of her own. She's strong-willed Robert – strong-willed."

"Yes sir, I've learned that too."

"A man needs a woman with backbone," said Micajah. "A smart man will recognize that."

"Yes sir, I believe that to be true."

Micajah put down his pipe, levered himself from the chair and approached Robert with his hand extended. Robert jumped to his feet.

"I'd be honored to have you as a son-in-law," said Micajah grasping his hand.

"Thank you sir, I won't disappoint you," he said, shaking Micajah's hand vigorously and turning to leave.

"Have you talked to Sallie?"

"No sir."

"Good luck."

---

When Robert woke on Sunday morning he reached over and pulled back the window curtain to see clear blue skies and autumn leaves drifting down from nearby maple trees. He took it as a good sign. Today he would propose to Miss Sallie McElroy. He didn't have an exact plan worked out about when and where he would pop the question. It pretty much depended on when he got up his nerve. He lay on his back, hands clasped behind his head, and pondered a plan of action. After church services he would invite her for an afternoon walk to Big Spring. Hopefully after hearing a sermon by the new minister, Reverend Louis S. Marshall, her heart would be filled with love and her mind receptive to his overture. Whew! The more he thought about it the more complicated it became. Things could go awry. Doubt began to creep in. What if she didn't attend church this morning? What if she didn't want to go for a walk to Big Spring? Or, what if she already had agreed to go picnicking with Hudson Sims? That young swain had been nosing around Sallie far too much.

He swung out of bed, stoked a fire in his Franklin stove and drew several buckets of water from the well, some of which he heated on top of the stove, the remainder he poured into a wood washtub. While the water heated, he shaved and brushed his teeth with salt and soda, sprinkled on a toothbrush he had fashioned from a hickory twig. When the water was hot, he poured it into the washtub and stirred it around until it was good and warm. He sat in the tub, knees pulled to his chest, and scrubbed himself with lye soap until his skin was pink. A woman likes a clean man, he thought,

112

then he scrubbed some more. After drying in front of the stove, he brushed his new gray pants and black waist coat then dressed and combed his beard and parted his hair. Just before walking out the door, it occurred to him that he hadn't eaten breakfast, but he was too nervous to eat. He felt in his right coat pocket for the ring. It wasn't there! He felt in his other pocket. No ring! "Where in tarnation is it?" he asked aloud. Just as he was about to panic, he remembered he had left it on the bedside table. He placed it in his right pocket and when he walked out the door, stopped and took a deep breath. It was the most beautiful autumn day he had ever seen. Yes, it was a good omen.

He walked south past the square then turned east on Washington Street toward Matthews School where the Methodists were currently meeting. Many people were walking to church services this morning. A warm breeze rattled pumpkin-colored leaves and sent them drifting down from above where they tumbled across the ground.

"Good morning Robert. Congratulations on becoming Postmaster," said a gentleman across the street.

"Thank you and good morning to you," he replied.

He looked for the McElroys, but didn't see them. Maybe they were already inside.

More folks than usual had already gathered in the log school house just across the street from the cemetery where the Methodist were currently meeting.

He took a seat near the back and looked around for the McElroy family, but didn't see them. Micajah didn't always attend church, but Mrs. McElroy and the girls seldom missed a service. His well-laid plan was already falling apart. A sick feeling welled up in the pit of his stomach. Where was she?

Robert couldn't keep his mind on the service. While opening prayer was offered, his mind wandered. Perhaps there was illness in the McElroy family. If so, it hadn't been mentioned. When the prayer ended, he had heard the back door open, then creaking floor planks. He looked over and saw Sallie and her mother and sister come in and take a seat. He relaxed, looked over their way and smiled.

Reverend Marshall's sermon "The Wiles of Satan" wasn't conducive to putting Sallie in an open and trusting frame of mind toward a man she had only recently met. It was the longest church service Robert had ever sat through, or at least that's the way it seemed to him. When the parishioners were finally dismissed, everyone walked out the back door to shake hands with Reverend Marshall and pass a few words.

Sallie, her mother and younger sister were standing in the front yard, conversing with other parishioners and enjoying the warm sunshine, when Robert walked over.

"Afternoon Mrs. McElroy," he said. "And afternoon to you Miss Sallie, you certainly look nice today."

"Thank you Robert."

"Do I look nice too?" asked Nancy. Robert blushed. "Why yes ma'am."

They walked toward town, Mrs. McElroy making small talk about the beautiful weather and the fact that Micajah wasn't feeling well.

"His lumbago is bothering him again. All that lifting building the courthouse hasn't been good for him," she said. "I'll be glad when the job is completed and we can return to Fayetteville."

"It's a mighty fine courthouse," said Robert. "I hate to see y'all leave Athens, but I know the day is coming."

Sallie changed the subject.

113

"Robert, I've never seen you so well-dressed, new suit and all. A girl might think it's a special day you're celebrating."

"Yes ma'am, it is."

"Oh! What?"

His heart raced. Should he tell her the truth in front of her mother and little sister? It wouldn't be proper, he decided.

"Being selected Acting Postmaster, I suppose."

"I heard about that," said Sallie. "Congratulations."

When they arrived at the front door, Robert's heart was really racing. "Miss Sallie, it sure is a beautiful day. I would be honored if you would walk with me to the Big Spring this afternoon, and uh, uh..." His words dribbled out. He couldn't think of anything else to say.

"Why, I'd love to," replied Sallie.

"Well, okay, say, about three o'clock?"

"That will be fine."

"Goodbye, see you at three," he said and departed jauntily. He couldn't believe how easy it had been. He still had no appetite and when he tried to take a nap, he was too excited to sleep. At three o'clock he knocked on the front door and Samuel asked him inside.

"I've come to call on Miss Sallie."

"Yah suh, Mr. Robert, I'll fetch her."

Robert was standing in the foyer with one hand in his pocket fingering the engagement ring, when Sallie entered. She was wearing her long black dress that came to her ankles and a white blouse with a collar that came up high on her neck. Sitting dashingly on her blonde head was a stylish bonnet and she was carrying a parasol. For a moment he was speechless.

"Miss Sallie, you- you are beautiful."

She batted her eyes. "Why thank you Robert."

He held out his arm. "Shall we go?"

She hooked her arm onto his and they walked out into the afternoon sunshine and strolled toward the Big Spring while Robert made small talk.

"I declare it's the finest autumn day I believe I've ever seen Miss Sallie. Don't you agree?"

"I hadn't thought about it."

Every time he was in Sallie's presence he became tongue-tied and couldn't think of anything intelligent to say. "Yes sir, it's a mighty fine day."

They walked over to Big Spring and sat on a rock that had been warmed by the sun. It was now or never. He took her hand and was about to speak.

"Robert, your hand is cold as ice," she said.

"Miss Sallie, I'm not very good at trying to be something I'm not. And I'm not eloquent like Hudson Sims and the other gentlemen. I'm just a plain fellow from Giles County. Every time I get nervous my hands get cold. I can't help it."

"Cold hands, warm heart, they say." She looked at him squarely in the eye for the first time. "Why are you so nervous Robert?"

He hesitated, and then stammered for a moment. "Well, I – I – I'll just tell you the God's truth."

"What?"

114

He palmed the ring and pulled it from his pocket and dropped to one knee. "Sallie, I've been planning this for a long time," he said meeting the gaze of her blue eyes. "I'll dress you in fine clothes and put you in a fine house and love and cherish you and care for you until the day you die and give you children – "

"And what Robert?"

"Will you marry me?"

Sallie smiled broadly and remembered what her mother had said about her own engagement. "Robert, get off your knee and kiss me."

He scrambled to his feet and took her into his arms and kissed her full lips. For an instant she was rigid, but her body quickly relaxed. She moaned slightly and kissed him back, but only for a moment. "Someone might see us," she whispered and giggled. "Oh Robert I've been praying this moment would come."

"So have I. I knew that I wanted you in my life since the first time I saw you come down the stairs at the Christmas Eve party nearly two years ago."

"I fell in love with you during the picnic on Independence Day," she said. "You were so humble and gentle yet manly – the very definition of a gentleman."

"Oh, I almost forgot!" said Robert, showing her the engagement ring, a modest gold one with a small solitary diamond. She held out her finger and he slid it on. "It's not much, but someday I'll buy you a real nice one."

"It's beautiful and I love it," she said, turning her hand and admiring the ring.

Shadows were lengthening when they started back to the house. There was so much to be discussed – making the formal announcement, the wedding date and place. But, the first priority was to share the wonderful news with her family.

"Goodness!" exclaimed Sallie. "I forgot to ask, have you talked to father?"

"Yes, and he's in full accord."

Robert was beaming as Samuel ushered Mr. and Mrs. McElroy and Nancy into the parlor.

"Would you please close the door?" asked Robert.

"Yas suh, Mistah Robert."

Robert looked at them, trying to conjure up exactly what he wanted to say and how he would say it. Nancy had a quizzical expression on her face that fell somewhere between expecting a death announcement and an invitation to a ball. Mrs. McElroy was expressionless except that he noticed she was rubbing her hands. A mischievous twinkle was in Micajah's eyes. All were staring at him. He nervously cleared his throat.

"I have an important announcement to make," he said boldly. "Sallie and I are to be married."

Mrs. McElroy uttered a barely audible sound and her shoulders went limp as she looked askance toward Micajah who was smiling broadly. He put his arms around her. "Robert and I have talked and I gave my permission," he said reassuring her.

"Let me be the first to congratulate you," Micajah said offering his hand. Sarah finally got her voice. "It's just that I was caught off guard," she said stumbling for words, then began sobbing. "My daughter is leaving me. I'm so sad, yet so happy for her. I'm sorry Robert, mothers sometimes get emotional about these things." She dabbed her eyes with a handkerchief. "Really, I'm so happy for both of you." And then she sobbed more.

"Look!" said Sallie, flashing her engagement ring trying to guide the conversation to a happier tone. "Isn't it beautiful?"

"Sister is finally going to jump over the broom," chimed Nancy, who until now had been silent.

"Mother, make her stop!" cried Sallie.

Sarah turned to Nancy. "Daughter, that is totally inappropriate! Negro women jump over the broom. Fine Southern ladies marry."

---

The ceremony took place on a clear and cold Saturday afternoon in late November at Ezekiel Smith's home where the McElroy's had boarded for the last two years. Reverend Louis S. Marshall of the Methodist Church officiated. The parlor was crowded with guests.

Micajah, his hair gray and thinning, hands gnarled from years of honest toil and slightly stooped from lumbago, was smiling. His once white shirt was dingy from too many washings and the floppy black cravat was just that – unorderly and floppy. He had brushed his old black waist coat until it shined.

Robert was nattily attired in his new gray pants, matching vest, white shirt and floppy black cravat and black waist coat.

When guests heard stair boards creaking, they looked up to see Sallie descending, blushing as she smiled at Robert.

Reverend Marshall conducted the ceremony with great solemnity, most of which didn't register with Robert. His mind was racing with excitement. "And now I pronounce you man and wife..." Those were the words that Robert had dreamed of hearing. "You may kiss the bride," said Reverend Marshall.

Robert raised the veil and kissed Sallie tenderly on her lips. The guests clapped. A reception followed.

When the eating was over and Sallie and Robert were preparing to depart to his house on their honeymoon, Nancy and several other unmarried girls gathered outside the front door.

"Stand behind me," said Sallie. The young women laughed and giggled. "Whoever catches it will be the lucky girl," said Sallie closing her eyes and tossing the bouquet of zinnias behind her. The women shrieked and scrambled for the bouquet.

"I got it!" Sallie turned and saw Nancy holding the bouquet against her breast and smiling. "Good luck sister," said Sallie.

After assisting Sallie into the buggy, Robert climbed in and pulled a blanket over their laps. Some of Robert's mischievous Masonic brethren had tied a trace chain to the back of the buggy which rattled, frightening the horse.

"Whoooooa horse, whoa!" exclaimed Samuel. "You better not mess up Mistah Robert's wedding." He popped his whip and they pulled off amid laughter, the chain rattling.

---

Finally, the courthouse was completed. Only one thing remained to be done. Samuel Crenshaw had made a clock at his foundry on Big Creek, near Elk River, and installed it in the cupola. Dedication was held on Trade Day and attended by the commissioners, elected officials and Mayor Tanner. Hundreds of county residents were present for the ceremony. Micajah, financially broke but proud of his accomplishments, was introduced to the crowd. "Aye, our little family has enjoyed living among you for

116

the past two years," he said. "In fact, so much that my daughter Sallie married your postmaster, Robert C. David. Now, my wife, Sarah and daughter, Nancy must return to our home in Fayetteville. I thank you for your kindness and hospitality and leave you with a fine courthouse that will hopefully last until Gabriel blows his trumpet... Well, maybe it won't last that long." Laughter from the crowd. "I bid you farewell," Micajah said and waved to the crowd. He eased to the background while the Stars and Stripes were raised above the cupola and Representative Nick Davis stepped forward and addressed the people.

The following morning was a day that Nancy had looked forward to, yet dreaded. Even the December weather had conspired against her. She walked out of the house into iron gray skies and biting north wind. Pausing, she turned and looked back at the house where she had spent the last two years of her life. She had reluctantly come to Athens as a sixteen year old child and now she was leaving a woman. So many wonderful memories were here – fighting with her older sister, meeting young men and growing up. She wondered if she would ever see Athens again.

She turned and walked toward the loaded wagons where the Negroes perched, hunched against the cold. Robert and Sallie were talking with her parents. Nancy walked up, her eyes welled with tears. "Ohhh sister, my heart is filled with sorrow. Will I ever see you again?"

"Yes, and please don't cry or you'll make me cry," said Sallie.

"I'm sorry I haven't always been a good sister and said unkind things to you. Will you please forgive me?"

They fell into each other's arms and wept. "I love you sister," said Nancy.

"And I love you," said Sallie. "Look at the bright side. You'll be home for Christmas. And you'll meet a nice gentleman that will fill up your life."

"Do you really think so?"

"I know it," replied Sallie.

The women hugged for a final time while Micajah and Robert shook hands. They climbed into the wagon, waved goodbye and pulled blankets around their shoulders.

"Git up!" commanded King Solomon. "We's be head'n back to de promised land."

117

# PART II

# 12 | A NEW LIFE

Summer, 1823.

Christian County, Kentucky.

James Daniel Barksdale was on the brink of making a life-changing decision. And a one-eyed bay horse named Andy was helping him make it. The soil was rocky, the row long and the sun was bearing down. The beast kept stepping on the corn stalks and snatching mouthfuls of the tender tops.

"Haw Andy!" He popped the leather plow lines on the horse's back. "By crackies, stay in the row!"

He was convinced the animal understood English, especially when it was feeding time, but not when it came to plowing a straight row. He had been plowing corn since daybreak and his stomach told him it was dinnertime. "Whoa… Andy." The horse stopped and snatched a mouthful of green corn shoots. Daniel squinted at the sun which hung almost directly overhead.

"DINNERTIIIME," he yelled to the Negroes, Luke, John and Big Pete, who were plowing nearby. They plowed to the end of the row where they unhooked the scratcher plows, looped the trace chains over the harness hames and drove the horses back to the barn. As soon as the harnesses were removed, the horses ran into the barn lot, rolled in the hot dust, then drank voraciously from a water trough made from a hollowed out oak log. Afterwards, the Negroes put out fodder and gave each horse several ears of corn.

Daniel entered his cabin, tossed his wide-brimmed hat, brown with dirt and sweat in the corner, plopped down at a crude table and mopped perspiration from his forehead. Lil' Alice dipped a bowl of pork stew from a blackened kettle that hung over the fireplace and set it before him. Even with all the doors open it was unbearably hot inside the house.

"Dis stew mighty fine Massa Dan'l. Betta eat fore de flies do."

"Sure smells good."

"Hoecakes be com'n up." She squatted in front of the fireplace and poured boiling water into a small bowl of cornmeal; let stand for a minute or so, then spooned dollops and fried until brown. She brought them to Daniel along with a glass of fresh sweet milk that was still warm from the cow's udders.

"When you git yoself a woman you won't be throw'n thangs in de floor," she said, picking up his hat and hanging it on a peg by the door.

"I'll never find a woman around here," he said and swallowed a spoonful of stew. "Ummm good. Now, if I could find a woman who can cook stew and hoecakes as good as you, I'd marry her in a minute."

"Dere be mo 'vailable women out dere than rabbits in a briar patch."

Daniel chuckled. Lil' Alice was like a mother to him. She had been with his family before they made the long journey from Virginia to Wilson County, Tennessee in 1804. When his mother was ill with fever, Alice had wet nursed him. She was short and thin, a mere sliver of a woman, but big hearted. When he turned age 21, two years previously, his parents had given him Lil' Alice and Luke and their two children. The fever had tragically struck their family, too, however, and one of their children had recently died.

After eating he retired beneath the shade of a large oak tree and took a quick

119

nap, but crab grass didn't rest. He was responsible for feeding five negroes, not to mention three horses, several hogs, two oxen, a milk cow, chickens, a dog and of course, himself.

Farming was never-ending work; break ground in the fall, work-up and plant in the spring and when the corn was about twelve inches tall, plow it as many times as necessary. And if the crab grass and weeds kept growing, chop them out with a hoe. In the fall, the ears had to be individually pulled until one's hands were sore to the touch. What remained of the crop after deer, corn borers and weevils had eaten their fill, he stored in the log crib where gophers grew fat. Most of the harvested corn was fed to livestock; the remainder was used for cornmeal. It was hard labor and for what? A hoecake for dinner? Raising tobacco was even more labor intensive, not to mention that it left the soil wasted. There had to be a better way to make a living. Daniel thought about it all afternoon as he plowed beneath a blazing sun. He wasn't complaining. To be only 23 years of age, his 218 acres of fair land on the west fork of the Red River was respectable. The Panic of 1819 and the miserable tobacco crops had impacted him hard. He needed to make a change, perhaps learn a trade. But more than anything, he craved adventure.

Saturday morning after breakfast he pulled on his hat and walked out on the porch where Luke had reined in Andy, saddled and swishing flies with his tail. Oliver, his big-boned red hound, was prancing around and howling, apparently thinking that a hunt was on.

Daniel mounted Andy's right side since he was blind on the left and skittish about any movement and noise on that side. Daniel looked down at Luke. "I'll be back Sunday night if the creeks don't rise and the snakes don't bite."

"Yassuh, tells Massa Daniel and Missus Polly that Luke say howdy."

"I sure will." Daniel nudged the horse and trotted off. The hound followed until Luke's holler sent him, tail tucked, slinking beneath the cabin.

The distance to his parent's home in neighboring Todd County wasn't far. He should arrive around supper time.

He hadn't seen his parents and siblings in several months and looked forward to the visit. He liked to listen to his father, whose name he carried, talk about the "good ol' days."

His father had married his mother, Polly Watson, in Prince Edward County, Virginia, on January 27, 1800. Before the end of the year, Daniel was born, and in 1804, the family pulled up stakes and traveled the Great Wilderness Road by ox-drawn wagons to Wilson County, Tennessee, just east of Nashville. His maternal grandparents, John and Grandmother Watson, had also made the journey.

Daniel's earliest memory was living on Cedar Lick Creek, where he had spent his formative years fishing and swimming in its waters. When he was sixteen years old his father sold out and moved again, this time to Kentucky.

The movement of Andy's long brown ears was a clear indication of what he was thinking, something that Daniel had learned from experience. At present, his ears were moving rhythmically back and forth which meant that everything was okay. The slightest noise from his blind left side would cause the ears to stop moving and point toward whatever disturbed him, which included grasshoppers, birds and squirrels. When his ears came together at the front – look out! When he pinned them back, it was time to grab the saddle horn with both hands and hang on. Sometimes he was tempted to sell the beast and purchase a less ornery horse, but Andy, named after General Andrew Jackson, had been given to him on his sixteenth birthday by his father. The horse would pull a plow like a draft animal and under saddle could trot, pace and single foot so smoothly that the rider could drink coffee without spilling a drop.

It was twilight when Daniel reined up at the picket fence in front of his parent's two-story log house. The light of a candle glowed dimly through a window. Dogs ran out barking. Soon, his father appeared on the front porch, squinting into the gray light. Peeking around the door was his sister and brother.

"Why it's Dan'l!"

"Hello Papa." Daniel dismounted and tethered Andy to the hitching post. His two young siblings came out on the front porch, waving and grinning.

"Good to see ya," said his father grabbing his hand. "Come on in, your mother will be glad to see ya too."

Daniel bounded onto the plank porch and greeted his young siblings.

His mother came out smiling and jabbering. "Dan'l I've missed you so much. Have you had supper yet? I can tell you hadn't. Look at you, you're wasting away to nothing. Ain't Lil' Alice cooking for you?"

"Mama, I'm doing fine," he said as she grabbed him around the neck. "Mama, I'm too old!"

"Don't back away from me. I'm your Mama and I want a good hug and kiss," she said, smacking him on the cheek. "Now come on in and eat some supper."

Annie, a scrawny Negro woman who had been with the family for years, was smiling and already hustling up food. "I declare, if it ain't Massa Dan'l and just as handsome as ever."

"Hi Annie, you still mak'n those delicious hoecakes?"

"I shore do."

Annie put leftovers on the table, pulled hot coals onto the hearth and fried cornbread hoecakes in an iron skillet.

Following a fine supper and good conversation, Daniel and his father adjourned to the front porch in search of a breeze. The mating calls of katydids, July flies, tree frogs and crickets filled the night. Lightning bugs flashed. His father filled his pipe with tobacco and passed the pouch to Daniel.

"It's pretty good. It's from last year's crop."

Daniel packed his pipe and fired it with a candle that Annie produced. Both men smoked in silence for a minute. The best part of a good supper was the first few draws on a pipe afterwards.

His father broke the silence. "What brought you over here, Daniel?"

This was the moment Daniel had dreaded. He rubbed his pipe stem across his front teeth, making a clicking sound. "Papa, I've been think'n about pull'n up stakes." He glanced over at his father illuminated in the tiny halo of candlelight through the window, and saw his chin drop.

"I'm sure you didn't ride all day just to ask my advice. Have you already made up your mind?"

"I'm ninety percent certain."

"I'm going to argue for the ten percent," his father said. "You may not realize it, but the Lord has blessed you with good land, Negroes and horses. My advice is to stay put and work the land. You won't make a good crop every year, but overall, you'll do alright. That's the way the Lord plans it. He doesn't give us everything we want when we want it. Be patient and thankful for what the Lord has given you."

"I know you're right Papa, but I've got this hanker'n inside me to move on and it won't go away."

"With an economic panic gripping the country, this isn't the time to be taking chances," his father said. "No tell'n what might happen."

"Fruit don't fall far from the tree," said Daniel. "I think a lot about your moving to Tennessee in 1804. That was mighty risky. You pulled up stakes, left parents and family and traveled hundreds of miles across a wilderness to the frontier. It took courage and determination. You left security in Virginia for the unknown in Tennessee."

"Aye, it was the impetuousness of youth."

"Papa, you were thirty-one years old at the time!"

His father pursed his lips. "I guess you're right."

"Do you regret moving to Tennessee?"

"Nay."

"Then you sold out again a few years ago and moved to Kentucky," Daniel added.

"You're right, but now is a bad time to make a change with money drying up and such."

"Papa, you hadn't asked where I'm think'n of going," said Daniel.

"Where?"

"Lincoln County, Tennessee."

"Why there?"

"I hear there's rich bottom land along the river and creeks. But mostly, it's a new and bigger place where a young man can start his life."

His father puffed his pipe. "Aye, I suppose it was only a matter of time before you struck out for someplace else. You come by it naturally. It's in the Barksdale blood, you know."

"What do you mean Papa?"

"Well, it's a long story," his father began. Daniel settled back in his chair. He loved to hear about the old days.

"Your triple-great-grandfather was William Barksdale. He was born about 1629, the son of Reverend Nathaniel and Dorothy Woodhull Barksdale of Worchester, England." His father relit his pipe, taking his time and letting the suspense build.

"About 1662, wanderlust grabbed 'im and he set sail with 116 people for the Colonies with Mosely and Hull Company, least that's what they say. He was 33 years old when he landed in Jamestown or Yorktown – I forget which; settled in Rappahannock County, Virginia and received a land grant." His father swatted at a mosquito. "Well, he died there in 1694, leaving two sons, William Jr., the oldest, who married Sarah Collins. They settled in Halifax County, Virginia. A second son married Sarah Daniel."

"That's interesting," Daniel commented and puffed his pipe.

His father continued. "Grandfather was Thomas, but folks called him Henry. He was born sometime after 1710 in Tidewater, Virginia, and married Judith Dudley the first time. After she died he married Judith Beverly." His father chuckled. "I suppose he was attracted to women named Judith. He bought and sold land in Prince Edward County and then moved to that part of Pittsylvania which later became Henry County, where he was a planter and traded in land. He died there in 1788, shortly after the Revolution ended."

"Did he serve in the Revolution?" asked Daniel.

"No, he was too old to fight the British, but your grandfather, Captain Dudley, and four of his brothers served. Uncle Claiborne served in the Charlotte County Militia; Uncle Beverly hauled military supplies and Uncle Henry Hickerson was a sergeant in Captain Joseph Martin's Company Militia. Uncle John was a captain in the Henry County Militia."

"What about Grandfather Dudley?"

"He was a captain with the Charlotte County Militia."

"And you Papa?"

"Too young. I was 3 years old when the Declaration of Independence was signed and too old – 39 – for the War of 1812. Thank the Lord those British devils are gone. And thank the Lord for His Excellency who persevered and brought us victory."

"His Excellency?" asked Daniel.

"Yes, General Washington. I never saw the great man. He died at Mount Vernon in Fairfax County about a month and a half before your mother and I married."

"Very interesting," Daniel commented.

"Aye. Well, when are you are leaving for Tennessee?"

"This fall after I gather my crops and sell out."

His father laid a hand on his thigh. "I wish you wouldn't go, Daniel," he said. "You have a comfortable life here in Kentucky. No tell'n what awaits you in Tennessee where you have no family and don't know a soul."

"I suppose that's what makes it excit'n."

"Well, you've always had a mind of your own," said his father, falling silent.

"Is anything wrong, Papa?"

"I – was – just thinking –" he said, voice quavering. "We might not – ever see you again."

"I'll come back and visit," replied Daniel.

---

Autumn, 1823.

Daniel sat at the cabin window looking at the harvest moon that rose large and orange above the tree line, bathing the landscape with soft light. A low fire flickered in the fireplace. He missed the presence of Lil' Alice scurrying around the cabin cooking, picking up after him and talking to herself. She and Luke and the little boy were like family. But he couldn't take them to Fayetteville and had sold them to his folks. Big Pete and the other Negroes had also been sold at the auction along with the livestock, chattels and land. All that he owned now could be carried on his horse, except for Oliver, his coon hound which money couldn't buy.

He turned in early and slept fitfully, too excited to sleep. At first light he saddled the one-eyed bay horse, carefully rolled his fiddle in a blanket and tied it to the back of the saddle and draped a sack containing venison jerky, bread and a few possessions around the horn. Hoisting his musket, he climbed in the saddle, clucked to Andy and rode south. He reached Nashville after dark, tired and chilly, and rewarded himself by stopping at a tavern for the night. A hot supper of bread and pork stew and a place in a bed cost 75¢; stabling and feeding cost for Andy was another 25¢. The dimly-lit tavern was smoky and crowded with all sorts of men, smoking, drinking and talking and enjoying the warmth of a fire. He found a seat.

"Something to drink?" asked the waiter. "Whiskey's a dime a pint and brandy's 18¢."

He was sorely tempted to celebrate his new adventure with a drink, but reasoned it wasn't prudent. He had heard too many stories of how brigands hung around taverns and, after unsuspecting travelers drank too much, robbed them. "No thanks," he told the waiter. He sat in the background listening to the men discussing politics. Some argued for a higher tariff, others for a lower one. Should America fight if Europe and especially if Spain began poking their noses in South America? Most agreed that James Madison was doing a good job as President but Andy Jackson, just sent to the U.S. Senate from Tennessee, ought to be running the country and probably would be following the next national election. Daniel found it all very exciting, but didn't' join in the conversation. He sat on the sidelines and listened. He could read and write but the availability of newspapers in rural Kentucky had been limited and his knowledge of national and world affairs was practically nil. The one thing he could do as well as any man or better was plow straight row and play a fiddle. When a fellow offered to engage him in conversation, he pretended not to hear. His whole future lay in the gold coins stuffed in the money belt around his waist and he wasn't about to risk their loss by revealing anything about himself. That night he shared a bed fully dressed, minus only his shoes, with a man who snored. His musket was within arm's reach and his money belt was strapped low near his groins. One light touch and he would be fully awake.

Departing at dawn, he was tempted to ride east and see his old home in Wilson County, where he had resided until age 16, but thought better of it. Anxious to reach his destination, he rode south on the pike to Franklin, then headed southeast to Shelbyville where he camped near the road, resolved not to fritter away his money at expensive taverns. Fall had brought chilly nights. While Andy munched nearby grass, Daniel sat around a small fire until late night, tired but too excited to sleep. Tomorrow night he would sleep in Fayetteville. What would it be like? Were the river and creek bottoms as fertile as he had heard? Would folks be friendly? Would he make new friends? Or maybe find a good woman? He was filled with uncertainty and yes – fear. He decided it was the fear of the unknown that made his adventure exciting. He slept little and was in the saddle at dawn, riding south and chewing on venison jerky for breakfast.

Late afternoon, he topped a gentle rise, reined Andy and surveyed the village of Fayetteville. Small, but picturesque, a red brick courthouse stood in the middle of town, towering over several small masonry buildings. South of the square, Elk River snaked its way through bottomland bordered by thick cane breaks and hardwoods. He felt good about what he saw. Fertile land and plentiful water and hard work offered the promise of wealth. If a young man worked hard he could acquire land. And land meant wealth.

Oliver's barking interrupted his thoughts. He twisted in the saddle and saw a barefoot boy walking toward him.

"Nice lookin' hound, mister," the boy said. "Is he any good?"

"The best," replied Daniel. "He can pick up a trail three miles away."

"What's his name?"

"Oliver."

"Howdy Oliver," the boy said and rubbed the hound's head. Oliver wagged his tail.

"Do you know of a cheap place where I can stable my horse and get a meal and a clean bed?" asked Daniel.

"I've heard Father say that Talbot's Tavern on the square is pretty good."

"Thanks." Daniel leaned in the saddle and offered his hand. "I'm Daniel Barksdale. I just arrived."

The boy smiled and shook his hand. "Thomas Joyce McClellan. My father is William. We live over on Cane Creek."

"Nice to make your acquaintance. Hope we meet again."

"Yes sir," replied the boy as Daniel rode off.

He would celebrate his arrival by eating a good meal and sleeping in a soft, clean bed. After stabling Andy and ordering hay and extra corn, he removed his fiddle and sack of possessions and entered Talbot's Tavern, a two-story log structure.

The room was crowded and noisy with a thick cloud of tobacco smoke hanging near the ceiling. He paid for his board, which was cheaper than it had been at Nashville, and took a seat at a long table where several men were seated, drinking, talking and smoking pipes.

A dark-haired damsel appeared and asked: "Whiskey, brandy or West India rum?"

"How much?"

"Good whiskey's twelve 'n half cents for half a pint; brandy is thirteen cents and rum is twenty-five."

A swig of whiskey would warm his insides and taste mighty good after a long day in the saddle, he thought, and he had the money to spend. It was time to celebrate his safe arrival in a new country. Then his mother's words rang in his ears. "Dan'l, always remember that the Good Book says that wine is a mocker, strong drink is raging and whosoever is deceived thereby is not wise."

"You're new in town, I can tell," said the young waitress.

Daniel met her brown eyes. "Yes, I just arrived."

"Which is it?" she asked.

"Bring me a glass of milk and a plate of supper."

He ate ravenously, wiped his mouth and quaffed down the warm glass of milk. Tomorrow he would explore around the area and get the lay of the land.

Over the next several days, he learned that thriving communities like Petersburg, Molino and Boon's Hill dotted the county of over 12,000 white inhabitants. According to the 1820 census, approximately 3,600 individuals were engaged in agriculture, and of that number 2,250 of them were slaves. Fayette Academy, deriving its support from state funds, had been in existence since 1815. Grist mills abounded up and down the creeks. Everything he had heard about Lincoln County was true. Here, he would plant his banner and become a wealthy man.

# 13 | LAND OF PROMISE

A feeling of freedom surged through Daniel. Today was the beginning of his new life. And decisions were to be made. First, he needed to leave Talbot's Tavern and find cheap quarters until he purchased his own place. Perhaps he could perform labor in exchange for bed and board. Secondly, he needed a job. The gold coins in his money belt were his grub stake for the future and must not be lightly spent. And while doing all of the above, he hoped to meet folks and make acquaintances – particularly single females.

Following a breakfast of salt bacon, hard bread and coffee, he explored the immediate area north of Elk River and discovered there were numerous creeks. Buchanan, Norris, Mulberry and Cane emptied into the river – Cane Creek being one of the largest – and gristmills were plentiful. Some were water powered, others were operated by a horse turning a sweeping arm to turn the milling stone. Working at a grist mill was laborious, but simple – something that he could do until he found a better job. He rode north on Cane Creek a short distance and stopped at a gristmill where an elderly man, beard was powdered white with flour dust, was working.

"Howdy," he said.

The man paused and looked up. "Whatcha have to grind, corn or wheat?"

"Neither," Daniel replied. "I'm new in town and look'n for a job and board."

"Know anything about milling?" asked the man.

"A hungry man learns fast."

The old man looked Daniel up and down for a moment then nodded his head. "Get down. I'm Nathaniel Blinkingham. This is my mill," he said, extending his hand.

"Daniel Barksdale from Christian County, Kentucky."

"I don't have much to offer," said Blinkingham. "Bed 'n board at my place for your labor. I expect hard work from sun up till sundown six days a week."

Daniel nodded and shook the old man's hand. "It's a bargain."

Daniel moved into a room in the nearby log house with Blinkingham and his frail wife and got to work – hard work – lifting heavy sacks of shelled corn and wheat from wagons and dumping them into an overhead hopper. Initially, his arms and shoulder muscles were inflamed and sore, but as the weeks went by they bulged against his homespun shirt.

At the outset, Blinkingham carefully measured out 1/8 of the customer's corn or wheat which was his percentage for doing the milling. Daniel poured the grain into a bushel basket, and then from it filled a wooden box that held 1/8 of a bushel.

"Be sure the box is filled to the top, shaken down real good, then packed real tight," Blinkingham instructed Daniel. Every extra kernel of corn that could be crammed into the box meant more profit.

One day a wagon carrying several sacks of shelled corn and driven by a Negro creaked into the mill yard and the oxen stopped. A redbone hound followed. An elderly man with shoulder-length thinning gray hair was seated beside him. Blinkingham came out and threw up his hand, "Howdy, Mr. McElroy, I's beginn'n to suspect you hadn't made any corn this year or else you had started doing business with my competitors."

"Aye, just saving up for one big load," McElroy replied.

The Negro clucked to the oxen and pulled near the mill hopper. Daniel stepped forward to unload the sacks of corn.

"King Solomon, give a helping hand to the young fellow," said McElroy.

"Yassuh, massa."

The shelled corn was poured into a bushel basket, an eighth measured and removed, then slowly poured into the hopper where it fell onto a millstone that turned around, grinding it into meal. Powered by water falling over a wheel, the millstone could be adjusted to grind the meal fine or coarse, depending on the customer's desire.

After the meal was ground and sacked, McElroy asked Blinkingham, "Who's your young helper?"

"Daniel Barksdale from Kentucky. He showed up here several weeks ago."

McElroy walked over to Daniel. "We're hav'n a corn shuck'n at my place next Saturday afternoon. I hope you can come."

Daniel shot Blinkingham a glance.

Placed on the spot, Blinkingham said, "If he don't, it won't be because I stopped him."

"Good," McElroy said and shook Daniel's hand.

True to his word, Blinkingham had worked Daniel six days a week from sun up till sundown and Daniel was anxious to relax, have fun and meet new people.

Saturday at noon, he departed the mill and went to his room. He scrubbed down, buckled on his money belt and dressed in his only decent outfit – homespun trousers and shirt. He slapped his brown hat against his leg, knocking off flour and corn dust, grabbed his fiddle, mounted Andy and rode north on Hamwood Road that ran east of Cane Creek. Stone fences bordered the road in places, marking boundary lines. He heard laughter and shortly saw dozens of horses, some hitched to buggies and wagons. A large, two-story log house with a chimney at each end stood in the clearing surrounded by hardwoods and cedars. It was a mighty fine house and no doubt constructed by an equally fine builder. A large crowd of folks milled around in the yard, talking and laughing. Daniel tethered Andy to a tree and loosened the girt. "Now stay out of trouble," he said and patted him on his neck.

He walked around, holding his fiddle and nodding to folks. In the backyard, Negroes were roasting several shoats over a spit. Tables made of boards resting on saw horses were laden with food where young Negro girls fanned flies away with cedar branches.

"Hello mister," said a youthful voice.

Daniel turned around and saw the young boy he had met on the road.

"Remember me? I'm Thomas McClellan."

"I sure do," said Daniel and shook his hand.

"Where's Oliver?" the boy asked.

"I left 'im at home."

An elderly man approached. "This is my father, William McClellan," the boy said.

"Glad to meet you," the elder McClellan said and offered a firm hand. "Welcome to Lincoln County."

"Thank you sir," Daniel replied.

"You must visit us sometime, on Cane Creek," McClellan said.

Micajah McElroy hobbled over, followed by a redbone hound, and said, "I see the two of you have already met. Come on young fellow, I'll introduce you around."

127

He introduced Daniel to his eldest son, Archibald. "He fought with Andy Jackson down in New Orleans; whipped the British for good."

"To hear Father tell it, we Tennesseans single-handedly won the war," said Archibald.

"Aye, you did," replied Micajah.

A fortyish-looking man walked up and offered his hand. "Howdy, I'm William McElroy. My wife Mary and I live here with Father. Welcome."

"Thank you sir, I'm glad to be here," replied Daniel.

Micajah said, "I'm proud of all my children, but William's the only one that has followed in my footsteps. We built the courthouse in Fayetteville."

"It's a mighty fine building," Daniel said.

"Aye, 'tis a fact. I also built the courthouse in Athens, Alabama," Micajah added.

The introductions continued and Daniel met another son, also named Micajah, who was married to Rachel Simpson of Madison County, Alabama; daughter, Abigail was married David Buchanan whom he had met, along with sons Ransom and Barney Linn McElroy. Daniel's head was spinning with names and faces. "My daughter Sallie married Robert C. David. They live down in Athens," the old man said. "My youngest daughter is here somewhere." He looked over the milling crowd and seeing her, beckoned. "Nancy, would you please come over here?"

An attractive woman wearing an ankle-length gray dress and with braided hair black as a crow's feather falling down her back approached.

"Nancy, please welcome a new neighbor, Mr. Daniel Barksdale," said Micajah.

Daniel accepted her offered hand with a slight bow and their eyes locked. He had never seen eyes so blue. A warm wave coursed through him.

"Welcome to our home," she said. Daniel didn't know if he should shake her hand or kiss it. It was soft and warm and he didn't want to let go. A quick glance at her other hand revealed no ring.

"Uh, uh, thank you Miss Nancy," he stammered. "I...I... I'm honored to be here."

"May I have my hand back?" she said.

"Oh! I'm very sorry," he said, embarrassed, and let it go.

"I'll be looking forward to hearing you play," she said, glancing at his fiddle, and then she turned and walked away.

After gorging himself on roasted pork, peas, boiled potatoes, corn pones, pickled beets and cucumbers and sampling every pudding on the table, Daniel drifted over to where the corn shucking contest was about to commence. Each contestant was standing behind a bushel basket filled with ears of corn. Micajah hobbled out front and announced the rules: "The man that shucks his bushel the fastest is the winner –"

"What's the prize?" a man asked.

"A sore hand," someone shouted. Laughter.

Daniel knew he wasn't going to sore his hands by shucking corn. He would save them for his fiddle. Anyway, after working at the grist mill six days a week, he was sick and tired of corn.

"The winner gets pick 'n choice to dance with these damsels," Micajah said. "Come on up ladies."

The crowd clapped and hooted.

128

Five giggling young women came forward, embarrassed by the attention. Nancy McElroy was one of them.

"Just a minute!" Daniel shouted and handed his fiddle and bow to young Thomas McClellan standing nearby and then trotted to join the contestants. He attempted to catch Nancy's attention, by waving at here but she was focused on another corn shucker, a tall red-headed fellow who was smiling at her.

Micajah pulled out his pocket watch and looked down at it. "Get ready, get set – go!"

The crowd hooted when Daniel grabbed an ear of corn and dropped it. He grabbed another one, stripping the shucks down to the stem, broke it off, threw the shucks in one pile and the yellow ear of corn in another. Soon, his right hand between the thumb and forefinger was sore and red. He switched shucking hands. He was determined to win this contest. He glanced at the red-headed fellow who was shucking like a machine – his was basket already half empty. Daniel sped up, but the faster he worked, the more ears he fumbled. *Concentrate and keep on shucking.* He didn't look around to see who was winning until the crowd began cheering. When he looked, the red-headed fellow was shucking his last ear. Daniel's basket was still half full.

"Dink Buchanan is the winner," announced Micajah. "Aye, I've never seen anybody shuck corn so fast. "Dink, were you in a hurry to rush home and split wood?" Loud laughter.

"No sir, I wanna dance with your Nancy. That's what I wanna do," Buchanan replied.

Grass and weeds had been chopped away to provide a smooth area for dancing. Guests gathered around as Dink walked over to Nancy and extended his hand. "Miss Nancy, will you honor me with the first dance?"

"Why I'd be honored," she smiled and took his hand.

"Don't trip and fall down Dink!" someone shouted. More laughter and hooting.

Micajah stepped up and raised his hand for attention. "Folks, we have a new neighbor on Cane Creek," he said. "He can't shuck corn worth a flip but his employer, Nathaniel Blinkingham, says that he can saw the strings off a fiddle. Daniel Barksdale, step up and play us a waltz."

Daniel, who was massaging his aching hand, almost fainted.

"But... but... Mr. McElroy."

"No excuses," said Micajah. "Folks, let 'im pass through."

Daniel walked forward, his mind reeling. *Waltz? What waltz can I play? Lord, please don't let me faint in front of my new neighbors.* He laid the bow across the strings and began playing *My Old Kentucky Home* as Buchanan placed his arm around, a beaming Nancy. When it was over the crowd applauded, cheered and whistled. Other contestants escorted their choice of ladies to dance area.

"Play us another waltz," said Micajah.

"That's the only one I know, Mr. McElroy."

"Then play it again."

Daniel played it several times until someone yelled: "Don't you know another tune?"

He broke into *Flop-Eared Mule*, a foot-stomping number that set folks to dancing and the redbone hound howling. Then he followed with *Turkey in the Straw* and *Possum up de Gum Tree.*

When he announced he was going to rest the crowd yelled, "MORE – MORE!" It took breaking a string and sawing through numerous horse hairs on his bow, for Daniel to finally say, "Folks, I've just about killed my fiddle. Thank y'all a lot." He tucked his fiddle beneath his arm and walked away to applause and back slapping. Another fiddler stepped forward.

Nancy McElroy was sticking to Dink Buchanan like a cocklebur on wool. Once when he caught her looking at him she quickly averted her eyes. He was tempted to ask her to dance but couldn't summon the courage. Instead he approached a redhead, bowed slightly and asked, "Miss, may I have this dance?"

She smiled and extended her hand. "Why, I'd be honored." Her hand was soft and inviting and when they danced close together he felt her warmness and inhaled her sweet and pleasing aroma. Dolly was her Christian name, but he didn't catch the surname.

Approaching darkness sent guests scurrying around gathering up children and bidding farewell to neighbors and the host, Micajah McElroy. Daniel shook the old gentleman's hand. "I've never had a grander time," he said.

"Aye, you must come and visit us again and bring your fiddle," said Micajah.

"I'd like that, sir."

It was dark and chilly when Andy, who had been tethered to a tree and was eager to limber up, began single footing down Hamwood Road. It had been a fun day and Daniel had met many of his neighbors. The only dark cloud in his life was working at Blinkingham's gristmill.

On cold winter nights after the Blinkinghams had gone to bed Daniel lay on his shuck mattress in the adjoining room, listening as the wind howled around the eaves and whistled through the log chinks and pondering his situation. He had been in Lincoln County four months and hadn't courted the first woman. All he was doing was working and sleeping which was tantamount to being a slave or being dead. He found some solace in playing his fiddle, but it wasn't as rewarding as touching the soft skin of a woman. He needed to scout around and meet a woman. But where? "Bye crackies, I know just the place!" he mumbled. He would need decent clothes. Homespuns are fine, but a woman likes a well-dressed man.

He left work early on Saturday afternoon and rode to Fayetteville. His first stop was I.H. Wallace - Shoe Maker, located off the square. The pungent aroma of leather was pleasing but the strong odor of dye made his eyes water. Wallace, wearing a leather apron and his hands stained with dye, looked up from his work bench at the man dressed in common homespun.

"Can I help ya?"

"I wanna fine pair of shoes," Daniel replied.

"A good pair'll cost plenty."

"I know," said Daniel and flashed a twenty dollar gold piece.

"Yes sir!" Wallace said and began measuring Daniel's feet and making notes.

"Black or brown? Price's the same."

"Black," Daniel said.

"They'll be ready next Saturday."

The next stop was at H. Worhsam's Tailor Shop.

"I want a black frock coat, matching pants, black vest and a good wool hat and whatever else goes with it," Daniel said, showing gold pieces. Worsham whipped out a tape measure and soap stone and commenced measuring.

"Say, ain't you that fiddler player that works for ol' man Blinkingham?"

"One and the same," Daniel replied.

"Planning a trip somewhere? I mean buying a fancy suit and all."

"To church," Daniel replied.

"You a preacher too?"

"No sir, just look'n for an eligible woman."

"Then I'd go to the Presbyterian Church," said Worsham. "You can meet some pretty young women there and get a dose of preaching at the same time."

"Now that's a bargain."

On Sunday morning, after clipping his hair and trimming his beard, Daniel dressed in his new outfit, pulled on his spanking new black wool slouch hat and stepped out into the coldness. In the distance, the pealing of church bells split the mid-morning silence. Not only was Daniel well dressed, but Andy was in fine form, also, showing off his mastery of single footing without breaking gait. Surreys and buggies were parked near the church building, some occupied by Negro drivers who shivered in the cold. Worship services had already begun when Daniel eased inside and sat down in a creaking pew, causing necks to crane to see the latecomer. The Pastor launched into a long sermon on the subject of lust which wasn't edifying to a 23-year old single male in search of a woman. Daniel's mind wandered. He shifted on the hard pew and made furtive glances at the mostly black-clad congregation. On his left he spotted red hair that spilled from beneath a gray bonnet. Dolly! She glanced at him but showed no sign of recognition.

Following services Daniel was welcomed by numerous people. An elderly man and woman, accompanied by Dolly, approached.

"Hello Miss Dolly," Daniel said.

"Have we met?" she asked, puzzled.

"Don't you remember me?"

"Should I?"

"We danced at McElroy's corn shucking."

Her eyes narrowed.

"I'm Daniel Barksdale – the fiddle player."

Her slate eyes brightened. "Oh my, I didn't recognize you." she said. "You look so different. What have you done to yourself, I mean, oh… I am so embarrassed."

"I bought a suit –"

"And trimmed your beard," she interjected.

"Yes and cut my hair."

"You look sooo nice," she cooed, then introduced her parents.

"Are you related to Dink Buchanan?" Daniel asked.

"He's my brother," said Dolly.

"You must come and visit us sometime," her father said.

"Yes, you must," Dolly quickly added.

That night Daniel reflected on the events of the day and decided that his investment in the new outfit had paid off handsomely. But he knew it would take more than clothes to catch a good woman, and he wasn't sure that he wanted to catch Dolly Buchanan. However, right now she was the only nibble at his hook.

The next Sunday following worship services he was invited to Dolly's for dinner.

The Buchanans lived north of Fayetteville, near the McElroys in a two-story log house. After two knocks, an elderly Negro woman opened the door. "You must be Mistuh Barksdale. Miss Dolly be just a buzzing 'bout you," she said. "Come in out of de cold fo' you freeze half to death."

Daniel handed her his hat and was immediately greeted by Mr. Buchanan and Dolly who escorted him into a large room where several people were gathered near the fireplace. Nancy McElroy looked straight at him for an instant, and then turned her head.

Mr. Buchanan made introductions. Reaching the black-haired Nancy, he said, "This is Nancy McElroy, Micajah's daughter."

"We've met – sort of," Daniel said, taking her hand and smiling. "My pleasure, Miss Nancy."

Their eyes met and Daniel felt the same warm feeling again.

"The suit is becoming on you," she said, her soft hand still in his.

---

Warm weather brought waxy green grass to the rolling hills along with blooming redbuds and much talk about Presidential politics. Just about everyone agreed that Andrew Jackson's time had arrived. It also brought Micajah McElroy back to the gristmill with a load of corn.

"Young fella, can you saw a straight line?" he asked Daniel.

"Truthfully, I've never done carpentry work," Daniel replied.

Micajah studied his answer thoughtfully for a moment and nodded slightly. "Aye, I like your forthrightness. I could use a good man. If you want to go to work for me, I'll teach you carpentry and pay you according to your work. It won't be much at first, but it will be a sight better than working here. There is no future in lifting and toting sacks of corn."

"You've just hired me," Daniel replied.

He boarded with Widow Larkin, an elderly woman in town chopping wood and doing chores in exchange for bed and board and a stable for Andy. During the ensuing months he performed manual labor alongside King Solomon, Green and the other Negroes. Micajah showed him how to shape a log with a broad axe so smooth that it looked like it had been sawed; use a draw knife and make shingles, level a foundation, saw a straight line, drill and peg. Micajah was a master at his trade and could convert a piece of wood into a thing of beauty. He offered to teach Daniel to carve but he was too busy learning arithmetic, calculating angles, roof pitches, etc. He liked his new trade and took pride in his work.

Life fell into a routine. Daniel rose before dawn six days a week and, after eating a breakfast of leftovers prepared by Widow Larkin, rode to the McElroy plantation on Hamwood Road to join Micajah in his shop. On Sundays, he attended worship service, followed by a visit to Dolly Buchanan's. Weather permitting, they often strolled or fished in the Cane Creek.

The McElroy plantation, consisting of several hundred acres, had its own unique rhythm. The Negroes, except for King Solomon and Moses, who were skilled craftsmen, and Annie, who worked in the big house cooking and cleaning, worked in the fields from sun up until sundown, singing their songs as they toiled. Rocks were picked up off the fields, loaded into ox-drawn wagons and hauled to build rock fences along the property line. Trees were girted and new ground cleared. The fertile creek bottoms were planted in corn, cotton, flax and wheat and some tobacco. Cattle, sheep, horses and oxen grazed on the rolling hills. Hogs were slaughtered in mid-November and hams, shoulders, sausage and great slabs of bacon were hung in the log smokehouse. Guineas roosted in the large trees that surrounded the houses and chickens scratched and pecked in the yard. It was a peaceful environment.

Then William McElroy returned home on a Saturday afternoon with a baboon tied in the back of the wagon. Daniel, who was in the shop behind the house, heard loud shrieks and went to inspect. The Negroes were standing far back staring suspiciously at the hairy beast. William's children ran out, excited.

"What is this thing?" young Sanford asked his father.

"A baboon, child. A creature from the dark continent of Africa... at least that's what the fella said who sold him to me."

Micajah hobbled over and looked the animal up and down suspiciously. "What in tarnation are you going to do with it?" he asked William.

"Baboons love eat'n lice more than we love blackberry pudd'n," William said. He motioned to the Negroes. "King Solomon, Moses, Big Annie, Sam – all the rest of you, line up and sit down."

The Negroes grumbled, but reluctantly obeyed.

"Father, can I do that too?" asked young Sanford.

"Sure."

William untethered the baboon and led him over to where the Negroes sat on the ground, trembling with fear. "All right, baboon, go to work," William said and gave the animal plenty of leash.

King Solomon's eyes were squeezed shut his mouth tight and a frightful grimace on his face as the beast sat in his lap picking through his hair looking for lice. Finding none, it moved to Green; found a louse and crushed it between his sharp teeth, and then smacked his large lips.

When it sat in Big Annie's lap, she was seized with fear and tried to get up. The baboon slapped her on the head. The Negroes prayed quietly as the baboon continued to forage for its dinner.

Each Saturday afternoon the Negroes were ordered to line up on the ground and the baboon picked over them looking for lice. If they moved, it slapped them on the head. They despised the beast and called him "Ol' Satan."

After several months the baboon began exhibiting signs of failing health. His enthusiasm for eating lice diminished. Young Ransom found the baboon in a barn stall on its back, feet stiff in the air. Dead. When the Negroes were questioned about the untimely death, King Solomon offered: "He be eat'n poke berries."

"Did you see him eat 'em?" asked William.

"Nassuh, but he could've."

The cause of death was never determined. Blood and Sam were ordered to dig a grave for the beast in the Negro graveyard nearby the house. All the Negroes were ordered to bury the baboon. After they threw the beast in the hole and covered him with dirt, they joined hands and danced on his grave, singing "Hallelujah, glory to God. We are glad you are gone." With the demise of "Ol' Satan," peace returned to the plantation.

---

Daniel was alone inside the shop, bent over a board he was planing when he heard a female voice.

"Can someone please help me?" He went to the door and saw Nancy McElroy holding a bucket of ashes to pour in the wooden hopper behind the carpentry shop. Daniel was used to seeing Big Annie doing this chore each Monday as she got ready to boil and wash clothes. The sight of Nancy, her long black hair braided, momentarily stopped him in his tracks.

"Well, don't just stand there, help me!"

"That's a mighty big bucket, Miss Nancy," Daniel said walking over to her. "Where's Big Annie?"

"Never mind where Big Annie is, but for your information she's sick. Just be a gentleman and help me."

"Yes ma'am." He poured the ashes into the hopper and handed her the empty bucket. "Next time don't fill it too full," he said.

"Thank you," she replied and their eyes met. He thought he saw a tiny smile on her lips. Again, that peculiar sensation swept through his body.

Later in the morning, Daniel looked out the door and saw Big Annie stirring clothes in the boiling kettle. *Huh health has greatly improved,* thought Daniel. Walking toward the clothesline was Nancy, her arms loaded with freshly-washed clothes. Daniel watched her drape clothes over the rail fence and clothes line. She stood between the morning sun and Daniel, and although he never meant to ogle at her, he did in fact see something that caused that peculiar sensation to run though him again. But, this time it was with greater force than before. Each time Nancy reached above her head the sunlight silhouetted the outline of her breast, her narrow waist and slender legs. Not only that, her reaching motions caused her skirt to rise to her calves. He couldn't take his eyes off her. Spying on a woman was wrong and he certainly wasn't doing that. It was an accident, he told himself. She wasn't aware that the sun was silhouetting her body and certainly not aware that he was watching her. Nevertheless he watched her until she had hung all the clothes. He returned to his work with a lot to ponder. During the ensuing week he thought about what he had witnessed and the meaning of it, if any.

Several beaus called on Nancy, but her primary interest was Dink Buchanan. Dink was a likable fellow from a good family who could dance his shoes off and beat any man shucking corn but, Daniel decided he didn't like Dink – even though he liked his sister. He didn't know the reason and he didn't need one.

Monday morning Daniel was in the shop planing boards, but keeping one eye looking out the door. Annie filled the big black kettle with water and started a fire beneath it, and then Daniel saw Nancy exit the back door of the house, her body leaning to one side, carrying a bucket of ashes. Daniel laid the planer aside and hurried toward her.

"Can I give you a hand, Miss Nancy?" he asked.

She smiled. "Why thank you, Daniel." He took the bucket of ashes from her and walked toward the ash hopper. When he lifted the bucket of ashes his heart was thumping so hard he knew it had to be pulsating against his shirt. *I'm so nervous! Either she will or she won't.* "Uhhh... Miss Nancy...." he stuttered.

"What?" she asked, looking at him.

*That look again.*

"I'm so nervous that...."

"Is something wrong?" she asked.

"Yes ma'am, plenty."

"What?" she asked with concern.

"Every time I see you I get a peculiar feeling... I was wondering if... you would like to go strolling tomorrow after church? That's why I am so nervous – afraid you might say no. I know you like Dink Buchanan and he's a nice person and all..." Daniel rattled on. "But I'm a nice person too and... well, I'd like to court you too."

"Dink and I are going riding tomorrow afternoon," Nancy said.

"Oh, I see," Daniel said, shoulders slumping.

"But, thanks for asking," she said and walked off.

*I've made a complete fool of myself. From now on, Nancy McElroy can tote her own ashes.*

---

Fayetteville.

Tuesday, July 4, 1826.

The nation's 50th birthday was a scorcher. It seemed to Daniel that most of Lincoln County's 12,000 inhabitants had turned out for the jubilee celebration. It was the largest crowd of people, horses and mules he had ever witnessed in one place. The horses and mules swished at flies with their tails. Homely women wearing bonnets and homespuns herded along thin brood of children while the more affluent paraded around in fine clothes shaded beneath fancy parasols as young boys ripped and romped through the crowd, hollering and chasing one another.

Parked on the courthouse lawn were two cannons the bags with powder stacked nearby. Blankets were spread on the ground along the north bank of the Elk River where young children napped and mothers fanned away flies. It was a festive occasion. There would be speech making, music and dancing.

Daniel pushed his way through the crowd toward the square where the stars and stripes fluttered above the courthouse. A fife and drum corps played *Yankee Doodle*. The Master of Ceremony reminded everyone that exactly fifty years earlier the Declaration of Independence had been signed in Philadelphia then read to the awaiting public. Lincoln County citizens, including Micajah McElroy, who fought in the Revolutionary War, were called out by name and applause.

The first salvo of a 21-gun salute caused a startle reaction and set babies crying and mules braying. Even though the Presidential election was a year off, Andrew Jackson's men were present, working the crowd and talking him up. Daniel wandered through the crowd, neck stretched, looking first one direction, and then another. Nancy McElroy was somewhere out there strutting around and probably with her arm hooked to Dink Buchanan.

"Look'n for someone?" asked a female voice from behind him.

It was Dolly Buchanan with her parents.

"Uh, hello Dolly – Mr. and Mrs. Buchanan," Daniel said, tipping his hat.

135

"You surprised to see me?" said Dolly.

"No, not at all."

She smiled and hooked her arm through Daniel's as they strolled along the river bank, nodding and greeting people they knew. Her parents fell behind them as they strolled ahead. "Is anything wrong?" Dolly asked. "You seem to be distracted."

He patted her hand. "No, not at all."

Fiddle music caught their attention. "Dancing is about to begin. Come on, let's go," she said.

Near the square, couples were lining up to dance. Dolly led Daniel into the circle as the fiddler played a lively jig. Daniel swung Dolly around and came face-to-face with Nancy McElroy, who was dancing with Dink Buchanan. She smiled, drilled him with her blue eyes for an instant, and then whisked away. Dolly, who hadn't seen Nancy, screamed. "Ouch! You stepped on my foot!"

That night Daniel lay awake, pondering the day's events and especially Nancy McElroy's smile and inviting eyes. What did she mean by that? The behavior of women puzzled him. At times she acted as if she didn't like him, then unexpectedly she gazed at him causing his insides to tingle. Right now he wanted her more than anything, including his fiddle, Andy and good fertile bottom land all combined. She was so close, yet so far away. He thought about her constantly; couldn't sleep and even lost his appetite.

---

It was mid-morning and Daniel was in the shop alone, bent over the work bench, his back to the doorway, carving pegs when he heard someone enter. He assumed it was Micajah.

"Good morning, Mister McElroy," he said.

There was no reply. He raised up and turned around to see Nancy standing inside the doorway, smiling at him. His heart fluttered.

"Morn'n Miss Nancy. Need some help with the ashes?"

"Nooo. I just stopped by to say hello."

Daniel's attention was drawn to her handsome face, full lips and long black braids that fell well past her shoulders. His eyes locked on hers.

"You – you look awfully pretty this morn'n," he stuttered.

"Why thank you, Daniel."

Without breaking eye contact, she slowly closed the door behind her. Daniel laid down the knife and walked toward her, gently pushed her against the door and kissed her full lips. She didn't resist. He kissed her again, this time harder.

"Why, Daniel Barksdale! You kissed me!"

Daniel backed away and dropped his head.

"I – I'm sorry Miss Nancy. I don't know what came over me. I – I had no right. Something just grabbed ahold of me and I couldn't resist. I hope I haven't soiled your honor and –"

"You sure do go on," she interrupted.

Daniel was confused. She wasn't angry. He was about to speak when she placed her finger on his lips.

"Shhh." She gently kissed his lips.

He took her into his arms, feeling her soft breasts against his chest, and kissed her long and lovingly.

136

"I've dreamed of this day since I met you," he whispered. She moaned softly. "Ohhh Daniel. Hold me."

The days that followed were the happiest Daniel had ever experienced. He was practically giddy and whistled while he worked – or tried to work. His mind wandered and he made inaccurate cuts in the wood; pegs weren't carved the exact dimension and more than once he hammered his thumb. Micajah took notice and several times Daniel caught the old man glancing at him, a quizzical look on his lined face.

When it became too risky for Daniel and Nancy to snatch intimate moments in the work shop, they began rendezvousing near twilight at the spring where Nancy went to fetch water.

Big Annie took notice. "Sump'n done come over Miss Nancy," she mumbled. "Use to be she wouldn't turn her hand, now she haul'n ashes, hang'n out clothes and tot'n water. Whatever it is, I sure wish some other folks would catch it too. I ain't never seen nobody get dooded up like her when she go to fetch water. Hmmm, hmmmm."

---

Twilight was approaching when Nancy nonchalantly announced she was going to the spring for water.

"Father likes good cold spring water with his supper," she said, picking up the bucket and departing.

"Hmmm – hmmm, ain't no spring water she be after," mumbled Big Annie.

Nancy had barely stepped out the door when her young niece, Mary Jane ran up. "Can I go too Aunt Nancy?"

"Not this time darling, you stay here and get ready for supper. I'll be right back."

Nancy hurried through the copse of hardwoods and across the soft leaves that had been dampened by a recent shower. Daniel was seated on a rock, his back to her, when she tiptoed up and placed her hand on his shoulder, startling him. "I was hoping you'd be here," she said.

He stood and faced her. "I've been thinking about you all day long," he said, taking the bucket from her hand and placing it on the ground. He pulled her into his arms and kissed her as she moaned softly.

"We can't keep meeting this way. It's wrong," he said.

"If it's wrong, then why does it feel so right?"

"I mean..."

"Look!" She pointed to the eastern horizon where a harvest moon was rising through the trees. "It's so lovely... and so romantic. Ohhh... Daniel I wouldn't trade this moment for all of the riches in the world."

"Nor I."

A twig snapped and both looked toward the sound.

"Mary Jane!" exclaimed Nancy. "What are you doing here sneaking around? I oughta give you a thrashing." The child took off running toward the house.

"Reckon she'll tell?" Daniel asked.

"She had better not."

Micajah was seated at one end of a long poplar board table he had made with his own hands and fastened together with wooden pegs. His wife, Sarah, was at the opposite end, and in between were the family and some of their grandchildren. Suppertime at the

137

McElroy house was when the family shared not only food, but fellowship and good conversation.

"The Lord has blessed us far beyond what we deserve," Micajah said as the family spooned helpings of food that Big Annie placed on the table. "All of my eight children are living and married except for Nancy and the way Dink Buchanan keeps coming around I wouldn't be surprised to hearing wedding bells soon," he said and looked at Nancy and smiled.

"I would," said young Mary Jane nonchalantly. Everyone stopped eating. Nancy, almost choking on her food, kicked the child under the table. "Ouch!"

"Daughter is there something going on that I don't know about?" Micajah asked.

"No – nothing."

"I saw 'em," said young Mary Jane calmly.

Nancy drilled the child with her eyes.

"Saw what?" asked Micajah.

"Aunt Nancy kissing Mister Daniel."

"What!" exclaimed her grandmother.

Nancy's face was red as the pickled beets on her plate. When her father looked at her, a tiny crack appeared at the corners of his mouth. "Is that a fact?" he said calmly. Silence at the table.

"Big Annie, pour me a glass of that good cool spring water?" said Micajah.

"Yessuh, I shore will."

---

Nancy was already at the spring when Daniel arrived – and without her bucket. "You're early," he said, embracing her. "Is something wrong?"

Nancy stepped back and searched Daniel's face and eyes. "Daniel, do you love me?" she asked, her voice quavering.

"Yes, with all my heart and soul," he replied without hesitation. "I've loved you since the first day I met you and held your hand at the corn shucking."

"Ohhh." She fell into his arms, her head resting against his chest. "Then squeeze me until I hurt."

He pulled her tight against him.

"Harder – harder. Ohh, that feels so good."

"Do you love me?" he asked.

"Yes, I do."

Without explanation he dropped to one knee and took warm hand, looked up and asked, "Will you marry me, Nancy McElroy?"

Remembering the story her mother told her when her father proposed, she smiled – almost laughed. "Yes, yes. Now get off the ground and kiss me."

---

Wednesday afternoon, January 24, 1827.

Andy's hooves beat a muffled rhythm on the snow that covered the ground and filled the branches of the cedar trees that grew alongside Hamwood Road. Daniel tugged his hat down and hunched his shoulders, making his head a small target for the falling flakes. He was anxious to reach his destination, but didn't want to arrive too early. He reined back on Andy. "Walk." Life could change in a flash, he thought. Two and a half years earlier he had ridden up this road, a stranger in the county, heading to a corn shucking at the McElroys. Now, he was about to marry his youngest daughter. The Lord certainly did work in strange ways. Slaving for old man Blinkingham at the mill was a dead end job, but if he hadn't been there unloading sacks of corn, he probably wouldn't have met Micajah; wouldn't have been invited to the party and wouldn't have met his blue-eyed daughter. It wasn't until he began courting Dolly Buchanan that Nancy showed the slightest interest in him. When a person can't have something, that's what they want. "It's just like you Andy," he muttered. "You know you're not supposed to eat the corn when you plow but that's what you want." The bay's ears perked up.

Dolly Buchanan had reacted to the betrothal first in shock, then with class. Not so with her brother Dink. Daniel had learned that getting married was stressful. The part that he had dreaded most, but turned out to be the easiest, was asking Micajah for his daughter's hand.

"I'm mighty proud to have you as a son," the old man said and shook his hand warmly.

Daniel noticed that Andy's ears were pointed forward. In a flash, both were pinned backward. Too late! He grabbed the saddle horn and caught the glimpse of a rabbit darting across the road as the horse bolted sideways, sending Daniel sailing into a snow bank. When Daniel got to his feet, the horse was running down the road, reins flapping against this neck, scaring him more. After knocking snow from his clothes, Daniel quick-timed after his mount, whistling and calling his name. "Bye crackies, I oughta take a stick and beat your good eye out!" he exclaimed angrily. Apparently Andy understood the threat, because each time Daniel got near, he backed away several yards and stood trembling with fear.

"Get over here Andy!" The horse ambled over and nuzzled Daniel's chest as if to apologize for his misdeed.

It was 2 o'clock, snow had stopped falling and the sun was partially out when Daniel reached the McElroy residence. Buggies, wagons and horses were tethered up and down the road. A fine black surrey, one that Daniel had never seen before, was parked in the yard. King Solomon and the other Negroes were assisting with the horses. It appeared that most of the neighbors of Cane Creek had turned out for the wedding.

"Afternoon Mistuh Daniel," said King Solomon smiling. "I sees afta yo' hoss. You goes inside and get yosef married. I've been know'n dat little gurl since she wuz a child. She be full of fire and vinegar, but she be a good woman."

"Thank you," Daniel said and handed his reins to King Solomon. He straightened his coat, took a deep breath. *Here goes.*

Blood, who was scrubbed clean and wearing one of Micajah's hand-me-down waist coasts, opened the door with a broad smile.

"Com'on in, Mistuh Daniel. Everybody be here, just awaitin'," Blood said.

Micajah made his way through the festive guests and grasped Daniel's hand. "I was beginning to think you got cold feet," he said.

"Sorry sir, but that confounded horse threw me in a snow bank, then trotted off," Daniel said.

"You haven't met my daughter, Sallie, and her husband, Robert C. David," said Micajah. "They drove up from Athens in their new surrey."

139

"Welcome to the family," said Robert David, extending his hand, then introduced his wife Sallie, a striking blue-eyed blonde.

"Fair warning. You getting yourself a handful," Sallie said and laughed.

After small talk about the trip, spending the night in Huntsville and the cold weather, Sallie said: "Nancy was my bridesmaid when I married Robert six years ago in Athens. Now, I'm her bridesmaid. Please excuse me so I can prepare to perform my duties."

Daniel scanned the crowd looking for his parents. He had written and invited them to the wedding, but they weren't present and he really didn't expect them to be here – too cold and too far to travel at their ages. Reverend W.C. Dunlap, Minister of the Presbyterian Church, called for everyone's attention and Daniel took his place and waited for the bride to enter. He breathed deeply, heart pounding, nervous, and watched the stairway.

"Here she comes," a lady said.

Daniel craned to see. "Isn't she beautiful?" commented another woman. Nancy appeared, wearing a gray dress that reached to the floor; her black braided hair falling nearly to her waist. The crowd parted to let her pass. Daniel's eyes never left her. When she was closer, her blue eyes locked on his and she smiled. A queer sensation swept through his body and he relaxed a notch and returned the smile. The next few minutes were a blur, his mind whirling, and he felt warm all over; fumbled for the ring and almost forgot his oath. Nancy, sensing that he was nervous as a goat, locked her soft eyes on his and smiled again.

"I pronounce you man and wife," Reverend Dunlap said. "You may kiss the bride."

"Smack her good," said a guest and everyone laughed. Daniel kissed her tenderly on her full lips. "I love you, Nancy McElroy," he whispered.

Clapping and cheering. It was over. He was married.

The afternoon was filled with eating, fellowship and good cheer. Furniture was pushed back and fiddle music began. Daniel led Nancy to the center of the circle of guests. "Now, I'm gonna have that dance that I was afraid to ask for at the corn shucking," he said.

It was late and cold when Daniel assisted Nancy into Robert and Sallie David's fancy surrey. They nestled warmly beneath a warm blanket while King Solomon drove them to Widow Larkin's house in Fayetteville. Daniel swooped Nancy into his arms and carried her across the threshold and into his room and gently placed her on his bed.

"Now, Mrs. Nancy McElroy, I have you in my lair."

"Correction. Mrs. James Daniel Barksdale, if you please."

# 14 | FULL OF HOPE

Fayetteville.
Late January, 1827.

Something cold striking his face woke Daniel. No light came through the chinks between the logs, but he could hear and feel the winter wind whistling into the room. He wiped his face. Snowflakes were blowing through the shingled roof. No work today. He tugged the blanket over his head and scooted against Nancy's warm body and tried to sleep, but he couldn't. For months he had been consumed with marrying her. Now, there were other matters to consider. She had been accustomed to a comfortable life and he would prove to her that she had made the right decision by marrying him. Hopefully, children would soon come and they would need a decent home.

Their wedding gifts had been few and practical. Her parents had given them a cast iron pot and skillet together with two pewter plates and forks. Micajah made a walnut bedstead. "If you want a mattress, you'll have to pluck your own goose feathers," he said. The gift that Nancy prized most was a pewter salter given to her by her sister Sallie and brother-in-law Robert David.

Daniel had marked their marriage by purchasing a large brown leather-bound Bible which came all the way from M. Carey & Sons in Philadelphia. It contained the old and new Testaments, the apocrypha chapters and a family section to record marriages, births and deaths.

Nestled against Nancy's warm body, Daniel finally drifted off to sleep, but when daylight crept around the curtains, he woke. A Christian man didn't lounge in bed – even when it was snowing – unless he was too sick to work. The Holy Bible said that "man goeth forth unto his work and to his labor until the evening." He got up and sat on the side of the bed. Nancy roused and turned over and rubbed sleep from her eyes.

"You can't work today," she said. "You may as well stay in bed where it's warm."

He yawned. "I'll find something useful to do."

He dressed warmly and lifted his musket from above the mantle. "Keep that pot your mother gave you warm," he said. "There'll be squirrel for supper."

"Good, I'll make some dumplings," said Nancy.

Snow covered the ground and Oliver quickly picked up fresh rabbit tracks that led to a hollow log. The hound bayed as Daniel cut a bamboo brier and inserted one end into the hollow log and twisted until it caught fur. He pulled the creature out squealing and fighting for its life. Fried rabbit drizzled with gravy was fine eating.

Hunting squirrels required patience. He located empty hulls beneath a scaly bark hickory tree, walked downwind several yards and sat quietly waiting for the furry creatures to appear. He bagged three by noon.

The squirrels boiled all afternoon in the blackened pot. Nancy rolled out dough, cut out strips and dropped them into the boiling pot and made squirrel dumplings, salted and peppered to perfection. Daniel smacked his lips. "Mighty fine, yes ma'am."

"Mother taught us girls to make 'em," said Nancy.

Daniel was happy. "What a blessed man I am," he said between spoonfuls of dumplings. "A comely wife and a fine cook all wrapped up in one. I've got the world by the tail on a downhill drag. Our future is full of promise."

Nancy beamed.

That day marked the last hunt Daniel had with Oliver. A few weeks later, Oliver dragged home with bloody chicken feathers around his mouth and bleeding from a gunshot wound in the belly. He died that night. Daniel moped around for days, missing the hound that had been his constant companion since his father had gifted him several years earlier in Kentucky.

"I'd sure like to know who shot 'im," Daniel remarked to Micajah at the shop.

"What's done is done," Micajah said. "If the dog is eat'n chickens, he oughta been shot."

"I'd like to know just the same."

Micajah departed without explanation and returned shortly cradling a puppy in his arms. "Aye, every man needs a good woman and a good dog," he said, handing the puppy to Daniel. "Uncle Abington McElroy gave me a red-boned hound years ago when he moved off to Georgia. This dog is out of the same stock. He'll make you a dandy hunting dog."

Daniel beamed. "Bye crackies, that's a fine looking puppy," he said. "I appreciate it."

He named the puppy Jack, after Andrew Jackson.

---

Early March brought not only the first hint of spring but also the first disagreement between the newlyweds. Daniel had turned a garden spot with oxen and was preparing to plant potatoes when Nancy approached him and asked, "What are you doing?"

"Gett'n ready to plant potatoes."

"It ain't the right sign," she said. "They won't make like they are supposed to."

"Aww, that's a bunch of nonsense."

Nancy stiffened. "It ain't nonsense, somewhere in the Bible it says there is 'a time to plant and a time to pluck up that which is planted.'"

Daniel didn't want to offend Nancy, yet at the same time he felt that knew more about planting potatoes than she did.

"That verse don't necessarily mean what you say it means," he said.

"I can't believe that you argue with scriptures –"

"I ain't arguing, I'm just saying –"

"Don't plant potatoes when the sign is in the feet," she said. "Else they'll have little toe-looking things all over them."

Daniel nervously scratched his head. "Well, when am I supposed to plant according to the sign?"

"On the first dark night."

"Night!"

"Yes, a dark night," she replied.

"Well, I won't do it! I'm planting today in the sunlight so I can see what I'm doing."

---

Summer, 1827.

The potatoes had bloomed and the vines were dying. It was time to dig them. Daniel harnessed Andy to a plow and was proceeding to the patch when he looked up and saw Nancy lifting her skirt hem and hurrying toward him.

"What's wrong?" he asked thinking there must be trouble at the house.

"You're digging at the wrong time. The sign ain't right."

"I know when to dig potatoes," he said.

"You dig the potatoes when the sign is in the knee and the feet during the last quarter of the moon so they'll keep longer."

"Today is the only day I have to dig 'em and bye crackies that's what I'm gonna do!"

Nancy stood back and watched in silence as the plow turned the potatoes to the surface. She picked up one and brushed away the dirt. It was covered with small nodules that looked like baby toes. She tossed it to Daniel. "I told you what would happen," she said.

He looked it over, put it in his pocket and kept plowing up potatoes.

"Daniel, you are a hard-headed husband," she said and tramped back to the cabin.

---

January 1, 1828.

Cold wind whistling through the chinks woke Daniel. The room was cold as ice. Nancy was lying on her back, her bulging belly resembling a large melon beneath the cover. She had groaned all night, keeping him awake. He lay still for a while thinking about the impending birth of their first child. He hoped it would be a boy, and then thought how selfish he was. Whether it was a boy or a girl, he didn't care. His first concern was that Nancy would be safe. Many women died during childbirth. That fear gnawed at him more as the birthing date approached. He closed his eyes and asked God not to punish him for being selfish then prayed hard that God would protect Nancy. Feeling somewhat better, he quietly got out of bed and went into the main room and pushed back the ashes in the fireplace, exposing red hot coals; laid on kindling and blew on it until a flame appeared, then added oak. Soon the room was warm.

Nancy approached, groaning and cradling her large belly with both hands. Daniel assisted her into a chair. "How much longer?"

"Any day," she said quietly. "And the sooner the better."

Daniel wrung his hands. "What do I do when the time comes?"

"Get Mother and Big Annie over here as fast as you can," said Nancy. "They'll know what to do."

After resting quietly for a moment, Nancy said, "Well, life don't stop every time a woman gets pregnant. There's work to be done."

"I'll do it," replied Daniel. "You sit here and rest."

"Daniel, this is New Year's. Our first since we married. I want it to be special. I'm going to get some of those black-eyed peas that Mother gave me and get 'em going over the fire. If you'll slice up some of that hog jowl, we'll have a fine dinner. Some folks claim it's luck to eat hog jowls and black-eyed peas on New Year's Day."

"Where did you hear –" Daniel stopped in mid-sentence. He was about to ask where did you hear such a foolish idea? But he thought better of it. After all she had been right about planting and gathering potatoes by the signs. And they needed all the luck they could get.

At dinner, then again at supper, they ate peas and hog jowls until the black pot was empty. Daniel rubbed his stomach and belched. "After eat'n all those peas I'll be the luckiest man in Lincoln County."

That brought a smile to Nancy's face.

---

January 24th. It was Daniel and Nancy's first anniversary. The weather had warmed to the low thirties and a few days earlier Daniel and Micajah had slaughtered more hogs. But, signs of cold weather were evident: wooly worms with heavy coats were crawling about.

Daniel was rendering lard in a large black kettle behind the cabin. Fat scraps had been trimmed from the meat and dumped in the kettle where it was boiled down into bubbling grease. The resulting pork rinds had been dipped out and saved for cracklings. For supper he would bake cracking cornbread for Nancy in celebration of their anniversary. He had just poured hot lard into a container when he heard Nancy cry out. "Daniel!"

He rushed into the cabin and into the bedroom. Nancy was on her back, moaning. "It's time," she said. "Get Mother and Big Annie!"

Daniel nearly panicked. "Will you be okay while I'm gone?"

"Yes, go."

Daniel quickly hitched Andy to a one-horse wagon and departed down Hamwood Road at a fast trot. Andy seemed to sense that time was of the essence and broke into a run. When they wheeled into the McElroy yard, dogs and chickens scattered. "Whoa... whoa!" Daniel pulled back on the reins and the brake pole, barely missing Big Annie, who was carrying a big armload of firewood toward the house.

"Laawwwddyy Mercy, Massuh Daniel, you shores be's in a big hurry dis morning."

Daniel jumped down from the wagon. "Nancy is about to birth. Where's Mrs. McElroy?"

"She be's sick with de flu."

"Run in the house and tell the folks what's happening and that you're going with me."

"Yes suh."

Soon the wagon was bumping and jumping ruts on the way to Daniel's cabin.

---

Nancy had never felt such intense and excruciating pain. It felt like someone was trying to hack out her womb with a dull ax. The room was dark and freezing cold. The only sound was wind whistling through the chinked logs. In her pain-demented mind, she first thought it was night, but later realized that a winter storm must be moving in. *Where are Mother and Big Annie?*

"Arrggghh, oh God, oh God help me!" She squeezed her fists and clenched her teeth. All she could think about was Susan Buchanan, who had recently died during childbirth. "I'm too young to die," she jabbered aloud. "Don't let me die, Please God, don't let me die."

144

The door flew open and in the dull light she saw someone in the room. "Big Annie be's here chile, you be's jus' fine,"

"Where's Mother?"

"She be's sick with de flu." Big Annie lit a candle that flickered when gusts of wind blew through the chinks. "How long you be's hurt'n?" she asked.

"Not long... aaarrrrgghhh!" and her voice died away.

"Dis may be's a long day,"

"Where is Daniel?" Nancy mumbled.

"He be's sitt'n by de fire smoking hisself to death."

---

Daniel went outside for more firewood and studied the clouds that moved toward him from the north. The oxen were behind the small log barn bunched together, their backs toward the approaching weather.

Back inside, he lay on more wood and got water boiling in the black kettle that hung over the fire, paced the floor; sucked on his pipe and waited. He heard Nancy scream. All he could do was pray. He sat down before the fire and closed his eyes and prayed like he had never prayed before. "Ohh please God, save my Nancy –"

The bedroom door opened. "Massuh Daniel."

Daniel jumped to his feet. "What?"

"Get some whiskey. De missus be's in lots of pain."

Daniel grabbed a pint of corn whiskey and handed it to Big Annie. "How is she?"

"She be's fine, but hurt'n awfully," said Big Annie and went back into the bedroom and closed the door.

Blowing wind caused the chimney to stop drawing and the room filled with smoke. Daniel peeked outside where snow was falling sideways. It had been hours and still no baby. What was wrong?

Late afternoon there was a knock on the door and in came Micajah, followed by his older daughter, Abigail Buchanan, who went directly to the bedroom to see after her younger sister.

"How is she?" Micajah asked.

"It's been several hours since she went in labor," replied Daniel. "She must be in trouble."

"She's in God's hands," said Micajah.

"I know, I've been praying all day," said Daniel. They sat by the fire and waited.

"Aye, I'll never forget when Arch was born," said Micajah. "I had been drafted by the militia and was away from home when he was birthed. I was worried to death when William was born. I was away again, fighting Tories."

"That must have been awfully hard on you," said Daniel.

"Aye."

A loud scream behind the closed door brought both men upright in their chairs.

"Push down child," they heard Big Annie say.

More screams.

"It ain't coming – it ain't coming," Nancy cried out.

145

Daniel heard the fear in her voice. Long silence. Daniel sat on the edge of his chair and nervously massaged his hand.

"It be's com'n," exclaimed Big Annie. "Push hard chile."

More loud screaming. Silence.

Daniel and Micajah looked at each other, their faces pensive.

"Shhh, listen," said Micajah. Daniel cocked his head. Yes, it was a baby crying. "Aye, I believe I've got myself a grandchild," said Micajah, smiling.

Daniel slumped in his chair and exhaled loudly. "Thank you, Lord."

---

Inside the cold room where a candle flickered, Nancy lay in a puddle of sweat and blood. Thank God the child was finally out of her body and alive! Abigail and Big Annie helped her out of bed and held her upright while the afterbirth dropped fell from her womb onto the board floor. Big Annie clipped the unbiblical cord and tied the end with a string.

"I'm weak and hungry," said Nancy, weakly. "And I need to go to the outhouse."

"I'll take you as soon as I clean you up," said Abigail. Big Annie cleaned the baby, wrapped it inside a blanket and carried it out to Daniel. "How is Nancy?" he asked.

"She be's jus' fine."

"What is it, a boy or a girl?"

"Massuh, you got yo'self a fine son," she replied and unwrapped the blanket.

Micajah hobbled over and viewed the baby. "He favors the McElroys," he said smiling. "Just look at those blue eyes and black hair."

They named the child George Edward. The same month Micajah was presented with another grandson, Micajah L. McElroy – "Mike" they would call him – born to William and Mary. It was a momentous year. In November, Andrew Jackson was elected the 7th President of the United States, defeating incumbent, John Quincy Adams. Jackson's wife, Rachel died in late December and "Old Hickory" refused to leave her gravesite at the Hermitage, near Nashville to travel to Washington to take the oath of office. Change was on the way.

---

Massuh, yo' dog Oliver wuzn't eat'n no chickens," King Solomon said quietly.

Daniel looked up from his work, puzzled by what the Negro man said. "I saw bloody chicken feathers on his mouth."

"Yassuh, but dey wuz put dere."

Daniel's face tightened. "Who?"

"I'se tell you, but don't ever tell I said so."

"Who?"

"Mistuh Dink Buchanan. I sees 'im shoot de hound, then smear feathers on his mouth."

Daniel clenched his jaw. "Thanks."

---

Fayetteville.
Early February, 1829.

146

They paid the crossing fee, nudged their mounts onto the ferry and crossed Elk river to the south side; rode down the Huntsville Pike a short distance, then turned west on Molino Road. Micajah led the way to the top of a ridge overlooking Fayetteville.

"The west line of the property begins at a point where a branch flows into the river," Micajah said, pointing. "Then runs along the riverbank 64 poles to a point, then south up this ridge to a point, then west, then north back to the river. It's a hundred and ten acres."

Daniel twisted in the saddle and surveyed the tract; first the fertile bottom land that would produce good cotton and corn, and then the forested ridge where ample hardwoods grew.

"It's mighty fine-looking land, Mr. McElroy," he said. "Course, it will require a lot of work to clear new ground and make it productive."

"Aye, Daniel, you'll find no richer soil in Lincoln County."

"How much?"

"Five hundred and fifty dollars," said Micajah. "And that's cheap."

Daniel whistled and faked shock, but he knew it was worth the asking price.

On February 5th, Daniel, Micajah, Archibald and William McElroy rode to the courthouse where Micajah executed a deed in the presence of his two sons and Court Clerk Brice M. Garner. Daniel counted out five hundred and fifty dollars in gold coins to his father-in-law and was handed the deed.

"Aye, you've made a wise purchase," said Micajah. "Take care of the land and it will take care of you."

"I sure hope so," he said, shaking his father-in-law's hand.

Daniel rode home, happy that he had made the purchase, but a little scared that he couldn't make the land productive.

"It's done!" exclaimed Daniel and showed a pregnant Nancy the deed. "This represents our future."

She shifted one-year-old George Edward to her other hip. "Let me see," she said excitedly. "Read it to me."

Daniel read the deed slowly, as Nancy nursed the baby.

"It sounds so wonderful. And it's ours."

"It's a fine piece of land," he said.

"I don't ever want to leave it," Nancy said.

"We won't. I'll build a house, clear the land and plant crops. We'll sink our roots so deep we can't ever be uprooted." He paused and smiled. "But, I'll need plenty of help."

She took his hand and placed it on her bulging belly. "I've got a feeling it's another boy."

"When?"

"July."

Daniel built a cabin on the land and purchased three Negroes to help farm it. Joe was about 45 years old and his 12 year old son, Green, cleared new ground while Judy, age 35, cooked and assisted Nancy with the baby.

True to her prediction, Nancy birthed a boy – James Greer born on July 22nd. Daniel duly it recorded in the big brown Bible.

Daniel did carpentry work when he could find it. The farm wasn't fully productive and his dream of raising cotton for a cash crop was fading. He borrowed money to make up the shortfall, bought on credit and gradually slipped into debt.

Another boy, William Coleman, was born on March 23, 1831. Nancy had her hands full caring for three babies, all three and younger.

---

Daniel had tethered Andy near the courthouse where several men rested on their haunches, whittling, chewing tobacco and spitting juice, when Dink Buchanan rode up.

"Well, if it ain't Dan'l Barksdale," he sneered.

Every time Daniel thought of Dink the veins on the side of his temples bulged out. He wasn't looking for trouble, but he wouldn't run from it either. He nodded. "Morn'n Dink."

"I hear you don't pay your debts," Dink said loud enough for the whittlers to hear.

Daniel bit his tongue.

"A man that don't pay his debts won't be around here for long," Dink said.

"I've never had a debt that I didn't pay," said Daniel. "Why don't you mind your own business, Dink."

"Well, I thought I might help ya out," said Dink.

"How's that?"

Dink eyed Andy. "I might take that horse off of your hands," he said. "You need money and I could use a horse."

"He ain't for sale."

"Everything's for sale when a man needs money – like you do," replied Dink.

Daniel's jaws tightened and the blood vessels on the side of his head pulsated. Dink was spoiling for a fight, but Daniel refused to rise to the occasion. There was more than one way to skin a cat.

"You're right, Dink, I owe money and I might consider selling this bay horse if the price is right. But this ain't no ordinary horse. He's real special."

The men stopped whittling and watched.

"Looks like any other horse to me, 'cept he has one eye," replied Dink. "That makes him about worthless."

"He can pull a plow, a buggy and wagon, trot, pace, canter and single-foot so smooth you can drink your coffee while rid'n 'em."

"I'd like to see that," Dink sneered.

"See for yourself."

Daniel untied the reins and handed them to Dink.

"Who has the coffee cup?" asked Dink and laughed. He had just grasped the saddle horn and hooked his foot in the left stirrup – Andy's blind side – when the horse bolted to the right, bucking and kicking.

"WHOA – WHOA!" Dink yelled, holding on for dear life and trying to climb aboard as Andy made one final buck sending Dink sprawling to the ground. The men whittling were bent over, guffawing and slapping their thighs. Dink got up and knocked the dirt from his clothes.

"Oh, there's one other thing I forgot to tell you," said Daniel.

"What?"

148

"He's a one-man horse." The men guffawed. "And he don't like dog killers either," added Daniel, his tone deadly serious.

---

Winter, 1831.
McElroy Plantation.

Micajah was teaching Daniel the finer skills of making shingles with a drawing knife and shaving horse in the shop when William McElroy returned from Fayetteville. He hitched his mount, flung open the door, letting a cold draft of air inside, and stamped snow from his feet.

"A letter for you, Father," he announced, offering it to Micajah.

"Who's it from?" asked Micajah, laying down the drawing knife and hobbling over to accept it.

"Sallie."

"Oh, I haven't heard from her and Robert in quite a spell. Wonder what the news is in Athens."

Daniel threw a log on the fire while Micajah ripped open the letter and walked to the window where sunlight spilled in. Daniel watched the old man as he read silently; his face reflecting the contents of the letter. At first, he smiled, and then as he read on, his lips parted, mouth opened and shoulders slumped. The arm holding the letter dropped to his side.

"Is something wrong, Father?" asked William.

"I warned 'em," Micajah said.

"Warned who?"

"I told the County Commissioners that there was too many springs nearby to chance building the courthouse where they wanted it," said Micajah, "but they said they would take the chance."

"What happened?" William asked, concerned.

"The foundation cracked," Micajah said solemnly.

"Can it be repaired?"

They are going to tear it down," Micajah muttered. "Can you believe it? After only a few years and they are destroying that fine building. Located anywhere else that building would have stood for hundreds of years."

William attempted to console his Father. "Everyone knows that you do excellent work."

"Yeah, but the County Commission will place the blame on me," Micajah said and slumped into a chair by the fire.

Daniel felt pity for the old man and walked over and laid a hand on his shoulder. "Can I do anything for you, Mr. McElroy?"

Micajah looked up, laid his hand on Daniel's and shook his head. "No, but much obliged for asking."

# 15 | TOUGH TIMES

Fayetteville.

Early March, 1832.

Daniel had slept little. Finally, at 3 a.m. he slipped out of bed, careful not to wake Nancy, built a small fire in the fireplace and fired his pipe. He stared at the dancing flames as though they were a crystal ball. He was drowning in debt. He had talked to his creditors and assured them that he would pay, but they weren't listening. They had debt too. The court was clogged with lawsuits. He knew that if he didn't pay his creditors soon they would sue him, obtain judgments and sell his property. There was no easy way out of the financial morass. The solution would be bitter medicine to swallow. Nancy entered, cradling William Coleman, and placed her hand on Daniel's shoulder.

"You rolled and twisted all night long," she said.

He patted her hand. "Sorry, did I keep you awake?"

"You, and this young'un."

She sat down and rocked the infant. Daniel took a last deep pull on the pipe, tapped ashes into the fire and looked up at Nancy, still beautiful after four years of marriage and birthing three babies. Telling her would be hard.

"We need to talk," he said. "When I bought this place from your father I promised you we'd never move –"

Her eyes narrowed.

"I may hav'ta break that promise," he said quietly. "It's just a matter of time before I'm sued. The only question is whether I sell for the best price I can get now or let the sheriff sell it to the highest bidder."

Nancy lowered her head. "Is that our only choice?"

"I'm afraid so," Daniel replied, not able to look at her.

"The sweat'n labor we've invested; cutt'n trees, clearing new ground, building a cabin, plow'n and plant'n – all for nothing," she said. "I had set my mind on spending the rest of my days here, raising my children and even dying here." She looked up at Daniel. "My heart and soul 'n this place."

"I know." She was heartbroken and it tore at his heart.

"I need to nurse this baby," she announced and abruptly went to the bedroom.

Daniel heard her weeping softly and went and brushed away her tears. "I'm sorry," he said and embraced her.

She sucked up and wiped her eyes. "I may cry, but I'm no weakling."

"I know."

Daniel squeezed her tight and said, "With God's help, we'll weather this storm."

---

On March 26th, Daniel executed a deed conveying the 110 acres, including the cabin and all improvements, to Keys Meeks for the sum of $450 – $100 less than he paid three years earlier. Alexander Akin and Company sued Daniel for debt. He hired a lawyer and fought the case, but lost. The jury verdict was for $75.94 plus costs. He appealed on July 27, 1832, not so much to overturn the judgment but to delay its execution.

Then Allen Urquhart sued and got judgment for $102 plus cost.

Daniel was worried. Carpentry work was scarce and gold and silver even more so. Paper notes were discounted, depending on which bank issued it. Micajah couldn't bail him out, even if he asked. The old man was suffering financially also – practically everyone was. He was 72 years old and hobbled around attempting to work, but his body was wearing out. His ankles were swollen and his breath was short. It was just a matter of time before he was confined to bed or worse.

A letter arrived from Sallie David in Athens telling about an outbreak of small pox in Limestone County. "It is thought to have come from New Orleans," she wrote, "in a child's willow wagon." People were fleeing town and using tar fire and other disinfectants.

It seemed that all news was bad.

---

When ol' Jack struck the hot trail of coon, Daniel quickly forgot about his problems. Negro Joe and his boy Green hunted with him and they never failed to bag a raccoon. Daniel tanned the hides and sold them for profit and gave the meat to Joe and his family, who loved it baked with sweet potatoes. It was dark when Daniel lifted his musket from above the fireplace and slung the powder horn across his shoulder. Nancy, pregnant again, waddled into the room followed by the babies and said, "It's an awfully bad night to go hunt'n with no moon out."

"There is never a bad night to go coon hunt'n," Daniel replied. He examined the musket in the candle light to determine if it was loaded with ball and powder. He couldn't remember reloading, but was pretty sure he did.

Outside, Joe and his boy Green waited with blazing pine knot torches. Ol' Jack was bouncing and yelping, eager to hunt. Daniel pulled the hound's ear and pointed to a wash tub leaning against the cabin. "Jack, I want you to tree a coon that big, you heah," he said.

The dog yelped and howled.

"Massa, ol' Jack, he be ready to go," said Joe.

"Put a leash on 'im," said Daniel. "We'll head up to Buchanan Creek. Coons oughta be out feed'n along the banks."

They tramped through the woods, stumbling over fallen logs and ol' Jack straining at the leash. Finally, he gave a long howl and almost broke free from Joe's grip.

"He be on a scent, Massa."

"Turn 'im loose," said Daniel.

The hound lunged forward, barking.

"De trail be hot, he be done treed a coon 'fore long," said young Green.

They tore out through the woods, following the hound with Joe and Green holding their torches high and lighting the way. The barking suddenly changed to a long baying sound.

"He be treed shore as de world," said Joe.

"Music to my ears," said Daniel. "Com'on. Let's go!"

They ran through bushes, gum thickets, and brier patches, arriving at the base of a beechnut tree where Jack sat back on his haunches looking up in the branches and baying.

"Hold your torches real high so I can see to shoot," ordered Daniel.

"I don't sees nut'n," said Joe. "I believe dat coon done crawled in a holla spot.

Daniel examined the base of the tree and saw that it was indeed hollow. "You're right. Gather some dry leaves and we'll smoke 'im out."

Joe and Green packed sticks and leaves in the opening and torched it. Smoke boiled out of a hole high in the tree.

"I sees sump'n whiz outta dat hole!" exclaimed Green.

"A big coon?" asked Daniel.

"Nassuh, it wadn't no coon."

"Had to be," said Daniel.

"Jack ain't baying like it be's a coon," interjected Joe.

"I sees his eyes," said Green pointing.

Daniel walked around the base of the tree trying to draw a bead on the animal. "He keeps moving around," Daniel said. "Green, get a stick and shimmy up there and knock that coon out."

"Yassuh." The boy found a sturdy stick and climbed up the tree.

"Do you see 'im?" shouted Daniel.

"Nash. He is moving higher."

"Keep climbing," said Daniel.

The boy grunted as he struggled higher in the tree.

"Do you see 'im now?" Daniel asked again.

"Nash, he be gone higher again, I heah 'em massuh, I believe ol' Jack done treed something wuzn't ta coon."

"Jack never makes a mistake," Daniel replied. It's probably an old she coon."

"Watch out below!" Green hollered. "I gonna knock 'im out."

The stick slapping against limbs brought a sound that Daniel had never heard before. And it wasn't a coon.

"Hear he come!" yelled Green.

There was more slapping of the stick followed by a crashing noise as the animal fell through the limbs. A loud scream.

"Hold up the torch!" yelled Daniel. "I'll shoot 'em when he hits the ground."

"Yassuh!" Joe had barely uttered the words when the falling animal crashed on top of him knocking the torch to the ground. Joe hollered, "Lordee, mercie! He be no coon!"

There was just enough light from the torch for Daniel to draw a bead on the animal. He cocked and squeezed the trigger. The gun didn't fire. The torches died and the night was suddenly pitch black. A snarling fight ensued. Daniel couldn't tell who was winning. From Jack's yelping, it sounded like the animal was victorious. Soon there was silence, except for Jack yelping in pain. When Joe got a torch ignited, Green was sliding down the tree and Jack was limping, cut, scratched and bloodied. "That's gotta be the meanest coon on Buchanan Creek," said Daniel.

"Beg pardon, massa," said Joe. "Ol' Jack done made a big mistake. Dat be's a bob cat or worse."

"Nassuh, dat was a worse," said Green. "Dat was a panter."

"Boy hush, you ain't never seen no panter," said his father.

"I has now."

"Massa, I wouldn't recommend show'n dat dog de washtub again," said Joe. "No tell'n what he might tree de next time."

---

February 22, 1833, was cold and blustery and the drinking water in the wooden bucket located just inside the back door was frozen solid. Daniel scooted his chair closer to the fireplace. Through the window he saw deep drifts of snow against the wood pile. If there were complications, it would be difficult to ride for help. He fidgeted.

The three boys sat on the floor near the flame and played with corn shuck toys that Daniel had made for them. A moan came from behind the closed door. The children looked up at their father, who jumped to his feet and poked his head inside the cold room where Nancy lay propped up on a pillow both hands rubbing her protuberant belly.

"Are you okay?" he asked.

She barely nodded.

"How much longer?" he asked Negro Judy.

"Won't be long Massa."

"What can I do?"

"You done did yo part, massa. It be up to the Missus and de Lord now."

Satisfied, Daniel closed the door and returned to the chair in front of the fire. He read from the Bible – and waited.

"What's wrong with Ma?" James Greer asked, "Is she sick?"

"Hush!" said his older brother, George Edward.

"You hush!" replied James Greer and looked up at his father, concern on his innocent face.

Daniel patted the child's head. "She's all right," he said.

Time passed. Daniel got up and paced the creaking floor. He felt helpless. It was taking far too long. And he was worried. Judy said she knew all about birthing. Yet....?

Moans from the bedroom. The door squeaked open and Judy poked out her head. Daniel froze in his tracks, staring at the Negro woman. "Had she?"

"Mo hot water massa."

Daniel sprang for the iron kettle that hung over the flames; poured a pitcher of water and hustled it to Judy.

"Everything be's fine massa."

Daniel paced. Shortly, he heard the unmistakable cry of a baby. "Thank God," he mumbled. He peaked inside the candlelit room. "Is everything okay?"

"Come on in Massa," said Judy.

Daniel hurried to the bed where Nancy lay, a tiny baby nestled against her breast. He stroked her forehead. "Are you okay?"

"Yes, and you have another fine boy," she said weakly.

It was their fourth child and they named him Robert Beasley Barksdale.

---

June, 1833.

Daniel was behind the cabin, chopping wood and sending chips flying, when ol' Jack's bark told him that a stranger was approached. He looked up and saw a rider on a big chestnut horse, approaching. His guts tightened and he lowered the axe. Every man in Lincoln County knew who rode that horse – Alfred Smith.

"Morn'n Sheriff. This a social call?" Instinct told Daniel that it wasn't.

"Wish it was Daniel."

153

"Well, get down anyway and visit a spell," Daniel said, resignedly.

Sheriff Smith slid from the saddle. They shook hands and passed a few pleasantries. "I've got papers for you," said Sheriff Smith and handed them to Daniel.

After the Sheriff departed Daniel read the document – a lawsuit filed by Robert Hairston. It also named Micajah McElroy as a party defendant. Daniel's stomach roiled. Then he remembered that when he had borrowed $110 from Hairston, Micajah had co-signed the note. With failing health, a lawsuit was the last thing the old man needed now.

The case was tried on July 16th in the courtroom that Micajah had constructed over two decades earlier. They lost the case and judgment was entered against them jointly for $110 plus cost.

Daniel knew that if the judgment wasn't paid within thirty days the court clerk would issue a writ of execution and the Sheriff would sell Micajah's property to the highest bidder to satisfy the debt. Daniel couldn't allow that to happen. He had no choice but to accept William Eason's offer. Eason had offered to lend Daniel $800 with the Negroes, Joe, Judy and Green pledged as security. He also required George Jude as surety. Jude, named after his father who was a revolutionary soldier and friend to Micajah, had agreed to co-sign the note. Daniel signed the deed of trust on July 17th before Court Clerk, F.L. Kincannon. The $800 was to be repaid on March 1, 1834, the following year. If not, the Negroes would be sold at the courthouse door to satisfy the debt. Daniel's plan was simple: Pay off his principal creditors with the proceeds and work like the dickens to repay Eason by March 1st. With the nation's economy deteriorating by the day, he knew it was a big bite to swallow.

---

Daniel was sharecropping cotton and corn on Micajah's Cane Creek bottom land where the plants were healthy and showing promise of a good crop – and Lord knows, he needed one. Then a big rain came and didn't stop for three days. The bottom land flooded and washed away the cotton and corn. Several weeks elapsed before the water receded, the driftwood removed and the soil dried. He had replanted. It was late in the season to replant and he knew that the crop might not mature before frost, but he had to take the chance. Then drought came in July and the cotton squares didn't mature. Hopefully, the corn would produce. Daniel walked over the field and saw that the ears were small – mere nubbins. If the plants received sufficient rain for the remainder of the season, there might be enough corn to make cornmeal and feed the oxen and horses for a few months. Might.

---

Saturday, February, 1834.

It was a day that Daniel had dreaded. He hurried through the morning cold to the Negro cabin where smoke curled from the chimney. He pounded on the door. Joe poked out his head.

"Morn'n Massa."

"Joe, hitch up the wagon and get all of your stuff together," Daniel said brusquely.

"What fer massa?"

154

"Just do as I say," snapped Daniel and returned to the house where Nancy was seated by the fire rocking the baby. He hovered over the fireplace and massaged his cold hands.

"You're awfully quiet this morning," she said.

"Yeah."

Nancy leaned to one side and looked out the window and saw Joe and Judy and their boy, Green, shivering in the cold by the wagon holding their few belongings.

"What's this?" she asked, her tone serious.

"I'm gonna sell 'em."

"Noo!"

"I don't have a choice Nancy, the $800 note to William Eason is due in a few days and if I don't pay it, he'll sell 'em on the courthouse steps. They might not bring enough to pay off the note."

"But –?"

"There'll be a lot of folks in town today," he said. "Maybe I can find a private buyer and get a good price." He buttoned his coat to the top and pulled down his hat and strode outside in the cold where the Negroes shivered and clutched a few items of clothing tied in a bundle.

"Y'all load up," he commanded. They didn't move.

"Massa, please don't sell us," Joe begged.

Grim faced, Daniel said nothing.

"You and the Missus be's good to us and we wanna stays with ya. Please massa."

Daniel looked up at the shivering threesome. Judy was clutching Joe's arms, her big black eyes wet and begging, her other arm wrapped around their boy.

"We work extra hard," continued Joe. "My boy be's strong and don't eat much and don't cause no trouble... and Judy... why, she de the best cook 'n housecleaner in de county. She just about be's the Mammie to yo' chillens."

"Please massa, Judy begged. "We be's real good."

"I have no choice," Daniel said. "I borrowed money and pledged y'all as security and if I don't find a private buyer y'all will be sold at auction to no tellin' who."

"Massa, I be's strong and be's a good worker," said the boy. I hire out and make money for ye."

"I've already considered all that," replied Daniel. "Truth is, I can't afford y'all any longer. Now load up in the wagon."

The Negroes huddled in the back of the wagon while Daniel climbed in the seat. He clucked to Andy and popped the reins on his back. Andy, old and worn out, strained against the harness and the wagon slowly creaked forward.

"JUST A DARN MINUTE!"

Daniel looked to his side and saw Nancy rushing toward him, William Coleman on her hip, and a fierce look on her face.

Daniel carried enough burdens without taking on one more from his wife.

"What is it, woman?"

"I got a say in this matter and I'm gonna say it," she said, her blue eyes hard as stones. "The note isn't due until March 1st and here you go jumping the gun –"

"– I hate doing this worse'n anything."

155

"I know you do," she said. "But a lot can happen between now and then. Maybe Mr. Eason will give you an extension."

"He won't do that."

"Well, ask him!"

"Bye crackies I know what I'm doing. Now go back to the house!"

She stepped in front of the horse. "Daniel Barksdale, you'll have to run over me and this young'un!"

Daniel exhaled loudly. "Okay – Okay."

He fretted and avoided Nancy for the remainder of the day. She had no right to interfere with his business.

That night, after the children were in bed and Nancy rocked the baby, Daniel lifted the large Bible and opened it to Genesis Chapter 3. He would be gentle with her, but she needed to be reminded of her place in God's scheme of things.

"God laid down the laws that govern a man and wife a long time ago," he said. She said nothing, looking straight ahead and continued rocking the baby.

"Listen to what the Bible says." Daniel leaned into the small circle of candlelight and began reading. "'Unto the woman he said, I will greatly multiply thy sorrow and thy conception; in sorrow thou shall bring forth children; and thy desire shall be thy husband and' – "now listen carefully," Daniel emphasized. "'He shall rule over thee.'" He closed the Bible and laid it aside. "I was doing what I thought was right and proper and you interfered. And in the presence of the negroes!" he added. They'll become uppity and won't do a thing I tell 'em. They'll run to you."

Nancy looked at Daniel, piercing him with her blue eyes. "Are you finished?"

"I guess so."

"I know what the Bible says about the duty of a woman to her husband. I also know what the good book says about how to treat our neighbors –"

"Neighbors? They're slaves!" Daniel exclaimed.

"As far as I'm concerned they're my neighbors. God made them in his image just like he made us. They have a soul just like we do –"

"But?"

"And we're also commanded to love our neighbors as ourselves," she continued. "Joe, Judy and Green are like family to me. Why, Judy delivered this baby! If it hadn't been for her, I might have died. I'm not going to stand idle and allow you to auction them off like livestock. They might be split up and that would be a terrible thing to live with."

The anger that Daniel had carried all day evaporated. Nancy was right. However, they were property – his property at law – that could be bought and sold. He didn't want to sell them any more than she did. Yet, what was he to do?

He watched Nancy rock their baby. *What if she were sold on the auction block and he never saw her again? Nor his baby?* It was too horrible to ponder. He walked over and stroked her hair.

"I know in my heart you're right and I love you even more for speaking the truth," he said quietly. "I'm sorry for being angry with you. I'm frustrated. I feel like a rat hemmed up in a corner staring at a dozen cats. I don't know which way to run."

Nancy looked up, her eyes now soft and loving. "I'm sorry too. I love you."

They talked and agreed on a course of action. Tomorrow, he would rise early and ride to Madison County to visit William Eason.

Daniel crossed Elk River by ferry and rode south across the Plateau of the Barrens to Madison County and to William Eason's plantation. He reined at the front gate. "Well, Andy, here we are. I don't know if horses pray, but if you do say one for me."

He was met at the front door by an elderly Negro woman.

"Massa be in de study." She ushered Daniel into a high-ceilinged room where William Eason sat before a fireplace, a book in his lap. He rose and greeted Daniel.

"Welcome, Daniel. You must be tired and cold. Warm yourself in front of the fire."

"Thank you sir," said Daniel. "It was a long ride."

Eason offered Daniel refreshments – which he refused – and inquired of his family, particularly Micajah McElroy.

"His health is failing," said Daniel.

"I'm sorry to hear that," said Eason. "He's a good man and a mighty fine builder." Brief silence. "I am quite impressed that you are here early to pay off the loan. With money being so tight, I frankly thought you wouldn't be able to meet the March 1st date. I sincerely congratulate you Daniel. And I assure you that I need the money. Will you pay with specie or with bank notes? If the latter, you know that I'll have to discount them."

Daniel shuffled his feet. "Neither, Mr. Eason. I didn't come to pay, I come to ask for an extension."

"Well – uh, I'm afraid that's quite impossible," Eason blustered.

Daniel felt his stomach plummet to his bowels. He had hoped for and, yes, prayed that Eason would work with him. He dropped his head. "The God's truth, Mr. Eason. I can't pay it. Can you just give me a little more time?"

Eason was suddenly very formal. "When a man makes a bargain with me I expect it to be carried out."

"Yes sir, I agree," replied Daniel. "I'm doing my dead level best to carry my end of the bargain. I work my fingers to the bone and you know how hard times are."

"I'm sorry that I can't accommodate you Daniel," said Eason, laying a hand on his back. "Please convey my regards to your family, and of course to Micajah."

Daniel nodded disappointedly as Eason accompanied him to the door.

"Just turn the Negroes over to me and I'll mark the note paid and satisfied," said Eason.

Several weeks passed and Daniel didn't hear from Eason. "I believe he's gonna give me an extension," he said to Nancy one evening.

"Ohh, I've prayed unceasingly for that to happen," she said. "Joe and Judy will be greatly relieved. They've been worried to death. They have feelings too, you know?"

"I know. Nancy – I know."

Saturday, April 19, 1834.

A dog barking woke Daniel. A horse neighed, followed by a voice and a loud banging on the cabin door. At 3 a.m. that spelled trouble. Daniel sprang from bed clad in his nightshirt and stumbled in the darkness to the front door. "Who is it?"

"It be's King Solomon, Massa Daniel."

Daniel lifted the latch and opened the door. "What's wrong?"

"It be's Massa Micajah," he said, voice quavering. "He be real sick. Massa William sent me to round up de family. He say hurry right along."

"Thank you King Solomon, we'll be right over."

Daniel shook Nancy, who was sound asleep on her side, one-year-old Robert Beasley nestled against her breast. "Wake up!"

She roused. "I'm plum wore out. This baby whimpered all night long."

"I know," said Daniel touching her face.

"What's wrong?" she asked.

"It's your father. He's sick."

She sat up in bed. "How bad?"

"Pretty bad," replied Daniel.

"Ohhh no!" She sprang up and quickly dressed. "Judy can stay here and see after the boys. I'll take Robert Beasley with me." she said.

Daniel hitched Andy to a one-horse wagon and soon they were bumping down Hamwood Road. The baby was crying. "Is he ailing?" asked Daniel.

"No, just hungry." She unbuttoned her blouse and after the baby suckled, he was soon asleep in her arms. The spring air was warm and balmy and the woodland seething with sweet aroma. Morning light was creeping over the surrounding hills when they reached the McElroy residence where several horses and wagons were hitched in the front yard. News had spread fast.

Inside, Micajah was in bed, his head propped up on a pillow and surrounded by family. His eyes were closed and breathing was labored. Mrs. McElroy was lovingly stroking his forehead and speaking to him. Nancy rushed over and took his father's hand and rubbed it gently. She leaned close. "Father, can you hear me? It's Nancy." Daniel thought he saw the old man's finger move.

"What happened, mother?" Nancy asked.

"He wouldn't eat his supper last night; said he had heartburns and he complained of pain in his arm and said his chest felt like it had a tight belt around it."

"It's probably his heart," whispered a daughter-in-law."

Family, friends and neighbors kept arriving until the room was filled and people spilled out into the yard. "Has anyone sent word to Sallie?" Nancy asked.

"Blood rode off earlier on my best horse," said her brother, Barney Linn.

"Good, I know she'd wanna be here."

Nancy left her father's side only long enough to nurse the baby and answer the call of nature. The old man labored for breath all day. Neighbors brought in food until the board table was piled high with roasted venison, ham, turkey, chicken and all sorts of relishes and bread.

Daniel returned home and gathered his three boys who were playing outside in the warm spring weather. "Children, get in the wagon."

"Where we going Pa?" George Edward asked.

"Your grandfather is real sick."

James Greer asked. "What's wrong with 'em?"

"When a man's time comes, it just comes," Daniel replied. He lifted three-year-old William Coleman onto his lap and slapped the reins and clucked to Andy. The trip up Hamwood Road was fast and bumpy.

158

Inside the McElroy home, Daniel lifted William Coleman into the crook of his arm and with his free arm ushered the other two boys over to Micajah's bedside. The children looked at their grandfather in silence. Finally, James Greer asked: "Is he gonna die?"

"Hush," scolded George Edward.

"It's all right," said Daniel. "All of us have our appointed time. I just wanted you to see him for a final time. He was a good man – a real good man." Daniel bit his lip and turned his head away.

Mrs. McElroy asked her second eldest son, William, to bring in the Negroes so that they might see their master for perhaps a final time. Family members stepped back as King Solomon lead a small delegation over to the bed where Micajah lay.

"You be's a good man, massa," said King Solomon, placing a gnarled hand on Micajah's arm and sobbing. "We all gonna miss you." Big Annie threw her arms over her head and wailed, "Laud, Laud, take care of massa."

King Solomon wiped tears. "Massa, King Solomon will se's you up in heaben. Maybe we build a new set of pearly gates up der."

After the Negroes were ushered out of the room, Micajah's children and grandchildren gathered around his bed and laid on hands. Daniel, standing back near a sister-in-law asked: "Has a doctor been out to see 'im?"

"Yes, he bled him twice, but it didn't seem to help."

Shortly after the mantle clock struck 2 p.m., Micajah gasped and slowly exhaled making a gurgling sound. Mrs. McElroy leaned over and placed an ear to his heart.

"Is he?" asked Nancy, hesitantly.

"Yes," her mother said quietly.

"Oh… no! Lord no! Father don't leave me!" Nancy was the youngest child and Micajah's baby daughter. Daniel knew that she would take her father's death hard. He held her close as she sobbed against his chest.

Micajah McElroy, patriot, pioneer, builder and father of eight children, was dead at the age of 73 years and 7 months. Only last month a letter had arrived awarding him a Revolutionary pension of $26.00 a year. It had made the old man proud.

Arch, the eldest son, walked outside and announced his father's death to those gathered. When King Solomon and Big Annie heard the news they moaned and wailed loudly. "I be jinin' you 'fore long, Massa," King Solomon cried out.

Immediately, Daniel went to the shop and began constructing a coffin the with cedar boards that Micajah had saved to make coffins for neighbors. Nancy and her older sister, Abigail Buchanan, washed their father's body and dressed him in his well-worn waistcoat and gray pants. His corpse was laid out in the parlor where neighbors came by droves, bringing food and viewing the body. The men folk kept vigil around the clock, smoking and quietly reminiscing.

The corpse began to bloat and discolor, but Mrs. McElroy wouldn't bury him until Robert and Sallie arrived from Athens. Meanwhile, King Solomon and the other Negro men dug a grave six feet deep, southwest of the house.

Finally, Robert and Sallie David's black surrey rolled into the yard. Sallie rushed inside the house and straight to her father's corpse where she lay her head on his chest and wept quietly until Robert pulled her away.

The following day, beneath a blustery sky, Micajah was laid to rest. Reverend Dunlap, who had performed Daniel and Nancy's marriage vows, made remarks. He

159

scooped up a hand full of dirt "The Lord formed man of the dust of the ground," he said solemnly, "and breathed into his nostrils the breath of life; and man became a living soul. In the sweat of thy face shall thou eat bread, until thou return unto the ground; for out of it wast thou taken; from dust thou art and unto dust thou shall return." He sprinkled the dirt on the coffin and concluded with a prayer.

All eight of Micajah's children surrounded their mourning mother while King Solomon, Blood and the other Negro men slowly lowered the coffin into the earth and then shoveled in dirt.

Daniel wrapped his arm around Nancy, the baby on her hip and the other boys clustered around them. "Children, a great oak has fallen," Daniel said. George Edward looked up, teary-eyed, at this father.

"What do you mean, Pa?"

"He was a good and great man; that's what I mean."

Daniel watched as the clumps of dirt pounded on the wooden coffin. The old man had given him a job and taught him a trade. He had been not only mentor, but a good friend; referred carpentry jobs to him; and encouraged him when he was depressed about finances. He would surely miss him.

Thomas Joyce McClellan, now in his 20's, walked over and offered his condolences to Daniel and Nancy. "A mighty fine man he was," said McClellan.

"Nothing will be the same without him," said Daniel.

"I fear for the future," said Nancy, squeezing Daniel's arm. Daniel looked at Nancy, patted her arm and reassured her. We'll be just fine."

The following day, Daniel went to Micajah's shop and began constructing a grave marker. It would be unique, he thought. Instead of stone, he selected an ash log from inventory, cut it into two 3-foot sections, placed them flat on all sides and fastened them with ash pins. On the front side he inscribed name, birth and death date. It certainly didn't measure up to what the old man could have fashioned, but he hoped he would have been proud, just the same.

---

Lincoln County.
Late April, 1834.

"Whooaa, Andy." The aged horse stopped in his tracks and snorted. Daniel leaned against the plow handles and looked across the field, pleased at what he saw. A few more days of nice weather and he and Negro Joe and his boy would have the Cane Creek bottomland ready to plant corn and cotton. A decent crop and he figured he could pay off a lot of debt.

He looked up and the sun confirmed what his stomach told him.

"DINNERTIIIME!"

Joe looked over at him and waved that he understood. When they reached the end of the field, they unhooked the animals from the plows and led them home. They were at the barn, Joe feeding Andy and the oxen fodder and corn, when Sheriff Smith rode up on his big chestnut, followed by a rattling wagon driven by a deputy. Daniel had a sinking feeling and steadied himself against a rail fence.

"Howdy Sheriff, won't 'che get down and have some dinner?"

"Much obliged Daniel but I'm on official duty. I've come for the negroes."

Daniel's legs grew weak. *Damnation, I knew it.*

160

"Can't you wait a week or so, Sheriff, I need 'em awfully bad to help plant my crops."

"Sorry Daniel, I've got a writ of seizure signed by the Judge," he said, handing it to Daniel.

"Since I hadn't heard from Mr. Eason, I figured he'd give me an extension," said Daniel, glancing at the writ.

"Reckon not. Just took him awhile to get this writ."

"LAWD HAVE MERCY!" exclaimed Joe. "I be pray'n hard dis wouldn't happ'n. Please massa, don't let de Sheriff take us."

Nancy and the children, along with Negro Judy ran out into the yard to see what the commotion was about. Sheriff Smith tipped his hat. "Afternoon Mrs. Nancy. Sure sorry to hear about Micajah's passing. Mighty fine man."

"What's this all about?" she asked.

"I've got a writ of seizure to pick up these Negroes," the Sheriff said. "After publication they'll be sold at the courthouse door."

"Lawd save us!" Judy wailed, raising her arms heavenward.

The deputy lifted iron shackles from the wagon and approached Judy, who clung to Nancy's waist and began to wail. "Please missus, don't let 'im shackle us. We won't run."

"Sheriff, you do you have to do that?" asked Nancy.

"Yes ma'am, I can't take any chances." He nodded at the deputy, who locked shackles on Judy, Joe and their boy and roughly loaded them into the wagon and drove off.

"Massa, help us!" yelled Joe, looking back.

It was the saddest, most forlorn look that Nancy had ever seen on a face.

"Don't worry!" she yelled back. "We'll think of something."

---

Downtown Fayetteville.

Saturday morning.

A warm spring breeze played in the treetops that shaded the crowd of mostly men who had come to witness the auction and, if the price was right, purchase a Negro.

Daniel and family sat in a wagon away from the gathering and watched as Joe, Judy and young Green were brought to the courthouse steps in leg irons and chains.

"Look at 'em, they're scared to death. I can't bear to watch this," Nancy said and looked away.

Daniel was tight-lipped.

"Why is Joe and them here?" asked young James Greer.

"Are you dumb?" said George Edward. "They're gonna be sold."

"Quiet! All of you," barked Daniel.

At exactly 11 a.m. Edward Douglas, trustee named in the chattel mortgage that Daniel had signed, mounted the courthouse steps, rang a bell and announced the terms of sale.

"Ladies and gentlemen, pursuant to a promissory note and chattel mortgage executed by Daniel Barksdale of this county to William Eason on July 17, 1833, and said note being due and payable on March 1st, instant, and the note being in default, the security has been seized by writ and will now be sold to the highest bidder to satisfy the

161

indebtedness. Payment will be in specie. If you pay by bank note, it will be discounted depending on the financial standing of the issuing bank." He paused. "Any questions?"

"Are the negroes to be sold as a family?" someone hollered.

"They'll be sold individually, and then offered together. If anyone wants to buy them as a family, they'll have to bid a minimum of 10% more than the combined individual bids."

"Are they sound?" yelled a man.

"They appear to be, but we are selling them as is," replied Douglas.

"Bring 'em out closer so we can look 'em over," another man said.

"How old is the woman?" asked a corpulent man wearing a wide-brimmed gray hat.

"Approximately thirty-six," replied Douglas. "Her husband is forty-four and the boy is twelve or thirteen years old."

"Can she reproduce?" someone else asked.

"Can't answer that," said Douglas. "Alright, here we go. We'll sell the young black buck first, then his mammy, followed by the man. Alright, who'll give a thousand dollars for the young buck?"

"ONE HUNDRED DOLLARS!" shouted the corpulent man.

"ONE FIFTY!"

"TWO HUNDRED!"

"TWO FIFTY!"

The bidding was spirited until it reached seven hundred dollars and stalled.

"Going once... going twice...three times," said the auctioneer. "Sold to the gentleman wearing the gray hat."

Judy, her wrist weighted down by chains, reached out to touch her son as he was led away. He looked back at his parents, terror on his face.

"MY SON – MY SON!" Judy wailed and looked begging Daniel and Nancy seated in the wagon. She mouthed to Nancy, "You promised me."

Nancy averted her eyes. "Can't you do something?" she asked Daniel.

"What?"

"When they were hauled off by the Sheriff, I promised I'd find a way to save 'em," said Nancy.

Douglas tugged Judy forward. "We selling the boy's mammy," he said. "She looks as healthy as a nanny goat in a briar patch." The crowd chuckled.

"Who'll give a thousand dollars?

"ONE HUNDRED FIFTY!"

"TWO HUNDRED!"

And so it went until the hammer fell at five hundred dollars.

"I can't look," said Nancy covering her face. "Did the man who bought Green buy her?"

"No," said Daniel.

Joe sold for nine hundred dollars to yet a different purchaser.

"The three negroes brought a total price of twenty-one hundred dollars," said Douglas. "If anyone wants to buy them as a family, it will require an opening bid of $2,310. Do I hear a bid?"

Silence.

"It's a nice healthy family, don't lose out."

162

Silence.

"Hearing no further bid, the negroes are sold individually as auctioned," he said and banged his gavel.

"Other than father's death, this is the worst thing I've ever experienced," said Nancy and wept quietly.

Judy was wailing loudly when Daniel slapped the leather reins on Andy's back and drove off at a trot.

---

Even though the debt to Eason was extinguished, there was little to rejoice about. With Joe and Green gone, Daniel was late planting cotton and corn. A torrential rain caused Cane Creek to overflow washing away the tender plants. After clearing away driftwood and trash from the field, he replanted, but it was late in the season. Drought came and the cotton was hardly worth plowing and the ears of corn were mostly shriveled nubbins.

Then his mother-in-law, Sarah McElroy died. In August, Samuel Doak of Bedford County sued him to collect a $250 debt and, that winter he was bedridden for days with flu. Perhaps 1835 would be a better year.

And it was. God blessed them with their first daughter, Sarah Ann, named after her deceased grandmother, Sarah McElroy. Money continued to be scarce across the country which had a devastating effect on commerce. The only thing that Daniel and Nancy weren't short of were children. Thomas Micajah was born on February 2, 1837.

Daniel didn't learn about it immediately, but he quickly felt its impact. On May 10, 1837, a financial panic was touched off in New York City when every bank there stopped payment in gold and silver. The bubble finally burst. Daniel looked for carpentry work, farmed, played his fiddle and coon hunted. And he worried.

On April 17, 1839, Dudley Richard, named after his great-grandfather, Captain Dudley Barksdale, was born.

Nancy was kept busy nursing babies, changing and washing diapers, cooking and cleaning.

"I have too much to worry about taking care of seven young'uns than to fret about what we don't have," she would often say.

But Daniel knew better. The sale of the Negro family had upset her greatly. Following the death of her parents she was often quiet for extended periods. A letter postmarked "Athens" brought her first smile in a long time. Dudley was on her hip and Sarah Ann and Thomas were clinging to her skirt.

"Oh my! It has to be from Sallie," she exclaimed. "Hurry and read it to me."

She sat down in a chair and holding the baby, closed her eyes. Daniel ripped open the letter. It was dated June, 1839 and written in pretty script.

"Dear sister, I trust that this letter will find you and yours in good health. Except for the usual fever and stomach ailments, Robert and I are enjoying good health for which we thank God daily –"

"Read slower," interrupted Nancy. "I want to enjoy every word of it."

"As you know Robert was elected a town trustee. What a wonderful man he is! And just think sister, I was such a reluctant suitor when he came calling when you and I were mere girls back in the twenties –"

"Ohh, I remember those days with fondness," interrupted Nancy. "It seemed only yesterday and we were so young and carefree."

Daniel continued reading.

"God has blessed us – not with children – but with a fine living. Athens is a place of opportunity. Remember how we laughed when Father told us that Athens was named after Athens, Greece? (Oh, how I miss Father.) A large two-story frame building has been constructed at the Female Academy. Many men of vision live her. The land is fertile and well suited for growing cotton from which many men are becoming rich."

Daniel lowered the letter and looked at Nancy, whose eyes were still closed.

"Why did you stop reading?" she asked, opening her eyes.

"I was just thinking about what she said – about cotton –"

"Well, read on."

"I know your roots are deep in Lincoln County, but oh sister, I miss you greatly. Father and Mother have gone to heaven and you are the closest family I have. I would love to see you more often and visit with my niece and nephews and would especially love to see the new baby, Dudley. Write often. Love, Sallie."

# 16 | PULLING UP STAKES

Lincoln County, Tennessee.

Late September, 1839.

The two loaded wagons set in the early morning pinkness, the horses snorting and pawing the ground and the oxen bellowing.

"Where's your Ma?" Daniel asked George Edward, who was perched in the driver's seat of a wagon.

"She went back in the house, Pa."

Daniel found Nancy in the parlor clutching the baby against her chest and quietly sobbing. He placed his arm around her shoulder and gently squeezed.

"So many good memories are here," she said, her voice breaking.

"No one can take them away," said Daniel. "We'll carry 'em with us."

She wiped tears. "Most of my babies were born in this house. Good – good memories..."

A lump rose in Daniel's throat. Nancy laid her head against his chest and sobbed quietly, her body jerking. He held her tightly.

"Oh... Daniel, I'm so scared."

"We'll... be just fine," he finally managed to say.

"We're leaving family and friends and going to the unknown."

"We'll raise our own family and make new friends," he said, trying to be optimistic. "Limestone County is a land of opportunity. I didn't see it when I was down there, but they say that cotton rows are so long that a person can't see the end without wearing spectacles. We'll make it big in Alabama. Just wait and see."

"A woman likes to know about her house. Tell me again about the place you rented."

"Well, like I said, it's a log house with two large rooms and a fireplace at each end, a loft is upstairs. It needs some fixin' up, but it's really a nice place."

"Is it really?" she asked, searching his face.

"You'll like it."

"She took a deep breath and exhaled. "I hope so."

"Are you read to go?" he asked.

"We're not spring chickens anymore," she said. "It's late in life to start over."

"Are you ready to go?" he asked.

"It's never too late to begin life anew." He wiped away her tears. "Now com'on, let's go. Tonight, we'll sleep in Alabama."

He assisted her onto the wagon seat, and then gave instructions to the children. George Edward, the eldest, would drive the second wagon pulled by oxen. Riding with him was James Greer, Coleman and Robert Beasley. The wagon was piled high with plows, farming equipment, tools, spinning wheels, kettles, salt, pots, personal belongings and a dinner bell that Micajah had given him long before he died. Rooting in the dirt was a hog that Daniel intended to fatten and slaughter come November. Roped to the back were a coop of chickens and a coop of carping geese, including a gander the children called Scratch. Tethered farther back was a heifer named Jezebel that Daniel had recently purchased.

"Keep a sharp look out and make sure we don't lose anything," said Daniel.

"Yes, Pa," replied James Greer.

Daniel climbed into the wagon seat next to Nancy, who was cradling five-month-old Dudley in her lap and holding the salter wrapped in a cloth – a wedding gift from her older sister, Sallie. Sarah, age 4, and Thomas, nearly 3 years old, huddled sleepy-eyed on a pallet just behind the wagon seat. Stacked and roped in the wagon was furniture, trunks, cooking pots, and in the back, stacks of fodder and a loose pile of corn ears.

"ALABAMA, HERE WE COME. MOVE 'EM OUT!" Daniel roared and popped the reins. A cheer rose from the children. The wagons creaked forward, the oxen struggling and bellowing to start the heavy load moving. They crossed Elk River by ferry, and then proceeded south and up the long grade to the Plateau of the Barrens.

Nancy looked back until Fayetteville disappeared from sight. "Home... I was just wondering if I'd ever see it again," she said quietly.

"Home is where the heart is," Daniel said.

"I was six years old when Father moved us here from North Carolina," she said. "And except for the two years we spent in Athens when he was building the courthouse, I've never been anywhere else. My roots are deep in this land."

Daniel laid a hand on her thigh. "We'll plant new roots in Limestone County that'll run so deep they can never be pulled up."

Nancy fell silent and the wagon rumbled southward. Daniel was scared about the future also, maybe even more so than Nancy, but he could never reveal that. He had utterly failed in Lincoln County. He didn't like to think about selling the Negroes, but truthfully it had been heaven sent. After paying William Eason, there was enough money remaining to pay off his remaining debts. Then Sallie's letter arrived extolling Limestone County. He had taken it as a sign from heaven. It was time to make a move. He had traveled to Athens the previous month and found it to be a fine place with rich soil and numerous creeks and branches. Many planters were becoming wealthy raising cotton. With the assistance of his brother-in-law, Robert C. David, he had entered into a sharecropping arrangement with James and Caroline Mitchell, who owned 40 acres three miles east of Athens. It was gray land, with a log house, that faced the Athens-Fayetteville Pike, and across the road in a deep cove was a fine spring of Limestone water.

Near twilight they reached a spring near the intersection of Limestone Road, a rutted, dirt pike that ran from Winchester, Tennessee, and perhaps on beyond, to Athens, Alabama. "We'll overnight here," Daniel said.

The boys unharnessed the oxen and horses and led them to the spring for water; fed them corn and fodder then staked them to graze. The hog rooted for acorns and the chickens and geese was fed a few kernels of corn. Daniel started a fire and Nancy cooked a supper of corn hoe cakes and fried sow belly. Daniel surveyed the western sky as pork sizzling in the iron skillet filled the air with its delicious aroma.

"We due a rain," he said. "I sure hope it holds off 'til we reach Athens."

The night was warm and the tree frogs and katydids were singing when Daniel fell over on his blanket and went to sleep. The baby crying woke him several times during the night. Each time he opened his eyes, Nancy was sitting up rocking him against her breast. He was still crying at dawn when the rooster crowed waking Daniel. He built a fire and started brewing coffee. Nancy looked exhausted. "What's wrong – colic?" he asked.

"No, he keeps rubbing his ears."

166

"Let me see."

Daniel pulled baby Thomas's ear out and looked to see redness in the canals. The child screamed even louder.

"He must have a sore," he said.

They traveled the Limestone Road, forded Brier Fork and Beaver Dam Creeks and sloshed through a swamp and, halfway to Madison Crossroads, the baby, exhausted, finally fell asleep. Nancy was bone tired, but there was no place to lay her head. She made conversation to stay awake.

"When I was sixteen years old we traveled this same road, except it was only a path back then, when Father took us to Athens to build the courthouse there. I'll never forget how unhappy Sallie and I were. We had wanted to remain in Fayetteville and live with William or Arch, but father would have none of it; said it would be scandalous. The day we drove into Athens it was raining and the streets were mud and mire. It was the most dismal-looking place I'd ever seen. We laughed when Father told us the town was named after Athens, Greece."

Nancy grew quiet for a moment. "I won't know a soul there except for Robert and Sallie."

Late afternoon, they passed through Madison Crossroads and reached Limestone Creek, where the slow-moving water was filled with dead leaves.

"There's still sunshine to burn, but the animals are tired," Daniel announced. "We'll overnight here."

The older boys unhitched the livestock, watered them at the creek and staked them to graze the tall grass in the bottomland.

"William Coleman, let the geese out to feed," said Daniel. "They won't be hard to catch."

"Pa, I'm afraid of ol' Scratch. He's the meanest gander that ever lived." "Aw, he's harmless."

William Coleman opened the coop door and ran.

Daniel was feeding Jezebel two ears of corn when he heard George Edward yell: "Last one in's a rotten egg!" He looked up and saw the older boys running toward the creek, shedding shirts and breeches.

"STAY OUT OF THE WATER! IT'S DOG DAYS!" yelled their mother.

Ignoring her, the boys splashed into the water. "Hold this baby," Nancy said to Daniel and began searching for a stick. "When I get through with 'em, they'll hear me next time."

"Ohhh, Nancy leave 'em be, they're just being boys," he said.

"The water is poisonous this time of year. One scratch and they'll get sores," she said.

A loud scream sent both parents running toward the creek.

"I CAN'T SWIM!" Coleman yelled, splashing around noisily.

"Yes you can," replied George Edward. "I'll prove it. SNAAAKE!"

Daniel and Nancy arrived just in time to witness Coleman practically walking on water toward the bank.

"What happened?" Nancy demanded.

"He threw me in, Ma," said William Coleman, gasping for breath.

"What kind of snake was it?" she asked George Edward.

"Oh Ma, I just said that to teach 'im to swim."

167

"You scared me half to death," she said. "I oughta give both of you a good switching." After the boys were dressed, Nancy inspected their feet and found a small cut on William Coleman's sole. "Don't ever get in the water during dog days," she scolded, dabbing tobacco on the wound.

"You boys catch the geese and put 'em in the coop," Daniel ordered.

In no time, William Coleman came flying around the wagon screaming for help with ol' Scratch the gander nipping at his heels.

Twilight brought swarms of mosquitoes. Daniel built a fire and threw on green foliage to create smoke. Nancy bent over the flames and fried more bacon and corn hoecakes. Smoke got in her eyes. The baby, who had been asleep in the wagon, woke and began crying.

"Sarah, rock that child!" she barked.

"Yes ma'am," the child replied.

"I'll be crazy before we get there," mumbled Nancy.

"What?" asked Daniel.

"I said I'll be plum crazy before we get to Athens. Six children under foot – one of 'em sick and me exhausted – I'll be crazy!"

"Hold on another day," said Daniel. "When we cross the creek in the morning, we'll be in Limestone County." He studied the western sky for a minute and decided he didn't like what he saw. "Barring trouble, we should reach our new home tomorrow afternoon." Several ominous signs of rain were present. He had noticed that birds had been flying low, earthworms had come to the surface of the ground and, most telling, the horn of the moon pointed down. Before turning in he cautioned George Edward once again regarding the milk cow, who had been stealing corn. "Be sure she's tied real good and don't let her get into the corn again. We'll need every ear come winter."

"Yes sir, I'll hog tie her if I have ta."

Daniel swatted mosquitoes and scratched and tried to sleep while Nancy rocked the crying baby against her breast. If the child wasn't improved when they reached Athens, he would take him to a doctor. Finally Daniel slept, but not for long. Rain drops woke him. He hadn't heard thunder and decided he must have slept sounder than he thought. He could smell the rain and hear it roar through the treetops as it approached. Then the bottom fell out. Everyone scrambled to get beneath the wagons where they were soon sitting in water.

"I've never seen such a hard rain," said Nancy, who was wet from head to toes.

"It'll pass on through directly," Daniel predicted.

At daybreak rain continued to pour. Daniel nervously eyed the creek where the water was rising fast. Nancy had noticed it too.

"The creek is too deep to ford," she said.

"Yeah, no telling how long we'll be stuck on this side – maybe days." He remembered having seen a drover's stand near Madison Crossroads, and when the rain had slowed to a drizzle, he began hitching up the wagons.

"Pa, that doggone heifer has been in the corn again," said George Edward.

"How'd she do that?"

"Gnawed the rope."

"No wonder she's named Jezebel."

They put up at the drover's stand, where they ate and dried out but slept little because of bed bugs. Two days later they forded Limestone Creek and late afternoon crossed Piney Creek five miles east of Athens. Everyone was exhausted.

"Two more miles and we'll be there," Daniel announced as the wagons rumbled out of the brown water and wobbled up the mud rutted road toward Athens. They topped a rise and Daniel pointed. "There it is!" The children stood in the wagons and craned to see. Ol' Jack was running in front, barking.

"Where, Pa?" asked William Coleman.

"The house on the right."

"Oh, I remember passing through here when I was sixteen years old," said Nancy, recognizing the area. "Father stopped at the spring across the road and remarked that it was good water.

They pulled into the back yard beneath several large white oak trees whose leaves were tinting yellow and orange.

"Whoooaa." The horses, hot and lathered, blew, sensing the journey having ended. Nancy surveyed her new home. There were large gaping holes between the logs where chinking had fallen out; wooden shingles were missing from the roof, and tall weeds grew around the house.

"Is... is this where we are going to live?" she asked Daniel, her voice barely audible.

"Yep, a little patching up and it'll look like new."

Nancy dropped her head in silence.

"Come on," he said and helped her down from the wagon. "Let's go inside."

The children tagged along, looking around in silence. There were two large rooms, a fireplace in each room, rough plank floors and a loft for the children to sleep.

Nancy was silent as she looked around at cobwebs and rat droppings. Daniel could tell that she was disappointed.

"I'll have it looking like a mansion in no time," he said. "Just wait and see."

A gopher rat skeetered across the room. Little Sarah screamed and grabbed her mother's skirt.

"A good cat'll solve the rat problem in no time," Daniel said.

They went back outside and entered the log kitchen that sat directly behind the house. It was about 16 x 16 feet with a brick fireplace. Sunlight poured through missing chinks and shingles, revealing a tangle of cobwebs in the rafters.

What remained of a fence was down with tall grass growing through the rails. A log barn that housed four stalls, corn crib and fodder loft sat farther north of the house and leaned slightly sideways.

There was no smokehouse. Daniel attempted to make the best of a dismal situation by pointing out the white oak trees that towered in the back yard. "I've never seen finer shade trees," he said. "Children, I want you to remember this day."

"Why, Pa?" asked James Greer.

"Just like those big oak trees, we're gonna plant our roots so deep in this soil that nobody can ever pull 'em out."

# 17 | STARTING OVER

Near Athens.

October, 1839.

Daniel was encumbered by neither debt nor money – only worry. Starting over at age 40 with a wife and seven children to support gnawed at his mind. Winter was coming on. They had arrived too late to plant corn and the small quantity brought from Tennessee would soon be gone. Where would he get cornmeal to feed his family? And what about the livestock? The hens weren't laying and Jezebel wouldn't come fresh until spring when she calved. Thankfully, he did have a hog to slaughter, but that wouldn't provide enough meat to last through the winter. Had he moved his family to this new land only to fail again? And there were other things to worry about. The log house had to be rechinked, missing shingles split and replaced, wood cut and laid up for the winter, new ground cleared, bushes cut and land broken to make ready for spring planting.

Strangely, there was something exhilarating about his predicament. Crisis brought not only danger but opportunity. He would find carpentry work. Yes, there was hope. If the family could survive the winter, God would send spring and the earth would bring forth plenty.

"I've seen hard times in the past, but nothing equals this," Nancy said, rocking the baby. "And it's so lonely. The only people I know down here are Robert and Sallie."

"The trip wore you out. When you get rested, you'll feel better and I'm sure we'll meet new neighbors," Daniel said, trying to lift her spirits. "Look at the bright side. We have shelter, good spring water and good health. Not only that, the woods are full of squirrels, rabbit and deer."

"I suppose you're right," she said. "The Lord has provided for us thus far."

As always, when he was troubled, Daniel found solace in God's word. He opened the Bible and turned to St. Luke, Chapter 12 and read verse 24. "'Consider the ravens: for they neither sow nor reap, which neither have store house, nor barn and God feedeth them; how much more are ye better than the fowls?'" He closed the Bible and put it aside.

"I needed to hear that," Nancy said. "Sometimes I forget that God is watching over us."

Daniel leaned over and placed a hand on her forehead and gently stroked her long, black hair as he had done on so many occasions. "You're a good and courageous woman, Nancy McElroy," he said.

"That's Nancy Barksdale, if you please."

They both laughed.

---

Saturday morning, several days later.

Daniel was splitting shingles with a draw knife while the older boys, their breeches legs rolled past their knees, were mixing straw and mud with their bare feet. The weather was fine and the temperature nippy enough to keep one from perspiring. A few more days of good weather and Daniel figured he could winterize the house.

Ol' Jack jumped up from his resting place beneath the large oak tree and ran toward the pike, barking.

"Look, Pa!" exclaimed James Greer, pointing. "Somebody's coming."

170

Daniel looked up just as a two-horse wagon, loaded with children, rattled into the yard. Seated beside the driver was a woman wearing a black bonnet and black dress and clutching a baby.

"Hello, neighbor," said the driver.

Daniel laid the draw knife aside and stood.

"Howdy."

"Are you Daniel Barksdale?"

"In the flesh."

"I'm Matthew Newby and this is my wife, Ann. Everyone calls her Nannie."

Daniel doffed his hat. "Morn' ma'am. Glad to meet ye."

The Barksdale children stared at the Newby children in the back of the wagon, the first that they had seen since moving to Limestone County.

"We come visiting and to lend a neighborly hand," said Newby.

Nancy came out the back door holding the baby, with young Sarah clutching her skirt. "For goodness sakes, Daniel, invite 'em in," she said, slightly scolding her husband.

The children bailed out of the wagon while Newby assisted his wife to the ground. "We live a mile south of here on Nick Davis Road," he said, shaking Daniel's hand.

Newby introduced his seven children. "James Martin is sixteen, George is twelve; Patrick Henry Dickerson is eleven; Susan, five; Joseph, three and Isabella is two years old. And the baby is Benjamin," he added.

Soon, the older Newby boys were barefoot and in the pit with the Barksdale boys mixing mud.

"We brought you a few things," Nannie Newby said to Nancy.

There was a sack of cornmeal, a side of bacon, relishes, dried beans and even milk and butter. Nancy was momentarily speechless. "I… I don't know what to say, except thank you."

"We're going to be neighbors so we might as well get acquainted," said Nannie.

Matthew Newby of Chesterfield, Virginia, 56 years of age, and Ann "Nannie" Brooks Newby, age 51, had been married in Virginia. They had come to Limestone County four years earlier and eventually settled on a parcel of high ground overlooking Swan Creek.

No sooner had Daniel and Newby set about replacing shingles when another wagon loaded with children, tools and bulging sacks rolled into the yard.

Daniel looked down. "Who'n the world is that?"

"Oh, that's William and Sarah Ann Fielding," replied Newby. "They live about three miles northeast of here."

"First you show up, then other neighbors," said Daniel with a suspicious tone.

Newby grinned. "That's what neighbors are for."

They climbed down from the roof and Daniel introduced himself and his family.

"We've come to get acquainted and help out," said Fielding, grinning. Mary Francis, an intelligent-looking seven-year-old, climbed down from the wagon, followed by Henry Rhodes, age 5, and 2-year-old Eppa. The baby, John Everett "Jack", was only 2 months old. William Fielding, age 49, born in Virginia, had served in the War of 1812 and had come to Alabama in 1818. In 1831, he married Sarah Ann Thompson and they settled seven miles northeast of Athens on the west bank of Piney Creek.

The Fieldings had also brought food — salt-cured ham, eggs, cornmeal, dried beans, relishes and several sacks of corn.

The children were having a grand time, daubing mud between the logs while the men folks shingled the roof. The women prepared a large spread of food and set it on a board table beneath the large oak trees. Nancy brought out her salter and placed it on the table.

"James Greer, go fetch a bucket of cold water," she said.

He grabbed a wooden bucket and, accompanied by James Newby, ran across the road to the spring in the cove and quickly returned with a sloshing bucket full.

"DINNERTIIIME!" Nancy called out. The children raced to see who could line up first behind their elders. Daniel prayed long and hard and thanked the Lord for sending good neighbors and good food to eat. After feasting on fried ham and eggs, relishes, and cornbread slathered with fresh butter and washed down with fresh sweet milk, Daniel declared it to be one of the finest meals he had ever eaten. The women adjourned to the house while the men rested beneath the trees and smoked their pipes and talked. Fielding, having lived in Limestone County for many years, knew much about the area, and Daniel was anxious to learn.

"'Course the county's named for its largest creek — Limestone — which flows into the Tennessee River on our southern border," said Fielding. "Elk River flows through the northwest portion of the county and most of the land there is hilly and not very productive. The best land for cotton lies between here and Mooresville. A lot of men are getting rich growing cotton. Naturally, they are large slaveholders — have to be. The 1830 census showed a total of 14,807 folks. Of that number, 6,730 were slaves. I suspect there's even more by now."

"There's a good market in England for cotton-wool," said Newby. "Some folks are making so much money from growing it, they call it 'White Gold.'"

"How's it delivered to market?" asked Daniel.

"By boat down the Tennessee River, up to the Ohio, then down the Mississippi to New Orleans and by ship to England," replied Newby.

"This place oughta make fairly good cotton," said Fielding. "I'd recommend planting between March 25th and April 1st."

Daniel filed the information away in his head.

"You need to know who the influential men are around here," Fielding said. "'Course Nathaniel Terry is State Senator. He moved here from Bedford, Virginia, in 1818 and has grown wealthy as a planter. John Wynn, Robert A. High and A.E. Mills are State Representatives. Some of the leading men are Nick Davis, Daniel Coleman and Dr. Joshua P. Coman."

"There's another fellow that arrived here about the same time I did," said Newby "I predict he'll be heard from in the future."

"Who's that?" asked Fielding.

"George Smith Houston. He was elected solicitor two years ago."

Fielding nodded. "I agree. Impressive fellow. I predict he'll go places."

Daniel's brain was spinning with names that meant nothing to him at the time.

"Daniel Coleman was one of our first as District Judge; operates a law school and is involved in about everything going on," said Fielding, "Including being alderman.

"Dr. Coman moved here about ten years ago and has been practicing medicine and dabbling in politics ever since. He's well-respected as a man and a physician.

Perhaps the most influential man in the county and one of the wealthiest is Nick Davis. They say he owns nearly 80 Negroes."

"I agree," said Newby. "The fact that the road I live by is named after him tells you something about his importance."

"He lives like a prince at Walnut Grove, his large plantation on Limestone Creek. Loves to race his blooded horses," said Fielding. "He represented the county when the State Constitution was framed and served as President of the Senate for several years. He carries a lot of weight around here. Sometimes there are forty to fifty guests at his house at one time."

"He's also the biggest Whig in these parts," added Newby. "He ran unsuccessfully for Governor and again two years ago, but you know Alabama is solid Democrat."

"He's a close friend of Henry Clay," added Fielding.

Late afternoon, when the sun hung low in the western sky and the breeze carried a chill, William Fielding announced it was time to go home and milk the cow. Newby likewise had a cow to milk. Daniel and Nancy thanked both families as they climbed into their wagons and drove off, the children waving to each other.

"Y'all come back anytime," Daniel hollered. He and Nancy stood in the yard watching until the wagons drove out of sight.

"We accomplished a lot today," Daniel said. "Repaired the roof and got the logs chinked."

"We accomplished a lot more than that," said Nancy.

"What?"

"Discovered we have good neighbors."

"That we did," Daniel said, wrapping his arm around her shoulder. She looked up at him and smiled. "I'm beginning to think I might like living here."

He squeezed her shoulder. "That makes me happy."

---

Sunday afternoon.

Daniel was seated in front of a small fire, Bible in his lap and nodding, when Ol' Jack's barking and the children yelling and scrambling through the house woke him.

"What'n tarnation is going on?" he asked Nancy, who was mending socks. William Coleman darted through the back door several steps ahead of James Greer.

"I'll tell 'em!" exclaimed James Greer.

"Naw, I saw it first, I'll tell 'em!" replied William Coleman.

"Pipe down, young'uns. Tell us what?" demanded Nancy.

"Uncle Robert and Aunt Sallie are coming down the road!"

"Looorrrdy!" Nancy put down her needle and thread and ran to the door just as a black surrey pulled by two matching black horses entered the yard.

Before Robert and Sallie could exit the surrey, it was surrounded by gleeful children, laughing, chattering and bouncing up and down.

"George Edward, you and James Greer tend the horses," ordered Sallie.

"Yes ma'am," they chimed.

"Coleman, you and Robert Beasley help me with these packages," she added.

"Yes ma'am!"

173

Aunt Sallie never visited unless she brought gifts for the children. And they knew it.

Inside, the children watched intently as Aunt Sallie slowly untied the string around wrapping paper, letting the drama build. "What do we have here?" she asked and lifted out a rag doll and handed it to 4-year-old Sarah, who grinned and pressed it to her bosom.

"Do I get a kiss?" Aunt Sallie asked. The child beamed and grabbed her Aunt's neck. "I lub you."

Everyone laughed. Robert Beasley, age 6, received a small pocket knife; Coleman, age 8, a pair of shoes; James Greer, age 10, a new shirt; and George Edward received a wide-brimmed straw hat. For the two babies, Thomas Micajah and Dudley Richard, Sallie gave toys. And there was candy for all. "Let me hold that baby," Sallie said taking Dudley Richard into her arms. "Ohhh, he's so sweet."

Robert David, an avid hunter, had noticed Jack, the red-bone hound, when he drove up and wanted to see him at closer range. He and Daniel walked outside. "A fine-looking hound," said Robert.

"He can pick up a trail three miles away," said Daniel.

"I've got an old bitch dog I'd like to breed to him," said Robert.

"Fine with me," said Daniel. "Bring her out when she comes in heat."

They strolled across the nearby field where Robert kicked up dirt with his booted foot. "This is fairly good soil and should be well suited for growing cotton," he said.

"I'm going to plant all that I can come spring," Daniel said.

"I don't know what practices you followed in Lincoln County, but it's a little different down here," said Robert.

"I'm listening."

"Around here the successful planters break the ground in November at least ten inches deep," said Robert. "That kills the insects, prevents rust and loosens the soil. In early March, go back and break up the clods and prepare the seed bed. Most prefer to plant between March 25th and April 1st."

Daniel looked out across the field, much of it grown over with weeds and young saplings. Much work remained to be done before it was white with cotton.

"I can't wait to get started," he said, "but I've got to earn some money in the meantime."

"One of the best carpenters around here is Emanuel Isom," said Robert. "I suggest you pay him a visit."

---

Daniel was still sitting in front of the fireplace when Nancy announced she was going to bed.

"You turn in," he said. "I'm going to have another pipe."

Soon, the house was quiet, with only the occasional crackle of the fire. He smoked his pipe and watched the flames grow lower. The truth was he was too excited to sleep. The last two weeks had been a whirlwind of emotions and activity. Failing financially and leaving Lincoln County had been hard on him. He had worried that life wouldn't be any different in Limestone County, but he had been wrong. Hope and prosperity lay ahead. And he couldn't wait to smell freshly broken earth, plant seeds and

174

visit the field early each morning to see if a tiny shoot had raised its head. He and the boys could begin cutting saplings immediately and as soon as the ground dried, he would begin breaking the soil. But first, he needed to pay Emanuel Isom a visit.

---

Daniel rode east on Nick Davis Road. When he reached the plank bridge that spanned Piney Creek, he nudged one-eyed Andy forward, but the animal panicked at the clattering sound of his hooves against the boards, pointed both ears forward and quickly backed off.

"Bye crackies Andy, you throw me and I promise to nail your miserable hide to the barn." Andy's ears perked. He understood. They went down the bank and splashed through the cold water. When they emerged, Andy shook, flinging water on Daniel and wetting him.

He rode south on Mooresville Road about a mile to George and Susannah Isom's log house, where he was greeted by a pack of barking dogs. A barefoot boy who looked to be about 9 years old stepped out onto the front porch, hands in his pocket.

"Morn'n," said Daniel. "Is this the Isom place?"

"Yes sir."

"I'm looking for Emanuel."

Before the boy could answer an older woman wearing a black dust cap and apron came out onto the porch. "I'm Susannah Isom, can I help you?"

Daniel doffed his hat. "Morn'n ma'am, I'm Daniel Barksdale. Rode over to talk to Emanuel."

"We heard that y'all had moved in the neighborhood. Glad to meet you," she said.

"Same here ma'am."

"I reckon Emanuel is with his Pa at the shop," she said and pointed to a rectangular-shaped log building that faced the road. "You might try there."

"Thanks," Daniel said, tipping his hat again, and rode to the shop, where he tethered Andy outside and entered. An older fellow was measuring and marking a board and a younger man who looked to be in this late 20's was planning wood.

The older man looked up. "Can I help ya?"

"Morn'n, I'm Daniel Barksdale from across the creek."

"I heard about y'all moving in. Welcome to the neighborhood. I'm George Isom and this is my son, Emanuel," he said gesturing toward the younger man.

They all shook hands. "Need something built?" asked Mr. Isom. "If you do, my boy can build it."

"No sir, I'm looking for carpentry work."

The old man chuckled. "So are we. Times are hard – real hard – but I've seen tougher ones."

"I guess we'll all survive if we don't die first," said Daniel and walked over to the work bench where Emanuel was building a four-panel door. "Here, let me help," he said and assisted with fitting the panels together.

"You do good work," commented Emanuel.

"Thanks, so do you."

"You know that Jesus was a carpenter," said Emanuel. "He taught folks to build a better world. One day I'm gonna build a church house so that folks will have a place to worship."

"Maybe I can help out 'n drive a few pegs," replied Daniel.

Emanuel smiled. "That would be mighty nice."

"Where did you learn carpentry?" asked George.

"From my father-in-law, Micajah McElroy in Lincoln County."

"Say, ain't that the fellow that built our courthouse – the one with the cracked foundation?" asked George.

Daniel nodded. "I'm afraid so."

"I can't judge your father-in-law's skills as a builder since I'm only a carpenter and cabinet maker. Anyway, I wasn't present. I'm of the opinion that the courthouse should have been built elsewhere, away from the springs. I suppose it was only a matter of time before the foundation cracked, no matter who built it."

A dinner bell pealed.

BONG – BONG – BONG.

"You might as well eat dinner with us," said George.

"Much obliged," replied Daniel.

George's other sons came from the field driving oxen. After they had washed their hands, he introduced them. William Stinnett, Matthew, George and James Monroe were all teenagers, the latter being the oldest. John and Bryant were in their mid-twenties. Sylvester, the barefoot boy who he had met on the porch, was the youngest.

"The Lord has blessed us with four daughters, said George and introduced Almeda Agnes, age 15. "Our other daughters, Mary Ann, Adeline and Lucinda Jane, are married. Mary Ann married John Hanks two years ago; Adeline married William Yancy this year and Lucinda Jane married Benjamin Gray last year."

Following dinner, young Sylvester bounded into the house and said excitedly: "Mister Barksdale, something is wrong with your horse!"

"What now?" muttered Daniel.

He went outside and found Andy lying down. "What's wrong with him?" asked Sylvester.

"I guess he's tired." With assistance, he got Andy to his feet and led him the six miles home.

Daniel reflected on the day's events. Although he was offered no hope of employment, he felt he had profited by meeting the Isoms. George had soldiered from Grainger County, Tennessee, against the British during the War of 1812 and his father, George, Sr., had fought in the Revolution. They were patriotic Americans, devout Methodists and certainly would be good neighbors in the years to ahead.

---

Early the following morning, James Greer rushed through the open back door. "Pa come quick!"

Daniel looked up from the open Bible. "What is it, boy? Did the cow calve?"

"No sir, it's Andy!"

Daniel closed the Bible and hurried to the barn, the boys trailing behind him. In the hallway, lying on his side, was Andy. Daniel sat down and lifted the horse's head onto his lap and stroked his neck.

176

"Is he alive, Pa?" asked James Greer.

"Barely."

"What's wrong with him?" asked William Coleman.

"He's wore out, child."

The boys fetched shelled corn and tempted Andy to eat but to no avail.

"What can we do, Pa?" asked James Greer.

"Make his last moments pleasant ones."

While Daniel stroked Andy's neck, the children rubbed his body. Daniel bent down low and whispered into Andy's ear, which perked up.

"What did you say Pa?" asked William Coleman.

"I told 'im I's joshing about nailing his hide to the barn."

The children looked at each other mystified.

Daniel was glassy-eyed. "I've had Andy since I was sixteen years old when Pa gave 'im to me. He's been ornery at times – even threw me when I was on the way to marry your Ma. I'll miss him a lot."

Andy died mid-morning with his head in Daniel's lap.

George Edward yoked the oxen and dragged Andy far away from the house where the boys piled brush around his carcass and set it on fire. Only a row of whited bones remained.

---

Saturday, early November, 1839.

Early morning coldness stung Daniel's hands and fingers as he harnessed the horses and hitched them to the wagon.

"Pitch some straw in the back of the wagon," Daniel instructed George Edward.

"Can I drive the team?" asked James Greer.

"You drove 'em last time," interjected George Edward. "Let me drive, Pa."

Daniel frowned and shook his head. "If you boys don't beat all. If we were going to the woods to chop firewood, neither one of you would want to go, much less drive the team."

"Please, Pa?" begged George Edward.

"All right, you can drive us to town and James Greer can drive us back."

The boys jumped with glee. George Edward climbed into the wagon seat, grasped the leather reins, clucked to the horses and drove them to the back of the house where William Coleman and Robert Beasley bounded out the door and piled into the wagon.

"James Greer, go see if your Ma needs help," ordered Daniel.

"Yes sir!" he said and ran to the house.

Shortly, Nancy emerged with the baby wrapped in a blanket and pressed against her bosom, followed by little Sarah leading Thomas, who was whimpering and rubbing his ears. The children were excited, jabbering and punching one another.

"Now settle down, young'uns!" barked Nancy. "Y'all act like you've never been to town before."

"You're in a good humor too, Ma," said William Coleman.

"Don't get smart alecky with me young'un, I'll let you know when I'm happy or not."

177

Daniel chuckled. Everyone was in high spirits. He sat huddled on the straw with his family, a blanket over their laps and his arm around Nancy's shoulder, as the wagon bumped down the frozen rutted pike, crossed the plank bridge spanning Swan Creek, and eventually rolled past the large, two-story frame classrooms recently completed at the Female College.

George Edward stood, gripping the reins as they neared the square.

"Now just look at him!" Nancy snorted. "He wants to be sure that everybody sees 'im."

Everyone's attention focused on the recently-constructed Methodist Church, a magnificent brick structure with a front staircase ascending between two columns and topped off by a tall spire.

"Look!" Robert Beasley pointed at the two-story, red brick courthouse that stood in the center of town. The children gazed upward in awe. The square was surrounded by frozen mud streets and drab buildings where horses, mules, wagons and buggies were tethered.

"Certainly no Fayetteville," remarked Daniel.

"My goodness! I can't believe how much it's grown since I was here as a young girl," said Nancy, looking around.

The children rubbernecked in every direction. "Except for Fayetteville, this is the biggest town I've ever seen," said William Coleman in all seriousness. Everyone laughed.

Dr. Coman's office was located just off the square and identified by a wooden sign shaped like a medicine bottle. "Dr. Joshua Prout Coman, Physician" was painted across it. George Edward and James Greer were ordered to remain with the team and wagon as Nancy herded the other children before her like a gaggle of geese. "When y'all get inside, behave, be quiet and mind your manners," she said pointing her finger at the children. "Understood?"

"Yes Ma'am," they chimed.

"We know he's a good politician, now we'll see what kind of doctor he is," Daniel said, pushing open the door and causing a bell to ring. Inside, the pot-bellied stove felt good.

A young man in his late 20's, wearing spectacles and a white ruffled shirt and black fluffy tie emerged from the back room.

"I'm Doctor Coman, may I help you?"

Daniel stood, shook Coman's hand and introduced Nancy. "I'll let her tell you," he said.

Nancy grasped Thomas's arm and tugged him forward. "This child has been crying and rubbing his ear since we moved here over a month ago," she said. "Several days ago he screamed all night long and then yellow pus ran out both ears."

"Let me take a look," said Dr. Coman. "Bring him over here in the sunlight." He pulled back first one ear and then another and peered into the ear canals for a long time. "Well, the child has had a severe infection, but it looks like it's clearing up. And that's the good news."

"What's the bad news?" asked Nancy.

"He may be left deaf or partially so," said Dr. Coman.

Daniel and Nancy looked at each other grim-faced. "What can we do?" Nancy asked, almost pleading.

178

"Nothing, only time will tell," replied Dr. Coman.

After they departed, Nancy was unusually quiet.

"I don't know how good his doctoring is," said Daniel, "But I like the fellow just the same."

"I won't have it – I won't," Nancy said, her jaw set. "No young'n of mine is going to be deaf and dumb."

"He didn't say he'd be dumb," said Daniel.

"If he can't hear, how do you think he can learn to talk?"

"I didn't think of that."

James Greer, now the driver, grabbed the reins. Standing in the wagon so that he could be seen by all, he circled the square once then drove to Robert and Sallie David's house, an unpainted clapboard dwelling one block north of the courthouse. The children jumped from the wagon before it stopped rolling and ran to their Aunt Sallie, who was standing in the doorway, her arms outstretched.

---

The winter of 1839-1840 was cold and bitter and money was in short supply, but it was also a happy time. When it was too cold to cut bushes and plow new ground, Daniel hunted squirrel and deer on Swan and Piney Creeks. He constructed a fine box in which to salt pork recently slaughtered, built a log smokehouse, split rails, erected a fence around the barn and mounted the dinner bell on a pole. Emanuel Isom occasionally referred carpentry work, which produced a small amount of income.

The happy times were marred when a letter arrived from Fayetteville just before Christmas announcing that Nancy's older brother, Archibald, had died at age 59. Arch had fought the British with Andy Jackson in New Orleans. The happiest news was when young Thomas began to talk, but it was obvious that his hearing was impaired.

The Barksdale, Fielding and Newby families visited frequently, and many long winter nights were spent by the men sitting in front of a warm fire, smoking their pipes and discussing the great issue of the day – slavery. Northern abolitionists were stirring the pot. The arch abolitionist was William Lloyd Garrison, Editor of the *Liberator,* whose motto was "immediate and unconditional emancipation. An anti-slavery society was organized in New England with a platform that "slavery is a crime." The Underground Railroad assisted fugitive slaves to escape into Canada. Southerners were incensed and railed against the North.

"The talking gets louder," said Newby. "One day someone will pick up a gun and there will be violence. Daniel wagged his head in agreement. "I dread the day."

Newby told of having witnessed the long, ragged line of Cherokees that had been routed from their mountainous homes in North Carolina and Georgia and sent to Indian Territory. Some of them came down the Huntsville Pike. "I've never seen such a ragged bunch of people in my life. It was a trail of tears and grief."

"The price of progress, I suppose," commented Daniel.

179

# 18 | THE GOOD YEARS

April 1, 1840.

"I've never seen Pa this excited," said George Edward as he and James Greer yoked the oxen.

"Yeah, he thinks we're going to get rich raising cotton," replied James Greer.

"Maybe we will."

"Can't you just see Pa riding around in a fancy carriage someday," said James Greer, "all dressed up and smoking big cigars and yelling at his Negroes to pick more cotton."

George Edward looked at him incredulously. "Naw, not Pa."

"Hurry up boys!" Daniel yelled from the barn. "Daylight's break'n."

The Eastern horizon was peach red and the morning warm. The boys hitched the oxen to a slide and dragged it across the plowed ground, breaking clods and smoothing the seedbed.

Daniel paused at the edge of the field. The ends of plow lines were tied and draped over his shoulders, his hands gripping the handles of the cotton planter. He sucked in the pungent aroma of freshly plowed earth. It bespoke life. He clucked and the horse moved forward. Cotton planting was under way. Keeping the horse walking in a straight line was challenging, but the weather was good and by late evening of the third day he planted his last row. He halted, removed his hat, wiped sweat from his face with a sleeve, surveyed his work and was pleased. Now, it was up to the Lord to do the rest.

Each morning, he rose early and walked across the field, looking for tiny green sprouts. Several days passed and a warm rain during the night created the miracle he had hoped for. The following morning when he reached the field, he saw green rows of sprouting cotton. He hurried back to the house.

"We've got cotton!" he exclaimed, bursting through the back door. "It's the prettiest field I've ever laid my eyes on."

The children ran out to see.

"Don't step on the plants!" Daniel yelled.

---

Robert Beasley rushed from the barn where he had been sent to search for breakfast eggs and bounded into the house. "Pa, she's gone!"

"Who's gone?"

"Jezebel!"

"How could she?" asked Daniel, puzzled.

"She pushed down the rails."

"If that don't beat all!" exclaimed Daniel, grabbing his wide-brimmed hat. The children, ever alert for adventure jumped up to accompany their father.

"Can I go Pa?" asked 5-year-old Sarah.

"I guess so, if it's okay with your Ma."

"Pleeeease, Ma."

"Okay, but watch your step – all of you – snakes are out crawling this time of year."

Daniel strode briskly, trailed by the children, to the barn lot enclosed by a rail fence where the heifer had been confined. William Coleman ran ahead and pointed to where the rails had been pushed down. Daniel inspected the destruction. "Bye crackies, she must've worked all night long doing that."

"Look, Pa!" exclaimed James Greer, pointing to tracks that led west toward Swan Creek.

"Just what I figured," said Daniel. "George Edward, grab a rope."

They followed the tracks, Ol' Jack bounding ahead and barking, eager to join the adventure. "Stay!" The hound slinked back to the house.

"Wait, Pa," yelled Sarah, who was falling behind. Daniel squatted down. "Wanna ride on my back?"

"Yea!" She jumped on her father's back and wrapped her arms around his neck. "Ohh, Pa, this is fun."

"Reckon where she is, Pa?" asked George Edward.

"I figure she's in the canebrake."

The tracks led to the creek where cane grew thick on each side. "Watch out for cottonmouths," Daniel warned. "They're aggressive this time of year."

He picked up a stick and walked into the canebrake, using it to part the tall green stalks. Many had been broken over. He held up his hand. The children froze in their tracks.

"What is it, Pa?" asked William Coleman.

"I see 'er." Daniel inched forward and halted. It was a perfect hideaway. Lying on a bed of broken cane was Jezebel, licking a brown calf with a white blaze on its forehead. Jezebel bawled menacingly, warning her uninvited guests to keep their distance.

"Can I pet her, Pa?" asked Sarah.

"Not yet."

Daniel put Sarah on the ground and carefully fashioned a rope halter, slipping it over Jezebel's head and gently pulling her to her feet. The calf nuzzled her underside, searching for teats; found one and sucked with much gusto while its mother licked and groomed its body.

"It's important the calf get that first milk," Daniel said.

Jezebel mooed and kept a watchful eye on the intruders.

"Can I name the calf, Pa?" asked young Sarah.

"I reckon."

"Trouble," said Sarah.

After the calf had nursed, Daniel led Jezebel through the canebrake and George Edward followed, cradling the calf in his arms.

Ol' Jackson howled loudly and bayed.

"I told that dog to stay home," groused Daniel.

Ol' Jackson was baying at a coiled snake, its head moving back and forth and tongue flicking.

"COTTONMOUTHH!" yelled Robert Beasley, grabbing a stick. Daniel saw that the snake's tail was slender and pointed, its head somewhat the same. "That's no cottonmouth," he said. "It's a chicken snake. Don't harm it. We'll put it in the corn crib to catch rats."

"I ain't afraid of snakes," bragged George Edward.

"Then catch it," said Daniel.

181

George Edward crept up behind the snake while it focused its attention on the hound and, quick as a flash, grabbed its head. "I got it!"

The snake instantly wrapped its body around George Edward's arm. He panicked, turned its head loose and ran screaming, flinging his arm in the air trying to dislodge the reptile.

"Don't hurt the snake!" yelled Daniel as George Edward ran in circles alternately screaming and pleading for mercy.

"Somebody catch 'im!" yelled Daniel.

James Greer and William Coleman chased their older brother down and rescued the snake, which was addled from being slung and whiplashed.

Back home, the snake was set loose in the crib and Jezebel was rewarded with extra ears of corn.

---

When the cotton stalks were about three inches high Daniel and the children thinned them five inches apart, leaving clumps of three, and chopped away grass and weeds. For a while it was a contest between which would outgrow the other – the cotton or the grass. They chopped a second time and Daniel plowed the cotton twice; hilling dirt around the stalks. On July 4th, he "laid by" the cotton. The waxy green stalks loaded up with squares that eventually bloomed, transforming the field into waving white and pink blossoms. Each morning Daniel walked through the tall cotton inspecting the green bolls and counting the number on selective stalks. If every boll produced, he would have a bumper crop.

The hot August sun worked its magic. One morning Daniel walked across the field and saw an open boll with cotton spilling out. He plucked it and took it to the house to show the children. "This is our future," he said. "Nancy, start sewing sacks. Before you know it, we'll be picking white gold."

The stalks were loaded with bolls and Daniel predicted a yield of at least a half bale to the acre. With cotton selling at over ten cents a pound, he figured he could earn a profit - barely.

September was dry and the hot days and cool nights opened more bolls. Daniel inspected the field of white. Tomorrow they would begin picking.

The older children were in the field shortly after sunrise with sacks and baskets. Daniel set quotas, "Fifty pounds a day and don't fall below it."

Bending over all day long, picking the fluffy locks, not only caused back pains, but the needle-like hull endings pricked the fingers, drawing blood.

Late afternoon, Daniel straightened and rubbed the small of his back and studied the western sky. And he was bothered by what he saw.

That evening, hearing the oxen bellowing, he went to check on them. They were bunched together in the corner of the rail fence, facing southwest where lightning was flashing low on the horizon.

It was near midnight when Daniel was awakened by loud pounding on the roof. Wind screamed through the big oak trees. Nancy squeezed Daniel's arm until it hurt. "Lord have mercy," she pleaded, "we're gonna be blown away." The house shook and wind whistled through openings in the chinked logs. Daniel got out of bed, clad in his nightshirt, and peered out. Flashes of lightning revealed what he had feared most. Hail!

Morning brought clear skies and a fresh, scrubbed earth. Daniel inspected the cotton field, accompanied by George Edward and James Greer. Hail had beaten the cotton locks from the bolls where it lay in brown mud.

"What are we gonna do, Pa?" asked James Greer.

Daniel didn't reply. He bit his trembling lower lip and quickly wiped his eyes.

---

Daniel studied the lay of the 40-acre farm.

The Athens-Fayetteville Pike cut diagonally across the upper portion, leaving the bulk of the land south of the road, where a clear stream bubbled from a large spring and ran through a deep wooded cove of poplar and chestnut trees toward Piney Creek. Beyond the cove were approximately twenty acres of well-drained gray land which produced average cotton in a good year.

He watched as a drover passed by driving livestock.

"How far to Athens?" hollered the drover.

"About three miles."

"Any place to overnight?" he asked.

"Not that I know of."

"*Hmmm, that's an idea,*" Daniel thought.

---

February, 1842.

Daniel was on his back and nearly asleep when Nancy crawled between the cold sheets and scooted over to his warm side of the bed.

"Daniel," she whispered.

His deep breathing jerked. "What?"

"I have something to tell you."

"Can it wait 'til morning?" he asked.

"I guess so."

Several seconds passed before his curiosity prevailed. "What?"

"I'm pregnant," she said casually.

He raised up on his elbows, fully awake. "You don't look it."

"A woman knows these things," She took his hand and rubbed it across the slight bulge on her stomach.

"When?" he asked.

"Sometime in September."

"The Lord continues to bless us," he said.

"I'm thirty-nine years old and my body ain't what it used to be. I don't look forward to carrying this baby."

July and August were especially hot and dry and the heat sapped what little energy Nancy had remaining after caring for the babies, cooking, washing, cleaning and tending to her family.

The morning of September 17th carried the hint of approaching fall as Daniel and the older children picked cotton in the field across the Fayetteville Pike. He looked up and saw Sarah running toward him lifting her skirt and knocking locks of cotton from the bolls.

"Pa, come quick!"

"What is it, child?"

She caught her breath. "Ma's about to have the baby!"

Daniel turned to James Greer and said, "Hitch up the small wagon and go fetch Nannie Newby. And hurry!"

Daniel hurried to the house where he found Nancy on her back in bed, groaning with pain. He stroked her forehead. "What can I do?" he asked.

"Send for Nannie and start water boiling."

"James Greer's on his way."

Sarah stoked the fire and filled iron kettles with water. Nancy's labor pains came more frequently and intense.

"Oh lordie!" she wailed.

Hearing his mother cry out sent 5-year-old Thomas, who was caring for baby Dudley Richard, scurrying to her bedside.

"What's wrong, Ma?" Thomas asked.

"She's going to have a baby," said Daniel. "You boys leave the room."

Time passed slowly. Labor pains came at regular intervals. Nancy was suffering and all that Daniel could do was hold her hand. He yelled at Sarah, who was tending the boiling water in the adjoining room. "Do you see James Greer coming?"

"No, Pa."

"Where is that boy?" he groused.

Nancy screamed and her water broke, soaking the bed between her legs with bloody fluid. The scream sent Sarah running into the room. When she saw blood, she froze and began to sway.

"Pa, I think I'm going to faint."

"Buck up, child. You may have to help deliver this baby."

"I see a wagon coming!" yelled Thomas from the adjoining room.

"Thank God!" Daniel looked out the window just as the wagon bounced and careened into the yard. Seated between James Greer and Nannie Newby was 8-year-old Susan Newby. Both women were clinging to the seat for dear life.

Nannie rushed into the room and straight to Nancy's bedside. She stroked her forehead, observed bloody sheets and began issuing orders.

"Everybody out, except Susan!"

Daniel paced and hot-boxed his pipe while the young children rubbed their hands and stared at the closed door, wincing each time their mother screamed. Finally, there was silence. The door opened and Susan asked Daniel to come inside. The children peeked around the door.

"Is she okay?" Daniel asked, rushing to Nancy's bedside.

A baby lay nestled against her breast. "I've given you six boys to plow and chop wood," she said weakly. "This one is for me." Looking up at Nannie Newby, she said, "I don't know what I would have done without you."

"Susan helped too," Nannie said placing her arm around her beaming daughter.

"Yes, thank you child," said Nancy.

They named the baby girl Cornelia.

---

Early December, 1843.

184

The children were already in bed when Daniel laid another log in the fireplace and loaded his pipe.

"When you're bothered you smoke more," said Nancy, who was rocking baby Cornelia in a squeaking chair.

"Not bothered, just thinking about something."

"You may as well tell me."

"I'm gonna buy this place." He drew deeply on the pipe and waited for Nancy's reaction.

"It won't produce any more cotton just because you buy it. We're barely gett'n by as it is. Going in debt is the last thing we need to do. Remember it was debt that drove us out of Lincoln County."

Daniel was sensitive about the subject. "I wasn't the only person head over heels in debt. Lots of folks were. The collapse of the banks and the national economy had a lot to do with it."

"Don't get so touchy," Nancy said. "You're the one who wants to talk."

"We can clear several more acres and plant it in cotton, and that will help us out. But you're right, we're not gonna get rich raising a dab of cotton. It takes too many hands to work it and it's subject to the whims of weather. I have a better idea."

Nancy grunted. She was rocking faster and the chair was squeaking louder.

"This place has several assets," he said. "It's close to Athens, the Fayetteville Pike runs right through it and one of the finest springs in the county is located across the road."

"That's true, but it hasn't made us any wealthier."

"Vision, woman – vision."

"My only vision is cooking, cleaning, spinning yarn, sewing, washing clothes and diapers and tending to nine young'uns," she said. "Truth is I don't like the idea of going into debt."

"Right now we're sharecropp'n on a yearly basis," Daniel said. "When I see the Mitchells in a few days and pay rent, they may decide not to rent to us next year. Then what do we do? Where do we go? We need to own our own place so that no one can kick us out. I'd sleep better knowing that."

"Well, I would too." replied Nancy. "But how do you know that the Mitchell's will sell? And where are you gonna get the money if they will?"

"I can't answer that. But, they're not getting much rent for this year and I figure this might be the right time to make an offer. After paying them their share of the rent, we'll have about a hundred dollars in savings."

"What's this vision you have?"

"Open a drover's stand."

"Where?"

"Right here."

"Who's going to cook for 'em?"

"Well.... you and the girls."

"I'm about worked to the bone already," she said, rocking faster. "I wish you'd repair this chair before it drives me crazy. You're a carpenter and surely you can do that."

"I'll fix it," he said quietly and returned to his pipe as Nancy stalked from the room.

---

185

It was cold and spitting snow when Daniel climbed in the saddle and rode to James and Caroline Golightly Mitchell's house in Athens. After visiting a spell and warming before the fire, Daniel said: "I come to pay rent. I was hoping to make a better crop, but it just didn't happen." He showed Mitchell his figures on cotton and corn produced and counted out his one-fourth share of the money.

"It's hardly worth the effort," mumbled Mitchell. "By the time I pay for my share of seed and pay taxes on the land, there isn't much remaining."

"I work the land hard and give it my best effort," said Daniel. "But I have no control over the weather."

"I didn't intend to imply that you don't give it your best effort," said Mitchell. "Perhaps if you would work more land in cotton and less corn, both of us would profit more."

"I have to raise corn to feed the livestock and my family," said Daniel.

"I should advise you that someone else is interested in renting the farm for the coming year," said Mitchell.

Daniel was momentarily at a loss for words.

"Would you be interested in selling?" he finally asked. "On credit?"

"Gold and silver," Daniel replied and pulled out his money belt, pouring its contents on the table. Mitchell eyed the shiny coins for a moment.

"That's awfully tempting, but I guess not," he said.

Daniel had ridden to the Mitchells full of optimism and armed with a dream. Less than an hour later his dream was crushed and replaced by a sense of hopelessness. Life can change on a pinhead. Instead of building a drover's stand, it appeared he would be searching for another place to live. Nancy would be upset. She liked the neighbors and was warming up to the old house.

He entered the house and went directly to the fireplace to warm his frozen hands and feet. "James Greer, unsaddle my horse and give him an ear of corn," Daniel snapped.

"Is something wrong, Pa?"

"No, I'm just cold, that's all."

Nancy eyed her husband.

"Why are you looking at me like that?" he asked.

"No reason, you'll tell me what happened by and by."

"Mitchell won't sell," Daniel said. "And he may rent to someone else."

The following day, Daniel and the boys were in the crib shucking and shelling corn preparing for a trip to the gristmill when Ol' Jackson ran toward the house barking.

James Greer looked out as a buggy rolled into the yard.

"Pa, it's Mr. Mitchell."

Daniel had a sinking feeling. Mitchell had come to tell him to move. "One step forward and two back," he mumbled and went to meet his landlord.

"Morn'n Mr. Mitchell. Cold day to be out buggy riding. Come on inside and warm yourself."

"Thank you Daniel. What I've come to say, I can say it here."

Daniel was prepared for the worst. "Well, let it fly."

"Caroline and I have decided to sell... that is, if you are still interested."

*Had he heard correctly?* "Sell?"

186

"Yes.

Daniel suppressed his urge to shout with joy and instead took on a serious tone. "Well..., I don't know. What are your terms?"

"One hundred dollars - payable in specie."

Daniel expressed shock. "That's a lot of money for this old run-down place," he said. "I'll give you fifty dollars."

"How about seventy-five?"

"Agreed," said Daniel, and they shook hands.

As Mitchell rode off, Daniel said to himself, "Yep, life sure can change on a pinhead."

On December 16th he met James and Caroline Mitchell at Probate Judge, Thomas T. Tyrus's office in Athens where the deed was signed, gold coins were passed and the deed registered.

---

Following Christmas, Daniel put George Edward and James Greer to felling chestnut trees in the cove and William Coleman trimming limbs.

"What's Pa up to?" asked James Greer, swinging the ax and sending chips flying.

"He has another idea for making money," replied George Edward. "Overheard him saying that cotton is too unpredictable."

"What's his idea?"

George Edward shrugged. "That's all he said."

After numerous logs were cut and dragged behind the house with oxen, Daniel took out pencil and paper made calculations and announced that enough logs had been cut. It was time to trim and notch. Transforming the round logs to flat-sided ones required skill with a broad axe. Each end was carefully notched so that it fit perfectly onto the one below it. An ell-shaped addition to the house rose slowly and extended some twenty feet north toward the barn. It was divided into two rooms, each with an outside door and roofed with white oak shingles.

When they were done, Daniel constructed a wooden sign and burned into it: "Drover's Stand – Room and Board," and erected it on the edge of the Pike.

Before opening for business, there were bedsteads, chairs and tables to be built, and mattresses to be filled with shucks and pillows with goose feathers. While Daniel and the two older boys built furniture, Nancy organized the children into two squads.

"William Coleman, you catch the geese and start plucking feathers," she said. "The rest of you young'uns help me shuck corn."

"Awww... Ma, you know I'm afraid of Ol' Scratch," whined William Coleman.

"Whoever heard of a 12-year-old boy afraid of a little ol' goose?"

"That goose is mean –"

"Don't argue."

"But.... you're afraid of the chicken snake."

"Don't get smart alecky, young'un. You'd better be afraid of me."

William Coleman found a stick and herded the geese into an empty stall, grabbed the first one he could catch, pulled a sock over its head, turned it on its back and began plucking soft down amidst much kicking and loud squawking.

187

Across the hallway, Nancy slowly opened the crib door, peeked in and carefully studied the inside for several moments. Satisfied there were no gophers, and particularly no chicken snake present, she leaned over and began selecting ears of corn with quality shucks handing them back to the children.

"Put the shucks in one pile and the ears in another," she said.

The geese were squawking loudly and raising a ruckus.

"How's it going?" she yelled to William Coleman.

"So far so good, Ma, I'm saving Ol' Scratch for last."

"See, there is no need to be afraid of a little ol' goose."

William Coleman cracked open the door and began herding the already-plucked geese out of the stall one by one. Seeing his opportunity to escape, Ol' Scratch attacked William Coleman, biting his leg. He screamed and kicked at the gander and climbed the wall. Ol' Scratch ran out the door and straight to Nancy, who was bent forward in the crib, her hem hiked up, carefully selecting ears of corn and ever mindful that a snake lived there. The children scrambled in every direction as Ol' Scratch charged Nancy's exposed leg, biting it.

"Lordee mercie, I'm snake bit!"

Terrified, she whacked at her unseen attacker with an ear of corn. Dazed and injured, Ol' Scratch stumbled away in retreat, Nancy chasing him with an ear of corn.

"You'll be in a pot before sundown!" she yelled as the goose ran for his life. "That goose is mean."

"I told you so Ma," yelled William Coleman.

---

February, 1845.

Daniel was turning land with oxen when he saw a lone rider approaching on a dapple gray horse.

"Whooaa." The beasts stopped, nostrils flared, tongues lolling out, and blew while Daniel squinted at the approaching stranger. Something glinted on the lapel of his black coat. A badge! Daniel flashed back to Fayetteville several years earlier when the Sheriff served him with papers. He went weak. "Please Lord, not again." But he owed no one, nor had done any man wrong.

"Howdy Mister Barksdale."

"Afternoon Sheriff."

After small talk, Daniel said, "I know you didn't ride out just to pass the time of day."

"No sir." The sheriff reached inside his great coat and brought out a paper. Daniel squeezed the plow handle and his heart pounded.

"What is it?" he asked.

"A summon to jury duty."

"Praise the Lord!" exclaimed Daniel.

The Sheriff seemed surprised. "I commend you for your enthusiasm to perform your duty as a citizen. Far too many men complain and offer excuses when I deliver a jury summons."

Daniel was speechless.

"Well, have a good day Mister Barksdale," said the Sheriff as he rode off.

---

188

March, 1845.

The Spring Term of Court brought a multitude of people to Athens. Some were parties to lawsuits, others were witnesses and potential jurors, but the majority were spectators who had come to be entertained by the lawyers.

It was near 8 a.m. and warm as birds chirped beneath a clear sky when Daniel hitched horse and wagon in front of Robert and Sallie David's house and proceeded to the courthouse. He needed to be home working, readying the land for planting or helping Nancy with the Drover's Stand, but he was glad to have a day off to visit Athens – something he seldom did.

The courtroom on the top floor of the courthouse was crowded with noisy people when he entered, removed his hat and took a seat on a back bench. The pungent smell of oiled floors, the creaking of benches and the presence of well-dressed lawyers beyond the railing made his stomach roil. He had experienced these feelings in Lincoln County where he had been sued and lost. He shivered at the thought and knew that he'd rather be home breaking ground. Shortly, court clerk, Robert Austin opened court.

"ALL RISE. OH YEZ – OH YEZ, THE LIMESTONE COUNTY COURT IS NOW IN SESSION. JUDGE DANIEL COLEMAN PRESIDING."

A slightly obese man wearing a black waistcoat and carrying several law books and court files tucked under his arm mounted the bench and asked everyone to be seated. After the pool of jurors were seated separately and administered the oath, Judge Coleman informed them that civil cases were to be tried. The first case was called and a young, well-dressed lawyer stood, introduced himself as Luke Pryor and said that he was representing the plaintiff who had brought suit on debt. "Have any of you ever been sued for debt?" he asked the jury pool.

A couple of veniremen raised their hands, including Daniel. Pryor asked questions relating to service on the jury, then asked: "Because you were a defendant in the past, are there any of you who don't like lawyers?"

Daniel raised his hand. "There are some I don't care for," he said.

"Why is that?" asked Pryor.

"Because they sued me."

Laughter in the court room. Pryor grinned. "Well, did a lawyer represent you in your case?"

"Yes sir."

"Did you like your lawyer?"

"No sir," Daniel replied.

"Why not?"

"Because he lost my case."

More laughter.

The Judge banged the gavel. "Order in the court room."

Daniel was struck and excused from further service. He walked out of the courthouse into bright sunlight, pleased with himself, and headed across the square to S. Tanner & Company Mercantile to purchase a sack of coffee and a plug of store-bought tobacco.

Samuel Tanner, the proprietor and several years older than Daniel, had served as Athens' first mayor. His son Peterson clerked in the store.

"Mornin' Daniel, what brings you to town?" asked Samuel.

"Jury duty."

"Were you chosen?"

"Nah, that fancy pants Luke Pryor struck me off when I said didn't like lawyers – which was just dandy with me," Daniel replied. "I'd rather be following farting oxen, turning land, any day than listening to lawyers blowing hot air."

Tanner chuckled. "I'll tell Luke what you said the next time I see him. He'll get a kick out of it. Changing the subject, how is the drover's stand coming along?"

"Business is good and a sight easier than raising cotton," Daniel replied. "But it's about to work Nancy to death - washing, cleaning and cooking for the drovers."

"Well, what can I do for you?" asked Tanner.

"Bag of coffee and a plug of tobacco oughta do it."

Tanner turned to his son, Peterson. "Fetch that, will ya?"

Peterson placed the items on the counter. "What else for you?" asked Samuel.

"Give me several pieces of that rock candy," Daniel said, pointing to a glass jar. He paid and gathered up his purchases and departed.

"Come back anytime," hollered Tanner.

Daniel had bit off a plug of tobacco and stepped off the board sidewalk onto the dusty street when he looked up and saw a man approaching that looked vaguely familiar.

"Don't I know you?" he asked.

The man stopped. "Why, Mr. Barksdale! How are you? I haven't seen you since you left Lincoln County." Thomas Joyce McClellan grabbed Daniel's hand and shook it vigorously.

"What are you do'n in Athens?" Daniel asked.

"We moved to Limestone County last year; living out on Limestone Creek near Nick Davis's Plantation."

They talked, catching up on their respective families. McClellan had married Martha Fleming Beattie in Lincoln County and they had five children – John, age 9; William Cowan, 6; Sallie, 4; Robert Anderson, a year and a half – all born in Lincoln County. Matilda is the baby," said McClellan. "She was born just last month out on Limestone Creek."

"I'll never forget the first time I saw you," said Daniel. "I had just rode into Fayetteville and was looking for an inn to spend the night."

"Nor I. You were riding a one-eyed horse and had a red-bone hound named Oliver."

"Back then I was full of piss and vinegar; not a worry in the world, except gett'n rich and find'n a good woman," said Daniel. He paused momentarily. "But when a man gets too big for his britches, life has a way of bringing 'im down. That's what happened to me. But the future looks good."

"Still playing the fiddle?"

"Oh yeah. It's in my blood."

The men shook hands again and agreed to stay in touch. Daniel headed across the square, a smile on his face. *Never a finer fellow than Thomas Joyce McClellan.*

A stocky, middle-aged Negro man standing in a wagon caught Daniel's eye. Leaning against a wagon wheel was a white man, arms crossed over his chest, wearing a wide-brimmed black hat. Daniel walked over and looked the Negro up and down.

"If ya look'n for a strong, healthy Negro, this is him," said the man.

Daniel grunted, showing only slight interest. The drover's stand was profitable but it was nearly working Nancy to death. She needed help and he could use a field hand to work cotton and corn, not to mention keeping firewood cut and split. "What's wrong with 'im?" Daniel asked.

"Nothing, sound as a dollar."

"Why ya sell'n 'em?"

"I trade 'n traffic 'n Negroes and just about anything else that will turn a dollar."

Daniel sized up the Negro like inspecting a horse before making a trade; first his bare feet which were large and flat; then he felt his muscled thighs and his bulging biceps and shoulders. The Negro stood stoically while Daniel felt and poked.

"How old is he?" he asked.

"'Bout forty."

"Does he have a family?"

"Not that I know of."

"How long have you had 'im?" Daniel asked.

"Not long. Like I say, I trade 'n traffic. Just look at them muscles; you can get your money's worth out of him. I guarantee it."

"How much you asking?"

"Thousand dollars."

"I ain't interested," said Daniel flatly. "I don't need another mouth to feed and certainly not at that price."

"I might drop it down a tad."

"Has he ever run away?" Daniel asked.

"No sir, he's a good ol' darkie."

"Show me his back."

The trader winced and lifted the flimsy cotton shirt, revealing crisscross white scars. "Them's from a long time ago," the trader said. "Back when he was a young buck."

"A man oughta never buy trouble," Daniel remarked.

"Mister, I'll tell you the truth, my wife's sick with a fever and my young'uns are hungry. I need money bad. I'll sell 'im for seven fifty. And I swear, he never give me an ounce of trouble."

"Five hundred and that's all," Daniel shot back.

"Mister, you just bought yourself a good hand."

Daniel looked up at his purchase and asked, "What's your name?"

"Stocky... Massa."

"Well come on Stocky, let's go home."

Stocky handled the team expertly on the way home and to Daniels inquiry stated that he could do not only farm work, but could do masonry and carpentry work and even cook.

Daniel was pleased with his purchase.

"The Missus is really gonna be surprised when I bring you in. You can be a lot of help to her."

Nancy was in the back yard bent over a large wash kettle of boiling water and dirty clothes, stirring the contents with a hickory stick, when young Thomas exclaimed: "Here comes Pa!"

191

Nancy straightened, mopped sweat from her brow and studied the approaching wagon.

"And somebody else is driving," added Thomas.

The wagon rattled up to the barn and stopped.

"Unhitch and let the team water," Daniel said as he climbed down from the wagon and walked over to where Nancy was washing clothes.

"You're home early," she said, glaring at the Negro man. "Did they throw you off the jury?"

"Nah, I threw myself off."

"Who is that?" she asked gesturing toward the black man.

"Oh, that's Stocky. I bought him mainly to help you out. He says he can do about anything including cooking."

"Hmmph, just another mouth to feed, if you ask me. Anyway, where is he gonna live?"

"I figure he can sleep in the kitchen where he can start the fire in the morning and help cook."

Nancy was less than enthusiastic.

"I thought you'd be happy to have some help," Daniel said.

"It's not that I'm not appreciative, I am. But bringing a Negro into our family, and especially one that we don't know, is asking for trouble."

"Ah, you're still heartbroken about what happened to Joe 'n Judy and their boy in Fayetteville," he said.

"I guess I am. They were like family and I still grieve about what happened to 'em."

"Don't worry about Stocky."

"Slavery is such a bad thing and evil always follows it," said Nancy.

A corn shuck mattress was thrown on the floor in the kitchen corner, which became Stocky's new home. He rose before daylight each morning, stoked a fire, got water boiling, then went to the barn and milked Jezebel, gathered eggs and fetched butter at the spring. Nancy was impressed with his industriousness and gradually let him help her cook family meals. But there was something about him vaguely familiar and it bothered her.

One morning, she appeared at the kitchen earlier than usual and discovered Stocky bent over the flickering firelight looking at a paper. When she entered, he quickly folded and placed it in his pocket.

"Can you read?" she asked.

"Just a tiny bit, Missus."

On another occasion when she misread the label on a medicine bottle, Stocky corrected her. He performed his chores around the house as instructed, but Daniel frequently complained that he was lazy in the field.

Daniel had Stocky build a cot and place it in the kitchen corner, where he slept on his shuck mattress. After completing his day's chores, he often played with the children.

"You seem to be warming up to Stocky," Daniel said to Nancy one evening as she operated the spinning wheel.

"I think he once had children," she replied. "Notice the way he plays with the kids."

192

Daniel looked up at her, surprised. "I hadn't thought of that."

"And if he has children, he has a wife somewhere," she added.

"I guess so."

"It bothers me to think about that –"

"Oh, you're still upset over Joe 'n Judy and their boy," replied Daniel.

"It's more than that. It's the whole evil business of slavery. It ain't right and furthermore, it's unchristian."

"Bye crackies woman! I can't change the way things are," Daniel said, irritated. "There's been slavery since the days of Christ – even before –and it's legal. I don't want to hear any more about it – at least tonight! Let's talk about something else."

Nancy was momentarily silent as her foot nervously worked the treadle on the spinning wheel. "All right, I'll change the subject."

"Good."

"I'm pregnant again."

---

Nancy bolted upright in bed.

"What is it?" asked Daniel, waking. "Did you have a nightmare?" he asked.

"Not a nightmare." She lay back down and soon Daniel was snoring.

She lay awake and pondered what had finally surfaced to her conscious. Tomorrow, she would learn if it was true.

She was at the kitchen earlier than usual – before anyone else was awake. She wanted to be alone with Stocky.

"Morn'n Missus," he said, gathering up the milk bucket and egg basket.

"Good morning Stocky." she said as he headed out the door. "Stubby wait!"

The Negro man froze in his track and slowly turned around. "Why'che did you call me dat name Missus?" his black eyes searched her face.

"I know who you are."

He dropped his head. "I'ze ain't been called dat in a long, long time. How'd you know who I was, missus?"

"I'm Nancy McElroy, daughter of Micajah. I remember he sold you for being lazy."

His black eyes brightened. "Massa Micajah sure wuz good to me and de Lord didn't give me enough sense to know it. When he sold me is when all my troubles started."

"I'm sorry to hear that," said Nancy.

"Dat overseer whupped me til I couldn't pull on a shirt; said he'd beat the laziness out of me. Just about killed me, he did."

"Just because you were lazy?" she asked.

"Dat and other things."

"What things?" asked Nancy.

"Said I'se uppity – trying to act like de white folks – reading 'n sich."

"Do you have children?" she asked.

"Yessum, I has a little boy."

"Where is he?"

"He be sold when my wife wuz."

193

"Oh, that's awful," exclaimed Nancy. "Maybe you'll see them again someday."

"Yessum, someday in heaven, I hope."

"Well, do your work and you won't be mistreated around here," she said. "By the way, why did your name change from Stubby to Stocky?"

"One of my owners started calling me Stocky and I just went with it," he said. "Please don't tell Massa Daniel 'bout me. Everybody is mighty kind around here to me and if he knows I was sold for laziness, he might sell me too."

"Well, work hard and do what you're told and everything will be okay."

"Yessum, I shore will."

---

Christmas Eve morning, 1845.

Nancy waddled into the parlor where a warm fire burned in the fireplace, both hands clutching her bulging belly.

"This baby ain't long in com'n," she said. "And I'll sure be glad when it gets here."

Daniel looked up, closed the Bible in his lap and stood. "Here, sit down and warm yourself."

"I don't have time to sit. I got cooking to do: cakes to bake and candy to make. I want this to be the best Christmas ever."

She looked at the cedar tree in the corner, decorated with pine cones and wrapped with popcorn rope. Several wrapped gifts lay beneath it. She smiled and said, "Tomorrow, we'll have the biggest Christmas dinner ever with all of our children gathered around the table like family oughta do."

"The Lord has blessed us, not only with good, healthy children, but with material things too," said Daniel, looking at her protuberant belly. "And he's about to bless us again. "You think I oughta send one of the boys to fetch Nannie Newby?"

"It won't come till after New Year's when the moon's full."

After warming, she wrapped a scarf around her head. "I'm going out to the kitchen and get Stubby – uh, I mean Stocky – started cook'n Christmas dinner. When Sarah gets up, send her out to help me."

Daniel leaned over and kissed her forehead and said, "Merry Christmas, Nancy McElroy."

It was their joke. "That's Nancy Barksdale, if you please," she replied and they both laughed. Daniel returned to his warm seat by the fire and was nodding when Stocky burst through the back door.

"Massa, massa come quick!"

Daniel jerked awake. "What's wrong?"

"Missus be hurt'n bad."

Daniel jumped to his feet and rushed outside to the kitchen where Nancy was seated in a chair, legs outstretched, grasping her belly.

"I think this baby's com'n early," she said. "Send after Nannie. And hurry!"

Daniel turned to Stocky. "Tell George Edward to hitch up the buggy and go after Nannie.

"Yessuh, massa."

James Greer appeared at that moment. "I'll go, Pa."

"Then be about it."

194

Daniel turned to Nancy. "We need to get you in bed."

The household was up and the children were scurrying around offering to help. Baby Cornelia was crying. Daniel snapped at Sarah, "Take care of that young'un!" He knew it was going to be a long day.

---

James Greer hitched Sweet, a 2-year-old bay sorrel filly, to the buggy and within minutes was bumping down frozen ruts toward the Newby residence on Nick Davis Road. The filly was feeling her oats and straining against the reins. She was "green broke" and James Greer knew if she got the bit between her teeth she would be gone in a flash and might wreck Pa's recently acquired buggy. He kept a tight rein. "Slow!"

Smoke was boiling out of both chimneys of the Newby log house when James Greer careened into the front yard, bringing out several barking dogs. He reared back on the leather lines. "Whoooooa!"

Sweet pawed the ground and nervously eyed the dogs. After Mr. Newby appeared and called off the hounds, he exclaimed, "Why it's James Greer! When I heard all the noise I thought the stage was coming. "Come in and warm yourself."

"Morn'n, Mr. Newby. I don't have time. Ma's about to birth and I've come for Mrs. Nannie."

Newby's face turned grim. "She's sick in bed with the fever."

Several of the Newby children had come outside to see what was happening. "Lordy mercy!" exclaimed James Greer. "What am I gonna do? Nobody at our place knows how to birth a baby."

Susan Newby spoke up. "I know how."

Her father turned and looked with surprise at his 11-year-old daughter.

"I helped Mama deliver the last baby Mrs. Barksdale birthed," she said.

Mr. Newby looked at James Greer in the buggy. "What do you say?"

"Tell 'er to grab her coat and jump aboard."

In an instant Susan ran out the door, pulling on her coat, and climbed into the buggy seat, a big smile on her face.

"God bless and good luck!" Newby yelled as the buggy rolled out of the yard and disappeared down the frozen road.

"Hold on," said James Greer, wanting to impress the pretty young girl. "We'll see what this filly can do." He gave Sweet rein and soon they were clipping along at a fast trot, the buggy bouncing across the ruts and Susan clinging to the seat with both hands.

"Do you really know how to deliver a baby?" he asked, somewhat impressed.

"I watched Mama deliver Cornelia."

"That was three years ago. Do you remember what she did?"

"Some of it."

"Lordy mercy!"

Sweet was trotting nicely when they rolled into the yard and stopped. Susan jumped down from the buggy and raced into the bedroom. Daniel was seated on the edge of the bed holding Nancy's hand, who was groaning with pain.

"Where's Nannie?" he asked.

"She's sick with fever," said Susan.

"Lord have mercy! What are we gonna do?"

195

"Don't worry Mr. Barksdale," said Susan. "I watched Mama when she delivered Cornelia. The first thing we need to do is get Mrs. Barksdale out of these clothes and in something that's fitt'n to birth a baby... let me think... yeah, get water boiling; find some washcloths and boil 'em real good."

"Y'all hurry," said Nancy, "This baby is coming soon, my back is kill'n me!"

Shortly, her water broke. Susan panicked. "Oh goodness – oh my goodness, what do we do now?"

"Child, I thought you knew what to do," Daniel said harshly.

"I'm trying to think," replied Susan, clutching her head with both hands.

"Place a pillow under me," said Nancy, "and help me get my knees up and legs open."

Daniel was beside himself. Many women died during childbirth. "Do you want me to leave?" he asked, flustered.

"No, stay!"

"What can I do?"

"Hold my hand," she said. "Oh Lordy... Lordyyy, the pain is awful."

Daniel clamped down on her hand like a vise.

"Not too tight."

"I see its head!" exclaimed Susan. "Push hard, Mrs. Barksdale – push hard. Oh Lordee! It's coming out!"

Nancy groaned with pain and pushed down with all her might while Daniel squeezed her hand. With assistance from Susan the baby grudgingly emerged from the womb, dragging with it the umbilical cord.

"It's a girl!" exclaimed Susan.

Daniel had never witnessed this part of baby making and looked away.

Although the room was cold, big beads of perspiration ran down Nancy's forehead. She looked at her husband and said weakly. "Men have the easy part."

Daniel could only nod. He mopped her brow and kissed it. "You okay?"

"Yes."

"Oh me, oh my!" exclaimed Susan, eyeing the umbilical cord. "I can't remember what Mama did with this."

"Cut it off and tie the end," Nancy said, her voice uneven.

Daniel performed the task while Susan cleaned and wrapped the baby.

"Help me out of bed," said Nancy, weakly.

Daniel helped her stand and bloody afterbirth dropped from her womb onto the floor. He'd never witnessed this part of baby making either.

"Lord have mercy!" he exclaimed. "Are you okay?"

"I'm fine," said Nancy, crawling back in bed. "Hand me my daughter so she can nurse."

---

On Christmas morning the children scrambled down from the loft and rushed into the parlor where Daniel sat by a roaring fire. They backed up to the fireplace and warmed, all the while eyeing the gifts under the tree.

Shortly, their mother wobbled into the room, weak, but smiling, the baby wrapped in a blanket and nestled against her breast. "Look what Santa brought last night," she said.

196

The children rushed over to see their new sibling. "Now, you have a little sister to play with," Nancy said to Cornelia.

"What's her name?" the child asked.

"I like Francis Caladonia," Nancy said, eyeing Daniel, who got up and took the baby in his arms, kissing her tiny head.

"Cal, you're the prettiest baby I ever saw and the best Christmas present I ever received."

Daniel opened the large Bible and duly recorded the birth of Cal.

---

It had been a good year – mostly – and the best Christmas ever. Robert C. David had given them a red-bone female puppy, off Ol' Jackson, that the boys named Dolly, after President Jackson's wife. On the national level, James K. Polk, a Jacksonian Democrat, was inaugurated President of the United States and Florida and Texas had joined the Union – all good news.

On the other hand, the price of cotton fell to 5¢ a pound and Stocky had grown lazier than ever and rebellious.

---

Spring, 1846.

Daniel was catching a Sunday afternoon breeze beneath the big oaks and restringing his fiddle when Sylvester Isom, now a strapping 16-year-old, rode up on a mule. When Emanuel needed help he usually sent his younger brother.

"Howdy Sylvester, Emanuel got work for me?"

"No sir, Mr. Barksdale, he sent me over to invite y'all to church next Sunday."

"Church?"

"Yes sir, he's organized a Methodist congregation and Sunday'll be the first meeting. He considers you a good friend and would be honored if y'all attend. There'll be preaching, singing and praying."

Daniel kept restringing his fiddle.

"And there'll be dinner on the ground and plenty to eat," added Sylvster.

Daniel looked up. "Where might this be?"

"In the cabinet shop next to the house."

"Bye crackies, tell Emanuel that good food and good friendship is enough to give any man religion. If Piney Creek don't rise, we'll be there."

"Well, I'se best get along and invite the Newbys, Fieldings and Hicks," said Sylvester nudging the mule and riding off.

The older boys were lukewarm about attending, that is, until they learned that the Newbys and Hickses had been invited.

Sunday morning dawned warm and clear. Daniel woke the household earlier than usual, but no one complained. Everyone was excited about attending church, especially Nancy, who seldom got to visit the neighbors and catch up on news. She flew to cooking her trademark dish of squirrel dumpling while Stocky prepared breakfast. The boys milked Jezebel and her heifer, fed the livestock and hitched the team to the wagon.

"I've never seen those boys this excited about attending church," remarked Daniel. "If I could get them this motivated about chopp'n cotton, we'd be done inside a day."

Nancy was issuing orders like a sea captain about to embark on a voyage. "Sarah, wrap up the baby real good and bring an extra blanket. It may be cool when we come home." She turned to Thomas and spoke loudly, "You hold the dumplings and don't spill 'em." And to Stocky she said, "Be sure 'n milk the cow and do your chores. It'll probably be dark when we get back."

"Yessum, missus."

Everyone was dressed in their finest outfits and anxious to get under way. Then James Greer and George Edward began arguing about who was going to drive the team.

"If you'll let me drive over there, I'll let you drive home, plus one other trip of your choosing," said James Greer, almost begging. George Edward relented.

"LOAD UPP!" yelled James Greer.

Nancy, clutching the baby, sat next to James Greer on the seat. Everyone else squeezed into the wagon where they could find space. The trip was bumpy but nobody complained. The children laughed and picked at one another. Robert Beasley fell off the wagon.

"Stop show'n out before you get hurt. And don't get dirty!" said Nancy, scolding him.

"Dudley shoved me, Ma."

"No he didn't," said Nancy. I saw what happened. I've got eyes in the back of my head. Now behave before I stop this wagon and give both of you a good switch'n."

Judging from the number of horses and wagons present, it appeared that a good crowd had turned out for the initial service. When they neared the cabinet shop, James Greer stood and popped the reins, causing the horses to suddenly break into a trot and nearly tossing Ma from her seat.

"Slow down young'un, you're going to kill us all!" she exclaimed.

When she noticed a cluster of young women chattering beneath a nearby shade tree, she needed no further explanation for her son's action.

Inside the log cabinet shop, work benches and tools had been pushed against the walls freeing space for newly constructed pews. The room smelled of cedar wood shavings and turpentine. The room buzzed with people leaning forward, talking to one another in low voices. Daniel and family crowded onto a pew in the rear, nodded to acquaintances and waited for services to begin.

When Emanuel stood, the crowd fell silent. "God has blessed us with a beautiful spring day to worship him," he said. "It seems to me that most Sunday mornings are always beautiful and maybe that's because God wants to encourage us to attend church and worship."

He thanked everyone for attending; recognized guests, including the Barksdales, Newbys, Hicks, Fieldings and other families. The list of eighteen founding members of the Methodist Episcopal Church was read off, which included Emanuel, Jim, Matthew, John, William, Bryant and Sylvester Isom – together with their sisters, Mary Ann Isom Hanks, Lucinda Jane Isom Gray and Adalline Isom Yancy. Reverend Ashburn was also named along with seven other individuals that Daniel hadn't met.

Following praying and singing; Reverend Ashburn mounted the newly-constructed pulpit and launched into a long sermon. Soon, Daniel's mind began to wander. He glanced out the window where dishes of food, covered with white sheets, rested on makeshift tables beneath the trees. Squirrel dumplings, ham, fried chicken, fresh wheat bread – for sure. Uh – uh. His stomach growled.

198

James Greer kept cutting his eyes at the Newby family across the aisle. George Edward was eyeing young Mary Hicks, who lived near them. Young children grew restless and whimpered. Nancy gently rocked back and forth as she nursed the baby. Cal fell asleep against her mother's shoulder with her mouth open and Daniel nodded and slapped at pesky flies that buzzed around his head. When he began snoring, Nancy elbowed him in the ribs and gave him a stern look. Finally, Reverend Ashby concluded his sermon, and Emanuel closed with prayer that also went long.

"Dismissed!"

*Praise the Lord,* thought Daniel.

Everyone filed out the door past Reverend Ashburn who was shaking hands and thanking folks for attending. "Mighty fine preaching, Reverend," Daniel said. "The second Sermon on the Mount, if I say so myself."

"Why, thank you sir, I consider that a compliment of the highest order," said the Reverend, pumping Daniel's hand even harder.

Nancy elbowed Daniel, looked at him and shook her head in dismay. "You beat all," she whispered, a tiny smile on her lips.

The covers were removed from the food and everyone rushed to beat the flies there.

Daniel ate fried pullet legs, peas, buttered sweet potatoes and dumplings until he almost didn't get a slice of apple pie down. While the older boys chatted with young ladies, Daniel and Nancy met the Yancys and Grays and Hanks families. Emanuel walked over and introduced his wife, Rebecca Virginia, to Nancy. She was a Gray and they had married some four years earlier. Two small children were in tow; Susan Agnes, about 4 years old and James Franklin, age 3. And Rebecca was pregnant again.

"Daniel, you've been a good friend ever since you rode over on that one-eyed horse. I can't imagine anything coming between us."

"I feel the same," Daniel replied.

Emanuel turned to Nancy. "I hope y'all will come back every Sunday and worship with us."

When baby Cal began to whimper and cry, Nancy tried to burp her. Then it was announced that afternoon preaching would begin shortly.

"This baby has colic," said Nancy.

"We need to get 'er home," said Daniel, taking advantage of the situation. The way he figured it, too much preaching was like eating too many chicken legs – not good.

They arrived home earlier than expected and when Nancy went to the kitchen to tell Stocky to start preparing supper, he wasn't there. She waited for a few minutes, certain that any moment he would walk out of the bushes, buttoning his breeches. When she glanced at his cot in the corner of the kitchen, it was neatly made, and then she noticed something that she hadn't seen before – fresh dirt beneath it. Getting down on her knees, she brushed back the dirt. Newspapers! And all neatly folded. She unfolded one and gasped. *The Liberator* – an abolitionist rag! "My heavens!" she exclaimed. What kind of person was Stocky to be reading such Northern trash?" He seemed so gentle and so good. Obviously, he wasn't what he appeared to be. Was he part of a slave uprising that would murder her family in bed? Fear shot through her like a cold knife. Her hands trembled as she quickly refolded the papers and placed them back in their hiding place. What should she do?

Shortly, Stocky arrived. "Sorry Missus, I didn't 'pect y'all home so early."

Nancy could barely conceal her fear. "Where have you been?"

"Just sauntered over to de Fielding place."

Nancy didn't sleep a wink that night. Should she tell Daniel what she had discovered?" There had to be a simple explanation. Finally, she decided she would speak to Stocky.

---

A storm had passed through overnight and Nancy woke to a warm day and a sky so blue that it hurt her eyes to look up. The men folks were in the forest cutting wood and Cornelia was watching after the young children. She took a deep breath and walked unsteadily to the kitchen. She had to know.

Stocky was bent over, stoking a fire under a pot of pintos, when she walked in. He looked up. "Mornin' Missus, soon as I'se get dese beans a cook'n, I'll get de washpot fired up."

Nancy partially closed the door, leaving enough space to escape, if need be. "Stocky, do you believe in the Bible?"

"Shore do."

"Then you know that liars are doomed to burn forever in a lake of brimstone and fire?"

"Yessum, dat's what de good book say."

"You'll tell me the truth, won't you?"

Stocky's eyes, black as a bottomless pit, narrowed. His face hardened. Nancy placed one hand behind her on the door latch, her heart racing. Her knees were about to buckle.

"Yassum... missus," he answered slowly, studying her face.

"Why do you have abolitionist newspapers under your bed?"

Stocky's shoulders went limp and he dropped his eyes momentarily. Then he lifted his head and stood erect – even proud – and looked her in the eye.

"Cause I wanna be free missus, just like you and all de white folks. I have dreams about being free and seeing my wife and boy someday."

"If it was up to me, I'd set you free right now."

"I knows you would. You be's a good Christian woman that practices the scripture, but Massa Daniel won't ever set me free."

Nancy nodded in agreement.

"He find out dat I been read'n abolitionist newspapers he'll have me whupped for sure – maybe even sell me."

"He won't whip you," said Nancy. "I'll guarantee you that. He's a good man; never had a Negro whipped in his life."

"He sell me and dat be worse'n whupping."

"He will if he learns about what you been reading. Anyway, he says you're lazy."

"My old body be wore slapdab out Missus. I be worked like a mule all my life; whupped and half starved to death. I can't work like I useta. The only thing I have to live for in this life is the hope dat someday I'll be a free man."

Nancy thought about what he said. "I'll pray about what I should do," she said.

---

200

The previous nights had been the same. Nancy stared at the rough-hewn ceiling boards illuminated by a shaft of moonlight that cut through an opening in the curtains, her mind seized by one thought – Stocky. She wished she had never discovered the abolitionist newspapers. He performed his work – though at a snail's pace – and never caused problems. He showed affection for her children and treated them kindly. And her heart ached when she thought about him being separated from his wife and child. On the other hand, it frightened her to think about what he might be thinking. Northern abolitionists had declared slavery a crime and were bent on stirring up rebellion among slaves. And if Stocky was reading about it, he could be a part of a conspiracy. Where did he obtain the abolitionist newspapers? Who gave them to him? And when? He didn't bring them here the day Daniel purchased him. So, where did they come from? And what was he planning to do? Her heart raced. No matter how innocent Stocky appeared, he was bound to be involved in some evil plot. And who was he seeing at the Fielding plantation? Were their Negroes a part of a plan to rise up and kill their masters? Her imagination ran unbridled. Stocky could easily walk into the bedroom right now with an axe and chop off their heads. "Save us Lord!" she exclaimed and pulled the covers over her and scooted close to Daniel, waking him. He grunted and asked, "You hav'n chills?"

She shot her arm over his chest and hugged him tight. "No, I'm okay."

He returned to snoring. Should she tell him about finding the newspapers? If she did, he would sell Stocky to the first slave trader he could find. *Oh Lord! What am I to do?* She prayed and asked the Lord to give her direction. Finally, she slept.

---

Blackberry winter came late. The children were in bed and a low fire burned in the fireplace. Daniel smoked his final pipe of the evening and eyed Nancy, who was operating the spinning wheel. She had hardly spoken a word all evening.

"You might as well tell me what's wrong," he said quietly.

Her head snapped around toward him. "Who said anything was wrong?"

"Your face does. You hadn't been the same since we got home last Sunday from Isom's Chapel."

She avoided his eyes, her lips tight and foot nervously pumping the treadle. Daniel watched her. She glanced at him a couple of times. Abruptly, she stopped her work, took a deep breath and faced him.

"You're right. Something is wrong."

"Well, it can't be that bad –"

"Daniel, I've been worried to death, can't think, can't sleep, knowing that I should tell you but afraid of what you might do."

"For heaven's sakes, woman! What?"

"When we got home last Sunday I went to the kitchen and Stubby – uh, Stocky – wasn't there. I noticed fresh dirt under his cot and brushed it back and found an abolitionist newspaper."

Daniel slowly removed the pipe from his mouth and stared at her, slack-jawed and in disbelief.

"Lordy mercy! I didn't know he could read."

"Better than me," she replied.

"He could be plotting to murder us all!" exclaimed Daniel.

"Shhhh, not so loud. If the children heard us it would scare 'em to death."

Daniel chewed on the pipe stem, his mind racing.

"Father brought 'im down from Fayetteville to build the courthouse," she continued, "but sold 'im for being lazy. We called 'im Stubby back then. He said his new owner had him whipped; that later he took a wife and had a son but they were sold."

"If he's reading abolitionist newspapers, he's dangerous," said Daniel.

"He said he just wanted to be free, like white folks – like us."

"Free! If he thinks like that, he's dangerous. He's property," said Daniel. "Why didn't you tell me about this earlier?"

"I'm sorry Daniel, I know it was my wifely duty to tell you, but my mind was in turmoil. One minute I was scared he would murder us and the next I felt pity for 'im. He begged me not to tell you; said we treated 'im well and if you sold 'im he'd be whipped and starved –"

"Traders don't starve 'em," said Daniel. "That'd be like not feed'n your plow horse."

"I couldn't live with myself if you sold 'im to someone who mistreated him," she said. "It's so wrong, so unchristian. On the other hand, I'm afraid of what he might do to us and our neighbors."

Daniel fell silent and stared at the glowing embers, chewing on his pipe stem. Finally, Nancy announced that she was going to bed.

"Maybe I can finally sleep tonight," she said. "A loads been lifted off my chest. You coming to bed?"

"No, I got a lot of thinking to do."

---

Stocky was splitting wood with a single-blade axe when Daniel walked up. "Morn'n massa."

Daniel grunted.

Stocky turned a block of wood on end and expertly brought the blade down the center, halving it perfectly. Daniel shuddered.

"When you finish what you're doing," he said, "shell some corn. We're running low on meal."

"Yessuh Massa."

After Stocky had shucked a bushel or more of corn and run the ears through a hand crank sheller, he sacked the kernels. Daniel hitched up the wagon and drove around to the crib.

"Load it 'n in the wagon and get in," Daniel said.

"I be going, massa?"

"Yeah, my back's bothering me."

Stocky studied Daniel's face for an instant, said nothing and climbed into the wagon.

Nancy stood at the back door and watched as the wagon turned toward Athens instead of the gristmill on Piney Creek a couple of miles up the road. If her guess was correct, she would never see Stocky again. She felt a sense of relief that the matter was finally resolved, and then sadness overtook her. What would happen to the poor creature? Stocky's only crime was wanting to be free. "Lord God, forgive us for we know not what we do," she whispered.

202

She watched as the wagon moved slowly away until she was distracted by the baby crying.

Stocky's instinct kicked in. Massa Daniel, usually jovial and talkative, was unusually quiet. Not only that, he had never accompanied massa to the mill – and, he had never known of massa going to any mill except the one on Piney Creek. They were headed to Athens where there would be a big Saturday crowd. All that Stocky could do was silently pray.

When Daniel turned north toward the mill on Swan Creek, Stocky was greatly relieved. The Lord had answered his prayers. Suddenly, he was happy.

"Shore be a pretty morn'n massa."

"That it is," replied Daniel.

They pulled up to the mill and before the wheels stopped rolling, Stocky jumped off the wagon and threw the heavy sack of corn over his shoulder and carried it inside.

The miller's beard and clothes was covered with white cornmeal dust, giving him the appearance of a ghost. The miller measured out his 1/8 share of corn, and ground and sacked the remainder for Daniel. Stocky set it in the wagon and they headed back to the pike. When they reached the road, Daniel reined the horses and stopped. He didn't say a word.

"Want me to take de reins, massa?"

Daniel didn't reply. He packed his pipe with tobacco, taking his time. Stocky watched him closely from the corner of his eye. Again, instinct kicked in. Danger.

Finally, Daniel fired his pipe and without looking at Stocky said, "I've got business in Athens." He slapped the reins and the horses moved toward town. Stocky's heart dropped into his stomach. He knew what lay ahead. When they neared the Female Academy, he summoned the courage to ask a question, "Massa, you fix'n to sell me?"

Daniel clamped down on his pipe stem and didn't reply.

"De Missus done tole you 'bout finding de newspaper and dat's why you gonna sell me. Massa, you treat me good and I don't wanna be sold. I make you a better hand dan ever before."

"I can't take the chance!" Daniel shot back. "There's no telling what you and the other coloreds have been up to. If you've been reading abolitionist newspapers, you can't be trusted."

"I likes to read 'bout being free someday – free like you and de missus and de other white folks."

"That's impossible."

"I can think about it and dream about it. I dreams about see'n my wife and boy. Den I wake up and dey be gone - just a dream. She ain't really my wife, but we jumped de the broom together and declared ourselves married. It was de best we could do since marriage among slaves is outlawed."

"Bye crackies, be quiet!" exclaimed Daniel. "I can't do a dratted thing about it. I gotta do what I gotta do."

"Please massa."

Daniel sold Stocky – Stubby, whatever his name, to an overseer of a plantation near Mooresville and hastily signed the bill of sale. As he climbed into the wagon seat, Stocky shouted, "Massa, tell de missus and de chill'n I love 'em 'n and I'll see 'em in heaven."

# 19 | CALM BEFORE THE STORM

Friday morning, January 1, 1847.

Daniel rose early and pulled back the ashes in the fireplace. He liked the quietness of early morning when his mind was clear and the only sound was the crackle of burning wood and the distant crowing of the rooster. New Year's was a good time to take stock and look to the future. Eight years earlier he had departed Lincoln County, broke and facing an uncertain future. Now, he owned 40 acres, was raising cotton profitably and was operating a drover stand. His nine children were healthy and Nancy was pregnant again. Another good cotton crop would put him on easy street. He grinned to himself. Footsteps.

"You wouldn't be grinning if you felt as bad as I do," said Nancy.

He watched her waddle toward the fire, her pregnant belly nearly tilting her forward. He found her a chair.

"I was just sitting here thinking about how the Lord has blessed us," he said and kissed her on the cheek, then he stroked her forehead and ran his hand down her long, black hair, braided and peppered with gray.

"You're a mighty fine woman."

She looked up, smiled and laid a hand on his. "I'm getting too old for this."

"When?" he asked.

"A few weeks."

"I'd better make arrangements with Nannie Newby ahead of time," he said. "The last time was too close a call."

"Poor Susan," Nancy chuckled. "That child was scared to death."

"What about me?" Daniel asked, grinning.

Nancy said, "I think Susan and James Greer have more than a passing interest in each other."

"Daniel was surprised. "Why James Greer is 18 and she's only –"

"Thirteen," interjected Nancy. "She a woman or nearly one."

"That shows you how little I know."

"And I'll tell you something else," added Nancy. "Your little girl Sarah has told me that she's gonna marry James Martin Newby one day."

"What! She's only 12 years old, he's almost twice her age."

"Right now, but she'll catch up," said Nancy.

"Well, bye crackies!"

"Our children will be grown married 'n gone before we know it," said Nancy sadly.

"We'll make more," said Daniel and patted her bulging belly.

"This is the last one – And I mean it!"

At 11:30 a.m. the family gathered around the dinner table for a New Year's meal of black-eyed peas, hog jowl and cornbread. After giving thanks, Daniel said, "This will give us luck in the coming year, so eat up." He spooned peas and hog jowl on his plate. Cotton is bringing more than it ever has," he added. "We're gonna have the best year ever."

"The Lord willing," Nancy added.

"Yeah, the Lord willing," said Daniel.

Everyone was eating in silence when 8-year-old Dudley casually said, "James Greer is talking about joining the militia and fight'n Mexicans."

"Hush," said James Greer and gave his little brother an icy stare.

Daniel almost choked on cornbread crumbs. "What's this?" he asked James Greer.

"Just because I talked to Colonel Jones doesn't mean I'm joining up," he said.

The United States had declared war on Mexico on April 16 the previous year and the State of Alabama had been requested to furnish troops. Colonel Egbert Jones, an Athens attorney who had represented Limestone County in the Legislature in 1844-45, was raising a company. Captain Hiram Higgins, an Athens builder and architect, was also raising a company.

"Boy, you get that notion outta your head right now," said Daniel. "The only thing you are gonna be fight'n is crab grass in the cotton patch."

James Greer kicked his young sibling's leg under the table.

"Pa, he's threatening me!"

"Hush!" said Daniel. "Y'all eat your peas and hog jowls and be thankful you have it."

---

Wednesday.

January 6, 1847.

It was late afternoon and cold when Daniel looked toward the west and studied the dark clouds.

"Snow," he said to George Edward.

"Looks more like rain to me, Pa."

"You boys bring in plenty of wood," said Daniel.

George Edward turned to leave when his father asked, "What do you know about James Greer enlisting to fight Mexicans?"

"Well, Colonel Jones and Captain Higgins are both scouring the county trying to raise two companies," said George Edward. "They tell a mighty convincing tale of high adventure."

"James Greer is 18 and old enough to fight, but I need 'im here help'n raise cotton. This could be the best year yet; that is, if the weather cooperates."

"I hope it's only a passing thought with him," said George Edward. "You know how eager young bucks are to fight, but he seems to be more interested in school. Says he wants to be a school teacher someday."

"A school teacher!" exclaimed Daniel.

"That's what he said."

That night a cold rain fell. When Daniel woke the following morning he looked out and saw that his prophecy had come true. Snow. The white stuff fell for several days.

The weather turned bitter cold. A guest at the drover's stand who had been to Athens said that on the night of January 20th the courthouse clock froze and stopped running.

Later, the ground thawed and the roads turned to deep mush, making it difficult for folks to travel. Daniel worried. Nancy's time was getting close. What if he couldn't get Nannie Newby over to help birth the baby? Another cold snap came. The roads froze, which was good, closely followed by bad news. A traveler who had stopped for the night reported that typhoid had broken out and folks were dying by the scores, especially Negroes on the plantations south of Athens.

Cotton prices had reached the highest ever.

---

Saturday morning, February 6, 1847.

"Send for Nannie!" exclaimed Nancy, holding her belly. "It won't be long."

"James Greer, hitch up the wagon and tie an extra mount to the back," Daniel barked. "If y'all get stuck in the mud Nannie can ride over here. Now hurry!"

It wasn't long before James Greer returned with Nannie and Susan, all of them splattered with mud.

Later that day a healthy brown-eyed boy was born. After he had nursed, Nancy handed him to Daniel and said, "I give you another son. You can name 'im."

"Achilles," said Daniel. "It's an old family name. Achilles was the Greek hero of the Trojan War. He'll be my little hero."

Spring came early. February 15$^{th}$ was one of the prettiest days that Daniel had ever witnessed. Neighbors were turning their garden plots and burning leaves, filling the blue sky with gray smoke.

He planted most of his corn and was counting the days to begin planting cotton when the weather changed. It began raining on March 5$^{th}$ and continued for several days. Piney and Swan Creeks were muddy and impassable. Daniel looked out the window and watched as top soil washed away. He worried. Even if the rain stopped, it would be days before it was dry enough to plant cotton.

"The price of cotton has never been this high and I can't get in the fields to plant," he said to Nancy. "If it was raining soup, my bowl would be upside down. And not only that, I'm out of smoking tobacco."

"What's wrong with the tobacco you raise?" she asked.

"I like store-bought tobacco."

After Swan Creek receded, he saddled Sweet and rode to Athens. Robert C. David was at his office on the north side of the square when Daniel scraped mud from his shoes and walked inside. Robert, a small man, and as, usual, well-dressed, looked up and peered over the rim of his spectacles.

"Well Daniel, it's good to see you. I was beginning to wonder if y'all had been washed away."

"I've never seen this much rain in my lifetime," said Daniel. "Can't get in the field to plow, can't do anything but wait and worry."

"It's the same all over the county."

They exchanged family news. Sallie was dying to see the new baby, Achilles. And Robert, a Democrat, had it on good information that President Polk would likely appoint him Athens Postmaster.

"Changing the subject," said Robert, "but does anyone in your neighborhood have the fever?"

"Not that I know of."

"Typhoid fever is raging through the county," said Robert.

The front door squeaked open and a nattily-dressed young fellow entered. Robert smiled. "Good morning, Thomas, how are you?"

"Fine, sir, and I hope that you are the same."

David introduced his brother-in-law to Thomas H. Hobbs, whom Daniel would later learn was one of Limestone County's most prominent young gentlemen. The son of Ira and Rebecca Maclin Hobbs, the family lived in a roomy house on Marion Street one block north of the square. They were the masters of "Slopeside," a large plantation eight miles south of Athens. Daniel immediately liked the articulate and soft-spoken young man.

Hobbs said that the Tennessee River was out of its banks. "I was recently at Brown's Ferry and the river was at least two miles across. No one living has ever seen a flood of this magnitude."

"If it don't dry up I won't be able to plant cotton," said Daniel.

"Yes, the farmers are suffering, and at a time when cotton prices have reached an all-time high," replied Hobbs. "However, the outbreak of typhoid is of greater concern. It's a new type of fever and physicians don't know how to effectively treat it. I'm told that there are as many as 20 cases each on many plantations. The fever is sudden in its attack and it kills quickly. Several children have already died. Bleeding and ingesting Calomel is ineffective. It's a dreadful disease."

"What are the symptoms?" asked Robert David.

"Fever, feeling weak, tired and chilly, headaches, back aches, loss of appetite and accompanied by diarrhea and in some cases constipation."

Contrary to his hopes, the visit to Athens had not cheered Daniel's spirits. Now, he had typhoid to worry about. By the time he reached home, he was pretty sure he had the disease.

"Doctors don't know what causes it or how to treat it," he said to Nancy. "Bleeding don't help. Pretty much, you either live or die."

"We need to stay home and away from people," she said.

Daniel looked up at her with sad eyes. "I'm feeling poorly, even feverish."

"You don't look sick," she said and felt his forehead. "You don't have fever."

"Whew. Thank the Lord!"

---

The rain stopped in the nick of time and sun came out, drying the earth. Daniel began planting cotton on April 1st and green sprouts popped out of the ground within days. The crop looked promising. Governor Joshua Martin issued another call for volunteers to fight the Mexicans. Thank God, James Greer didn't enlist.

Daniel was in Athens on May 29th when Captain Hiram Higgins and his company departed for the war via Florence. A brass band accompanied them across Town Creek to the bottom of Edmonson's Hill. It was quite a show. On June 16th, the *Democrat Herald*, Athens' second newspaper, debuted. Athens was growing.

Daniel was back in Athens on September 30th, standing in front of Robert C. David's office observing Captain Egbert Jones's company preparing to leave for the Mexican war. The men stood in formation on the courthouse green, while friends and family looked on weeping. Rev. Thomas Scruggs, Methodist minister, gave a brief talk encouraging them on their journey. It was a sad parting. After final farewells, the company marched off toward Waterloo to board a boat. And again the band accompanied the soldiers to the bottom of Edmonson's Hill, playing rousing martial music.

Daniel knew that young men had to fight the nation's war, but he silently thanked God that his sons weren't among them.

---

Daniel's "little Greek hero," Achilles, was one year and 4 days old when the Treaty of Guadalupe Hidalgo was signed on February 2, 1848, ending the Mexican War and establishing the Rio Grande as the boundary between the two countries. New Mexico, which included Arizona, and also California were ceded to the United States. Now the nation stretched from sea to sea.

Achilles' favorite place was his Pa's lap. Daniel taught him his numbers and boasted to anyone who would listen that he was the smartest child in Limestone County.

"I've got some fine-looking boys," he often said. "But this young'un is the handsomest of the lot. He's got those McElroy blue eyes and Barksdale black hair."

It gave Nancy joy to see them together. "I've never seen him this fussy about a child," she told her older sister, Sallie David.

Daniel often sat Achilles astraddle his neck and took him on long walks along Swan Creek. When a frog croaked, he would say "frog." The child would repeat the word. In this manner he taught him to recognize the sounds of crow, dove, bobwhite and other birds. When Daniel rode Sweet, he set Achilles in the saddle, his arms enveloping the child as he held the rein. Often, he rode the child on his knee beneath the shade of the big oaks where bluejays fussed in the branches above. Daniel sang a dittie: "Jaybird, jaybird, sitt'n on a limb, he winked at me and I winked at him."

The child laughed, "Sing again."

Life was good. The older boys did most of the farming while Daniel enjoyed his days with his new son.

News came that President Polk, during the last days in office, had appointed Robert C. David Athens Postmaster. That fall General Zackary Taylor, a Whig and hero of the Mexican War, was elected President.

---

Late July, 1849.

What Daniel read in the local newspaper struck fear in his heart. A cholera epidemic was sweeping the nation and taking lives by the thousands. The symptoms were vomiting, diarrhea and dehydration, often followed by death within hours. President Zackary Taylor designated the first Friday in August as a day of fasting, humiliation and prayer. Daniel thought about it. The cotton and corn crop had been laid by and the family could afford to take a day off and rest. He made the announcement at supper on Thursday night.

"Cholera's kill'n so many folks across the country that President Taylor has declared tomorrow a day of fasting, humiliation and prayer," he said. "There's plenty of work to be done around here, but I've studied the matter and decided we'll participate. The Good Book says that the prayer of the righteous availeth much."

"Pa sure knows his Bible," said Cornelia, beaming at her father.

"It wouldn't hurt if all of y'all studied it more," he said.

"Why do we have to humiliate ourselves?" asked Dudley, puzzled.

Daniel broke off a hunk of cornbread and pondered the question a moment. "To rid ourselves of pride, that's why."

He scooted away from the table, retrieved the big brown Bible, turned to Proverbs and read: "Pride goeth before destruction, and a haughty spirit before the fall." He closed the Bible. "We've become too big for our breeches in this country and the Lord has sent the plague to cut us down to size."

"How are we gonna humiliate ourselves, Pa?" asked Dudley, still puzzled.

"There'll be no boasting, no arrogance and no pride all day long," he replied. "We won't dress up and brush our hair for one thing. We won't laugh and joke and tell stories. Just engage in serious reflection."

"And we can't eat anything all day?" asked Thomas.

"Nope. Y'all better dig in tonight."

"That makes me hungry just to think about it," said Dudley.

The older boys were happy that they wouldn't have to go to the forest and cut firewood in the sweltering heat and the girls were excited about not having to help wash clothes, spin, clean house and do a multitude of other chores that Ma always found for them to perform.

Next morning, Daniel walked outside at daybreak. Not a breeze stirred. It was going to be a real scorcher. No smoke curled from the kitchen chimney; no aroma of perking coffee, frying ham and baking biscuits wafted past his noise. He was already hungry. He needed to get his mind off food and on the Lord. He placed two ladderback chairs beneath the trees for himself and Nancy, sat down and quietly meditated.

Sarah and Cornelia appeared with little sister Cal in tow. When they saw Pa and their brothers disheveled, they stopped in their tracks and stifled a giggle. Daniel's hair and beard was a tangled, scrambled-up rat's nest, pointing in every direction, and the boys looked no better.

"What's so funny?" he asked, giving them a stern look. "You oughta see yourselves in the mirror." He made a short speech about how the Lord had blessed the family and seen them through hard times.

"Y'all bow your heads and let's pray," he said. James Greer stood and joined hands with George Edward and Coleman. The other children followed suit. Daniel stood and held Nancy's hand. Touched by the scene, Daniel's chest tightened and a wave of emotion gripped him. James Greer bent to his knees and the other children did likewise. Daniel fell to his knees, dropped Nancy hand and put his arm around her frail shoulders and pulled her against his chest. With voice breaking, he prayed hard that God would protect his family from "this disease that comes like a thief in the night and kills the innocent and the just." There was much sniffling and wiping of eyes.

It had been a moment of great release and Daniel felt cleansed. Achilles climbed in his lap and pulled at his scraggly beard.

"Pa looks funny," he said.

The girls stifled giggles. The boys wiped smiles from their faces and Nancy turned her head away. Finally, Daniel burst out laughing and the whole family joined in cackling and guffawing. Afterwards, they fell silent, each deep in their own thoughts. At 11:30 a.m. the bell at the nearby Hicks farm tolled dinner time. Everyone looked in that direction. Daniel's stomach growled. He looked at Nancy and asked, "What do you think?" She nodded.

"A half day of pray'n and fast'n, if done properly, is as good as a whole day," Daniel declared. "And starv'n for no good reason won't save one life from cholera. Let's eat!"

"Yippee!" exclaimed Cornelia and a cheer went up.

Nancy and the girls whipped up a fine meal and everyone ate voraciously, picnic-style beneath the shade trees.

Afterwards, Daniel got his fiddle out and played *Home Sweet Home*. The children grew quiet as the melodious strains filled the stillness.

Nancy looked at him with tears in her eyes and said, "Sooo beautiful."

When the fiddling was over, Thomas said, "Pa, it sure would be cool in the creek."

"Can we go?" asked Dudley.

"Welll…"

"Please Pa," begged Dudley.

"I guess it wouldn't hurt."

The boys hitched up the wagon and they drove down to Piney Creek and played in the cool water that rippled and gurgled beneath the shade of overlapping trees. On the return trip home, 7-year-old Cornelia asked, "Pa, can we humiliate ourselves and pray again next month?"

Robert Beasley laughed so hard that he again fell off the wagon.

---

The following Tuesday, Daniel and George Edward, who had just turned 21, went to Athens and voted. There was a crowd in town, but not as many as Daniel had expected on Election Day. Many folks had remained home, he figured, afraid they might catch the plague. Daniel didn't tarry long. On the return trip, George Edward said, "Pa, I've put in for a job driving the stage."

The announcement caught Daniel by surprise. "I need your help on the farm," he said.

"I know, and if I get the job, I'll still help out when I'm not working."

"Well, what brought on this big change?" Daniel asked.

"I'm a man now and it's time I started making my own way. No woman is gonna marry a man who can't provide a living."

"You thinking about gett'n married anytime soon?" asked his father.

"Welll…"

"Anybody I know?"

George Edward only grinned.

---

Saturday afternoon, July, 1850.

Daniel sat in the shade of the large oaks, the leaves burned and curled up at the ends. Occasionally, a hot breeze would create a dust devil in the nearby cotton field and rattle the dry foliage. He had never seen it hotter nor dryer. The cotton and corn was wilting and without rain soon, the crop wouldn't be worth harvesting.

A cloud of dust on the Pike approaching from the direction of Athens caught his attention. It was a buggy and moving fast. He stood and squinted. Someone was in a big hurry.

"Why, it's George Edward!" he exclaimed.

The buggy careened into the back yard and stopped. Sweet was lathered white and blowing hard.

"Is the devil chas'n you?" he asked, irritated that his buggy horse was overheated.

George Edward jumped down, smiling. "Good news, Pa!"

"What?"

"I got the job! I'll be driving the stage from Athens to Fayetteville."

Daniel was speechless. "Ain't you happy for me Pa?"

"Well sure, I just wasn't expecting it so soon."

"I start right away," said George Edward.

Daniel took his son's hand and squeezed it. "Son, I knew the day would come when you'd grow up and move on in life – that's the way it's supposed to be. I just kept hoping it would be later. I'm proud of you and I'm happy for you."

George Edward's eyes grew glassy. "Thanks Pa, I needed to hear that."

He reached in the buggy and handed Daniel the most recent edition of the *Athens Banner* and then headed toward the house to share his good news with Ma and his siblings. Daniel unfolded the newspaper and began reading. Zackary Taylor had died in office and a Whig lawyer from New York named Millard Fillmore was now President of the United States. Congress was debating the slavery issue; more than 40 million dollars in gold had been extracted at Sutter's Mill in California in 1849 alone and the citizens had petitioned for statehood as a free state. News was as scarce as rain. Daniel read every word from front to back, and then read it again.

---

With a cotton hoe over one shoulder, Thomas led the way across the dusty cornfield where the green leaves had wilted and turned brown. Dudley followed carrying a grain sack.

When they reached a wooded area bordering Swan Creek, Dudley asked, "Do you reckon this'll work?"

"Huh?"

"I declare Thomas, you can't hear thunder. I said, reckon this'll work?"

"Not so loud, you'll scare 'em off."

When they reached the creek, Thomas looked back at his younger brother and placed his finger to his lips. "Shhh." He tiptoed forward and flipped over a rock with the hoe.

"There's one!" exclaimed Dudley. The frog jumped just as Thomas whacked him with the hoe.

"He's just addled. Put 'im in the sack," said Thomas.

Dudley bent over to pick up the frog. "Don't let 'im pee on you," Thomas said, "or you'll get warts."

Dudley hesitated. "You pick 'im up."

Thomas frowned and said, "If you don't wanna to do your part and help Pa, just go home."

Using two fingers, Dudley carefully lifted the addled frog and dropped him in the sack.

"Now let's find some more," said Thomas.

After an hour or more the sack took on a life of its own as frogs leaped from side to side trying to escape.

"They sure are heavy, don't we have enough?" asked Dudley.

211

"Huh?"

"Nothing."

Thomas whacked more frogs. "That's too many," said Dudley.

"Huh?"

"THAT'S TOO DANG MANY!"

The sack was about to jump out of Dudley's hands. Thomas studied it a moment then declared, "I think it's just about the right amount."

Dudley threw the sack of frogs over his shoulder and staggered across the cornfield to a location where Thomas dug a deep hole.

"Now, dump 'em in real fast while I cover 'em up," said Thomas.

Dudley poured the frogs into the hole which Thomas quickly covered with dirt.

After the frogs had been buried alive, Thomas said, "If it don't rain tonight we'll bury some more tomorrow."

"That's too many already," said Dudley.

It didn't rain that night and they buried more frogs the following day.

It was past midnight when Dudley was awakened by thunder that shook the house. Lightning cracked and wind howled through the oak trees. Dudley elbowed Thomas, who was snoring. "Wake up."

"Huh?"

"Listen."

Rain came in torrents, the wind blowing it under the shingles and soaking everyone in the loft. Someone lit a lamp downstairs. "Loordy mercy we gonna be blowed away!" It was Ma. She was running from one end of the house to the other, praying aloud and gathering up the children.

Dudley looked at Thomas, who was soaking wet and scared, and said, "I told you we buried too many frogs."

Next morning, Thomas and Dudley followed Pa outside. It was cool and the sky was deep blue. Rain had washed deep gulleys across the cotton and corn field, carrying off stalks and top soil. Pa looked over the damage and shook his head. "I was praying for rain," he said, "but the Lord has sent entirely too much."

Thomas elbowed Dudley ad whispered, "Don't dare tell Pa what we did."

"I told you we buried too many frogs."

"Yeah, you're right. If I'd known Pa was praying that hard for rain, I'da cut way back on 'em."

---

August, 1850.

It was sweltering hot and breezeless in the tall corn patch where Daniel and the older children were stripping and bundling fodder. The stagecoach horn sounded.

"Look! Yonder comes George Edward," exclaimed Coleman and pointed at an approaching cloud of dust on the Pike. They paused and waved as the coach, pulled by four stout horses, creaked and swayed past. George Edward waved back and cracked a long bullwhip over the horses, causing them to bolt forward. "Now that's the kind of job I'd like to have," quipped Thomas as he watched the coach disappear from sight. "Just sitt'n and rid'n all day long and enjoy'n the breeze."

"Well, you don't," said Daniel. "Y'all quit looking and get back to pull'n fodder."

When George Edward returned from Fayetteville he was filled with news which everyone was anxious to hear, especially Nancy.

"Did you see any of the McElroys?" she asked.

"Ma, I spent the night with Uncle William and Aunt Mary on Hamwood Road-"

"You didn't!" she blurted. "My home. Oh how I sometimes think about it. That's where me and your Pa were married. Looorrrdy, that's been so long ago. I can just see Father standing there in his old waistcoat... and... your Pa here, all dressed up in his black coat and gray pants, handsome as he could be and nervous as a cat."

The children giggled.

"I wasn't nervous," Daniel deadpanned. "I's scared to death. Went blank and couldn't remember my vows."

Everybody laughed.

"Who else did you see?" Ma asked.

"Mike and Rufus Cooley – they're still at home, but courting heavy," said George Edward. "I met John Adams – they call 'im Jack."

"Who's that?" asked Ma.

"Their younger brother. He was born after we left Lincoln County."

"Well, I'll declare," said Ma. "I sure would like to see 'em all." She fell silent for a moment. "The only McElroy I've seen in the past 23 years is Sallie. I sure miss 'em."

Daniel laid a hand on her shoulder and squeezed. "I know you do. I know how you feel. I hadn't seen any of my folks in over 27 years."

---

One week later.

Daniel finished his supper and pushed back from the table and lifted Achilles on this lap. George Edward cleared his throat and said, "Everybody, I have an important announcement to make."

Everyone at the table stopped eating and looked at him.

"Speak it," said Daniel and held his breath.

"I want to build a cabin down the road aways," said George Edward.

Daniel exhaled, relieved. "That's all! I thought you were going to tell me you were gett'n married."

Ma spoke up. "You mind your own business. He's old enough to get married if he wants to and besides I like Mary Hicks. She's a fine woman. I'm ready for some grandchildren."

George Edward said, "Why Pa, Mary thinks you're hung in the moon."

"Most women do," Daniel deadpanned.

"Just listen to 'im," exclaimed Ma and drew back her hand in jest. "I oughta slap the pride out of 'im."

"Don't hit Pa!" exclaimed little Achilles.

The children cackled.

---

October 27, 1850.

213

The older boys were felling poplar trees across the Pike and dragging them by oxen to a site east of the residence where George Edward's cabin was being constructed. The foliage was yellow, orange and rust-colored set against a deep blue sky and the air nippy. Daniel was swinging an axe and notching the logs. He paused and wiped his brow, sucking in the beauty of fall.

"Remember this day that Lord has given us," he remarked to Dudley, who was assisting him.

"Why's that, Pa?"

"Because there ain't many like it."

The cabin would be a rectangular room with a loft and a fireplace at one end. Although small, it could be easily enlarged by adding more rooms.

Daniel was bent over a log, expertly shaping its side flat with a broad axe, when he heard yelling. He looked up and saw Sarah running toward him, eyes wide, face contorted and lifting the hem of her long black skirt.

"PA... PA... COME QUICK!"

She ran up to Daniel, heaving for breath.

"What is it child?"

"It's Achilles!"

Daniel's heart skipped a beat and the axe slid from his hands. He hobbled toward the house as fast as his old legs would carry him, Sarah and Dudley by his side.

"What's wrong with 'im?" Daniel asked Sarah, gasping for breath.

"He's real sick, Pa."

Daniel charged through the back room and rushed into the bedroom where Achilles was lying on his side, vomit dribbling from his mouth and soiling the sheet. The stench of diarrhea was strong. Nancy was seated on the edge of the bed wiping his face with a wet cloth.

"What's happened?" asked Daniel.

"He's got the fever," she said, looking up at Daniel, whose face was white as a ghost.

"Oh Lord God no!" Daniel bent over and laid a hand on his son's forehead. It was hot. "Achilles darling, it's Pa. Everything is gonna be okay."

The child barely cracked an eyelid.

"Poor baby, he's so weak he can't turn over by himself," said Nancy.

"When did he get sick?"

"It come on real quick. After y'all went to work, I heard him groan and went to check on 'im. He was vomiting and had diarrhea. It's been nonstop ever since. I gave him milk, but he threw it up. He can't keep anything down."

"Somebody go fetch Doc Coman," said Daniel. "Hurry!"

"I'll go," volunteered Dudley, who hitched Sweet to the buggy and took off at a fast trot headed to Athens. Daniel pulled a chair to the edge of the bed and tenderly held Achilles small hand. "You'll be alright little fellow," he said. "Doc Coman is on his way."

An hour later Dr. Joshua P. Coman entered the room, black bag in hand, and went directly to Achilles. After he had examined the child, he stood up and said, "He has all the symptoms of cholera."

"What can you do?" asked Daniel, panic in his voice.

"I can bleed him but that hasn't helped in other cases I've treated," replied Coman. "Dehydration is the real danger."

"Well, do something!" exclaimed Daniel.

"Mr. Barksdale, he's in the Lord's hands," Coman said, solemnly.

Daniel moaned and dropped to his knees by the bed, clutching his baby's hand. "Dear God, don't take my little boy from me. Please God, please spare his life." He was oblivious to Dr. Coman departing. He never stopped praying and he never got off his knees. The clock on the mantle was striking 5 p.m. when Nancy pried Daniel's hand from the child's. "He's gone, Daniel," she said quietly and then broke down and wept.

"My son, my son – oh God, my son," wailed Daniel. He stood and pulled Nancy into his arms, her face buried in his chest. They both clung to one another and wept for a long time.

"Just last night... he was sitt'n in my lap... and laugh'n," said Daniel, his voice breaking. "Now, he's gone – gone forever."

George Edward led his weeping parents from the room. "I'll tell the neighbors," he said quietly.

Sarah spoke up. "I'll clean 'im up, Ma."

Nancy wiped her eyes. "Dress 'im in that pretty little blue outfit that Sallie gave him."

"Yes ma'am, he'll look real pretty in that," said Sarah, before bursting in tears.

Word of Achilles' death spread quickly. Widow Hicks' family was the first to arrive. Mary Hicks, who was courting George Edward, helped Sarah wash and dress the child. Later, the Newbys, Fieldings, Holts and Isoms arrived, all bringing food.

Emanuel Isom grasped Daniel's hand and said, "Daniel, I have some nice cherry wood I've been saving. It would make an awfully pretty coffin."

Daniel, barely able to speak, nodded. "I'd like that."

By 9 p.m. the yard was filled with horses and buggies and wagons and the crowd had spilled out into the yard where the men leaned against the big oaks, some sitting on their haunches, smoking their pipes and quietly conversing. Achilles' corpse, scrubbed clean and dressed in the little blue outfit, was laid out on a makeshift bed in the parlor where neighbors kept an around-the-clock vigil. Several times during the night Daniel rose from his bed and went and stood silently by his blue-eyed baby.

It was late the following morning when Emanuel Isom arrived with the coffin. "I hope you like it," he said to Daniel. "I stayed up all night building it."

The sight of the coffin and the thought that his good friend had constructed such a beautiful object brought more tears. "Thank you... Emanuel... for everything. I'll always be grateful."

"It's what friends are for," said Emanuel, patting Daniel's back.

That afternoon beneath a blue sky the small coffin was placed on the back of a wagon and the family set out for the Athens Cemetery, a caravan of wagons and buggies following.

George Edward and James Greer lifted the coffin from the wagon and set it down by the open grave as folks gathered near. Daniel removed his old and worn black slouch hat, huddled his family together and looked across the open grave at Emanuel Isom. "Emanuel, I'd appreciate it if you would say a few words."

Emanuel took a small testament from his pocket and read the Twenty-Third Psalm. Following comforting words and prayer, the four older brothers, using leather

215

plow lines, lowered the small coffin into the earth, and then covered it with red dirt. Sarah and her two younger sisters placed fresh-picked wildflowers on the grave. The crowd pulled back, leaving Daniel and Nancy standing alone by the fresh grave. Daniel placed his arm around Nancy's frail shoulders and pulled her against him.

"It's so hard to give 'im up," he said, his voice quavering. "He brought laughter and joy to my old heart."

Nancy wiped away tears and said, "Death comes so quickly. One minute he's laughing and playing and the next he's gone."

A cold chill came on as the sun dropped below the horizon.

"It's time to go home," she said.

"I know." As they walked to the wagon Daniel turned and looked at the flower-covered mound a final time and muttered, "I'll never forget you."

During the days that followed, Daniel was unusually quiet and spent more time than usual reading his Bible. While James Greer was away during the day teaching school and the young children were attending classes, Daniel worked on the cabin. It was good therapy. One night Nancy noticed him writing in the Bible. The next day she read what he had written.

"Achilles W. Barksdale was borned February 6, 1847, died October 27, 1850 – age 3 years, 8 months and 21 days."

---

December 5, 1850.

One month and nine days had passed since Achilles' death. There was a noticeable bounce in Daniel's step. And it wasn't caused by cold weather. Nancy had been the first to rise and was scurrying around the kitchen preparing dumplings and issuing instructions to the girls about making apple pie crust.

Meanwhile, George Edward saddled up and rode to Athens and was waiting at the courthouse when Probate Judge Thomas Tyrus arrived at his office.

"You're mighty early," said Judge Tyrus. "Have a deed to record?"

"No sir, I need a marriage license."

"Congratulations. Who is the fortunate young lady?"

"Mary E. Hicks," replied George, "daughter of Widow Hicks. They live not too far from us."

"Yes, good folks," said Judge Tyrus and filled out the form. "Who's gonna marry you?"

"Mr. Johnson; that is, if we can get 'im there today."

George rode directly to Justice of the Peace, John A. Johnson's home on Nick Davis Road near Piney Creek and confirmed the ceremony at 3 p.m.

"It's a mighty cold day to be outside, but I'll do my darndest to be there," said Johnson.

When George Edward arrived home he went to the fireplace where Daniel sat and thawed out.

"I hate to see you grow up'n leave home," said Daniel. "But I'm happy for you. It was a cold day in January when me and your Ma married. You remember old Andy –"

"Who could forget that horse?" responded George Edward.

"That confounded animal threw me in a snow bank on the way to my wedding," said Daniel. "Then run off, causing me to be late."

George Edward chuckled. "I bet Ma was getting nervous."

"Everything went off as planned and you were born exactly one year later. Your Grandpa McElroy said you favored his family – blue eyes and black hair and all. I guess he was right."

At 2 p.m. the boys hitched up the wagon and buggy. "Y'all wrap up real good," ordered Ma. "I don't want any sick young'uns."

She and Daniel went by buggy and the rest of the family rode in the teeth jarring wagon.

Widow Hicks, the same age as Daniel, welcomed everyone inside her house while her 19-year-old son William placed another log on the fireplace.

Her oldest daughter, Sarah, disappeared into another room to assist the bride. Everyone huddled around the fireplace and made small talk while George Edward stood at the window looking out.

"Don't worry," said Daniel, "If Judge Johnson don't show, I'll marry you myself."

"That's not funny, Pa," said George Edward. "It wouldn't be legal and you'd end up being a Grandpa to a little bastard."

The clock struck 3:00 p.m. Judge Johnson still hadn't arrived.

"I see a buggy coming!" exclaimed Dudley.

Judge Johnson entered the room, nose red and dripping. He massaged his cold hands over the fire, and then the ceremony got under way. Daniel stood proudly next to his eldest son. Mary's older sister Sarah was bridesmaid and her brother William gave her away.

Mary, a comely but small woman with black hair and brown eyes, beamed as she took her place next to George Edward. Following the ceremony and a sumptuous meal, Daniel unwrapped his fiddle and picked up the bow.

"Pa's brought his fiddle!" exclaimed James Greer.

"Start pushing back the furniture."

The children slid the furniture against the wall and Daniel struck up *Turkey in the Straw*. George Edward pulled Mary onto the floor and the fun began.

---

Mid-June, 1851.

Daniel noticed that Nancy had been acting strangely, even mysteriously all day. That evening she invited George Edward and Mary over for supper.

"Pa, I have a wonderful announcement," said Mary, beaming.

Daniel looked up from his plate of beans. "You had a vision last night that the Lord is sending rain?"

"Nothing like that," she said. "But he's sending you a grandchild."

Daniel laid down his fork – speechless. Everyone around the table stopped chewing. Tears welled in Daniel's eyes. His lip trembled. Nancy reached over and patted his hand. He looked at her and asked, "You knew?"

"Yes, but we wanted to be sure."

He wiped his eyes with the back of his hand and a smile spread across his lined face. "By crackies, that's the best news I've heard in a long time."

Sarah, who hadn't seen her father smile since Achilles' death, beamed. "Oh Pa, this is wonderful!"

"Well, when is it?" asked Daniel.

"January," replied Mary.

---

It didn't rain a drop in June nor July. The ground cracked, gardens wilted and died, corn stalks turned brown, cotton squares dropped off, branches turned to mere dribbles of water and wells dried up. The earth was brown and grass made a crunching sound underfoot. Daniel had never seen a drought to match this one.

One day, he casually said to Thomas and Dudley, "You boys need to bury some more frogs."

The two brothers looked at one another, but said nothing.

"You boys can't hide anything from me," Daniel said. "I know about y'all burying them frogs before we were nearly washed away last year."

"Pa, we were just trying to help out," offered Thomas.

"I told 'im he was burying too many," said Dudley, shifting blame to Thomas.

Daniel grinned. "Well, y'all bury all you want to," he said. "And hang a few dead snakes over the fence too."

They did, but still no rain came.

It seemed to Daniel that the earth had died. The sun blistered plants and turned the soil to dust. Hardly a breeze stirred. Nights were worse. Trying to sleep in a pool of sweat was impossible. Everyone was growing irritable.

On August 4th he rode to Athens and voted in the election. Nick Davis, Jr. and Nathaniel Davis were elected to represent Limestone County in the Alabama Legislature. Nick Malone was sent to the State Senate.

Finally, rain came, quelling the heat. Temperature dropped and the first frost fell on September 28th, killing what few gardens that had survived the drought. It had been a depressing year. The family could use some good news.

And it came when William Coleman unexpectedly announced at Sunday dinner that he and Eliza Harvey were going to be married. "She's a wonderful girl," said Nancy.

Daniel hadn't expected the announcement. "Well, I'm losing a good hand," he said.

"Yeah, Pa," replied Coleman. "But you are gaining a new daughter."

On December 22nd the family loaded up – the children in the wagon and Daniel and Nancy in the buggy – and drove east five miles to Hansel and Patsie Harvey's home on Johnson's Branch.

"Why does our family always choose the dead of winter to marry?" groused Daniel.

"Because it's too cold to do anything else," replied Nancy.

Sweet perked her ears and neighed. Daniel turned and looked behind him and saw a buggy approaching fast. "My eyes ain't that good, but that looks like the Newby horse and buggy."

"It's James," said Nancy.

"Who's the woman with 'em?"

"Your daughter, Sarah," said Nancy, casually.

"Sarah!"

"Uh huh."

"Unchaperoned?"

"For goodness sakes, Daniel. They're right behind us."

"I didn't know she 'n James were court'n that heavy," said Daniel.

"I've known it for a long time."

"She's only –"

"Sixteen and a woman," said Nancy.

Eliza Harvey, age 18, was a mite of a woman, so slight in stature, thought Daniel, that a good breeze could blow her away. He knew her parents only slightly. Hansel Harvey was 59 years old, a farmer and a native of North Carolina. He had been in Limestone County since 1827. Patsie was age 56 and born in Virginia. Eliza had a younger sister, Elizabeth, age 16; an older sister, Jane, who was 24; and a brother, Martin who was 22 years old. Only family members and a few neighbors were in attendance. And again, Justice of the Peace John A. Johnson was so late arriving that Daniel quipped to Nancy that he might run for JP himself. He was in a jovial mood.

"Do you remember our wedding night?" he whispered in her ear.

"No, now hush and behave!"

They both looked at each other and smiled.

Following the wedding, the newlyweds resided with the Harveys on Johnson Branch.

---

January, 1852.

Daniel wrapped up against the cold, pulled on his old black slouch hat, walked the short distance to George Edward's house as he did each morning after breakfast, and peeked in the backdoor.

"I've come to check on Lil' Mama and the young'un," he said.

Mary smiled and invited him inside to warm.

"He's about to kick me to death, Pa," she said.

"He?" Daniel's face brightened.

"Mama says girls don't kick like boys do."

Daniel chuckled. "What de ya know? A grandson!"

"I'm not for sure, so don't be disappointed if it's a girl," Mary quickly added.

Several days later Daniel selected some of his best white oak boards and began constructing a small wagon with wooden axles and wheels.

George Edward was away driving the stage to Fayetteville when Daniel looked up from constructing the wagon and saw Mary waddling toward the house holding her bulging belly.

Daniel put down the saw and walked to meet her. "What's wrong?" he asked.

"I'm going in labor Pa."

James Greer was absent teaching school and Robert Beasley had gone to Athens. Daniel sent Thomas and Dudley by buggy to fetch Nannie Newby. Shortly all three returned.

Daniel waited outside the closed bedroom door for most of the day. He had held many vigils awaiting the birth of his own children, but this was different. His first grandchild.

Later, George Edward arrived and began pacing in front of the fireplace.

"You were born in January too," Daniel said to George Edward. "In fact it was me and ya Ma's first wedd'n anniversary."

219

The muffled groans of labor pain behind the door abruptly ceased. Daniel and George Edward looked at each other, faces pensive. Then came the unmistakable cry of a baby. Shortly, the door opened and Ma emerged holding a baby wrapped in a blanket.

"Welllll," asked Daniel. "Which is it?"

Ma opened the blanket and spread the baby's tiny legs, "See for yourself."

A wide smile spread across Daniel's face. "By crackies, I've got me a grandson! Can I hold 'im?"

Ma glanced at George Edward.

"Let him go first Ma," he said.

Daniel cradled the child in his arms and gently kissed his forehead. "Would you look at that black hair and them brown eyes. No doubt about it, he favors me."

They named him James Rufus. "'Salute Rufus, chosen of the Lord,'" Daniel said, quoting scripture.

---

To celebrate the birth of his first grandchild, Daniel and Ma sponsored a Saturday night social and invited their neighbors. The Newbys, Fieldings, Hickses and Isoms were present, along with Robert C. David and Aunt Sallie. Robert brought a puppy off his redbone coonhound as a gift to baby "Rufe," as they called the child. "The boy and the pup can grow up together," he said. They named the puppy Luther.

Ma and the girls cooked a large pot of chicken stew, throwing in plenty of potatoes, onions and corn. Eaten with cornbread it was supreme. Apple pies cooled in the kitchen.

Cold wind whistled through the chinked logs, but the fire was hot and the fellowship warm. After choking down a large slice of apple pie, James Martin Newby spoke up. "Mr. Barksdale, everyone sure would like to hear some good fiddling."

"Yeah - yeah." Much clapping.

Daniel retrieved his fiddle and while he tuned up the young folks pushed furniture against the wall.

"George Edward, you call," said Daniel and opened with a rousing, foot stomping rendition of *Turkey in the Straw*.

"Everybody grab a partner," said George Edward, "and let's do-si-do."

James Newby walked over to Sarah Barksdale, who was bunched in the corner with her younger sisters, Cornelia and Cal, along with Mary Fielding, Susan Newby and her younger sister, Isabelle Jane Newby, whom everyone called "Sweet."

"May I have the honor, Madam?" Newby asked Sarah and offered his hand.

Sarah batted her blue eyes and smiled. "Why, I'd be delighted, sir."

James Greer Barksdale pulled Susan Newby to the floor just as she was about to bite off a slice of pie. Everyone laughed. Then John Everitt "Jack" Fielding and "Sweet" Newby took the floor. Dudley Barksdale swung 7-year-old Sarah Jane Isom around to the delight of the guests. Soon, all of the young folks were dancing and laughing. Even Emanuel Isom was cutting a rug with his wife, Rebecca. Thomas, who didn't dance, threw another log on the fire.

George Edward was calling the dance and mopping his brow. "Somebody open the door," he yelled between calls. "Thomas is about to burn us alive."

"I've never seen our young folks have so much fun," Ma remarked to Nannie Newby. "Especially your James and my Sarah."

220

"I've never seen a finer pair," remarked Aunt Sallie David who claimed to be soothsayer about such matters. "And I'll tell you something else," she continued. "Keep your eyes on James Greer and Susan Newby."

The party broke up near 11 p.m. when Emanuel Isom announced that he had to depart and prepare remarks for Sunday worship service.

"After dinner we're having all day singing," he said. "All y'all are invited to attend."

James Newby turned to Sarah Barksdale and asked: "Will you accompany me to the singing?"

"I'd love to if Pa will let me." She walked over and asked her father for permission.

"Unchaperoned!" exclaimed Daniel.

"Pa, I'm 17 years old now."

Daniel thought about it a moment. "I like good singing myself," he said. "I'll follow you and James in my buggy."

"Pa!"

---

Isom's Chapel Methodist Church.

Sunday afternoon was cold and gloomy with the threat of snow looming.

Ma had elected to remain home as she wasn't feeling well. After the singing ended, Daniel watched as James Newby assisted Sarah into his black buggy. Darkness was coming on. He waited several minutes, giving them the opportunity to get a head start, and then he clucked to Sweet, "Take us home ol' gal."

He threw a blanket over him and was soon warm. Each rock and sway of the buggy made his eyelids heavier. He followed well behind the Newby buggy, giving the young couple plenty of privacy. When the black buggy went past the regular turn-off to his home Daniel, became concerned. "Now where'n Sam Hill are they going?" he mumbled. By now there were several buggies on the road, both coming and going and he wasn't sure which one was Newby's. *He deliberately took off and left me. No telling what he's up to.* Daniel was getting more upset by the moment. *Wait till I see 'em.* "I'm going to give 'em a piece of my mind and I'm going to wear Sarah out with a razor strap when I get home.* His bile was up. Arriving home, he charged through the back door and directly to the fireplace to thaw out his fingers where Ma sat nodding.

"What 'n the world is wrong with you?" she asked.

"They deliberately run off and left me!" Daniel said. "Just wait till I see James Newby. And Sarah has a lot of explaining when she gets home. I'm gonna wear 'er out. She knows better!"

"Calm down," said Ma.

"My daughter's out in the middle of the night alone with a man and you tell me to calm down. Bye crackies, I'm gonna get to the bottom of this right now."

"James brought her home a long time ago," Ma said casually.

"I wouldn't have thought James Newby would've done such a thing –"

He stopped in mid-sentence. "What'che say?"

"Sarah is home."

"She is?"

"Yes," said Ma. "You obviously followed the wrong buggy."

221

Sarah entered the room. "Pa! Where've you been? Ma and I were worried to death."

Embarrassed, Daniel blurted out. "It was that damn horse's fault."

Ma chuckled. "Blame the horse, huh?"

Sarah giggled. Daniel cracked a grin. "Aww, I guess that is pretty funny," he said. "Me, making a fool of myself."

"I'd say so," said Ma.

---

Two days later.

Daniel had just pushed away from the supper table when the dogs barked, followed by a knock on the front door.

"Must be a drover want'n to bed down for the night," he commented.

"I'll see who it is Pa," said Dudley, jumping up and going to the door.

James Martin Newby, dressed in his finest Sunday go-to-meeting clothes and holding his hat in front of him, entered.

"Evening, Mrs. Barksdale – Mr. Barksdale. How y'all?" he asked and nodded to the children.

"Get James a plate, Sarah," Ma barked.

"Thank you, but I'm not hungry," Newby replied.

"Sit a spell," said Daniel.

"I've come to talk to you Mr. Barksdale... in private," said Newby, hesitantly.

Ma shot Sarah a glance. Daniel escorted Newby into the parlor, closed the door and they sat before the open fire. Newby fidgeted with the brim of his hat.

"You going to a preaching tonight?" Daniel asked.

"No sir, I've come to ah, ah, ah, I'm nervous as a cat walking on hot coals."

Daniel filled his pipe with tobacco.

"Sir... ah sir... I've come to ask permission... your permission to marry Sarah."

In the adjoining room Ma and Sarah pressed their ear to the parlor door. Sarah crossed her fingers.

"Oh Ma, I'm so nervous I'm about to pee on myself," whispered Sarah.

Ma squeezed her hand.

"Has he asked Pa yet?"

"He just did," replied Ma.

"Ohhh..."

Daniel fired his pipe, took a few puffs and satisfied that it was burning, looked up at Newby. "Sarah is my eldest daughter," he said. "She's barely 17 years old and you're –"

"Twenty-nine, sir."

"I never thought there was any man good enough to marry my daughter," said Daniel, "but I guess that's how all fathers feel. I know you can provide for her well, but the question is: Do you love her?"

"Oh, yes sir, with all my heart," Newby said without hesitation. "I'll never forget the day we came over to help y'all out right after y'all moved here. Sarah was just a small child and hanging on to Mrs. Barksdale's skirt. I never thought the day would come when I'd want to marry her. But, over the years my love has grown for her and I

222

love her with all my heart. She's a fine woman and I'll love and take good care of her 'til we die."

Daniel put down his pipe and stood and took Newby's hand. "James, you're a fine man and you'll make a fine son-in-law."

"What did Pa say... what did he say?" whispered Sarah, from her hiding place behind the door.

Ma pressed her ear closer. "Pa said James would make a fine son-in-law."

"Oh, Ma, I think I'm gonna faint."

---

On a cold January 22, 1852, James Martin Newby married Sarah A. Barksdale at her parent's home with Justice of the Peace John A. Johnson solemnizing the vows. The couple resided with the Newby's on Nick Davis Road.

---

The first day of fall brought not only colorful foliage, cool days with blue skies and chilly nights, but frightening news. The fever was rampant through Limestone County and taking lives by the scores. It brought Daniel horrible memories of the death of Achilles. He lived in fear that death would claim his grandson.

Later in the fall, when Emanuel Isom sent word that a "log rolling" and dinner on the ground was planned to erect a church building to replace the old cabinet shop Daniel was reluctant was attend.

"Oh Pa, let's all go," said Mary. "We can't hole up forever. Anyway, I'm ready to get out and visit folks."

"Child, you don't understand."

Mary, whose father had died several years earlier, had found a replacement in her father-in-law. She laid her head against Daniel's shoulder and looked up at him with begging brown eyes. "Please Pa, we'll have so much fun."

"You just want to show off your new baby," he quipped.

A crowd had gathered on Saturday morning at Isom's Chapel where hewn logs lay on the ground, ready to be hoisted in place. Emanuel and other brethren of the congregation had cut the timber from his farm and shaped them. Not only that, but Emanuel and his wife Rebecca had deeded an acre of land to trustees, Emanuel Isom, John Johnson, John Saxon, Ruben Clem, James Isom, A.E. Meadows and T.B. Isom.

While the men fitted the logs in place, the women gossiped, showed off their babies and talked about quilting. Makeshift tables were laden with food where young girls shooed away flies with sassafras branches and eyed boys.

Mary had been right, the autumn day was been filled with good fellowship and delicious food. Yet Daniel worried. What caused the dreaded fever that produced a horrible death? Cholera and typhoid came all seasons to claim a life. Influenza visited mostly during cold months and "the fever" during warm months. There was death for all seasons.

On a cold January 6, 1853, death struck close to home. James Newby's 70-year-old father, Matthew Newby, the first neighbor to offer help when Daniel moved the family to Limestone County, died. He was buried on a ridge near his home overlooking Swan Creek.

---

Athens.

Monday, January 24, 1853.

The slave auction brought the largest crowd of people to town that Daniel could remember. Robert Beasley guided the team of horses down muddy Marion Street, as they strained to pull the wagon loaded with two 500-pound bales of cotton. The iron-rimmed wheels cut deep ruts in the soft earth. Scores of wagons, many also hauling bales of cotton, were parked along the street leading to the square. Thin clouds of steam rose into the morning coldness created by fresh horse droppings lodged in muddy ruts. Mules brayed and dogs barked. They tethered the team off the square and walked to the east courthouse lawn where a large crowd milled about talking and laughing, waiting for the auction to begin. Fancy carriages driven by Negroes and occupied by gentlemen planters were parked across the street, their overseers standing nearby. They had come, no doubt looking for a good buy on slaves. Many county folks – small farmers like Daniel – were also present, perhaps also looking for a good bargain on a single Negro. And, there was the usual hard-drinking, boisterous riff-raff who had come looking for excitement.

Daniel and Robert Beasley edged closer where scores of Negro men, women and children stood in a ragged line on the courthouse yard, facing the crowd who were in a festive mood. They were talking and laughing, some pointing toward the Negroes, obviously discussing their physical attributes.

Shortly, the auctioneer, a skinny man wearing an oversized gray, rumpled waistcoat and black wide-brimmed hat stepped up and rang a bell. When the crowd grew quiet, he spoke. "Gentlemen, welcome to the biggest auction of negroes ever held in Limestone County. I'll be sell'n the finest hands that can be bought anywhere. All are ready to go to work and prepare the ground for spring plant'n as soon as weather permits. I've just learned that cotton's bring'n seven 'n half cents a pound. With good, stout Negroes you can make your fortune.

"Terms is cash on the barrel head," he added. "You'll receive a bill of sale and good title. Any questions?"

"Are they in sound condition?" someone asked.

"As far as I know. If you see a Negro you're interested in buying, you'll have a chance to inspect 'im before bidd'n starts." He looked over the crowd and said, "If there are no more questions, let's start the auction."

A stout, healthy-looking Negro was pushed forward. "This here young buck's about twenty years old and strong as an ox," the auctioneer said. "Gentlemen, whata I hear. Who'll give fifteen hundred dollars?"

"Eight hundred!" someone shouted.

"Nine."

"One thousand!"

The auctioneer said, "Gentlemen, this young buck is worth more'n a thousand dollars and all of you know it. Look at his hands. Why, he can pick a bale a day."

Laughter.

An overseer leaning against a black carriage yelled: "Eleven hundred!"

The bidding resumed and the hammer fell at thirteen hundred dollars.

"My word!" Daniel exclaimed. "A man havta make... uh....uh." He mentally calculated a five hundred pound bale of cotton times seven and a half cents. "Why, a man would havta make about thirty five bales of cotton at the current price to pay for 'em," he said to Robert Beasley. "And that don't count housing and feeding 'em."

But Daniel hadn't come to purchase Negroes. He had come to sell his cotton crop – that is, if he could get a good price. The farm had produced only 12 bales and at the current price his gross profit would be about $435.00. From that sum he had to deduct the cost of guano. Expense of the horses, plows and human labor to plant and harvest the crop wasn't included. He needed to sell his cotton to finance his forthcoming crop. He figured the price would rise. Of course, prices could fall. It was a shot in the dark. Cotton buyers from Decatur were present and when the auction ended, they would be moving around haggling over prices and attempting to purchase.

Female slaves didn't generally bring as much as males. Older females sold for the lowest price. A 65-year-old woman fetched $130; a 40-year-old brought $700, and the highest price was brought for a 19-year-old who sold for $1,150.

Robert Beasley tugged at Daniel's arm. "Look yonder, Pa." He pointed to a Negro standing in line waiting to be sold.

"Stocky!" exclaimed Daniel.

Stocky was standing straight as a poker, chin up, a defiant look on his face.

"He don't look happy," muttered Robert Beasley. They watched as Stocky was pushed forward, and turned around several times so that the bidders could look him over.

"Show us his teeth!" somebody yelled.

"A mighty fine negro, he is," the auctioneer said. "He works in the field, cooks better 'n a woman, does masonry and carpentry work and is strong as an ox. What d'ya bid?"

Stocky was beginning to show his age, and his grizzled hair was streaked with gray causing the bidding to be less than enthusiastic. When he spotted Daniel and Robert Beasley in the crowd the stoic look on his face gave way to almost a smile.

"Pa, he's want'n you to buy 'im."

Daniel averted Stocky's eyes, "Let's go sell some cotton," he said and abruptly turned away.

When the auction ended and the crowd had thinned they drove the wagon loaded with cotton bales to the square and parked. Shortly, a man walked over and introduced himself as a buyer for J. Collins of Decatur. "Those bales for sale?"

"If the price is right," said Daniel.

The man pulled out a pocket knife, slashed open a small section of the burlap wrapping around the cotton bale and extracted a wad of lint. He slowly pulled the lint apart with his fingers, eyeballing its length. "Well, the staple ain't that good and the lint is dirty," he said. "All I can pay is 6₵ a pound."

"I just heard that cotton was bringing 7½ cents," said Daniel.

"That's long staple, clean lint and delivered to Decatur."

"I believe the price will rise," Daniel said. "I'm gonna hold my cotton." He turned to Robert Beasley and said, "Let's go home."

As they drove off, the buyer yelled, "And prices may fall."

"I'll ride the market down to nothing before I give my cotton away," Daniel shot back.

---

On miserable winter days when it was either too cold or too wet to work outside, Daniel sat in front of the fireplace, reading his Bible and, when he could obtain a copy, Thomas Hobbs' newspaper, the *Athens Herald*. Railroad fever had seized Limestone County. Hobbs, through his newspaper, was promoting it. The plan was to build tracks from the Tennessee line 17 miles south to Decatur, where it would link up with the Memphis and Charleston line running east and west, the latter having been under construction since 1851.

The price of cotton didn't rise as Daniel had hoped and he was forced to sell his 12 bales and market price. He knew he would never get rich raising cotton. It took a lot of fertile land and cheap labor to make money and that meant slaves. His work force was reduced when George Edward and Coleman married and moved out. It wouldn't be long before James Greer and Robert Beasley did the same. That would leave Thomas and Dudley to do the hard labor. He was getting old, his bones creaked and the day would come when he couldn't work in the fields. It was depressing. Then he would pull his grandson Rufe around in the little red wagon and his world would brighten.

---

March, 1853.

Loud banging on the back door woke Daniel. It opened and slammed shut.

"PA – MA!"

It was George Edward. Daniel's heart jumped to his throat. Trouble. He threw back the cover and hurried to the parlor where George Edward stood holding a lantern. Little Rufe was asleep on his shoulder.

"What's wrong?" he asked.

"Pa, it's Mary, she's awfully sick."

Ma entered and overheard. "Why didn't you let us know sooner?" she asked.

"When she got a headache I wasn't concerned, but she got worse," George Edward said. "She's burning up with fever."

Daniel and Ma quickly dressed and hurried down the path to the cabin where Mary lay in bed, the light of a lamp flickering and sending shadows up the white-washed log walls. Ma bent over and felt Mary's forehead, "Somebody get a wet cloth, this child is burning up," she said.

Daniel noticed her yellowish skin. Her eyes were shut. He bent over close to her and said, "Lil' Mama, it's Pa. Can you hear me?"

No response.

Daniel and Ma looked at each other knowingly. George Edward was beside himself with concern.

"I've been pray'n that it ain't the fever," he said.

"We're all pray'n," said Daniel.

They maintained vigil by Mary's bedside through the night and up into the morning, when she lapsed into a coma. Late afternoon, she stopped breathing while George Edward held her hand. Daniel held the other one while Ma gently stroked her forehead. "Is she...?" asked George Edward, his voice quavering.

"Yes son, she's gone," replied Daniel.

"Oh Mary – Mary! Don't leave me," wailed George Edward, throwing himself across her lifeless body. "You're a good woman and fine wife. I'm sorry I didn't tell you that every day."

Big tears ran down Daniel's cheeks into his grizzled whiskers. "And I never thanked you, Lil' Mama, for giving me my first grandson."

Daniel and George Edward constructed a coffin with cherry wood Daniel had been saving in case of a neighbor's death. He never considered that his only daughter-in-law would occupy the first one.

"It's beautiful, Pa," George Edward said. "Mary would be pleased if she could see it."

On a stormy Sunday afternoon they loaded the coffin on the back of a two-horse wagon and made the slow journey to the cemetery. The Hicks family and neighbors followed. Loved ones gathered around the open grave as men folks, using leather plow lines, lowered the coffin into the damp earth. Again, Emanuel Isom was present and said a few comforting words. Dirt was shoved into the hole, making a thudding sound as it struck the wooden coffin. George Edward stood over the grave for a long time, wiping his eyes and holding little Rufe in the crook of his arm.

"Ma-Ma," the child uttered and pointed toward the grave.

"Yes son, Mama," his father said. "She's gone to Heaven."

The family came together around George Edward, now a widower with a baby to raise. George worried. "I don't know what I'm gonna do."

"Don't you worry one minute," said his Ma. "I've raised ten young'uns already and one more won't make any difference."

---

Tuesday, January 1, 1856.

New Year's brought both happiness and worry. But that's life, thought Daniel as he enjoyed the warm fire and early morning solitude. He had risen early, just as the first dull light of dawn eased its way past the bedroom curtain. It was an iron gray, cold day. The cup of water by Nancy's bedside was frozen solid. He opened the Bible and read from James, Chapter 4. Verse 14: "Whereas ye know not what shall be on the morrow. For what is your life? It is even a vapor that appeareth for a little time, and vanisheth away." Yes, life was fleeting, Daniel thought. The last two years had gone by in a flash. He had reached the old age of 56 and figured he didn't have many years remaining. The Lord had blessed him – so far. While others around him had been slain by the grim reaper, the Lord had spared him and his family, except of course, Achilles and his daughter-in-law, Mary. He had a lot to be thankful for. Grandson Rufe was 4 years old and remained the apple of his eye. Perhaps it was because he lived in the household while George Edward was away driving the stage. Coleman and Elizabeth had given him two more grandchildren, Ophelia, born on September 27, 1853, and Robert Coleman "Bob" born March 16th, two years ago. Nevertheless, he was bothered. James Greer was courting Susan Newby and no doubt they would soon marry. George Edward, a widower, was pursuing Mary French, daughter of Amos. Robert Beasley was spending an unusual amount of time in Madison County chasing Lucy Rairty Gidden of the New Market community. Dudley was 17 years old and would soon find a girl, marry and move out. When that occurred, he and Thomas would be the only two remaining to farm and make a living for the family. It hadn't happened yet, but he was already feeling abandoned. He looked out the window at the big oaks, leafless and stark in the coldness and pondered what worried him most. The slavery issue was being stoked to a white heat. Eventually, something was bound to happen.

"Morning, Pa," said James Greer cheerfully, entering the parlor carrying his shoes.

Lost in thought, Daniel looked up at his smiling son. "What's got you in such a good humor?"

James Greer laced his shoes. "I was going to wait until dinner time to make the announcement when everyone is here. But, I'm so happy I just can't contain it."

"Did you discover gold?" Daniel asked.

"Pa, last night I asked Susan to marry me and she consented."

"Why don't all of y'all just go and desert me and your Ma and get it done with."

"Pa! I figured you'd be happy for me," said James Greer, disappointed.

Daniel exhaled audibly, rose from the chair and placed an arm around his son, "It ain't that," he said. "I've been expecting it any day. It's just that I hate to see you go. It won't be long before all my boys marry and move out. It makes me happy, yet sad. Susan is a fine woman from a fine family. All the Newby's are good folks – the salt of the earth."

"I want you to be happy for us Pa."

"I am, son. Y'all can live here as long as you like. Have you told your Ma yet?"

"No sir."

"Ohhh Lord!"

Coleman and Eliza and the two babies arrived mid-morning by wagon and nearly frozen. Nancy and the girls were out in the kitchen were hog jowl and black-eyed peas bubbled in an iron pot. Nancy was singing, happy that her family would be together.

George Edward appeared just before dinnertime with Mary French by his side and apologized for being late. I went over to French Mill and picked up Mary," he said.

"It shouldn't have taken that long," said Robert Beasley ribbing his brother.

"Well, we took our time," said George Edward, smiling.

The family squeezed around the table where large pones of cornbread sat. After Daniel had returned thanks, Ma passed around a big bowl of hog jowl and black-eyed peas. There was table talk about the price of cotton – it was good, the weather, typhoid fever and finally what Daniel called the approaching war over slavery.

"Loorrdyyy!" exclaimed Ma. "When he's not worried about one thing, he's worried about something else."

"If you knew what's happening in this country you'd be worried too," snapped Daniel.

"I can't do a dratted thing about it," Ma said. "Let's talk about something pleasant."

James Greer cleared his throat and said, "Everyone, I have happy news." The chatting stopped.

"Now that's what I'm talking about," Ma said. "Tell us son."

"Susan and I are going to be married," said James Greer, beaming. "Isn't that wonderful?"

Ma's jaw dropped. Speechless. Cornelia and Cal squealed with delight and clapped their hands. "What did he say?" Thomas asked, confused.

"Have you set a date?" asked George Edward.

"The latter part of January," replied James Greer.

228

"I have wonderful news also," George Edward said. "Mary and I are gett'n married too. She'll be a wonderful mother to little Rufe." More clapping from Cornelia and Cal.

"Ohhh Lorrrdddy!" Ma wailed.

"Now ain't this something," interjected Robert Beasley. "Lucy 'n me are getting married too."

"Oh Lordy…. Lordy… Lordddyy!" Ma exclaimed and burst into tears. "All my babies are leaving home. Booo hoooo hoooo."

James Greer rushed to his mother's side and said, "Ma, I thought you'd be happy for us."

George Edward and Robert Beasley also tried to console her. Mary French sat stone-faced, not knowing whether to excuse herself from the table or jump up and run home. Daniel came over, wrapped his arms around her shoulder and said, "Welcome to the family, Mary. You'll make George Edward a fine wife and Rufe a good mother. Don't pay any attention to Ma, she'll get over it."

"This is the worst New Year's I've ever had," said Ma, her voice jerking, and then she burst into tears again.

---

James Greer Barksdale, age 27, married Susan B. Newby, age 22, on a cold Wednesday, January 30th, at the home of her sister, Ann Newby. Presbyterian Minister Reverend George W. Mitchell performed the ceremony before a large crowd of family and neighbors.

Their happiness was marred several days later when George Edward brought news back from Fayetteville that Ma's older brother, William McElroy, age 75, had died at the family home on Hamwood Road of typhoid the same day of the wedding. He was buried next to his father Micajah in the McElroy cemetery.

"So many wonderful memories in that house," Ma said, mournfully. "That's where I fell in love with you Pa and we were married."

Ten days later, on Sunday afternoon, February 10th, George Edward, 28, married Mary French, age 18, at the home of her father, Amos French. Justice of the Peace John A. Johnson performed the vows as he had done at George Edward's first marriage to Mary Hicks. Mary was the granddaughter of Amos French, Sr., a colorful old man of 73 who had commanded a company of Alabama Volunteers under General Jackson at New Orleans. It was said that Captain French was drinking coffee just before the battle when Ol' Hickory walked up and knocked the cup from his hand with his sword. Whatever happened down there, Amos French developed a dislike for Jackson and became an ardent Whig and supporter of Henry Clay for President.

Robert Beasley Barksdale, age 23, broke a family tradition by marrying during the hottest part of the year. He and Lucy Rarity Giddens, age 21, were married by Magistrate J.C. Elliott on Thursday afternoon, July 17, 1856, at the Locust Grove Baptist Church located at Hay Store, at Deposit in northern Madison County. Lucy's mother, Nancy, was married first to Samuel Lewis and birthed six children. Lewis died and Nancy married a second time to John Gidden in 1836, but she died in late 1840 leaving four infant children, including Lucy Rarity Gidden. Robert Beasley and Lucy set up housekeeping with her father, John Gidden, a widower and respected citizen and landowner of Madison County. Robert Beasley helped his father-in-law farm. It was a two-day trip by wagon from Athens to Hay's Store in scorching weather.

"I know I'll regret not attending the wedding," bemoaned Ma, "but I ain't fit to make the trip."

Nannie Newby, who had helped deliver several of Nancy's babies, died three weeks later.

---

The ensuing four years quickly flew by, bringing much change in the Barksdale family, the town and the nation. The newly marrieds were producing babies faster than rabbits. William Coleman and Eliza had four children; James Greer and Susan Barksdale, one; James and Sarah Newby had three and Robert Beasley and Lucy Rarity Barksdale had a daughter named Mollie Beasley.

"I'll soon have to work full time just to make enough hickory whistles and corn cob dolls for Christmas presents for my grandchildren," complained Daniel.

"Well Pa, that's what happens when you become a grandpa," said Ma. "As for me I enjoy cook'n and fix'n for my family."

Daniel frowned. "You've never called me Pa before."

"Well, that's what we've become – Ma and Pa."

Sadness spread across her face. "Poor Thomas," she said quietly. "No woman will ever want 'im because he's nearly deaf."

Meanwhile Daniel had acquired an additional hundred acres of land and his holdings now stretched all the way south to Nick Davis Road. State Senator Luke Pryor and State Representative Thomas H. Hobbs had been successful in persuading the Legislature to enact a railroad tax and by November 1, 1859, tracks of the Tennessee and Alabama Central railroad had been completed from Veto to Decatur.

The U.S. Supreme Court, in the *Dred Scott* decision, declared that blacks are not citizens of the United States and couldn't sue. And radical abolitionist John Brown had raided Harper's Ferry Arsenal, attempting to trigger a slave rebellion.

# PART
# III

# 20 | THE APPROACHING STORM

Sunday, January 1, 1860.

Daniel Barksdale usually slept late on Sunday mornings, sometimes even past 5 a.m., but on this particular Lord's Day he had been awake since the clock on the parlor mantle struck 3 a.m. Rheumatism discomforted him, but mostly he was worried. In fact, he worried a lot these days. It used to be that he could shut off his mind and go back to sleep, but since he turned 60 years old, it wasn't that easy anymore. And there was plenty to worry about.

He leveraged out of bed, being careful not to wake Ma, and shuffled across the cold plank floor to the parlor where embers still glowed beneath the back log in the fireplace. The room was cold and dark. He fumbled around in the wood box until he found kindling and laid it on the hot coals and blew on them. Soon, a small flame ignited and he laid on more wood until the flames were leaping around the back log, casting light into the room. After slipping on his shoes and buttoning his shirt, he backed near the fireplace, enjoying its warmth, and resumed his worrisome thoughts – the ones that had interfered with his sleep.

Limestone County was in an uproar. The secession issue had split the county asunder politically like a broad axe busting open a block of white oak. Some people, especially slave-owning planters in south Limestone who raised lots of cotton, were promoting secession. If a state could choose to join the Union, they argued, then it had the right to leave the union. Many others, especially working people, and particularly Mr. A. B. Herndon, editor of the *The Union Banner,* opposed secession. Only time would tell who was right, or, more importantly, who would prevail.

He didn't own any slaves at the present, not because he thought it was wrong to have them – it wasn't. They were property, just like a yoke of oxen or a buggy, and the law protected the owner's legal right to them. The reason he didn't own slaves was because they were too darn expensive and too much damn trouble. Ol' Stubby had taught him that. There had been slavery since Old Testament days, and even when Jesus walked the earth. The New Testament endorsed slavery. In Ephesians it says: "Slaves, obey your earthly masters with fear and trembling." And again in Titus: "tell slaves to give satisfaction in every respect." It's just the way it was. But deep in his soul he knew it wasn't right. Slavery was a pox on America. Northern Abolitionists, many whose ancestors had brought them to America, wanted them freed immediately on moral grounds. Southerners clung to them because they were valuable property. And no one had a workable solution to the problem.

But that wasn't what worried him the most. That gangly, long-armed Lincoln fellow from Illinois and his abolitionist supporters were stirring the pot and planting dangerous ideas in Negroes. Folks in Limestone County were frightened and rightfully so. Of the county's 15,306 residents, 8,091 were slaves. The previous year, abolitionist John Brown had attempted to stoke a slave rebellion at Harper's Ferry, Virginia. He was captured and hanged, but with more than half of Limestone County's population being slaves, an uprising was a real fear.

And that thought got in bed with him every night.

As he often did when troubled, he lifted the large brown leather-bound Bible from a nearby table, opened it to the Twenty-Third Psalm and began reading. He was thinking about the Psalm when Ma padded into the room and backed up to the fireplace.

232

He looked up and said, "Morn'n, you're up awfully early for a Sunday morning."

"So are you. I heard you get up earlier. Is something bothering you?"

"Just gett'n old," he said. "What about you?"

"I've got to get an early start."

"Doing what?"

"Pa, It's New Year's Day!"

"By crackies, you're right, I completely forgot."

"Everyone is coming over for dinner," she said, beaming. "I just can't wait to see 'em."

Daniel put up his Bible just as son-in-law James Newby wandered in, shoes in hand, yawning. "Morn'n Mr. Barksdale, how you?"

"I forget."

Newby chuckled. He and Sarah and their three children lived in the ell addition of the house where, until recently, drovers had frequently put up for the night. He helped Dudley and Thomas work the family farm.

"Well, I better wake up Cal and Cornelia and get to cook'n," said Ma, leaving the room.

Thomas and Dudley wandered in, warming up in front of the fire before going to the barn to feed the livestock.

Soon, the household was up and hog jowl was simmering in a big pot of black-eyed peas out in the kitchen.

Near 11 a.m. ol' Luther barked long and lonesome, announcing the arrival of Coleman and Eliza and their four children all piled in a one-horse wagon. Pa walked out and greeted them. The children were wrapped in quilts and lying on a pallet in the back of the wagon.

"You're just in time for dinner," Pa said. "Y'all get out and come in."

Then George Edward, Mary and Rufe, who lived nearby, sauntered in. Ma was elated. She was happiest when she was cooking and feeding her family. "I wish Robert Beasley and Lucy and lil' Mollie could be here," she said. "I really miss seeing 'em. I don't know why they have to live way over yonder in New Market. I don't like it one bit."

The old house was packed with people. Babies were crying, children were running and yelling and the women were all talking at the same time.

"All this commotion makes a man thirsty for a chew," Pa said. Just as he reached in his pocket for a plug of tobacco, Ma called out, "DINNERTIME!"

The adults squeezed around the large table and the children found a niche wherever they could. Pa stood silently at the head of the table until the chattering ceased.

"Your Ma and me have been married for uh, let's see…"

"Thirty-three years," said Ma.

"I knew that," Pa replied, smiling. There was chuckling around the table. "Anyway, it's been a good life. All of you are a blessing to us; our children are all present except for Robert Beasley and of course little Achilles who would've been thirteen years old, had he lived. Our children are good, honest, law-abiding Christians that have never brought shame on our family. Your Ma and me are real proud of you. And we're proud of our daughters-in-law too." He looked at them. "Eliza, Mary, Susan, and our son-in-law, James. We love all of you. You have blessed us with fine grandchildren. This is the Lord's day and we should be mindful that our Lord and Savior, Jesus Christ, died for

233

our sins. No matter how tough life gets we can always go to 'im in prayer. We are beginning a new year and it brings with it great uncertainties. I pray that one year hence we can again gather in peace and harmony as we are today."

He looked over at James. "James, will you return thanks?"

After the prayer, Ma said, "We've been eating hog jowl and black-eyed peas on New Year's Day since we were married, but I've got a surprise for you today. Thomas killed a mess of squirrels yesterday." She lifted the lid on a pot and James Greer peeked in. "Squirrel dumplin's!" he exclaimed. "Ma makes the best in the county."

Big pones of hot cornbread, fresh butter, sweet milk, buttermilk, coffee, molasses, pickles and relish festooned the table, along with the squirrel dumplings, hog jowl and black-eyed peas.

"The Lord has blessed us not only with good health, but a bountiful harvest and good food. We are truly blessed," Pa said.

"Amen to that," said James Greer.

"Eat'n hog jowl and black-eyed peas on New Year's Day is supposed to bring luck," Ma said. "I think we're gonna need all we can get, so eat up."

Following dinner, the men gathered around the fireplace to smoke, chew and talk. Politics was the primary topic. Pa bit off a hunk of store-bought chewing tobacco, put it in his jaw and passed the twist around. "I haven't seen this country in such danger since the War of 1812," he said. "I's only twelve years old at the time but I remember it well. The British burned our capital. And by crackies, if it hadn't been for Andy Jackson and his Tennesseans at New Orleans we'd be bowing and scraping to a British King today." He paused and spat a stream of brown juice in the fire, then continued as it sizzled.

"After we defeated the British we truly became one nation. As long as we stick together we'll remain strong against outside meddlers. Now, there's talk of secession. I tell ya, no good will come from it."

"Pa, we can't continue to live peacefully in a country where one region is trying to destroy the other," said George Edward. "And that's what the North is doing. They want to destroy the South. Slavery is only an excuse. It's all economics, I tell ya."

School teacher James Greer joined the conversation. "The North enacts high tariffs that work a great injustice against the south. The higher the tariff, the more protection it gives to Northern industries —"

Thomas leaned close to hear. "How come?" he asked.

"Well, it works like this," said James Greer, turning to Thomas. "A tariff is a tax on certain goods that are imported into the country from abroad. The higher the tax, or duty as it's called, the more it cost the consumer and the more revenue that flow into the government treasury. Most of the revenues are spent developing the North. Not to mention that it protects Northern industries against competition. Thomas wrinkled his brow. "I think I understand," he said.

"The South exports more goods than the North — mostly cotton which is shipped to Europe," said James Greer. "In turn, the southern planters have to buy plows, equipment and manufactured good from Europe in order to raise the cotton. If there is a high tax on those goods, the southern planter earns less profit."

"Like, I said, it's all about money," chimed George Edward.

"No matter what the reason, we need to work out our differences," Pa said.

"Radical northern Abolitionists are stirring up the brew," James Greer said.

234

"They can't expect slave owners to voluntarily give up their property without compensation. Course, I don't own any, but they are property. It's legal to own slaves and always has been. Why, it's in the Bible!"

"Cotton is the South's main resource and it can't be worked profitably without slave labor." James Newby said. "If slavery is outlawed, our economy will crash."

Thomas cupped his ear. "Y'all speak up," he said.

"Talk of secession is disturbing enough," Pa said, "but right now I'm more concerned about a slave insurrection. More than half of this county's population are slaves. They're a whole lot smarter than folks give 'em credit for. Remember Stocky? I didn't even know he could read, but he was read'n an abolitionist newspaper and that was thirteen years ago. No tell'n what they got up their sleeves now. We live in dangerous times, I tell ya."

"Everything hinges on the outcome of the election this November," said George Edward. "If the Democrats win, I feel that the South will be treated fairly."

"What will happen if Lincoln is nominated by the Black Republicans and they win?" asked Dudley.

"The South will secede," said George Edward.

"Good," replied Dudley. "The Union be dammed!"

Pa shook his head. "Dudley, you don't know what you're say'n."

"It's not our family's fight," said James Greer. "Maybe we can remain out of the dispute."

"Eventually, we'll have to choose sides," Pa said.

---

Winter faded into spring which came with all of its usual glory in North Alabama. Redbuds and dogwoods bloomed in the hedgerows and forests bordering Swan Creek and the sweet aroma of honeysuckle filled the air. Early mornings Pa listened to doves coo and at twilight he sat beneath the big oak trees in the back yard and listened to whippoorwills call. It was peaceful.

Although the future was uncertain, he felt blessed. He was in fair health and owned 140 acres of land, debt free. He hadn't been in such good financial shape since departing Kentucky. And cotton was bringing over twelve cents a pound!

---

October 23, 1860.

Pa's arms were tired, but he didn't mind. He'd been playing the fiddle all afternoon was friends and family celebrated. Friend and neighbor, John "Jack" E. Fielding had just married James Newby's sister, Isabelle Jane "Sweet" Newby. James and Susan hosted the gay occasion at Daniel Barksdale's home, and he had been coaxed into playing.

Meanwhile, everyone in the neighborhood was buzzing about the Niphonia Fair that began on the day of the wedding and lasted through Friday, October 26th.

Cal and Cornelia begged Ma to attend.

"There is a large floral hall for exhibits and even a silver cornet band from Nashville," Cal said to Ma.

"Ask Pa to take us," Cornelia added. "Please Ma?"

"Y'all ain't interested in seeing exhibits," said Ma. "Y'all are interested in

235

seeing fellows."

"Well, what if we are?" asked Cornelia.

Ma convinced Pa to attend and early Friday morning the family loaded up in the two-horse wagon and headed to the new fairground a quarter mile northwest of the town square.

The Limestone County Stock and Agricultural and Mechanical Association had spent five thousand dollars developing the 60-acre fairground designed by Athens architect, Hiram Higgins, who had also designed the Female Institute and the courthouse. The main building was two stories and contained three additions that could seat two thousand people. There were judges' stands for livestock and a mile long race track. Four wells had been dug and hand pumps installed.

An ad in *The Limestone News* had bragged that "the grounds are beautifully laid off, the buildings are decidedly the most costly and commodious in the South; the track is a mile, and the best one at any fairground in the Union."

When the team of horses reached the newly-laid railroad tracks that ran north-south through Athens, they abruptly stopped, smelled the iron rails and refused to cross.

"What's wrong with 'em?" asked Dudley.

"They've never seen anything like this," Pa said.

Thomas slapped the leather lines and clucked, "Git up," but the horses were suspicious. They pawed at the tracks and neighed and refused to budge. Dudley jumped out of the wagon and gently led the horses across the tracks, while Ma craned her neck, looking up and down the tracks. "How 'n world does it work?" she asked.

"The engine pulls cars," Pa replied.

"Well, I don't see anything," she said.

"That's because they ain't here," Pa said. "They say the train will make its first run in a few days."

"Lordeee, what is this world coming to?" responded Ma.

When they passed the Luke Pryor home, Cal and Cornelia were speechless as they pointed at the large and beautiful two-story house. A grove of trees bordered the long driveway that ran from the railroad tracks to the front of the house. A cupola with glass windows, resembling a look-out tower, crowned the roof.

"Close your mouth Cal," teased Dudley. "You may swallow a fly."

"A fine man and a good lawyer, that Luke Pryor," commented Pa. "See that building on the south side of the house?"

Everyone gawked.

"Well, that's his law office."

At the fairground, wagons, buggies, carriages and gigs of all sorts were parked. A large crowd of folks had turned out for the event. Thomas tied up the horses and the family unloaded. Martial music was playing in the distance. Piles of steaming horse droppings littered the ground as they entered the ornamental archway gate. Ma immediately took notice of the racetrack and launched into lecturing Thomas and Dudley. "I better not hear of y'all gambling on horses," she said, shaking her finger at them.

But Dudley was more interested in the military cadets from LaGrange College who were stepping smartly on the parade ground to rousing martial music; that is, until his jaw dropped when he spotted some of the beauties from the Athens Female Academy parading around beneath parasols.

"Now, you close your mouth," teased Cal, "else you may swallow a fly."

Thomas was anxious to strike out and soak up the adventure.

"Ma?" asked Cornelia. "Can Cal and I go to the exhibit hall by ourselves?"

"Not unescorted, young ladies!" said Pa, who had overheard their request. "Y'all stay with us."

Ma and Pa, with the girls in tow, walked around the grounds, taking in the hub bub, music, laughter and sucking up the sweet aroma of food. Knots of men gathered and talked of war.

"It's so exciting," said Cal.

"Lordee, I've never seen this many people gathered in one place," Ma said, latching onto Pa's arm. "It's so much fun."

"Enjoy while you can," replied Daniel. "There ain't no telling what the future holds."

---

The upcoming presidential election was the main topic of conversation among folks. James Donnell's *Union Banner,* edited by Mr. A.B. Herndon, was whooping it up for John Bell who was a candidate of the Constitutional Union Party. Bell was favored by Whigs and many of the planters. He promised to protect slavery and push for its protection on the Federal level. On the other hand, the *Athens Herald,* owned by Thomas Hobbs, a Democrat, supported former Vice-President and Kentuckian, John C. Breckenridge. Breckenridge was a break-away Democrat and favored protecting slavery. Northern Democrats nominated Stephen Douglas of Illinois, who was against slavery but a "cooperative" for preserving the Union. The Republicans nominated Abe Lincoln. It promised to be an election of momentous consequence.

---

Tuesday, November 6, 1860.

Daniel rose early morning, an uneasiness resting in the pit of his stomach. Half hope – half fear. He peered out the window at a blanket of white frost on the ground. The day was cold and bleak as the leafless white oaks that stood stark and bare against morning's first light. A good opportunity to sit by the fire, read scriptures and nurse his old bones. But that would have to wait. It was election day. And Ol' Scratch himself couldn't keep him away from the polls. Today's vote would determine the future of the South. And that's the reason his stomach was uneasy.

Mid-morning, Thomas hitched the team to the wagon and brought it around.

"Wrap up real good," said Ma, fussing. "I don't wanna hear you complaining all week about your rheumatism. You oughta stay home since your vote won't make any difference anyway. The politicians always do what they wanna do."

"That's a bad attitude and a good reason women ain't allowed to vote," Pa said.

"Keep covered up and be careful," she said, ignoring his comment.

James Greer, George Edward, Dudley and James Newby were aboard the wagon when Pa emerged from the house.

"Dudley, you ain't registered to vote," Pa said. "You stay home and watch after your Ma and the women."

"Aw Pa, I was count'n on going to town," he said, climbing down from the wagon.

"Maybe you can go tomorrow."

237

Thomas clucked to the team and slapped the leather reins on their backs and the wagon lurched forward down the Fayetteville Pike toward Athens.

"There's no need to cancel out each other's vote," Pa said. "We need to decide which horse we're gonna ride 'n this race."

"I like Bell of Tennessee, but he has no chance of winning," Newby said.

"That's leaves Douglas and Breckenridge," replied Pa.

"I like Breckenridge," said George Edward. "But he's a regional candidate and he won't be elected."

"Stephen Douglas is the only candidate that has a chance of defeating Lincoln," said James Greer.

"I agree," Pa said. "He's a northerner but he stands for the Union and is will'n to accommodate the south."

"Who are we voting for, Pa?" asked Thomas, straining to hear.

"I'm voting for Douglas," Pa shouted. "And I hope y'all do the same. He can defeat Lincoln and the Black Republicans. He's the South's only hope. All that Bell and Breckenridge will accomplish is split the Democrat vote."

No one commented. Pa continued. "Young people, hear what I say. Breckenridge talks a good game, but he'll take us outta the Union and that's the last thing we wanna happen."

As they neared Athens, described as "shabby" by a northern reporter, blue smoke curled from every chimney, creating a pall that hung over the town. Athens had a population of 887 people, and it looked as if every one of them had braved the cold weather to come vote.

Thomas tethered the team beneath a tree off the square and they walked toward the red brick courthouse where the Stars and Stripes fluttered above a crowd of men who milled about the yard, talking loudly. In spite of the early hour, the taverns were full of boozing men and boisterous noise spilled out onto the street. No doubt, Sheriff John Johnson would have his hands full breaking up fist fights between drunken supporters of the different political factions. A cluster of Bell supporters hooted at a group of Breckenridge men across the square. A large assembly of Douglas men milled about, trading insults with both groups. Daniel threw up his hand and spoke, "Morn'n," as he and the boys walked between the groups, entered the courthouse and voted. After marking his paper ballots for Douglas, Pa turned and said, "Well boys, I've done my part to save the Union. I hope y'all done the same. We'll come back tomorrow and find out who won."

They agreed upon a time to meet at the wagon. While the boys wandered around town, Pa visited his brother-in-law, Postmaster, Robert C. David, on the north side of the square. David rented out upstairs rooms and used the ground floor as a post office. He was standing in front of a tall desk sorting mail into cubby holes when Pa walked in.

"Mornin' Robert."

David looked up, smiled and adjusted his wire rim spectacles. "Hello Daniel. What brings you by?"

"Just to pass the time and soak up some heat," Pa said, going directly to a wood heater to warm his hands. After exchanging information about the welfare of their respective families, David said, "This is a momentous day in our nation. What happens at the polls today will determine the direction of our country, perhaps for generations to come."

"I agree. I've done my part to save the Union by vot'n for Douglas," Pa replied. "He's not a southern man, but the only candidate that has a chance of defeat'n Lincoln. We can't abide with Lincoln. He's dead set on giving us a dose of medicine that the South won't swallow."

"Sometimes, I think there is no resolution to the problem," replied David. "I'd say that most people in Limestone County desire to remain in the Union, but a powerful and vocal minority are clamoring for secession. Our State Representative, Thomas Hobbs, and his planter friends won't be happy until Alabama secedes. Thank God there are level-headed men like Congressman George Smith Houston who ain't afraid to speak out for the Union."

"Well, it's outta our hands," Pa said.

The following morning, Pa was determined to return to Athens and hear the returns. Thomas remained home and Dudley drove him and the boys to town by wagon. Scores of buggies, wagons and horses were hitched around the frozen mud-rutted square and side streets. It looked like the entire county had turned out to hear the election returns. Dudley hitched the team in front of Uncle Robert and Aunt Sallie David's house, and with north wind to their backs, they walked to the courthouse. Pa learned that Stephen Douglas had carried Athens with 231 votes; Bell had received 165 and Breckenridge 136. There was hope. Then the county boxes began reporting. The hard drinking on election day had subsided as many of the boozers were long-faced and hung over.

Pa stood in the cold, his old black felt hat pulled down to his ears, hands jammed deep inside his pockets, and listened as the results were read. Stephen Douglas came in dead last with 325 votes. Breckenridge carried Limestone County with 522 votes followed by Bell with 368. Pa was disappointed, but he knew that Limestone County wouldn't decide the presidency. There was still no word on how Douglas was running nationwide.

The following day, Pa sat at home in front of a warm fire, despondent, while a crowd assembled at the southwest corner of the square in front of Mayor Press Tanner's place. They were anxious to hear how the Nation had voted. The telegraph wires from the North began humming down at the depot and the news they brought wasn't good. Lincoln had won!

Soon the telegraph wires were humming again, bringing news that the South Carolina Legislature was resolved to secede from the Union. Ten days later they did so.

The *Union Banner* advised its readers that, "every good citizen should suspend the formation of an opinion adverse to or in favor of his (Lincoln's) administration (and) the idle speculations of secessionists respecting the evils of his election... can only incite the pity and contempt of men of sense and nerve. We cannot but advise those who are opposed to secession to unite quietly but effectually on a policy that will show these secessionists that there is a power and influence which... will hold them... as aliens and foreigners."

Powerful men in Alabama – planters, slave holders and politicians – pushed Governor A.B. Moore of Perry County to call a Constitutional Convention to consider secession, which he did on December 6. He ordered that a special election be held on Christmas Eve to select delegates to attend a January meeting in Montgomery.

The Barksdales supported State Representative Thomas Joyce McClellan and

State Senator Dr. Joshua P. Coman, who ran on a platform of cooperation to seek a way for Alabama to remain in the union. Both were elected. Pa had known McClellan since he was a child living on Cane Creek in Lincoln County. "He was the first person I met when I rode into Lincoln County over thirty-seven years ago. He was just a boy then." He had confidence in McClellan's courage to oppose the secessionists. Dr. Coman, of course, had been his physician since moving to Limestone County.

Secession and war talk didn't hinder Ma from cooking a big New Year's dinner for her family. No matter what, they came first. Salted ham shoulders, great slabs of bacon and sacks of sausage hung in the smoke house and she cooked plenty of each to eat with her customary black-eyed peas. All of her children and grandchildren were present except for Robert Beasley, and wife, Lucy and lil' Molly. She was irritated they hadn't made the trip form their New Market home.

After dinner the men gathered around the fireplace, smoked and talked politics.

"I hope that McClellan and Doc Coman can stand up to the firebrands in Montgomery," Newby said.

Pa lit his pipe, took a deep pull and blew smoke. "I don't know about Doc Coman, but I have no doubt that McClellan can and will. He's solid as an oak. If he says he won't vote for secession, then he won't. I knew the family when they lived on Cane Creek. We moved here in '39 and the McClellans moved here about five years later and settled on Limestone Creek. Accommodations need to be reached with the North and Alabama must remain in the Union."

"That's like marrying a tomcat to gopher rat," said George Edward. "There are extremists in both camps. Abolitionists will never agree to anything less than complete emancipation of slaves."

"And the firebrand secessionists will never agree to anything!" exclaimed Pa. "They love slavery over the Union."

"Slavery is a blight upon our land. But it's legal and states do have the right to secede," George Edward said.

"Just because they have the right don't mean they should exercise it," Pa replied.

School teacher James Greer threw in his two cents worth. "This Nation is not an empire where all power is concentrated in a central government," he said. "We are a Union of free and independent states where all power resides, except for those few and limited powers specifically granted to the Federal Government. Alabama and every other state has the absolute right to withdraw from the Union."

The Barksdale family seemed as divided on the subject as was the nation.

---

Friday, January 11th, 1861.

Pa and the boys were preparing to slaughter more hogs just as soon as the weather warmed. If it was too cold the meat would freeze, too warm and it would ruin. The scalding vat was in place and ready for use. Dudley had gone to Athens to purchase salt. Pa and Thomas were in the crib shucking and shelling corn, readying for a trip to the grist mill, when Pa looked up and saw Dudley coming fast, the buggy wheels bouncing over ruts. Sweet was panting and lathered. Dudley jumped down.

"Pa, I just heard about it!" he said excitedly.

"Heard what?" asked Pa.

"Alabama has voted to secede!"

240

Pa, stunned, dropped the ear of corn. "How do you know?"

"I saw Uncle Robert at the post office and he said that the news come over the telegraph." Dudley said. "The Secession Ordinance passed this afternoon by 22 votes."

"Lord help us," said Pa shaking his head. "We were never given a chance to vote on the issue. Mark my word, there'll be trouble: The Holy Book says, 'He that troubleth his own house shall inherit the wind.'"

---

Athens,
Saturday, January 26, 1861.

Iron gray clouds hid the sinking sun and cold north wind whipped through the buggy and bit at Pa's face. The Athens-Fayetteville Pike was deeply rutted from a recent rain and the mud had frozen the ground causing the buggy wheels to wobble and bounce almost pitching Pa from his seat. Emanuel Isom pulled back on the reins and slowed, allowing other bouncing buggies, wagons and riders on horseback to pass.

"I ain't never seen this many folks headed to town on a late Saturday afternoon, especially with it being so cold," Pa said.

"Folks are stirred up and rightly so," replied Emanuel.

Pa blew hot breath on his hands. "When the sun sets it'll really get cold."

"I know it's a bad time to be out in the weather, but I knew you would want to show your support for the Union," Emanuel said. "We've got to show Thomas Hobbs and his slave-owning friends that we value the Union over slavery."

"I'm glad you dropped by and picked me up," said Pa. "But by crackies, if I don't freeze to death, this bouncing buggy will for sure kill my piles."

Emanuel chuckled. "Daniel, I've know you for nigh twenty-five years and you've proven to be a good friend. "I'm grateful the Lord sent you my way."

Pa looked over at Emanuel, his gray mutton chops fluttering in the cold wind. "Same here," he said.

When they reached the Methodist Church, one block north of the Courthouse, Marion Street was already clogged with buggies, wagons, carts and horses. Nearer to the public square, scores of people milled about. Music was playing.

"Drive over to Robert David's and park in front of his house," Pa said. "He won't mind."

At the David residence, Emanuel tethered his little mare to a metal hitching post and tied a feed bag filled with a handful of corn to her muzzle. Robert C. David stepped out the front door and, recognizing his brother-in-law and Isom, spoke: "Daniel, y'all come in and warm up."

"Much obliged, but me and Emanuel are going to the rally against secession. You com'n?"

"In spirit only," David replied. "Being Postmaster I need to pursue a neutral course – or at least make folks believe that."

"This isn't the time to sit and do nothing," Emanuel said. "It's the time to stand up and save our Union."

David dropped his head. "Y'all go on."

When Pa and Emanuel reached the square, people were still arriving from all directions. Darkness was fast approaching. Blazing pine torches bobbled among the crowd. Brass horns and drums played nearby. Shortly, a fife and drum struck up *Yankee*

*Doodle.* Pa and Emanuel pushed through the crowd toward the courthouse where a man mounted in the back of a wagon was speaking. Emanuel nodded to A.B. Herndon, Editor of *Athens Banner,* who was standing nearby taking notes.

"Who's that fella?"

"Green is his last name," replied Herndon. He's an Irish tinner. Some say he is an abolitionist. I don't know that. But he's a Union man through and through."

"It's easy to slander anyone," Emanuel said.

Green's voice was deep and full of Irish. "Working people, mechanics, craftsman, small farmers and just plain folks who don't earn their daily bread by the sweat of other men's labors are against secession," he said.

"Yes – yes!" the crowd roared.

"It's the silk stocking, slave-owning, plantation gentry that don't raise a hand except to feed themselves or whip a negro that has taken Alabama out of the Union. We won't have it. The Union now! The Union forever!"

The crowd took up the chant THE UNION NOW – THE UNION FOREVER."

"The delegates should be recalled and instructed to vote against secession," Green continued. "No money should be spent out of the Treasury to support its enforcement."

Green reached inside his great coat and retrieved a flag, which he unfolded and displayed to the crowd. "Thirty-three beautiful white stars representing the purity of our Union, and when the traitors who sold us out are brought to justice and the rebellious states restored to the Union, it will still be thirty-three stars."

The crowd roared its approval.

"Who will gain the honor and run up this glorious flag of our Union?" Green cried out.

"I will – I will," several shouted and pushed forward to grasp the flag. A young man tore the flag from Green's hands and ran toward the flag pole and attached it to a rope and hoisted it upward.'

"Long may it wave!" someone shouted.

"When the flag reached the top of the pole, a voice cried out: "Nail it to the pole!" "STAND ASIDE!" someone from behind bellowed. Pa turned around just as a column of men shouldering muskets marched through the crowd and took up a position on the courthouse yard, six men in front and six behind.

"A twenty-gun salute to the flag," someone yelled.

"A hundred or nothing," cried another voice.

The first line unshouldered their muskets and held them at ready.

"Aim!" they raised their barrels high over the waving flag.

"Firrre!"

"POW... POW... POW..." The firing was ragged as red flames leaped from the rifle muzzles. The crowd erupted with loud hurrahs while the first row of men knelt to reload, the second line fired and so it went until 100 shots had been fired.

"Music," Green said.

When the little band struck up *The Battle Cry of Freedom*, a spirited martial number, the crowd went wild with cheering.

"Maybe when the Secessionists see that people don't want to leave the Union – there will be accommodations made," Emanuel said to Pa.

"What's done is done," Pa replied.

"There's always hope," said Emanuel.

"Folks must fight for what's right. And the Union is right!"

There was a big commotion behind the crowd and people turned to look. "Make way – make way!" The assembly parted as a two-wheel "stick gig" pulled by a mule rolled up near the wagon where Green stood. In the passenger seat was a stuffed dummy dressed in ragged frock coat and top hat. A sign was pinned on the front: "WILLIAM YANCEY – ARCH TRAITOR."

"The arch traitor has paid us a visit," Green shouted. "What shall we do with him?"

"Burn him!" someone shouted. After the gig made a loop around the square, the stuffed dummy was hanged on the end of a pole and hoisted upward and burned in *effigie.*

"Burn Thomas Hobbs too. He's no different than Yancey," someone said.

Pa watched as flames licked around the material and finally burst into a hot fire when the straw ignited.

"Daniel, what would our ancestors who won our independence from Britain and gave us the Union think about it being destroyed?" Emanuel said.

"I've wondered the same," Pa replied quietly.

---

A couple of days later, Pa opened his copy of the *Union Banner* and read A.B. Herndon's account of the event.

"Yancey in pickle – On Saturday night last, Yancey, the notorious secessionist and agitator was publicly humiliated by a portion of the populace of Athens. A large crowd assembled on the public square: the honorable gentleman was rigged up a *la effigie*, escorted around town in an old fashioned stick gig and finally consumed by a more devouring element, than that, with which southern hearts are fired. These doings are unmistakable evidence of a feeling of a part of the public of Athens, and foreshadow a resistance to secession and its ring leaders, which we presume nothing else but a backing down from some of the recent acts of the Convention was served to eradicate. The idea of governmental oppression very justly served to rekindle the fire of patriotism in the working man's breast, in hence these outbursts of expression among the bone and sinew of our land."

Across Elk River, in the Lentzville community, folks gathered and threatened to secede from Alabama. Neighbors and family were split on the issue. Pa had been correct, there was bound to be trouble.

On February 4th, Congressman George Smith Houston rose on the floor of the U.S. House of Representatives and wept as he withdrew the Alabama Congressional Delegation. "The causes which, in the judgment of our state, rendered this action necessary, we need not relate," wrote Houston in a note to Speaker of the House. "It is sufficient to say that duty requires our obedience to her sovereign will, and that we shall return to our homes, sustain her action, and share the fortunes of the people." Then he departed by train to Athens. Two weeks later, Jefferson Davis was inaugurated President

243

of the Confederacy in Montgomery.

Pa knew that the good years were about to come to an end. Whether an individual was for secession or against it no longer mattered. The die had been cast. The only thing that mattered were the consequences.

"Matters are only gonna get worse," he told his family.

---

Athens.

Monday, March 4th.

Noisy citizens filled every seat and lined the walls of the courtroom on the top floor of the Limestone County Courthouse. Pa squeezed in and found standing room in the back. Looking around, he saw Emanuel Isom and his two younger brothers, William Stinnett and Matthew, standing nearby, a pensive look on their faces. He nodded at them and spoke. "How y'all?" They returned the nod.

Seated in front at counsel table were several well-dressed gentlemen, the most recognizable being former Congressman George Smith Houston, Luke Pryor and Jack Nicholas Malone. Seated on the opposite side of the room was State Representative Daniel Coleman, Dr. Jonathan McDonald and several other men Pa didn't recognize. The stated purpose of the meeting was to bring harmony to the different political voices about secession. Dr. McDonald stood and stepped to the front. The crowd grew quiet.

"Citizens, we have gathered here today for the purpose of harmonizing the various political complexions of the county," he said, "I call to the chair one of our own distinguished attorneys at law, Honorable Matthew Redus."

Redus, nattily dressed in a split-tail coat, rose, thanked everyone for attending, and then recognized State Representative Thomas H. Hobbs, a frail man of slight frame.

"Mr. Chairman," said Hobbs, rising to his feet, "I move that Honorable Daniel Coleman be appointed as secretary."

There being no other nominations, Coleman was appointed, and sat down at counsel table. Chairman Redus addressed the crowd. "The object of this meeting is to correct the impression that has gone abroad, that we are in a state of hostility at the actions at our convention recently held in Montgomery, and to try to harmonize the different elements of the county."

Afterwards, Hobbs was again recognized. "Mr. Chairman, I move the appointment of a five-member committee to draft a resolution to be presented to the meeting.

"Mr. Chairman, I further move the adoption of the following resolution," added Hobbs, unfolding a sheet of paper and commencing to read. There was so much coughing, shuffling of feet and creaking of wooden benches in the room that Pa couldn't hear everything that Hobbs read, but he did hear him say, "...that whatever may have been our individual preferences as to the proper method of resisting Black Republican rule, now that the state has taken action, we acknowledge that our allegiance is due her and that we will stand by and sustain her...."

The last part of the resolution supported the submission of the permanent Constitution of the Confederate States of America to ratification or rejection by the voters by the state.

John Nicholas Malone was recognized and took the floor and offered a second resolution. His voice was strong and carried well.

"WHEREAS, the people should be heard and their wishes obeyed, both in destroying and building up Governments. And whereas the Ordinance of Secession by which the State of Alabama was withdrawn from the Union was not submitted to them for consideration and the great principle of self-government thus ignored –" Cheered by the crowd, Malone waited until the assembly grew quiet and continued. "Therefore, resolved that the Constitution for the Confederate States of America should be referred to the voters of this State for ratification before it becomes binding on the people, and in the event of its reference to the State Convention this day assembled in Montgomery according to its own adjournment. Our delegates are to use all proper efforts to have it referred to the people for action. Resolved, that while we disapprove the means used and the policy adopted in passing the Ordinance of Secession, yet, as the State of Alabama, has by that act been made to assume a position outside of the Union of the United States, we declare our purpose to assist in her defense against force or coercion on the part of the Federal Government, sharing the responsibilities and dangers of our fellow-citizens. At the same time we avow our desire for a reconstruction of the government in the event the non-slaveholding states will give us proper and satisfactory constitutional guarantees. Resolved, that we approve the acts of our delegates, Coman & McClellan, touching the Ordinance of Secession and thereby avow our confidence in them as our representatives."

"No!" someone shouted.

Pa agreed with most of Malone's resolution, but not with the part approving Coman and McClelland signing the secession ordinance.

After reading the resolutions, Chairman Redus appointed a committee of Dr. J. N. McDonald, Thomas H. Hobbs, Dr. C. J. Massenburg, E. W. Grigsby and Edward Hatchett, Esquire to consider them and hopefully reach a consensus. Hobbs then moved that John Nicholas Malone be added to the committee, which was done. After the committee departed to consider the resolutions the room erupted in loud debate. Pa leaned against the wall and kept his counsel as, the committee members filed in and Chairman McDonald raised his hand for quiet.

"Pleeease. Gentlemen, may I have your attention? I am pleased to report that the committee has unanimously adopted the two resolutions offered by Major Hobbs and also the third resolution by Major Malone."

Loud talking erupted. Chairman McDonald raised his voice: "I urge you to seriously consider these resolutions –"

A man jumped to his feet and yelled, "Why weren't the citizens of Limestone County given the opportunity to vote on secession? The majority of people don't want to secede. It's only the planters and politicians who want it – like Major Hobbs."

Dr. McDonald tried to quiet the crowd. "Please, let's remain orderly and civil," he said, almost begging, then recognized Malone.

Malone rose and walked to the front of the judge's bench, grasping the lapels of his coat with both hands. "Gentlemen, what is done is done," he said. "Whether the people should have been given the opportunity to vote is past history – it's water over the dam –"

"RECALL!" someone shouted.

"–our beloved Alabama," continued Malone, "has left the Union and it becomes our solemn duty to support her during the crisis that looms ahead. What has been done cannot be changed."

"HOUSTON!" someone shouted.

245

"We want to hear Houston!" exclaimed one of the Isom brothers.

"HOUSTON… HOUSTON… HOUSTON…" the crowd chanted.

George Smith Houston, at least six feet tall and tending to fatness, nattily attired in a dark suit, fluffy white shirt and black cravat, had been sitting quietly, but he rose to his feet and approached the jury railing. The most striking physical characteristic about him, Pa decided, was his large, partially bald head. The crowd fell silent. He spoke quietly, but eloquently, for several minutes, thanked the citizens of Limestone County for permitting him to serve in Congress and told of his deep sadness when he heard that Alabama had seceded from the Union and how it became his duty to withdraw the Alabama Delegation from Congress. "I confess to you that my heart was never heavier nor my eyes wetter when I learned that my beloved Alabama had left the Union.

"I speak against these resolutions now before you. They do not say enough. I want a resolution that says if the North will give us proper guarantees the Union will be reconstructed. The South cannot sustain itself. We have neither the industry nor the resources –"

"Which side are you on?" someone yelled.

"If you do not yet know, sir, I despair of enlightening you, and will permit you to grope in the dark," replied Houston.

Loud applause and cheering. After speaking at length, Houston sat down.

"PRYOR! LET US HEAR PRYOR," someone yelled.

Luke Pryor, of average height with light hair and beard, took to the floor and spoke against the proposed resolutions and against the newly-established Confederate Government. "It is a government without the consent of the governed," he said.

Loud cheering.

Thomas Hobbs again took the floor and spoke eloquently in defense of the resolution. "It is the highest compliment that General Houston and Mr. Pryor have addressed the meeting with lengthy speeches and found no objection to the report," he said. "My only object is conciliation and harmony – to throw oil upon troubled waters. I love my state and have served her proudly in the past. It is my sincere hope that we can obtain harmony."

Houston jumped to his feet. "I strongly object to the word 'proper' in your resolution. Your side, Major Hobbs first brought up the reconstruction subject and your President Davis and his newspaper have taken bold action against it –"

"State what position your paper and your President took?" asked Hobbs, followed by laughter and cheering.

Houston looked Hubbs squarely in the eye. "Sir, do you insinuate that I am a follower of Lincoln?" he asked. "You have done something unworthy of yourself."

"I make no insinuation," replied Hobbs. "I only ask a question."

It appeared to Pa that a row was about to erupt between Hobbs and Houston. Luke Pryor, Dr. McDonald and Malone jumped to their feet and rushed between the two men to keep them apart. The meeting adjourned without voting on the resolutions. Nothing was settled.

Pa exited the courtroom with the Isoms and they walked outside into the brisk March wind.

"Look how proudly she waves," Emanuel Isom, said looking up at the flagpole where the Nation's symbol was stiff in the breeze. "It breaks my heart that our dear old flag will soon be taken down and replaced by a Rebel one."

"I suppose it's just a matter of time," said Pa.

"Daniel, mine and your ancestors paid a high price in blood, hardship and fortune to build this Union, but hotheads won't be content until it's destroyed." His eyes teared. "It's an awful thing they're doing, may God have mercy on all of us."

"What are you going to do, Mister Barksdale?" asked Matthew Isom.

"What's done is done and I can't change it," Pa replied. "I intend to raise cotton and corn and take care of my family and mind my own business, just like I've always done."

"Somewhere down the line you'll have to choose," Emanuel said.

"I sure hope it don't come to that."

---

Athens.

Early March, 1861.

The muffled "clop-clop" of Sweet's hooves striking the dusty street and the creaking of buggy wheels were the only sounds, except for a rooster crowing somewhere in the distance. It was early morning and a weekday and the citizens of Athens had yet to come alive. Pa looked to the west where most bad weather comes from and saw ominous clouds building. Spring always brought the unpredictable storms. Ordinarily, he wouldn't have been in Athens on a weekday and, especially this early in the morning, but he had broken a point on the plow which he needed to plant Irish potatoes. Ma said the sign was right to plant now and he didn't argue with Ma about the signs. He smiled to himself. She had to be the most hard-headed, strong-willed female that God put on Earth – not to mention, she was a wonderful mother and awfully fine wife. So, he did what she said.

The black buggy rocked and swayed up Marion Street toward the square and when he came within sight of the courthouse, he looked up and saw Stars and Stripes stiff in the early morning breeze. A pretty sight. Alabama had left the Union in January, but no one had taken down the "old flag," which was just dandy with him.

Some folks were saying that Athens was a "damned Union hole" and ought to be "sunk into hell" and that the flag should be taken down. Folks were stirred up on both sides of the issues. Other than that, Athens was pretty much like it had been before secession – quiet and far removed from the conflict.

After purchasing a plow point and a twist of store-bought tobacco at S & P Tanner's and Sons, he ambled over to the post office. Perhaps a letter from the McElroy's had arrived from Fayetteville. That would tickle Ma to death.

He peeked through the dusty window and saw his brother in law, Robert C. David, sorting mail into cubby holes of an upright desk. He pushed open the squeaking door and entered. David looked up and over his wire-rimmed spectacles and smiled. "Well-well, if it isn't my favorite brother0in-law. "How are you Daniel?"

"I forget."

David chuckled.

Pa gestured with his head toward the courthouse. "I see that Old Glory is still flying. Ain't she pretty?"

"Yeah, but it's just a matter of time before some hot-head tears it down. That'll set off trouble."

"Who are you working for now? Lincoln or Jefferson Davis?" asked Pa.

247

"Both 'til I'm told differently," David replied. "I'm going to concentrate on getting the mail out and try not worry about which government I work for."

"Any mail for us?" Pa asked.

"Nope, sorry."

The squeaking front door caught their attention. A well-dressed gentleman who appeared to be about 30 years old entered and spoke to David.

"Captain David sir, I haven't seen you in several years. I trust you are doing well."

"Goodness, Judge Hundley. I heard that you were practicing law in Chicago."

"That I was sir, that is, until Alabama seceded. Came back home to Hundley Hill to take care of my aging parents and operate the plantation."

David introduced Pa, and then asked Hundley: "What can I do for you?"

Hundley produced a letter from inside his coat and handed it to David. "I'd like to mail this to Chicago."

David collected the postage due and stamped the envelope.

"Sirs, have a good day," Hundley said and departed.

"Who is that dandy?" Pa asked.

"Daniel Robinson Hundley," replied David. "He was born and raised near Triana and went off to Harvard and got a law degree and set up practice in Chicago. His father, Dr. John Hundley, is getting on in years. Good folks. Judge Hundley is a nice fellow. Smart too. Wrote a book called *Social Relations in the Southern States*. It's his answer to *Uncle Tom's Cabin* by that Yankee woman."

"Lawyer, huh," quipped Pa.

"Yep, and they say a darn good one."

"Hmmm, that's all we need, another lawyer." Pa said. "Every time I get around a lawyer, something bad happens to me."

---

Monday evening, April 1.

It was Dudley's 22$^{nd}$ birthday and Ma was using the opportunity to feed her family. While she and the women were busy in the kitchen cooking supper, Pa and the menfolk were seated in the back yard, smoking and enjoying a warm spring breeze. In the distance whippoorwills called and across the road at Cove Springs frogs croaked.

"Sure is a fine evening," Pa remarked. "So peaceful."

"Yeah, we had better enjoy it while it lasts," replied George Edward.

"Whether secession was right or wrong, and I believe it was dead wrong," Pa said, "the issue has been settled. It's in the past and we must look to the future."

"The next move is up to Lincoln and the Black Republicans," said James Newby. "We have no voice in the decision they make."

"Don't leave out Jeff Davis and the Confederate Government down in Montgomery," added James Greer. "There's no telling what some of those hotheads might do and we have no more influence with them than we do with Lincoln."

"Pa, what do you think will happen?" asked Dudley.

Thomas leaned forward and cupped his ear trying to follow the conversation. "Speak up."

Pa reflected for a moment. "I wish I had a crystal ball," he said. "Somewhere down the line there's gonna be fight'n. The Abolitionists won't be satisfied until every

248

slave is free and the slave owners ain't gonna give up valuable property. People will fight to protect their property. They always have and they always will."

"I'm ready," said Dudley.

"You don't own any property, brother," deadpanned George Edward. Everyone chuckled.

"You know what I mean," replied Dudley. "If war comes, I'm enlisting."

"I wouldn't be too eager to get myself killed," Pa said. "Let's hope that war don't come."

"One Southern man can whip three Yankees any day," said Dudley. "We can out fight 'em any day of the week."

"Why can't they just leave us be?" Pa asked, shaking his head. "We ain't bothering 'em. Why'd they have to bother us?"

"They won't leave us be," said George Edward.

"Your grandpas on both sides of the family fought in the Revolution against the tyranny of King George," Pa said. "And so did yours," he added, looking at his son-in-law, James Newby. "I wonder what they would say if they could speak today? Which side would they be on?"

Before anyone could respond, Cal stepped out the back door and yelled, "SUPPER TIIIMMMMME!"

Eleven days later, General P.G.T. Beauregard fired on Ft. Sumter at Charleston, South Carolina. Talking had ceased. President Lincoln called for 75,000 volunteers to put down "what he termed a "rebellion."

# 21 | INSURRECTION

Near Mooresville, Alabama.

Saturday, May 18, 1861.

Daniel Robinson Hundley was still reeling from news delivered by a member of the Triana Vigilance Committee. Their worst fear had materialized. Slaves in southeast Limestone County were planning an insurrection.

He gazed out the window of "Hundley Hill," the large frame house his father had built on a gentle knoll north of the Tennessee River, and watched the rider disappear into the lengthening shadows of twilight. Hundley was saddle worn and tired, but this was no time for rest. Tonight he would patrol. Before supper, he wrote in his diary:

> "May 18 Saturday. Startling! I just learned that a vigilance committee
> in Triana has ferreted out a most hellish insurrectionary plot among the
> slaves and in consequence I expect to go out patrolling tonight – a thing
> I never did before. I've ridden about 30 miles today but I do not expect
> to close my eyes tonight."

After having supper with his wife and parents, he took his father into the study and told him the disturbing news. Dr. John Henderson Hundley was 65 years old and the master of Hundley Hill, a red land cotton plantation that sloped off toward the river a mile or more to the south.

"Who are the leaders of this insurrection?" asked his father.

"We don't know yet, but we'll find out."

"Surely, our negroes wouldn't be a part of this devilish plot," said his father, brows wrinkled.

"I don't think so, but we must be vigilant, nevertheless."

Afterwards, Hundley dressed in hunting garb, pulled on riding boots and lifted a revolver from his desk drawer. It was an 1860, 44-caliber Colt "Army" revolver that fired six rounds. After determining that it was fully loaded he slid it behind his wide leather belt and walked out to where a Negro held a saddled horse. He mounted and rode off at a gallop into the darkness.

Hundley was a 29-year-old lawyer, a graduate of Harvard Law School. After marrying his cousin, Mary Hundley of Virginia, they settled in Chicago where he practiced law and authored *Social Relations in the Southern States*, considered by some to be a response to *Uncle Tom's Cabin*. Following Alabama's secession on January 11th, they came to Limestone County to live with his aging parents.

He knew the countryside like the back of his hand. As a boy, he had fished the river, hunted rabbit, deer and wild turkey in the woods and trapped in Beaver Dam Swamp. He rode east a short distance over into Madison County where he rendezvoused with members of the Triana Vigilance Committee. He knew them all – Fletcher Henderson, Harry Pemberton, Egbert Hargrove, Sykes Moore and Miles Monroe. They patrolled the area without incident until approximately 2:30 a.m.

"I see someone!" exclaimed Henderson.

"Where?"

"He ducked into the woods," replied Henderson.

"Get 'im!" yelled another.

They spurred their mounts forward. Moonlight cast a soft glow on something beside a tree. The men rode up fast. It was a Negro man trying to hide.

"Who are you? What are you doing here?" demanded Henderson, drawing his revolver. "Step out here in the moonlight."

The Negro stepped from behind the tree, trembling with fear.

"I asked, who are you?"

"I'se Ben and I'se belongs to Massa Tate."

"He's from the Tate plantation," declared Hundley and turned to the Negro and asked, "What are you doing out here this time of night?"

"I'se lost."

"You're under arrest," said Henderson. "Bind 'im."

After two men had tied his arms behind his back, Henderson cocked his pistol and pointed it at the Negro's head. "Now tell us, who were you going to meet?"

The Negro fell to his knees sobbing. "Lawd, don't shoot me massa, please...."

"Talk."

"Mistuh Lincoln, he gwineuh set us free."

"Who told you that?"

"Parson Mudd, be da one who say it."

---

Hundley arrived back at Hundley Hill early morning, exhausted, and sleepy. Before he took a nap, he wrote in his diary.

"May 19 - Sunday. Returned home just after daylight. Was gone nearly all night, but owing to a change of plans only succeeded in arresting one Negro. We arrested him about half past two o'clock."

Hundley didn't sleep for long. Action was needed. He spent Sunday afternoon meeting with other planters in the neighborhood, planning a course of action.

"May 20 - Monday. Today I became a member of the Committee of Public Safety to investigate into the insurrectionary movement of the slaves in the neighborhood of my father's residence. We have punished several and the testimony elicited is very startling. The whole servile population appeared to be disaffected and the falsehoods everywhere pass current among them.

May 21 – Tuesday. Our committee continues its labors to date, and the developments are utterly confounding. It seems that the Negroes have concluded that Lincoln is going to free them all and that they are everywhere making preparations to aid him when he makes his appearance.

May 22 – Wednesday. Engaged all day in the labors of the vigilance committee. Similar committees are being organized in every neighborhood.

May 23- Thursday. So far as our investigations have not extended, we are led to believe that Peter Mudd, Andrew Green and Nicholas Moore, slaves, and one or two free Negroes, aided by base white men, are the leaders in the proposed servile insurrection."

Friday morning, Hundley and the Committee of Public Safety rode to the Rice Plantation at nearby Mooresville. Information gathered indicated it was a hot bed for insurrection. Bentley, the overseer, had the Negroes assembled near a small office building where the committee examined each one in private. The first slave brought in was a young female. Her eyes darted around the room nervously at the five white men who sat silently staring at her.

"What's your name gal?" demanded Harry Pemberton, a committee member.

"I'se Ann."

"We know there are those among you who are talking about freedom. You have heard that talk, of course."

"Yassuh."

"Who was talking about it?"

"I'se can't remember," she replied her voice quavering with fear.

"TELL US NOW!" ordered committee member Egbert Hargrove, slamming his fist against the desk. "Be quick about it."

She began to sob and wail. "They tole me nots to tell."

"Who told you?" asked Hundley.

"Big Joe be the one."

After further questioning she was dismissed and the overseer ushered in Big Joe, a large, muscular, barefoot and sullen Negro about thirty years old.

"We know that you are involved in a plot against white people," said Hundley.

"Nahsuh. I'se ain't done no such thang, I just repeat what someone else say."

"Who said it?"

"He be a free man named Jacob. He come over here one night when de white folks done gone to bed."

Committee members leaned forward listening intently. "What did he say?" asked Hundley.

"He say Mistuh Lincoln gonna come down here and free all de black folks and de black folks will hav'ta help 'em out."

"Help by doing what?"

Big Joe dropped his head.

"Tell us."

"Kill dey masters." The men looked at each other in disbelief as color drained from their faces.

"Who else was at the meeting?" asked Hundley.

"Well ol' Stubby he be dere and Jake... and Zeke."

"Why didn't you report this meeting to your master?" demanded Hundley.

"Dunno."

"What did Stubby, Jake and Zeke say?"

"Zeke and ol' Stubby say dey would kill."

"What about Jake?"

"Nassuh, he didn't say dat."

252

Big Joe was immediately arrested and shackled. Zeke was brought in, but was sullen and silent and was arrested and shackled. Jake couldn't add anything to the testimony of Big Joe.

"Bring in Stubby," said Hundley to the overseer. A few minutes passed and he returned empty-handed.

"Sir, no one has seen him since last night."

Following the interrogation of the slaves, the committee discussed what action to take.

"Big Joe should be tried," said Hundley.

The committee agreed.

"And Zeke also," added Hundley.

"Definitely," said one and all agreed.

"I suggest that Jake be whipped," said Pemberton. "It's lawful and will set a good example for the rest of the Negroes to cease this devilish nonsense."

Bentley the overseer had Jake's shirt removed and shackled him to a whipping post in the back yard. Bentley unfurled a bull whip. The slaves watched in silence as Bentley drew back the leather whip and brought it forward, the tip end tearing away Jake's flesh. Initially, Jake was silent, gritting his teeth and recoiling as the leather tore his skin. Blood mixed with sweat flowed down his muscular back. The pain became too intense. He screamed and begged, "Mercy – mercy – Lord have mercy!" Bentley was proficient with his whip, tearing and ripping skin until Jake's back was crisscrossed with bloody whelps. After 40 lashes Jake was untied from the post and he collapsed to the ground. Two other males who admitted they knew something about the plot were also whipped. "Let this be a warning to y'all," said Bentley, coiling his whip. "Now get back to work!"

Afterwards, the committee reassembled in the office. "What do you know about Stubby?" Hundley asked Bentley.

"He's been here a lot longer than me. I heard that the Rices bought him back in the early 1820s, sold 'im to Dan'l Barksdale, then bought 'im back several years ago."

"He must be rather old," commented a committee member.

"It's hard to say, but I'd guess he's about 60. He's a bad 'un too. I tell you he's been whipped several times but it never done any good. I don't know why Mrs. Rice didn't stay rid of 'im."

"We need to locate him," said Hundley.

"May 25 – Saturday. By invitation, members of the several committees met with Triana committee in Triana. This committee has already hung one free Negro named Jacobs and today had an old English abolitionist who for lack of proper evidence was sent to Huntsville jail to await the future action of the committee."

———————————

It was Thursday near midnight when Stubby eased from bed and pulled on his well-worn floppy hat. Lil' Mary roused and sat up and blinked.

"Where you gwine dis time a night?"

"Shhh, hush woman. I gwine on import'n bizness. Go back to sleep."

"You gonna be back by daylight?"

"Naw, I be gone for good."

"Run away?"

"Freedom woman. I gwine be free."

"When Mistuh Bentley finds you'se gone he'll put de hounds on yo trail and when he catches you he'll whup de hide off yo back."

"He ain't gwina catch me unless you tell. Now hush."

Stubby cracked the cabin door and peered into the moonlit night. It was warm and near perfect for his mission. He walked quietly past a row of slave cabins and followed the tree line around fields where cotton had recently been planted and continued on toward Beaver Dam Swamp. Once in the swamp, he figured the tracking hounds wouldn't be able to follow his trail. Not many people dared venture into the swamp at night since it was known to be a haven for cottonmouth moccasins. He found a spot of dry ground and sat down on a rotting log, slapped at mosquitoes, listened to croaking frogs and waited. Pretty soon he would be a free man. And he was willing to do whatever it required, including killing white folks. His hair was grizzly white and his old joints ached most of the time, but he wasn't too old to fight for his freedom. Nawsuh. He couldn't remember when he hadn't been worked like a mule. He didn't know who his parents were or where he was born. He did remember when old man McElroy bought him in Fayetteville, Tennessee, when he was a young man and brought him to Athens to build the courthouse and then sold him to Massa Rice. A slave trader sold him to Daniel Barksdale who sold him and he eventually ended up back at the Rice Plantation and had been there ever since.

He would hide in the swamp and meet Parson Mudd.

At daybreak, he walked deeper into the swamp, wading through brackish water and scaring away cottonmouth moccasins by beating the water with a long stick. He located a dry spot and sat down on the ground, nibbled on a hunk of cornbread and waited for nightfall. Pretty soon, he would be a free man. Mistuh Lincoln was coming down and freeing all the darkies. Stubby figured he was no different from white folks. Why should he have to work like a mule and be treated like a dog? White folks say they are fighting for freedom. Why shouldn't he do the same? If a man wanted to be free, he had to fight for it.

After darkness had gathered he sloshed through the knee-deep water and around banyan trees toward the rendezvous point. Frogs croaked and crickets chirped. Approaching a tiny clearing, he saw lantern light, then three men huddled together, peering through the darkness looking his way.

"It be ol' Stubby," he said with a low voice.

The men relaxed as he splashed out of the water onto dry ground. He knew Andrew Green and Nicholas Moore.

"Dis be Parson Mudd," said Green whispering. "He be get'n de darkies together for our freedom."

They sat on a log and lowered the wick of the lantern and spoke in hushed tones.

"De committee of safety be prowl'n everywhere," said Mudd. "We has to be careful. But dere is good news. Mistuh Lincoln gonna free de slaves."

"When's he gonna do dat?" asked Stubby.

"Any day," said Mudd. "But we has to help 'im."

"How we gonna help?"

"We need folks we can trust on every plantation and when Mistuh Lincoln come, we rise up like Samson against de Philistines and slay our masters. Den we's be free."

"Are you shore Mistuh Lincoln be coming?" asked Stubby.

"He say he will and he done sent out an army to free us. He'll come alright," said Mudd. "We has to be ready to rise up."

"We's don't have guns," said Stubby. "How we gonna kill our masters?"

"Chop off dey heads with an axe or use a –"

"Sshhhh, I hear sum'in," whispered Green.

"I'se hear it too," said Stubby. "Turn off de lantern."

Moore put out the light and they sat quietly and perfectly still in the darkness, afraid to move. Shafts of moonlight filtered through the tops of the tall banyan trees bathing the swamp with a dull glow. From the darkness came more sounds. A horse snorted.

"I'se scared," whispered Green.

"Sshhssh, don't twitch a muscle," said Mudd.

"I'se get'n outta here," said Moore and jumped to his feet and ran splashing through the swamp.

"I SEE 'EM!" someone yelled from the darkness. "RUN 'EM DOWN."

"There must be others there. Circle around," someone shouted.

Horses splashing through water grew louder.

"I'se gett'n outta here too," said Stubby.

"Don't move and they won't see us," whispered Mudd. "De Lord, he protect us."

Green jumped and ran.

"THERE GOES ANOTHER ONE!" a horseman shouted. "CATCH 'EM."

Horses splashed through the swamp, drawing closer. Stubby was frozen by fear. He panicked. At first his legs wouldn't work. Then flight took over and he bolted into the swamp, wild with fear, sucking air and making animal grunting sounds as he fled through the maze of bushes and banyan trees. Loud splashing behind him. Coming closer. Horses. He ran as fast as his old legs would carry him; his heart about to explode. Faster – faster. He turned his head and looked behind him. He didn't see a horse. "Hallelujah, de Lord has delivered me." He heard a cracking noise followed by excruciating head pain, then nothingness.

"I got one of them," someone yelled. "The devil run into a tree and damn near killed himself."

Overseer Bentley dismounted, pistol drawn, and reached down and pulled Stubby to his feet.

"It's ol' Stubby," he said, looking up at Hundley.

"Bind him securely," replied Hundley.

The other Negroes fled into the swamp.

Dawn was cracking Saturday morning when the committee arrived at the Rice Plantation with Stubby in shackles. Threatened with a severe whipping, he reluctantly gave the name of Parson Peter Mudd, owned by Dr. John Pickett, as the leader of insurrection. After breakfast, Hundley announced that they should impanel a jury and try Stubby. Overseer Bentley was assigned the responsibility of finding "twelve good and lawful men" all of whom had to be slave owners. After a jury was impaneled and sworn, the trial commenced in the shade of a large oak tree. Hundley acted as prosecutor.

255

Jake was called as the first witness and testified that he had attended a meeting where Stubby was present.

"What did you hear Stubby say?" asked Hundley.

"He say Mistuh Lincoln wuz com'n down to free de black folks and we had to rise up and hep 'im."

"Did he say he would help?"

"Yassuh."

"How?"

"Kill dey masters."

Hundley gave Stubby the opportunity to cross examine. No response.

Next, Lil' Mary was called. "Are you Stubby's wife?"

"Yassuh, we jumped de broom."

"Where were you when Stubby ran away?"

"I'se in bed asleep. He woke me rattl'n around search'n for his ole hat. I say's 'Stubby, where in de world are you gwine.' He say he was gwine to freedom. I'se tole him if he was caught that Mistuh Bentley would whip de hide off his back. He tole me to hush up and I did."

Following the testimony of several other witnesses Hundley rested his case. He informed Stubby that he had the right to call witnesses, cross examine and testify in his own behalf but he couldn't be forced to do so. At the conclusion of the evidence Hundley charged the jury with the law of the case.

"Gentlemen, the defendant has been charged with insurrection and rebellion against his master in violation of the Act of 1812. If convicted, it can carry a death sentence if, you, the jury so decide." He collected his thoughts and continued.

"In all felony charges such as this the law provides that it must be presented to the Grand Jury to determine if probable cause exists that a crime has been committed. However, these are exigent times and every dot and tittle of the law cannot be adhered to. I have no doubt that a grand jury would have indicted the defendant.

"Now it is your duty to determine the facts. Has enough evidence been presented to convince you beyond a reasonable doubt and to a moral certainty that the defendant is guilty of insurrection and rebellion? The burden of proof is on the prosecution to convince you of that. The fact the defendant offered no evidence and did not testify is not to be taken into consideration of his guilt or innocence as the Constitution provides that a person charged with a crime is not compelled to testify.

"Although I acted as prosecutor, I make no comment on the evidence. It is up to you twelve citizens to determine if the defendant is guilty beyond a reasonable doubt and to a moral certainty of the crime so charged." Hundley continued for several minutes. At the conclusion, he looked over at Stubby. "Do you wish to say anything?" Stubby didn't reply.

"Now retire somewhere to consider the evidence," said Hundley to the jury. "When you have reached a verdict, which must be unanimous, let us know."

The jury walked off several hundred feet and disappeared behind a building. Shortly, they returned.

"Gentlemen, have you reached a verdict?" Hundley asked.

"Yes, we have," replied the foreman.

"What is your verdict?"

"Guilty as charged and we recommend hanging."

256

"Is your verdict unanimous?" asked Hundley.

"Yes," they said in unison and nodded in agreement.

"Will the defendant please stand," said Hundley. Stubby strained to get to his feet, his hands and ankles heavy with the weight of the iron shackles.

"Do you have anything to say before I pronounce sentence?" asked Hundley.

"Nassuh, 'cept all I ever wanted wuz to be free like de white folks."

"Very well, a jury of twelve good and lawful men has found you guilty of insurrection and rebellion as charged, and recommended that you be hanged by your neck until dead."

Stubby dropped his head. "Massah, don't hang me. I ain't done nut'n but talk, I ain't hurt nobody."

Hundley looked at the overseer. "Mr. Bentley, the defendant has been duly convicted. "Carry out the sentence, sir."

"With pleasure." Bentley threw a rope over a low-hanging limb on the big oak tree; unlocked the ankle shackles and with assistance, heaved Stubby on horseback, and threw a noose over his head.

"MERCY LORD, HAVE MERCY!" Stubby cried out.

Bentley slapped the horse's flank hard. It bolted from beneath Stubby. He screamed, choked and grunted. The assembled Negroes cried out in anguish, "Lordy-Lordy, mercy." Stubby kicked his legs in the air as if trying to find something on which to plant his feet. His neck stretched like rubber, eyes bulged. Then his body grew still and gently swung like a pendulum on a clock.

The Negroes murmured, praying.

"Ol' Stubby finally free," said Lil Mary.

Bentley faced the Negroes. "This is what happens when you break the law. Now get back to work."

Hundley recorded committee progress in his diary.

"May 26 – Sunday. They hung one Negro of Mrs. Rice's slaves in Mooresville yesterday. A jury of twelve men, selected by his overseer, was allowed to hear the evidence against him, and afterwards, bring in their verdict – it being the desire of the citizens to preserve the spirit of the law at all events, although it may be necessary in these exciting and dangerous time to override the letter thereof.

May 27 – Monday. Our committee renewed its labors again today and we had a very exciting session owing to the fact that Dr. John Pickett had run off Peter Mudd, one of the ring leaders in the conspiracy. We sent our committeemen after the fugitive and were informed by telegraph that the police had secured him in Memphis.

May 28 – Tuesday. Our committee today visited the plantation of Mr. Sam Moore. On yesterday, Andrew Green, one of the instigators and leaders of the conspiracy, was hung at Triana. He had made a partial confession.

May 30 – Thursday. We had an exciting time in the committee today.

257

First, we tried a free Negro, who was sentenced to the penitentiary for life. We then tried Parson Peter Mudd. Peter was proven to be one of the principal conspirators, but the influence of his master's family in his behalf was great – however, he was found guilty by the jury and was hung about half an hour after sundown.

May 31 – Friday. We met the Triana committee again today. Two Negroes were tried but the final decision in their case was postponed for one month. In the meantime they were to remain in the Huntsville jail. We also tried the case of Bob Williams – white man. He was given until Christmas to settle up his affairs and leave the country.

June 9 – Sunday. The committee seems satisfied with their labors thus far and by apparent consent are doing nothing more about the rumored insurrection."

# 22 | WAR

Athens.

Three days earlier, Thursday morning, June 6, 1861.

Dudley Barksdale hitched his little sorrel mare, Sweet, to the buggy. Ordinarily, he would have been plowing cotton or corn this time of day, but the ground was still wet from a recent rain. Cotton grew fast on these hot days and cool nights, but so did weeds and grass.

But today, he wasn't worried about crab grass. He was going to Athens. Ma wanted to visit Aunt Sallie David for a spell while Pa bought tobacco, salt and plow points. Sisters Cal and Cornelia were going shopping for cloth and buttons to make new dresses. It would be a fun trip. If it had rained countywide, Athens would be crowded.

He pulled the buggy to the rear of the house where ol' Luther was barking and wagging his tail, no doubt thinking that a coon hunting trip was imminent. Cal and Cornelia came out the back door, wearing their best dresses and bonnets, followed by Pa pulling on his old black felt hat. A horse fly was buzzing Sweet's rump and she was stamping and swishing her tail, anxious to get under way.

"Where's Ma?" asked Dudley.

"She's sacking up some apples and peaches for Sallie," said Pa.

Shortly Ma emerged, straightening her bonnet and carrying a cloth sack filled with fresh fruit. They squeezed into the buggy.

Dudley clucked to Sweet and the buggy creaked out onto the muddy Fayetteville Pike and headed to Athens. Ol' Luther, disappointed, ambled back to his shady spot beneath the oak tree.

"Lotta folks going to town," remarked Ma, noticing other buggies on the road.

"It rained last night," Pa said.

"I know that," she said, mildly irritated. "I mean there are more than the usual number of folks going to town after a good rain."

"Capt'n Hobbs' company is leaving today for the war, Ma," said Dudley.

"Now how do you know that?" she asked.

"His company marched past the house Monday on the way to Clem Spring to encamp, then yesterday, they marched back headed to Athens," said Dudley. "I hollered at Eppa Fielding and asked why they were returning to Athens and he said they were shipping out today for the war. I sure wish I was with 'em."

"If Eppa Fielding wants to go off and get killed that's his business," Ma said. "I don't want my boys fight'n. The Yankees ain't bother'n us. Anyway, it's a pretty day, let's talk about something besides war."

The weather was warm and balmy with only a few clouds. Honeysuckle was blooming and their sweetness filled the air. They crossed Swan Creek, and then passed "The Cedars" where Jim Henry Malone lived. "That's the prettiest place in the county," said Ma, gazing at the large two-story frame house that sat back in a grove of cedar trees.

"Just as soon as I make a decent cotton crop, I'm gonna build you a house just like it, only larger," Pa said with a twinkle in his eye.

"Huh," harrumphed Ma. "You spend all of our money on tobacco."

"Ma's sure feeling her oats this morning," said Dudley, laughing.

"Young'un, hush your mouth and mind your own business," she replied and playfully swatted him on the back on the head. "Just because you're twenty-two years old don't mean that I won't give you a switch'n.''

The girls giggled. "And that goes for y'all too," she said. It was all in good humor, of course. Everyone was happy to be going to town. Sweet trotted the three miles to Athens and was lathered when they tethered her in front of Uncle Robert and Aunt Sallie David's house a block north of the square.

Ma and the girls disappeared inside the house, while Pa and Dudley walked up town.

Scores of carriages, buggies, wagons and horses were hitched around the square. Streets were muddy and cut with deep ruts. The plank sidewalks were crowded with people, laughing and seemingly in no hurry.

Pa and Dudley walked down to Samuel Tanner & Company Mercantile on the square. Pa preferred stopping there first and, if he couldn't find what he wanted, he usually went to Peterson Tanner & Son Dry Goods on the northwest corner or George Mason's Store on the northeast corner. As usual, several men were sitting on a wooden bench chewing tobacco, smoking pipes and whittling, engaged in animated conversation.

"Morn'n," said Pa. "How y'all?"

They briefly looked up. "Howdy Mr. Barksdale," replied a fellow.

Samuel Tanner, the proprietor and Athens first Mayor appeared behind the counter. "Good morn'n Mr. Barksdale – Dudley. Can I help y'all?"

"I need a little salt and some tobacco and plow points if you have 'em," said Pa.

Shortly, Tanner returned with the order and plunked it on the countertop and tallied the charges in his head. Pa handed him a Confederate note.

"What's got 'em excited?" asked Pa, looking at the huddled men.

"The slave insurrection," said Tanner. "You didn't hear about it?"

Pa was momentarily stunned, "Nooo."

"Yeah, the committee on safety hung some negroes down at Mooresville the other day that they caught plotting to kill their masters," said Tanner. "One of 'em was ol' Stubby that was owned by Mrs. Rice," Tanner paused. "Say, didn't your father-in-law, Mr. McElroy, own him at one time?"

The color drained from Pa's face. "And so did I. Lordy mercy!"

"As bad as it was to hang 'em, it will serve as a warning to others who might be thinking of rebellion," said Tanner.

Afterwards Pa and Dudley walked to the post office on the north side of the square and chatted with Robert David.

"I guess you heard about them hanging a bunch of Negroes down in Mooresville," said David.

"Yeah, Samuel Tanner told me about it a while ago," Pa replied Daniel.

"It's a good thing they uncovered their devilish plot – one of 'em they hung was ol' Stubby, the one you owned several years ago," said David. "I remember when Mr. McElroy brought him here in 1819 to build the courthouse. He was a rebellious young buck even back then."

"He was lazy but never give me an ounce of trouble," Pa said. "I wouldn't have sold him except for finding abolitionist papers he was hid'n. At first I had misgivings about selling him, but now I'm glad I did. Why he could have killed us all! It gives me the jitters just to think about it." Pa hesitated. "Robert, we're liv'n in mighty dangerous times."

"Yes, we are," replied David. "I'd say that over half of the county's population are slaves. If they got organized and rebelled, no woman or child would be safe. It makes me shudder to ponder it."

"And the Yankees are stirr'n the pot," interjected Dudley. "Until we whip 'em good things will only get worse."

"That's easier said than done," replied David.

"I'm rar'n to go fight," Uncle Robert Dudley said.

"He won't be happy 'til he joins up and gets himself killed," added Pa.

"I wish I was leaving with Capt'n Hobbs Company this afternoon," said Dudley. "Once we give the Yankees a good thrashing they'll quit and go back home where they belong."

"I wouldn't count on that," said David. "I'm afraid we're in for a long hard struggle."

Meanwhile, Aunt Sallie, considered to be the fashion queen of Athens, took the girls shopping for calico dress material. They returned near noon with cloth and new bonnets that Aunt Sallie had purchased for them at Peterson Tanner & Son Dry Goods.

At 1 p.m. most of Athens walked down to the depot where a large crowd had gathered near an idling locomotive that was pulling several rail cars.

"I'll declare," said Ma. "I haven't seen this many people in one place since the Niphonia Fair last year."

They moved closer and craned to see. One hundred men of newly-organized Company F, 9th Alabama Infantry Regiment, stood in formation dressed in gray uniforms, knapsacks on their backs and haversacks hanging to their sides. Rifles were stacked. Captain Thomas H. Hobbs, splendidly dressed in gray pants and a matching double-breasted frock coat, was standing in front of them.

"Look, there's Eppa!" said Cal, pointing at their neighbor, Eppa Fielding. "Isn't he handsome?"

Just then Reverend A.F. Lawrence, a Methodist pastor, stepped in front of the formation, Bible in hand, and cleared his throat. Talking died down.

"Sshh, listen girls," whispered Ma.

"Brothers and sisters in the Lord," said Reverend Lawrence, raising his arms toward heaven. There was silence except for the idling locomotive hissing steam. "We are gathered on this solemn occasion to bid farewell to sons, brothers, fathers, husbands and kinsmen. They depart for Virginia, the ancestral home of many of us gathered here. They do not go to a strange and inhospitable land. Though we are sad to see them leave, I can assure you they will find outstretched hands eager to assist them. They will be met with open arms. They go to defend our beloved southland and are to be placed upon a pedestal and honored for their bravery. You are looking at the finest example of manhood in God's Kingdom. Some are young; others are graying. Yet, all have unsheathed the sword and picked up the musket to defend our liberty as free citizens. To them we shall be eternally…grateful…" His voice broke and tears streamed down his cheeks. Women wept. Men stared stoically ahead, perhaps afraid to do otherwise lest they break down and cry. Reverend Lawrence wiped away his tears with a handkerchief and continued. "Just as God walked with Joshua in biblical times he will be with our Army. God told Joshua to march around the city of Jericho seven times. There were doubters. But Joshua had great faith and did what God commanded him to do. We must have the same degree of faith. There will be doubters, as there was in those ancient times, but, we must keep faith with God. So, I say lift up your faces toward heaven from

261

whence cometh our help and keep faith; keep faith in God; keep faith in our brave men and keep faith in yourselves for we know that faith moves mountains. I bid thee farewell, brave and noble men."

Following a prayer, Reverend Lawrence, assisted by Reverend George W. Mitchell of the Cumberland Presbyterian Church, gave each soldier a Bible.

Afterwards, Mayor Samuel Tanner stepped forward and, following introductory remarks, presented each officer and the four sergeants a company roll. He spoke movingly and concluded by making an appeal for pocket change. "A few of these noble and brave men are wholly without funds to purchase food along the way," he said. "Our county has already given hundreds of dollars, but I ask you to reach deep in your pockets and hearts and share once more."

Someone placed a hat nearby on the ground and the crowd surged forward and tossed in coins. The ceremony was concluded by the reading of a proclamation drafted by Daniel Coleman, former editor of the *Athens Herald,* now a private standing in the ranks.

"Resolved: That the prayers of the ministers and members of the various churches of Limestone County be earnestly requested for the safety of our company, from the danger of the field, and the temptations of the camp, and for the speedy and complete triumph of the cause of the South."

The crowd roared its approval.

Then it was over. The men fell out of rank and hugged loved ones. Mothers and wives sobbed, children clung to their fathers' legs and it ended only when Mr. Harrison, the engineer sounded the train whistle. The men scrambled aboard, the whistle sounded again and the railcars lurched forward and slowly moved down the tracks no faster than a walk. Loved ones followed beside the cars, tears flowing and hands extended, offering farewell, perhaps their final one. Families and friends wiped tears and watched as the train slowly moved out of sight.

---

That night, Pa opened all doors and windows in an effort to catch a breeze, but none stirred. He rolled and twisted in bed and couldn't sleep.

"I'm going to make a pallet and sleep on the porch," he said to Ma and rolled out of bed.

"It don't seem that hot to me," she said. Pa carried his pillow and a quilt to the porch and made a pallet and lay down. He still couldn't sleep. The discovery of the planned slave insurrection was seared on his brain. One half of the county population were slaves. Even more now since more white men had departed for the war. There was no telling what the Negroes might do. They had rebelled before in 1831 when Nat Turner led an uprising in Virginia and killed 60 whites.

Footsteps. In the moonlight, he saw Ma, a pillow and quilt in her arms.

"I thought I'd join you," she said and made her pallet next to him. "It ain't that hot. Something is bothering you."

Pa pondered whether he should tell her the recent news. It would upset and scare her, but he knew she'd hear about it later anyway.

"The Vigilence committee hung ol' Stubby at Mooresville a few days ago."

262

"Ohhh, Lordeee mercy. No!"

"He's part of a planned rebellion; gonna kill whites and join Mister Lincoln."

"I hate to hear it," Ma said, more sad than fearful.

"He was gonna kill white folks. Don't you understand, woman?"

"I know, but I feel sorry for him. He told me that he just wanted to be free – like us. I guess desperate people do desperate things."

"I say, feel sorry for 'em," said Pa and rolled over.

---

Early August, 1861.

The front door of the Athens Post Office was wide open when Pa walked in and saw his brother-in-law, Robert C. David, mopping his brow with a handkerchief.

"Hot enough for ya?"

David looked up. "I've never seen it hotter or drier."

"You must be forgett'n the summer of '51," Pa said. "Didn't rain a drop in June and July."

"You know how it is, current misery is always worse than past misery," said David.

"I stopped at Tanner's to buy tobacco and everyone was talking about the big battle on July 22$^{nd}$ near Washington," Pa said.

"Oh yes, a huge victory for General Beauregard at Manassas, Virginia," said David. "Southern newspapers reported the Yankees threw down their arms and ran all the way back to the capital. Details are dribbling in; lots of men killed and wounded on both sides. One newspaper reported that the Confederates had lost about 2,000 killed and wounded and the Yankees more than 3,000."

"Any casualties from Limestone County?"

"Several," replied David. "Thomas Joyce McClellan stopped by yesterday and had received a letter from his boy who barely missed the battle. He wrote that Colonel Egbert Jones of the 4$^{th}$ Alabama was killed along with about 100 of his men; said James Bailey was wounded and Lieutenant Robert Hughes was killed."

"I hate to hear it," Pa said. "I was in Athens the day that Colonel Jones marched off to fight the Mexicans. James Greer was jump'n up and down to enlist."

"Now that the Yankees lost at Manassas, some people are saying that Lincoln will make peace," said David. "But, I think the war is just getting started."

"Let's pray it don't come here," Pa said.

263

# 23 | RARIN' TO GO

Athens, approximately one year later.

Early March, 1862.

It was a warm and windy Tuesday morning with the threat of thunderstorms when Dudley Barksdale saddled Sweet and rode to Athens. The mare's hooves clattered rhythmically as she trotted across the plank bridge spanning Swan Creek, swollen and muddy after a recent rain. Spring was in the air. Even Sweet seemed to sense it.

Dudley sucked in a lung full of fresh air filled with the sweet aroma of spring and freshly plowed earth. Ah, he loved that smell and he loved farming, but no glory came from trudging from sun up till sun down behind a farting horse. It wasn't something that impressed young women. He was one month shy of his 23$^{rd}$ birthday, stood 5 feet 10 inches and had his Mother's sparkling blue eyes – McElroy eyes she called them – and he figured he was reasonably handsome. But, he was a common farmer – a clod buster. Henceforth, he would cover himself, not with dirt, but with glory.

It was too early in the season to plant cotton and corn. Anyway, brother Thomas and brother-in-law James Newby could plant the crops in his absence. Some folks said the war wouldn't last long and he figured he'd probably be back home in time to help pick cotton and pull corn. And the $50 bounty paid for enlisting would come in handy, enough to purchase a new pair of shoes, all of the tobacco he could smoke in a year and still have money remaining, not to speak of receiving eleven dollars a month pay.

It had all started when little red-headed Jesse N. Holt had stopped by the house several days ago on the way to Athens and said he was going to enlist in the company being organized by John W. West. Holt, not an inch over 5 feet, with bright blue eyes, lived several miles north of the Barksdale farm on the west bank of Piney Creek. He was 28 years old and limped, caused by a deformity to his left leg due to a childhood fracture.

"You oughta join up too," he said to Dudley. "I ain't no bigger 'n a chicken mite, but I can shoot out a squirrel's eye with my musket and do the same to Yankees. Anyway, it'll be a lot of fun."

Dudley didn't require much convincing.

In Athens, the streets were muddy and cut with ruts. Horses, buggies and wagons were hitched around the red brick courthouse where the Confederate flag snapped in the warm breeze.

He tied Sweet to the hitching rail and entered the east door of the courthouse where a score of mostly young men milled about, smoking their pipes, chewing tobacco and talking loudly.

"We'll show them Yanks how to fight," bragged a red-headed fellow with a scraggly beard.

"They come down here mess 'n with us and we'll send 'em back 'cross the Mason-Dixon Line with a butt full of lead," bragged another fellow.

Shortly, 35-year-old Athens merchant John W. West, splendidly clad in a butternut gray uniform, stepped into the hallway from an adjoining office.

"Boys, can I have your attention?" The men fell silent.

"Many of you know me. I'm Captain John West," he said. "I'm recruiting a company that will be made up of Limestone Countians. We'll all remain together and we'll fight for each other –"

"How long?" someone hollered.

264

"Three years," West replied.

"It won't take three years to whup them Yankees," said the red-bearded fellow. "More like three months."

Everyone agreed.

"Enlist for three years," said West. "And you'll be paid a $50 bounty and given a hunting license to shoot Yankees that come down here to spoil our southland."

"Where's the line begin?" asked the red-headed fellow.

"Right here," said Captain West, raising an arm over his head. The men jostled in line, laughing, some bragging about how many Yankees they were going to kill.

---

Dudley pondered the experience as he rode back home that afternoon. Enlisting in the Confederate Army had been simple. Captain West had asked him a few questions, like name, birthday, parents, etc. He signed a document, was handed a fifty-dollar Confederate note and told to report to Cambridge Campground the following Friday with a weapon – if he had one – and be prepared to march. He was a soldier – well pretty soon he would be, just as soon as he took the oath. No more plowing and following a horse's rear end from can 'til can't. Henceforth, he would be like a knight of ancient times, charged with the sacred duty of protecting home and hearth from Yankees that might have the audacity to venture down here. He straightened in the saddle. From now on, he would have to be more conscious of his military bearing.

He dreaded breaking the news to Ma and Pa. Ma would cry and beg him to reconsider and Pa would tighten his lips and shake his head with disapproval and say little. He'd rather they pitch a fit and get over it.

Thunder rolled in the west and he wondered if the roar of cannon would sound the same. "Com'n Sweet," he clucked, kicking the mare in the flanks. "We better get home before that storm hits."

He unsaddled Sweet in the barn and turned her loose in the pasture, and then hurried inside the house where everyone was gathered at the west window, watching the approaching storm.

"I's worried 'bout you," said Ma. "Where'n the world have you been?"

"I joined the Army," he said nonchalantly.

Silence. Pa frowned and dropped his head. Ma tried to speak but no sound came forth immediately. Finally, "You didn't!"

Cornelia smiled broadly and ran gleefully to him. "Oh brother, I'm so proud of you!"

"I knew it was coming," Ma interrupted. "I suppose I shouldn't be so shocked."

Cal hugged his neck and exclaimed. "My brave brother!"

"Who's gonna help me put in the crop?" asked Thomas.

"I won't be gone for long," replied Dudley.

"Why 'n the world do you wanna leave a nice home, a soft bed and good food and march all day and sleep on the ground?" Ma asked. "To say nothing of gett'n shot at."

"I'll see new places and meet new people," replied Dudley. "It'll be a great adventure all the while chasing them Yankees back home. Them that don't fight for the cause will be sorry they didn't when we win the war."

"I wish you had waited, at least until the crops had been planted," said Pa.

265

"I'll be fighting for our independence, Pa," said Dudley. "Just like grandfather Micajah fought for our Independence against the British. I'll make you proud of me."

Pa placed a hand on Dudley's shoulder. "Son, I'm already proud of you and you don't have to do a thing to prove yourself."

The storm slammed with a ferocity that Dudley had seldom seen. Rain lashed the house and the wind sent shingles flying from the roof and shook the log structure. The family huddled in the corner of the house as the wind howled through treetops. Pa squeezed his eyes shut as if to block out what he saw. Each time the thunder clapped, he thought of cannon fire and saw Dudley marching into battle. An awful storm that came on the day his youngest son enlisted was not a good omen, he decided. He reached over and lovingly squeezed Dudley's shoulder.

---

Thursday evening. Dudley couldn't wait to tell Sarah Jane Isom that he had enlisted. She would be surprised. After feeding the horses corn and fodder and doing his chores, he freshened up, dressed in his Sunday go-to-meeting clothes and saddled Sweet. "I'm riding over to Sarah Jane's," he remarked casually to Ma, who eyed him suspiciously.

"Is there a meeting going on at Isom's Chapel?" she asked.

"No ma'am, I just thought I'd ride over and say good-bye before I ride away off to war."

"I'd be mighty careful about what I said in front of her Pa," interjected his father. "You know how cranky ol' Emanuel is about the Union."

"Yes sir, I'll keep that in mind."

He clucked to Sweet, told ol' Luther to "stay" and rode east on the Nick Davis Road toward the Isom homestead across Piney Creek. Hooves clattered on the plank bridge and the water beneath it ran swift and muddy from the recent rain. A mile south on Mooresville Road, he reined in front of the Isom log house. Dogs ran out barking.

James Franklin, a year younger than Sarah Jane, stepped out on the porch in the gathering darkness and scolded the dogs.

"Hello Jim," said Dudley. No one ever called Jim by his full name.

"Why it's Dudley Barksdale! What brings you across Piney Creek on a week night?"

"Just visiting."

"Get down and come in," Jim said.

He ushered Dudley into the parlor where Emanuel Isom sat by a flickering lamp reading the Bible while Mrs. Isom sat nearby, rocking an infant.

"Look what the cats drug up," Jim said.

Mr. Isom, his hair graying and thin on top and with fluffy mutton chops down to his chin, looked up, mildly irritated. He laid the Bible aside and stood and extended his hand. "Evening Dudley."

"Evening Sir – evening Mrs. Isom," said Dudley.

"Please have a seat," Mr. Isom said and gestured toward a black couch.

"Can I fix you something to eat?" asked Mrs. Isom.

"Oh, no ma'am, thank you."

Several children peeked around the corner to see their guest. After making inquiry about the Barksdale family, Emanuel said: "I know you didn't ride over here to

266

visit with me and Rebecca." Dudley shifted on the couch. *That old man makes me nervous as a cat.* "Well, no sir... I mean... It's good to see both of you... but I come calling on Miss Sarah Jane."

"Ohhh myy, she's visiting with her cousin," her mother said.

Dudley felt the air leave his sails. Now he was stuck with old man Isom, a devout Methodist who was a dead ringer for what he figured Job must have looked like – stern and dead serious. Mr. Isom fixed his eyes on Dudley, who hoped the old man wasn't a mind reader too, because if he was, he'd know that Dudley had spent a lot of time recently thinking about his daughter's warm, soft body. Dudley twisted on the couch; anxious to depart, he reached for his hat.

"Well, it's getting late, I guess I need to get going," he said and stood to leave.

"Just a minute," said Emanuel. The old man took Dudley's hand. "I want to commend you for your decision."

*Surely he wasn't being congratulated for joining the Confederate Army.* "What's that sir?"

"Since the terrible war started many misguided young men from this county have flocked to enlist in the Confederate Army to help destroy the Union that our ancestors created. I'm glad to know that you haven't done that. I congratulate you for using good judgment."

Dudley was speechless, his mouth suddenly dry as dust. Beads of perspiration popped up on his upper lip. He shuffled his feet and licked his lips. "Well... uh... that's not exactly the case Mr. Isom."

Emanuel's brows knotted, his brown eyes unblinking. "What are you saying Dudley?"

"Well... uh... the reason I rode over tonight was to tell Miss Sarah Jane goodbye –"

"Goodbye?"

"Yes sir, I've enlisted in the Confederate Army."

"You didn't!" exclaimed Mrs. Isom.

Emanuel's face fell and his mouth opened but no sound came forth. He shook his head with disapproval. "I'm sorry to hear that," he finally said. "It's a kick in the guts to hear it. Our grandfathers fought in the Revolution to win Independence from a Royal Monarch and my father and your Uncle Arch and Mike fought the British in the War of 1812 to preserve that Union. There are those among us – mostly the privileged planter class I might say – that love their slaves above the Union. They are hell bent on destroying the Union."

"But... but sir, it seems to me that if we voted to voluntarily join the Union, then we can vote to leave it," Dudley said. "That's freedom of choice, that's liberty."

"The Union first, then liberty," retorted Emanuel. "Without a strong Union, we cannot enjoy liberty. Our overseas enemy will divide and conquer us. Dudley, I fear you have been deceived. At all costs we must preserve our Union. The scriptures say, 'If a house be divided against itself, that house cannot stand.' Seeds of our destruction are being sown; the Confederacy will fail and the harvest that we reap will be desolation."

"I think I need to go," Dudley said. Bidding farewell to Mrs. Isom, he pulled on his hat and departed.

------

Early Friday morning.

Dudley saddled Sweet and tied her at the back of the house and then went inside where Ma handed him a sack stocked with socks, underwear and an extra pair of pants that she had made. Cal and Cornelia had baked biscuits and filled them with thick slices of salt cured ham, layered with molasses.

The family gathered in the backyard to bid Dudley farewell. Brother George and Mary and their four children who lived nearby were present along with brother-in-law James Newby, sister Sarah and their two children, Luke Pryor and Oscar. And of course, brother Thomas, sisters Cal and Cornelia, along with Ma and Pa, stood there. It was a somber occasion. He shook hands with George and James Newby then spoke to each child, hoisting the small ones up in the air like a sack of cornmeal. "Be good, say your prayers and mind your Ma 'n Pa, ya heah?"

"Uncle Dudley, are you going to kill Yankees?" asked young Luke Pryor Newby.

"If I have to, I will. Now you be a good boy, ya heah?" he said and tousled his hair. He turned to his sister Cal and kissed her on the cheek. "Take good care of Ma and Pa."

"Oh Brother! I'm sad to see you leave." Her voice quavered as she hugged him tightly. "May God protect you."

Then he kissed Cornelia. "I'm proud of you Brother," she said and began to sob. He held her close for a moment and lovingly patted her back.

He shook his father's hand, gnarled and rough from years of honest labor. "Goodbye Pa."

"Farewell son," his voice breaking and eye sockets filling with tears. "I know... you'll do us... proud."

Dudley couldn't stand to see his father weep. He threw his arms around him and pulled him close and he felt him heave. His own chest was about to explode. "I'll make you proud Pa."

"I know you will."

Bidding farewell to his mother was the hardest of all. She was biting her lip and holding back tears. "I can't bring myself to say goodbye," she said, her voice trembling.

"Don't cry Ma, it ain't goodbye. I'll be back, I promise."

She kissed him on the forehead as she had often done when she put him to bed when he was a child, then sucked up and wiped away her tears. "Be careful and don't forget your raising and stay away from sinful men and alcohol and gambling and –"

"Don't worry Ma." He squeezed her tightly. He knew he must depart before he burst out crying. Ol' Luther, his coon dog was standing nearby wagging his tail. Dudley reached down and gently tugged his long, brown ears.

"Y'all take good care of Luther, ya heah?" His voice cracked. He swung in the saddle and rode off – never looking back – he couldn't. He was weeping. Thomas followed behind on another horse and would lead Sweet back home where she would be needed for spring planting.

Cambridge Campground was located a few miles slightly southeast of Athens, across Piney Creek. At one time it had been a bustling community and had vied with English Spring and Athens to become the county seat. Athens won over English Springs by only two votes. Presently, the Methodist Church, where people flocked by the hundreds to attend revivals, was the centerpiece of the community. A large, cold spring located nearby made it an ideal campground.

When Dudley topped the rise overlooking the campground, he was surprised at what he saw. The several acres were speckled with tents and teaming with scores of men marching back and forth. A few shouldered muskets, but most were unarmed. Officers wearing swords scurried around barking orders. Near the center of the encampment the Confederate flag flapped in the breeze. It was very exciting.

Dudley reined his horse and unsaddled. "Well Thomas," he said, looking up at his grizzled older brother, "I guess this is where we part."

"I'll miss you Dudley."

"I won't be gone for long," said Dudley. "I'll be back before you know it. Take care of Ma 'n Pa." Dudley threw the sack over his shoulder, shook Thomas's hand, turned and walked toward the bustling encampment.

As Dudley soon learned, two companies were bivouacked on the grounds. Company G, recruited by Captain West, had mustered 86 men. Company D, raised by Dr. William Tell Sanders of "Nubbin Ridge" had raised 79 men. The latter called themselves the "Mollie Walton Guards" in honor of Miss Mary "Mollie" Walton of Mooresville, who had generously outfitted each man with a uniform.

Dudley saw Jesse Holt limping toward him, all smiles.

"I heard you joined up," he said. "Glad you did. Now I know somebody close to home. Com' on, I'll show you to our camp."

An air of excitement prevailed. Sergeants shouted commands and men marched, out of step and sometimes in opposite directions, provoking the former to fume and swear.

"Your other left foot! Dammit!"

Dudley was issued a blanket and knapsack in which to carry his belongings. He was still getting his bearings when a bugle sounded and someone shouted: "FALL IN..."

Dudley looked at Holt, puzzled. "That means we're to get in company formation," said Holt and limped off.

The same tall, red-headed fellow with the scraggly beard and snaggle-teeth that he had seen on enlistment day stood next to Dudley.

"Howdy, I'm Dudley Barksdale."

"Howdy to ye'self. I'm Junior Bill Pendergrass from over Elk at Lentzville."

"Good to meet 'che," Dudley said.

"ATEN---HUT!"

The men came to attention and Captain West, impeccably dressed in a sparkling new gray uniform, hat and boots, stepped in front of the formation and addressed the men.

"Men of Limestone County, you have enlisted in a great and noble cause. We will soon show the tyrant Lincoln that free people will fight for their liberty. As Thomas Jefferson said, 'The tree of liberty must be refreshed from time to time with the blood of Patriots and tyrants.' We will pick up the gauntlet that has been thrown at our feet and drive the invaders from our sacred Southland; land our forefathers hewed from a wilderness. We will not flinch; we will not waiver; we will not retreat. We shall cover ourselves with glory."

A hurrah went up from the company. Dudley gazed at the Confederate flag that rippled in the breeze. He liked the flag, a pattern of stars and bars. When he returned to Athens, he wouldn't be a mere dirt farmer, he told himself. He'd be covered with glory.

A few days later, camp was struck and both companies marched by way of downtown Athens, toward LaGrange, some 40 miles west, near Tuscumbia. The "Mollie Walton Guards" led the long column of men. When they neared the courthouse a band struck up *Dixie* and the two companies marched around the square where several hundred people stood cheering them.

Dudley saw Thomas standing in the throng of people that lined the street, waving his hand.

"Goodbye Dudley," he yelled.

Dudley straightened and threw him a quick salute. He'd never felt more alive nor proud. When they reached the bottom of Edmundson Hill at Town Creek, the band stopped playing and turned back.

"You heard the Capt'n say 'we'll cover ourselves with glory.' Well he was talk'n to me," Dudley said to Junior Bill Pendergrass, who was marching beside him.

Junior Bill spit out a stream of brown tobacco juice. "Naw sir, he wuz look'n squarely at me, I tell ya he wuz. I said to myself and told Earline after I jined up, 'Earline, I'm gonna bring you a set of Yankee ears.'"

"Who's Earline?" asked Dudley.

"Earline McLemore, she's my galfriend from over Elk."

"She wants Yankee ears?"

"Aw naw, that 'uz my idea," replied Junior Bill.

After marching for a while, Junior Bill said, "Heck, I figure we can outshoot 'n outride any Yankee any day of the week."

"If you hadn't noticed, Junior Bill, we ain't riding, we're walking."

"But if we wuz, we could do it better 'n 'nem."

The column of 165 men, officers riding and the men walking, marched west to LaGrange Military Academy. A few miles east of Tuscumbia, Lagrange overlooked a wide green valley from atop a lush mountain called Lawrence Hill. Tuscumbia was a few miles to the west. It was there that the 35th Alabama Infantry Regiment consisting of about 750 men recruited from Franklin, Lawrence, Limestone, Lauderdale and Madison Counties, had officially come into existence. Each man was issued a haversack, cartridge box, canteen and eating utensils.

A week earlier on April 6th, while the recruits drilled daily and learned to load and fire the academy muskets, a big battle erupted around Shiloh Church a few miles north of Corinth, Mississippi. The Confederates carried the first day, but were driven back the following day. Approximately 24,000 men were killed, wounded and captured, including Confederate Commander General Albert Sydney Johnston, who was shot in the leg and bled to death. The Confederate Army of Mississippi, now under the leadership of P.G.T. Beauregard, fell back to Corinth.

---

Monday evening, April 14th.

Unknown to Dudley and the men in ranks, General Omsby Mitchell had unexpectedly pounced on Huntsville and sent troops to capture Tuscumbia. When it was learned that Federal troops were approaching LaGrange in an attempt to capture the 35th,

270

the regiment pulled out without equipment or arms and marched toward Corinth. And just in the nick of time. The Yankees occupied Tuscumbia two days later.

In spite of the danger the men sang and bragged about how they would whip the Yankees. They halted about six miles southwest of LaGrange and made camp. The next day they marched through Russellville, cheered by crowds that lined the streets.

They slogged down a dusty road where scores of horses, hundreds of men and dozens of wagons had ground the dirt into a fine powder that enveloped them, stifling their breath and irritating their eyes.

"I can't breathe and my dogs are kill'n me," said Junior Bill.

"Mine too," replied Dudley, limping. "I've got blisters on both feet."

"I didn't jine this Army to walk all over Dixie, I jined up to fight," said Junior Bill.

"I'm pulling off these shoes," said Dudley.

"Me too."

They stepped out of the column, sat by the road side and were removing their shoes when an officer rode up. "Get back in formation and close up!"

Junior Bill looked up at the Lieutenant. "Now, how can I git back 'n formation and take off my shoes at the same time?"

"Private, what's your name?"

"Junior Bill Pendergrass from over Elk, what's you'rn?"

The Lieutenant spun his horse around and galloped off.

"Unneighborly fella, ain't he?" said Junior Bill.

"We better hurry up and get back in formation before this fella causes us trouble," said Dudley.

They tied their shoes on their knapsacks and ran limping to catch up with the company.

"There ain't too much glory going on right now," said Junior Bill. "All we doin' is walk'n and gett'n blisters."

"There'll be a lot of fight'n directly, just as soon as we reach the Yankees," said Dudley. "I want Pa to be proud of me. He wasn't for secession and he wasn't for the war."

"My Pa was strong against secession too," said Junior Bill. "Most everybody in Lentzville wuz. Old man Solomon Lentz has even organized about twelve union families in a home guard. I don't give a hoot 'n hell about slavery, state's rights or the union. Yankees come down here uninvited and I'll fight 'em till they leave."

It rained all day on April 19th and ankle-deep mud replaced dust.

The Company organized into mess groups consisting of four to eight men. Dudley and Junior Bill paired with Jesse Holt, Earl Jackson and Tyler Thornton.

"Jackson 'n Thornton are from over Elk," Junior Bill said. "So they gotta be mighty fine folk."

"Who's gonna cook for the first week?" asked Dudley.

The men looked at one another but no one volunteered. Junior Bill produced a deck of cards. "Let's us draw high cards and whoever gets it will be eliminated and we'll keep draw'n till all but one fella is left and he'll be the cook."

"Why don't we draw just once and whoever gets the high card will be cook?" asked Thornton.

"That won't be nearly as much fun," replied Junior Bill.

271

The men agreed except for Dudley. "That's gamblin' and gamblin's a sin–"

"We ain't play'n for money," said Junior Bill.

"Yeah, but it's taking a chance and the scriptures speak against it," replied Dudley.

"Which scripture?" asked Junior Bill.

"I can't quote chapter and verse, but it's in there somewhere."

"Doggoneit!" exclaimed Thornton. "We ain't sinning, we just talking about who's gonna fry sow belly and make hoe cakes."

Dudley relented. "I sure would hate for Ma to find out I've been draw'n cards."

The men drew cards until everyone was eliminated except for Junior Bill.

"Does it make any difference that I can't cook?" he asked.

"Doggoneit, you'd better learn fast," replied Thornton.

"Don't tell Earline I've been cook'n," said Junior Bill, "or she'll have me doin' the wash and milk'n the cow when I git back home."

Their mess had been issued a skillet, coffee pot and stew kettle, and each man was given a tin plate and cup, knife, fork and spoon. Rations were salt pork, corn meal, salt, molasses and at first, coffee.

Fried bacon, hoecakes, molasses and coffee was standard fare until Junior Bill learned to make coosh. He fried bacon, added cornmeal and water to the greasy mixture and cooked until it turned into a thick brown gravy. "Now that's mighty fine eat'n, if I do say so myself," he said.

"What's in it?" asked Dudley.

"I ain't tell'n," replied Junior Bill. "If you don't like it, don't throw it out."

"You know why he cooks coosh all the time, don't ye?" griped Thornton.

"Why?" asked Dudley.

"'Cause he don't have no teeth to chew real food."

Blisters became the regiment's enemy, not Yankees. At Burleson they halted and rested for two days before continuing to Jacinto, Mississippi, where they again encamped.

Officers campaigned for election, visiting the men, shaking hands, slapping backs, making speeches and offering food and a nip of whiskey.

My hand is squished plum blue," said Junior Bill. "And I've et so many election cakes my belly's ach'n."

"Who you gonna vote for captain?" asked Thornton.

"I'm gonna dance with the man that brung us to the ball and that's Capt'n West," replied Junior Bill.

Captain West was elected Commander of Company G, but more importantly, the 35th was issued .54 caliber Belgian rifles. They were ready to fight Yankees.

They reached Corinth on April 23rd and that night, Dudley sat by the camp fire, sharpened a lead pencil and with paper resting on his knapsack, wrote his first letter home.

April 23rd.

Dear Ma and Pa and all,

Well, I'm finally a soldier and I really like it. I'm in good health and doing fine except my feet are killing me from walking all day and mosquitoes and chiggers are feasting on me. Sure wish I had some turpentine to rub on. We march rain or shine and sleep on the ground. At first I didn't sleep well, but now I sleep like a baby except when I'm scratching. We left LaGrange in a hurry on April 14th because Yankee cavalry was coming for us.

We reached Corinth this afternoon and were told that we were placed in Breckenridge's Brigade which made me proud. General Breckenridge, you'll remember, carried Limestone County in the last Presidential Election. I hadn't been in any battle yet, but I know with General Breckenridge leading us we'll whip the Yankees.

I've met some good men and made friends with Junior Bill Pendergrass from across Elk River near Lentzville. Junior Bill is about my age and is what Ma would call a real handful. Poor little Jesse Holt is so small and crippled, you know, that he gets run over by others. I have agreed to write letters for Junior Bill and read the ones he receives. Tell Cal and Cornelia I send my love and for them to behave themselves like young ladies should when attending church meetings and such. Ma, I love you and want you to know I don't gamble or drink like some of the men. Pa, I'm going to make you proud of me. Tell Thomas that he's missing out on a great adventure.

Give my love to Jim, James and all the kids. Tell Thomas to pull Ol' Luther's ears for me. I'll send this with the next person that leaves for Athens. Write Soon.

Your Loving Son,
Dudley.

Fayetteville, Tennessee.

Earlier, Tuesday, April 8, 1862.

Spring marched up from the south, bringing warm breezes, blooming redbuds and new leaves on the numerous oak trees that studded the rolling green hills of Lincoln County. It also brought Yankees down from the North.

A column of blue-clad soldiers, some 7,400 in all, and hundreds of horses and mules – scores pulling creaking supply wagons, others ridden by cavalry and smartly dressed officers – stretched for miles along the dusty Shelbyville Pike. The U.S. Third Division was headed to peaceful Fayetteville. They had been well received in Shelbyville, thirty miles north, and expected no less in Fayetteville.

Brigadier General Ormsby M. Mitchell, Division Commander rode with his staff behind Turchin's Eighth Brigade that spearheaded the column. North of town he ordered a halt, and while his men pitched camp he sent two of his staff officers into Fayetteville on horseback carrying a white flag of truce. Their mission was to inform local leaders of his impending arrival. The Lincoln Administration was following a policy of reconciliation with Southerners. Firm, but nice. The emissaries barely escaped with their lives, finding refuge in a hotel. General Mitchell's bile was up. The following day he ordered local citizens to assemble on the town square.

Rufus Cooley McElroy and two of his brothers, Jack and Mike, sons of William and grandsons of Micajah, rode to town to see what the ruckus was about. Roads were crawling with union troops. They hitched their horses and joined the sullen crowd that stood far back, staring in stony silence at several blue-clad officers on horseback. In the center, mounted on a fine-looking black gelding and immaculately dressed in double-breasted blue uniform and sword, was General Mitchell, a slim man with unruly blonde hair that tumbled from beneath his hat. He was called "Old Stars" by his men and looked more like the New York mathematician and astronomer that he was than a Brigadier General who had graduated from West Point in 1829. He was in a foul mood. In his opinion, the Lincoln Administration policy of conciliation toward the South was pure nonsense and a failure. You don't cater to Rebels. You make them feel the sting of war. If he had his way, there would be no more coddling of these people. He raised high in the saddle and bellowed at his sullen audience.

"PEOPLE OF FAYETTEVILLE! YOU ARE WORSE THAN SAVAGES. EVEN THEY RESPECT A FLAG OF TRUCE. I'm General Mitchell, Commander of the Third Division. You shamefully and publicly insulted my soldiers that I sent here as a matter of courtesy. You are not worthy to associate with honest men. Those of you who are loyal to the Union need not be concerned with our presence. Those of you who are Rebel supporters and have picked up arms against your duly-established government should be concerned. It is my duty to put down the rebellion and I assure you that I will do my utmost to carry out my duties. Go to your homes and remain there until I give you permission to come out." That said, General Mitchell wheeled on his horse and he and staff galloped off.

The McElroy brothers witnessed the spectacle and didn't like it one bit.

"Who do they think they are?" mumbled Rufus. "They invade our country with an army and expect us to welcome them?"

"Yeah, he's done more today to recruit rebel soldiers than Ol' Jeff Davis could do in a year," added Mike.

Also observing was Rev. Milus E. Johnston, a tall, bearded, Methodist minister of the Fayetteville circuit, which included the flock at tiny Mulberry community up the road. He was minding his own business, which was God's business. He prayed for all men's salvation and prayed hard that God would preserve the Union, but he was arrested and dragged off to jail for no good reason.

He was told he could preach in downtown Fayetteville, but he was forbidden to tend his parishioners at Mulberry. To worsen matters, Yankees took his horse.

The Yankees didn't tarry long in Fayetteville. The main force marched south thirty five miles and at daybreak on April 9th Turchin's Eighth Brigade struck an unsuspecting Huntsville, Alabama.   They captured 170 Confederate recruits, 16 locomotives and 100 cars.

General Mitchell marched east to destroy the railroad bridge near Bridgeport. Col. John Turchin went west to burn the bridge at Decatur. Finding that the Rebels had already torched it and fled, Turchin extinguished the flames and continued west toward Tuscumbia, which he occupied on April 16th.

Turchin received information that Confederate forces in strength were advancing from the west.   He pulled back to Decatur, burned the bridge over the Tennessee River and fell back to Huntsville.

Born Ivan Vasilevitch Turchininoff in St. Petersburg, Russia, Colonel John Basil Turchin was a stocky man with a short black beard and hard eyes.  Called the "Mad Cossack," he saw his first action at age 19 as a member of the Tsar's Army in the Russian Campaign that helped the Austrian Empress suppress the Hungarian Revolution of 1848. The Hungarian leader, Louis Cossuth, described the Tsar's Army as "a hoard of looters, rapists and mongerers."

Turchin graduated from the Russian Senior Military Academy in 1852 and served in the Crimean War before moving to Chicago in 1859 to work for the Illinois Central Railroad. But his true love was the life of a soldier.

On April 29th, the 28th Ohio Regiment, Turchin's Brigade, commanded by Colonel Timothy R. Stanley, readied to move out for Athens some twenty-five miles to the west. General Mitchell, knowing the strong Union sentiment there, assured the Ohioans their mission would be easy. "The locals will raise the flag of our Union the moment you enter town," he told them.

Although small, Athens was strategically important because of the Nashville & Decatur Railroad that ran through town and connected with the Memphis & Charleston at Decatur.

Colonel Stanley's Regiment was also charged with guarding the railroad from Athens to Limestone Bridge in Belle Mina where Limestone Creek flowed beneath the railroad in south Limestone County.

Stanley, age 51, a lawyer and furnace manufacturer from Marietta, Ohio, had no military experience but had been successful enough to raise a voluntary regiment.  He arrived in Athens on Tuesday evening, April 29th, and lodged with Mayor William Presley Tanner. Company E moved out to guard the railroad bridge over Limestone Creek. Company I went north approximately thirty miles to Pulaski, Tennessee. One-half of another company rode on the trains and the remainder of the regiment, approximately 300 men, came to Niphonia Park, a few blocks north of the courthouse.

Niphonia Park was a 60-acre fairground that had opened on October 23, 1860, and featured a mile-long race track, a two-story L-shaped building and three auditoriums able to seat 2,000 people. There were three large livery stables, 40 stalls on the ground and stalls for livestock. Four large wells fitted with iron pumps provided water. According to a newspaper ad, "the buildings are decidedly the most costly and commodious in the South." Col. Stanley decided it was perfect for his encampment.

Athenians didn't raise the Stars and Stripes, as Gen. Mitchell had predicted. But peace and quiet did prevail – at least for a little while.

Two days earlier, Sunday, April 27th, Mary Fielding, Daniel Barksdale's neighbor, recorded in her diary:

> "Well, I've seen some of the Yankees, at last seen the elephant, have a good view of the animal, and come to the conclusion he's rather sheepish. Five of them came to Sunday School this morning and there were several at church. They had the impudence to join in the singing with us, thought they look sheepish and mean. I couldn't help but thinking all during the sermon, how I do wish that Captain Morgan or some other boys of ours would come galloping into town! How I would like to see you all scamper. But vain were all my wishes; they sat quietly through the services."

---

Thursday morning, May 1, 1862.

Athens Postmaster Robert C. David was at home enjoying his usual breakfast of two fried eggs, bacon, gravy and biscuits.

"More coffee?" asked Sallie.

"Please."

She poured black coffee to the rim of the china cup.

The childless couple, affectionately called "Uncle Bob" and "Aunt Sallie," married for 41 years, resided in a fine house one block north of the square near where Robert had lived in a log house when he proposed to Sallie in 1821. Miss Sallie McElroy of Fayetteville was the most beautiful woman he'd ever seen and in his mind, she still was. When he arrived in Athens in 1817, his goal was to become a good citizen and a successful businessman. He had accomplished both. Postmaster, off and on, since 1821, he had served as Alderman, was a founding member of Masonic Lodge #16, a lay leader in the Methodist Episcopal Church and a generous supporter of the Sabbath School. If he had a vice, it was coon hunting. The baying of any one of his coonhounds sent chills up his back. He had accumulated a considerable estate consisting of farms, town lots and railroad stock. Sallie always had plenty of cash on hand. She was without dispute the leader of fashion in Athens. No lady even thought of buying a fine dress or a new bonnet without first consulting with Aunt Sallie.

David pulled a watch from his vest pocket and flipped open the cover. It was almost 7 a.m. He wiped his mouth with a napkin.

"I'd better get to the post office and be sure the mail goes out."

"Be careful," said Sallie. "Yankees are everywhere."

"Oh, they appear to be a decent lot. We've had no trouble so far and I don't expect any." He kissed Sallie on the forehead, said goodbye and departed.

276

When he neared the square, he heard pistol shots ring out west of town where Federal pickets were posted on the Florence Road. Inside the Post Office, he peered out the front window. Shortly, he saw a company of Federal troops headed west in the direction of the pistol shots. When they didn't return, another company of soldiers went in the same direction. Musket fire rolled toward Athens. He stepped outside to better observe. Cannon fire boomed from the west, rattling office windows and bringing out curious townspeople.

Then Federal troops coming from Niphonia Fairground passed through town at double quick time, minus their usual equipment. It was obvious to David that for whatever reason, they were skedaddling out of town. Spectators loved it and began shouting and hooting at them. Women derisively waved handkerchiefs and jeered at the fleeing soldiers until they were gone.

No sooner had the last soldier disappeared when David heard the thunder of hoofbeats and loud shouting from west of town. Momentarily, 150 to 200 Confederate soldiers came running up the hill from Town Creek, hollering and giving the rebel yell. Behind them were at least 200 cavalrymen. The loud shouting scared many of the citizens and sent them scurrying back to their businesses and houses.

Colonel John S. Scott's First Louisiana Cavalry had sent the Yankees fleeing. When citizens learned it was Confederates, they poured into the streets, shouting and waving handkerchiefs and hats. There was great jubilation.

Colonel Scott, a broad-shouldered man with black mustache and stubby beard and long black hair that fell past his shoulders, reined his big bay horse on the east side of the square. He doffed his hat to the ladies and inquired of the whereabouts of Union troops.

"Hightailing it outta town," someone shouted and pointed south.

Ladies at a tavern produced a Confederate flag and presented it to Colonel Scott. He ordered that a company of his men proceed to the fairground and seize all Union equipment that could be used and put everything else to torch. Numerous Yankee knapsacks were distributed to Negroes and children.

Colonel Stanley's Federals marched south, parallel to the railroad, where they met a stopped train carrying General Mitchell en route to Athens. Mitchell had also heard the gunfire. He ordered retreat until the regiment met reinforcements. The train chugged away in reverse.

Stanley's regiment turned southeasterly, closely followed by a band of local citizens. At Piney Creek the locals struck. A firefight ensued, killing one Federal and wounding two.

Colonel Scott sent a company of Confederates to Belle Mina where the Memphis & Charleston R.R. crossed over Limestone Creek. They burned the bridge. Two trains were caught at the bridge and 20 cars were burned, including two Union soldiers of the 18th Ohio who were trapped inside. The train was torched and 25,000 rations were lost.

In Huntsville, General Mitchell's blood was up. He summoned Colonel Turchin to his headquarters and ordered him to Athens.

"Leave not a grease spot there," he said

"Yes sir," replied Turchin, grinning.

"I will build a monument to those soldiers who were killed on the site of Athens," said Mitchell. "I have dealt gently enough with those people. I will try another course now."

Turchin couldn't have been more pleased.

---

In Lincoln County, Tennessee, Reverend Milus Johnston, his wife and children departed Fayetteville by buggy for Vienna on the north bank of the Tennessee River in Madison County, Alabama. Rev. Johnston wanted only to be left alone to farm and preach God's word. But it wasn't to be. His family was burned out by Yankee troops on three occasions. Finally, Johnston fled across the river into "Dixie," where he put down his Bible and picked up a sword.

# 25 | ATHENS SACKED AND PILLAGED

Athens.

Friday, May 2, 1862.

It was one of the prettiest spring days that Daniel could remember. The earth was warm and pulsating with new life. New foliage on trees was thick and waxy green and grass was lush and fat. The freshly-plowed earth where he and Thomas planted cotton was soft, rich and pungent and offered hope and the promise of a good year. It was a perfect morning and the planting was going smoothly; that is, until the planter broke.

Three miles away in Athens, residents woke to the rumble of cannon wheels, caissons and the clatter of hoof beats on the dusty streets. Colonel Turchin marched the 19th Regiment, Illinois Volunteers to "Pleasant Hill," the mansion of J.W.S. Donnell a few blocks south of the courthouse, and positioned cannon on the front lawn. It was an event that would be etched in the minds of Athenians until death.

Leaving Thomas in the field preparing the seed bed, Pa drove his buggy to Athens to purchase a replacement part on the cotton planter at Mayor Press Tanner's store. He hitched Sweet at the courthouse fence at the southeast corner of the square, patted her on the neck and walked across the dusty street toward the livery stable, intending on turning and walking west to Tanner's. The noise of many horses and rumblings from the east caused him to stop and turn around. A long column of blue-coated Federals were headed directly toward him. The lead horsemen reined up at the livery stable.

"Come over here!" yelled one of the mounted soldiers to two black men standing nearby. "Take care of Colonel Turchin's horse."

"I don't vant no negroes to take care of my horse," the Colonel said in his thick Russian accent. "I have a notion to make some of these white men rub him down. They would as soon cut all of your throats as not."

Pa observed as cannon, caissons and limbers rumbled past and began setting up at the southwest corner of the square, directly in front of Mayor Press Tanner's store and residence.

It was high ground and covered the approach of the Florence and Brownsferry Roads. Soldiers broke down a board fence, cut peach trees and trampled through Tanner's garden. Colonel Turchin, along with several officers, walked around the square where the two-story red brick courthouse sat in the center, enclosed by a board fence. Citizens watched in sullen silence.

"Go to your home!" Turchin ordered.

Pa got a good look at Turchin, a stocky, heavily-built man with black whiskers and dark eyes.

Just then, Walter C. McKinney and his partner, Rogers, both carriage makers, hearing the commotion, came out to see what was going on and sat down on the fence.

"Go home!" Turchin ordered.

McKinney and Rogers got down and headed home.

"Double-quick!"

McKinney looked back at Turchin and smirked.

"None of you laughing and jeering," Turchin said. "Arrest that man!"

Two soldiers grabbed McKinney and led him into the courthouse.

279

Not wanting to be arrested, Pa immediately climbed in his buggy and departed for home. News of what happened spread like wildfire. Robert C. David, who had witnessed the aftermath, gave Pa a full account gained from reliable sources. The 19th Illinois had stacked arms in the street, followed by the 18th Ohio. Turchin had sat down on the courthouse door step, stood up and said loudly, "I vill turn my head vor two hours."

Hearing this, the soldiers scattered and the plundering and pillaging began. After watching for a while, Turchin went to the Davidson's Hotel near the train depot where he and his wife Nadine were staying. He had dinner and rested.

---

Mrs. Milly Ann Clayton, a widow, was at her home on that Friday afternoon when two Union soldiers appeared at her door.

"Do you have arms?" one asked.

"There are none here."

"You are a goddamn liar," one soldier said and turned to the other one. "Hand me your revolver. I'll shoot her."

He didn't shoot her, but they did trash her house, pilfering boxes and trunks and carrying off the contents and clothes. The following day, more soldiers showed up and attempted to rape her servant girl.

Postmaster Robert C. David was home when he heard a loud ruckus uptown. He grabbed his coat and hollered to Sallie, who was in the back of the house. "I'm going to the post office, lock the door."

"Please be careful, Robert."

He walked briskly to the square. Bluecoats were swarming through the streets and in and out of stores. No telling what was happening at his office. He picked up his pace. At the northwest corner of the square he was stopped by a sentinel carrying a rifle.

"Halt! You can't pass," he said brusquely.

"I'm the postmaster and I need to go to my office and attend to business," said David.

"You'd be in danger. Now turn around and leave," ordered the sentinel.

David returned home, where he worried and paced the floor. Not only were there books and Bibles in his office, there was also cash.

He had cause to worry. While he paced, a squad of soldiers broke open the front door of David's office located on the north side of the square and pillaged it.

Soldiers entered the home of Mrs. M.E. Malone and Mrs. S. B. Malone and destroyed furniture, stole money, jewelry, plates and valuable ornaments and generally trashed the house. For six to eight hours troops occupied the dwelling of Thomas S. Malone, broke open desks and stole and destroyed valuable papers worth $4,500. They were rude and violent toward the women present. The same party entered the drug store owned by William D. Allen and destroyed medical equipment and dental instruments.

Madison Thompson's store was broken open and $3,000 of goods and merchandise was carried away. Next, they entered his stable and hauled off corn, oats and fodder.

"Give me a receipt for what you took," demanded Thompson. The soldier laughed.

"This place should support us," one replied. No receipt was given.

280

J.F. Sowell's office was broken open and a microscope and surgical instruments and books were carried off and destroyed.

Soldiers broke into the home of John F. Malone, where they forced open locks, broke open all the drawers of bureaus, secretaries, sideboards, wardrobes and trunks. Cursing the women present, they stole silverware, jewelry, gold watch and chain. After trashing the house they went and broke open Malone's law office and destroyed his safe and damaged his books. Several of the soldiers went to Malone's plantation and lived with his slaves for weeks, debauching the women and riding over the countryside plundering and pillaging.

A mob of Yankee soldiers broke open Samuel Taylor's store and stole sugar, coffee, books, shoes, leather and other merchandise.

Troops broke into the R.S. Irwin dwelling and ordered Mrs. Irwin to cook dinner for them, while they made sexual advances toward her servant girl in the presence of the family.

They fired into J.B. Hollingsworth's home and threatened to burn it down. Their language was so violent that Mrs. Hollingsworth miscarried her baby and subsequently died.

Soldiers broke open an iron safe belonging to J.A. Cox and destroyed and stole valuable papers, then took family clothes. Soldiers also broke into the brick store of P. Tanner and Son and destroyed and stole nearly all the stock, including breaking open the safe and taking $2,000 in cash.

Colonel Mihalotzy of the 24th Illinois Volunteers entered the J.H. Jones mansion a few blocks south of the square and quartered a company of men in the parlor. They stole food, clothing and spoiled the parlor carpets by cutting bacon on them; chopped bacon joints on the piano with an axe and the men slept in the beds with muddy boots and generally trashed the house.

George G. Peck's store was pillaged, the safe broke open and $940.90 cash and $4,000 of notes were taken. John Turrentine's store fared no better. Soldiers cut open his iron safe and stole $5,000 in notes and destroyed law and religious books.

Mrs. Charlotte Hines, a widow, lived by herself seven miles southwest of Athens. Her only son was away fighting with the Confederate Army. On Saturday, May 3rd, several Union soldiers came to her house and demanded hams.

"I can't spare any," she said.

"I guess we'll have some," said one soldier.

Mrs. Hines unlocked the smokehouse door to prevent them from breaking it open.

"You have a lot of meat," one said.

"I have a large family to eat it," she said, referring to the Negroes on her plantation.

The party took three hams and departed, but later, another group of soldiers arrived and took all the hams, including about fifteen hundred pounds of bacon.

---

Saturday morning, May 3rd.

Robert C. David gulped down coffee but skipped his usual leisurely breakfast and hurried to his office. When he rounded the corner he was shocked at what he saw. Businesses had been broken open, window shutters and soiled merchandise lay in the dirt. The town had been sacked. He reached his two-story building on the north side of the square and found the door broke open. Inside the post office everything was torn to pieces, furniture had been broken and scattered about, pictures pulled from the walls, papers strewn on the floor and worst of all, nearly 200 Bibles were missing. A few lay trashed on the floor. A thousand dollars was missing, along with his spectacles. He went upstairs to check the room occupied by four young men. Their wardrobes were missing, together with bed clothing, pillows, bolsters – everything was gone except the feather bed.

That afternoon at his residence David heard loud banging on the front door. He peeked out and saw three Union soldiers. "Get in the back of the house," he said to Sallie. "Hurry!"

More loud banging. He opened the door.

"May I help you?"

"We've orders to take all your firearms," said a corporal.

"I have nothing except a double barrel shotgun which I use for hunting."

"Our orders are to take all firearms."

"Surely, I can keep my shotgun. It's only for hunting," said David.

"Sorry sir."

"Please let me keep it."

"Sorry, go get it."

"Won't you please reconsider?"

"You might get it back in a day or two but I've got orders to take it."

David turned over his shotgun.

Other soldiers plundered his barn, taking 220 to 230 bundles of fodder, a great deal of corn; they threw down his rail fence, cut and hauled off thirty loads of clover hay and never gave him a receipt and never paid him a nickel.

Later, David walked over to check on the John N. Malone family, where nine intoxicated soldiers were busy trashing the house. Bureau drawers were open and the contents were scattered about the house. One soldier had a shawl draped over his arm.

"Give me that!" commanded David and tugged at the shawl, but the drunken soldier held on and cursed him. They caroused and cursed the women before heading off with two loads of molasses.

Sunday morning at about 11:00 a.m. Mrs. Charlotte Hines was seated on her front porch reading when she saw three soldiers coming across the field brandishing guns. They went directly to the Negro quarters close by and began talking to the females and running their hands down their bosoms and making sexual advances. Afterwards, they walked over to where Mrs. Hines sat on the porch.

"Do you have any guns?"

"I'm a lone woman and have none," she said.

They barged inside the house and ransacked drawers, looking for valuables, then went back to the Negro quarters. All the women had fled except for one and her 14-year-old daughter who was nursing a baby.

"How old are you?" one of the soldiers asked.

"I don't know how old I is."

"Put down that child; I want to use you."

Her mother ran to Mrs. Hines and begged her to save her daughter. The young girl cried out for her mother.

282

"Goddamn you mammy, we'll have you next," threatened a soldier.

Mrs. Hines ran out in the yard just in time to see one of the soldiers raping the young girl. When he was finished, another soldier raped her.

---

It was near suppertime when Thomas Barksdale unhitched his team of matching sorrels, a mare and a gelding and led them into the barn. The trace chains clanged as he hung them on a peg in the hallway. He slipped off the harness and draped them over a peg then removed the big leather collars and did the same. Before removing their bridles, he brushed both of the horses while they stamped their feet and whinnied, anxious to be free. Ordinarily, he would let them drink and roll in the dust before stabling them, but today was different. There were too many Yankees roaming the countryside, stealing, robbing and pillaging. They called it foraging, he called it thieving.

Ol' Luther began barking; probably treed a squirrel in the back yard, thought Thomas. He opened the stable doors and the horses walked inside. He fed them several ears of corn, gave each a bundle of fodder and provided water.

He had just reached the end of the barn hallway when he saw four men on horseback riding through the open gate. A fifth man remained at the gate. Yankees! Thomas hadn't heard them ride up. Dad gum it!

"You a secesh?" asked a corporal riding the lead horse.

Thomas didn't understand what he said. The soldier rode closer. "I'm talking to you," he said in a belligerent tone. "Are you secesh!"

"If I'se a secesh, I'd be in the Confederate Army, now wouldn't I?"

"Do you support the Union Army?"

Thomas glared at him.

"Will you take the oath?"

"There is no need for me to take an oath," replied Thomas.

"You're a secesh all right," said the corporal. "Get outta my way." He lifted his foot from his stirrup and shoved Thomas backward onto the ground.

"Let's see what he's got in the barn."

Thomas scrambled to his feet. "No, please don't take my team," he begged. "I need 'em to make a crop."

The corporal drew his revolver and pointed it at Thomas. "Reb, we need your horses for our Army so we can save the Union." The soldiers laughed.

"Check the barn, Private Julaski," ordered the corporal.

Shortly, he returned. "Fine pair of horses; lots of fodder in the loft, corn in the crib and a milk cow with her bag full."

"Send for a wagon," ordered the corporal. "Private Parsky, look in the smokehouse. I'm a hankering for some good ham and bacon."

He turned to another private and said, "McNeil, check out the house."

"Yes sir." The soldier dismounted, went to the back door and, without knocking, barged inside. Shortly he emerged, clasping something shiny. "Look here what I found."

Ma was at his heels. "Give that back to me you thief!" she said and grabbed for the silver salter. The soldier stepped sideways and pushed her away. "Shut up, old woman. Don't you know that to the victor belongs the spoils?"

Thomas watched as the soldiers loaded the wagon to the brim with corn and fodder and emptied the smokehouse. They tied hams and slabs of bacon on his horses. As an afterthought, the Corporal ordered one of the men to check the house for cornmeal. He returned with a sack over his shoulder. "We'll eat Rebel cornmeal tonight," he said and laughed.

"I want a voucher for my property," Thomas demanded.

"Shut up. The only thing you'll get is a bullet," hollered the corporal.

"Get the cow," the corporal ordered. "Nothing better than good cornbread and fresh milk."

"Please don't take our cow," Thomas begged. A soldier tethered Handful to the back of the wagon.

As they rode off, Thomas stood watching, trembling with anger, but also with fear. How would he make a crop and support Ma and Pa and the family? Thank the Lord that Sweet was back in the woods or they would have stolen her.

He turned and saw his mother wipe her eyes.

"That meant so much to me," she said. "It was a wedding gift from Sallie."

Thomas wrapped his arms around her and patted her back. "Aw Ma, don't cry. We'll get you another salter someday."

"But it won't be that one."

---

The following morning, Thomas discovered Handful standing in the hallway of the barn, bawling and waiting to be milked. The rope that dangled from her halter had been chewed through. Pa walked up, examined the rope and chuckled.

"If I had one, I'd give a Yankee dollar to seen a Yankee trying to milk ol' Handful."

Thomas grinned. "Yeah, I bet by the time she got through hook'n, kick'n and slapp'n, them Yankees were ready to turn 'er loose."

"The Lord always provides," Pa said.

# 26 | COURT MARTIAL

Athens, Alabama.

July 7, 1862.

Colonel John Turchin felt much older than his forty years as he trudged up the wooden stairs to the courtroom on the second floor of the Limestone County Courthouse. A thick-set man, he paused to catch his breath and briefly glanced out the window toward the east side of the square. The few trees that surrounded the red brick courthouse were limp in the scorching heat and the leaves were caked with brown dust. Below, he saw sentries that were posted to keep unauthorized civilians away from the courtroom. He took a deep breath and continued to climb. Today, he wasn't checking on Rebel prisoners. He was attending his own court martial.

He entered the courtroom, which was mostly empty, except for several Union soldiers and civilians who had been subpoenaed. His eyes searched for his wife, Nadine. She was seated on the front bench. He nodded to her and she smiled. He walked to the counsel table which faced several tables that had been slid together end to end, removed his hat and placed it on the table, tugged at his blue army coat and sat down.

It was hot and humid and the open windows offered little relief from the oppressive heat. It was the same courtroom where in March of the previous year, former congressman George S. Houston had argued eloquently for reconstruction of the Union and Thomas H. Hobbs had argued just as eloquently for secession. This morning, blue-coated officers were assembling for a far different purpose. The dogs of war had been loosed and it was their responsibility to deal with its consequences. It appeared that justice had finally caught up with Turchin.

Turchin sat alone at the small wooden table, dressed smartly in a blue uniform and white shirt. Silver eagles designating the rank of full Colonel perched on his shoulders. He sat erect in the chair and looked straight ahead, moving only to wipe away the sweat that beaded on his broad forehead and mustached lips. Much was riding on the outcome of these proceedings. On May 26th, he had been ordered to Fayetteville, Tennessee, and one month later he had been recommended for Brigadier General. His army career had been doing well, that is, until Commanding General, Don Carlos Buell, a by-the-book West Pointer, had ordered an investigation of his conduct in Athens. Now, this court martial.

Just before 10 a.m., members of the court martial filed in and seated themselves behind the tables. A few minutes later an officer announced "A-Ten-Hut!" Everyone rose, including Turchin, as Brigadier General James A. Garfield strode into the room and stood behind the tables at the front.

"At ease, please be seated," Garfield said and banged a gavel. There was a rustling noise and creaking of wooden benches as everyone was seated.

"This court martial will come to order," said Garfield, a tall, strong, Ohioian with short blondish whiskers. He had worked his way through school and took great pride in being a "self-made man." Garfield sat down and lifted a document from a stack of papers in front of him and read in a clear voice.

"Special orders. No. 92. Headquarters Army of Ohio Huntsville, Alabama, July 5, 1862." He cleared his throat and continued.

"A General court-martial is hereby ordered to assemble at Athens, Alabama at 10 a.m. on the 7th day of July or as soon thereafter is practicable, for the trial of Col. J.B.

Turchin, 19<sup>th</sup> Illinois Volunteers, and such other persons as may be properly brought before it."

Garfield droned on, reading the names of the six colonels who had been detailed for the court martial and were seated on each side of him.

Captain P. T. Swaine, U.S. Infantry, Judge Advocate, had been designated to prosecute Turchin. He wasn't present, having been detained at Headquarters of the Army of Ohio regarding matters relevant to the court martial. Taking note, Garfield banged the gavel. "Court is adjourned until 10 a.m. tomorrow morning."

The following morning when the court martial reconvened, Colonel Turchin was absent and the court adjourned until 10 a.m. the following day. After reading the order convening the Court, the Judge-Advocate asked Turchin if he had any objection to any member named therein.

"No sir."

The Judge Advocate proceeded to swear in the members of the Court and then he was sworn by General Garfield.

The accused will now be arraigned," Garfield said. "Will the defendant please stand?"

Turchin slowly leveraged his large body from the chair.

Captain Swaine read the charges. Charge I listed nineteen separate specifications of pillage. Charge II listed two specifications of conduct unbecoming an officer and a gentleman, to-wit: Failure to pay his bill at the Davidson Hotel and failure to prevent disgraceful behavior of his troops.

Charge III alleged disobedience of orders, to-wit:

Violation of order 13(a) – "peaceful citizens are not to be molested in person and property; failure to pay fair compensation for property or give vouchers; took forage and animals without absolute necessity and permitted his wife to remain in camp."

General Garfield looked at Turchin and asked, "Colonel, how do you plead to the charges?"

"Not guilty to all charges and specifications," Turchin answered in a strong voice. "Except for permitting my wife to remain in camp to which I plead guilty."

"Duly noted," Garfield said.

"May it please the Court," Turchin continued. "I request the privilege of introducing my counsel and move for a postponement until July 10<sup>th</sup> to enable him to reach Athens and be present at the commencement of the evidence."

The Court members briefly conferred. "Granted," said General Garfield. "This Court will be in adjournment until 10 a.m. on July 10, 1862."

When the court reconvened, Turchin was absent. Assistant Surgeon D. S. Young had sent a written statement to the court which stated that he found Turchin suffering from a severe fever and headache the night before and "it would be imprudent for him to leave his quarters in his present condition."

General Garfield passed the note to other members of the court and said, "I find this unsatisfactory." They agreed.

Dr. Young was summoned to Court and placed under oath. "Would his coming here endanger his life?" asked Judge Advocate, Swaine.

"It would not," replied Dr. Young.

"Is it an ordinary case of chills and fever?"

"It is an ordinary case," said Dr. Young, "although all of its stages are not

286

thoroughly marked."

The Court concluded that Turchin hadn't proven his motion and he was ordered to immediately appear.

Finally, Turchin showed up, not appearing nearly as cocky as before. He had one more trick up his sleeve. He raised a novel legal argument.

"I move the Court to require each witness who will testify against me be required to take the Oath of Allegiance to the United States Government before he or she be allowed to testify."

General Garfield wasn't persuaded. "Motion denied. But the Court will permit you to ask proper questions on cross examination that inquire about the loyalty of any witness against you."

Turchin's lawyer still hadn't arrived in Athens.

"I move that the trial be postponed until my counsel arrives," said Turchin.

"Motion denied. Captain Swaine, call your first witness," said General Garfield.

A good prosecutor always calls his best witness first. Postmaster Robert C. David, brother-in-law of Daniel Barksdale, was sworn and took the witness chair.

"Narrate what you know in regard to the conduct of the troops of Colonel J. B. Turchin's command when they entered Athens," said Captain Swaine.

David cleared his throat and slightly straightened. "Well, on the 2$^{nd}$ day of May, they broke open my office, the Post Office – the front door of it. I tried to come to the office. A sentinel was stationed at the corner who ordered me back saying I would be in danger. It was the next day before I got in my office; then I found everything torn to pieces, they had taken about a thousand dollars and many other things of value, among which was the wardrobes of four young men who occupied the office upstairs and all the clothes belonging to the beds, under beds, pillows, bolsters and everything, except the feather bed.

"They also took my spectacles, for which I had offered twenty dollars reward. The next day three of them came to my house and demanded my firearms. I had nothing but a double barrel shotgun. I pleaded very hard with them to let me keep it, but they said their orders were to positively to take all them up. They said perhaps I might get it back in a day or two, but I have never seen it since.

"I saw them take my corn and fodder, for which they never gave me a receipt – one bag of corn and 220 to 230 bundles of fodder. They threw down the fences on my farm, letting the cattle on it three weeks. In other portions of my farm they cut and hauled off hay and clover, not less than 30 loads."

"Were there any books damaged or destroyed?" asked Captain Swaine. "And if so, what where they?"

"About 200 Bibles and Testaments," replied David. "Nearly all Bibles, some very nice ones, were missing from my office. I saw some of the pieces afterwards in the neighborhood of the office but not immediately." David further testified that he didn't know if Turchin was aware of what was going on and that he, David, didn't notify proper officers so they could stop the pillaging. He also stated that he didn't receive money or vouchers for property taken from him.

Captain Swaine gave a satisfied nod and sat down. Now it was Turchin's turn to cross examine.

"Did the money taken from your office belong to the Southern Confederacy, or to yourself?" asked Turchin.

287

"The larger portion belonged to me," said David. "I was Treasurer of the Athens Masonic Lodge. About $130 belonged to the Lodge, about $160 or $170 belonged to the American Bible Society. Between $17 and $30 belonged to the Confederate Post Office. The balance belonged to me."

"Are you a Postmaster of the Confederate States or the United States?" asked Turchin.

"I was acting for the Confederate States at that time."

"Are you now a Union man or a secessionist, and if you are a Union man, are you willing to take the Oath of Allegiance to the United States?" asked Turchin.

"I have always called myself a Union man. As to the other part of the question, I would not be willing to take the Oath of Allegiance to the United States, as I do not think there is any necessity for it."

After a few more questions, the Court adjourned at 5:30 p.m. to meet again the next morning at 8:00 a.m.

The following morning, Mrs. Mildred Ann Clayton, a widow who lived four-and-a-half blocks from the courthouse, was sworn in and took the stand. She testified that two Federals came to her house, called her a "Goddamn Bitch" and threatened to shoot her. They pilfered and trashed her house and attempted to rape her servant girl.

"Did you notify some of the officers about the outrage?" asked Turchin.

"No, I went to a friend to know what to do and he said he would get me a guard, but I got none."

Robert J. Mendum, the next witness, was at the livery stable at the southeast corner of the square when Turchin and his troops rode up.

"One of his men called up two negroes to take care of Turchin's horse," he testified. "He seemed much excited or mad and said they didn't want any Negroes to take his horse; that he had a notion to make some of these white men rub him down, they, being the citizens, 'would as soon cut all your throats as not.'"

"What did you do?" asked Swaine.

"I left then as I did not feel like rubbing him myself."

The court martial dragged on for days. Prosecutor Swaine put on one local citizen after another that testified to pillaging, thievery and debauchery by Turchin's troops. Swaine was slowly building his case. Turchin, whose lawyer still hadn't arrived, asked few questions. Most were directed to whether the witness supported the Confederacy and whether they had seen him present when the pillaging was ongoing.

On July 15th, the prosecutor called 1st Lt. Robert G. Chandler to the stand. He was with the 1st Regiment Michigan Artillery and wasn't a local with an axe to grind.

So far, no witness had placed Turchin positively at the scene of the crime.

"I was ordered to plant my guns to command a certain hill," said Chandler. "And to do so, it became necessary to take down the fence of Mr. Tanner, on the corner of the square. "The 19th Illinois stacked arms in the street by orders from its commander, which I heard, I do not know whether the rest of the brigade stacked arms or not. A great number of soldiers dispersed in town, and I saw some of them appear afterwards with citizen's clothing, caps, hats and etc. – such as would naturally come from stores. I also saw a great number of Negroes carrying away a variety of articles, and I heard a great noise in town as a pillaging.

"Afterwards, when speaking to Colonel Turchin on duty in regard to sending away a gun as ordered and about rations, I found him talking to someone and he

288

remarked that the affairs then going on, 'that he did not care so long as they did not take what they did not need,' or words to that effect."

The Court recessed during the middle of the day and instructed Lt. Chandler to reappear before the Court at 4:00 p.m. Failing to appear, he was sent for at his quarters where he was found asleep. After waiting an hour the Court directed the arrest of Lt. Chandler for contempt of court, and Captain Swaine then informed the Court that Lt. Chandler was too drunk to be arrested.

The following morning the court reconvened, and this time Lt. Chandler was present to take the witness stand. He had gone to his hotel room for dinner and drunk a bottle of wine the previous afternoon, he said. Before taking a nap, he also took a dose of morphine for a neuralgia. "I was too stooped to awake," he said, "and was totally unconscious of it."

The Court found his condition was not intentional disrespect for the Court and he was released from arrest.

Joseph E. Arnold, bass drummer of the 18th Ohio Regiment was called to the stand. He said he saw Turchin sitting on the door step of the courthouse.

"Was there much plundering directly in front of Colonel Turchin where he sat at the time?" asked Captain Swaine.

"Yes. All the stores and shops over there were open as many soldiers as could were going in and out. Those coming out were bringing goods, and the noise was so great that if a person had not seen it, if he had ordinary hearing, would have had his attention drawn to it."

Private Joel C. Stevens of Company D, 18th Ohio, was with Colonel Stanley when he retreated from Athens.

"How has your regiment been treated in the town by the citizens?" asked Captain Swaine.

"It was treated very well. I never saw any soldier misused in anyway," said Pvt. Stevens. "When we retreated from town I saw several citizens – several ladies – wave their handkerchiefs, but the men did nothing out of the way. He further testified that this regiment was the last to come back into Athens on May 2nd and stacked arms. The other troops also stacked arms in the street and dispersed and commenced pillaging the town.

"The pillaging was general, and there was considerable noise," said Stevens. "The soldiers would take what articles they could find and break the doors open with them. I was on guard and sitting on the fence at the courthouse."

"Did you see Colonel Turchin while this was going on?"

"He came from the depot on horseback," replied Stevens. "Some soldiers were with him. He took a road passing on one side of the square."

The following morning Madison Thompson, an Athens citizen, testified that troops broke open the back door of the store and "nearly all of my stock of dry goods and groceries were gone – or about $3,000." His stable and crib were entered and corn, oats and fodder were taken, together with some lumber.

George L. Peck, a clerk at Peck and McAllister's Store was upstairs looking on at the plundering on May 2nd. The soldiers rushed over and burst in the door and stripped the store of all of its contents. An iron safe was broken open in his presence with about a half a dozen sledge hammers and axes. "A Lieutenant assisted in this until he got tired," said Peck. "They robbed the safe of $140 of Peck and McAllister's money and other money placed there on deposit."

"Were no steps taken to put a stop to this plundering?" asked Captain Swaine.

"No, none that I saw. The total value of goods taken was about $4,800."

Turchin's lawyer rose to cross examine. "When the soldier first broke into the store, did you ask the commander of the troops or some commander of some regiment to protect your property?"

"I saw an officer riding around the square," said Peck, "He witnessed what was going on right under their noses. But I did ask one Captain who came to my door and he answered that 'we were treated no worse than we deserved.'"

J.S. Sowell, a local citizen, testified that he went to his office and found soldiers there destroying its contents. "They destroyed and carried away some books of my library, some of the volumes were scattered about the floor and they were broken, also a fine microscope, some surgical tooth instruments and some glassware was broken." He further testified that soldiers went to his dwelling and took some bedding for the wounded that they had in a house nearby where he went to help dress the wounds and never got paid for any of the items nor was he given a receipt.

T.J. Cox was recalled as a witness and testified that he was present at Niphonia Fairground on May 1st when Colonel Scott's Confederate Cavalry gave orders to burn the property of the 18th Ohio that could not be carried away in wagons. "Someone suggested that the knapsacks which were piled up be given to the Negroes. And, the soldiers of the Scott's Cavalry gave the Negroes knapsacks and clothing which they carried away."

"Do you know that some of the prominent citizens of Athens refused in the beginning to sign a pledge against guerilla warfare," asked Turchin's counsel, "which had been submitted by General Mitchell for the signatures to discontinue the same?"

"I do not," said Cox. "It was presented to me and I signed it."

Peterson Tanner testified that troops broke into Peterson Tanner and Sons on May 2nd between 10 a.m. and 12:00 and destroyed and carried away nearly all of their entire stock of goods. After recalling Private Joel C. Stevens and bass drummer, Joseph E. Arnold, who testified that it was the 8th Brigade commanded by Colonel Turchin who came into Athens, the prosecution rested after calling 19 witnesses.

Defense counsel rose. "May it please the court, I move the case be continued for two days to give me time to prepare a defense and await the arrival of witnesses."

"Granted, the court will reconvene Monday morning, July 21, at 10 a.m.," Garfield said and banged the gavel.

The witnesses were unaware, but while they testified about the pillaging of Turchin's troops, an order was being signed promoting him to Brigadier General. The message was clear.

Five days earlier, General Nathan Bedford Forrest raided Murfreesboro, Tennessee, capturing 1,400 Federal troops. It was feared that Forrest would pounce on Athens at any time. General Buell moved the court martial to Huntsville, where it resumed in the courthouse on July 21st.

Lt. William B. Curtis, 19th Illinois Regiment testified that soldiers of the 18th Ohio stated that they had received insults from the men and women of Athens when they were driven out, being called "Goddamn sons of bitches," and women had spit on their faces. This was pure hearsay.

The defense called fourteen witnesses. Turchin didn't take the stand and subject himself to cross examination but he was allowed to present a written statement. "The more lenient we are to secessionists, the bolder they become," he wrote. "And if we do

290

not change our policy and prosecute this war with vigor, using all means that we possess against the enemy, including the emancipation of slaves, the ruin of this country is inevitable."

The court martial adjourned at 7 p.m. on July 29th. Next morning the verdict was rendered. Guilty on 22 of the 25 specifications. Not guilty on failure to pay the hotel bill; not guilty of taking forage and animals without necessity and not guilty on conduct unbecoming a gentleman.

Turchin was sentenced to be dismissed from the Army. On August 12, 1862, he telegraphed his friends and family in Chicago that he would catch a train home the next day. He arrived to a thunderous welcome.

On August 16th, General Buell felt constrained to carry the sentence into effect and affirmed the court martial's decision.

On August 26, 1862, when the 19th Illinois was retreating towards Nashville, part of the Athens business district, the east side of the square and the Niphonia Fairground were set fire.

On September 25th Lincoln gave Brigadier General Turchin a new command. General Buell was mustered out of the volunteer service as well as General Mitchell. The policy of conciliation was dead.

# PART
# IV

# 27 | DUTY CALLED

Lincoln County, Tennessee
Saturday, November 1, 1862.

Rufus Cooley McElroy, age 32, woke early. It wasn't because of the soft snoring of his wife Amanda, or the fact that her arm and leg was draped over him. He liked to feel the warmth of her body. She was 26 years of age, the mother of his two children, Constant, age 5, and Martha, 1 year old, and a very desirable woman in all respects. The room was cold and north wind whistled beneath the door and around the chinks in the log house. Any other Saturday morning he would have sunk deeper in the warm feather bed and nudged closer to Amanda, perhaps waking her for a moment of intimacy before the children woke. But today was different. He quietly climbed out of bed, stood barefoot on the cold plank floor, and pulled on his breeches and with shoes in hand, hurried to the parlor where he finished dressing then stoked a fire in the fireplace. Dawn came clear and cold. He stared at the flames, deep in thought, and smoked his long-stem corncob pipe. He hadn't rushed to join the "Glorious Cause" as some called it, when Tennessee had seceded from the Union in April, 1861. Neither had his brothers. Like many folks, the McElroys believed in the Union. Their grandfather Micajah had fought the British to establish a free and independent Union and their Uncles Arch and Mike had fought them again in the War of 1812. They waited on the sidelines, hoping that the North would see the error of its ways and leave Tennessee and the South to mind its own business. The way they viewed it, Tennesseans had voluntarily joined the Union and as free and independent citizens they had the right to leave it.

Then in April, 1862, General Ormsby Mitchell invaded middle Tennessee and marched into Fayetteville and threatened the citizens of Lincoln County. Free citizens won't long abide such arrogant behavior and threats. Yankees stole practically every horse, mule, chicken and turkey in the county, not to mention smokehouse meat, corn and fodder. The war had moved closer. The Union Army of the Cumberland was headquartered in Nashville and the Confederate Army of Tennessee was at Murfreesboro, only fifty miles up the road. It was only a matter of time before a major battle erupted. If Confederate forces prevailed, the Yankees would be driven from Tennessee, hopefully for good. Every able-bodied man was needed.

His father William had died from typhoid fever approximately seven years earlier. Death was always lurking – stopping a bullet to save the Southland was preferred to the fever.

A bumping noise interrupted his thoughts. A door opened and slammed. Footsteps.

"You up mighty early," said his younger brother, Thomas, who sat down in front of the fireplace, yawned and pulled on his shoes.

"I got things on my mind," replied Rufus.

Thomas glanced out the window where wind swayed the cedar trees. "Another cold and windy day," he said.

Rufus grunted and puffed his pipe in silence. Shortly, he looked over at his brother and said, "Tom, I'm enlisting."

Tom reflected for a moment, and then sighed. "If anyone goes it outta be me, I'm twenty-one and single. You need to stay here with Amanda and the kids."

"Duty calls and I must heed its summons. I want you to stay here, at least for a while, and take care of the family. Seeing after them is as important as fighting Yankees. I've talked to Mike and Jack and they're going to enlist too. We figure if the Yankees can be defeated in Tennessee, they'll be gone for good."

"Have you told Amanda?"

"Not yet."

"Told me what?" Amanda entered the room, rubbing sleep from her eyes, and backed up the fireplace to warm.

Sensing that he needed to absent himself, Tom stood and announced, "I'm gonna feed the livestock."

After Tom departed, Rufus looked up at his young wife. "Amanda, I've decided to enlist."

Her eyes dropped and face tightened slightly as she nodded. "I've known it was coming for a long time. In fact, I've been knitting wool socks for you," she said, lip trembling. "It has to be done. Don't worry about me and the children. Tom can plant the crop and oversee the Negroes and we'll be okay, but I'll worry about you."

Rufus stood and pulled her into his arms. "You're a mighty fine woman, Amanda, and I love you more than I can speak it."

She looked up, teary eyed. "I'm proud of you."

After breakfasting on fried sowbelly and cornmeal mush, Rufus warmed his hands at the fireplace momentarily before striding out the back door to the log stables. Vapor streamed from Jackson's nostrils as Rufus slipped a bridle over the big chestnut gelding's head and threw on the saddle. He cinched the belly band tight. "Don't swell up on me Jackson," he said quietly. He waited for the horse to exhale and then notched it tighter. He swung into the cold saddle and clucked to the horse. The animal was eager to warm up and soon they were trotting south down Hamwood Road toward Fayetteville, hooves clattering on the frozen earth.

John Adams, his 21-year-old younger brother who everyone called "Jack," had agreed to meet him at the courthouse around nine o'clock. Today, he didn't have to avoid Yankee patrols as he had done in the recent past. With the Confederate Army up the road, they had high-tailed it out of Fayetteville. Town was crowded as it was most Saturdays, many purchasing supplies, others present to visit and catch up on the latest news. Numerous horses and buggies were hitched around the courthouse that his father and grandfather had built, and he suspected that some of their owners were there to join the Confederate Army.

He spotted Jack standing beside his mount, blowing on his fingers and stamping his feet. He rode up and reined.

"Mornin' Jack, how are ya?" he asked, swinging from the saddle.

"Cold. Where's Mike? Ain't he enlisting?"

"He's gonna kill hogs first," replied Rufus.

"It sure is a bad time of the year to leave home," said Jack. "But I'm ready to whip some damn Yankees."

"Where is he?"

"Inside," said Jack, gesturing toward the brick courthouse.

They entered the courthouse and stood in line behind several other men who were enlisting, most of whom they knew. There was much bravado among the younger ones who seemed eager to fight Yankees.

Shortly, a man wearing a gray uniform with Captain insignia came to the door and motioned Rufus inside a small office. Jack followed.

"I'm Captain Francisco Rice, Starnes' Fourth Tennessee Cavalry Regiment," he said, offering his hand to Rufus.

"Good to meet you sir. I'm Rufus McElroy and this is my brother, John Adams. We call 'im Jack."

After shaking Jack's hand, Rice asked, "You men here to enlist?"

"Reckon so, unless the war has ended," quipped Jack.

"Hardly the case," said Captain Rice. "A big fight is shaping up near Murfreesboro and we need all the men we can find."

"We don't wanna walk, we wanna ride," said Rufus.

"Can you men ride and shoot?"

"Both. And at the same time," replied Jack, proudly.

"Do you own your own horses?" asked Rice.

"Sure do," the brothers chimed.

"Good, the government will allow you $24.40 for their use," said Captain Rice. "How long do you want to enlist?"

"'Til we're dead or the Yankees leave us alone," replied Jack.

Captain Rice glanced at Rufus. "Your brother is enthusiastic. I like that."

"That's youth, Capt'n. As for me, I'm more interested in living."

"Have y'all seen action?" asked Jack.

"Very little. We were ordered to Chattanooga and attached to General Kirby Smith. At the time we were armed only with shotguns. We skirmished at Wartrace in April and again at Readyville in June.

"On August 4$^{th}$, this year, we were ordered to report to General Nathan Bedford Forrest in middle Tennessee. Currently, the regiment is on the outskirts of Nashville with General Forrest."

"Ain't Forrest the one who refused to surrender at Fort Donelson back in February?" asked Rufus.

"Yes, when the commander decided to surrender, Forrest replied, 'to hell with that. I didn't come here to surrender.' And he didn't. He cut his way out of the fort and escaped to Nashville. He's making a name for himself."

"Show me where to sign," said Jack.

It didn't take long for Captain Rice to fill out the forms. "Men you have done the honorable thing," he said. "Report to Company K, Starnes' Regiment at Murfreesboro where you'll be sworn in and paid for the use of your horses." He stood and shook their hands. "Congratulations and may providence guide our noble cause."

---

Monday, November 20$^{th}$, near Molino Post Office.

Micajah L. "Mike" McElroy, named after his grandfather, rose at first light and walked outside his log house near the south bank of Elk River and studied the weather. It was cold, but not freezing. And the moon was shrinking. Just right. Old timers said that November 20$^{th}$ was "hog killing day." If the moon was shrinking the meat produced a lot of lard and grease.

Inside, after placing a back log in the rock fireplace and stoking a fire, he lifted his musket from above the mantle together with a powder horn and lead shot; poured powder down the barrel; dropped in a shot and wadding and tamped it down with ram rod.

Outside, Amos and Paul, Negroes who belonged to his brother Rufus, were placing a metal scalding vat over a trench filled with firewood.

"Fill it about two-thirds full before you start the fire," ordered Mike.

"Yassuh, massa," replied Amos.

After the vat was positioned over the fire hole, the Negroes drew water from the well and poured it into the vat, then started a fire beneath it.

Mike went to the crib and got several ears of corn and called the hogs.

"Heah piggie – piggie, heah... heah." He made noise by rubbing the corn ears together. Soon, four large hogs waddled toward him, squealing for the corn. Mike locked them inside the rail pen; shouldered the musket, took dead aim at a hog's snout and fired. The hog toppled over dead. He quickly reloaded and killed the remaining pigs, then slit their throats and let them bleed.

The Negroes dragged the hogs over to the vat. As soon as one hog was lifted out and hung upside down by the heels on a tree limb by using block and tackle, another hog was lowered into the vat. After the hair was scraped off with knives, Mike slit open the hog's bellies with a sharp butcher knife, letting the guts fall into a tub. Those would be given to the Negroes for chittlins. The stomach, lungs and bladder, he sliced out and tossed to the salivating dogs that sat nearby on their haunches. Each hog was dressed, the fat trimmed away from the hams, shoulders and middlins before they were placed inside the salt box. The tails, feet, heads and most of the brains, he gave to the Negroes.

"Massa, ain't no better eat'n than scrambled hog brains 'n eggs," said Amos.

Mike cut off several slices of tenderloin and handed them to the Negroes. "Yeah, but this is the best," he said.

Nearby, Amos' wife, Lizer, heavy with child, had a hot fire going under a large cast iron kettle, where fat trimmings were cooked and lard rendered. After the trimmings had cooked down they would be placed in a cloth sack to drip dry and eaten later in cornbread. Cracklin cornbread was mighty fine eating. The grease in the kettle was poured into stands and would become lard. By suppertime, sausages had been ground and meat was stored in the salt box where it would remain for six weeks, then hung in the smokehouse and smoked for flavor.

For supper, Mattie fried tenderloin and scrambled hog brains and eggs. Biscuits were baking in a Dutch oven. They sat near the fire and ate in silence. Except for rabbit and squirrel, it was the only meat they'd eaten since the Yankees cleaned out their smokehouse and stole their chickens in the spring. They ate sweet tenderloin until they had gorged themselves.

"Will you be here for Christmas?" asked Mattie.

Mike wiped grease from his whiskers. "No, I'll be leaving in a week or so."

She nodded stoically. A small, pretty woman – a Whitaker of Lincoln County – they had been married for two years and one month.

---

Monday, December 1st.

Mike hunched his shoulders against the cold as he rode east. There was silence except for the soft crunching of the mare's hooves on the frozen snow and her occasional snorting that spooked a rabbit to jump and run. A cold snap had followed hog killing.

Snow drifts lay against the rail fences bordering Molino Road. Tranquil. But he knew it was only temporary. Soon, he would hear the thunder of cannon and the crackle of rifle fire. He was a livestock trader, not a warrior. He didn't look forward to making the change. He wished that he had departed for the Army with his brothers, but it wasn't to be. He had to provide food for his family. In the distance, smoke curled from scores of chimneys, creating a gray cloud that hung over Fayetteville. He rode over the newly-constructed stone bridge that spanned 450 feet across Elk River, iron shoes clanging on the limestone, and into Fayetteville where he met Lt. Adams recruiting for Captain Rice at the courthouse.

Mike enlisted in Company K with his brothers. It was quick and simple. Lt. Adams asked several questions and filled in a printed form: "Micajah L. McElroy, age 35, 6'1" tall, hazel eyes, auburn hair and ruddy complexion."

"Sign at the bottom," said Lt. Adams, handing him an ink pen. Mike hesitated.

"What about my horse?"

"At Murfreesboro, you'll be sworn in and paid $24.40 for the use of your mount."

---

Tuesday morning. Mike rose early. Murfreesboro was fifty miles north. If he rode hard, he could be there in time for a late supper. After starting a fire, he went to the barn and fed his dapple gray mare, giving her extra fodder and corn. The weather had turned colder and by the time he returned to the house, his fingers were numb. Mattie was up, quietly placing freshly cut biscuit dough into a Dutch oven. He reached for a drink of water and the dipper was frozen in the wooden bucket.

""Darn it's cold," he remarked.

"I've knitted wool socks," she said; wiped flour from her hands and went to the bedroom and returned with three pairs. She was teary-eyed.

"I can't bear to think of you being cold and hungry," she said, wiping her eyes, "I'm frying up some tenderloin. It will taste good between biscuits –"

He pulled her into his arms, feeling the warmth of her body against him. Her chest heaved and her words came out in jerks. "I prayed that... I would be strong... that God would give me the strength... to stand behind you, but I can't hold back... any longer."

"It's okay, honey," he said, stroking her hair.

"I'm so afraid." Then she broke down and wept.

"Everything'll be okay." But he knew it was a lie. Men were dying not only from bullets, but from disease and malnutrition. Those fortunate enough to come home often returned without arms and legs. He had enlisted for the duration of the war. And it was probable that he wouldn't return home alive. With death lurking in his future, he suddenly had a primitive desire to copulate and reproduce. They had coupled during the night, but now he wanted her again. He swooped her up in his arms and carried her to the bedroom.

"Mike!"

"What?"

"The biscuits!" she exclaimed, looking back over her shoulder.

"They'll wait."

Afterwards, he lay on his back with Mattie cuddled against him.

"I smell something," she said, raising up. "The biscuits!" She leapt from bed and ran to the fireplace. He entered, pulling on his breeches.

"I don't think they're too burned to eat," she said.

After breakfast he dressed warmly and went to the barn and saddled the mare and led her around to the front door. Mattie was waiting with a sack. "Inside are extra socks and some biscuits and tenderloin. And here is something special that I knitted for you." She handed him gloves and draped a wool scarf around his neck. "Wrap it around your ears and think of me."

He kissed her softly on the lips. "I'll be back." With musket in one hand he swung into the saddle and nudged the mare forward.

"I'll have hot biscuits waiting," she yelled and waved.

"Can we burn 'em?" he hollered.

----

It was near midnight and barely enough starlight to see the road when Mike and the other recruits neared Murfreesboro. His feet, hands and nose were numb, maybe even frostbitten. He swayed in the saddle, not sure if he was going to sleep or dying from hypothermia. The mare's nervous behavior woke him. She sensed danger. The other horses were acting strangely also.

"HALT! WHO GOES THERE?"

The mare bolted sideways, nearly toppling Mike from the saddle. Standing in the road were two shadowy figures.

"I said halt or we'll fire!"

"Whoa..." said Mike reining his horse.

"Who goes there?"

"We're headed for Murfreesboro," replied Mike.

"Are you Rebs or homemade Yankees?"

"Depends on whose asking," replied Mike.

"You'd better hope you Rebs," said one, rifle raised.

"We're looking for Starnes' Fourth Tennessee Cavalry," said Mike.

"Why didn't ya say so? They're somewhere in that direction," said the picket, pointing.

Camp fires lit up the night. When Mike located headquarters he was nearly frozen and a soldier assisted him from the saddle. It was then that he learned that K Company wasn't present.

While thawing out over a blazing fire he munched on biscuit and tenderloin. He was loaned an extra blanket and rolled up in it near the fire and was soon sound asleep.

Someone shaking his shoulder woke him before daylight. He heard a bugle.

"Get up trooper, - it's *reveille*." Mike cracked his sleepy eyes and saw a man wearing a gray coat and a gray slouch hat standing over him.

"Who are you?"

"Sergeant Knowles, Fourth Tennessee."

"I'm too old for this," said Mike. "Every bone in my body aches. I rode fifty miles yesterday and got here a few hours ago. I'm half froze to death."

"You just got started. After formation and breakfast, you and the other recruits are to join K Company with General Forrest in Columbia. Now get up, private!"

Mike was sworn in, paid $24.40 for the use of his horse, issued an extra blanket, slouch hat, overcoat, canteen, knapsack, haversack, bacon and a 12-gauge, double barrel sawed-off shotgun. Each barrel fired a 12-pellet round of buckshot. The Quartermaster Sergeant eyed Mike's old musket. "Reckon that thing will hurt a Yankee?"

"If his head ain't no harder than a hogs, it will," replied Mike.

---

It was a bitter cold and exhausting fifty-mile ride to Columbia. But when he was reunited with his brothers, he quickly forgot about his misery. They invited him to their mess.

"Jack's our cook," said Rufus.

"When did he learn to cook?" asked Mike.

"He hasn't," teased Rufus.

In truth, his brothers were gaunt-looking, having lost weight since he last saw them a month earlier.

That night wood was added to the fire for final time before they rolled up in their blankets and slept on the frozen ground. Later, Mike woke up cold and saw that the fire had burned down to ashes. His brothers were snoring. He rolled out of his blanket, got wood and rekindled the fire and tried to sleep, but couldn't. Too damn cold. And the ground was too damn hard. He thought about Mattie and wondered if she was lying awake in her warm feather bed thinking about him. He hoped so, but doubted it. He dozed off and was awakened when someone jerked his blanket back.

"Wake up McElroy!" Mike sat up and blinked.

A short, middle-aged man with wide shoulders and a bushy black beard hovered over him.

"Damm. Absalom Powell!"

"That's right."

"What 'n hell you doin' here?" asked Mike.

"I'm First Sergeant of Company K."

Mike cleared his throat and spit. "Who made you a sergeant?"

"The same authority that made you a private," replied Powell. "Now git up and report to Company Headquarters for guard duty."

December 10<sup>th</sup> dawned bitter cold and with much activity in the camp. They were moving out. Finally, the McElroy brothers would get a crack at Yankees.

General Nathan Bedford Forrest's command rode west. The McElroy brothers rode together near the rear of the regiment in Company K, one of the seven companies of the Fourth Tennessee commanded by Colonel James W. Starnes, a black whiskered medical doctor by profession. . All total, there were approximately 2,000 troopers.

Artillery caissons lumbered along, pulled by horses, together with numerous supply wagons pulled by mules. As long as the ground was frozen traveling was easy, but when it thawed thousands of hooves and wheels churned the road into knee deep mud.

Gen. Braxton Bragg, Commander of the Army of Tennessee, headquartered at Murfreesboro, had ordered Forrest to west Tennessee to draw Federal troops out of north Mississippi and relieve pressure against the Confederates there. Forrest departed for battle without tents and firing caps for shotguns and pistols. The men grumbled. "What are we to fight with?" asked a trooper.

"Use your gun as a club."

Mike considered his younger brothers veterans and listened to their advice.

"Ole Bedford is ornery as a sore tail cat," said Rufus. "Stay out of his way and don't cross 'im. And be damn sure you take good care of your mount. He's liable to show up at any moment and inspect her feet."

Forrest, born in poverty near Chapel Hill, Bedford County, Tennessee in 1821, moved to North Mississippi at an early age. Although, he had no formal education, he had become a Memphis millionaire engaged in planting, real estate and slave trading. A little more than a year before, he was a private in the ranks. Now, he was a Brigadier General, commanding a brigade. Folks were taking notice of him.

Mike fell into camp routine. After a long day in the saddle the company stopped, gathered wood and started fires. Horses were brushed, fed corn and oats and cared for.

Jack started cooking supper, which was the same as the day before – sow belly and cornbread hoecakes.

"What's that racing around in the cornmeal?" asked Rufus.

Jack bent over and squinted. "Weevils. Good for you."

"We're down to living on noth'n," said Mike.

"Don't complain to me, I just cook it," said Jack.

"The horses eat better than we do," said Rufus.

"I can parch some corn if you'd rather have it," replied Jack.

"Forget it."

When it rained, they ate leftovers, if they had any, and shivered while water ran down their backs. And there was always guard duty, two hours on and four off, especially for Mike, which Sergeant Absalom Powell always made sure of. Reveille came before day light. After feeding horses, they usually breakfasted on sow belly and hoecakes washed down with spring water, that is, if a fire could be kindled. The campsite was filthy. Troopers often relieved themselves where they stood.

The weather turned miserable and freezing rain began to fall. The men rode wet and cold all day and at night they slept on hard ground under the stars and near a fire, that is, if they were lucky enough to get one started. And they pushed on. Mike saw Forrest up close for the first time when they forded Buffalo River west of Hohenwald.

At least 6 feet two inches tall, 180 pounds with wavy black hair, short mustache and black chin whiskers, he wore an old slouch hat, pinned up on one side, gray coat and pants, and sat erect in the saddle. He carefully eyed each horse that came out of the water.

"Trooper, your horse is limping. Rein up and wait," he ordered a soldier.

When Mike drew nearer he noticed Forrest's penetrating dark gray eyes and even white teeth.

"Fine-looking mare you're riding," said Forrest to Mike.

"Thank you suh."

A cold rain continued for days. On December 13th, they reached the east bank of the icy Tennessee River at Clifton. The men crossed the 300-foot-wide icy waters in two flat boats that were shuttled back and forth for three days. The horses swam. Once across, the boats were sunk for future use. General Forrest obtained 50,000 caps for pistols and shotguns. Now, the men were not only eager to fight, they were prepared to do so.

They rode northwest toward Lexington, where a large force of Federal troops was stationed. At first, it was reported to be more than a thousand Yankees, but as they rode nearer the rumor mill ran wild.

"I heard a Lieutenant say there're two thousand blue bellies dug in up there just wait'n on us," said a trooper.

Before nightfall the rumor mill had increased the Union force to five thousand. The usual banter among men ceased as they thought about what lay ahead of them. Many of the men, like the McElroy brothers, had no combat experience. Mike felt a tightness in his gut and a rumbling in this stomach. Fear was creeping in. He had experienced the same feeling before when he was a young man confronted by a bully like Absalom Powell. *The sorry son of the Devil.* When the time came, he wondered if he would measure up.

They reached the outskirts of Lexington on the evening of December 17th and pitched camp. The officers ordered the men to build numerous fires and someone beat on a kettle drum for most of the night to give the impression of a large infantry force present.

The brothers huddled around their fire while Jack cooked coosh, a mixture of fried sow belly, grease and cornmeal, then prepared enough rations of hoecake and sow belly for two days. Rufus swallowed a spoonful of coosh and set his plate aside.

"No offense Jack, but I'm not hungry."

The usual chatter among the men at nearby campfires had ceased except for an occasional utterance of false bravado. The men sensed the impending danger.

Rufus sat near the fire and wrote a letter to Amanda. Finished, he folded it carefully and placed it inside his hat. "Mike, if something happens to me be sure Amanda gets this letter."

"Don't talk like that."

"I'm serious," said Rufus. "Promise me."

"I swear it Brother."

Jack hadn't spoken a word in the last hour.

"You okay?" asked Mike.

Jack swallowed and nodded. "Yeah."

They scrunched together close to the fire and spent another cold, miserable night on the ground.

The bugler blew reveille at 4 a.m. After the horses were fed and cared for, shot guns, muskets, and pistols were inspected by the officer and ammunition was issued - shells for the double barrels and rounds for the muskets.

"PREPARE TO MOUNT!"

"MOUNT!"

Saddles creaked as the troopers mounted.

General Forrest rode to the front of the formation on Roderick, his favorite mount. Mike strained to hear.

"Men of the South. Remember, you are here to defend the honor of your mothers, daughters and wives. And remember them. And, remember your once-happy homes as you go into battle. Upon your bravery hinges the destiny of our sacred Southland, our homes and our loved ones. Drive the enemy from our land. Keep up the skeer!"

A thunderous shout went up from the ranks.

"FORWARRD!" bellowed Forrest and the brigade moved out.

They advanced toward Lexington, driving in the Yankee pickets. General Forrest split the brigade into three forces. The smaller one would assault the Union center while the two larger forces would swing around and strike their flanks.

Starnes' Fourth Tennessee would attack the flank. The seven companies lined up, horses prancing, neighing and pawing the ground, sensing the impending danger.

On Mike's right was Rufus, calmly sitting on his big chestnut gelding reins in one hand, a double barrel shotgun in the other. On his left was younger brother Jack, face pale as death, also cradling a shotgun.

"How are ya?" Mike asked.

"Scared," mouthed Jack.

"Me too Brother. Let's all stay together and watch each other's back and we'll be okay."

"When I enlisted I never figured it would be like this," said Jack. "I knew there would be fight'n, but it didn't seem real at the time. This is real. We could all die."

"Keep your nerve Brother," said Mike.

Colonel Starnes, dressed in gray, rode to the front of the regiment on a 16-hands black gelding, a sword hanging at his side. The regimental colors fluttered in the breeze. His words were measured. "Men, remember your families back home. And remember what the Yankees have done and what they will continue to do until we drive them from our soil. We were at peace until they invaded our land, stole our property, plundered our goods and killed our neighbors and members of our families. And remember that you are Tennesseans. Tennesseans have always fought for their liberty. Let us do our duty. Sweep the field of Bluecoats."

Mike nervously checked his shotgun; both barrels were loaded with buckshot. The tightness in his stomach had turned into a knot and moved to his dry throat where it was stuck. His heart pounded and he had an urge to defecate and empty his bowels. Suddenly, he had something else to worry about. Would he soil his pants? He was saying a silent prayer when cannon thundered at the Yankee front. They seemed to fire forever, giving him too much time to ponder his mortality. Now he had to urinate.

Finally, he heard the rattle of small arms. The battle had opened. Colonel Starnes raised his sword. "MEN, LET'S SHOW 'EM HOW TENNESSEANS FIGHT!"

Sergeant Powell took over and gave the command in a loud, clear voice, "Reg-i-ment—For-warrdd!"

The phalanx of horsemen moved forward at a walk. The trooper looked left and right, lining up, careful not to get too close to the horse in front.

"TROT!"

Rufus nudged his beg chestnut gelding with spurs and the horse jumped to a trot, wanting to go faster. He pulled back on the reins and spoke to him. "Trot-Jackson-trot."

They trotted closer to the enemy. Equipment rattled, horses blew and hooves clattered.

"GAL—LOPP!"

Rufus spurred his mount. The regiment lunged forward at a faster pace. Closer and closer they came. The horses were anxious to go. Rufus pulled the rein tight. "Easy Jackson." Colonel Starnes was in front. Closer and closer.

"CHARRGGE!"

The bugler sounded the charge and the horses ran forward, hooves thundering and flinging dirt into the air.

Someone gave the Rebel Yell. "E-E-E-E-E-E AAAAAAAARA!"

Others joined in and the fiendish sound erupted from hundreds of throats, drowning out the thundering hooves, as the men, eager for retribution, charged forward. There was no turning back, it was kill or be killed. Mike glanced to each side and saw his brothers, faces distorted, screaming the Rebel yell. He joined in until his voice was hoarse and no sound would come forth. They crashed into the Yankee flank, shotguns blazing and pistols barking. The Federals whirled and fired. Adrenaline shot through Mike's body, his only thoughts being to save himself. Curses, screams, guns blazing, shotguns blasting, swords hacking at human flesh. Blood spurting, horses falling and men dying. He took no note of his brothers.

Finally, the blue line buckled, then broke. When the firing ended, Mike sat in the saddle for a moment, surveying the destruction. His hands trembled. Men and horses were dead and wounded, some men begging for help, others praying. He had survived and he hadn't soiled his pants. *Where were Rufus and Jack?* He looked around and saw Rufus with his arm around Jack, who was bent over his saddle puking. In some bizarre way, Mike felt exhilarated by the horrible experience. Never before had he lived this close to death.

That evening, sitting around a warm fire, the brothers discussed their experience.

"It's strange," said Rufus. "At first, I was so scared I didn't hear a word that Colonel Starnes said to us. All I could think about was dying. What would happen to Amanda and the children if I was killed? Then I thought about what would happen to them if we didn't drive those blue devils from our land. I prayed that God would give me strength to do my duty. Then a feeling of inner peace swept through me."

"Yeah, I was scared too," said Mike. "But I think I was more scared of running, than dying. I'll tell ya, I didn't know if I would run or fight. And I was praying too. It helped a lot. But when I looked over at you sitting calm and collected in the saddle it gave me confidence. When we plowed into them Yanks, all I could think of was surviving. I didn't give a damn if I killed a dozen blue bellies and went to hell for it. It was them or me –"

"I know what you mean," said Rufus. "And after it was over I felt like I had won the county wrestling match and was ready to fight again."

Jack listened in silence. "I'm a coward and I know it," he said quietly.

"Cowards run," said Rufus. "You fought just like we did. And remember not every man is the same."

"I was scared to death," said Jack. "Couldn't think. I barely remember what happened." He held up his trembling hands near the glowing fire. "Just look at this."

"All of us were scared and everyone deals with his fear in his own way and that's the way it oughta be," said Rufus, putting his arm around Jack's shoulder. "You did your duty and that's all that's expected of any man."

The surrender provided fine pistols and rifles to the Confederates. Now, the men were adequately armed and ready to carry on the fight. The command moved toward Jackson, mopping up Federal pickets, destroying railroad tracks and creating havoc. Finding the town heavily defended, they moved around it. Starnes' Fourth Cavalry was ordered to Humboldt while General Forrest advanced on Trenton.

Rufus slept very little, not only because he kept thinking about killing other humans – men like him who had wives and children – but more so because of the bone-cracking cold. He had scooted close to the fire, but only one side of his body warmed, so he turned over and warmed the other side.

He rose early, laid on more wood and hovered over the flame, warming his hands that had turned blue.

The camp was coming alive. He woke his brothers. "I've never been so dadburned cold in my life," said Mike, leaning close to the fire.

Jack quietly rolled out of his blanket and warmed before cooking breakfast.

"Jack," said Mike. "I'd like some tenderloin, battered in flour and sprinkled with plenty of salt and gently fried until it breaks apart. And bake some biscuits as big as my fist and I'll have a big steaming pot of coffee too."

"Hush Mike!" exclaimed Rufus. "You're just making me hungrier."

"How 'bout some coosh?" asked Jack.

"We had that yesterday.... and the day before," said Mike.

Horses were fed and, following breakfast, the men fell in formation. Captain Rice addressed them. "Men, I'm proud of you and honored to lead this company. Yesterday you showed your manliness and bravery. Every time we capture or kill a Yankee, that's one less that we'll have down here bothering us. Today our regiment has been ordered to capture Humboldt. If you perform as gloriously as you did yesterday, we'll send the Yankees fleeing back home. Now remember your families and make them proud. Saddle up and check your ammo and weapons and get ready to ride."

The morning sun was sending warm rays across the treetops as the column of mounted men moved out, saddles creaking and the men in high spirits and talking optimistically about whipping Yankees. Thanks to the Federal government, they now had good guns and plenty of ammo.

Outside of Humboldt, Colonel Starnes divided his men into three separate units intent on repeating the Lexington victory.

Company K would dismount and advance in infantry style toward the Federal front. Two larger forces would attack the flanks. Before forming the attack, Captain Rice addressed his men a final time. The McElroy brothers stood side by side. "Every

304

seventh man will be a horse holder and remain back out of sight with the animals," said Rice. "Now count off."

The soldiers sounded off. "One-two-three-four-"

"Five," said Mike.

"Six," said Jack, his voice barely audible.

"Seven," said Rufus.

He looked over at Jack, pale as bread and stepped into his place in line.

"Now, you're number seven," he said.

Jack and the other holders hid with the horses at the rear as the rest of the troops stepped off briskly toward the Yankee center, rifles at port arms. Captain Rice was in front, his sword raised in the air.

The bugler blew charge.

"CHARGE!"

The men rushed forward as rifle fire crackled and minie balls snapped around their heads. The Rebel yell went up and they returned fire. At the same time the men on horseback charged the Union flanks, throwing them in confusion. The battle was short and violent. After taking more than one hundred prisoners they began destroying nearby railroad tracks.

The Fourth Tennessee was ecstatic – two victories in as many days. Forrest had taken Trenton, along with four hundred Federal prisoners, three hundred Negroes and a large quantity of arms and supplies.

That night the troopers ate good Yankee food until their stomachs were stuffed. And even had real coffee! Jack poured Rufus's tin cup full of the magical elixir, looked up at him and said, "Thanks for taking my place."

"Glad to, Brother." Then he turned up the cup and took a long swig – the first coffee he had drunk in weeks.

"Boys, this Yankee coffee is worth fight'n for," he said, smacking his lips.

On December 21$^{st}$ they struck Union City where 100 Yankees surrendered without firing a shot. Then the troopers rested for a few days. The brothers sat around a warm fire, ate Yankee beef and hard tack soaked in coffee and talked about home.

The evening wore on and the fire burned down. In the distance horses occasionally snorted and nearby troopers talked, laughed and played cards. Rufus silently stared at the leaping flames.

"You're awfully quiet," Jack said. Rufus barely acknowledged him.

"Thinking about Amanda and the children?"

"That too," replied Rufus. "I was mainly thinking about the men that died – men that we killed. He looked up at his brother. "Some of 'em surely had wives and children too. They'll have a sad Christmas."

"I try not to think about it," added Mike. "It's war. If they weren't down here they wouldn't be killed. Anyway, we've lost men too. What about their families?"

"I know," said Rufus. "It bothers me just the same."

"Speaking of Christmas, I wonder what the folks back home are doing?" said Jack, changing subjects. "Just think how nice it would be to wake up on Christmas morn'n to a warm fire and the children rush'n to the Christmas tree, holler'n and laugh'n."

"Yeah, I'd give anything to be home on Christmas morning sunk deep in a warm feather bed and scooted up close to Amanda," said Rufus. "Then I'd build a rip roaring fire and get the children up and watch 'em look in their stockings, then breakfast on country ham, fried eggs, biscuits, thick'n gravy and coffee so hot and stifling it would scald my tongue –"

"Dammit! Stop that kind of talk," exclaimed Mike. "I'm freezing my ass off and all I can think about is bedding Mattie. Let's talk about something else."

"Reckon what plans ol' Bedford has for us on Christmas Day?" asked Jack.

"Resting and feasting on Yankee vittles, I reckon," said Rufus.

"All we been doing is rid'n, fight'n and freez'n," said Jack. "We've covered at least twenty miles a day."

General Forrest had other plans. The troopers were up early, building fires, thawing out and feeding and brushing their mounts. After breakfast they rode to Union City and began destroying railroad tracks that ran to McKenzie. The men lined up along the tracks, removed the iron spikes and, then, in unison, lifted the rails and tossed them onto burning crossties. Afterwards, the heated rails were bent around trees.

Federal troops began closing in on Forrest. He moved southwest toward Jackson as a cold rain began to fall, turning the road to mud. A bridge over the Obion River partially collapsed and the men labored all night in sleet mixed with rain to get the artillery and wagons across.

Meanwhile, Biffle's Regiment was ordered to Trenton. Starnes' Regiment and the McElroys rode toward Huntingdon, east of Trenton. Their purpose was to shield Forrest's main force.

While absent, Forrest attacked Federal forces near Parker's Crossroads.

Heavy fighting had been ongoing for nearly five hours and Forrest was driving the Yankees when the McElroy brothers and the 4th Tennessee reached the fight. Yankees were talking surrender when a large Union force came up behind Forrest. Suddenly, he was in a squeeze, fighting a two-front battle. When informed of his predicament Forrest exclaimed, "Charge both ways!" He ordered Colonel Dibrell's regiment to retreat, which they did with great difficulty. Many of the horse holders were captured.

The 4th Tennessee arrived on the field in the nick of time. Colonel Starnes quickly formed his troopers and they moved toward the Yankees at a trot. As always, the McElroy brothers rode side by side, Jack in the middle. Rufus looked over at Jack and gave him encouragement. "Keep up your nerve, Brother." The bugler sounded charge and hundreds of horses lunged forward, their thundering hooves throwing up dirt and drowning out the crackle of musketry. Bullets snapped in the air. Men sagged in the saddle and some fell off. Onward they rode. The Rebel yell went up from hundreds of throats and drowned out all sound. Mike glanced at his brother Jack, who was white as biscuit dough. Rufus, his red face contorted, was yelling fiendishly when his brown slouch hat suddenly flew backward. Rufus grabbed his head.

"I'M KILLED!" he exclaimed.

Mike reached over and grabbed the bridle on the big chestnut gelding and pulled back. "Whoaaaa." He knew the rule and he could be shot for violating it. Never stop to tend the wounded. *The Devil with rules.* This was his brother. He reined back and the rest of the troopers, including Jack, thundered toward the Yankees. Rufus swayed in the saddle. Mike leaned over and examined his head. He laughed.

"I'm dead and you're laughing," said Rufus, confused.

"You ain't dead Brother. You got a haircut – a pretty close one at that."

A minie ball had sliced off a sliver of scalp and grazed the skull, leaving an indenture.

"A dab of lard on the cut and you'll be fine," said Mike.

"I thought I was dead for sure," said Rufus. "Where's my hat?"

The Federals were driven back, allowing Forrest time to extricate his artillery and men from between the opposing forces.

It had been a close call and the losses were significant. At least 100 troopers were killed, 300 captured, and three cannons lost along with six wagon loads of ammunition. But they had given as much as they had received. Blue bellies lay scattered on the field.

General Forrest regrouped and headed back toward middle Tennessee. In Clifton, they raised the sunken flatboats and began crossing the Tennessee River at noon on New Year's Day. Using a canoe, a man led a horse into the water and started it swimming toward the east bank. Over one thousand horses were herded into the river and followed. The McElroy brothers had crossed the river only two weeks earlier as raw recruits. Now, they were veterans. They had seen "the elephant."

# 29 | CALL TO ARMS

East of Athens.

Christmas Eve, 1862.

James Greer "Jim" Barksdale was troubled. Ordinarily, Christmas Eve would have been a happy occasion at his home on Piney Creek, where he and Susan lived on eighty acres and reared their two young sons, Waddie, age 2, and Benjamin Dudley, who had just begun to walk. But these weren't ordinary times.

Men were leaving every day for the Army – and some were being killed. Recently, Uncle Robert C. David had informed him of the July 22$^{nd}$ death of Captain Thomas H. Hobbs of Athens, wounded in the leg at Gaines Mill outside Richmond on June 27$^{th}$. A fine man, that Captain Hobbs. Barksdale had recently learned that three of his McElroy first cousins in Lincoln County had enlisted in the cavalry.

Barksdale felt blessed. Since marrying Susan Newby she had given him two fine sons; he owned land and earned extra income by teaching school. He had a good life.

Then the fat hit the fire. Alabama seceded from the Union and General Beauregard fired on Ft. Sumter and nothing had been the same since.

Initially, not much changed in the county until Federal troops invaded North Alabama early May, 1862, and sacked Athens. Money dried up. Now, every week brought news of some family being burned out, livestock stolen and citizens dragged from their homes and mistreated. People were living in fear.

Christmas Eve promised to be no different from the preceding days – wet, muddy and cold. *When would the dratted rain end?* Barksdale waded through an ankle-deep muck of water, mud and manure in the barn lot. The temperature was just above freezing. What a blessing if it dropped and froze the mud. He gathered several ears of corn and a bundle of fodder from the crib and headed off down to Piney Creek, where he had hidden his team of horses in the woody bottom from prowling Yankees. There were none nearby that he knew of, but they could suddenly appear out of nowhere. They had just about stripped folks of their stock. If he didn't have a team available come spring, he wouldn't be able to plant, and if he couldn't plant, his family wouldn't eat.

The horses were skinny, but if he could keep them alive until spring, they would fatten up on the new grass. He fed them, checked their hobbles and then trudged back up the hill toward the log house, where he grabbed the ax and headed toward a grove of small cedar trees. "The children need to have good memories," she had said. Jim smiled, knowing that it was she, not the babies, who really wanted a tree. He selected a cone-shaped cedar about seven feet tall and chopped it down; threw it over his shoulder; and walked home. After squaring off the trunk he nailed a stand.

The drizzle had stopped and the sky was clearing in the west. Maybe James and Sarah would come over after all. They had promised to spend Christmas Eve with them, and on Christmas Day the two families would walk to his parents' house on the Athens-Fayetteville Pike.

He had become good friends with James Newby when the latter married his sister, Sarah, and then the friendship deepened when he, in turn, married James's sister, Susan. They were more than brothers-in-law, they were like brothers.

He looked up the muddy road several times, hoping to see them coming but to no avail.

He carried the tree inside the cabin, which was warm and smelled of cooking food. Susan was dicing potatoes and onions into a bubbling black kettle that hung over the fireplace. Boiling inside was an old Rhode Island Red rooster whose neck he had wrung before it finally croaked of old age. Chicken stew eaten with hoecakes and black molasses would make a fine dinner.

His sister-in-law, Jane Newby, was tending Waddie and Benjamin Dudley.

"Oh Jim, it's beautiful," Susan gushed when she saw the tree.

"Where do you want to put it?"

"In front of the window," she said.

Jim stood the tree and backed away. "Looks good to me."

"Well..."

"What?" Jim asked.

"It's a bit too tall, don't you think?"

No need to argue. He dragged the tree out to the porch, sawed down the trunk, re-attached the stand and came back in to set it in front of the window.

"What'che think?"

"Well... It's still too tall, don't you think?"

Jim frowned. "If you say so, darlin'."

"Oh Jim, I love you," she said and hugged his neck. "The tree is beautiful just like it is and I love you just like you are. Ohh Jim!"

"What?"

"Ohh Jim, I love you," she said and wiped her eyes.

"Is something wrong?"

"No, I'm sorry. I'm just acting like a woman."

Barksdale backed up to the fireplace to warm his backside and smoke his pipe.

"How are the horses?" Susan asked.

"Bad shape. I'm praying I can keep 'em alive 'til plant'n time."

There was loud bumping against the plank floor, then barking as the hounds ran from beneath the log house.

"Somebody's coming!" Jane exclaimed.

"I hope it's James and Sarah," Susan said, hurrying to the window. "It is! Oh, thank the Lord, I so want to see 'em."

Barksdale walked out on the front porch, called off the dogs and watched as his visitors approached. James was carrying Oscar and Sarah was yelling at Luke Pryor and Worley to stay out of the mud holes.

"Merry Christmas," Barksdale yelled as they entered the front yard.

"And Merry Christmas to you," Newby replied. The two boys ran across the yard and bounded onto the porch.

"Hi, Uncle Jim," Luke said. "Guess what Worley and I have?"

"No tell'n."

"A pet squirrel," blurted Worley. "Grandpa says if the Yankees don't hurry up and leave, we may have to eat it when it grows up."

Barksdale laughed and gave each boy a masculine slap on the back. "Y'all look like you're half frozen to death," he said to his guests. "Com'n inside."

They entered the house, red-faced and cold, just as Susan and Jane came from the kitchen.

"Let me see that precious baby," Susan said, lifting Oscar from her brother's arms. "Ohhh, isn't he precious?"

309

Barksdale soon had a roaring fire going in the parlor, where he and Newby repaired to smoke a pipe and talk while the women prepared food in the kitchen and bragged about their children.

The rooster stew proved to be a big hit, outdone only by the molasses and hot buttered hoecakes.

"Sister, I believe this is the best stew meal I ever ate," Newby said to Susan. "Well, except Sarah's of course," he quickly added and everybody laughed.

After dinner Barksdale and Newby settled in front of the parlor fireplace and smoked their pipes while the women and children remained in the kitchen washing dishes, talking about their children and catching up on local gossip.

"I've never seen harder times," Newby said. "Some folks don't want to accept Confederate notes and Yankee dollars are scarcer than hen's teeth. If you're lucky enough to get your hands on a dollar, it won't purchase much. Since the Yankees showed up prices have shot through the ceiling." He shook his head. "I don't know what we're to do."

"You know that I was against secession like most folks around here," Barksdale said. "I don't own slaves and never will. But none of that matters now. They're down here stealing, burning, raping and killing. Look what they done to Athens! That devil Turchin and his kind must be stopped. I won't be a bond servant to Mr. Lincoln. No sir! They leave us no choice but to take up arms. James, we have to protect our families."

"I agree."

"I'm thirty-three years old and hate like the dickens to leave Susan and the children and go off and fight," Barksdale said, "but I feel I have no other choice. If we don't stop 'em, they'll completely destroy us. Anyway, the conscript law was amended back in April, raising the age to thirty-five."

"What are you saying?" Newby asked.

"I'm going to enlist before I'm conscripted. I understand if I enlist I'll receive a fifty dollar bounty. That's a lot of money. And we can sure use it."

"Have you mentioned it to Susan?"

"Oh no!" Barksdale said. "She knows nothing about it. I'll tell her after New Year's."

Newby sucked deeply on his pipe and slowly exhaled. "Jim, we've been best friends since we were children and you know I won't let you go by yourself."

Barksdale reached over and laid a hand on Newby's knee. "James, I was hoping you'd say that."

Newby's youngest brother, Benjamin Benton Newby, had enlisted with Captain Hiram Higgins' Company in August, 1861 at age 21. "Have you heard from Benjamin?" Barksdale asked.

"All I know is he is somewhere with the 40th Tennessee Regiment."

Later, the women popped corn and strung it around the Christmas tree.

"Where are the presents?" young Luke Pryor Newby asked.

"Santa will leave them over at Grandpa Barksdale's house," replied Newby.

"Why?"

"He can't get down the chimney here."

"Oh," Luke Pryor replied, unconvinced.

Susan spread a quilt pallet on the floor close to the fireplace.

"You young'uns go to sleep before the sandman comes," she said.

310

They woke to a hard freeze on Christmas morning and, after breakfast, the two families set out walking the three miles to Daniel Barksdale's home. Mud holes were frozen solid and the boys had found a new sport.

"Young'un, stop sliding on the ice," ordered Sarah Newby. "You'll fall and break an arm."

They were cold and tired when Luke Pryor, who had run ahead, called out, "I see Grandpa's house!"

Blue smoke curled from both chimneys of the log house. What a welcome sight. Ol' Luther ran from beneath the porch barking, which brought Daniel Barksdale out on the front porch. "By crackies, look what the cat dragged up," he exclaimed. "Merry Christmas. Been expect'n y'all. Com'on in and warm up."

Inside the house was warm, crowded and noisy. George Edward Barksdale and his family were already there.

Ma came in from the outside kitchen, wiping her hands with a cloth. "I was afraid the weather would be too bad for y'all to come," she said. "Thank the Lord you're here." After hugging her grandchildren and welcoming everyone, she returned to the kitchen.

Stockings hung from the mantel. A Christmas tree stood in the corner of the parlor with a few gifts beneath it, which the children eyed with great curiosity until ushered into the adjoining bedroom to play.

While the women prepared the meal the men folks gathered in front of the fireplace and discussed the subject on everyone's mind – the war. Union General Rosecran's Army of the Cumberland was occupying Nashville, his supply base. Less than 40 miles to the southeast Confederate General Braxton Bragg's Army of Tennessee was concentrated at Murfreesboro which was his supply base.

"There's gonna to be a big fight there," predicted George Edward. "It's just a matter of time. I heard that Rosecran had already moved out of Nashville with some 44,000 troops headed toward Murfreesboro."

"How many men does Bragg have?" Newby asked.

"Best estimate is 34,000 plus cavalry," replied George Edward.

Thomas leaned forward, cupping his ear. "Four thousand?"

"Thirty-four thousand, Thomas," replied Pa. "Bye crackies, I believe his hear'n is get'n worse every day."

"I heard," Thomas said. "I hope our boys run every dad gum Yankee all the way across the Mason-Dixon Line."

"It's going to be a crucial fight," George Edward said. "If Bragg wins, we'll clear Tennessee and north Alabama of Yankees. Let's pray that our boys prevail."

Everyone nodded in agreement.

"A lot of boys from around here are up there in Bragg's Army," George Edward said. "They're suffer'n too. Here we sit in front of a warm fire about to enjoy a hot meal and they're out in the freez'n weather eat'n only god knows what."

"Lordy mercy," Pa exclaimed, "the thought of it makes me shiver. I was talking to Robert David last week at the Post Office and he had heard that some of the McElroys boys in Fayetteville had enlisted."

"Which ones?" Thomas asked. "I hadn't heard that."

That's because you can't hear thunder," Pa said.

"I can't help it Pa."

311

"Rufus, Jack and Micajah or Mike as they call him." Pa said. "They're William's boys. Hadn't seen 'em since we moved away in '39."

It was early afternoon when Ma entered the parlor and announced dinner.

The family crowded around the table where a large bowl of squirrel dumplings sat. Pa stood at the head of the table and cleared his throat, which was a signal for everyone to be silent. The children were in the adjoining room playing noisily.

"Hush up, young'un," Ma commanded. "Mind your manners." They fell silent. None of them wanted to get their grandmother riled up.

"The Lord has blessed our family mightily," said Pa. "Even though our land is overrun with evil men bent upon no good, we are all alive and safe. Except for Dudley off fight'n, and William Coleman's family, and of course, Robert Beasley's over in New Market, we're all here. I was hoping that William Coleman and Eliza and the kids could come over, but I guess it's too cold and the roads are too bad.

"I want this to be a special Christmas. No matter how dark the days may come, we still have each other and that's something that no Army can take from us." Tears welled in his eyes. "And let's all remember our boys off fight'n and especially Dudley... and the McElroy boys too. They may be hungry and cold and..." His voice broke. After blessing the food and praying for victory at Murfreesboro, they sat down to eat. The mood was somber.

"Times can't be too bad when we're din'n on Ma's squirrel dumplings," said George Edward, lighthearted.

"We wouldn't be eat'n my dumplings if it hadn't been for Thomas kill'n the squirrels," Ma replied.

Thomas heard his name. "What 'che say, Ma?"

"Ma said you killed Rebel squirrels that were near starvation," said George Edward, "and that you should've shot fat Yankee squirrels."

Laughter. Thomas didn't catch the humor. "Huh?"

More laughter and the somber mood lifted.

"I hate to eat Luke and Worley's pet squirrel, but it sure is good in dumplings," George Edward said.

Worley, who was about to take a mouthful, lowered his spoon and burst out crying.

"George Edward!" his wife exclaimed. "You've made him cry. Shame on you."

"I was only kidd'n Worley," George Edward said. "Your pet squirrel ain't in the dumplings."

"Everybody behave," Ma said. "And I mean it."

After the meal, as the family munched on tea cakes sweetened with molasses, Pa announced that presents would be opened. The grandchildren rushed to the tree, where he handed out homemade hickory whistles to the boys and corncob dolls for the girls.

"Shucks, it's the same thing I got last year," Luke Pryor said, disappointed. His mother grabbed his shoulder and shook him. "Luke Pryor Newby, you'd better mind your manners! Now, what do you say?"

"Thank you Grandpa, I'm sorry."

That evening Jim sat with the men in front of the warm fire while the children laughed and played. After the women had cleaned up the kitchen, they joined the semi-circle around the fireplace and got out their knitting needles and balls of wool. Pa sat

312

down in his rocking chair and lifted the brown leather-bound Bible from a nearby table and asked the children to settle down and listen. They gathered close and grew quiet as he opened the book.

"Children, Christmas is about the birth of our Savior," he said. "Now listen as I read about his birth. It was on a cold winter night such as this way back yonder when he was born in a barn in faraway Jerusalem. I'll read from Luke Chapter Two. 'And it came to pass in those days, that there went out a decree from Caesar Augustus, that all the world should be taxed.....'" Pa read on as the children listened and flames cast dancing shadows on the wall.

Jim studied the peaceful scene, listened to the sounds and sucked in the familiar smell of home and family. He knew it could be his last opportunity to do so for a long time – maybe forever.

Pa closed the Bible and everyone grew quiet. George Edward broke the silence. "Silent night--- holy night," he sang low and gently. Cal joined in, followed by Cornelia and others. Jim reached over and took Susan's hand and squeezed it. This could be their last Christmas together. He fought back tears as he looked around at his family – perhaps for a final time.

---

Early January, 1863.

It was unusual for George Edward to come over late at night, especially when it was so cold. He barely spoke to his father when he stormed into the parlor and held his hand near the fireplace.

Pa looked up from his chair near the fire. "Anything wrong?"

"That damn Lincoln has finally showed what a devil he really is," George Edward said, agitated.

"What now?"

"He freed the slaves!"

"What!" Pa sat forward, hardly believing what he heard.

"Yeah, I heard about it in Fayetteville this morning before I left," George Edward said. "It's in all the Yankee papers. He issued an Emancipation Proclamation on January 1$^{st}$ freeing all slaves in states engaged in war against the Union –"

"What about other states where there's slavery."

"It don't apply to them," George Edward replied. "And it don't apply to the border states of Kentucky, Maryland, Tennessee and Missouri. It's nothing more than a weapon of war to stir up the Negroes to murder white people."

"Did the Yankee Congress pass it?" Pa asked.

"No sir! It was all Lincoln's own doin'," replied George Edward. "Even though it has no legal authority, can't you see what can happen? I've heard there's over 4 million slaves in the South. Half of the population of Limestone County is slaves. If they rise up they'll slaughter men, women and children."

"I've been worried about an uprising for years," Pa said. "Lincoln's got us backed in a corner now. We've got no choice but to fight them devils and we've gotta win. I don't want back in the damned Union."

"I never thought I'd live to hear you say that, Pa."

"Mister Lincoln is a tyrant."

---

Breaking the news to Susan wouldn't be easy. Jim Barksdale sat near the fire, staring at the flame and puffing his pipe while Susan knitted.

"You've been awfully quiet the last few days," she said. "And more attentive toward me than usual."

He removed his pipe and eyed her nimble hands working the knitting needle like a machine. He nodded.

"Something on your mind?" she asked.

Before he could answer, she continued. "Jim, I've been married to you long enough to know what's going on in your head." He smiled lovingly at her.

"Maybe you don't know half as much as you think you do."

"You're determined to enlist and the devil and all of his angels can't stop you."

He pursed his lips and wagged his head. "How did you know?"

"A woman knows these kind of things about the man she loves. I've known for a long time."

"Is that why you were crying when I put up the Christmas tree?"

"Yes, and I've already knitted three pairs of socks for you.... And I want you to know..." her voice quavered and she teared up. "...that I'm proud of you... and the children and I will be just fine. Is James going too?"

"Yes."

He got up and put his arm around her shoulder and squeezed. He was about to cry. She laid her knitting aside and stood. "I know how you feel darling," she said. "It's hard for me, but it's doubly hard for you. I can't bear to think of you wet, cold and hungry and in danger. I want you to know that I support your manly decision and I'll write you as long as there is paper and ink."

---

Monday, February 26, 1863.

Two days before Jim Barksdale was to depart for the Army he busied himself with final preparations. Susan and the two children would move in with Ma and Pa together with his sister, Sarah Newby, and their three children. It would be crowded but Pa said they could live in the ell at the back of the house where overnight lodgers usually stayed.

He walked around the barn, making sure that nothing had been left behind. He had already hauled the small amount of corn and fodder over to Pa's along with a turning plow, planter and cultivator and the chickens. He stood beneath the iron clouds and massaged his hands. He'd never seen a bleaker nor colder day. The thought of leaving Susan and his babies was almost too much to bear. *Dear God, I pray this bitter cup will pass from my lips. Maybe the war will end before I have to depart.* He shivered in the cold like a wet dog shaking off water, ridding himself of such foolish thoughts. The war would not magically end and save him from the ordeal that lay ahead. Of course, he didn't have to enlist, but he knew he would probably be conscripted. "Lord, how do we get ourselves into such predicaments?" he asked aloud. Satisfied that everything was in order, he entered the back door of the house and stamped his feet to knock off mud. "Duty is hard," he said. Susan, who was heaping coals on a Dutch oven that sat in front of the fireplace, stood and fell into his arms.

314

"Oh Jim – Jim," she said. "I can't stand to think of you cold and hungry."

They remained locked in each other's arms for a long time. Then, he smelled something cooking that caused him to temporarily forget his misery. "What is that I smell?"

"Something special for you," Susan said.

Jim released her and walked over to the Dutch oven and started to lift the lid.

"Don't you dare!" Susan scolded him. "Warm yourself while I finish supper."

Jim leaned over the fire and massaged his cold hands, all the while eyeing the Dutch oven.

Susan put supper on the table, the same as the day before – fried potatoes, pinto beans and cornbread. After he had eaten, she removed the lid from the Dutch oven. "Now, close your eyes and don't peek," she said.

Jim complied as she spooned food onto his plate. "Now, you can open them."

"Good gracious!" he exclaimed. "Where did you get the makings?"

"I had dried peaches and butter and your Ma gave me and a pinch of flour and molasses for sweetening." Jim ate all the cobbler and then sopped the bowl. He smacked his lips and declared: "Mmm, now this is a real send off."

Susan looked at him with a twinkle in her eye. After putting the babies to bed, she emerged from the bedroom wearing a gown and went directly to Jim, who was standing in front of the fireplace. He pulled her close, feeling her soft breasts against him. The thought of possibly not returning from war triggered within him a primordial instinct to copulate. He swooped her up in his arms and carried her to the bed, next to where Waddie and Benjamin Dudley slept.

"Jim, they'll hear us," she said, but not convincingly.

"They're asleep." The room was dark as pitch and cold. He quickly undressed and slid beneath the quilts and scooted up to Susan's warm and soft body.

"Love me," she whispered. He kissed her and felt hot tears run down her cheek. "Don't cry," he whispered.

"You may never return home Jim."

"As God as my witness, I'll be back. I want to live, not die."

He pulled her into his arms and she clung to him until he hurt.

"I don't ever want to let go," she said.

He rolled over and mounted her and they made love. Susan moaned and the bedstead squeaked.

"Jim, the children will hear us," she whispered.

"Should I stop?"

"No – no." When they finished, they made love again until both were exhausted.

"Jim, I'll think of you daily and pray that a merciful God will deliver you back into my arms."

"Please do," he said and instantly fell into a deep and satisfying sleep.

The following morning Jim loaded the remainder of the household furniture into the wagon behind the bony horse; tied the milk cow to the back and assisted the children aboard. He looked at the house a final time and slapped the reins. "Git up."

Susan sat nestled against him, holding the baby in her lap, as the wagon bumped and rattled down the road.

---

315

Saturday, February 28, 1863.

It was a bitter cold and gloomy morning when Jim Barksdale pulled on his coat and hat and bade farewell to his family. He turned to his father, "Pa... if something happens to me, promise that you'll see after Susan and the children."

Pa teared up and nodded. "I, I will son – I will," and his voice faded.

Then Jim hugged his mother to his breast and felt her hot tears on his cheek. "Goodbye Ma..." he choked up. All he could do was squeeze her tight. He lifted both children in his arms and kissed them on their cheeks. "Papa will be absent for a spell and I want both of you to obey your mother and help her out. Okay?"

He was thankful that they were too young to know that he was leaving for war and might not return, still, they sensed danger. They hugged his neck tightly and Waddie began whimpering which started little Benjamin Dudley crying. Jim's heart was in his throat. *Oh Lord, let this cup pass from me.* He kissed them again and set them down and they clung to his legs as he pulled Susan into his arms. He hugged her for a long time, feeling her beating heart against his chest as he fought back tears. He kissed her on the forehead, both cheeks and finally on her lips. "I love you Susan. No matter what happens always know that I love you more than anything on this earth."

"Ohhhh Jim!" She squeezed him hard. "And I love you darling."

"I'll be back."

"Take this and remember me," she said and handed him a lock of her hair. He carefully placed it in the left pocket over his heart, kissed her once more and walked out the door. He looked back and she was standing on the front porch waving at him. "I love you Jim."

"And I love you. I'll be back," he said and walked off.

Barksdale and Newby slipped quietly out of Athens and enlisted in Company B, 15th Battalion of Hawkins Sharpshooters, 16th Alabama Infantry Regiment.

They went to Huntsville and it was there that Hawkins Sharpshooters departed by rail in April, headed for action in middle Tennessee.

The 16th Alabama Infantry Regiment was organized in Courtland, Alabama on August 8, 1861 and had seen action at Shiloh before Barksdale and Newby enlisted. The two recruits wouldn't have long to wait before smelling gunpowder and hearing minie balls cracking the air around their ears.

---

On a breezy April day Barksdale and Newby arrived near Tullahoma, where General Bragg was headquartered after the Army of Tennessee had fallen back following the Battle of Murfreesboro. The vast array of white canvas tents standing in line after line reminded Barksdale of a cotton patch ready for picking. Quartermaster issued each of them a canvas knapsack in which to carry their belongings; haversack, wooden canteen, eating utensils, blanket, brown slouch hat, cartridge box and a muzzle-loaded Enfield rifle.

Sergeant Rayburn Meadows, a tall, gruff man with a thick black beard, escorted them to a tent where three men sat outside on their haunches around a small fire fanned by the April breeze.

"Men, y'all meet Privates Barksdale and Newby from Athens, Alabama. They just arrived and will be joining your mess unless you have some strong objection,"

316

Meadows said, emphasizing "strong." That said, he stalked off.

A boy with light brown hair protruding from beneath his hat and who didn't look a day past 17, with fuzz still on his face, stood, spat out a stream of tobacco juice and offered his hand. "Howdy, I'm John Henry Terry from Moulton. Glad to meet ya. If you didn't bring ya own lice, don't worry, we have plenty and you can borrow some of ours, can't they, Skinny?"

"That's right," said a tall, sunken chest-fellow, about 19 years old, poking out his hand. "I'm John Copeland from near Moulton. They call me Skinny. Glad to have ya. Don't pay no mind to John Henry. He tells every recruit the same thing. We don't have no more lice on us than the rest of this miserable army."

"And this here's Worm," said John Henry, gesturing toward a clean-shaven man wearing spectacles who appeared to be in his early twenties.

"He's a book worm, always read'n and write'n, so we call him Worm for short."

"Good afternoon, Gentlemen," said the man and warmly shook their hands. "I'm Carter Poole of Florence. Welcome to our mess. I'm sure you will find this group quite interesting, and feel free to call me Worm because I don't mind. In fact, I'm honored. Someone in this mess needs to know how to read and write."

Barksdale and Newby learned that John Henry had been appointed permanent cook, not because he knew how, but because he was willing to undertake the unwanted task – for a price that is. He expected to be compensated with tobacco.

That night, he fried strips of sow belly in a skillet, added cornmeal to the grease and after it had cooked for a while, poured in water and stirred it until the mixture turned into a brown gravy. "Hold out ya plate, Grandpa," he said to Barksdale, "and have some good ol' coosh."

"He calls it coosh, I call it sow belly slop," Skinny said.

"We use to have good stews, but John Henry traded our cooking pot for tobacco," Worm said.

"Naw, somebody stole it," John Henry replied.

"About the time our pot went missing is when you ended up with a sackful of tobacco," Skinny said.

John Henry had a nickname for everyone in the mess and quickly dubbed Barksdale "Grandpa" and James Newby "Mister Nubbin," perhaps because it sounded similar to Newby.

*Taps* blew at 10:30 p.m. and Barksdale and Newby slept inside a tent, rolled up in a blanket on the cold, hard ground. Barksdale didn't sleep a wink, partly because Newby and Skinny snored loudly. *Reveille* blew at 5:45 a.m. and Barksdale, stiff and sore, was slow rising. Following a breakfast of more sow belly slop, they fell in formation and drilled for most of the day. The drilling was easy compared to plowing all day behind an ornery mule, but the lack of sleep was slowly grinding him down to exhaustion. The second night he bedded down outside the tent near the fire and away from the unharmonious snoring of Newby and Skinny.

The following day there was more drilling. That night, as the men sat around the fire eating sow belly slop, John Henry said, "Grandpa, army life takes a spell gett'n used to, eat'n no good food and sleep'n on the hard ground and all, but this is your third night and I predict you'll sleep like a newborn baby tonight."

Barksdale noticed John Henry glance at Skinny, who grinned. "Yep, just like a baby," Skinny said.

Following *Taps*, Barksdale pitched an extra log on the fire, rolled up close to it in his blanket and fell into a coma.

He and Susan were buried deep in the feather bed. She snuggled close, her warm back and buttocks spooned against him. He draped his right arm over her and pulled her closer, her brown hair tickling his nose and the aroma of her body heavenly and so inviting...

"BOOOOM!"

Barksdale jumped from reflex, but still in his dream. Something hot was on his face. He woke slowly from the stupor, realizing that the loud boom wasn't a dream and the hot on his face were ashes.

"RUN FOR YOUR LIVES! THE YANKEES ARE ON US. RUUNN!"

Barksdale shot straight up, attempting to untangle himself from the blanket, looking for his rifle.

"RUNN!"

Barksdale sprang to his feet and screamed, "JAMES, WHERE ARE YOU? WE'RE BEING ATTACKED!"

Newby crawled out of his tent, panic on his face, looking in all directions. "Where are they?"

Jim slowly realized that he hadn't heard gunshots, roll of drums or bugles sounding. And where were John Henry, Skinny and Worm? Why weren't they fleeing? Uproarious laughter interrupted his thoughts. John Henry and Skinny were bent double laughing. "Oh God, you should have seen yourself... scrambling to get out of that blanket," said John Henry, hysterical.

"Oh Lord... that was funny," said Skinny, bent over slapping his knees, laughing and coughing. Barksdale took a deep breath and smiled. He and Newby were victims of a prank.

"It's part of the initiation," Worm said. "They threw five powder bags into the fire and had to chase me down half way back to Florence."

"You fuzzy-face little whippersnapper," Barksdale exclaimed. "If I was a cat with nine lives, I'd be dead from fright."

From then on John Henry was called Fuzzy.

Adjusting to army life was difficult for Barksdale and Newby. Both had fine wives who cooked good, tasty meals and kept a clean house as well as themselves. Camp food was barely edible, consisting mostly of pork, rancid beef and cornmeal. Instead of quaffing down a gourd full of pure, cold water from Cove Spring across the road from Pa's house, he drank from a hole where the water stank so badly that he had to hold his nose to drink. There were sinks ("latrines") for the men to use, but most often they relieved themselves outside the tent. Many of the men were sick with dysentery and they defecated where they stood. The camp was a filthy, stinking mess.

There was no soap and no baths. To compound the misery, lice, fleas and mosquitoes tormented them night and day. It seemed that half of the regiment was sick with measles, flu and pneumonia. When Barksdale thought life couldn't get worse, he came down with itch. He sat around the camp fire and scratched.

"I've never been this miserable in my life," he said.

"The way to deal with itch is to scratch it," said Fuzzy chuckling, a wad of tobacco lodged in his jaw.

"When you catch it, we'll see how funny you think it is," Barksdale replied.

318

"I can tell you my Mama's cure for itch," Worm said.

"I'm listening."

"Let me think," said Worm. "Mix about two ounces of elder flower ointment and flour of sulfur together with a half a dram of peppermint; take a bath then rub the compound over your body for three nights before you go to bed."

"Thanks Worm, but where do I get those compounds?" Barksdale asked.

Three nights later, Fuzzy showed up with elder flower ointment, sulfur and peppermint. "I just happen to be near the surgeons' tent when the Lord spoke to me and said, 'Oh, thou good and faithful servant, enter that tent and fetch needed supplies from the pharmacy.' I always obey the Lord," said Fuzzy.

The ointment cleared up Jim's itch.

East Limestone County, Alabama.

Early March, 1863.

On Johnson Branch, William Coleman Barksdale was wishing that spring would hurry up and arrive. It had been a cold and wet winter. The branch behind his log house, along with other area branches, had been running high for a long time and it was nigh impossible for folks to ford them. As a result he had been stuck at home, which gave him plenty of time to think. He climbed the rail fence walked across the field just west of his log house.

It was an iron gray, blustery day. Winter wasn't quite over, but spring wasn't far behind. He had turned the field last fall and it would be ready for planting cotton, corn and a patch of sorghum cane as soon as the earth warmed. Each year, he had girded trees and cut bushes, creating new ground and expanding the field. It was satisfying to watch his field grow. That meant he could raise more cotton, which, after the war began, was bringing a good price.

His log house sat on high ground overlooking the branch. With help from Pa and his brothers, he had built the house shortly after he and Eliza had married twelve years earlier. The cabin was 30 x 30 feet, constructed from hewn yellow poplar logs with a puncheon floor and half loft accessible by ladder. The cabin faced south, where a dirt road meandered in front, and a well was located behind the cabin near a detached log kitchen. Several hundred feet north of the kitchen was a log barn and a split rail chestnut fence that angled off northeasterly across a meadow and down to the branch. An ox, horse and milk cow grazed in the meadow. His hogs ran wild and mostly lived on acorns and roots they rooted up in the surrounding forest.

Coleman liked what he observed. It was no plantation, but it was his little piece of earth it and fed his growing family. The little cabin was bulging with his brood of five children. Robert Coleman (Bob), age 9, was the eldest son, followed by James Daniel (Jim Dan), age 5. They were old enough to help clear new ground, drag brush, carry wood and do light farm work. Emmitt was 2 years old and barely walking. Ophelia, the oldest child, was age 10, LouElla was 7, and, the Lord willing, Eliza would give birth to their sixth child in June. He was proud of his little family and what he and Eliza had accomplished. They had been happy – this is, until last May when Yankees came to Limestone County like a hoard of locusts destroying everything in their path. They broke into homes and stole what they wanted, raped negro girls, carried meat from smoke houses, took horses, mules, corn, fodder and anything else they desired. When asked to give a receipt they only laughed. He didn't own slaves, didn't vote for secession and the way he saw it, he had nothing to do with bringing on the war. He had done no wrong to Yankees, yet they had come down to Northern Alabama and made war against people. They were invaders. He had to protect his family, his home and his land. And God willing, he would do so. He had no other choice. If they didn't choose to leave voluntarily, he would help see that they were buried here. Just a couple of months earlier, Lincoln had issued a Proclamation freeing slaves which was calculated to make war against men, women and children.

There was a limit to what good folks would endure. Grandpa McElroy had fought the British for the same reasons and Uncles Arch and Mike had fought them again at New Orleans. You don't tell free-born people what they can and can't do.

320

Men were leaving every day for the war. Last month, his older brother, James Greer (Jim) and James Newby enlisted and departed for Tullahoma. He had hoped the war would pass him by, but it was only wishful thinking.

In less than two weeks, he would be 33 years old. It would be difficult to leave Eliza and the children at home while he was off fighting, knowing that he might never see them again. But he felt he had no choice.

They had plenty to eat. He and the two eldest boys had planted Irish potatoes and sowed turnip greens, and hanging in the log kitchen were salted hams, shoulders, fatback, middlings and sow belly. The milk cow was giving milk; the hens and geese were laying eggs; and there were molasses in the barrel, corn in the crib and fodder in the barn. The only thing that remained to be done was to cut a big pile of firewood.

That evening after the children were asleep, he and Eliza sat in front of the fireplace as he smoked his last sack of tobacco.

"Well, after this sack, I'll be smoking rabbit tobacco or corn silks," he said and spat in the fire. "Money wise, we're poorer than Job's turkey."

"If the war don't hurry up 'n end and the Yankees go home," said Eliza, "folks won't be able to pay their taxes and they'll lose their land."

"They ain't leaving until we drive 'em out," said Coleman, puffing his pipe. "That's the reason I've decided to enlist," he said quietly. "Lincoln says he has made war against the South to save the Union, yet he seeks to destroy us. He's willing to kill us to save us."

Tears welled in her eyes. "I knew it was coming. I hate it, I really do, but I know you have no choice."

"Now, don't cry Eliza," he said, patting her shoulder.

She sniffed and dried her eyes. "I'll be all right. A few good cries and I'll be just fine."

"I'll worry about you," said Coleman. "I won't be here when you give birth."

"Don't worry, Mama will come and stay with me. Anyway, I've had plenty of experience birthing children."

"I'll worry about you just the same."

"No need to do that, Bob and Jim Dan can put in the cotton, corn and sorghum crop. We have plenty of meat and we'll plant a big garden."

You'll need to keep the horse hid in the woods so the Yankees won't find 'em," said Coleman.

"We'll do that."

"I sure hate tell'n the kids."

"They gotta know sometime," said Eliza.

"In the morning, I'm going to Athens and enlist. When I return I'll tell 'em," he said.

---

On Tuesday morning, March 10th, Coleman set out walking the five miles to "The Cedars," home of Captain James Henry Malone, located halfway between the courthouse and his Pa's place on the Fayetteville Pike. Captain Malone had organized the Limestone Rebels when the war broke out but had resigned the following year due to health problems. Command was handed over to Captain John B. McClellan, a school teacher. He liked McClellan, not solely because his family lived less than five miles east of him on Limestone Creek, but because both of them had been born on Cane Creek in Lincoln County only five years apart. That gave them something in common. They were neighbors, so to speak.

When he reached his parents' house he stopped. Ol' Luther ran out from beneath the porch barking his head off. Pa came out on the front porch, fiddle in hand, to see what the ruckus was about.

"By crackies, if it ain't Coleman. Com'on in."

"Hi Pa," said Coleman, grabbing his hand. "You goin' to a square dance or someth'n?"

"No," Pa chuckled, "just limbering it up to stay in practice."

Ma heard the commotion and came to see who it was. "Lorrrrdy! It's Coleman. Come in and warm up. It's sure good to see ya. Give me a hug. Where've you been so long?"

"The creek's been up, Ma."

Cal and Cornelia dashed into the parlor. After hugging and catching up on family news, Coleman joined his father in front of the fireplace.

"What brings you visiting?" Pa asked.

"I'm head'n to Capt'n Malone's to enlist."

"I've been wondering when that was coming," said Pa. "Jim and James left about two weeks ago."

"I heard about it."

"Yep, they enlisted in Capt'n Coleman's company. Haven't heard from 'em since they left to join Bragg's Army in middle Tennessee. There was a big battle at Murfreesboro and we hear there is another fight shaping up."

"Maybe I'll get there in time to pitch in and help," Coleman said.

"The last we heard Dudley was somewhere in Mississippi fight'n with the 35$^{th}$ Alabama," Pa said. "I saw Robert David several days ago at the post office and he said that Rufus, Jack and Mike McElroy enlisted in Lincoln County back in November and are rid'n with General Forrest. "Bye crackies, if I wasn't so old, I'd enlist myself."

Coleman chuckled and asked about his brother, Robert Beasley, who lived in Madison County.

"As far as I know he's still home, but I don't know for how long," Pa said.

"I sure would love to see 'im," said Coleman.

"Yeah, me too. Lil' Molly will be grown and married before I get to see her again."

They both fell silent for a moment.

"Coleman, you need to be careful and watch your step. We've got a lot of homemade Yankees around here and they're snoop'n on folks and report'n to the soldiers. They say Emanuel Isom and his two brothers are the main ones. If they learn you've enlisted, they'll be at your house robb'n and burn'n."

"Yeah, I've heard that myself, but I hadn't told anyone about my intentions."

Pa nodded. "See that you don't."

Ma brought Coleman a cup of coffee and a warmed-up biscuit.

"Un uhh, I haven't had a cup of coffee in so long I don't remember what it tastes like," he said and took a sip. "Mighty fine, yes ma'am. Thank ya."

"It's made from used grounds. Enjoy it, it's the last we have," Ma said. "You can't get anything anymore – coffee, salt, sugar – unless you got a pocketful of Yankee

322

dollars and we don't."

Thomas, who had been at the barn, entered with mud and manure on his shoes. He hadn't gotten over the Yankees taking his team of horses back in May of the previous year.

"I guess I'm lucky they didn't take Sweet," he said. "I figure if she can pull a buggy, she can pull a plow. I'm not planting much cotton come spring, just corn and sorghum. At least we'll have cornbread and molasses to eat."

"They took our milk cow, Handful," Pa added and chuckled. "But she was back the next morning. I'd like to seen them Yankees trying to milk her."

---

"The Cedars" was a two-story, six-room frame house with a balcony that sat on a knoll in a grove of cedar trees on the north side of the Fayetteville Pike about a mile and a quarter east of the Daniel Barksdale home. The house had been built in 1846, seven years after Coleman and his family had moved to Limestone County in 1839. He was eight years old at the time.

He stepped on the front porch, banged the metal knocker at the front entrance and waited. Shortly, an elderly Negro woman opened the door.

"Yassuh.... Why it's Mistuh Coleman! Ain't seen you in ages. Come on in."

Coleman removed his hat and stepped into the front hall onto wide oak boards.

"I've come to see Capt'n Malone," he said.

"Jest a minute," said the woman. "Let me take yo' hat."

She waddled off toward the parlor as Coleman looked around. Two stairways rose off to each side of large, high-ceilinged, plastered rooms that he guessed were at least 19 by 23 feet. It was warm inside and no wonder, he's heard that all six fireplaces were kept going.

The Negro woman returned and ushered him into the parlor where Captain James (Jim) Henry Malone, age 51, sat by a window reading a book. He rose and shook Coleman's hand warmly.

"Coleman, it's been much too long. It seems you should still be a teenager. How is Eliza and the children?"

"Fine, under the circumstances," replied Coleman. "And your family, sir?"

"Tolerable," replied Malone. "Please be seated." They talked mostly about the war and the Battle at Murfreesboro back in January. Then Coleman got down to business. "Capt'n, I wanna enlist in Capt'n McClellan's company."

"The South needs every good man it can find and I congratulate you for your patriotism," Malone said, "but I'm afraid that Captain McClellan is no longer with the company."

"Oh?"

"He lost an arm at Murfreesboro."

"I'm sorry to hear that."

"Captain William Richardson of Athens has assumed command. He's an awfully fine officer and you'll be proud to serve with him," said Malone.

"I know Capt'n Richardson in pass'n," Coleman said.

"He was wounded at Shiloh and taken prisoner, but he escaped," said Malone. "However, he was captured a second time while in the company of that spy James Paul and was to be executed on the morning when he was rescued by General Forrest. And just in the nick of time! His captor ignited a fire in the jail and attempted to burn him alive." Malone shook his head. "Oh the evil that dwells in some men."

"Those people must be driven from our land," Coleman said.

Captain Malone gave Coleman directions where to meet other recruits who would be leaving for middle Tennessee immediately.

---

That evening Eliza cooked supper instead of Ophelia, who usually did. The family sat down to fried ham, scrambled eggs, gravy, molasses, butter and piping hot biscuits baked in a Dutch oven. She had even managed to find enough used coffee grounds to brew a cup for Coleman.

"Whose birthday is it?" asked little Lou Ella.

"No birthday," replied her mother.

"Is it Sunday?"

"No, Lou Ella, hush and enjoy your food," said Eliza.

The older children glanced at each other across the table. Something was awry. Instead of joy and laughter at having such a feast, everyone was somber.

Coleman ate in silence and on the verge of tears. He had a good wife and five fine children that he loved more than himself. Yet, he was about to leave them and go to war and the likelihood was that he wouldn't return. Who would take care of his family? They would be left to fend for themselves in a desolate land overrun by thieving, murdering Yankees. It was unbearable to think about. Yet, he had to go. He had to fight to protect them from the invaders. Why did the Lord place such a burden upon his shoulders? It was a supper fit for a king, but he wasn't hungry. He nibbled on the ham and ate a half a biscuit with molasses before pushing his plate aside.

After supper, he filled his pipe with the leftover coffee grounds and lit it while the children watched.

"This is the saddest day in my life," he said haltingly. "I've enlisted. I'll be leaving home in the morning –"

"Oh Papa!" exclaimed little Lou Ella and began to sob. The boys wiped their eyes and Ophelia wept openly. Eliza was stoic as tears flowed down her cheeks.

Coleman wiped his eyes with his sleeve and continued, his voice unsteady. "There are times when we have to do our duty no matter how hard it is. This is one of those times. I want y'all to be strong and brave. Y'all have to pull together and help out. I'm depend'n on y'all to pitch in and help your Ma. Bob, you can cut firewood and Jim Dan can help you carry it into the house." He eyed his daughters. "Lou Ella, you're only five, but grown enough to help your Ma. Ophelia, you're in charge of milk'n and help'n cook and doing anything else your Ma tells you to do.

"Keep the horse hid in the woods and hide the musket in the hayloft. Maybe Yankees won't come this way. I hope not. The rest of you kids stay out of the way and don't cause trouble. I love all y'all... and ... Lord, this is the hardest thing I've ever had to do."

"Papa, we'll be fine," said Ophelia, jumping to her feet and racing to her father. She wiped his tears and kissed his cheek.

"Don't worry, Papa, we'll take care of everything," Bob said.

The children gathered around their father. "I love all y'all," he said. "The first chance I get, I'll come back and check on you."

A combination of coffee and worry kept Coleman turning and twisting in bed most of the night. Near 3 a.m., while Eliza slept, he kissed her gently on the forehead and quietly slipped out of the house.

He walked through darkness toward the rendezvous point east of Athens and tried not to think about his family or what lay ahead of him. The choice had been made and there was no looking back. Duty, he decided was a hard task master.

He joined several other recruits, and riding double, they departed for Tullahoma, where General Braxton Bragg's Army of Tennessee was headquartered after falling back from Murfreesboro.

On arrival, Coleman was sworn in as a private and assigned to Company E, 26th Alabama Infantry Regiment, which had been organized at Corinth, Mississippi on April 3, 1862. Its designation was later changed to the 50th Alabama Infantry Regiment. The Regiment had earned its keep at Shiloh the previous April, where approximately 24,000 men, both Union and Confederates, were killed, wounded or captured. At Murfreesboro, the regiment had fought with conspicuous gallantry, losing 80 men – killed and wounded. Coleman was issued a gray felt slouch hat, rubber blanket, canvas haversack for his rations, wooden canteen, knapsack, blanket, cap pouch, leather cartridge box and muzzle-loaded .557-caliber 3-band British Enfield rifle. The musket weighed over nine pounds, was 55 inches long and because of its rifled bore was fairly accurate at a thousand yards. He was equipped to kill Yankees.

Army life came as a shock. Instead of sleeping on goose feathers and curled up against Eliza with warm embers glowing in the fireplace, he slept on the ground inside a canvas tent. The weather was warming each day, but the ground was cold and hard at night. His days were filled with bugle calls. The first one was *Reveille* at 5:45 a.m. when he rolled out of his blanket and got ready to begin a day of tiresome drilling led by Sergeant Hardy Thompson of Athens. There were bugle calls for housekeeping, assembly, sick call, meals, dress rehearsal, tattoo and finally Taps at 10:30 p.m.

A man wasn't allowed to load his rifle his own way.

"There is only one proper way to load a musket," bellowed Sergeant Thompson, "and that's by the manual – the Army way."

Instead of loading as fast as he could – like when he was hunting and missed a shot – there was an 8-step procedure barked out by the Sergeant Thompson. "LOAD. HANDLE CARTRIDGE. CHARGE CARTRIDGE. DRAW RAMMER. RAM CARTRIDGE. RETURN HAMMER. PRIME. READY – AIM, FIRE!"

Loading took twenty seconds, if not nervous and flustered, while standing elbow to elbow and taking fire. Foolishness, thought Coleman. A darned good way to get killed in an actual fight.

He sorely missed Eliza and Ophelia's breakfasts of salt cured ham, eggs and hot biscuits. Now, he was in a mess with four other soldiers, none of whom could boil water. Tom Baker, a twenty-year-old from Elkmont, volunteered to cook. Their diet was primarily fried beef, often rancid, accompanied with cornbread hoecakes. If they didn't have meat, they ate captured Yankee hard tack soaked in water.

"A man needs squirrel teeth to eat these things," said Peavine Romine, a tall lanky fellow about 30 years old from Mt. Rozell in Limestone County.

"What are they made from?" asked Coleman. "Creek rocks?"

"Wheat," said Tom Baker.

"I never seen wheat this hard," replied Coleman.

After duty, the men played checkers and cards, gambled, swapped yarns and wrote letters home. Coleman liked Peavine right away and, except for the latter's liking of strong drink, they had a lot in common. Both were close to the same age, married and had children. Peavine was a veteran of Shiloh, and Coleman figured he was a fellow to stick close with in battle. They spent many evenings sitting around a campfire, smoking their pipes and talking about home and what they were gonna do after vanquishing the Yankees.

Young Tom Baker from Elkmont figured that would be fairly easy to do. "One Southerner can whip five Yankees any day of the week," he said.

Peavine was amused. "If that was true, we'd whipped 'em in Shiloh with one hand tied behind our backs." He paused and sucked on his pipe. "Naw sir, it's gonna be a long, hard struggle."

"Why so?" asked Tom, who seemed offended.

"They got plenty of good weapons, powder, food to eat and an unlimited supply of men. If we kill ten, twenty will step up and fill their shoes."

"Then we'll kill twenty," Tom said.

"Maybe if we kill enough they'll grow tired and leave us alone," Coleman said. "They don't have any business down here. Why don't they leave us be? I've got a family to raise. If they will leave me alone, I'll leave them alone."

"I want to go back to Mt. Rozell and my Rebecca and my family," said Peavine. "Get me some good Sugar Creek bottomland and plant cotton. Cotton's the future of the south."

"I just want to go home," Coleman said.

Somewhere in the 46,000 men of the Army of Tennessee was Coleman's brother Jim and brother-in-law, James Newby. The first chance he got, he would seek them out.

Coleman was barely adjusting to Army life when it began raining in late June. Water ran through the tent and across the ground where he slept, soaking his blanket. They drilled and carried on their usual duties until the ground became ankle deep in mud. Water ran off the brim of his slouch hat and down his back. It became impossible to start a fire to cook and they ate hardtacks. Remaining dry had long since become impossible and Coleman soon succumbed to a state of wet misery and accepted it as a way of life. At least he had a tent to sleep in at nights and, though continually wet, he was thankful.

There were clashes with Union troops but Coleman wasn't engaged. He didn't know which he feared most – that he wouldn't get into the fight or that he would.

# 31 | STREIGHT'S RAID

Saturday, April 25, 1863.

The McElroy brothers had been riding hard, fighting and eating dust since departing Springhill, Tennessee, early Friday morning. A long gray column of mounted men stretched for a mile or more down the dusty road that snaked south around the rolling green hills of middle Tennessee. General Nathan Bedford Forrest rode his white horse at the front with his Escort Company. Following them were Dibrells's Eighth, Biffle's Ninth and DeMoss' Tenth, all Tennessee Regiments. Captain John Morton's 8⁻ gun battery rumbled along, the iron-rimmed wheels clanging against rocks and grinding up dust. Trailing the artillery were numerous supply wagons pulled by teams of braying, cantankerous mules, and bringing up the rear of the long column was Starnes' Fourth Tennessee, currently commanded by Colonel W. S. McLemore due to the illness of Colonel Starnes. All total, there were some sixteen hundred men.

Since returning to middle Tennessee in January, Forrest's Cavalry had been fighting continuously. Ol' Bedford had bristled when placed under the command of General Joseph Wheeler, a much younger man, and had considered the recent attack on Dover to cut off Union supplies coming up the Cumberland River ill advised. Afterwards, he reportedly told Wheeler he would be in his coffin before he again fought under his command. Apparently, it was true, since Wheeler went one way and Forrest the other. Rufus, Mike and Jack McElroy had participated in the Dover Battle, as well as at Thompson Station and Brentwood.

The winter had been long and hard and the only ray of sunshine that entered Mike's life was a letter he had received from Mattie dated March 15th. He kept it handy in his left shirt pocket near his heart. He had unfolded and read it so many times that the paper had broken at the creases. He knew its contents by heart.

*"Dearest Husband –*

> *The only time I'm not thinking of you is when I'm asleep, then I dream of you. Sometimes I wake and reach across the bed to touch you and realize that you aren't there. My heart pines for you. Every time I hear hoofbeats I run to the window and look out thinking it is you home at last. I pray unceasingly that you are safe and will return home safely after this terrible war is over. Otherwise, I am in good health and all of us have plenty to eat. We still have meat hanging in the smokehouse but I worry about the coming winter. We have plenty of hogs to kill, but salt is not to be found anywhere. And if it could, it's so expensive folks couldn't buy it. You remember that when you left home in December that Lizer was pregnant. Well, she had a fine baby boy that looks just like Amos. They named him Lonnie. Negroes are running off every day to follow the Yankee Army, but Lizer and Amos are loyal as two little puppies. They take care of me and pray that 'Massuh Micajah will be safe and soon be home'.*

> *Darling, I'll cook biscuits when you come home and I promise they'll be burned. Remember? Be safe and think of me.*

327

*Your Loving Wife, Mattie.*

Mike daydreamed and smiled at the thought of seeing Mattie. Perhaps when they returned from wherever they were headed he could obtain a furlough and go home.

"What's our big brother all grins about?" asked Jack.

"You mind your own business," snapped Mike.

Jack laughed, removed his hat and slapped it on his leg, knocking away dust. "Why do we always have to bring up the rear?"

"Cause we're the best," replied Rufus. "Ol' Bedford trusts us to keep Yankees off of his tail. Be proud."

"Dad blame it, I don't know if I'm chew'n tobacco or a mud ball," said Jack.

"I'm pray'n for a shower to settle the dust," Mike said.

The day before they departed, Edmondson's Eleventh Tennessee had been sent ahead to cross the Tennessee River at Bainbridge Ferry near Florence, Alabama where he linked up with Colonel Roddy's Fourth Alabama Cavalry.

When word spread that Forrest's Cavalry was approaching, people gathered along the road and gawked. Old men raised their hats and hurrahed, women exclaimed, "GOD BLESS YOU!" and young girls offered a hunk of cornbread and a few eggs here and there. But it wasn't a parade. The men had been skirmishing and pushing their way south since early Friday morning.

It was a fine spring day and a lungful of fresh air laden with the sweet aroma of fresh blooms was enough to cause one to forget about the dust. The low hills were arrayed with waxy green hardwoods interspersed with blooming dogwoods and redbuds. New grass was tall and plentiful, and the hungry horses snatched it by the mouthfuls when offered an opportunity. Late afternoon, the column halted near a creek where they unsaddled the horses to let them drink and eat shelled corn carried in saddlebags. Rufus stretched out on the ground, pushed back his hat and stroked the bald groove on his scalp.

"The reason hair don't grow there," said Mike, "is 'cause you keep rubb'n it off."

"If that minie ball had been a gnat's tail lower I wouldn't be here today," said Rufus. "I'd be deader 'n a doornail. I don't understand why I lived, and so many of our men have died."

"Pure luck," said Mike.

"No, it's purely the Lord's doin's," said Rufus. "Scripture says that every hair on our head is numbered."

"Maybe life is one big crap game," said Mike. "Sometimes we crap out 'cause of where we are and what we're doing."

"Won't you listen to our brother," Jack said. "He's turned philosopher."

"It makes sense to me that if you are asleep in your bed and not fight'n Yankees, you ain't gonna get shot," said Mike. "Anyway, I don't know how much time the Lord spends manag'n the foolish affairs of men."

Sergeant Absalom Powell walked up, interrupting the conversation. "Men, you know the routine," he said. "Check your mount's feet carefully. I'd hate to be the poor soul that Ol' Bedford caught riding a lame horse."

"Absalom, where we head'n?" asked Mike.

Powell glared back.

"I beg your pardon, uh… Sergeant," added Mike, frowning.

"To kill Yankees, but I don't know where. I don't ask foolish questions, I just carry out my orders," Powell said and stalked off.

"Why do you go outta your way to rile 'im up?" asked Rufus.

"I don't like 'im, nor his dog," Mike said, "He'd better never get between my sights and a Yankee."

"He just makes it hard on you," added Jack. "How many times have you pulled extra guard duty?"

"So many times I can't remember."

"I know he don't like nobody," said Jack, "but he singles you out."

"Yeah, I bested 'im in a horse trade several years ago," Mike said, "and I guess he ain't forgot it."

"All that over a horse trade?" asked Rufus.

"Well, that 'n other things," Mike said.

"What other things?" asked Jack.

"He heard me say at a social years ago that this here woman I'd danced with was uglier than a jackass and couldn't dance no better'n one."

"Why's that got 'em riled up?" asked Jack.

""How'd I know it was his sister?"

The men gnawed on hard tacks and rested. Within the hour the bugler blew "mount up" and they were back in the saddle riding south.

They rode through the night as clouds gathered hiding starlight. Early Sunday morning rain fell in torrents, turning the dirt road into mud. The long column entered Limestone County, Alabama, on Sunday afternoon and that evening they halted, drenched and tired, on the north bank of the Tennessee River at Brown's Ferry. They had been in the saddle for 36 hours, except for short breaks while watering and resting their horses.

General Bragg, headquartered at Tullahoma, having recently learned that a large Federal force of approximately 9,500 men commanded by General Grenville Dodge was moving toward Florence, Alabama, had ordered Forrest south to assist Colonel Phillip D. Roddy and his greatly-outnumbered Fourth Alabama Cavalry.

On Sunday night, before crossing the river on two old ferries during a downpour, Forrest split his forces, sending the Eighth and Ninth Tennessee to Florence to assist Colonel Roddy with taking that city while he proceeded to Courtland.

Unknown to Forrest, while he rode to confront Dodge, Colonel Abel Streight and 1,600 infantrymen mounted on mules broke away from the main force and headed south to Russellville, then rode east to Moulton on a secret mission. On Monday morning, Forrest's exhausted and wet troopers slogged into Courtland, where they skirmished with Federal forces. Rain fell steadily all day and darkness came early. After caring for their horses, Jack sat down with his brothers on the water-soaked ground and leaned against a large oak tree, the branches providing a small measure of protection from the rain. Wet to the bone, and water running off the brim of their slouch hats, they ate hard tack for supper.

Rufus pulled his hat lower and gnawed a hard tack. "Well Mike, you prayed for a shower to settle the dust, but I believe you prayed too hard. I'm about to drown. How about pray'n for fair weather?"

"I'll put it on my list, but right now I'm pray'n for something decent to eat."

329

"I've never been this wet and tired 'n my life," said Rufus. "Three days in the saddle has worn my old body down to a nub."

"Whew, me too," Mike said. "If It don't quit rain'n and I don't get outta the saddle, my piles are gonna take root."

Rufus chuckled. "Now that'll be a sight to see."

Jack ate in silence. Mike looked over and asked, "You com'n down with fever?"

"No, just that –"

"What?"

"I don't know how much more of this I can take," said Jack. "My nerves are shot. Every time I hear a horse fart, I jump."

"When I think I can't go any further," Rufus said, "I think of Uncle Arch and Mike down in New Orleans with Andy Jackson, stand'n in swamp water to their knees; cottonmouths as big as your arm and hungry gators swimm'n around, as they watched Redcoats com'n at 'em with fixed bayonets. They didn't quit and we ain't quitt'n either."

He stretched out on the wet ground and pulled his hat down over his eyes. "Well brothers, I'm off to sweet dreams. I could sleep on a bed of horseshoe nails."

"Me too," Mike said, stretching out beside Jack.

---

On April 28th Forrest was encamped at Courtland when he learned that General Dodge's movement was a fient to cover Streight's true goal, which was to make a beeline to Rome, Georgia, and cut the rail lines. If successful, much-needed supplies and ammunition would be denied Confederate forces around Chattanooga. Forrest wasted no time in reacting.

Something kicking Mike's booted foot woke him from a deep sleep.

"Wake up your brothers, McElroy. We've got things to do." It was Sergeant Absalom Powell. The bugler was blowing *Reveille*.

"What's the rush, sergeant?" asked Mike, still in a stupor.

"You already know McElroy. I don't make the rules –"

"Yeah, I know, you just carry 'em out," replied Mike.

"Mooove!" commanded Powell.

Rufus and Jack were awake and shivering in their wet clothes.

"Now, why did Powell have to come over and personally wake me?" growled Mike.

"Cause you're special," Rufus replied, laughing.

"Have you noticed, Mike?" asked Jack. "No matter how bad the situation is, Rufus always finds something good about it."

"It's a McElroy trait, I guess," Rufus said, grinning.

"Well, how come I didn't get any?" snorted Mike.

The camp was a beehive of activity with men and animals sloshing through mud, preparing to move out. Hot flames roared from the portable forage; blacksmiths' hammers clanged pounding metal into horse shoes; farriers reshod mounts and the ever-cantankerous mules brayed and kicked. Several days' ration of shelled corn was issued to each man to carry in his saddle bags. Three days ration were cooked. General Forrest moved among the men, cautioning them to keep their powder dry and checking mounts and inspecting their feet. Around midnight, the bugler blew "saddle up" and the tired

330

troopers mounted.

"MOVE 'EM OUT!" commanded Sergeant Absalom Powell and the long column of men and horses departed for Moulton. Rain ceased and stars twinkled.

Colonel Roddy's Fourth Cavalry and Edmondson's Eleventh Tennessee had rejoined the command, bringing Forrest's troop level to two thousand men.

Streight's 1,500 men on mule back had cut an easy trail to follow. If they could be caught before reaching Rome, Forrest's hardy fighters were men who could do it.

Near midnight the gray column of two thousand men rode south eleven miles toward Moulton. A short distance from town, they began a long and gradual climb up Courtland mountain. The rhythmic swaying of the saddle and the creaking leather was more than Rufus could resist. He was sleepy. His head fell forward and just before he pitched from the saddle, he woke and jerked himself upright. He had to do something to stay awake. Talk.

"Hey Mike – Jack, what are y'all gonna to do when the war's over?" he asked.

"First of all, I'm gonna make love to Mattie all night long," Mike replied. "Then I'm gonna eat a big breakfast of tenderloin, hot biscuits dripp'n with butter, half a dozen fried eggs, sunnyside up, thick'n gravy and drink a whole pot of black coffee."

Rufus was not only awake now, he was salivating. "Did you have to say that?" He asked. "Let's talk about something besides food. What are you gonna do, Jack?"

"I'm going to Texas," he said casually.

"Texas! What's out there?" Asked Mike.

"I don't know. That's the reason I'm going. I wanna find out."

"If that don't beat all," said Mike. "Of all the things in the world to do, he wants to trot off to Texas."

"That makes my butt hurt just to think about it," Rufus said. "As for me, I'm not gonna sit in a saddle for six months and I'm not going anywhere 'cept the bedroom, kitchen and outhouse. I've seen all the world I wanna see from the top of a horse."

They rode into Moulton before daylight on April 29th and stopped one hour to pull off the saddles and feed the horses shelled corn. The Bugler blew, "Saddle Up" and the saddle-worn and sleepy men mounted and formed a column. General Forrest, astride his white horse rode to the front and called out, "MOVE UP MEN!"

The troopers, inspired by the sight of their leader, raised their hats and gave the Rebel Yell.

The main column, with Forrest leading, rode south in hot pursuit of Streight. Starnes' Fourth and Biffle's Ninth were sent on a parallel road in an effort to get in front to Streight.

Dawn revealed a countryside that was relatively flat and wooded except for small farms marked by broken rail fences. Rufus didn't see a single mule or horse at the farmsteads, no doubt because they had been stolen. He did see dead and near dead-mules abandoned by the advancing Yankees.

To the south, a green mountain rose up some four hundred feet from the green valley. They halted briefly at a creek and watered the horses, then continued the pursuit, the horses blowing, nostrils flared, sucking air and dripping sweat.

"They say this is Sand Mountain," Jack said, reaching over and punching Mike, who was reeling in the saddle.

"You woke me up just to tell me that?"

"You were about to tumble off your horse. Wake up, talk to me," said Jack.

331

"I don't wanna talk, I wanna sleep."

Thursday morning, April 30th, Forrest was awakened at daybreak and informed that Streight's mule mounted infantrymen were only four miles ahead at the crest of Days Gap. He gathered his troopers and charged up the dirt road, the men giving the Rebel yell. Streight held the high ground and quickly formed his men in battle line. Cannons roared. There was charge and counter charge. The Yankees overran a battery and captured two of Forrest's cannons. The battle see-sawed back and forth while many men dropped, dead and wounded.

A courier rode up fast and reined before Colonel McLemore, acting commander of Starnes' Fourth Tennessee. They, along with Biffle's Ninth were ordered to the front immediately.

"Brothers, it looks like we're gonna to see the elephant again," Rufus quipped.

"One day my time is gonna run out," replied Jack. "Why did he have to select us?"

"Honor, brother," replied Rufus.

"If it wasn't for the honor of dying, I'd just as soon stay alive," said Jack.

They arrived at the front around 3 p.m. and dismounted. Jack grabbed the reins of seven horses. Sergeant Absalom Powell barked at Jack, "Grab your rifle, McElroy, and come with me."

"I'm holding horses, Sergeant."

"I've been keeping my eye on you, McElroy. Tie those horses to trees and let's go!"

Jack's hand trembled as he clutched his Enfield and struggled up the mountain to catch his regiment. Starnes' Fourth Tennessee was ordered to the far right; Edmondson's Eleventh on the left and Biffle's Ninth and Roddy's Fourth Cavalry to the center. When they reached the crest, the Yankees were gone. The Confederates hastily remounted and gave chase overtaking Streight's rear guard at Crooked Creek where they had stopped to water their thirsty mules. Forrest struck with a fury. Streight fell back about two miles to Hog Mountain and placed his men and artillery in line.

The McElroy brothers and the Fourth Tennessee were placed at the far right next to the Escort company, with Biffle in the center and the Scout Company on the left. Night was falling when Forrest rode before his exhausted men, his face flushed. "Men, give 'em no rest. If you see a blue uniform, shoot. Keep up the skeer."

Forrest led the charge up the hill, followed by his tired and grim-faced men. Cannons thundered, emitting great shards of fire, and hundreds of muskets spoke, their muzzle flashes illuminating the night. It was an eerie scene of destruction as men and horses went down; mules braying; men screaming, praying, and begging for help and water. Forrest's white horse was shot from beneath him. The fight lasted for three hours until Streight, leaving his wounded and dead under the care of his assistant surgeon, pulled out for Blountsville. Forrest pursued, the Scout Company riding point.

Near midnight Streight set up an ambush along the road. The night was bathed with soft moonlight, the only sound being the muffled clomp of hundreds of horse hooves on the dirt road and the rattle of equipment as the sleep-walking animals carried their somnolent riders.

Rufus, Mike and Jack were bent forward in the saddle, asleep, heads half resting on the necks of their mounts. Rifle fire cracked. Startled, half-asleep mounts jumped sideways. Jack pitched from the saddle.

332

"AMBUSH!" someone yelled.

Rufus and Mike straightened in the saddle, their muddled brains unable to immediately comprehend.

"Jack's been hit!" exclaimed Mike, unsaddling and rushing to his younger brother who was on the ground, struggling to get to his feet.

"Where ya hit Jack?"

"I ain't dead, I fell outta my damn saddle."

The scouts discovered the ambush and lying low in the saddles on their fast mounts thundered back down the road to warn the main column. Forrest halted his troopers and ordered Starnes' Fourth, supported by cannon, and Biffle to get behind the Yankees.

Jack held horses while his brothers and the other troopers of Starnes' Regiment sneaked up on the Yankees. Cannons and muskets opened up at near point-blank range, sending the Yankees' rear guard skeedaddling toward their main column. Forrest followed, keeping up the pressure.

Near 2 a.m. Streight set up another ambush at a stream crossing. It resulted only in waking up the Confederates, who were tired but more alert than the Yankees, who had been given no time to pause and rest. Forrest could sense that his quarry was weakening. Around 3 a.m. he halted his exhausted men. They tied their horses to trees, unsaddled and fed them corn, then collapsed asleep on the ground.

Streight continued toward Blountsville. At daybreak Forrest and his men were back in the saddle. Forrest allowed some of his men to rest while he and the Escort Company and part of Starnes' Fourth Tennessee pursued Streight. Streight paused in Blountsville to rest his men and mules and cook breakfast. They had barely settled down when Forrest, riding at the head of his men with part of Starnes' Fourth Tennessee, galloped into the small village, giving the Rebel yell and firing pistols, sending the Yankees scurrying.

At the Black Warrior River, Streight formed skirmishers on the west bank to protect his men and pack mules while they forded the swift stream. A hot fight erupted, the Yankees using artillery and well-positioned riflemen to push back pursuing Confederate cavalry.

Jack was holding horses in the rear and had a good view of the action. The last of the pack mules laden with crates splashed across the fast-moving waters. In the noise and confusion, one mule lost his footing on rocks and fell against another mule, knocking it down. Both were braying and pawing the water trying to find their footing, but to no avail. The strong current quickly carried them downstream.

By five p.m. all of Streight's Raiders, including the rear guard, were across the river, and headed toward Gadsden, twenty-five miles away.

Forrest's exhausted men forded the stream and encamped on the east side. Both horses and men were weak from hunger and exhaustion. Forrest sent some of Biffle's men ahead to nip at the Yankees' heels and keep up the pressure. He walked around the encampment talking to his men, checking horses and equipment. After horses had been tied, saddles removed and shelled corn fed to them, the men were bugled to formation. Forrest rode to the front of his men and spoke, his voice strong and steady. "Men, you've rode and fought continuously since we left Spring Hill nine days ago. We've lost friends, some killed, some wounded. You kept going. I know you are hungry, sleepy and exhausted. Some of you may wonder why we don't stop. I'll tell you why. Our foe is in worse condition than you. We hadn't allowed him to rest, sleep and eat. His animals are dying. If we let off the pressure now then he will forage the countryside, plundering and stealing from women who can't protect themselves. He's worn out. It's just a matter of time until he quits." Forrest paused for a moment, looking at his bedraggled men, then raised in the saddle. "Who will continue with me?"

There was momentary silence as the men gathered their strength, followed by a loud Rebel yell as they removed and waved their hats.

After arranging their campsite on the riverbank, the men collapsed, some asleep before they hit the ground.

"I'll be back directly," Jack said to Rufus, who was positioning his saddle for a pillow. "Where ya going?" asked Mike.

"For a little stroll." Jack hurried downstream in the direction that the mules had floated. He figured that something valuable was in the crates; otherwise them Yankees would have already discarded them along the way as they had done with many other items. There were two things they wouldn't abandon – ammunition and food. His thin body had begun eating itself. Since departing Spring Hill he had lost weight and was feeling light-headed, and when he wasn't dodging bullets, his mind was occupied by food. He followed the river bank for a mile or so when he heard voices. "There they are!" someone shouted. Jack rounded a bend and saw three men splashing into the water. Two mules were lodged against boulders, drowned, their limp necks moving up and down in the current. The crushed crates had slid off into the water where the swift current rippled over them. The hungry men were cutting savagely at the pack ropes when one exclaimed, "Crackers!"

Jack scrambled down the bank and jumped into the water, joining the men tearing at the ropes and crates. He grabbed a crushed box, clamping it tightly against his chest as he waded out of the water, and walked to a clump of bushes where he sat down, exhausted, and tore into his precious cargo, ripping away the paper. The crackers were wet and mushy and full of black mule hair. He picked out a few strands, but soon reasoned that it was harmless and gouged a handful into his mouth. He sat chewing and enjoying the wonderful sensation of food as it settled into his empty stomach. Filled, he hurried back to the camp to share with his older brothers.

Both were asleep on the ground. He shook them to no avail, and then lay down beside them, clutching his precious food.

Meanwhile, Forrest accompanied by his Escort Company and Scouts rode off to relieve Biffle, who would bring up the remaining troops after resting a spell. Someone shaking his shoulder woke Jack. "Wake up brother, we're mov'n out."

Jack looked up through matted eyes to see Rufus standing over him, eyeing the crushed carton.

"What's that?"

"Hard tack. Have some."

"Where did you find 'em?" asked Mike.

"On a dead mule."

Rufus tore into the wet package like a dog digging for a bone; ripped away paper and ate the soggy dough. Mike grabbed a handful. Rufus gagged and spit out a mouthful into his hand. "What's in it?"

"Mule hair," replied Jack casually.

"Never tasted better," Rufus said and continued eating.

It was Saturday, May 2$^{nd,}$ and warm when the remainder of Forrest's 600 troops rode east toward the rising sun.

"I do believe that was the best mule hair breakfast I ever ate," Rufus said to Jack.

"That was surely a sorrel mule," commented Mike. "I think I like bay mule hair better."

"I'll keep that in mind for future breakfasts," said Jack. "Now y'all be quiet and let me go to sleep."

The roadside was littered with discarded blankets, clothing, coffee pots, tin plates and stolen booty the Yankees had thrown away to lessen their load. Several elderly Negroes who couldn't keep up with Streight's column straggled behind and darted into the brush on seeing the men in gray. No one cared.

Soon they crashed into Streight's rear guard that had crossed a bridge over Black Creek before torching it. The McElroy brothers were in the saddle watching the timbers burn when Forrest galloped up. Federals were on the opposite side of the creek. A young girl they later learned was 16-year-old Emma Sansom appeared at the gate of a nearby farmhouse.

"Can you tell me where I can cross the creek?" asked Forrest.

"Yes sir. We herd our cows across up yonder above the bridge," she said, pointing.

At Forrest's request, she mounted behind him and they rode off toward the ford. Having found a passage across the creek, Forrest positioned artillery and pounded the Yankees as the McElroy brothers and Starnes' Fourth led the way across the creek.

Streight's force continued toward Gadsden, arriving around 10 a.m.; got fresh mounts; burned the bridge over the Coosa River; then continued east toward Blount's plantation. There he stopped to rest and feed his men.

During a sharp skirmish, Pvt. Joseph Martin of Starnes' Fourth Tennessee made a 600-yard shot that killed Colonel Gilbert Hathaway, Commander of the 73$^{rd}$ Indiana Regiment. Streight pulled out toward Rome.

"I don't know who is gonna to outlast who," complained Jack. "I'm near 'bout dead."

"I gotta give the devil his due, the Yanks are tough," said Rufus, "but we'll outlast 'em."

"There you go again. Always optimistic," said Jack.

"I just feel it in my bones," Rufus said.

Two of Forrest's Regiments were at Russellville, two at Somerville and one near Guntersville.

That night they encamped near Blount's plantation and slept ten hours. They woke early Sunday morning rested and eager to catch their quarry. When Forrest rode out before his mounted men, now dwindled down by death, wounds and illness to a mere 475, they burst forth with the Rebel yell.

"Move 'em out!" commanded Forrest. The gray backs sat a little higher in the saddle. Upon reaching the Chattooga River they found that Dykes Bridge had been burned. The men dismounted and waded across the water, holding ammunition over their heads. The two cannons were pulled across the river bottom with ropes. There was no time to waste. Near Gaylesville, around nine a.m. they slammed into the rear of the Yankees who had paused to rest and cook breakfast. Many were asleep on the ground.

Starnes' Fourth and the McElroy brothers were sent around to the left and Biffle's Ninth swung to the right. Forrest and the Scouts covered the center. They opened fire on the Yankees, who were too exhausted to fight. Many couldn't wake.

Forrest sent Captain Henry Pointer under a flag of truce with a demand to surrender. Streight wasn't persuaded. Then Forrest employed a ruse that he would use successfully in the future. He paraded the same two cannons and men over a hill crest, making it appear that his force was much larger. Starnes' Fourth and Biffle's Ninth took turns marching in front of Streight who was too far away to see that they were the same men. Streight hesitated and pondered.

"What's tak'n the Yankees so long to surrender?" asked Jack.

"He may be on to Ol' Bedford's bluff," replied Mike. "And if he is we're in a fix. They could whip us handily."

At noon, Sunday, May 3rd, after a running battle that had lasted for a week, Streight surrendered his 1,450 men and stacked arms.

"I feel like celebrating," said Jack.

"How ya gonna do that brother?" Rufus asked.

"With a good chew of tobacco."

"You don't have any tobacco," Mike said.

"I will after I do a little foraging amongst the Yanks."

---

The McElroy Brothers and Forrest's cavalry returned to Springhill, where they fought at Franklin and Triune. On June 30, Col. Starnes died of wounds incurred at Bobo's Crossroads south of Tullahoma while his brigade was screening the withdrawal of the Army of Tennessee from Tullahoma to Chattanooga. Col. W. S. McLemore assumed command of the Fourth Tennessee.

In Middle Tennessee the Union Army moved south toward Tullahoma on June 24th with 65,137 troops. Fearful of being flanked, General Bragg began a retreat to Chattanooga some fifty miles to the southeast across the rugged Cumberland mountains. Roads were few and the progress was slow and difficult. Many of the men were wearing the same clothes they wore when they departed home. And rain continued to fall. The Army was stretched out for miles and thousands of foot soldiers, horses, wagons and caissons turned the narrow dirt roads into sucking mud. Rations were short.

William Coleman Barksdale, was hot, wet, tired and hungry. Chiggers, ticks and mosquitoes, not to mention poison oak, tormented the men, but they plodded on.

The Army reached the Tennessee River at Chattanooga, but it was unfordable. With General Bragg growing fearful that his Army might be pinned against the river, they marched to Bridgeport just south of the Alabama line, and crossed the river on pontoons. Coleman kept track. It had rained for fifteen days in a row.

The McElroy brothers and Forrest's Cavalry rode rear guard protecting the retreating Army as it crossed the Tennessee River on July 6th.

Federal troops occupied Chattanooga, an important rail center for the Confederacy. On July 4th, the same day that General Lee lost at Gettysburg, Vicksburg fell. The fate of the Confederacy had never looked bleaker. All eyes of the South were now on General Bragg and the Army of Tennessee.

# 32 | BACK ON JOHNSON BRANCH

Limestone County, Alabama.

June 17, 1863.

It wasn't the loud croaking of bull frogs on Johnson Branch that woke Eliza Barksdale near midnight. It was the recurring pain in her womb. Having already birthed five children, she knew what it meant. If only Coleman were home, like he was when the other children had been born. No telling where he was or what danger faced him. She hadn't received a letter from him in several weeks. But that didn't mean he hadn't written since it took a long time for a letter to get through. She would be strong and brave.

"LouElla – LouElla!" The child roused, slightly lifted her head then fell back onto her pillow. Her mother shook her again, much harder this time. "Wake up child!"

LouElla sat up in bed and rubbed her sleepy eyes. "What Mama?"

"Go wake Ophelia then wake Bob and tell 'em to come down here. HURRY!"

"Are the Yankees coming?" asked LouElla, fear in her voice.

"No child, I'm gonna have a baby." She laid LouElla's hand on her bulging stomach. "Feel it kick?"

Yes, Ma'am." She swung out of bed, woke Ophelia who was sleeping with baby Emmit. "Mama said get up right now. The baby's coming!"

She then scrambled up the ladder to the loft where Bob and Jim Dan were sound asleep. She shook Bob's shoulder. "Wake up, Bob!"

Moonlight poured past open shutters. When he saw that it was his little sister, he turned over. "Go away."

"Get up now, Mama said," and she shook him again.

"No."

"You better do what Mama says cause she's gonna have a baby."

He sat up. "Why didn't you say so?" He scrambled around in the near darkness, found his breeches, slipped them on and practically slid down the ladder. Ophelia had already lit a candle. He rushed to his mother's bed.

"What, Mama?"

"Ride over to your Grandma Harvey's and tell 'er 'n Papa that the baby's coming. She'll know what to do. Now hurry along."

"Yes ma'am," Bob tore out barefoot to the barn, grabbed a bridle and ran to the woods where the horse had been hidden from prowling Yankees. He slipped on the bridle, swung on bareback and galloped off.

His maternal grandparents Hansel and Patsie Harvey lived nearby, across a copse of woods. The skinny mare was panting hard when Bob reined in the front yard, a pack of barking hounds running out to meet him. "Quiet!" The dogs recognized him and retreated back to the breezeway between the two large log rooms. He hammered on the front door once and his aged grandfather opened it.

"Grandpa!" he gasped.

"What young'un? Have the Yankees come?"

"Mama's hav'n a baby!"

"Right now?"

"She's about to have it. Said y'all would know what to do."

"While I'm waking your Grandma, you hitch up the buggy then go back home and tell Eliza we're on our way."

"Yes suh."

Bob mounted and rode like the wind back home where to find his mother in pain and children awake and scared.

Shortly, his grandparents drove up in their buggy and came inside. Grandma Harvey surveyed the scene and immediately took charge. "Jim Dan, get a hot fire going. Ophelia start boiling water. The rest of you young'uns get outside and don't come back in till I tell ya. And if I catch one you peek'n through the window, I'll tan your hide. Now go!"

Eliza cried out in pain as the contractions came more frequently. It was near daylight when Grandma Harvey ordered Grandpa and Bob outside. "You stay, Ophelia," she said. "It's time you learned about birthing."

Grandpa Harvey hobbled outside, followed by Bob, to witness an eastern sky glowing pink. LouElla was rocking back and forth on her feet, holding a crying baby Emmit. Stretched out on the ground and sound asleep was Jim Dan. A rooster crowed.

"What's wrong with little Emmit?' Grandpa asked.

"He doesn't understand what's happening and is scared to death," said LouElla. "And I'm scared too."

"Your Mama is fine, child; nothing to worry about," he said and paced back and forth in the yard.

He nudged Jim Dan's foot, waking him. "Hide the horses in the woods, and give 'em each an ear of corn." He turned to Bob. "After the baby's born, we'll celebrate with a fine breakfast. Gather some eggs and milk the cow. Now y'all hurry along."

Bob and Jim Dan walked off together. "Grandpa is wound tighter than a five-string banjo," remarked Jim Dan.

It was mid-morning and already stifling hot when a loud scream came from inside the cabin. The children jumped to their feet, LouElla clutching baby Emmit, who had cried himself to sleep. They stared at the house. Grandpa hurried over and put an ear against the door, brows wrinkled, lips pursed. More screams. Then came the barely audible, but unmistakable, cry of a baby.

"By golly, she's finally had it!" exclaimed Grandpa, smiling.

"Thank the Lord," added Bob.

The children relaxed and laughed. "I hope it's a girl," said LouElla.

Shortly, the front door opened and Grandma Harvey poked out her head. "Hansel, you've got yourself another fine grandson."

---

Near Chattanooga.
Early August, 1863.

The Army of Tennessee was positioned on the southeast side of the Tennessee River, stretching from north Georgia to well above Chattanooga. Thousands of ill-clothed, underfed, sweaty men, many sick with dysentery, were strung out as far as the eye could see. Stinking latrines and hundreds of mules and horses creating mountains of manure produced a stench to which Coleman Barksdale had grown accustomed. A blazing sun cooked the earth, damp from recent rains, turning the valley into a steam cooker, but Coleman didn't complain. At least it wasn't raining. Mosquitoes that they called "Gallinapper" buzzed around his head at night and sucked his blood. Then there were lice, chiggers, ticks and poison ivy that drove him to the brink of madness. But what tortured him most was worrying about his family. Nights he lay on the ground, swatted mosquitoes and looked up at the stars and thought about Eliza and the children. *Had the baby been born healthy? Was the family in good health? Had the corn, cotton and sugar cane been planted? Were Yankees occupying Athens?* He agonized over these matters.

Lice laid nits in the seams of his clothing, particularly around the waistband and arm pits. The tiny whitish-looking eggs hatched into nymphs in one to two weeks and fed on his blood. To rid them, Coleman held his clothes over a flame, but it was a losing battle.

"I laid my shirt down last night and when I woke this morning, it was gone," said Peavine as the men sat around morning mess eating coosh.

"Somebody steal it?" asked Coleman.

"Yeah, lice. They walked off with it."

On Sunday afternoon Coleman went to regimental post office and inquired about mail. The corporal thumbed through the stack and handed him a letter.

Coleman eyed the return address: "Shoalford, Alabama." Eliza! A letter from home was something to savor like sipping coffee or smoking good tobacco. He found a shade tree, sat back and carefully unfolded the letter.

"Dear Coleman:                                    June 20, instant.

Wonderful news. We have a brown-eyed boy born mid-morning on the 17th and is in good health, as we all are. How is your health? I think the baby should carry your first name of William. What do you think his middle name should be? You would be proud of the children. Bob rode over to Ma and Pa's and asked them to come. Ma is an old hand at birthing. Ophelia helped out too. The cow is giving milk and the garden has produced plenty of peas. The hogs are getting fat rooting around in the woods. Hopefully we'll have plenty of meat to eat this winter. The corn and cotton crop look pretty good if the worms don't eat it up. We are knitting socks and will send them to you in a few days. The Yankees haven't bothered us yet, but they are robbing and stealing from other folks and we live in fear they will show up here one day. I sure would like to see you. The children miss you very much and pray for your safe and quick return home. Every time the dogs bark we run to the door thinking it might be you. When can you get a furlough? If you can't come home, please write.

Your loving wife, Eliza.

He carefully folded the letter and put it inside his hat. "Peavine, I got me a fine boy!" exclaimed Coleman. "Tomorrow, I'm gonna talk to Capt'n Richardson."

---

They rode south to near LaFayette, Georgia, then turned west, crossed Lookout Mountain and headed northwest toward Decatur. The shortest route to Athens would have been due west, keeping on the less traveled roads that ran through the mountains bordering the Alabama-Tennessee line. But it was far too dangerous. Yankee troops were thicker than fleas on a dog back north of the Tennessee River, but they seldom ventured south of the river to "Dixie."

Coleman and Lieutenant Adams had been in the saddle for two days when they reined their horses in a wooded area near the south bank of the Tennessee River. The water was gray and moving lazily.

"Home's over there," said Lieutenant Adams, pointing across the river. "Mooresville is downstream only a short distance. There are probably Yankee sentries patrolling so we'll wait here until nightfall."

Coleman hid the horses in a patch of tall grass, and while they grazed he sat beneath a shade tree and thought about events of the past days. After receiving Eliza's letter, he had requested a furlough from Lieutenant Adams, who wrote out the request and passed it on to the company commander. It wasn't forthcoming. The Army was idle and many men had gone home to check on their families. Just when he had decided to grant himself "French Leave," one evening a courier rode up and told him to report to Captain Richardson.

"Lieutenant Adams is being sent back home to recruit and I'm granting you a 15-day furlough to check on your family," said Captain Richardson. "You can accompany him. He'll provide a horse for you."

"I really appreciate it," said Coleman.

Captain Richardson signed the document and handed it to Coleman, "Good luck."

Coleman straightened and saluted.

"Thank you, sir."

Coleman was excited about seeing Eliza and the children. It had been six long months since he left home. Now, all he had to do was successfully cross the river, ride north approximately 15 miles and he would be home.

Lieutenant Adams came over, sat down and passed tobacco to Coleman. They smoked and talked, waiting for darkness. "The moon won't come up until later, which is good," said Lieutenant Adams. "Hopefully, we won't be detected."

Coleman hadn't seen a boat and was becoming concerned about how they would cross the river. Perhaps, they would float across on a log while holding the horse's reins. He had waded across Johnson Branch in water up to his waist during flood stage; even ridden his horse across Piney Creek and Limestone Creek, but the Tennessee River was a daunting body of water. It was wide and deep and he wasn't a good swimmer.

"Sir, how we gonna cross?" he asked.

"Swim."

When darkness came, Lieutenant Adams rode his horse to the river bank and Coleman followed. "Do what I do," whispered Adams. He spurred his horse and went into the water with a loud splash. The horse attempted to return to the bank, but Adams wouldn't permit it. When the horse headed toward the opposite bank, Adams slid to the rear and clutched the saddle.

Coleman took a deep breath and kicked his mount. They splashed into the murky water and followed Adams. Coleman slid off the saddle, grabbed the back and held on for dear life. He hoped the horse was a better swimmer than he. And he hoped Yankees weren't waiting with cocked rifles. His horse was swimming steadily and in a straight line. Coleman decided it was easy and fun. Suddenly, driftwood struck the horse in the flank and she lunged. Coleman lost his grip on the back of the saddle, slid into the

340

water, flailing. He tried to grasp something, found the horse's tail and hung on with both hands. The horse kicked, trying to dislodge Coleman. He let go with one hand, trying to get to the side and away from the horse's kicking hind legs. Drowned or kicked to death? Coleman decided drowning would be less painful. Just as he decided to let go the animal found his footing and scrambled onto the bank. Coleman pawed at the water until he grabbed a tree root and climbed out, dripping wet. His horse gave him an evil eye before shaking off and sending a shower of water on him.

"If Yankees didn't hear that commotion, they ain't here," he whispered.

"Shhh, follow me," whispered Lieutenant Adams. They let the horses pick their way through the woods and into open country, then traveled north up Mooresville Road. When they reached Nick Davis Road, they parted, Coleman riding east, wet and chilled, toward Johnson Branch.

It was past midnight and the moon out when he rode up to the cabin and dismounted. Samson and the other hounds dashed out barking, but hearing his voice, began whining and slapping their tails. No sound came from inside the cabin. *They probably think its prowling Yankees.*

The front door flew open. "It's Papa!" Bob exclaimed and bolted toward his father.

"Papa... Papa!"

Coleman dropped the reins and ran to meet his eldest son. "It's good to see ya son." Someone lit a candle and Coleman bounded into the cabin. The kids were running toward him, arms open, screams of joy. He hugged and kissed each one; looked up and saw Eliza, clad in her nightshirt, a baby pressed against her breast.

"Coleman... oh Coleman. Thank God you're home!"

He embraced her, feeling the baby soft against him. Afterwards, she looked him up and down. "Just look at you, you've lost weight, your clothes are rags, you're wet and need a bath." She issued orders to Ophelia. "Heat bath water and get your Papa dry clothes."

"Yes ma'am."

"Let me see 'im," said Coleman. "Bring a candle." He held the baby in the flickering light until he began to cry, and then handed him back to Eliza. "So, you've decided to name him William," declared Coleman.

"Yes, after you."

"What about William Matthew?"

"After the Apostle Matthew who walked with our Savior? Yes, I like that," said Eliza.

Then Eliza told him about Emanuel Isom and his brothers, Matthew and William Stinnett. "Folks say they're run'n tell'n the Yankees when a Confederate comes home or furlough. You gotta be careful."

"Not the Isom's!" exclaimed Coleman.

"It must be true," said Eliza. "Papa said he heard it from several folks."

"I can't believe it," said Coleman. "I knew he was against secession – a lot of folks were – but I never thought he'd join forces with the Yankees."

It was near daybreak when the candle was snuffed out and everyone finally settled in bed. After the children were asleep, Coleman scooted close to Eliza's warm body.

"It's been a long time," he whispered.

341

"Yes." She placed the sleeping baby to her side, pulled Coleman close and they made love.

Later, a crowing rooster woke Coleman. It was the sweetest sound he ever heard. No bugles, no loud commands, no swearing, just a rooster crowing. "Ahhh, peace."

He was about to roll over and go back to sleep when he heard the cow bawling, wanting to be milked. Then the baby began crying, wanting to be nursed. He rolled out, tired and sleepy, but fulfilled and at peace.

Ophelia prepared a sumptuous breakfast of fried eggs, fat back, biscuits, thickening gravy and molasses.

There was much to be done before he returned to the Army. He walked between the green rows of cotton stalks loaded with white and purple blooms. The crop looked good. They might make a bale or more. The corn crop needed the buck grass chopped out as did the sorghum cane. While the children chopped grass, he and Bob went to the woods with a cross cut saw and ax. The family would need plenty of firewood to cook with and keep them warm during the winter months. There wasn't enough meat hanging in the smokehouse to last until hog killing time on November 20th. The few chickens were still laying eggs as well as the geese and there was a barrel of molasses, but very little corn remained in the crib. The garden would produce until frost. Afterwards, they would have to tighten their belts until the corn crop was gathered and hogs were killed. If worse came to worse, the boys could trap rabbits and hunt squirrel, which was mighty tasty eating. But he worried. There were six mouths to feed, seven counting Eliza.

After toiling from sun up till sundown, chopping grass and cutting wood, the family had supper, and then adjourned to the front yard to catch a breeze. Crickets chirped and bull frogs croaked. The children laughed and chased lightning bugs. Jim Dan had tied a string to a June bug which was flying around his head.

Eliza nursed the baby. Coleman savored the peaceful scene, knowing it wouldn't last much longer. The day was fast approaching when laughter would be replaced by the thunder of cannon, the rattle of musketry and the cries of wounded men.

His heart had never been heavier than when he mounted and rode off to only God knew what awaited him.

---

Two weeks later, September 27th to be exact, a milestone would be reached in Ophelia's life. She would be one decade old. Already, she was doing woman's work; washing clothes and cooking for the family, taking care of children, and most recently, helping birth a baby. In addition, she worked in the field and gardened, chopped wood and shelled corn. It was hard work, but she readily accepted the responsibility. It made her feel important.

Walking from the branch back to the kitchen carrying a jug of sweet milk and butter that was kept cool in the water, she thought about what her father had said to her just before departing to rejoin the Army.

He had laid his hand on her shoulder and said, "Ophelia, pretty soon you'll be ten, the oldest child and I'm depending on you to fill your Mama's shoes until the baby is older."

"Papa, I'll do my best," she told him.

Before going to the kitchen, she peeked inside the house at her mother, who was in the bedroom rocking the baby and knitting socks and quietly singing, "Swing Low Sweet Chariot…"

"Mama, I'm gonna start supper."

"Bob and Jim Dan are in the woods checking their snares," said Eliza. "Fried rabbit sure would taste good."

"I thought I'd stew some potatoes and fry fat back and make cornbread."

She walked across the backyard to the log kitchen; stoked the fire in the fireplace; peeled potatoes and dropped them in a black pot of boiling water. After mixing cornbread batter, she pulled hot coals into a pile and placed the Dutch oven on top then spooned in a dollop of lard. She poured the batter into the Dutch oven that sizzled with hot grease, placed on the lid and heaped hot coal on top. Shortly, delicious cornbread with a thick brown crust would be ready to eat. There was nothing that tasted any better than hot cornbread soaked with fresh butter and drowned with molasses. She liked to cook, especially when she did it alone. It gave her time to think, which was difficult to do with her mother and children under foot. Sometimes, she liked to imagine what the world was like beyond walking distance. She had been to Athens a few times, but the majority of her life had been spent on Johnson Branch. She had heard about faraway places and read about them in old newspapers that her father had brought home, but the closest she got to them was in her imagination. Maybe a handsome beau on a white steed would gallop up someday when she was picking blackberries and fetch her up behind him and ride off.

Rheubin Isom was handsome, but he was only a child and even younger than she. She had seen him at Isom Chapel's Church at the summer meeting. His family lived near Piney Creek and it was said that his Papa, old man Matthew Isom was a Union man. She was far too young to be thinking of a man, but one day she would be grown and cute little Rheubin would grow up too. She was pretty sure Rheubin wouldn't be riding a beautiful steed in the future. Most likely, he would be following an old plow horse or a mule. One thing for sure, if the war didn't end soon, all of the good men would be dead or crippled.

Barking dogs interrupted her daydreaming. Someone was approaching and the way Samson and the other dogs were raising Cain, she knew it wasn't a visiting neighbor or her Grandpa Harvey. The hair on the back of her neck tingled. She laid down the spoon and rushed to the front door. Yankee soldiers! She stepped back inside the door, certain they had seen her. She saw her mother standing at the door of the cabin holding the baby, Emmit clinging to her skirt. The dogs continued barking and growling.

"Call them dogs off or I'll shoot 'em," said a corporal on a white horse.

"No, please don't!" pleaded Eliza. "Samson, Moses, Zeke, hush!" The dogs backed away, still growling.

"Where's the man of the house?" asked the Corporal.

"He ain't here."

"Where is he, off fighting in the Rebel Army?"

Eliza didn't answer.

"You can bet your boots they're secesh," said one of the men.

"Search the place," ordered the Corporal.

The soldiers dismounted. One walked to the back of the house; one pushed Eliza aside and entered the front door and one went toward the barn. Another trooper headed straight toward the log kitchen. Ophelia froze, her heart pounding. There was no place to hide. Papa had put her in charge and she had to be strong. The soldier entered the kitchen, startled when he saw Ophelia staring at him. His black eyes locked on her, and then he gave a crooked smile.

"Well-well, what do we have here, a young Rebel tart? How old are you gal?"

"Ten."

"I bet you have a Rebel boyfriend."

Ophelia didn't respond. She was weak-kneed and her heart was about to explode, but she was trying to keep a brave face. The soldier hollered out the door, "Hey Corporal, I've found a little Rebel gal in here."

The Corporal entered the kitchen and glanced around. "What's cooking in the pot?" gesturing toward the Dutch oven.

"Cornbread."

"My men are hungry and so am I," he said. "You got any ham?"

Ophelia nodded.

"Cat got your tongue?"

"No."

"Fry up some meat. That would taste mighty good with cornbread," he said. "If we're gonna save the Union, we need to be well fed and strong, don't you agree?"

Ophelia said nothing as she cut off several slices of ham that hung from the rafter, placed them in a big black skillet and set it on hot coals, where it was soon sizzling.

She removed the cornbread from the black pot and placed it on the table. The Corporal tore off a hunk of the bread, broke it open and laid on fried ham.

"Now, that's good," he said, mouth full and grease dripping down his chin. Two more soldiers entered and began eating.

The Corporal wiped grease from his mouth with a sleeve and grinned at Ophelia, revealing crooked yellow teeth.

"You're a pretty good cook," he said, "and pretty good looking to be a secesh." He grabbed her arm and pulled her toward him. "How about a little kiss?"

The men laughed. Ophelia's free hand shot to the handle of the iron skillet containing hot grease and grabbed it. She slung the grease at the men, some splattering on the Corporal. He screamed and dropped her hand. Ophelia backed away, wielding the skillet as a weapon.

"I ought to kill you!" screamed the corporal.

The scream brought Eliza running into the kitchen, clutching the baby to her chest, Emmit and LouElla close behind her. "Leave her alone!"

The soldier who had gone to the barn entered the kitchen and saw Ophelia backed in the corner with the uplifted skillet. He looked at her and she thought she saw a hint of kindness on his face.

"Aww, leave her alone, Corporal," he said. "She's just a child."

The Corporal wiped grease from his uniform. "What did you find in the barn?"

"Nothing much. Very little corn, some fodder and an old oxen and a cow grazing in the meadow."

"How 'bout horses and mules?"

"Didn't see any."

"The Union needs the corn and fodder," said the Corporal. "Fetch a sack and get as much as you can. Take the hams and bacon, middlins too… and take the butter and molasses."

"What about the ox and cow?" asked another soldier.

"Shoot 'em."

"No, please don't," begged Eliza.

The soldier with a kind face spoke up. "Aw, Corporal, there's no need to do that, they'll starve to death."

The Corporal stared at Ophelia for what seemed like forever. Then he turned up the jug of sweet milk, drank several gulps, and then passed it around to his men.

"Okay men, let's get outta here."

After watching the last soldier ride out of sight, Ophelia wobbled over to a chair where she collapsed.

# 33 | CHICKAMAUGA

North Georgia.

Saturday morning, September 19, 1863.

James Greer "Jim" Barksdale woke cold long before reveille, an uneasiness roiling in his stomach. It could be another bout of dysentery coming on but it didn't feel the same. It had frosted during the night. The vast encampment of soldiers were mostly quiet, except for men snoring and coughing and in the distance the whinnying of horses and lowing of livestock. The weather had been unseasonably hot and dry and the roads were bowls of dust. His throat was parched. From the nearby creek came a soothing gurgling sound. The previous evening he had gone to there and filled his quart canteen with its cold, clear water. It reminded him of Swan Creek back home, except that it was about forty feet wide and flowed faster. Indians, he was told, called it Chickamauga, which meant dwelling place. The creek meandered northeasterly out of the mountains of north Georgia through rough, broken terrain before emptying into the Tennessee River north of Chattanooga. Listening to the water brought a measure of peace to his troubled soul.

Lying next to him on his back, hat down over his eyes, mouth open and snoring, was his brother-in-law, James Newby. If anything bothered Newby, he never revealed it. Approximately one week earlier, on September 11th, both of them had "seen the elephant." Their battalion, 15th Hawkins Sharpshooters, had been sent to Pigeon Mountain where they attacked Federals coming through Dug Gap. That was their first and only combat experience since enlisting more than nine months earlier.

They had performed well. "The sharpshooter Brigade, under the gallant Major Hawkins," it was officially reported, "advanced in handsome style, driving the Yankee pickets and skirmishers." Barksdale was proud of their performance and the honor accorded them, but he was more elated by the fact that he and Newby were still alive. Unlike some of the youngsters who sought honor, his goal was less noble. He wanted only to return home alive to see Susan and their two children, Waddie and Benjamin Dudley.

The Union and Confederate Armies had marched and counter marched since Murfreesboro trying to outmaneuver each other. Now, they were face to face, but neither side knew that fact with certainty because of the thick forest and undergrowth between them. Approximately 60,000 Yankees were west of the LaFayette Road that ran south from Chattanooga on the opposite side of Chickamauga Creek. Almost 55,000 Confederates were east of the road and creek. Barksdale didn't know those facts at the time, but his primal instinct was sending out loud warning signals. It wasn't dysentery that caused his stomach to roil. It was fear.

When the Bugler blew *Reveille* Newby sat straight up.

"Welcome to the world, James," said Barksdale. "You've been saw'n logs all night."

Newby massaged his lower back. "I'm gett'n too old for this. We need to whip them Yankees once and for all and go home."

Barksdale was silent for a spell. "Home, how wonderful that sounds."

The day was breaking cool and clear but he knew it would soon be hot. The regiment came alive and men moved about, coughing, grumbling and making ready for another day in the Army. Fires were stoked.

Sergeant Meadows appeared and, without greeting, said: "Men, prepare three days ration. And be quick about it!" Then he abruptly departed.

"Wonder who put a cockle burr in his underwear?" asked Skinny.

"Don't worry, we ain't gonna fight," said Fuzzy Terry. "The vittles are for eat'n while we retreat. We retreated from Murfreesboro, we retreated from Tullahoma and we retreated from Chattanooga. For just once I'd like to see blue bellies show'n tail instead of gray backs."

Fuzzy, the cook, was from Lawrence County, Alabama. He called Barksdale "Grandpa" and the latter affectionately addressed him as "Fuzzy." Fuzzy had three known talents: talking, cooking and gambling. He had been appointed permanent cook, but for a price. The five men in the mess compensated him with tobacco, which he smoked and chewed with relish. He had lost or, more than likely, thrown away the skillet because he didn't want to carry it. Using gunpowder, he had blown open a Yankee canteen which he flattened with a stone and fashioned into a skillet.

He laid sow belly on the flattened canteen and placed it on hot coals. In addition to cooking, he was developing another talent – stealing, which he called "foraging." He had managed to acquire flour and made baked bread by throwing the dough balls into the ashes.

Barksdale warmed by the fire and watched Fuzzy turning the sizzling bacon.

"Grandpa, I'm cook'n something you hadn't eat since yesterday," said Fuzzy.

"Lordy mercy Fuzzy, if I have to eat one more slice of sow belly I'll be grunt'n and root'n around for acorns."

"Reckon we gonna fight today?" asked Fuzzy.

"Yeah, I feel it in my bones," replied Barksdale.

"I hope we do," said Newby, joining the conversation. "I'm gonna dine on Yankee food tonight."

After breakfast, ammunition was passed out, 40 rounds to each man. The men cleaned their rifles, checked equipment and filled their canteens with cold water from Chickamauga Creek. Barksdale and Newby wrote letters to Susan and Sarah which they carefully folded and placed in the crowns of their hats. Some of the men played cards and others shot crap when Sergeant Meadows wasn't around. Later in the day, Lieutenant Richard Coleman of Athens came by to buck up the men. "Boys, I hear that the Yanks have so much food stacked in wagons that mules can't pull 'em. All we have to do is whip 'em and we'll eat well."

"There are three things I want," said Barksdale. "A hot cup of coffee to drink, a slab of beef dripp'n with brown gravy and a pair of shoes without holes in 'em."

"Fight hard, and you'll get all three," said Lieutenant Coleman.

Heavy firing broke out to the distant front. Barksdale's nerves tightened, his heart beat increased and his mouth became cotton dry. Waiting to go in battle was torture causing the body to do strange things to itself. Barksdale suddenly had the urge to empty his bladder and bowels again. He was watching the sunset behind Lookout Mountain when in the distance the long roll of drums sounded. The company bugler blew "assemble." He didn't budge, but kept staring at the reddish orange color spreading across the western horizon.

"Fall in, Jim!" yelled Newby.

"I'll be along directly; I just want to get one last glimpse of something beautiful."

347

The roll of the drums was incessant and bugles were sounding, summoning the soldiers to harm's way. Men grabbed their rifles and hurried along to assemble. There was no need to hurry toward death, thought Barksdale. It would come soon enough.

"Come on Jim!" Newby yelled.

After falling in formation, they dressed down the ranks and were given the command, "at rest." Shortly, Major Hawkins rode up on a fine-looking chestnut horse.

"A—TEN HUT!" Commanded Sergeant Meadows.

The men snapped to attention.

"At ease," said Major Hawkins. "Men, our battalion, together with Woods' Brigade and several other regiments, has been ordered to cross Chickamauga Creek. There will be fighting on the other side and plenty of it. I am confident that you will give your best effort. You are brave and honorable men. You demonstrated that at Dug Gap. Remember that you are fighting for your parents, your wives, your children and your homes. Home is beyond Lookout Mountain and Yankees are blocking the way. I know that you will do your duty. May God bless our arms and may God bless the Confederate States of America and our struggle for independence." He removed his hat and made a sweeping bow to his men. They responded with a loud hurrah.

At six p.m. Woods' Brigade began wading across the chilly waters of Chickamauga Creek. Barksdale and Newby held their rifles and ammunition pouches over their heads, and when they climbed onto the opposite bank they were dripping wet and cold. They moved through the brush and around trees until they came to Jay's Mill Road, where they halted and dressed up the formation. Cleaburne's entire division was formed on the road with Polk's Brigade on the right and Deshlers' on the left. Barksdale knew that a major battle was shaping up.

The temperature dropped and men shivered in their wet clothes. Barksdale's teeth chattered and he shook uncontrollably from the cold and from fear. He was glad that it was dark and the men couldn't see him. He had never envisioned dying in this manner – cold, hungry, scared and far from home. But, if it was time to die, he would do so honorably and like a man, fighting to protect his home and family.

The bugler sounded "Forward" and the brigade marched forward in darkness across a field toward the Yankee line. Newby marched at Barksdale's right elbow. The shuffle of thousands of feet, many barefoot, the rattling of canteens and the squeaking of equipment drowned out the snapping sound of the regimental colors flying somewhere out front. Barksdale tensed and waited for the first volley that was certain to come any second. He saw red muzzle flashes and heard the simultaneous roar of rifles. Minie balls cut through the cool crisp air, snapping limbs and knocking off leaves; whirring like demons from hell, one snapping near his head. Some made sickening thudding sounds as they impacted into flesh and men cried out and crumpled to the ground, but they continued to advance. The bugler blew "Commence firing" and the graybacks let loose a sheet of fire. The night was ablaze with red muzzle flashes. It seemed that the earth was on fire. Bullets whizzed near Barksdale's head and the deafening roar of gunfire sounded like the devil stoking up hell. Barksdale's instinct was to flee in search of cover, but he fought to resist that urge and anyway, there was no place to hide. He wondered if other men felt the same. They kept moving forward and firing. Insanity! The bugler sounded "Charge," and someone yelled, "TAKE 'EM BOYS! CHARGE!"

The men responded like water gushing from a hole in a dam. The Rebel yell pierced the night as they moved forward toward the Yankees, who were located behind a

348

breast work of rails and logs. The Confederates crashed into the Yankee line with ferocity, firing, bayonetting and clubbing the Yankees. It was a fratricidal free for all. The gray backs released their pent-up anger in a savage bloodletting. After an hour or so, the Yankees had enough and withdrew, but without their brigade commander, Colonel Baldwin, who was dead.

When the bloody mess ended, the Confederates sunk to the ground and slept on the blood-soaked soil among the dead and the dying; both friend and foe. The last voice that Barksdale heard before falling asleep was Newby's.

"Jim, thank God we're still alive."

Sunday morning came early for Barksdale, who was awakened from his stupor by a faraway voice, "Mama, Mama."

At first, Barksdale thought he was dreaming. Then he heard it again. "Mama, Mama."

The coldness that he felt to his bone marrow was no dream, and the pain of inflamed muscles and stiffness of his body was real. He ached all over. Now, he remembered where he was. He cracked an eye and saw Newby, asleep and breathing. Thank God, he was alive.

"Mama, Mama."

Barksdale sat up and squinted through the dingy dawn light at the grim scene around him. Nearby, men slept on the ground, some rolled up in blankets, others covered with frost. Numerous bodies, both Confederate and Yankee, lay in grotesque form, blood congealed around gaping wounds. Some had half of their heads blown off and brains spilled onto the bloodied ground; others had been mangled with shots. Wounded horses stood with their heads nearly touching the ground; others lay dead and stiff, some with their feet sticking straight out. The wounded moaned, some crying out for help, others for their mothers and some praying that God would end their pain. Barksdale placed his filthy hands over his ears and tried to drown out their cries. Men walked among the strewn bodies looking for the wounded. It was a sickening sight. Barksdale retched and closed his eyes to shut out the horrible scene of carnage. He lay on the cold earth and heaved with emotions. But closing his eyes didn't stop hot tears from flowing.

"Almighty and merciful God, thank you for saving my life," he whispered. "I'm cold, hungry and scared and have nothing left but faith in thee. Give me strength and courage to endure his horrible ordeal. If you see fit to spare my miserable life, I will serve you all the days of my life." He lifted his head and looked to the east where the sun was rising in a clear sky. He'd never seen a prettier Lord's Day.

"Mama, Mama," came the plea again.

Barksdale sat up and wiped his eyes and looked across the battlefield. The voice had come from behind the Yankee earthwork. He stood and walked unsteadily toward the pleading voice, careful not to step on a corpse or sleeping soldiers. Several blue-clad soldiers were grotesquely draped over the logs rail and breastwork.

"Water...please."

Several yards away, Barksdale saw a man, lying on his back, his hand slightly above his chest. It appeared that he had dragged himself away from the earthwork, perhaps trying to rejoin his unit. Barksdale walked over to where the man lay and knelt down. He was a mere kid. Blood oozed out of his chest onto his soiled blue jacket. The boy's eyes danced with fear.

"I'm not going to hurt you, Yank."

"Water Johnny, water."

Barksdale took out the boy's canteen, lifted his head slightly, held it to his parched lips and let him sip.

"Thanks Johnny."

"How old are you son?"

"Seventeen."

"You oughta be home with your folks," said Barksdale. "All you Yanks oughta go home where you belong and leave us be. You don't have any business down here."

The boys breathing grew shallow and tears formed in his eye sockets and ran down his dirty cheeks, creating rivulets of white.

"Pleeeaaase hold... my hand... Johnny."

Barksdale grasped his bloody hand and the boy squeezed hard.

"I don't... want... to be ... alone."

"I've got it son. I won't leave ya."

"My... pocket," said the boy, eyes lowering toward his chest.

Barksdale reached inside his blue coat and into his shirt pocket and extracted a folded paper. It was a letter bearing a forwarding address.

"Will you... see... that?"

Barksdale choked back tears. "Yeah, I will."

"Thanks Johnny."

"What's your name son?"

"Henry..."

"Don't talk."

"Johnny... I'm ... going... home." He coughed several times and went limp. Barksdale gently lowered the boy's head to the ground. He felt as though he had known him all of his life. In the last few minutes they had become friends. He wept.

Barksdale unfolded the letter and a small daguerreotype dropped out. He picked it up and examined it. It was a photo of an older woman. He blinked away tears and read the letter.

"Dear Ma,

By the time you receive this letter I will be in heaven with Pa.

You have been a good mother and I thank you for giving me a good life and lots of love. I have carried your picture over my heart since I departed home and knowing that you were close to my heart gave me great peace and comfort. I love you and will see you in heaven someday.

Love, your only son, Henry."

"Damn this war to hell!" exclaimed Barksdale. He folded the letter and placed it in the front pocket of his threadbare trousers and returned to where Newby slept.

———————

Morning sun was welcomed by the chilled and exhausted men of Hawkins' Sharpshooters. They breakfasted on leftover wheat bread and cold sow belly caked with

350

grease that had turned white. It didn't fill a growling stomach but it was a sight better than eating parched corn that would crack a man's teeth. At 10:00 a.m. the snare drum rolled and bugle sounded. The men grabbed their rifles and fell in formation.

"We're com'n at'che again blue bellies!" exclaimed Fuzzy with bravado. "And I'm gonna get me some."

Barksdale looked over at Newby and said, "Fight'n sure has a way of focusing a man's attention."

"How's that Jim?"

"There is nothing in the world to worry about 'cept surviving for the next second."

"I figure there is either a bullet with my name on it or there isn't," replied Newby. "And no matter how much I worry, I can't change that fact."

Barksdale was still pondering that theory when the bugles sounded "Forward." He barely noticed that a pretty day was in the making. The brigade moved forward with General Leonidas Polk's troops on the right. Woods' Brigade obliqued to the left and Polk obliqued to the right. Into the gap marched Deshler's Brigade, which joined Woods. Thousands of gray back advanced across Poe Field toward LaFayette Road which ran north-south. Yankees were hidden in the timbers across the road with itchy trigger fingers, waiting. When the Confederates came closer they ripped their ranks with enfilading fire and sent them reeling backward.

But the Confederates weren't ready to quit. At 11 a.m. Woods' Brigade, including Hawkins' Sharpshooters, advanced forward again, aided by artillery, and attacked the Federal forces positioned behind rail barricades west of LaFayette Road. Confederate cannon roared from the rear and shook the ground. Major Hawkins was leading his sharpshooters, mounted on his big chestnut horse. Lieutenant Coleman was walking beside the men, encouraging them onward. The regimental flag fluttered in the breeze. Skinny was in the first line of the column and over his shoulder Barksdale saw Confederate artillery ripping into the Federal position, sending fence rail and blue-clad men flying into the air.

Barksdale set his jaw and continued forward; glanced to the right at Newby, his rifle resting on his shoulder, a look of grim determination on his dirty face.

"James, tell me there isn't a bullet with my name on it," said Barksdale.

Newby looked at him and opened his mouth to speak when all hell broke loose. Cannon thundered from across LaFayette Road and rifles rattled, sending a hail of lead and iron tearing into the Confederate ranks. Major Hawkins toppled from his saddle. Lieutenant Coleman dropped to the ground. Bullets and artillery tore through Confederate ranks. The front line fired and knelt to reload. The second line fired. While Barksdale and Newby were reloading, a bullet ripped into Skinny, sending him falling backwards, his head resting near Barksdale's foot.

"Grandpa... I'll miss you," Skinny said and rolled back big brown eyes, then went limp. Men were dropping like autumn leaves. The bugler sounded "retreat." Someone screamed "Fall back! Fall back!" They returned to their starting position. It was all for nothing. The Sharpshooters had suffered the severest losses of Woods' Brigade. Afterwards, the living went to the bloody field and retrieved the dead. Lieutenant Coleman's Negro carried his body off and would soon return him to Athens. Barksdale and Newby located Skinny, his head lying in a puddle of dark blood caused by a minie ball that had severed a neck artery.

"He was a good fellow," said Barksdale, his voice quavering. "I would have been proud if he had been my brother. I'll miss him." He wiped away tears.

"Yeah, me too," said Newby.

Barksdale bent over and grabbed Skinny's feet and Newby got his arms and were carrying him from the field when Fuzzy and Worm walked up.

"Have you been through his pockets?" Fuzzy asked.

"Not yet," replied Newby.

"I'll write his folks a letter and send his things," said Worm.

"We need to get his tobacco 'fore someone else does," Fuzzy said.

---

Coleman Barksdale and the 50th Alabama Regiment, Deas' Brigade, about 500 strong, marched toward the battlefield, but didn't arrive in time to fight on Saturday. That night they waded across Chickamauga Creek and slept damp and cold on the ground east of the LaFayette Road.

Coleman woke early Sunday morning and breakfasted on hard tack, but ate only a few bites. Butterflies fluttered in his stomach. The men made nervous talk. He checked his rifle a dozen times to make sure it was loaded.

At 11:15 a.m., they waded through thick brush, stopped and waited for orders to advance. Coleman had been in a skirmish or two before, but they didn't compare to what this was shaping up to be. Waiting for order to move forward was nerve wracking and gave him time to ponder what could go wrong. The Yankees were dug in somewhere to the front, behind logs, rails and earthworks. All they had to do was wait, take aim and fire at the advancing Confederates. It would be like shooting fish in a barrel. And a host of Confederates would never see home again. Even if he wasn't instantly killed, a minie ball could rip away muscle, arteries and bones. A quick and painless bullet to the brain was better than slow death from infection that was sure to follow a wound.

Skirmishers were thrown out to the front, and to their right rifle fire was crackling.

Generals Longstreet and Buckner rode to the front of the regiment and reined their horses. Longstreet had recently arrived by rail from Virginia with 12,000 needed reinforcements.

Longstreet looked out to the front and gestured with his finger toward the forest. "The enemy is somewhere in there," he said.

Brigade Commander, General Deas called his Alabamians to attention, and rifles clanged as the men snapped to and Longstreet and Buckner rode away. At 11:30 a.m., the 50th Alabama stepped across the LaFayette Road, and when the bugler blew "quick time" they picked up their pace and moved toward the thick forest and bushes. Some 600 yards in front of them the enemy lay hidden and waiting behind breastwork. As they got closer, the bugler sounded "double quick time". Someone spotted the Yankee skirmishers and hollered, "THERE THEY ARE!" Simultaneously, the bugle blew the "run." The Alabamians bolted forward like they had been spring loaded. Someone gave the Rebel yell and instantly the throats of hundreds of men bent on killing Yankees joined in. A loud blood curdling scream went up. "E-E-E-E-E-E AAAAAARA!" Southern muskets spoke. Quickly they were on top of the Yankee skirmishers who fled back to the main line of breastwork. The Confederates charged. The Yanks opened fire. The gray backs were slowed, but not stopped. They charged again, giving the Rebel yell; took

352

another volley, but kept going. The Yankee line broke. Some ran, others threw down their rifles and surrendered. The remaining Yankees were driven over the high ground west of Craw Fish Spring Road.

The brigade moved to the right and that afternoon at about 3:30 charged up Snodgrass hill. They fought for nearly two hours before having to fall back to the foot of the hill. At 4 p.m. the brigade formed into a ravine west of the Vittetoe House and assaulted the spur of the hill again. They were eventually driven back to the base of the hill. Later, launching a third attack, they found that the enemy had slipped away. The price of victory was high. The 50th had lost 100 out of 500 engaged. Coleman Barksdale was unscathed.

---

The Yankees had fought hard, but not good enough. Running low on ammunition and men, they couldn't hold out any longer. After nightfall, they retreated to Chattanooga. Both sides had paid a heavy price. The Yankees had lost 16,170 men and the Confederates 18,454. It would prove to be one of the bloodiest battles of the war.

Bragg's Army of Tennessee had finally scored a victory, or so it seemed. Instead of following and destroying the retreating Union Army, General Bragg let them escape to Chattanooga. He occupied the high ground, blockaded the river and lay siege to the city. The Federal troops slowly starved. They survived on a few grains of parched corn and hard tacks each day. Over 10,000 horses and mules died. They were too weak to fight and soon, Bragg surmised, they would be too weak to run. Then they would have no alternative but to surrender. Bragg neglected to consider one important fact: the Yankees had the rail lines.

---

The savagery ended as abruptly as it began. For days every nerve in Jim Barksdale's body had been wound tighter than banjo strings. Adrenaline had surged through his veins, gearing him to fight. Fear had seared his brain. Now, he found there was nothing to do. He reverted to mundane things like scratching lice, staying warm, trotting to the bushes, squelching hunger and thinking about home. When the regiment was organized in Courtland two years earlier there were approximately 1,000 men standing in the ranks. Now, there were less than 400. Enthusiasm for the war had evaporated and enlistments were few. Camp life was boring for a 33-year-old married father who had no interest in that gambling that occupied the time of most of the men. He and Newby were seated on the ground, their backs against a tree, writing letters home while Fuzzy Terry organized a weevil race. Fuzzy, who would wager on anything, had spread weevil-infested cornmeal on a blanket and was taking bets on which weevil could outrun the other one.

"Hey Grandpa! Come on over and put your money on the fastest weevil," he yelled.

Barksdale looked up, laughed and waved him off. In the distance, an approaching figure caught his attention.

"James, is that who I think it is?"

Newby watched for a moment. "It sure favors his walk."

The man was thin as a rail, barefoot with a scrawny beard and wore a brown slouch hat.

"Well, blow me down," said Barksdale jumping to his feet. "It is! It's Coleman!" He ran to meet his brother, Newby following.

Coleman spotted his older brother and ran toward him, crashing into his open arms.

"Thank God, you're alive," said Jim, hugging him. "I didn't know your regiment was here. Let me look at you. Lordy mercy, you look like forty miles of bad road."

"Yeah, and I feel like it too," replied Coleman then howdied Newby and slapped his back.

"Have y'all heard from home?" he asked. "How's Ma and Pa and the family?"

"Not a word," said Jim. There was much catching up on news.

That afternoon the three men hiked to the top of Missionary Ridge, a twenty-mile-long hump of land that ran north-south and rose some 400 feet above the valley floor. Crestline Road bristled with Confederate artillery. They turned around and gazed west across the valley toward Lookout Mountain, which was also occupied by Confederate forces. Down below was Chattanooga, nestled against a great bend of the Tennessee River, and what remained of General Rosecran's Federal Army.

"We got them blue devils by the short hair," said Coleman. "I hear they're starv'n."

"I don't know who's got who," replied Newby. "We're sitting up here surviving on goober peas and blue beef brought up from Georgia. Some of those cows are so weak and poor it takes three men to hold 'em up to shoot 'em. I don't know who's gonna starve first."

"Those railroad tracks you see down there brought General Longstreet here with 12,000 men from Virginia just 'n time for the Chickamauga battle," Jim said. "They can also bring Yankee troops."

"I hadn't thought of that," said Coleman. "'Course, they don't pay me to sit around 'n think 'bout such things."

---

Union Secretary of War Stanton had other plans. He persuaded President Lincoln to transfer two corps of General Meade's Army out of the Potomac. In less than two weeks, 25,000 Union troops, equipment and 3,000 animals were transferred by rail to relieve the besieged Federal Army at Chattanooga. They threw a pontoon bridge across the Tennessee, down river, out of range of Confederate guns on Lookout Mountain, and came up behind them.

# 34 | A TIME FOR DECISION

McLemore's Cove.

Friday, November 20, 1863.

It was well past midnight and John Adams "Jack" McElroy was wide awake. It wasn't because of the cold hard ground or the flimsy blanket that offered little warmth to his body or even his empty stomach that constantly growled. Something else ate at Jack McElroy – and it was getting worse.

The fire had burned down to coals and the only sound in the camp was snoring and an occasional horse snorting. Jack stared up at the star-studded heaven and pondered his dilemma. Nowadays, any unexpected noise – the clanging of a skillet or crack of a twig – brought him upright, heart racing. Every gunshot stretched his nerves tighter. And a man's nerves could be stretched only so much until they snapped.

For a year he had been in the saddle fighting, living on practically nothing, baking under the summer sun, freezing during the winter, sleeping in the rain, wearing rags, eaten by chiggers, ticks and poison ivy, and drawing no pay – except for the occasional near-worthless Confederate note. And worst of all, he was ill with diarrhea.

Since General Forrest had been transferred to Mississippi in October and the Fourth Tennessee Regiment had been placed under Wheeler's Cavalry Corps, the little confidence Jack had of surviving the war had vanished. The boys trusted Ol' Bedford to pull them through thick and thin. Now he was gone. The talk around camp fires was that following Chickamauga, Ol' Bedford had marched into General Bragg's headquarters tent, stuck his finger in his face and given him a tongue lashing, threatening that if he ever interfered with him or crossed his path it would be at the peril of his life. There wasn't a man in the outfit that wouldn't have given a plug of tobacco to have had his head under the tent and witnessed that scene.

Jack was wide awake when *reveille* sounded. Mike struggled to his feet, rubbed his low back, stretched, tossed a stick of wood on the dying embers and warmed his hands. Rufus rolled out, yawned, moving slowly in the coldness, and looked at Jack, who lay motionless staring at the sky.

"Morn'n brother," Rufus said. "You 'bout let the fire go out last night."

Jack didn't reply. Rufus looked over at Mike, who merely shrugged.

"Better roll out," Rufus said to Jack. "Or Absalom Powell will be along raising cane."

Jack sat up and mumbled, "I've had a bellyful of him too."

The fire caught up and Rufus broke a fence rail in half and pitched it on. Mike chopped hunks of salt pork in to a skillet and set it on the hot coals. Soon grease was popping and meat was sizzling, giving off a sour odor.

"Is that pork gone bad too?" Rufus asked.

"Yeah," replied Mike. "But don't worry, I'll cook it real good." He added cornmeal and water and stirred until the mixture turned into thick gravy. Jack reached for his cup but couldn't grasp it. His right hand trembled uncontrollably. It had trembled before but now it was worse – much worse. He pocketed his right hand and used his left. Mike noticed and asked, "What's wrong?"

"Nothing."

"You've been quieter 'n a mouse for the past several days," added Rufus. "Let me see that hand." He reached over pulled it out of Jack's pocket. Jack jerked it free.

355

"Okay, I'll show you. Look, it's shaking like a leaf and won't stop."

Rufus and Mike's eyes met. "Aww, don't worry Jack," said Mike. "It'll go away, here have some coosh. It'll make you feel better."

He dipped a cupful and gave it to Jack, who smelled it and gagged.

"I can't eat it," he said and handed it back.

"You need to eat," said Rufus.

"I've had the runs for days," Jack said. "Eat'n more green meat will make it worse."

Jack looked up and, seeing Sgt. Absalom Powell, pocketed his right hand.

"Men, cook two days' rations," Powell said. "We're moving out. Been a lot of Yankee movement around McLemore's Cove."

Jack never looked up and turned his head and spat on the ground as Powell departed.

Shortly, the regiment, down to a few hundred men, was riding north through the wooded landscape of north Georgia. A cold north wind blew down McLemore's Cove, which lay east of Missionary Ridge and west of Pigeon Mountain. The intersection of two main roads cutting through the gap made it important to Union forces concentrating in the area. And that's the reason Starnes' Fourth was there. At mid-morning they clashed with Yankee pickets who fired on the column and then pulled back. Pickets always shield a larger force. Somewhere behind the leafless trees that blanketed the mountains were Yankees and plenty of them, no doubt working their way north where Bragg's Army was positioned.

Jack winced at every shot. They halted behind a low ridge. Sgt. Powell rode back selecting skirmishers to send forward.

"McElroy, you come with me," he ordered Jack.

Jack goosed his horse and rode forward with a squad of men who dismounted and formed a skirmish line. They spread out and advanced on foot cautiously through the heavy timber. Jacks' heart was racing and his right hand trembled so bad that he could hardly hold his musket. Somewhere out front were Yankees watching and waiting. The first warning of their presence would be gunfire and bullets. Jack squinted into the gray light looking for any sign of the enemy as they moved forward into the woods. A startled rabbit jumped and ran. Jack's heart sprang to his throat. Sharp diarrhea pain struck. Any moment gunfire could erupt, but it didn't. He relaxed a notch. Maybe the blue bellies had pulled back.

"POW." A thud and a recent recruit dropped to the ground.

"SNIPER!" someone yelled.

"POW." Another man fell.

Jack dropped and hugged the ground.

Sgt. Powell ran up and screamed, "ON YOUR FEET MCELROY!" Jack lay on the ground shaking. He tried to rise but couldn't.

"GET UP COWARD!" Powell yelled, holding a cocked revolver in his hand. Jack raised his head and saw blue bellies approaching. A minie ball snapped past his ear and he heard a dull thud. He glanced back and saw Sgt. Powell crumple, the revolver dropping from his hand. Blood gushed from his neck – a severed artery.

"Help me McElroy. Don't leave me," pleaded Powell, who was lying on his back. "Pleeeeease help me."

If he jumped up and ran out now, he could escape the advancing Yankees, Jack

356

thought. He owed Powell nothing.

Yet…

"Hold on Sarge," Jack said, ripping away Powell's shirt and cramming a piece of it into the gaping wound.

Finally, Jack's dilemma had been resolved. He tossed his rifle to the ground and stood with arms raised and watched as the Yankees advanced. One slammed the butt of his rifle to Jack's head, knocking him down. When he came to, the rest of his squad was gone. Only he and Powell remained. And Powell was dead.

For Jack the war was over. His enthusiasm for the cause had long since evaporated.

"I'm tired of fightin' you Yanks," he said to a Union Sergeant. "I'm ready to quit and take the oath."

He was sent to east Tennessee and eight days later on November 28th he signed an Oath of Allegiance to the United States.

# 35 | DEFEAT AND RETREAT

Missionary Ridge.

Tuesday, November 24, 1863.

Coleman Barksdale turned and gazed up at the series of gully-cut hills that undulated to the top of Missionary Ridge.

"I betcha we could see all the way to Athens from up there," said Peavine.

"I wouldn't climb up there if I could see Pharaoh's Tomb," Coleman replied. "I'm so dad-blamed hungry I hardly have enough strength to tie my shoe laces."

"Coleman, you ain't wear'n no shoes."

"It's just a figure of speech, Peavine."

The 50th Alabama, Dea's Brigade, was positioned near the base of Missionary Ridge on the far right wing of Bragg's Army, next to Vaughn's Brigade that was at the tail end of the line. The sun dropped behind Lookout Mountain to the west and it grew much colder. A small fire was stoked and the men in Coleman's mess gathered around it to warm.

Sergeant Thompson stomped up. "Men, we're moving up top after dark. Cook three days rations," he said brusquely and went on to the next line.

"What are we supposed to cook, our belts?" groused Tom Baker. "The only thing we have to eat is a few ears of corn."

"I'd like mine without the shuck, please," said Peavine.

Kernels were shelled from the cob and fried in lard to soften them. "If I was a mule this would be right tasty,' said Peavine, cracking kernels between his teeth.

Coleman knew there was only one reason for moving to the top of the ridge. A Federal attack was imminent. The previous day, Federals had seized Orchard Knob, a swell of high ground in front of Missionary Ridge. He figured a large force would assault the front while the main force would attack both flanks in an attempt to roll up the Confederate forces.

The 50th, down to 400 men, climbed up the brushy, rock-strewn ridge passing through two lines of rifle pits manned by cold and hungry Confederates.

"You boys retreating?" asked a Reb in a rifle pit.

"Naw, we've been invited to dine on ham and biscuit with General Bragg," replied Peavine. Coleman chuckled. Peavine was never at a loss for words.

The climb was strenuous and the men were exhausted and cold when they finally reached a dirt road that ran down the spine of the ridge where General Bragg's headquarters were located. After taking up positions, Coleman rolled up in his blanket and collapsed on the cold ground and slept.

Next morning, he woke shivering, his hands and bare feet freezing. A cold north wind swept unabated down the ridge, tearing at his tattered clothes. Pulling the blanket tightly around him, he faced the rising sun and lifted his face toward the warm rays. He prayed silently, asking God to let him live to see his children and Eliza, whose last letter had informed him that she was again pregnant.

Sunlight bathed the valley. Chattanooga was located below, nestled against the Tennessee River which wound like a giant silver snake between the mountain and ridges.

After breakfasting on parched corn, they threw up dirt embankments, took their positions, checked ammunition and waited.

"Let 'em come," said Peavine. "They'll never take this ridge. In war hold'n the high ground is what counts."

"Peavine has gone from plow'n a mule to an expert on war," mused Baker.

"We whipped 'em at Chickamauga and we'll whip 'em again," Peavine shot back.

Clouds drifted over the sun and a cold wind barreled down the ridge. Coleman massaged his hands, his eyes searching across the valley. Waiting was gut wrenching. He wished the Yankees would hurry up and appear. He thought about Eliza and the children and wondered if they had enough wood for the winter and plenty of meat in the smokehouse.

It was mid-afternoon when Peavine, who was hunkered nearby, asked, "Reckon when this doggone war is gonna end?"

"When they're all dead or we're all dead, I reckon," said Coleman.

"Look!" exclaimed Peavine, pointing.

Coleman strained to see. His heart leapt. "Yeah, I see 'em."

Across the valley thousands of tiny blue specks emerged from the tree line. They looked like rows of harmless ants. The roll of drums was barely audible. The soldiers formed a long blue line, followed by a second line only a few feet behind them. They marched forward, followed by a similar line until companies, regiments and finally brigades were in place. The Stars and Stripes and regimental colors whipped in the wind. It was a sobering sight. There were so many troops that he couldn't see where the line began or ended.

"I reckon they gonna parade for us," Peavine said, breaking the tension.

"From up here, they look pretty all lined up with their flags," added Coleman.

"BOOOM – BOOM – BOOM!" Yankee cannon fired in rapid secession. Coleman's raw nerves made him jump, then duck. He suddenly felt warm all over. Shells were exploding lower down the ridge near the first line of the rifle pits, sending up showers of rock, dirt and debris. Following a pounding cannon barrage, the long blue line moved forward across the valley.

"Here they come!" exclaimed Coleman, his throat dry as dust in August.

"Let the devils come, we'll send 'em to hell where they belong," Peavine said.

When the Yankees neared the middle of the valley, Confederate artillery positioned on top of Missionary Ridge opened with a deafening roar, shaking the ground. Shrapnel tore holes in the Yankee formations, decimating men by the scores. Others stepped up and they kept coming. They were caught in a killing zone, exposed to the deadly artillery. For an instant Coleman felt a tinge of pity for them.

Suddenly, the soldiers broke and ran, but not backward – forward! They ran pell mell toward the base of the ridge. Confederates manning the front rifle pits opened up with muskets up and down the line, sending out thousands of smoke puffs. Yankees dropped by the dozens. Smoke drifted upward from the valley floor and it was difficult to see but what Coleman saw next struck fear in his heart. Confederates were fleeing up the ridge! The first line of rifle pits had been overrun and many Confederates were fleeing and surrendering. Unbelievable! The Federals kept coming and screaming, "REMEMBER CHICAMAUGA!" The second line of rifle pits fired with effect, but blue bellies kept coming, bent over climbing, stopping only to fire. The Confederate cannon on the ridge couldn't fire effectively downward and were useless. Confederates fled up the ridge, and down below Coleman could see that many had their arms in the air.

How could this have happened? They were flush with victory after

Chickamauga and now held the high ground, but somehow they had lost.

---

Wednesday, November 25, 1863, 8:30 a.m.

James Greer "Jim" Barksdale and James Newby shivered and waited in their cold rifle pit near the base of Missionary Ridge.

What remained of the hard-bitten veterans of Hawkins' Sharpshooters were dug in with the 16th Alabama Infantry Regiment, Woods' Brigade. Several hundred feet above them was a second line of rifle pits. Fuzzy Terry and Worm Poole were several yards to Barksdale's left. He looked over and saw Fuzzy chewing a plug of tobacco. Worm had his nose stuck in a small New Testament.

Barksdale hadn't seen his brother Coleman in weeks and briefly worried about him before pondering his own misery. He blew warm breath on his numb fingers and massaged them. Not only was he cold, he was scared. Just about now thousands of blue bellies were swarming in the trees across the valley checking their ammunition and snapping on bayonets. As always, he was scared senseless right before battle, but once he was engaged, the fear dissipated and instinct took over. Waiting was hard. It gave a man too much time to think and right now he was thinking of Susan and his two baby boys, Waddie and Benjamin Dudley, back in Athens. It was far more comforting to think of his loved ones than those blue devils. He reached inside the left pocket of his tattered shirt, pulled out the lock of brown hair that Susan had given him the day he departed home and brushed it across his nose. He'd swear he could still smell her sweetness. He thought about the night just before he left home, back in February, and the peach cobbler Susan had made – and then what happened afterwards. He closed his eyes and saw her body pressed against him – and then the ecstasy of love making. Newby's voice jarred him back to reality.

"Look at 'im. You're smiling and we may be dead in thirty minutes."

Barksdale opened his eye and looked at his dirty and bedraggled brother-in-law. "Ah, I's just thinking about eat'n a big helping of Ma's squirrel dumplings," he said. "She makes the best in Limestone County."

Newby looked at Jim suspiciously. "Squirrel dumplings don't make a man smile like that," he said. "But speaking of 'em, oh what I'd give for a plate of 'em and a hot fire right now. I'm about to freeze." He rubbed and blew hot breath on his hands.

"Yeah, me too," replied Barksdale then returned to day dreaming.

"Booom – Booom – Booom – Booom – Booom!"

Union artillery fired in rapid succession, interrupting Barksdale's daydream. He squinted across the wooded valley where bluecoats were emerging by the thousands. Suddenly his hands weren't cold anymore. He nervously fingered the trigger on his rifle and uttered a silent prayer. *Dear God, see me through this ordeal and if I don't make it, please watch over Susan and my precious children.*

"I've never seen so many Yanks in my life," exclaimed Newby.

"They're coming straight at us," said Barksdale.

Fuzzy stood, shook his fist and shouted, "Com'on ya blue belly bastards."

Barksdale remembered something and removed his old gray slouch hat, where a folded letter was resting in the crown. "James, if something happens will you see that Susan gets this?"

Newby nodded. "Same here," he said pointing to his hat.

Twenty-five thousand Yankees, stretching a mile wide, advanced in parade fashion toward Missionary Ridge. When they were midway a hundred Confederate cannons posted on the ridge crest fired, sending a hail storm of iron shrapnel into their ranks. Blue coats fell like wheat before a scythe. They closed ranks and kept coming.

For a moment Barksdale took pity on the unfortunate men who were being slaughtered. They were caught in an open killing zone with nowhere to run except forward. A few Yanks bolted toward the base of the ridge trying to escape the slaughter pen. Others followed, then whole squads, and companies until a tidal wave of blue coats were surging toward the rifle pits. They had run past their officers who were behind them yelling, "Follow me!"

Barksdale and Newby laid their rifles across the dirt embankment, took aim and waited. The Yanks weren't stopping. In the pit of his stomach, Barksdale knew this wasn't going to be another Chickamauga.

"Give' em the dickens boys. FIRE!" yelled a Lieutenant.

Thousands of muskets spoke at once, creating black clouds of smoke and sending forth a blizzard of lead. Blue coats dropped by the scores but more took their places and they kept coming.

"REMEMBER CHICKAMAUGA!" they yelled, disregarding their officers and sweeping toward the ridge. There was no stopping them. Minie balls snapped near Barksdale's ears. He heard Fuzzy swear and looked over and saw him raise up to take aim, then a minie ball sent him reeling backward.

"Grandpa, help me!"

Barksdale jumped up and yelled, "Hold on Fuzzy. I'm coming!" A minie ball tore into his left shoulder with a thud, spinning him around, rifle falling from his hands. "I'm hit!" He clutched his shoulder.

He had wondered what it would feel like to catch a ball. Now he knew. It was like being walloped with a hickory stick.

Newby looked over and saw blood oozing between his brother-in-law's fingers.

"Run James before they kill you!" yelled Barksdale over the thunderous roar of musketry and whining bullets splitting the air.

"I'm not leaving you, Jim!" exclaimed Newby, breathing hard; he reached into his cartridge pouch, extracted one, bit off the paper end, poured powder down the barrel, inserted the ball and ramrodded it home. Barksdale looked down the battle line and saw Confederates running up the ridge toward the second line of rifle pits. Many had thrown down their rifles and thrown up their arms. Panic. The Confederate left buckled, and then broke. Men were running to the rear. Before Barksdale and Newby had time to ponder what to do, angry, screaming blue coats were within pistol range. They had climbed straight up the ridge and overwhelmed the Confederates.

"They got us Jim!" exclaimed Newby.

Both men threw down their weapons and climbed out of their pit and raised their arms. "We surrender," exclaimed Newby. "He's wounded," nodding toward his brother-in-law.

Several Yankees ran up and jabbed at them menacingly with bayonets.

"Keep your hands up, Rebs, and move down the hill," said a corporal, poking at them with his bayonet.

Barksdale glanced to the rear and saw thousands of blue coats, bent over, climbing higher toward the second line of rifle pits, firing as they went. Confederates were dropping their weapons and surrendering. *How did this happen?* They were dug in and held the high ground. They had the advantage, but somehow had lost it.

The battle was over by 4:30 p.m. The sun was sinking behind Lookout Mountain as Barksdale and Newby were herded down the ridge along with other prisoners. Twilight cast an eerie light on the scene of death and destruction. Trees and bushes had been shredded by shot and shell but the most disturbing sight was the crumpled bodies. Scores of Confederates, many shoeless and most wearing tattered clothes, lay in grotesque positions of death. Strewn among them were dead Yankees. Death was no respecter of ideology. Whether the Union remained or was eventually dissolved now depended on lead and gun powder, not eloquent arguments. The wounded groaned with pain and pleaded for water.

"How bad is it Jim?" asked Newby, looking at the wounded shoulder.

"It hurts like the dickens, but it's only a flesh wound. I don't think it severed a blood vessel."

"You've won your red badge of courage," said Newby.

"If it wasn't for the honor I'd just as soon forego it."

Newby ripped the tail off his shirt and handed it to Barksdale. "This will help stop the bleeding."

Barksdale pressed it against the wound and groaned with pain.

When they reached the valley floor the scene of death was far more ghastly. Scores of Yankees lay dead, some killed by minie balls, others by flying shrapnel that tore away limbs and chunks of flesh.

A Yankee private poked Barksdale with his bayonet. "Empty your pockets." Jim pulled out Susan's lock of hair.

"You won't be needing that where you're going, give it here," said the Private and snatched it away.

"Please, it is my wife's."

The soldier spat. "What else you got? Barksdale removed the folded letter from his front pocket and handed it to the soldier.

"Well – well, what have we got here?" The soldier unfolded the letter and perused it. "Who is this, your Ma?" he asked, looking at the tin picture.

"It belonged to a Union soldier –"

"Robbed the dead, eh? I ought to cut your bowels out."

"It's not what you think," said Newby.

"Shut up, Reb. No one asked you a darned thing."

A Sergeant walked over and inquired, "What's going on?"

"This Reb robbed one of our dead, Sergeant," the private replied and handed him the letter and tin photo.

"Why that's Henry Jackson's Ma! I've seen the picture a dozen times," exclaimed the Sergeant. He locked his cold dark eyes on Barksdale. "Reb, you better have a good explanation for having that or you'll be dead before you can say John Brown's body."

"Is a good deed to be punished?" asked Newby.

"Speak."

Barksdale explained what had occurred and how he had given the boy water and promised to send the letter to his mother.

The sergeant eyed him carefully, weighing what Barksdale said.

"The picture has no value to me and certainly not the letter," said Jim. "Don't you think I know the consequences for being caught robbing the dead? I could have easily thrown it away after the boy died and he wouldn't know the difference."

The sergeant nodded slightly and his cold black eyes brightened.

"Can I have my wife's lock of hair back?" asked Barksdale.

"Private, give it back to 'im," said the sergeant. "Hey, let me look at that wound."

"Thanks, Sergeant, but it's only slight. I'd rather more severely wounded men be treated."

The sergeant slapped Barksdale on the back. "All right, move along Johnny Reb."

Later, the moon came up in a clear sky. It appeared to Barksdale that the entire Confederate Army had been taken prisoner. When the pain in his shoulder eased somewhat, he became aware of another discomfort: his hands and feet were freezing. His clothes were threadbare, barely enough to keep his thin frame decent, but not enough to ward off the cold. Thankfully, he did have shoes – such as they were. Most of his compatriots were barefoot and most were, like him, wearing tattered rags. He had lost his blanket guaranteeing that the night would be long and cold. The cold, hard earth was their bed and he and Newby scrunched together and shared their body heat. Before falling asleep, Barksdale wondered about Coleman. Was he dead, a prisoner or had he escaped?

---

Meanwhile, Coleman and the exhausted and demoralized men of the 50th Alabama pulled out and marched south down the ridge to Shallowford Road where they crossed Chickamauga Creek. They had lost 45 men, most captured.

Between November 23rd and 25th, the Confederates suffered 6,667 losses, including 361 killed, 2,160 wounded and 4,146 captured and missing. They had killed 753 Federals, wounded 4,722 and captured approximately 349. But losses couldn't be measured solely by the number of dead and wounded. The Army of Tennessee had been driven from the field and suffered a bitter defeat. The doorway to the South had been blown open. General Bragg began falling back south to Dalton, Georgia where the Army would winter and lick its wounds.

363

Missionary Ridge.

Thursday, November 26, 1863.

Throbbing pain and hunger woke Jim Barksdale long before daylight. He was cold and stiff. Newby was curled up in a ball and sound asleep. Barksdale lay still, wondering what fate held for him. Prison for sure. The thought of being sent north with winter coming on was sobering. Now, it would be Ol' Abe's responsibility to feed and properly clothe him. Whatever awaited him couldn't be much worse than serving in the Confederate Army. A steady diet of salted sow belly, stringy beef, cornmeal and parched corn was barely enough to keep a soul alive. If he hadn't found acorns, hickory nuts and walnuts to crack and eat, he would have already starved to death.

At dawn everyone was roused to their feet and ordered in formation. A Union doctor barely looked at Barksdale's wound and walked on. The gray line of Confederate prisoners was so long that he couldn't see the beginning or the end. After a breakfast of Yankee hard tack and water, they marched to Chattanooga.

Approximately 5000 prisoners were herded to the Memphis and Charleston Railway Station in Chattanooga where they milled about, shivered and waited. "Well, at least we won't be walk'n," deadpanned Newby. "I'm beginn'n to like this Yankee Army. They wear decent clothes, eat real food, have shoes and ride the train."

Later, the Yankee doctor moved through the crowd of prisoners checking for wounded. He stopped in front of Barksdale, examined the wound and sprinkled on sulfur powder.

"You'll be okay," he said.

"Can I have a handful of sulfur?" asked Barksdale.

The doctor poured some into his hand and walked away. Barksdale put the sulfur in his front pocket.

They spent another cold and miserable night. Frigid north winds blew unabated across the Tennessee River nearly cutting them in half. Thank God Newby still had his blanket, shredded as it was. They shared it, but it offered little comfort when the temperature dropped well below freezing.

Barksdale tore a sliver of cloth from his shirt tail and covered it with sulfur powder.

"What are you doing?" asked Newby.

"Watch." Where the minie ball had torn a ragged hole in his flesh, he inserted a cloth and pulled it through. Grimacing with pain, he sprinkled the bloody cloth again with sulfur and pulled it back through the wound.

The men stood around the following day, stamping their feet and blowing into their hands trying to keep warm. Rumors were rampant.

"They say if we take the oath they'll pardon us and we can go home," said one soldier.

"I wouldn't take their damn oath if it meant I'd freeze to death," replied another.

"You may get your chance," someone else said.

"I hear that a prisoner exchange is being worked out," said another. "We'll all be released as soon as the details are ironed out."

"Don't you men read newspapers?" asked a Lieutenant. "Grant doesn't exchange prisoners."

"Listen to him!" exclaimed a soldier. "Who in the world has seen a newspaper, much less read one?"

"What's gonna happen to us, Lieutenant?" asked a soldier.

"They'll ship us north to a Yankee hellhole where, if we're lucky, we'll freeze to death before dying slowly of starvation and disease."

The men fell silent, shivered and coughed and hacked up phlegm.

"I'd give my right arm for a chew of tobacco," said Barksdale.

"Shoot, I'd give both arms for a plug or a smoke, I don't care which," said Newby. "I could eat a whole plateful of tobacco."

The long, lonesome whistle of a locomotive sounded in the distance. Shortly, a steam engine chugged into the station, pulling a string of boxcars. The guards hustled the men in formation and they were divided into groups for boarding. Barksdale and Newby stayed close together as they were herded and jostled into a railcar. An armed guard slammed the door shut.

The men were crammed into the car like animals. The engine sounded two shrill whistles and the cars lurched forward, causing some of the men to fall. Soon the train was rolling through the night, the car rocking gently from side to side, iron wheels singing "clickety-clack" on the steel rails.

They were on the Nashville and Chattanooga line headed northwest. Frigid air whistled through the railcar, numbing face and hands. The train stopped and started a lot, switching tracks. There wasn't enough room to stretch out on the floor and the men sat back to back, legs pulled to chest, sharing body heat and what few blankets that were available. Barksdale and Newby sat side by side and pulled a single blanket around their shoulders, but there was no escaping the cold. Barksdale's wound was painful, but it was trivial compared to the bone-crunching cold that numbed his body and mind. He caught snatches of sleep and dreamed of Susan and family. They were sitting in front of a roaring fire at Ma and Pa's house on Christmas Eve when Susan announced supper. Tom had killed a mess of quail and Susan was frying the sweet meat in a skillet of sizzling grease. The dream vanished when he was awakened by a man next to him coughing. As time passed more men were coughing.

During the night they rolled through a city that someone said was Nashville. Early morning they slowed to a creep and crossed a river.

"It's the Ohio, boys," said one. "We're in Louisville."

There was no stopping to eat, drink water or empty bladder or bowels. Men soiled their pants. And it grew colder. They chewed hard tack in silence, no doubt thinking the same thing that Barksdale was pondering. *I may never see the sunny southland again.*

The two guards were warmly dressed in great coats and government-issued wool blankets draped over their shoulders. A prisoner asked one of them to pull open the door for a moment so he could see where he was. The guard complied. Frigid air gushed into the car. Men begged him to close the door. He laughed. "You Rebs wanna see out, now look all you want to."

"Animal," whispered Newby, clouds of vapor streaming from his mouth and nostrils.

"I'm afraid it'll only get worse," replied Barksdale.

The farther north they traveled the colder it got. Barksdale had experienced cold in north Alabama, but nothing compared to this.

365

They rattled through Indianapolis. More men were sick. Coughing was incessant and many had diarrhea and dysentery. One man died, perhaps froze to death.

The train stopped in Chicago and the bitter cold weather was indescribable. Many of the men had frostbitten fingers and toes. Icicles hung from the railcar.

*Dear God, how can we survive this?* Barksdale silently prayed that God would see him and Newby through this awful ordeal. He was starving and freezing. The only thing he had left was hope and faith. And both were evaporating. It prompted a man to think about what was important in life. He didn't own a single slave and didn't enlist in the Confederate Army until the Yankees invaded North Alabama. A man had to protect his home and family, didn't he? He hadn't done anything to northerners. *Why can't they just leave us alone?*

The train rattled westward beneath gray skies and bitter cold. On December 3$^{rd}$, just before 4:00 p.m., with the thermometer at 32 degrees below zero, the train slowed, crossed the Mississippi River and jerked to a stop. The men sat huddled and shivering, not knowing what to expect.

"Welcome to Rock Island, Rebs," said a guard and laughed.

The box car door screeched open letting in a blast of frigid air.

"Now git out! And be quick about it."

The prisoners slowly climbed down, many sick and weak from hunger, and looked around in confusion. They were on an island in the middle of the Mississippi River. Civilians were standing around gawking at them as they fell in formation. Barksdale glanced at his compatriots, a barefoot ragtag group of dirty, hungry and sick men. The train journey had taken a heavy toll on them.

Then the long, drawn-out task of processing began.

"Step forward four paces," said a sergeant, beckoning to Barksdale. He complied and was searched.

"Name?"

"James Greer Barksdale."

"Home state?"

"Alabama."

After the information was recorded he was ordered back in formation where he shivered and waited for what seemed an interminable time while the other prisoners were processed.

The prisoners were assigned to barracks and marched through the gate where they again waited in formation. The compound was surrounded by a twelve foot plank fence with a parapet on the outside where armed guards patrolled and looked over into the yard. Located twenty-five feet from inside the fence was a wire. The Provost Marshall pointed it out after he had read aloud the prison rules.

"Any man that steps across the 'dead line' will be shot on the spot. Any questions?"

The prisoners gazed at the unremarkable stretch of wire but said nothing.

"Sergeant, take these prisoners to their quarters," said the Provost.

"Yes sir."

The prison occupied 25 acres, located on one end of the island. Set in the middle of the open waters, the wind screamed unabated across the island. The barracks was 20 x 100 feet, one of 84 roughly-constructed wooden shanties that had been hastily thrown up, each to house 120 men. A kitchen and eating area was located at one end of each barracks.

Once inside, the men rushed to start fires in the two-coal burning stoves, and then they huddled around. It was a small improvement over the outside, but offered very little heat unless you were close to the stove. Five feet away and it was bitter cold. Wind whistled through the walls and Barksdale knew the reason. The building had been constructed of green wood and when cold weather came, the boards contracted, leaving cracks. Three tiers of wooden bunks with wire stretched across the tops lined the walls. None had mattresses or blankets. Barksdale and Newby, knowing that heat rises, selected top bunks.

Another trainload of prisoners arrived two days later followed by several thousand more over the next several days, all ragged, hungry and half frozen. The prison was overwhelmed and not prepared to accommodate so many men. There were no blankets and clothing available. In the beginning, the only potable water was drawn from dug wells. Outdoor toilets served the men, but many were too sick to plough through the snow and frigid weather to use them and others didn't see the need. They relieved their bowels and bladders wherever they happened to be at the time.

They gradually adapted to camp routine. The barracks were inspected each morning and the roll was called three times a day. The bitter cold weather was unforgiving. The Mississippi River froze and the cold seeped into the barracks where men six feet from the stove suffered frostbitten feet and ears. On January 1st, the temperature dropped to thirty below zero. The men slept by relief so that someone was always awake to stoke the fires.

Men began dying. Pneumonia took victims, and then came dysentery, turning a man's bowels inside out until he was dehydrated. When they thought that misery couldn't get worse, it did.

"Smallpox!" exclaimed a prisoner rushing through the doorway. The men stared at him in silence, knowing what it meant. Smallpox was the scourge of mankind. And highly contagious.

"How do you know?" asked someone.

"I heard a guard talking about it. He said they were building a pest house to isolate the sick."

Newby looked around at the miserable disheveled men, including his brother-in-law who had dysentery, and said: "The first symptom is a high fever, then puss filled sores appear on the skin. I've seen it and it's a slow and horrible way to die. The yanks don't care about us so we have to look out for ourselves. If symptoms appear, let the rest of us know about it. Isolation is the only way to prevent its spread. If we ever expect to get out of this place alive, we'll have to work together."

The rumor mill brought news daily of men coming down with smallpox. During January, 1864, 232 prisoners died from multiple causes, including smallpox, typhoid and simply freezing to death.

The *Argus*, published in nearby Rock Island, Illinois ran a story on January 2, 1864 that, had the prisoners been able to read it, would have heartily concurred.

> "…it is a shame that, in this enlightened age of the world, white men, our own countrymen, should be confined in a pen, fed on such scanty and improper food, and reduced down almost to starvation point, until disease and death ensue… if done by order of the administration it is a

shame and a disgrace to them. There is no excuse for this deliberate torture of human beings, and the hand that does it or the heart that prompts it is hardened against the common instincts of humanity."

Stories of the atrocities at Rock Island also appeared in the *New York Daily News,* which described the rations.

"1/3 lb of bread and 2" square of meat – supplemented when possible by dog, rats and mice. Many are nearly naked, bare-footed, bareheaded and without bed clothes. They are thus exposed to the ceaseless torture from the chill and pitiless winds of the Upper Mississippi River. Death is the only comforter and he appears frequently."

Conditions at Rock Island grew worse. The filthy conditions brought on lice and itch, which tormented the men to the edge of insanity.

Barksdale and Newby decided it was time to save themselves. But they needed a plan.

Private James G. Dement, a 29-year-old Limestone Countian whose home was located west of Athens on the Elk River, was also a prisoner. Dement had served with Company F, 9th Alabama and he too was interested in returning to the sunny southland as soon as possible.

---

Meanwhile, down south at Dalton, Georgia, William Coleman Barksdale and the men of the 50th Alabama were also suffering. Disease was rampant, food was lacking, but most of all, it was bone-chilling cold. Yet, they persevered.

Finally, the boys in gray heard good news: Bragg resigned and was replaced by General Joseph E. Johnston. There was much jubilation in camp. Most of the men despised Bragg.

"I think I'll resign too," said Peavine.

"Only officers can resign," replied Coleman. "If you quit – and that's what it is – you'll be executed for desertion."

"Well, it ain't fair," said Peavine and spat into the fire.

General Johnston immediately set about to raise the morale of his Army. Because of bad conditions men were deserting by the thousand. Johnston saw that his men were properly fed and clothed. Even sugar, coffee and flour were issued. He gave furlough to 1/3 of his troops at a time. Shortly, Johnston was as loved by his men as much as they despised Bragg. When spring arrived, the Army retreated, following Western and Atlantic Railroad tracks toward Atlanta, engaged nearly every day in a fight with General Sherman.

While Jim Barksdale and James Newby were sitting out the war in Rock Island prison, William Coleman Barksdale and the 50th Alabama were fighting and retreating.

# PART V

# 37 | A TIME FOR GLORY

Approximately 18 months earlier.
Wednesday, May 29, 1862.
Corinth, Mississippi.

A bugle sounding *reveille* woke Dudley Barksdale at 5:45 a.m. as it had done most mornings since the 35th Alabama Infantry Regiment had arrived at Corinth a month earlier. Another boring day of drilling lay ahead. He looked over at tent mate, Junior Bill Pendegrass, asleep on his back, mouth open, snoring loudly and unrhythmically. He poked his ribs.

"Rise 'n shine Junior Bill."

Junior Bill grunted and opened his eyes. "What fer. I'm gett'n mighty bored with this Army life. First it was noth'n but walk'n and now it's noth'n but drill'n. This heah war is gonna be over 'fore we get to plug our first Yankee."

"I'm hungry, get up and cook some breakfast," Dudley said.

Messmates, Tyler Thornton and Earl Jackson stoked the fire while Junior Bill cooked coosh as he had done every morning for the past week.

"Doggoneit, Junior Bill, I'm gett'n mighty tired of eat'n coosh every day," complained Thornton. "Don't you have any other recipes?"

"How'd ya like to have some fried rabbit covered with brown gravy?"

"Doggoneit, I'd like it."

"Fetch me a rabbit and I'll shore cook it."

"What kinda coffee are we drinkin?" asked Earl Jackson.

"Parched cornmeal," replied Junior Bill.

"Not again," groaned Jackson.

Coffee had long since disappeared. A substitute was made by parching rye, cornmeal or wheat which was ground, roasted and boiled. The favorite was sweet potato coffee. The tuber was cut into small pieces, dried in the sun, parched, ground and boiled.

After falling in formation and answering roll call, Sergeant Estes Patterson ordered, "Rest," and addressed the men of G. Company.

"Boys, the Yankee army is moving south of Pittsburg Landing and headed straight toward Corinth –"

"Let 'em come!" yelled someone from the ranks and others chimed in

"–but we ain't gonna fight 'em," Patterson added.

A loud groan went up.

"I reckon that General Beauregard has decided this ain't the place nor the time to fight," said Sergeant Patterson. "The brigade has been given orders to fall back to Tupelo. So, break camp and get ready to move out."

The men spent the day striking tents and packing food, ammunition and supplies while locomotives switched cars and made up a special train. All night they loaded the railcars with supplies, horses and livestock. Mules brayed and kicked as they were pushed and pulled into box cars by sweaty men both cursing and cajoling them aboard. Wagons and ambulances were pushed up ramps onto flat cars and roped in place. Cannon, caissons and limbers were loaded. Near dawn the tired stinky soldiers crowded into boxcars with no room to stretch out. Many, including Dudley and Junior Bill climbed on top. Daylight was breaking when the whistle sounded and the cars jerked forward and moved slowly toward Tupelo, some fifty miles to the south.

A deafening roar went off, startling Dudley, causing him to almost fall off the moving boxcar.

"What was that?" he asked.

More explosions.

"Lookee yonder!" exclaimed Junior Bill, pointing back toward Corinth. The dawn sky was eerie red and great pillars of smoke rose from burning warehouses. Beauregard was destroying the Confederate arsenal and supplies.

"Folks are hungry and need food 'n clothes and they're burn'n 'em," said Dudley.

"Yeah, but at least he Yankees won't get it."

Yankee cavalry pursued the retreating Confederates who fought a rear guard action, clashing violently near Booneville where some 2000 graybacks were captured. Later in the day the train rattled into Tupelo where the Army encamped.

When the men weren't drilling, they fought boredom by hunting, playing cards and shooting bull.

"Junior Bill, I have a question," said Thornton.

"Yeah, what?"

"With snaggle teeth, how you gonna bite off the cartridge paper and load your rifle?"

"You don't worry 'bout it," replied Junior Bill. "I'll gum it off if I havta."

"Be careful you don't swallow the powder and blow us up," quipped Earl Jackson.

Everyone laughed.

Soap was unavailable. Dudley washed his clothes in wet weather branches which did little to clean them. After the branches dried up the men dug holes in the ground which they called "springs" to trap drinking water. As a result many became ill with fever and diarrhea.

At twilight when rabbits came out to feed, Dudley and his mess mates went hunting. They spread out in the piney woods with sticks and beat the grass and bushes. A rabbit jumped and ran. They gave chase, barking like hounds with Junior Bill leading the pack. The frightened rabbit darted into a hollow log. Junior Bill and Dudley howled like tracking hounds while Thornton and Jackson located a bamboo brier which they inserted inside the hollow log and twisted until it caught the rabbit fur.

"I've got 'em!" exclaimed Thornton, and then carefully pulled the rabbit from the log.

After enjoying a small but tasty meal of rabbit, Dudley and Junior Bill sat in front of their tent beneath the stars picking and sucking their teeth.

"I thank about Earline all the time," Junior Bill said.

"Yeah, I think about Ma and Pa and Thomas and my sisters a right smart too," Dudley said.

Junior Bill eyed Dudley and asked. "You gotta favorite gal?"

"Well, I sorta like one of the Isom girls that lives near home but I never told anyone that except my sisters – and now you."

"What's her name?"

"Sarah Jane."

"How old is she?" asked Junior Bill.

"Ohh, about sixteen."

371

"Is she purty?"

"Sure is," replied Dudley.

"Have you writ 'er?"

"Naw, her Pa's a Union man and that could cause big trouble."

Junior Bill loaded his pipe and pondered his friend's dilemma. Finally, "Wahl, this heah war won't last forever. Anyway, you won't be snuggling up to her Pa. I'd write 'er."

"I hadn't thought about it that way," Dudley said.

"As for me, Earline's the purttiest gal 'cross the river. I've had my eye on 'er since she started fill'n out and look'n like a woman." Junior Bill sucked his pipe. "But she probably wouldn't want me."

"Why not?"

"The McLemores are right smart better off 'n my folks. We jist plain dirt farmers. Anyhow, all that talk about sending her Yankee ears was just spout'n off at the mouth. And to tell ya the truth, I ain't never courted 'er. Shoot, I can't even read'n write."

"I can teach you to do that," said Dudley.

"Folks have tried, but it ain't happened yet."

"You gotta have a learning attitude," said Dudley. "A mule is born to pull and plow, but he can also be taught to pull a buggy."

"Hmmm, you gotta point," said Junior Bill. "I'd be much obliged if you'd teach me."

"Have you told Earline how you feel about her?" asked Dudley.

"Aw naw!"

"How would she know if you ain't told her?"

"Waal she's bound to know by the way I strut 'round 'er."

"If I had a girl like her, I'd sure tell her before somebody else whispers sweet nothings 'n 'er ear," said Dudley.

"Ummm, that's sump'n to smoke 'n my pipe."

Before tattoo was sounded, Dudley began teaching Junior Bill the alphabet. "There's twenty-six letters in the alphabet," said Dudley.

"Why ain't there more'n that?"

Dudley pondered the questions. "I don't know and ya don't need to know either. Just accept it."

That night, while Junior Bill snored, Dudley lay on his back and thought about Sarah Jane Isom. The last time he had seen her was nearly two years earlier, at the fall revival, held at Isom Chapel Methodist Church. At the time he was 21 and she was going on fifteen. Her father, Emanuel Isom, had donated land for the church building and the family lived next door, where Mr. Isom farmed, made cabinets and did carpentry work. His younger brothers, Matthew and William Stinnett Isom also lived nearby. It was said that all three brothers were Union men. Anyway, that didn't detract from Sarah Jane's appearance. She was pretty as a picture and had black hair and brown eyes. Junior Bill was right. One day this war would be over. And a man needed a good woman, even if her family were homemade Yankees.

---

June 19th.

372

To prevent Federal forces from outflanking him, General Beauregard retreated to Vicksburg by train. The men grumbled – they had enlisted to fight, not run like rabbits. They encamped in a low-lying area where many men became ill with fever and diarrhea. Forty percent were unfit for duty. Then good news came on June 27th – General Beauregard was replaced by General Braxton Bragg. Hopefully, Bragg would fight. Federal gun boats lobbed shells into civilian homes located on the bluff overlooking the Mississippi River and the Confederates replied chasing them away. Otherwise, days were filled with drilling, cleaning weapons and shooting bull.

---

A boy-faced fellow wearing a gray forage cap and new uniform walked up to where Dudley and his mess mates sat whittling and shooting bull.

"Hello, I'm Holder Spotwood," he announced. "Sergeant Patterson sent me over to ask if I can join your mess."

Junior Bill eyed him from head to toe. "Where ye from son?" he asked, spitting out a stream of brown juice.

"Huntsville."

"How old are ya son?"

"I just turned sixteen," he said. "I enlisted to fight for State's Rights."

"Waal, that's a high-falutin reason, but I'm fight'n for a better one," Junior Bill said.

"What's that?"

"'Cause they down here fight'n me," said Junior Bill. "You have any tobacky?"

"I don't use it."

"Waal, can you cook?"

"If he can boil water he's a whole lot better cook than you Junior Bill," offered Thornton.

"Waal, I guess that qualifies ya," said Junior Bill. "I sure would love some good ole fried snipe for breakfast."

"Snipe?" Spotwood asked, puzzled.

"Yeah, they're a ground bird – sorta like quail – that runs in the woods down here."

"Doggoneit, they're better eat'n than quail," offered Thornton.

"Where does one find these snipe?"

"I'se hoping you'd ask that," said Thornton. "They come out only at night."

"You'd be a mighty big hit with us boys if ya caught and cooked us some," added Junior Bill.

"Well let's do it!" exclaimed Spotwood.

"Now, I like a man who's ready to try new things," said Junior Bill.

After dark Dudley found an empty cornmeal bag and the boys led Spotwood deep into the dark piney woods.

"Now you stand right chere'n this low spot and hold the sack open and call them snipe while we go up chere 'n herd 'em toward you," Junior Bill said.

"How does one call snipe?" asked Spotwood.

"Just whistle every once 'n a while and say 'heah-heah.'"

"I can do that," Spotwood said confidently.

"Now, don't move," said Thornton. "It may take us awhile to find 'em and run 'em your way. And be rea-all quiet."

Spotwood held open the sack and called out, "heah snipe, heah-heah," then whistled. Dudley and his messmates skedaddled back to the campsite, giggling. They were sitting around a low and smoky fire to drive away mosquitoes, when Spotwood ran up, dragging the sack, wild-eyed and breathless; his new uniform muddy and torn by briers.

"How many did ya catch?" asked Junior Bill.

The men roared with laughter and slapped their legs.

"I've been made a fool," Spotwood said.

"Naw, you wuz already a fool, we just took advantage of it," replied Junior Bill. The men howled.

Dudley walked over to Spotwood and poked out his hand. "Welcome to our mess."

---

On July 27th orders were received to board a train for Tangipohea, Louisiana, located just south of the Mississippi line, where they were to reinforce Confederate forces under threat near Camp Moore. When they arrived at the depot there were only a few railcars available and everything except for ammunition had to be left behind.

They offloaded at Tangipohea and slogged for miles through sucking mud and rain. Spotwood carried the mess's only skillet, tied to the end of his rifle barrel. When it wasn't raining, it was sizzling hot and humid and clouds of hungry mosquitoes made their lives miserable, not to mention chiggers that gnawed on their groins.

Shelter had been left behind in Vicksburg and they slept and ate in the rain and mud, causing many of the men to become ill. As it turned out, there were no attacking Yankees.

On July 30th they fell in formation and Colonel James W. Robertson announced that the regiment was to march to Baton Rouge – and battle. "Men, we will be in the thickest of things," he said solemnly.

The 35th Regiment had started out with about 750 men on April 14th, now three months later because of measles, dysentery, flu, typhoid, pneumonia and fever; they were down to only 200 fighting men. But, at least they were going to fight, not retreat.

It would be Dudley's first chance to cover himself with glory.

---

August 5, 1862, 4 a.m.

Baton Rouge was blanketed with heavy fog when the 35th Regiment formed a line of battle east of town. Forty rounds of ammunition had been issued to each soldier. Dudley had hardly slept, not so much because he bedded down in rain and mud and swatted mosquitoes all night, but because he kept thinking of what lay ahead of him. The usual joking and bantering among the men who were bragging the previous night about how many Yankees they were going to kill had ceased. They were quiet and pensive. For once, Junior Bill was quiet. Dudley had wondered how he would feel when this moment arrived. His chance for glory lay just a few hundred yards in front of him. And somewhere out there, a Yankee was waiting to kill him. He wasn't nearly as certain of himself as he had been when Colonel Robertson had announced that they would be in the

374

"thickest of things." Doubt had crept into his mind. *What if a minie ball found its mark and he never got to see Ma and Pa and his family again? Worse, what if he lost his nerve?* His mouth was dry as cotton, heart pounding, knees weak, hands slightly trembling. There was much clearing of throats in the ranks. Fear. A knot was lodged in his own throat.

"I'm nervous as a billy goat," he whispered from the corner of his mouth to Junior Bill. "Say something encouraging."

"Kin I have ya tobacky if you get plugged?"

"What?" asked Dudley, shocked.

Junior Bill gave a snaggle-tooth grin. Dudley laughed and tension drained from his body.

"I knew I could count on you, Junior Bill."

When dawn broke they were given the command "forward" and advanced across an open pea patch, the regimental colors in front popping in the breeze. It was eerie quiet except for the crunch of feet tearing through pea plants and men coughing trying to expel fear from their throats. Most of the boys like Dudley hadn't been in battle. He glanced at the kid, Spotwood, who had a fierce look of determination on his face. Junior Bill was shifting his plug of tobacco from one side of his jaw to the other, brown juice running down his scraggly red beard. So far, no Yankees. Dudley half-hoped they had pulled back. Maybe tomorrow he would feel better about fighting. He was feeling more relaxed. Suddenly, Yankee skirmishers opened up with rifle fire, sending a torrent of minie balls ripping through gray ranks. Men crumpled to the ground and moaned. Yankee artillery thundered, but the rounds fell short. They were trying to find the correct range and elevation. The next barrage would be on top of them.

"HIT THE GROUND!" shouted Sergeant Patterson. The men dropped and Confederate artillery replied, shaking the earth, sending a storm of iron overhead toward the Yankees.

"CHARGE 'EM BOYS!"

Dudley lay on the ground paralyzed with fear.

"Let's go Dudley!" shouted Junior Bill. "It's glory time."

Dudley scrambled to his feet. Someone gave the Rebel yell and others picked up the cry. Dudley yelled to the top of his lungs, expelling the fear from the throat. They ran toward the Yankee skirmishers yelling and firing, driving them backward, quickly followed by the main enemy line that fell back to their camp in a wooded area. The 35th charged ahead, overrunning the camp; halted and took cover behind a rail fence so that another regiment could catch up and the line straightened. Dudley's heart was pounding sending adrenaline into every corpuscle. Fear was gone, replaced by something else. Maybe it was the spirit of the Lord. Meanwhile, the Yankees regrouped and Dudley looked out to his front and saw a hoard of blue coats coming toward him.

"HOLD YOUR FIRE BOYS," commanded Sergeant Patterson. The Yankees came closer – closer. Dudley found a target, a big fellow wearing a blue forage cap.

"FIRE!" Dudley closed his eyes and squeezed the trigger. A deafening roar erupted. When he opened his eyes the big Yankee was down. Others were dropping like autumn leaves. He quickly reloaded and fired again. The Yankee line slowed, and then buckled. Confederate infantry and cavalry flanked them. Lt. Col. Goodwin lifted his sword above his head. "CHARGE!" The regiment sprang to their feet and ran toward the Yankees firing and giving the Rebel yell. The Yankees turned tail.

"Look at 'em, they're runn'n like rabbits," yelled Junior Bill.

They pushed them to the Mississippi River and under the protection of their gunboats where they waited.

The 35th torched the Yankee camp. They had been lucky. When the Yankees launched their last charge the Confederates were down to one cartridge per man.

---

The sun was searing hot at 10 a.m. when the battle ended. The men's first priority was to find water then collect their wounded and dead.

"Barksdale, you and Spotwood come over here," said Sergeant Patterson, beckoning to them.

They compiled.

"I'm detailing both of you to remove our dead from the field and bring them here," he said.

Dudley and Spotwood walked across the pea patch and began their gruesome task. The first corpse they saw was on his back, legs and arms grotesquely spread out. He was already bloated and green flies were swarming around him. In the middle of his forehead was a large round hole. It was Pvt. Smith from Moulton. Dudley had seen him many times in the past. When he picked up his shoulder to carry him off, his head fell sideways. Dudley dropped the body and retched.

"Lord God almighty!"

"What?" asked Spotwood.

"His brains are running out on the ground," said Dudley, retching up bile. Nothing came up but pure bile.

The next body was mangled, an arm torn off and the head hanging on the shoulders by a strip of skin. The poor man had been hit with grapeshot. Dudley didn't recognize him. One soldier's leg was blow, off at the hip – he probably bled to death.

He counted four dead. Later, he heard that 21 had been wounded and one was missing out of a total of 180 men.

That night Dudley wrote his name and address on a piece of paper and pinned it to the inside of his shirt. If killed, at least someone would know his name and could tell Ma and Pa.

"The Regiment lost heavily and displayed the superb character of its officers and men," it was later written.

The Yankees abandoned Baton Rouge and retreated to New Orleans. The 35th marched a few miles north of Baton Rouge and began shoveling dirt to fortify Port Hudson and prepare it for cannon emplacement. The rumor among the men of the 35th was that ol' Abe Lincoln had relieved the Yankee force and was replacing it with 15,000 women to take Port Hudson. At least one-third of the Confederates were barefoot and most were still wearing the same clothes they left home in. Rain, mud and sweat had reduced them to tatters.

---

"Dudley, you set muh mind to think'n about Earline," said Junior Bill. "You're right, if I don't' tell her sweet things somebody else is liable to do it. I pet my ol' hound and tell 'im what a good dog he is, and I ought to do no less toward Earline."

"I agree."

"I'd be obliged if you would pen a letter to 'er for me. Will you do it?"

"Heck yeah," Dudley said.

Dudley sharpened a pencil and laid a piece of paper across his knapsack and looked up at Junior Bill. "What do you wanna say?"

"I ain't much at this... but here goes: 'Dear Earline, how 'r ya? As for me I'm fine and dandy, mostly. Have y'all had plenty of rain? I hope so. How is your milk cow? I hope she's giving plenty of milk –"

"Junior Bill, that's thoughtful, but when you talk to a woman you need to be romantic. They don't care about rain and crops 'n such," said Dudley.

"Waal, what ya suggest?"

Dudley stroked his chin and pondered, then started the letter over. "Dear Earline. I have been thinking about you every day since I left Athens. Sometimes when I smell blooming honeysuckles along the march, I'm reminded of your sweetness –"

Junior Bill interrupted. "Earline don't smell sweet."

"It's just love talk. Poets say things like that all the time."

"Waalll..."

"Thinking of you gives me the strength and courage to keep on fighting. So far we have whipped the Yankees every time. At first, I thought the war would be over soon, but it may last a while longer. So when you go to the church and socials and such, remember that I'm thinking of you every day. I'll be home one day when you least expect me, covered with glory. I hope that you are doing fine and in good health. Write me soon.

Devoted, Junior Bill.

p.s. I'm learning to read and write."

"I like it, Dudley, but do ya thank we're lay'n it on too thick?"

"Nah."

Junior Bill took a deep breath, smiled and started to make his x.

"Today, you're gonna sign your name for the first time," said Dudley.

"Ya thank I kin do it?"

"I know you can," said Dudley. "Take the pen and I'll guide your hand."

He scrawled his name, and then reared back. "You know sump'n Dudley. When this heah war's over I'm gonna marry that gal."

---

Following the battle at Baton Rouge on August 5, 1862, the regiment marched back to Tangipohea, rested, and then entrained to Jackson, Mississippi. On September 11th, they moved to Holly Springs, Mississippi, re-equipped and on the 27th marched toward Corinth and another big fight. North of Corinth they encountered Union skirmishers who fled and vacated their camp, leaving their equipment. The Confederates took what they needed and burned the rest. That night they slept on the ground in battle line. At 4 a.m. the next morning they moved out toward Corinth. Soon firing erupted. The Yankees were in rifle pits on the south side of the railroad tracks with artillery firing from high ground. The entire Confederate division advanced forward with the 35th bringing up the right side of the line.

Charge was ordered and the regiment sprang forward, running, firing and giving the Rebel yell. They were met with grape shot and canister. Captain Felton of Company B was instantly killed.

"Fix bayonets boys!" yelled Captain Ashford of Lawrence County, now in command. "Don't stop until we carry the breastwork."

They rushed through smoke and bullets toward the Yankees positioned behind breastwork. Fighting was vicious and close. Just when the 35th needed help, the 7th Kentucky arrived and they drove the Yankees from the field.

Darkness ended the fighting and the 35th spent a foggy night in the Yankee fortifications. The next morning, they advanced with a division south of the railroad, toward more Yankee breastwork, but couldn't take it.

The Army fell back, retreating southward, its long column of supply wagons, caissons, limbers and bedraggled men slogging through cold rain and sucking mud, passing through Ripley, Mississippi, on October 7th. The 35th Regiment arrived at Holly Springs the following day and was ordered to nearby Grenada for wintering. The fighting was over, at least for a while. Colonel James W. Robertson fell ill and Lt. Colonel Edwin Goodwin took command of the regiment.

The cold, rainy weather brought more misery. Field officers were housed in wall tents in which they could stand and use cots and stools. The men had no such luxuries. The few fortunate ones had "A" tents – canvas stretched over a horizontal pole and pegged in the ground. The less fortunate men, Dudley and his mess mates among them, slept on the cold and wet ground. They were huddled beneath the boughs of a red oak tree trying to stay dry and broiling strips of beef over a damp fire when Dudley said, "Junior Bill, if you'll find a canvas, I'll build us a house with a fireplace."

Junior Bill spit a mouthful of tobacco juice into the fire. "Waall when do you wanna start?"

"Just as soon as I can get this green beef down my gullet," replied Dudley.

While Junior Bill was out foraging for canvas, Dudley laid out the cabin site in a rectangle; Thornton and Jackson located small pine trees and cut them into poles and Spotwood brought in hunks of moss. The pine poles were notched at the ends and stacked in log cabin fashion and high enough so that a man could stand.

Junior Bill arrived after dark with a canvas cover.

"Doggoneit, what took ya so long?" asked Thornton.

"I had to do some military reconnoitering."

"Where'd ya find it?" asked Thornton.

"I ain't say'n."

They stretched the canvas across a roof pole and secured it, and then they stuffed moss in the openings between the poles and daubed it with mud. They built a fireplace of sticks and mud at one end of the cabin and they constructed double bunks of saplings along each wall, complete with pine boughs mattresses. This new home was crowded, but warm and dry.

Their first Christmas away from home was cold and rainy. Spotwood roasted corn kernels in an iron skillet and pounded them into grounds for ersatz coffee. Thornton had traded for some onions and potatoes and they made beef stew. Junior Bill wiped his mouth with his sleeve and declared it to be the best stew he had ever "et." Afterwards, the men smoked and grew silent, no doubt thinking of home. About now, thought Dudley, Pa was sitting in front of the fireplace smoking his pipe and reading from the large leather-bound Bible that rested on a nearby table; Ma and his sisters were out in the kitchen cooking. The children were laughing and eyeing a few small gifts beneath the cedar tree that Thomas had cut along the fence line. Brother George and his family

378

would soon arrive and the old log house would be abuzz with activity. His daydreaming was interrupted when Thornton began humming *Silent Night*. Jackson joined in. Spotwood, who had a good voice, sang the lyrics and they all joined in as tears ran down their grizzled cheeks.

"Ol' Santa has brung ye' a gift," said Junior Bill to Dudley. "So close ya eyes."

It was a whistle made from a hickory tree branch. "That's for learn'n me to read 'n write."

Following Christmas, when the weather was cold and miserable and the wind wailed in the pine trees, Sergeant Patterson brought a replacement to the rude long shelter. Dudley and his messmates were hovering in front of the stick and mud fireplace.

"Men, this is Jonah Wales," said the Sergeant. "See if you can squeeze 'im in."

Dudley looked up and said, "Sergeant, we're pretty cramped already."

"Do the best you can," replied Patterson and walked off.

Junior Bill spit in the fire, creating a sizzling sound, and eyed the blue-eyed, blond-headed boy.

"How old are you, Jonah-in-the-belly-of-a-whale?" he asked.

The men chuckled.

"Sixteen," the boy said enthusiastically. "Well, don't tell, but I'm really fifteen. I told 'em I's older."

"Where ya from?" asked Tyler Thornton.

"Winston County."

"I thought they 'uz all Yankees down there," said Thornton, remembering that when Alabama seceded from the Union, Winston County seceded from Alabama. Many Winston County men had joined the Federal Army.

"I guess you wanna fight for States Rights too," said Junior Bill, glaring over at Holder Spotwood.

"Nawsir –"

"You don't have to say 'sir' to me," replied Junior Bill, "I ain't no damn officer. I'm just a webfoot dirt packer."

"Yes sir – uh, I mean alright."

"Look at 'im," said Earl Jackson. "He ain't old enough to even grow fuzz yet."

"I don't care nothing about States Rights or keeping Negroes," said Jonah. "I'm old enough to fight. I enlisted to kill Yankees and I'm gonna kill every one I can."

"Waal – waal," mused Junior Bill. "Jonah-in-the-belly-of-a-whale wants to kill Yankees. What got ya so fired up, boy?"

"Mainly, because they killed my Pa, that's why." His story poured out. The Wales family was one of the few farming families in that neck of the woods that supported the Confederacy. Jonah's two older brothers had enlisted in 1861; one was killed at Shiloh and the other one was killed somewhere in Tennessee. "One night, the Yankee home guard rode up to our house and the hounds were bark'n and raising Cain. They called Pa out. He was standing on the front porch, I's right beside 'im, holding a lantern, and the Yankees started shoot'n our dogs. Pa asked 'em not to shoot his dogs. 'We know you got a boy in the Rebel Army and we're gonna shoot you!' one of 'em said to Pa. Then he shot Pa in cold blood and torched our house. I held Pa in my arms, but he was dead. They burned us out. Ma moved over to Franklin County and I enlisted. The Yankees killed my brothers, my Pa and my dogs and I'm gonna kill every damn one I can."

379

The men were silent, their faces hard and serious.

"Doggoneit," said Thornton. "We'll squeeze you in somewhere."

Dudley stepped forward and introduced himself and the other men did likewise.

From January through April 3rd, Dudley took on extra duty in the field as a teamster. He cracked his whip over the heads of exhausted and often reluctant mules as they struggled through mud, strained up hills and across swollen streams pulling supplies and ammunition. He received an extra 25¢ for his duties.

---

On a cold and rainy night as the messmates huddled in front of the fireplace smoking their pipes, Spotwood lifted a book from his haversack and began reading by firelight.

"Whatche read'n kid?" asked Jackson.

"Blackstone."

The men looked at each other with puzzlement.

"What'n tarnation 'n that?" asked Jackson.

"A law book," replied Spotwood. "When the war is over I'm going to read law and become a lawyer."

Junior Bill spit into the fire, creating a sizzle. "Now that's what the South needs," he quipped, "another dratted lawyer suing folks 'n stirr'n up trouble."

"Doggoneit, if you get in trouble with the law," said Thornton, "you'd be glad to have a good lawyer."

"I don't take it personal," said Spotwood. "Many people don't appreciate how essential lawyers are to our system because they don't understand how our courts function. I'll be proud to be a lawyer someday. Thomas Jefferson, who drafted our Declaration of Independence, was a lawyer as well as many of its signers. It was lawyers that created our Constitution and lawyers who led our country –"

"Ain't ol' Abe a lawyer?" interrupted Junior Bill.

"He is," replied Spotwood.

"I rest my case."

Everyone chuckled.

"Maybe you oughta read law when this war's over," said Thornton to Junior Bill.

"Naw, I'm gonna get me a piece of Elk River bottom land, marry Earline McLemore and raise corn and a passel of young'uns."

Dudley, who was listening with interest, said, "Yeah, me too. Pa has some pretty good cotton land and I'm gonna buy a good team of mules. Cotton's where the money is. The richest people in Limestone County are cotton planters. No matter what happens, folks have gotta wear clothes and clothes are made from cotton. That's the future."

"I'd find me a woman 'fore I started look'n for mules," quipped Junior Bill.

"I figure I'll get started farming cotton first," said Dudley. "A woman wants a man who can support her. A fine team of mules and a good cotton crop is pretty good woman bait."

"As for me," said Thornton, "I may go to Texas or Arkansas. I've heard that land is cheap out there and anyway, there won't be any damn Yankees around to bother a man. I ain't livin' amongst Yankees." The men wagged their heads in agreement.

"Amen to that," said Jackson. "When this war is over I'm goin' back home 'cross the river on Sugar Creek and I' ain't leavin'."

"Whatcha gonna do for a livin'?" asked Dudley.

"Do what my Pa did and his Pa before him did: stir 'n the dirt, hunt, fish, trap 'n whatever."

"None of our dreams will come to fruition until we win this struggle," said Spotwood. "If we don't prevail, the consequences are too dire to contemplate. The Yankees will overrun us like locust, take over our government, raise our taxes, deprive us the right to vote and occupy our land with troops."

"Waall, they gotta kill us first," said Junior Bill.

---

On January 31, 1863, the regiment moved out by train to Jackson and the defense of Vicksburg. They were shifted to Port Hudson, then sent north to Tullahoma, Tennessee, then ordered to Meridian, Mississippi.

On the night of April 28th near Enterprise, the regiment, exhausted from campaigning, slept on their guns and were sound asleep when the order to "fall in" was given.

"THE YANKEES 'R ON US!" hollered Junior Bill jumping up and grabbing his rifle. Dudley scrambled to formation. Instead of Yankees, Colonel Edwin Goodwin informed them that General Reuben Davis, a cousin of President Jefferson Davis, was at the hotel in nearby Enterprise and would honor them with a speech.

"He woke us up 'n the middle of the night just to hear a politician blabber," groused Junior Bill.

Colonel Goodwin was elated that his men were to hear such an important person and he gave specific instructions on how they were to conduct themselves. "There must be good order and you must conduct yourselves as gentlemen," he said. "We will march up to the front of the hotel where I will call out, 'Halt,' and then give 'Order Arms!' At this time, I will call out, 'Davis! Davis!' then the regiment will join me in calling, 'Davis! Davis! Davis!'"

The regiment marched to the front of the hotel and stood at order arms while Colonel Goodwin called out for General Davis. Some of the men did as ordered, but not Junior Bill. "COME OUTTA THERE REUBEN!" he shouted.

I KNOW YOU'RE IN THERE," someone else hollered out. "GET THROUGH AS QUICK AS YOU CAN, I'M MIGHTY SLEEPY."

General Davis appeared on the balcony and launched into his speech complimenting the regiment and sharing "good news" from Richmond about the imminent recognition by foreign governments and breaking the Yankee blockade. The men had heard those worn-out stories before.

"THOSE SURE ARE SLOW BOATS," someone shouted. "THEY'VE BEEN ON THEIR WAY SINCE THE WAR STARTED." The speech was abbreviated and the men soon returned to their bed on the ground and much-needed sleep.

On May 16th, they fought at Champion's Hill and two days later at Baker's Creek. The engagements had been costly to Confederates; 7,400 men killed, wounded and captured. The 35th Regiment had lost a third of its men.

---

East bank of Big Black River.

July 4, 1863.

Confederate Cavalry that had been probing Grant's defenses around Vicksburg rode into camp with disturbing news. "Vicksburg has fallen!" Over 30,000 troops were captured. The Mississippi River was now open to Union gunboats from New Orleans to St. Louis. The Confederacy was being choked to death.

The army fell back to Jackson, fighting a rearguard action. Days were filled with fighting, no rest, and very little food. The war dragged on.

On September 3rd at sundown, the regiment marched through rain and mud to Canton where they wintered and built cabins. It was wet and they spent much time trying to stay dry and warm. They wore rags, but at least they had shelter.

Dudley's idealism had been replaced by trying to stay alive. He hadn't been home for more than a year and a half and he thought of Ma and Pa and his family almost constantly. Reckon the Yankees had stolen Thomas's fine horses? He'd love to see the old home place, sit under the shade tree in the evening listening to the Whippoorwills on Swan Creek and walk across the road and get a cool drink from Cove Springs.

He wondered if brother George Edward was still driving the stage from Athens to Fayetteville. So far as he knew, he hadn't enlisted in the army, and Dudley couldn't blame him for not doing so.

He had heard that Coleman's regiment had been in a big battle near Lookout Mountain and at a place called Missionary Ridge and that General Bragg had retreated into north Georgia. He had a feeling they would soon be sent there.

---

Near Grenada, Mississippi.

Winter, 1863.

Dudley warmed his hands over the flames, then did the same with both of his feet; grabbed his musket and made ready to report to the corporal of the guard. Tonight, he would be on two and off four.

"There ain't a Yankee within 100 miles," he said to Junior Bill. "Pulling guard is a waste of time."

"More danger of freez'n to death than being attacked by Yankees," said Junior Bill.

Dudley's feet and toes ached with an intensity he had never experienced. Frost bitten, he figured. He wore no socks and his leather shoes were so worn and thin they provided no protection from the cold. It was his fingers on his right hand, the one gripping the musket, that hurt him the most. They were frozen in place. Pulling guard duty on a night like this was more deadly than marching into battle among a hail of minie balls. A bullet might miss, but the cold weather would kill a man for certain. When he went on duty at 6 p.m. it wasn't biting cold, but when he returned to his post at midnight the temperature had dropped like a falling rock. Now, it was bone-cracking cold. He pulled his left hand from his trouser pocket and pried open his frozen fingers, then switched the musket to his left side and blew warm breath on his stiff fingers. Not only was he slowly freezing to death, he was sleepy. All he wanted to do was lie down and drift into a peaceful sleep. Freezing to death in this Army was permissible, but sleeping on guard duty would get a man shot. His mind wandered to Ma and Pa and the family gathered in front of the fireplace, Pa smoking his pipe, Ma knitting socks and his sisters,

Cal and Cornelia, spinning and carding lint. *Why did I leave a warm, loving home to fight in this miserable war?* Occasionally, he peeked off into the distance to see if anything moved. No light was present in this cold weather, much less a Yankee. *Where is Jonah Wales?* He asked himself. *My two hours is about over.* He came to a large pine tree and leaned against it and stamped his numb feet on pine needles. They were soft - like a bed. He stood still, back against the tree. So relaxing. *Sleep – sleep – God, please let me sleep.* His head dropped. He jerked awake. *Can't sleep. Must remain awake.* It was becoming more difficult to keep his eyes open. He felt himself slowly sliding down the tree trunk and into the soft pine needles. *Ahh, just for a moment. No one will ever know.* He was at a dance and Pa was fiddling when he looked across the room and saw Sarah Jane Isom stealing a glance at him. She was beautiful and wearing a pretty calico dress. His eyes met hers and he walked across the room and offered his hand. "May I have this dance?" She smiled and grasped his hand and they moved to the dance floor and he put an arm around her waist. She was soft and smelled heavenly and – Footsteps. Dudley woke from the dream. *My God, I've been asleep.* He jumped to his feet and shouldered his musket. Footsteps coming closer.

"HALT. WHO GOES THERE?"

"Corporal of the Guard," came the reply.

*Thank God.*

The corporal and Jonah Wales appeared.

"Heard or seen anything?" asked the corporal, eyeing Dudley suspiciously.

"No – no," replied Dudley. He wondered if the corporal had seen him stand up. Dudley said to Wales, "Stay warm."

"And stay awake," added the corporal, walking off.

Dudley had hardly rolled up in his blanket when reveille sounded. When the company fell in for roll call, Wales wasn't present. Sergeant Patterson stepped to the front of the shivering soldiers. "Men, Private Jonah Wales has been arrested," he said and paused, letting the message sink in. "For sleeping at his post." The men were silent. They knew the punishment. If Wales was convicted, he would be shot.

That evening, the men huddled around the fire on their haunches and sopped up a measly plate of coosh. Finally, Junior Bill spoke. "I'm gonna miss Jonah-in-the-belly-of-the-whale. He 'uz a right smart good fellow."

"Doggoneit, he's just a kid," added Thornton. "He volunteered to kill Yankees and look what they are going to do to him. Kill him."

"You don't know for sure," said Jackson. "Court martial may find him not guilty."

"Hmp," harrumphed Junior Bill. "They'll make an example of 'im. When officers git scared and sick of this damn war, they resign. If an enlisted man does the same he'll be shot for desertion. Like they say, it's a rich man's war and a poor man's fight."

Dudley was quiet.

"What's on your mind?" asked Junior Bill, looking at him.

Dudley looked up. "I went to sleep too, but I didn't get caught. I'll live and Wales will die."

"They won't kill that boy, he's too young and innocent, said Jackson."

---

Three days later.

The bugle blew "assemble" and the regiment fell in formation and were informed that Wales had been found guilty of sleeping at his post and been sentenced to death by firing squad. A murmur rose in the ranks.

"They gonna kill 'im to sceer us," said Junior Bill.

"If he deserves to die, so do I," said Dudley.

"Doggoneit, shut your mouth," Thornton said. "We can't do a dang thing about it."

"It ain't right. No sir, it ain't right," said Jackson and spat.

"Damn the Confederate Army," Dudley added.

"Quiet in the ranks," commanded Sergeant Patterson.

The men of Company G stood quiet and sullen as they watched a mule-pulled wagon hauling a wooden coffin pass in front of the regiment. Seated on the coffin was Wales. His eyes found Dudley, terror written on his face. The wagon stopped near the center of the assembled troops and Wales remained seated on the coffin while soldiers dug his grave. When the grave was completed, a wooden post was anchored in the ground and the guards pulled Wales off the wagon and led him to the post. His eyes darted with fear and when a guard grabbed Wales and attempted to bind him to the post, he broke loose and fell to his knees begging and praying for his life. "Please don't shoot me... please."

The firing squad took its post. Dudley turned his head and closed his eyes. They could order him to stand in formation but the forces of hell couldn't make him watch.

"READY – AIM – FIRE!"

The muskets fired. Dudley flinched. When he opened his eyes, Wales was sagging at the post, blood running from his shirt.

---

The 35$^{th}$ was ordered to Dalton to assist in the defense of north Georgia. The 27$^{th}$ and 35$^{th}$ Regiments departed immediately. Their route of march took them through north Alabama where they would recruit, look for deserters and visit their folks.

They arrived by rail in Demopolis on February 24, 1864 and set out walking north. Col. Charles Goodwin had died of illness and Lt. Col. Samuel Ives of Center Star, Alabama, was promoted to full Colonel. They happened upon a Yankee detachment near Moulton and sent them scurrying, leaving many of their horses behind. They marched to Russellville and it was there that Dudley received the best news he'd heard in two years. He and most of the men were given a short furlough home.

---

March, 1864.

It was a windy morning when Dudley and Junior Bill departed for Limestone County riding captured Yankee horses. They had been away from home for exactly two years. They rode past LaGrange Military Academy – or what use to be LaGrange Academy – where they had been sworn in as members of the 35$^{th}$ Regiment. The only thing that remained of the once-proud school were fire-gutted buildings and blackened rubbles of bricks. The 7$^{th}$ Kansas Federal Cavalry had burned the buildings to the ground the previous year.

384

Weeds, bushes and briers grew where they had once drilled and paraded. Where some of Alabama's finest young minds once studied, rabbits, raccoons and possums lived.

"We've lost a lot of good boys since we marched away from here two years ago," Dudley said sadly.

"Yeah, we started out with over 750 men and now we're down to less 'n two hundred fifty," replied Junior Bill.

"I feel like I've been to hell and back," said Dudley. "I keep thinking ol' Abe will see that he can't whip us and make peace."

"It's gonna get worser and worser," predicted Junior Bill.

"I don't see how it can," replied Dudley. "We're already outnumbered, barefoot, wearing rags and living on noth'n."

"Just wait 'til winter comes on."

Have you ever thought about quitt'n?" asked Dudley.

"Naw, I ain't quittin' until I'm dead or they leave here. I'll fight in hell if I havta," said Junior Bill and spat.

Yankee cavalry was combing the countryside and they kept off the main roads. If caught on Yankee horses they would be shot, no questions asked. They forded the Tennessee River at the Shoals and rode east, stopping only long enough to water and rest their horses and let them graze. Late afternoon they came to a narrow and isolated section on Elk River near Stewart Ferry where they halted.

"Waal, I reckon this is where we part company," said Junior Bill. "I'll see ya in Lentzville 'n about a week."

Dudley leaned over and shook Junior Bill's hand. "Be careful and watch out for Yankees." He nudged his horse and rode down into the river; pulled his feet up on the saddle and gave the mare her head as she carefully picked her way across the water and climbed up on the east bank. Barring trouble, he should be home by late night.

The sun set and the temperature dropped, making him wish he had a blanket or, better still, a decent coat to wear. Shivering, he hunched his shoulders forward and rode on. The moon came out making it easy to follow the road. He wondered what had changed at home. Was the old home place still standing? All along the way he had seen blackened chimneys standing like lone sentinels where once-proud homes had stood. The Yankees had torched and pillaged the county.

When he neared Athens he left the Florence Pike and rode south of town. He didn't know if Federal troops were in Athens, but he assumed they were present guarding the railroad and if that was the case, sentinels would be posted. He saw a light blinking in the window of Daniel Coleman's mansion on top of Coleman Hill. There was just enough moonlight to see the courthouse. He had been told that Grandpa McElroy had built the first brick courthouse in Athens; that the foundation had shifted and it had to be reconstructed but, as far as he knew, the present courthouse was just like the one Grandpa had built. It was a comforting sight.

It was dangerous to be in town, but curiosity overcame caution. He reined the mare to a slow walk. It was late night and no one stirred. Brick buildings on the east side of the square had been gutted by fire. When he reached the railroad tracks, he dismounted and after waiting a few moments, looked in both directions to determine if a sentry was present. Seeing no one, he quickly crossed the tracks, remounted and rode east on the Athens - Fayetteville Pike, hearing only the soft clump of a horse's feet on the dusty road.

385

After he crossed the plank bridge over Swan Creek, he saw a log house silhouetted in the moonlight. Home!

Tears welled in his eyes and his chest ached. He kicked the mare and sped off at a gallop. One never knew when spying Yankees were around so he rode into the backyard beneath the trees where it was pitch black. Just as he reined and slid off the mare ol' Luther ran out from under the front porch barking and growling.

"It's me, Luther, hush!"

The liver-colored coon dog whined and wagged his tail, trotting over to smell Dudley's hand.

The back door flew open and someone was holding a lantern aloft and peering into the darkness. It was Thomas.

"Who's there?"

"It's me – Dudley."

Thomas ran into the yard, holding the lantern outstretched to shed light, and squinted at the strange-looking fellow.

"It is! It's Dudley!" exclaimed Thomas, grabbing his hand and pumping it. Dudley loosed his free hand and pulled Thomas to his chest, his eyes burning with hot tears.

"How's Ma and Pa?" he asked, voice quavering.

"Tolerable," said Thomas. "Come on in."

The barking and commotion had awakened his father and when they entered the house Pa was standing in the living room, holding a flickering candle.

"Who is it, Thomas?"

"Pa!" Dudley blurted out and ran to his stunned father, hugging him for a long time.

"Dudley, my boy! The Lord has answered my prayers."

"Yeah Pa, I'm home."

"Wake up your Ma, Thomas."

Ma entered the room and froze in her tracks. She hardly recognized her boy. He was dirty, wooly with hair, wearing soiled and tattered rags and looked much older than his 25 years. She burst into tears and ran to him, arms outstretched. "My son – my son." Tears flowed down her cheeks.

"Ma – Ma, don't cry."

Soon the whole household was awake. Cornelia and Cal entered the room, clutching the collars of their gowns.

"Brother!" screamed Cal and ran to him and threw her arms around his neck. Cornelia, now 19, was more reserved. She came over and grabbed his arm and hugged his shoulder. "You look awful, brother."

Everyone was awake. Dudley's older sister, Sarah Ann, wife of James Newby, entered the room with little Luke Pryor and Worley tagging along behind her, yawning and rubbing sleep from their eyes. Oscar, now 3 years old, had learned to walk since Dudley last saw him. Thomas went next door and woke George Edward and his family and they hurried over.

Ma flew into action. "Somebody stoke the fire," she said. "The Yankees just about cleared out our smoke house, but I managed to hide a ham. Cal, you and Cornelia get it out and slice off a big slab for Dudley. Thomas, go to the barn and find some eggs –"

"Huh?"

"I said find some eggs! I declare his hearing is getting worse by the day." She looked at her grandson, Luke Pryor Newby. "You run over to the spring and fetch our milk and be quick about it."

"Yes ma'am," he wheeled and flew out the door, honored at being selected for the important mission.

Soon the house was filled with the aroma of sizzling ham and hoecakes cooking in a skillet of popping grease.

"Uncle Dudley, how many Yankees have you killed?" asked young Luke Pryor Newby.

Ma drew back a threatening hand. "Young'un hush that talk! There's been too much killing and I'm tired of hearing about it, especially in my house."

Everyone was bubbling with news. Brother Jim and James Newby were prisoners at Rock Island and safe and sound as far as they knew.

"What about Coleman?" Dudley asked.

"Last time we heard he's in Georgia fighting with General Johnston," said George Edward.

"When the Yankees pulled out of Athens and headed to Nashville about two years ago," said Pa, "they set fire to the east side of the square."

"And burned Niphonia Fairground too," added George.

Thomas leaned forward, hand cupped to his ear. "And they stole two of my best horses."

"And Handful too," Pa added. "But she escaped or they turned her loose."

There was other news. Captain Thomas H. Hobbs, who had organized Company F, 9th Alabama in Athens was killed at Gaines Mill on June 27th, right after Dudley had enlisted. Many good men from the county had been killed or wounded and the telegraph brought news almost daily of more deaths.

Dudley wolfed down salt-cured ham, fried eggs and hoecakes washed down with the sweetest milk that he had drank since leaving home.

They sat up until near daybreak talking and visiting. His stomach full, but tired and exhausted, Dudley piled into bed with Thomas. It was first time in two years he had slept on a mattress in a real bed. Thank God. He was home at last. And then he slept the sleep of the dead.

When he woke late morning and walked outside he saw the awful state of things. Where once fertile fields of corn and cotton grew were briers and bushes. The countryside was no different from what he had seen in northern Mississippi – burned, abused and grown over with vines, bushes and brambles.

---

Thomas was turning land in a patch behind the house with the little mare, Sweet, preparing the soil to plant corn in April, when Ma announced dinnertime.

"Can I ring the dinner bell, Ma?" asked young Luke Pryor Newby.

"I reckon," she said. "I'll declare that child had rather ring the bell than eat."

Luke Pryor ran to the back yard, followed by his younger brother, Worley, and tugged hard on the bell rope. "BONG – BONG – BONG."

Thomas never looked up, but the little mare did. She bee-lined to the barn, Thomas clutching the plow handles, trying to keep up and hollering, "Whoa-whoa Sweet,

387

whoa!" When they reached the barn lot, the mare stopped and snorted. Pa and Dudley witnessed the event.

"By crackies, it beats anything I ever seen," Pa said. "Every time she hears the dinner bell she heads to the barn knowing she's gonna be fed. One of these days I'm gonna break 'er from the dinner bell."

"How you gonna do that?" asked Dudley.

"I'll figure something out."

Later, finding a moment of privacy with Cal, Dudley inquired about Sarah Jane Isom.

"I saw her at a church meeting at Isom's Chapel but didn't speak. Folks say her Pa is cooperating with the Yankees."

"What's he done?" asked Dudley.

"They say when Confederates slip home to visit their folks – like you – he runs and tattles to the Yankees. Sheriff McKinney has threatened to go out and hang 'im."

"Well, if you see Sarah Jane, tell 'er I asked about 'er... and if it's okay I'd like to write to 'er."

---

Shades of night were falling and frogs were croaking across the road at Cove Springs when Thomas saddled the bay mare and led her to the back of the house where the family waited in the shadows.

"You look a sight better leav'n than you did com'n," said Pa, attempting to inject levity into the sad occasion. Dudley was clean, hair cut, beard trimmed and was wearing freshly-washed pants, shirt, socks and patched-up shoes.

Thomas walked up and handed him his coat. "Here, I don't need this. It just gets in my way."

Cal and Cornelia, who were sobbing, had prepared a sack of food which Dudley hung over the saddle horn. "There's dried apples and peaches, cornbread, potatoes and an apple pie," said Cal. The sisters hugged his neck, sobbing.

Dudley bid farewell to everyone and finally to Ma, wearing her ever-present bonnet, lips trembling. She buried her face against his chest, heaving and sobbing. He stroked her back, "Ma, I'll be okay."

"Remember to call on the Lord daily and he'll see you through this awful war. Here, take this testament and carry it over your heart and read it daily," she said and placed it in his shirt pocket.

"I promise, Ma."

Dudley tugged ol' Luther's ears. "Y'all take care of 'im, ya heah." He mounted and rode off into the night, ol' Luther following.

"Be careful," Pa called out.

Dudley threw up his hand. "I will. Love y'all." Then he scolded ol' Luther. "Get back home." When he rode a short distance he broke down and sobbed. Then his thoughts turned to Junior Bill at Lentzville.

---

Ol' Luther barking and growling near midnight woke Pa. Cal tiptoed into the dark bedroom and whispered, "Pa – Pa, wake up. Somebody's outside."

"Who is it?"

The way ol' Luther was growling spelled trouble. BAM-BAM-BAM. Someone was at the door.

Pa got up, lit a candle, padded to the window and peeked out.

"Be careful," whispered Ma. "Whoever it is, is up to no good."

"Yankees!" exclaimed Daniel.

"Oh Lord, help us," Ma wailed.

BAM-BAM-BAM. "OPEN UP!" Pa opened the door and held out the candle. A Yankee sergeant holding a pistol was on the porch. Mounted men were in the edge of darkness. Ol' Luther stood at the door near Pa, hair bristled and growling.

"Are you Daniel Barksdale?" asked the sergeant.

""Yeah, what ye want?"

"You got a son named Dudley in the seceesh army?"

"Yeah, but he's a grown man and makes his own decisions."

"We've heard that he's home," said the sergeant and took a step forward. Ol' Luther intervened and snarled. "You better call that mongrel off before I shoot him."

Pa reached down and patted the dog's head. "It's okay," then addressed the sergeant. "Dudley ain't here."

"You won't mind if we see for ourselves?"

The sergeant turned to his men and commanded them to search the barn and outbuildings. He and a private entered the house.

"I FOUND HIM!" the private hollered, then shoved Thomas out on the front porch as he was trying to get into his breeches.

"Where'd you find him?" asked the sergeant.

"Asleep in bed."

"What's going on?" asked Thomas, sleepy and confused.

"Is your name Dudley?"

"Huh? What's going on Pa?"

"He's nearly deaf," Pa told the sergeant, "He ain't in the army and has never been."

Disappointed at not finding Dudley, the sergeant shoved Thomas backward. Ol' Luther, teeth out, lunged at the sergeant's cavalry boot. The trooper kicked, striking the dog in the head. Ol' Luther whimpered with pain and let go of the boot. The sergeant lowered his pistol.

"No. Don't shoot 'im!" yelled Pa, just as the pistol spoke, emitting a tongue of fire. Ol' Luther yelped loudly and dragged himself off the porch.

"Why'd you have to do that?" asked Thomas.

"Shut up Reb," threatened the sergeant, sticking the pistol barrel under Thomas's chin and cocking the hammer.

"No. Please! There has been enough violence," Ma pleaded. The sergeant thought it over and let the hammer down. "Yeah, you're right."

They searched all rooms including the attic, even looked under the house. Finding nothing, they rode off toward Athens. Ol' Luther had dragged himself under the porch where he lay in a puddle of blood. Thomas got him out and laid him on the porch, and while Ma held a lamp, Pa located where the ball had entered near his hip. "All we can do is doctor him with tar and say a prayer," Pa said.

Afterwards, Pa turned to Ma and said, "By crackies, somebody is talk'n to the Yankees and I know who it is. It's that Union-loving Isom bunch."

389

"Now, the Isoms are good Christian folks, good neighbors and our best friends. Don't be accusing unless you know for sure," said Ma. "Remember what the Good Book says about bearing false witness."

"Hmp," harrumphed Pa. "I'm in no mood to hear you defending 'em when our boys are dying at the hands of Yankee invaders." He went back inside and sat down in his rocker. Ma followed.

"James Daniel Barksdale, you need a good talking-to," she said.

Pa frowned. When she called him by his full name, he knew what was coming. "I ain't interested in hearing a lecture from you, woman."

"You're gonna hear it anyhow. Now hush up and listen. You study your Bible and quote scriptures, but you don't always listen to what you say –"

"Now don't start –"

"Hush up for a minute," Ma said. "Have you forgot that Emanuel is one of your oldest and dearest friends? That he befriended us when we moved here from Tennessee, referred carpentry work to you –"

"I know," said Daniel holding up his hand.

"That when little Achilles died Emanuel was here and sat up all night long, that he built his coffin with his own hands," said Ma choking up.

Daniel wiped away tears.

"And he preached his funeral," Ma added.

Pa nodded his head in agreement and again wiped away tears. "I know," he whispered. "You're right." He stood and walked to Ma and pulled her thin body into his arms and squeezed her tight. "Oh God, this dreadful war is destroying all of us, when will it end?" And they wept on each other's shoulders.

---

It was past midnight when Dudley forded the river below Elk River Mills and rode dripping wet into the Lentzville community. The Pendegrass cabin sat on high ground silhouetted by the moonlight. A chimney was at each end, a breezeway in the center with a porch across the front. A stranger approaching a house unannounced at this hour of night in these violent times was dangerous. He halted in the road where a pack of dogs ran out barking and growling, frightening his mount.

"WHO IS IT?" someone yelled from the darkened porch.

"Dudley Barksdale. Looking for Junior Bill Pendegrass."

A man walked out into the moonlight carrying a musket, eyed Dudley carefully then called off the dogs. "I'm his Pa, get down and come in."

Mr. Pendegrass lit a lamp and said that everyone was asleep. "Junior Bill attended a social last night at Cairo and wobbled in soused on white light'n. He's asleep in yonder," he said gesturing. "I'll take care of your horse. You go find a spot in bed."

A beam of moonlight poured through the window, illuminating the room where bodies were piled on two beds, all snoring. Junior Bill was fast asleep, lying on his back, mouth open and snoring louder than the rest. He smelled like a whiskey still. Dudley punched him in the ribs. "Scoot over!" he said and crawled into bed. Hearing Junior Bill's familiar snoring gave him a small sense of security. He had walked through hell with this man and they had become as close as brothers.

Dudley was awakened next morning by someone punching his side.

"Who in tarnation is he?" a voice asked. Dudley cracked an eye and saw a half a dozen boys staring down at him. Junior Bill was still asleep and snoring.

"What ya doin' in our bed?" asked a tall, lanky boy with a shock of red hair.

Dudley sat up and placed his feet on the floor. "I'm Dudley Barksdale."

One of the boys shook Junior Bill, finally getting him awake. He raised up on his elbows, blurry-eyed and rubbing his temples.

"Who's he?" he asked, staring at Dudley.

"Why Junior Bill, it's me, Dudley."

Junior Bill eyed him closely then grinned. "I didn't recognize you all shaved and cleaned up." Then he collapsed on the bed and began snoring.

A rider came up fast and reined in front of the cabin.

"The word is that ol' man Solomon Lentz and his Yankee home guard heard that Junior Bill was home," said the rider. "Tell 'em to skedaddle outta here fast!"

---

Junior Bill was unusually quiet as they rode back to their regiment encamped at Russellville.

"Every time this horse takes a step my head feels like it's exploding," said Junior Bill.

"I didn't know you were a drinking man," said Dudley.

"I ain't."

"Did somebody hold ya and pour whiskey down ya?"

"Naw, I was celebrating my engagement."

"You're engaged!" exclaimed Dudley.

"Well, almost, I asked 'er to marry me and she said she'd thank about it. Yep, that letter you wrote done the trick. Earline said it was almost as romantic as reading Songs of Solomon in the Good Book."

# 38 | WE'LL DIE TOGETHER

April 1, 1864.

Rock Island Prison.

The sound of cracking ice in the Mississippi River meant that warmer weather was approaching. It offered hope. The prisoners at Rock Island were permitted to write one letter a week not exceeding one page, which was censored. Absolutely no criticism of the prison was permitted.

James Greer Barksdale and James Newby hadn't received mail from home since their arrival and refused to believe their folks weren't writing them. Then on April 1st, Jim received a letter from Susan. He climbed on the bunk and lay back, first looking at the handwriting on the envelope for a long time, then smelling the letter. He was sure it smelled like home. He opened the envelope and read slowly, savoring every word.

> Athens, Alabama.
>
> March 16, 1864.
>
> Dearest Jim –
>
> Your letter of January 2nd, instant, was just received. I have been worried sick about you and brother, James. Has your wound completely healed? Uncle Robert and Aunt Sallie have been checking the list of killed and wounded each day at the railroad station and since y'all's name didn't appear, we figured y'all were captured near Chattanooga after the big fight there in late November. When I received your letter and learned y'all are alive my heart was filled with unspeakable joy. I fell on my knees and thanked a loving and merciful God for saving both of you. I pray unceasing for you and our brave boys who are likewise suffering.
>
> Ma and Pa are doing tolerably well, the same for George and Thomas. Thomas hunts squirrels about every day on Swan Creek and Ma made some of her famous squirrel dumplings yesterday. It was delicious but I could hardly swallow a bite for thinking that you, my darling husband, might be hungry and cold. Are you getting enough to eat? Do you manage to stay warm? We sent you and James each a blanket together with socks, underwear, pants and shirts. I assume you received them. Ma is knitting socks every day; says she can't bear to think that her boys might be cold. We just heard from William Coleman, he's alive and fighting somewhere in Georgia. No word on Robert Beasley. Pa says Ma is going to wear out the spinning wheel making clothes for her boys, but if she does, he said he'll get her another one somehow.
>
> Since you didn't mention it in your letter, I assume that you are well fed and warm. I pray that you are. Little Waddie and Benjamin Dudley are doing fine and miss their Papa. When I tuck them in at night, they pray that God will send them "their Papa home pretty quick."
>
> Dudley came home on furlough a few days ago. He looked so awful that it took ol' Luther a minute to recognize him. He said his

392

regiment was down to 240 men and most of them were sick with dysentery and flu. Each day brings news of our boys being killed and wounded. When will this terrible war end so that I get to see you again? The Yankees care for no one. They burn, pillage and steal our food. But don't worry about us darling, as we are doing fine. Pa and Thomas are readying the ground for planting corn, potatoes, peanuts and turnip greens. They have an old sow with pigs hid in the woods on Swan Creek. If the Yankees don't find them then we'll have plenty of meat to eat this coming winter provided we can find salt to cure it. Thomas has dug and removed the dirt beneath the smoke house and we are busy boiling it to separate what little bit of salt there is in it. Cornelia and Cal are knitting socks and making clothes for our boys and send their love. They say they will write soon. Do you have shoes, my darling? Sarah has written letters to James. Hope he has received them. Write soon. I love you.

      Your devoted wife, Susan.

Hot tears ran down Jim's cheeks. He kissed the letters.

"Thank the Lord that my family is alive," he muttered.

After re-reading the letter several times he passed it to his brother-in law, James Newby, then found pen and paper.

      Rock Island Prison
      April 1, 1864
      Dearest Susan:
      When I received your letter, I first thought it was an April Fool's joke. But no darling, it was real. Oh, my heart yearns to hold you and our precious children. My wound has healed. No, we didn't get the blankets and clothes. We had a rough winter, but don't worry, we are doing tolerably well. I've been sick with flu and dysentery, but am feeling much better. Send tobacco as James and I are starving for a chew. Write me each day darling; send all my love to Ma and Pa and Thomas, George, Cal and Cornelia and all the children. James keeps my spirits up along with other southern men. We don't get much news. How is the war going? Are you and the family getting plenty to eat? All my love to you, Waddie and Benjamin Dudley and all of the children. Your lock of hair is still over my heart and sometimes I smell it at night. Oh darling Susan -
      Your loving husband, Jim"

In April, guards began firing on prisoners in the barracks or while they walked outside and particularly when they went to relieve themselves. The toilet ditch was located near the "dead line" and several prisoners were shot and killed while defecating. On May 12th it was ordered that no prisoner was to be outside the barracks after *Taps*. The following day, an order was posted that "any prisoner shouting or making a noise will be shot." The cruelty grew worse.

In July, the 108th U.S. Colored Infantry arrived for guard duty. They were freed slaves recruited from Kentucky and some of their former masters were now incarcerated. They fired indiscriminately on prisoners.

Barksdale made a mental note of their atrocities. Prisoner shot on April 27th; man killed and one wounded in leg on May 27th; June 9th, Franks of 4th Alabama Cavalry killed when he was about to step from barracks into street; On July 22nd, two men from Georgia who were on work detail in a ditch, stopped to drink fresh water brought to them when they were shot. There were so many shootings that he lost count.

The prisoners were finally furnished straw mattresses and even sheets, but on June 1st rations were officially reduced to 12 oz. of cornbread and 4 ½ oz. of salt beef daily. The bread, delivered daily, was a loaf of cornbread shaped like a brick and nearly as hard. Meat was issued every ten days and was rank and unfit for human consumption. The explanation given for cutting rations was in retaliation for mistreatment of Union prisoners by Confederates at Andersonville, Georgia. However, the prisoners uniformly believed it was because of the capture of Ft. Pillow by General Nathan Bedford Forest on April 10th when several hundred colored troops who refused to surrender were killed.

In reality, the actual rations were only 4 oz. of green beef and 8 oz. of bread daily – a recipe for slow starvation.

It was late July, hot and muggy, as Barksdale and Newby sat in the shade of the barracks carving on clam shells that came from the river. Barksdale was carving buttons and Newby was fashioning trinkets that could be worn as a bracelet which they hoped to sell to guards or fellow prisoners for currency. It was one of the few privileges they were allowed.

"That's a nice breeze Jim," remarked Newby, taking note of the gentle wind that swept across the river.

"Yep."

"You're awfully quiet Jim."

"Yep."

"Whatcha thinkin'?"

"How delicious a mouthful of Ma's squirrel dumplings would taste right now," replied Barksdale. "I dreamed last night that I was home and Ma was in the kitchen rolling out dough with a whiskey bottle while squirrel meat boiled and bubbled in a black pot over the fire. She cut out strips of dumplings and dropped 'em in the pot and added salt and pepper and –"

"I've never been so hungry in my life," interjected Newby. "I can taste those dumplings right now."

"All I think about is food," said Barksdale.

"Jim, we've gotta get outta this place before we starve. Winter will be coming on and if we don't starve, we'll freeze to death."

Barksdale stopped carving and looked up at his brother-in-law. "Maybe the war will end soon and we can go home."

"It will end someday, but we may be dead before that time comes," said Newby, and then added, "Of course one way outta here is to take the oath and enlist in the Union Army."

"I'd rather die first."

"Yeah, me too," replied Newby.

They continued carving in silence. Momentarily, Barksdale paused and looked at his brother-in-law. "How are we going to get outta here James?"

"I've been thinking about it," said Newby. "We have to get enough to eat so that we are strong enough to escape. And we need money. We can sell these trinkets and raise money for bribes and to purchase food."

"Uh huh, that sounds sensible, but who's going to sell us cornbread and beef?"

"No one," replied Newby. "We're going to buy a dog from the suttler or one of the guards."

"A dog!"

"Yep."

"In that case, I'd like to put in an order for a greyhound."

"A greyhound!"

"Uh huh, I figure if I eat greyhound meat I might be able to outrun Yankee bullets."

Newby chuckled. It had been a long time since he had witnessed his brother-in-law exhibit humor.

"Let's suppose we get over the wall, then what?" asked Barksdale. "How are we gonna get across the Mississippi River and get home?"

"Swim."

---

A dog wasn't to be purchased. There were over 8,000 prisoners and all of them were hungry. Then the Lord sent them manna just as he had sent manna to the children of Israel when they were wandering, starving and destitute in the wilderness. But, this manna didn't fall from heaven. It had a long slick tail and ran on four feet.

"I don't know if I can eat a rat," Barksdale said.

"It'll keep us alive," said Newby.

Several prisoners enlisted to participate. They located the rat holes which were in the kitchen and barricaded all of them except one which was in a corner.

It was near midnight and most of the prisoners were snoring, some coughing, others too sick and weak to care. Barksdale and Newby were wide awake. They heard rats squeaking and scrambling over the pots and pans in the kitchen, searching for crumbs of food.

"All right boys, it's time," whispered Newby.

Half a dozen prisoners quietly exited their bunks, sticks in hand and tiptoed into the kitchen. They had no candle, but the Lord had sent them a three-quarters moon that cast light through the window. Newby carried a stick in one hand and a brick in the other. He rushed to the open rat hole and placed the brick over it. The rats, sensing danger, fled toward the hole that was now blocked. The men moved in. Panicked, the rats screeched and ran wildly sliding across the floor in every direction trying to escape as the men whacked them with sticks. One huge gopher was backed up in the corner, reared up on his hind legs hissing when Barksdale bashed his head. Another rat ran up a prisoner's pant leg. When the slaughter was over, twelve good-sized gophers lay dead in puddles of blood.

They skinned and gutted the rats, cut off their heads, feet and tails and dropped the carcass in a kettle of boiling water. The men hovered around the kettle and salivated as the meat cooked. When it was done, Newby divided it, two to each man.

Barksdale bit into the soft meat, gagged and retched. "Jim, just think of it as a squirrel with a shaved tail," said Newby.

395

That worked and Barksdale ate ravenously like the other men.

---

July dragged into August and the men had been unsuccessful in purchasing a dog. Even rats were scarce.

"I say we act now," said Heck Simpson of Georgia. "Once we get across the river we're bound to find food." Barksdale, Newby, James Dement and Richard Green of Mississippi, all members of the escape party, continued carving on clam shells. Green spit a stream of tobacco juice into the dust and wiped brown stain from his chin. "But, what if we can't find food? Then we'll be in a real fix. I got a better idea."

The men stopped whittling and looked up at Green. "We won't buy a dog, we'll steal one," he said.

"From who?" asked Simpson.

"The driver of the bread wagon," replied Green. "He's got the fattest old yellow mongrel I've ever laid eyes on."

The men looked at each other and nodded in agreement.

"It's a shame that while men are starving to death that dog is so fat that he couldn't catch a rabbit if he had to," said Newby.

The plan was that Green would feed the dog scraps of boiled gopher meat for a few days to gain its confidence, then lure it behind the barracks, cut its throat and hide it under the building until night fall.

---

"Dog ain't that bad," said Green, gnawing meat off a hind leg.

"Tastes good as tenderloin," added Dement. "Especially when you're hungry."

The four men fell silent and ate voraciously tearing off the meat, mouths full, grease dribbling down their chin, table manners forgotten. When they were gorged Newby whispered, "We'll start at 2 a.m. Now let's get some rest."

Barksdale was too keyed up to sleep, but when Newby whispered, "Jim, it's time to go," he knew that he had dozed because he thought he was home and Susan had told him to bring in some wood and stoke a fire in the fireplace. He shook cobwebs from his mind and rubbed his eyes. Today, he would be either a free man or be with the Lord. He quietly exited the bunk, pulling off the sheets as he went. The five men tiptoed out of the barracks into a moonlit yard, keeping in the shadows of the buildings, and moved quietly toward the plank fence. Newby gave a low whistle. The guard that he had given $25.00 worth of jewelry to unlock the sewer whistled back. "Everything's dandy," whispered Newby. "Twist the sheets and tie good knots."

The men remained in the shadows, tying their two sheets end to end.

"Let's go," said Newby.

The men skeetered across open space, crossed the "dead line" and ran twenty-five feet to the wall where they catapulted each other to the top, slipped a knotted end into the board slats then quietly lowered themselves down.

"So far... so good," said Newby, gasping for breath. Barksdale could feel his heart pounding against his chest. He kept looking over his shoulders, expecting to hear the crack of a rifle and feel a lead ball slap into his back at any moment. How could the guard be trusted? he wondered. They ran to the sewer, opened the top and quietly dropped down and on their hands and knees and crawled toward the opening near the river. The stench of feces and urine was overpowering.

"Com' on boys, we'll be in Dixie before you know it," exclaimed Simpson.

"Listen! I hear water," said Green. Everyone froze and listened.

"It's gushing!" shouted Dement. "The guard has played us false."

"GO BOYS GO!" yelled Newby and the men scrambling forward on hands and knees.

No sooner had he uttered the words when they were slammed by a wall of water that sent them tumbling through the sewer. Barksdale closed his eyes and held his breath until his lungs were about to explode. He was drowning. Suddenly, he shot out the end of the sewer. When he cleared the water and feces from his face and eyes, he looked up and saw guards standing over him laughing and with rifles pointed.

"Going for a swim Rebs?" asked one and the others laughed uproariously.

---

"I'm getting outta here even if I die doing it," said Newby shifting his body on "Morgan's mule," a thin board turned up and mounted between two poles about five feet in the air. The weight of one's body pressing against the edge of the board gradually cut into the crotch, decreasing circulation and causing great pain. Barksdale, Dement, Green and Simpson had been placed astraddle the board as punishment. Simpson grimaced. "We'll all die here," he said. "It's a wonder they didn't shoot us like dogs when we popped outta the sewer."

"Count me in," said Green. "I'd rather die try'n to get outta here than slowly starve and freeze to death."

"What about you Jim?" asked Newby.

"Yeah, I'm in."

"Heck, what about you?"

"I've had enough. I'm out."

Dement shifted and groaned with pain. "I'm in."

---

It was mid-September and fall was fast approaching. Winter came early and brutally in this northern country. The men knew if they stood a chance of making it home before cold weather they had to act promptly.

Barksdale had never seen a darker or wetter night as he, Newby, Dement and Richard Green edged along the side of the barracks toward the "dead line." Green, who had previously counted out the footsteps and knew exactly where to turn in the murky darkness, was in front. If the Lord intended the men to escape, this was the night. It was late and the colored guards were sleepy and not alert. Not only that, they were trying to stay dry and not walking their post as usual.

"How do we know we can trust 'em?" whispered Newby, whose resolve was growing less certain. At first he had been excited about the plan, now he was conflicted.

"He says he don't care about the Yankees, he just needs the money," whispered Green. The guard, according to Green, was from Kentucky and had fled his master and joined the Union Army when Federal forces came through the area. He claimed he needed money to buy his wife's freedom and didn't care where or how he obtained it.

Crossing the "dead line" was the most dangerous aspect of the escape plan. If a guard other than the one to be bribed spotted them, he would shoot them down like rabbits.

They approached the "dead line" where a latrine ditch ran along the outside of a wire. Green was in front, then Newby, Barksdale and finally Dement bringing up the rear. Barksdale suddenly had a bad feeling. Many prisoners had been shot and killed for getting near the "dead line." It was a death warrant to step across it. "I don't like it," he whispered to Newby. "I don't like it at all."

"I don't have a good feeling about it either," replied his brother-in-law, "but we have to take a chance if we ever expect to get outta here."

"Shhh," shushed Green. "Wait here. I'm going to sneak across the 'dead line' and pay the guard. Then I'll whistle when it's okay for y'all to run across."

Green jumped over the ditch and ran across no man's land toward the plank fence that enclosed the prison. The men waited in the soaking rain for the signal.

POW! The blast of a rifle pierced the rainy night, its muzzle flash clearly visible only a few yards in front of the waiting men.

"He's played the devil," said Newby. "Run!"

They bolted toward the barracks, running as fast as they could. Green had been shot in cold blood, perhaps killed, but maybe they could get back in bed before anyone learned they were gone. Barksdale lay in bed, wet and scared, expecting any moment the guards to burst through the door and jerk him from bed, drag him outside and kill him.

The next morning he heard that Green was dead – shot through the heart. The guard had accepted the bribe and killed Green in cold blood.

"Green made a deal with the devil," said Barksdale. "James, we're gonna die in this hell hole."

"Then we'll die together," replied Newby.

# 39 | BLOOD AND MUD IN GEORGIA

North Georgia.

Tuesday, May 24, 1864.

The railcars rattled and swayed as they rumbled down the tracks toward Atlanta, black smoke boiling from the engine's stack sending a shower of soot back into the cars. For once Dudley was glad he wasn't riding on top. The 35$^{th}$ and 27$^{th}$ Regiments consolidated had boarded in Montgomery, the cars crammed with horses, mules, wagons, cannon, limbers and supplies. The journey was slow with frequent stops to inspect the tracks, take on water and fuel and to care for the officer's horses. Night fell as Dudley and Junior Bill sat squeezed inside a car, their knees pulled to their chest. Dudley closed his eyes and thought about the events of the past six months. Following Colonel Goodwin's death from illness in Columbus, Mississippi, Colonel Samuel S. Ives had taken command of the two regiments. The men liked Ives. Twenty-eight years old and born at Center Star in eastern Lauderdale County, Alabama, he had initially enlisted as a private in the 9$^{th}$ Alabama in 1861. Wounded in Virginia, he was discharged and later joined the 35$^{th}$ Regiment at Florence in the spring of 1862. He had been shot so many times in battle that Junior Bill swore that he rattled when he walked. Dudley grinned to himself. *Good ol' Junior Bill.* He was sound asleep, snaggle-tooth mouth hanging open as usual and making more noise snoring than the locomotive chugging through the night.

Following their furlough home, he and Junior Bill had participated in a raid across the Tennessee River near Tuscumbia on the night of April 12$^{th}$, attacking an encampment of 9$^{th}$ Ohio Cavalry. They killed three troopers, captured three officers and 39 enlisted men, and took 65 horses and mules. Mounted, the regiment rode south of Decatur, which was occupied with Union troops, then proceeded to Montgomery where the enlisted men gave up their horses and boarded the train for Atlanta to join General Joseph E. Johnston's Army of Tennessee. General William T. Sherman, with his army of 100,000 Federals, was knocking at the door of the rail hub city.

Near nightfall on Wednesday, the train screeched to a stop north of Marietta, where they hastily unloaded and marched westward in stifling dust to join a big fight under way at a place called New Hope Church. Two main roads intersected where the small Methodist Church stood. Assigned to Scott's Brigade, they were immediately sent to the front, issued pick-axes, spades and shovels, and began digging rifle pits to be topped with head-logs. A violent thunderstorm rolled in, producing torrents of rain and lightning that crackled and popped and illuminated their work. They stood knee-deep in mud. Dudley swore that for every shovel full of mud they pitched out, two slid back into the trench. Spotwood leaned on his pick handle and squinted through the darkness at the Federal entrenchments where Yankees were no doubt wearing slickers and snacking on real food.

"You see them Yankees over there, Spotwood?" said Dudley, pausing from shoveling mud.

"Sure."

"Well they ain't want'n to just take your States Rights, they wanna kill ya. Now start swing'n that pick-axe."

They dug and shoveled until near dawn before sliding down into the mud, sleepy and exhausted. Unknown to Dudley, his older brother, William Coleman, was also digging rifle pits somewhere along the Confederates line. Thunder shaking the ground woke Dudley. At first he thought another storm had rolled in, and then he realized it was cannon fire. The two armies were sending tons of shot and shell into each other's ranks. Shortly, hordes of blue bellies appeared from the northwest. Dudley lay in mud behind the head-log, sighting down his rifle barrel, watching as they came closer, marching in step in parade fashion. For an instant he admired how impressive they looked in their blue uniforms, and then he realized they were coming to kill him. His mind had never been so sharply focused. Spotwood might be fighting for States Rights but he was fighting for survival. All of his high-falutin reasons for enlisting meant nothing to him now. Glory be damned! He wanted to live.

"FIRE!" Hundreds of muskets rattled and blue bellies dropped. Dudley and the regiment reloaded and sent out another blizzard of lead. Though outnumbered, the gray backs turned back every charge. Many good men fell in the red mud, made redder with blood. The ground was littered with not only men, but dead and dying horses, and the trees and saplings had been blown away.

"It ain't nut'n but blood and mud!" exclaimed Thornton.

When the battle ended, the Confederates, though hungry, muddy and exhausted, had refused to budge. It continued to rain for over two weeks. They had lost 900 men, but the Yankees who called the place "Hell Hole" had lost approximately 3,000 men.

When General Sherman shifted his Army east in an attempt to flank the Confederates, the 35th Regiment took up a position near the base of Kennesaw Mountain. June 27th was a day that Dudley would never forget. Blood and guts! Approximately 100,000 blue coats tried to dislodge 40,000 Confederates. They failed. When the firing died and the smoke cleared, 9,000 Federals were dead or wounded. Only 808 Confederates were lost, including Corps Commander General Leonidas Polk. Generals Polk, Joseph Johnston and Hardee had climbed to the top of Pine Top Mountain to observe Union movement when a single cannon ball ripped through him and exploded against a tree. The fighting Episcopalian bishop never knew what killed him.

General Sherman, unable to dislodge the Confederates, pulled out on July 2nd. His plan was obvious; march around the Confederates and take Atlanta. The 35th Regiment shifted to entrenchments previously constructed that surrounded outer Atlanta and began digging deeper. News came that Sherman had burned Roswell, northwest of Atlanta, and ordered every factory worker – about 400 – taken prisoner and shipped north. Sherman crossed the Chattahoochee River by pontoon bridge northeast of Atlanta, again flanking the Confederates and forcing them to pull back into the outer fortifications that protected Atlanta. There was one more fall back line. If the Yankees took that one, Atlanta would be lost.

---

Back in Athens, Daniel Barksdale was oblivious to the bloody fighting that was trying the souls of his two sons at Atlanta. He was busy hitching up Sweet to plow his patch of corn a final time before "laying by." And he had a plan.

His grandson, Luke Pryor Newby, was assisting.

"Luke Pryor, I got a plan to break Sweet from the dinner bell," he said.

"You have!"

"Yessiree. By crackies, when I'm finished with my plan this horse will be totally dinner bell broke."

"Nobody has broken 'er yet, Grandpa."

"I'll need your help," Pa said.

Luke Pryor grinned from ear to ear. "Yessiree!"

"Now here's what I want you to do," Pa said. "Just before Ma rings the dinner bell at 11:30, you find a rock about the size of your fist and position yourself at the barnyard gate —"

"A rock?"

"—a nice big 'un. When Sweet hears the dinner bell, she'll take off to the barn like she always does. When she comes through the gate, you haul off and hit her right between her eyes and ears. That'll break her for good."

"What if I miss, Grandpa?"

"You won't. Now run along and find a rock."

Thomas plowed corn until near 11 a.m. when Pa took over. "You go to the house and I'll plow 'til dinnertime," Pa said and draped the plow lines over his shoulder. It was a cloudless day and a scorcher. Sweet kept snatching tender corn shoots from the young stalks. Pa jerked her bit and yelled, "Stop eat'n my corn!"

At 11:30 a.m., Ma walked to the dinner bell attached on top of a post behind the house and yanked the rope several times. BONG – BONG – BONG.

Pa was ready. Sweet's ears pointed toward the sound and she headed to the barn, cutting across the corn, knocking over stalks.

"Whoa – whoa!"

Sweet paid no attention. Luke Pryor was standing at the barn gate, a rock in hand.

"Are you ready?" Pa yelled.

"Yessir."

Just as Sweet approached the gate, Pa said, "You won't forget today, you daughter of Satan."

Luke Pryor aimed the rock at Sweet's head as instructed and let it fly. At this very moment, the mare lowered her head. The rock whizzed between her ears, striking Pa on the head, knocking him to the ground.

"GRANDPA!" Luke Pryor ran to his grandfather, who was lying on his back, rubbing his forehead.

"I didn't mean to hit you, Grandpa. Are you okay?"

"You made a fine throw, son, but you were supposed to hit the horse, not me."

---

July 17th.

The news swept through the regiment like wildfire.

"You won't believe it!" exclaimed the bearer. "Johnston has been replaced with Hood!"

"I won't fight for Hood," responded an Alabamian. The men were despondent and grumbled mightily.

"Why would ol' Jeff Davis remove his best General in the face of the enemy?" asked Thornton.

"He wants somebody who'll fight, not fall back into trenches," said Dudley. "And fight'n means dying. A bunch of us boys are about to die."

At 6 feet 2 inches, 33 year-old John Bell Hood, a Kentuckian, was a Davis favorite with a reputation for fighting. No one questioned his courage. He had lost the use of his left arm at Gettysburg and his right leg at Chickamauga. When mounted, he had to be strapped to his saddle.

The once-mighty Army of Tennessee, now ragged and vastly outnumbered by Sherman's forces, lined both sides of the road and watched as the well-dressed man on horseback galloped past them. Dudley had never seen the President of the Confederacy. Jefferson Davis, though of average height and wiry frame, was dressed in a black waistcoat, gray pants and boots, and struck an imposing sight as he reviewed his bedraggled men.

"Hoorah… Hoorah!" shouted some of the men.

Others weren't as appreciative. "Take away Hood and give us back Johnston!" someone shouted.

Hood immediately took the offensive, feeding troops into the Yankee killing machine, but with no gain. He pulled his army back toward Atlanta, where breastwork had previously been constructed. Sherman pressed closer, mounted siege guns and began bombarding Atlanta. Dudley and the men of the 35th lived in trenches which were knee deep in stinking and stagnant water with a scorching sun overhead baking their brains.

On July 28th, the 35th Regiment moved out of Atlanta with Loring's Division and took up a position near Ezra Methodist Church to attack Union forces and prevent them from cutting the last railroad connection to the outside. The men fought hard, but the plan was ill conceived. Approximately 5,000 men, including 27 from the 35th Regiment, were lost. Bombardment of Atlanta continued. Citizens fled the city and those that remained lived in caves and holes. Buildings were demolished. Food was scarce. The once-proud city was rubble. Sherman tightened the noose and prepared to cut the last railroad connection. Hood was about to be trapped. He had to act fast.

Chaos triggered by panic prevailed among the citizens of Atlanta. Great clouds of smoke rose from the burning city. Citizens fled in buggies and wagons piled high with their belongings. Others galloped past on horses and mules, choosing to leave their possessions, but most walked, carrying a few items with small dirty children tagging along behind them. Dudley watched the exodus as they passed through the fortifications and headed south away from the approaching Yankees. Atlanta, an important railhead and great city, was about to fall. How could it be?

He hunkered down in his filthy, muddy hole and watched as large shells roared overhead, exploding with great force that shook the ground. It was hell on earth.

---

Near Atlanta. Early August, 1864.

A sharp pain in his gut woke Coleman Barksdale in the middle of the night. In the fog of sleep, he first thought he had rolled over onto a rock, and then the pain came again. It was no rock. It felt like a gopher gnawing on his bowels. The pain came regular and closer together, much like a woman in labor. Suddenly, he had the urge to defecate. He threw back his thin blanket and trotted toward the nearest clump of bushes, barely making it in time. *It was something I ate, I'll be okay in a day or so just like before. Drink lots of water and flush out the body.*

At the morning formation, he was weak and barely able to remain in the ranks without trotting to the bushes. Over the following days, the stomach pain increased and he noticed mucous in his stools. He had the worst case of trots he had experienced since joining the Army.

Peavine Perkins took notice. "You got the flux," he said. "You oughta report to sick call."

"I'll be okay in a couple of days."

He'd improve, he told himself. No need of complaining. After all, he'd had the trots before, but never this bad. Following the defeat at Missionary Ridge and subsequent 30-mile retreat to Dalton where the army had wintered is where he first experienced symptoms. When he had fought at New Hope Church back in May, and Peachtree Creek and Ezra Church in July, his symptoms had worsened. He was ill, but so were many other men.

As time went by the pain grew worse and he grew weaker.

Finally, he reported to sick call and waited in a long line to see Dr. Malone, the regimental surgeon. When his time came, Coleman entered the wall-tent and stood before a camp table where a small wiry man with a pipe hanging from the corner of his mouth sat writing. He finally looked up at Coleman with tired eyes and removed the pipe.

"What's your problem, soldier?"

"Got a bad case of trots."

"How long has it been going on?" asked Dr. Malone.

"A long time, but it's gett'n worse."

"You have dysentery or flux as most people call it," said Dr. Malone. "Nothing unusual. A third of the brigade has it. More men die from dysentery than Yankee bullets. I'm going to give you a purgative to clean you out. If you don't get better I'll try something else." He handed Coleman a substance, which he ingested, but it gave him no relief over the ensuing days.

The march south to Atlanta through piney woods and down sun-baked roads that burned his bare feet was arduous, and if Peavine hadn't carried his rifle for him, he couldn't have made it.

"I don't believe Doc Malone knows what he's doing," Coleman said to Peavine. "Whatever he gave me is giv'n me a worse case of trots. All I'm doing is runn'n to the bushes and I'm so weak I can hardly stand up. I need something to plug me up, not open me up."

Peavine looked at Coleman, barefoot, ragged, hollow-eyed and skinny as a rail. "You need a different kind of medicine," he said.

"Yeah, I do."

Coleman remembered that when he was a child and had stomach ailments Ma made a tea from sweet gum bark. And sweet gums were plentiful in north Georgia. Peavine gathered bark and boiled tea for Coleman, but it wasn't the magic elixir hoped for. He grew weaker. The only bright spot in his miserable life came on August 1st when he received a penciled letter from home.

"May, 1864 –
Dearest husband – I hope this finds you in good health and fine spirits. I am doing fine and all the children are well except for Jim Dan who has measles. I'm looking any day for the rest of the children to come down with them. William Matthew is almost a year old. Pa claims he favors him, but he don't. He has the Barksdale nose and brown eyes. Right after you left last year the Yankees come and cleaned out the

smokehouse. We have hogs to kill this winter but we don't have salt to cure the meat. Salt can't be found anywhere and if it could it would cost too much. We'll try to smoke the meat, I guess. We've been living pretty good off rabbits and squirrels and vegetables. I worry about you. The other night I dreamed that I saw you but I didn't recognize you at first. You looked sick. I pray to God constantly that you'll be all right and will return to us. Your Ma and Pa are tolerable. Thomas rode out several days ago to check on us. He said that Jim and James Newby were taken prisoner at Missionary Ridge and sent to Rock Island Prison. Dudley is with the General Johnston's Army somewhere in Georgia. I guess you've seen him. Darlin' I'm hanging on waiting for you. Come home when you can. The children send their love.
Your loving wife, Eliza.
P.S. The cow went dry."

Coleman read the letter three times and smelled the paper before carefully folding and placing it inside the pocket over his heart. He squeezed his eyes shut to keep tears from flowing. Would he ever see his family again on this earth? If not, he would surely see them in Heaven. He was going to die – he could feel it. He had served God's purpose and now he was about to leave this earthly domain to be with Jesus where the streets are gold, the water cool and people are at peace. He wondered if there would be food in heaven. Ahhh, food. He would willingly die if he could eat a good meal. But if he had to die he didn't want to shit himself to death. He'd prefer a Yankee bullet instead. Before that happened, he decided he was going home – even if he had to desert.

One morning, following formation he was ordered to report to Doc Malone.

"Private Barksdale, a detail is leaving in the morning for Athens to recruit and round up deserters," he said. "I'm sending you home on sick furlough. You are to report back to the Army as soon as you are well." He signed a paper and handed it to Coleman.

When the half dozen men led by Lieutenant Adams departed for Athens early morning on horseback, it was already hot. They followed the same route he had taken the year before, fording the Tennessee River near Mooresville on a moonless night to avoid Yankee gunboats, then rode north on dusty Mooresville Road. When they reached the intersection of Nick Davis Road, they halted. Coleman was shaking with fever and reeling in the saddle.

"Can you make it home by yourself?" asked Lieutenant Adams.

"I can walk barefooted through hell if I haveta."

"Just the same, I'm going to give you a little help," he said and roped Coleman to the saddle. "Good luck and better health."

"Thanks Lieutenant." Coleman nudged the gelding forward and rode east toward Johnson Branch. Dawn was breaking and the rooster was crowing when he rode into the yard, triggering a pack of hounds to emerge from beneath the cabin, barking and snarling. The front door of the cabin cracked open and Ophelia peeked out into the murky light. "Mama, it's somebody on a horse!"

"Who is it?" asked her mother.

"I don't know." Soon all of the children were peeking out the door; baby William Matthew clinging to Eliza's black skirt. One of the hounds whined, tucked his tail and smelled Coleman's leg, then began flapping his tail.

"It's Papa!" cried Ophelia. The door flew open and the children rushed out, Eliza grabbed the baby and followed.

Eliza's hand flew to her mouth. "Lordy Mercy! He's near death." Frightened by the sight, some of the children began to whimper and sob.

"Hush, young'n and help me," commanded Eliza.

They assisted Coleman from the saddle, helped him inside the cabin and placed him on a bed. Eliza flew to action.

"Ophelia, get water boiling." Then she turned to Bob and Jim Dan. "Y'all get plenty of wood for the kitchen and draw some water. Lou Ella, you stay and help me. The rest of you young'uns quit gawking and clear outta here. Can't you see that your Papa's sick?"

She touched Coleman's forehead. "Lordee, he's burning up with fever." She removed his tattered shirt and said, "Lou Ella turn your head." Then she pulled down his stinking pants, soiled with feces and blood.

"He's got lice. LouElla, burn those rags in the kitchen fireplace," she said holding his clothes at arm's length. "And try not to touch 'em any more than you have to."

He was filthy and his feet were black and the soles were as hard as shoe leather. His groin was a red mass of chigger bites. He mumbled, "hom----"

"Yes darling, you're home."

LouElla returned. "Run down to the branch, young'n, and get a bucket of water. And hurry! I gotta bring down this fever."

Lou Ella ran out the door and soon returned with a bucket of cool branch water. Eliza soaked a cloth in the water and laid it across Coleman's forehead.

"You keep his brow cool and turn your back and don't look," said Eliza. "I'm gonna clean 'im up." After scrubbing his body with warm water and lye soap she rubbed turpentine on the chiggers. His Ma always declared that turpentine was sovereign for chiggers and she reckoned it to be so. Then she covered him with a sheet and permitted the children to gather around the bed. They looked down teary-eyed at the emaciated man whom they hardly recognized.

Mid-morning, Coleman opened his eyes and saw Eliza hovering over him, gently rubbing his face, and then he saw his children. He smiled and tears welled in his eyes and ran down his grizzled cheeks.

"I'm home," he said weakly. "Thank God, I'm finally home."

"Oh Papa!" exclaimed Ophelia and ran to him. The children crowded around and laid their hands on their father.

"Don't worry Papa, we'll take good care of you," said little Lou Ella.

"Dogwood tea and whiskey is what he needs," said Eliza.

She sent Jim Dan, now fully recovered from measles, across the woods to Grandpa Harvey's to fetch a pint of whiskey and ordered Ophelia down to the branch to gather dogwood bark. The children pitched in, excited to be helping their father. After the tea had boiled several minutes in the black pot over the kitchen fireplace, Eliza dipped out a half cup and poured in whiskey. She helped Coleman sit up in bed.

He looked at the black liquid. "What is it?"

"Never you mind. Drink all of it," said Eliza.

He drank it down in one long gulp. "Lord God have mercy!" He grabbed his throat and screwed up his face. "You've poisoned me."

While Coleman slept the children gathered vine-ripe tomatoes, fresh cucumbers, yellow squash, green beans and okra from the garden. When he woke at twilight a sumptuous feast of freshly cooked vegetables festooned the table.

Ophelia came from the kitchen smiling and holding a hot skillet of cornbread. "I made this special for you Papa."

"Thank you kindly daughter but I've been livin' on cornmeal so long that I never want to eat another hoecake or corn pone as long as I live."

---

A barking dog sent children scrambling to the front window to peer out.

"It's Grandpa and Grandma!" exclaimed Lou Ella.

"Don't just stand there young'un, go out and invite 'em in," said Eliza, rising from behind her spinning wheel and going to the door.

"Y'all come in and see what the dogs dragged up," she said as her father helped her mother down from the buggy.

Shortly, Hansel and Patsie Harvey entered the cabin. Coleman struggled to rise from his chair and noticed the shocked look on their faces. Mrs. Harvey came over and laid a hand on his shoulder. "Now, you just stay put, there's no need for you to stand up, you being a sick man."

Mr. Harvey walked over and poked out his hand. "Lordy mercy, it's good to see you Coleman," he said. "How are you doin'?"

"I'm getting' better every day," he replied. "Eatin' fresh vegetables and fried rabbit that Bob and Jim Dan trapped is puttin' me on the road to recovery – that'n dogwood tea. If it don't kill ya, it'll sure cure ya."

They all laughed.

Eliza believed in feeding her guests, no matter whether they were hungry or not. "Y'all plan to stay for supper," she said then turned to Ophelia. "Put extra plates out for your grandma and grandpa."

While Eliza and her mother visited, Coleman talked with Mr. Harvey, who was anxious for news. Coleman told him about the siege of Atlanta.

"Have you heard what happened since you left?" asked his father-in-law.

"No."

"Atlanta fell. They say that Hood's Army is falling back to the North."

"What's the situation in Athens?" asked Coleman.

"Yankees'r thicker'n chiggers in a briar patch. They're everywhere. They constructed a fort on Edmondson Hill overlooking Athens – call it Fort Henderson. Bunch of Negro troops there.

"The Yankees are ridin' high in the saddle these days – they and their sympathizers. You gotta be careful, Coleman. If they learn that you're home they're liable to come out here and arrest you and burn y'all out."

"They won't know I'm home unless someone tells 'em," said Coleman.

"Folks say it's the Isoms."

"Which ones?'"

"Old man George Isom's bunch – Emmanuel, Matthew and William. I don't know that for a fact, but I do know they're Union sympathizers and don't care who knows it."

406

"It's a wonder someone hasn't paid 'em a visit," said Coleman.

"Sheriff McKinney has threatened to catch 'em and hang 'em, but as long as Federals occupy Athens, they're safe."

---

In the following days, as Coleman drank dogwood tea and whiskey, and ate fresh vegetables and fried rabbit, the flux slowly disappeared and he gained weight.

He didn't talk about the war, but in the back of his mind it was always present.

While strolling along Johnson Branch in the afternoon, Eliza squeezed Coleman's hand and said, "I've never seen a finer day."

"Nor a more peaceful one."

The fever was gone and now a different kind gripped him.

"Let's go to the Blue Hole and take a bath," he said.

"Someone might see us."

"Then let's walk up the sedge field," he said, looking in her eyes.

"Let's."

The yellow sedge grass swayed in the warm breeze. A rabbit jumped and ran. They walked behind a clump of blackberry briers and sat down. Coleman kissed Eliza gently, and then said, "I've been thinking about this moment ever since I left home." They kissed again – longer this time. Eliza moaned. "It's been so long my darling," she said.

"Too long," Coleman replied and gently pushed her back on the ground.

Afterwards, Coleman lay on his back, head resting in laced palms with Eliza nestled next to him. The sky was clear and the sun warmed their faces as a gentle breeze swayed the brown grass. Down by the branch crows cawed and blue jays argued.

"A man don't know how blessed he is until he's been to hell and lived to talk about it," said Coleman.

Eliza nodded.

"God blessed me with land, a good wife and fine healthy children and I left that to go off to fight. And for what?"

"For the cause–"

"Who's cause? My cause is you, the children and this land. Men with power stirred the pot to a boil and brought this war down on our heads. And we common folks are paying a high price for it. A rich man's war and a poor man's fight, they say. All I want to do is farm this land and be left alone with my family–"

"They won't leave us alone and you know it," she interrupted.

"Yeah, I know."

"Are you going back to the Army?" she reluctantly asked.

Coleman didn't answer for a long time. "Yeah, but not right away. There are more men absent from the Army than present. They've gone home to see after their families. Some have deserted."

He raised up and looked at Eliza. "Eliza, this war's lost."

"Don't say that."

"It's true. Men are sick, hungry, wear'n rags and march'n barefoot. The Yankees are well fed and equipped. It's just a matter of time before the end."

"Oh Coleman! You have suffered so much."

"I fear the worst is yet to come." A long silence.

407

"I want to see Ma and Pa before I leave," he finally said.

"It's too dangerous to go to Athens," said Eliza. "I'll send Bob and tell 'em you're home."

---

Atlanta. Thursday morning September 1, 1864.

Sergeant Patterson scurried along the trenches, passing the word, "The Army's moving out, but the 35th Regiment will bring up the rear."

"If it wasn't such an honor to stay and get killed, I'd just as soon get outta here right now," quipped Junior Bill.

Supplies and munitions were loaded onto wagons and the once-proud Army of Tennessee vacated Atlanta. The 35th and Stewart's Corps were the last to leave. All supplies that couldn't be hauled away were burned. Confederate cavalry blew up 81 railcars of arms and ammunition, flattening every building within a quarter-mile radius.

On September 2nd, Union forces marched into Atlanta unopposed.

Dudley and the 35th caught up with the army near Palmetto. On the 25th, President Davis, who had come to confer with Hood, had the men assembled for review. He rode past them in red mud, followed by Hood and staff. Dudley caught only a quick glimpse of the President but on this occasion he didn't look quite so impressive. In fact, he looked haggard. What Davis saw must have shocked him. Gaunt-faced men in dirty, tattered rags stared back at him as he rode past. They were hungry, exhausted and sick. Many were ill with dysentery and scurvy and most were barefoot. A diet of parched corn only whetted a man's appetite. There were few cheers. After the review, Davis gave a speech. The men didn't want to hear words; they wanted food and something else.

"We don't want a speech," someone yelled. "We want ol' Joe back."

The grand strategy, Dudley later learned, was that the army would move northwest, cross the Tennessee River and eventually seize Nashville, tearing up tracks and disrupting Sherman's supply line along the way. Hopefully, this would force Sherman to leave Georgia. If they captured Nashville, Federal warehouses bulging with food, clothing and equipment would be theirs.

On September 29th Hood's Army moved out of Lovejoy Station and marched northwest; crossed the Chattahoochee River; and intersected the Western and Atlantic Railroad tracks, which they began destroying for miles as Sherman's forces nipped at their heels.

Georgia peanuts had been added to the diet of parched corn. "Doggoneit, a body gets mighty tired of eating goober peas," groused Thornton.

"Yeah, but at least they won't crack your teeth like eat'n mule corn," replied Dudley.

Spotwood had memorized a song about goober peas and taught it to his messmates. There were many occasions, as they slogged down a dusty road that he would break out in song, joined by the boys.

*Sitting by the roadside on a summer's day*
*Chatting with my messmates, passing time away.*
*Lying in the shadows underneath the trees-*
*Goodness how delicious, eating goober peas.*

*When a horseman passes, the soldiers have a rule.*
*They shout out at their loudest, 'Mister, here's your mule!"*
*But another pleasure enchantinger than these*
*Is wearing out your grinders eating goober peas.*

*Just before battle, the general hears a row.*
*He says 'The Yanks are coming! I hear their rifles now!'*
*He turns around in wonder, and what do you think he sees?*
*The 35th Alabama eating goober peas!*

*I think my song has ended: it's lasted long enough.*
*The subject's interesting, but the rhymes are mighty rough.*
*I wish this war was over, when free from rags and fleas*
*We'd kiss our wives and sweethearts and gobble goober peas!'"*

Everyone jumped in on the chorus:
*Peas, peas, peas, peas, eatin' goober peas.*
*Goodness, how delicious, eatin' goober peas!*

The long column of hungry gray backs continued north, tearing up railroad tracks and destroying block houses. They reached Dalton on October 13th and the 35th attacked a fort, capturing 400 Negro troops and supplies of the 44th U.S. Regiment.

The landscape gradually changed from rolling hills to heavily timbered ridges and finally the more daunting Appalachian foothills, which they struggled mightily to cross. They had consumed their rations of goober peas and had been subsisting mostly on parched corn. A few handfuls a day barely kept a man alive. Dudley's feet were bruised and bleeding from stepping on briers and sharp rocks but so were the other men's. He didn't complain.

Autumn had come with all its usual glory. The oaks, maples and hickories shimmered with orange and rusty red foliage interspersed with yellow poplars and beechnuts. They drank from cold, clear streams that roared down the mountain and saw blue sky and felt the unique coolness that comes to the humid South only in the fall of the year.

On October 18, west of Dalton, where the country was mountainous and walking arduous, Sgt. Patterson came down the ragged line and announced: "Boys, Colonel Ives said that according to his calculations we crossed into Alabama few miles back."

A loud cheer went up from the men. "Ala-a-bama, how wonderful the sound of that name," Dudley said to no one in particular. He stepped out of the column and walked off into the bushes to relieve himself. Many of the men were sick with flux. After straining an empty gut he fell to his knees and kissed the earth. He was on Alabama soil and practically home. He wasn't particularly religious, but he prayed if God would deliver him from this hell on earth he would never leave home again and go whoring for glory. He would be contented with what God had given him.

The Army turned southwest toward Gadsden to avoid Union troops in Huntsville, and then headed to Guntersville to cross the Tennessee River. But there were too many Federals there. They continued toward Decatur, arriving nearby on the evening of October 26th. That night Dudley and his messmates were warming by a fire when Sgt. Patterson came by and informed them that the 35th had been assigned the honor of spearheading Loring's Division in assaulting Decatur.

"It'll be a feint to keep the Yankees occupied while the main army marches to Courtland and crosses the river," said Patterson.

"Every time they start talk'n honor a bunch of us get killed," quipped Junior Bill.

"Why doggoneit, we must be the most honorable regiment in the whole dang Confederate Army," added Thornton.

Sergeant Patterson frowned, shook his head and walked off.

"Right now, I'd trade all my honor for a hunk of cornbread and some of Ma's squirrel dumplings," Dudley said.

---

Friday, October 28th, 3:00 a.m.

A dense fog hung over the Tennessee River and enveloped Decatur as Dudley and the men of the 35th felt their way through darkness and pea soup toward the Federal entrenchments. They had been awake since 2 a.m., checking their rifles, drawing ammunition and wolfing down a few handfuls of parched corn. Loring's Division would demonstrate against the Federals while hood's main army marched to Courtland.

Dudley couldn't see his hands in front of him. If he bumped into a Yankee, he wouldn't know it. The only consolation was that the enemy couldn't see any better.

POW-POW-POW! Bullets whined and snapped past Dudley's head and he heard the unmistakable thud of a minie ball when it struck flesh. Someone moaned and crashed to the ground.

"It's Spotwood!" yelled Junior Bill.

"Damn!" cursed Thornton.

*A good kid. His dream of becoming a lawyer was dead like he probably was – or would be soon. Can't think about it. Too many people already dead. Damn the Yankees, damn this miserable war. Dudley kept moving forward.*

Yankee pickets increased their firing.

"DRIVE 'EM!" yelled Sergeant Patterson. The men shouldered their muskets and returned fire. The Yankee pickets fled back to their secure entrenchments. The 35th took possession of a ravine about 300 yards from the Federal line and began digging rifle pits that would soon be filled with sharpshooters.

Junior Bill leaned on his shovel handle and looked at Dudley, who was swinging a pick axe. "How fur do you reckon it's to hell?"

Dudley paused and wiped his brow. "About half way down in the earth. Why?"

"I figure if I stacked every hole I've dug end-on-end, since jinn'n the Army, I've dug fur enough to reach hell," said Junior Bill. "And that makes me feel mighty good."

"Good?"

"Yessire, that means if I chance to go to hell – and I hope I don't – I can dig my way out."

"I foresee a problem with that," Dudley said.

"What?"

"You'd have to dig up, not down. Where you gonna put the dirt?"

"Waal, I hadn't thought of that."

410

They went back to digging, avoiding talking about what was on everyone's mind.

Finally Dudley asked: "Reckon Spotwood's dead?"

"Maybe he got the Red Badge of Courage and he'll be sent home," said Jackson.

"He's deader 'n a doornail," said Thornton.

Silence.

"Nice boy," said Dudley. "Mighta been Governor someday."

"Him and his State's Rights," added Jackson.

"Damn fool kid. I ain't worry'n about it," said Junior Bill, turning his back, and flailing the earth with his pick axe. "Y'all get to digg'n. We got Yankees to kill. Anyway, he weren't such a good cook."

At 9 a.m. when the fog lifted, the Confederates were dug in with artillery in place, forming a semi-circle in front of the Yankees, whose backs were to the river.

"We got the Yanks in a hard spot," said Thornton, peeking toward their entrenchments while Confederate sharpshooters began taking shots of opportunity.

"I don't like it," said Dudley. "It's too quiet. They're up to something."

Suddenly, firing broke out on the Confederate left intermingled with yelling and it wasn't the Rebel yell.

"They flanked us!" Junior Bill shouted over the noise of rifle fire.

Dudley looked to his left and saw Confederates scrambling out of their rifle pits and running away. Blue coats were thicker than a nest of hornets and coming toward them.

"Let's git while we can!" shouted Junior Bill and climbed out of the rifle pit. Dudley, Jackson and Thornton were on his heels. They ran through a blizzard of lead. Federal artillery opened, sending grape shot and shells exploding over their heads. The morning sky was filled with descending iron and flying lead.

Dudley grasped his rifle with a death grip and ran as fast as his wiry legs could carry him. He looked back over his shoulders and saw men dropping. Others who couldn't run fast enough had their arms in the air, surrendering.

Confederate artillery returned fire. Dudley and the messmates watched from safety as Federal gunboat "Stone River" steamed up the Tennessee and blasted the Confederate batteries.

When night fell, fog again enveloped Decatur, bringing hostilities to a close. Cold settled in. Dudley hunkered in his hole, a tattered blanket around his shoulders, and shivered. His messmates were unusually quiet – rattled by what they had experienced.

"Doggoneit I ain't never seen our boys run like that," Thornton said.

"Yeah, we were running like rabbits," Jackson said.

"We done the right thing," added Junior Bill. "We're alive to fight another day."

"I guess that's a good way to look at it," said Jackson.

"We lost a lot of boys today," said Dudley. "We're lucky. We've been together since April, 1862 and are still alive while a bunch of others have been killed, wounded or captured."

"Doggoneit, one day our luck is gonna run out," Thornton said.

"I don't wanna hear it," said Junior Bill. "Anyhow, I wish you'd quit say'n 'doggoneit' all the time, it gets on my nerves."

"It's my bye word," said Thornton.

"Can't you find anuthern?"

411

Dudley lay back on the cold earth and closed his eyes. He was less than 15 miles from home. He'd give anything to see Ma and Pa if only for a few minutes and he'd love to see Cal and Cornelia and his nieces and nephews and even ol' Luther. He'd love to pull his long ears and hear him whine. Would he ever see his family again? Would he be killed by a minie ball like Spotwood or cut to shreds by grapeshot and canister? He didn't dare say it, nor did the men, but any fool could see that the war was lost. Instead the men spoke with their feet. They simply went home. He had lived through hell for almost three years, sick, hungry, scratching lice, chiggers, poison ivy and mosquito bites. Life couldn't possibly get any worse. But, he didn't go home.

During the night, Loring's Division began quietly withdrawing with the 35th Regiment bringing up the rear. They plodded toward Tuscumbia where the main army was encamped having decided to cross the river there. The 35th and 27th consolidated had lost 35 men, killed or wounded at Decatur. Yankee newspapers reported that 140 Rebels had been captured with a total loss of 1,200. Whomever one believed one fact was for certain: a lot of good men had fallen.

The Army of Tennessee had been whittled down to approximately 38,000 effectives. Death, wounds, disease, stragglers and deserters had taken a toll. Over 62,000 men were absent from that Army. The Army encampment stretched from Leighton to Tuscumbia, where the men rested, foraged for food among a friendly populace, and waited for Forrest's Cavalry to arrive.

Dudley and Junior Bill walked south foraging while Thornton and Jackson went north toward the river. In spite of constant carping the messmates had again chosen Junior Bill as their cook. They owned one skillet – a prized possession – which Junior Bill kept tied to his knapsack.

"Tonight this here skillet'll be sizzl'n with fried chicken,' he bragged.

"I guess you've been invited to supper with ol' Jeff Davis himself," replied Dudley.

"Shorely, some of these good folks'll have some chickens they'll share with us," said Junior Bill.

"How many chickens have you seen running around?" asked Jackson.

"Come to think of it, not any."

The wide valley that stretched between the Tennessee River on the north and the low mountain country to the south was some of the finest farm land that Dudley had seen anywhere. A lot of cotton remained in the fields, unpicked, with long white locks hanging out of the bolls and touching the ground. Acres of brown corn stalks sagged under the weight of ungathered ears. He saw few horses, mules and cattle. Crops had been planted, but slaves to gather them had fled. Roving Yankee cavalry had taken livestock and burned many fine homes.

They approached a two-story frame house located in a grove of cedar trees and stopped at the front gate.

"Halloo!" Junior Bill called out.

Shortly, an elderly man appeared on the front porch and inquired, "Can I help you?"

"We're looking for something to eat," Dudley said.

The old man hobbled to the gate and looked them over. "Y'all Confederates?"

"Yessirreee, and darned proud of it," replied Junior Bill.

"Well, it isn't hard to figure out. Yankees are fat and Rebels are half starved,"

412

said the man. "Appreciate you asking instead of coming and stealing what you want. Between thieving Yankee cavalry and thieving Confederates, I've just about been cleaned out. The smokehouse was cleaned out long ago with the chickens."

"I shore had my mind set on fried chicken for dinner," said Junior Bill.

"We have sweet and Irish potatoes and, of course, corn," the old gentleman said. The crib is empty but y'all are welcome to pick all you want in the field. There's turnips and beets in the garden. Take a few of 'em but please leave us some."

"We sure appreciate it," said Dudley.

They stuffed their knapsacks with potatoes, beets, turnips and ears of corn and found a spot by a meandering stream where they built a small fire. While sweet potatoes baked inside a mud crust in hot coals, Dudley and Junior Bill gnawed on raw turnips.

"If the Confederate government expects us to gnaw food like a squirrel they oughta issue us a file so we can sharpen our teeth," said Dudley.

Later, they cracked the mud shells from around the sweet potatoes revealing soft, orange meat inside.

"All we need is a spoonful of fresh butter and they would be just like Ma makes 'em," Dudley said.

"Earline makes the best sweet potato casserole I ever et," said Junior Bill. "Butter'n sugar stirred in sweet potatoes and cooked in the oven till the sugar forms a crust on top. Uhm humm, now that's good eatin.'" Junior Bill grew quiet as he ate the potato. "I'd give a Yankee dollar to see Earline," he finally said.

"Yeah, I'd like to see my folks too," said Dudley. "We're so close to home."

"I love to hear you say 'home,'" said Junior Bill. "There ain't nuthin' like it... 'cept when I hear Earline's name. Jest as soon as this here war's over, I'm gonna marry that gal." Junior Bill looked east toward Limestone County and smiled. "Yessir, I gonna do it."

ER-ER-ER.

Dudley cocked his head and listened. "Did you hear that?"

"Hear what?"

"It sounded like a rooster crowing."

ER-ER-ER.

"It's a rooster!" exclaimed Dudley.

"That old man lied to us," said Junior Bill. "He's got chickens. Com'on!"

They grabbed their knapsacks and took off running toward the sound. In a clearing, perched atop a rail fence, was a Rhode Island Red rooster with a big red crown and long droopy tail feathers. Dudley held up his hand to halt. "Shhhh, there he is," he pointed.

"Fried chicken tonight," Junior Bill prophesied.

"Okay, we'll flank him," whispered Dudley. "I'll sneak around behind 'im and when I'm ready, you charge from the front."

They found sticks. When Dudley was behind the rooster, Junior Bill approached from the front. The rooster watched Junior Bill while Dudley crept up behind him, raised the stick over his head and came down with a mighty blow. The rooster jumped sideways just in time to avoid the stick.

"Don't worry, I'll get him!" exclaimed Junior Bill, taking a swing at the feathered fowl.

The rooster dodged, jumped from the rail and took off running and zigzagging

413

as Dudley and Junior Bill ran behind him flailing with sticks. The rooster ran through woods, into a cornfield, through a cotton field and doubled back to the rail fence as Dudley and Junior Bill swung at him with sticks.

"STAND AND FIGHT YOU COWARD!" yelled Junior Bill. Suddenly, the rooster turned, jumped into the air and spurred Junior Bill on the thigh.

"No rooster attacks me and lives to crow about it!" exclaimed Junior Bill and swung his stick. The agile rooster jumped and took off running. Dudley and Junior Bill were gasping for air as the rooster steadily gained ground on them. They stopped, bent over with hands on knees, trying to catch their breath.

"Maybe we should have offered him some corn first, then whacked him," said Dudley.

"Or shot 'im!" Junior Bill added.

"Now, why didn't' we think of that?" asked Dudley.

Later, they dragged into camp, tired and disappointed and found Thornton and Jackson with a five-pound catfish hanging from a hickory stick threaded through its gills.

"What'd ya trade for that?" asked Junior Bill.

"Now, what would we have to trade 'cept lice, chiggers and fleas? I caught it," said Thornton.

Junior Bill laughed.

"You don't have hook'n line. What'd ya do, outrun it in a foot race?"

"He grabbed it," said Jackson. "Got down in the river and stuck his hand up on a rock crevice and caught that fish. Shore did."

"Git the skillet Junior Bill," said Thornton. "We gonna eat fried catfish for supper."

When Junior Bill went to his knapsack the skillet was missing. "I lost it," he said almost in a whisper.

"Doggoneit, don't joke us," said Thornton.

"I ain't joking."

The men stared at Junior Bill in disbelief. "How'd you lose it?" asked Jackson.

"Chasing a rooster."

"Well doggoneit, if that don't beat all," Thornton said.

After gorging themselves on roasted catfish they sat around the fire and passed a pipe.

"Stop fretting Junior Bill," said Jackson. "Losing our skillet was just bad luck."

"Yeah, this Army's been plagued with bad luck ever since Hood took command," commented Thornton.

Dudley thought he heard singing in the distance and cocked his head and listened, "Shhh" he said. The men grew quiet.

Yes, it was singing. Others joined in and it became louder. The men were singing "Home Sweet Home" and the beautiful and sad melody was picked up by other camps until the entire Army was singing. Dudley fought back tears as he remembered the hot August day back home when he was only 10 years old and the family fasted and prayed and Pa had played "Home Sweet Home" on his fiddle. Now, he could only listen. Home was so near, yet so far away. When the men tried to sing only a few halting words came forth. They listened and choked back tears.

414

# 40 | RIDING WITH BUSHWHACKER

Hayes Store, Madison County, Alabama
August, 1864.

Robert Beasley Barksdale at age 34 was slim and straight as a rail, his body hardened by shocking hay and fodder and working from can 'til can't plowing, cutting firewood and clearing new ground. Married for 8 years, he was doing his dead-level best to mind his own business and remain out of the fratricidal conflict that raged around him. He figured his business was taking care of his wife Lucy and their 7-year-old daughter, Mary Beasley, whom they called "Mollie." His father-in-law, John Giddens, a prominent citizen and former Tax Assessor of Madison County, had died two years earlier and he and Lucy continued to live on the family farm near New Market. Except for the damnable Yankees, Robert's life was as good as could be expected under the circumstances. North of the Tennessee River, Bluecoats were thicker than mites on a chicken. They came like locusts destroying everything in their path, invading houses and stealing quilts, bedspreads, eating utensils and jewelry. They took horses, mules, hogs and livestock; cleaned out smokehouses; arrested citizens without legal cause; plundered; burned and killed. If a son was serving in the Confederate Army, Union soldiers burned down the family homestead. They dragged citizens from their homes if they were suspected of feeding guerillas and shot them in cold blood while family members looked on, begging and pleading.

In December, 1863, four members of the Roden family who lived five miles upriver from Guntersville, along with Charles Hardcastle, on leave from the 50th Alabama Regiment, went to Buck Island in the middle of the Tennessee River to check on corn and horses kept there. Captain Ben Harris, a local homemade Yankee, arrested the men, lined them up, shot them in cold blood and tossed their bodies in the river. Hardcastle, though wounded, played dead and escaped to tell the story.

That was unsettling enough, but when Robert heard about the recent Davis murder it shook his very foundation.

Patrick Davis, a seventeen-year-old who lived in the Brownsboro community with his widowed mother and numerous siblings, was hauled before Colonel Edward Anderson and asked to take the oath of allegiance. He refused. When he was asked which Army he would choose if he had to enlist, he said that he was taking care of his mother and her family and he wouldn't go in either Army. But, if he was forced to enlist, he would go in the Southern Army. Colonel Anderson kept him locked up overnight before giving him a pass to go home. Anderson sent out a squad of men with orders to kill him. They tied Davis to a tree near Maysville and pumped 14 bullets into him and carried his body into the mountains and threw it into a sinkhole.

The murder touched Robert's core. Enough was enough.

August was the hottest and driest month of the year. Grass and weeds were scorched and the leaves on the large oak trees in the yard had turned brown and curled at the end. It was twilight, Robert's favorite time of the day when the earth began to cool and doves cooed and whippoorwills called. The family was sitting on the porch hoping to catch a breeze as they watched the last streaks of red disappear below the horizon while the hounds lazed about, flicking flies off their long ears.

Robert filled his pipe half full of tobacco, being careful to conserve his small remaining supply, fired the contents, took a deep pull and looked vacantly toward the gray mountains in the east. Lucy slowly rocked back and forth, the runners creaking on the boards, and quietly played a pat-a-cake hand game with young Mollie.

Robert couldn't erase the Davis murder from his mind. Perhaps because it had occurred so near home – Brownsboro was just down the road – or maybe it was because the boy was so young. How would the widow Davis survive with her boy dead? What if Yankees came here and dragged him out and jailed him? Or worse, shot him? Lucy and Mollie would be cast onto a harsh world. Perhaps, the wisest course of action was no action at all; keep his mouth shut, continue minding his own business and scratching a living out of the soil, and hope that the damnable war would soon be over. Farming for profit was nigh impossible. He worked a few acres of corn with a bony bay horse that he kept hidden in the woods; raised a few hogs and chickens for food, but just as he was getting ahead, foraging Yankees came through and took what they wanted.

Sitting on the fence and doing nothing while the world around him collapsed didn't meet his standard of manhood. Duty tugged hard at his mind. Someone had once said that evil triumphs when good men do nothing. And it was true. His grandfather Micajah McElroy had fought the Tories in North Carolina; Uncles Arch and Mike McElroy had battled the Redcoats at New Orleans; his brothers, Dudley, James Greer and William Coleman were currently fighting Yankees – exactly where, he didn't know – and three of his McElroy cousins were riding with Forrrest. The Confederate Postal system barely functioned and it was next to impossible to correspond by mail. He hadn't heard from Ma and Pa over in Athens for so long he couldn't remember.

He figured the only way to stop evil is to destroy it.

"A penny for your thoughts," Lucy said.

"I was thinking about the Davis boy – so young to die like that."

"I think of poor ol' Mrs. Davis too," said Lucy. "With a houseful of kids, how in the world will she survive?"

"It'll be hard." Robert sucked on his pipe and retreated to his thoughts. Prospects of winning the war had dimmed. When word got out that he had enlisted, Yankees might burn out his family. Where would they go? To whom would they turn for help? Lucy had relatives in the area, or perhaps they could go live with Ma and Pa in Athens. He had no answer. But, he knew one thing for certain: doing nothing wouldn't stamp out the evil.

That night while Mollie slept, Robert discussed his dilemma with Lucy.

"I can't get it off my mind," he said quietly. "Men with families just like me are fight'n and sacrific'n–"

"–and you feel guilty about being at home –"

"That's part of it," he said, "but mostly I feel it's my duty to protect my family and my home and not depend on someone else to do it."

"A man must follow his heart," Lucy said.

Robert nodded. "Yeah, the call of duty is hard to ignore."

"You do what you think is right and I'll support you proudly," she said.

---

Shocking news came in early September. Atlanta had fallen to Sherman! The South had suffered a mighty blow. Nevertheless, on a crisp Saturday morning, October 1st when trees on the high ridge were turning orange and yellow, Robert saddled Johnnie and rode to Concord Campground, near Hazel Green and enlisted for the duration of the

416

war in a company organized by James M. Robinson. A few days later, he rose early in the morning, pulled on his sweat-stained black hat, fed his horse fodder and two ears of corn, and walked around the homestead. The sow and her litter of pigs were already out in the woods rooting for acorns and the chickens were running free and scratching for food. Hopefully, the Yankees wouldn't find them. Several cords of wood had already been cut and stacked and a turn of cornmeal was in the bin.

After breakfast he saddled Johnnie and led him to the front yard. Lucy handed him a sack containing food, socks, and a change of clothes, which he tied to the back of his saddle.

He hoisted little Mollie into his arms and kissed her on both cheeks, then hugged her tightly for several seconds as she clung to him.

"Papa will be gone for a little while," he said. "You take care of your Ma and help her out. Okay?"

"Yes Papa."

He broke away her clinging arms and put her down and looked at Lucy, who was fighting back tears.

"Don't worry about me," he said. "I'll be back and check on you when I can. Take care of yourself and Mollie." He hugged her tightly then kissed her and turned and mounted his horse and rode away. His heart ached. Would he ever see the old home place again and hold his Lucy and romp with little Mollie? He didn't want to think about it.

He was assigned Company A, 7th Alabama Cavalry and ordered to join the main Army at Shelbyville, Tennessee. Third Lieutenant, B.W. Roseborough of Lincoln County, Tennessee, rode with him.

When they neared Old Salem, Lt. Roseborough eyed the bony bay horse that Robert rode and said "I believe that's the ugliest horse I've ever seen. His ears are almost as long as his legs."

"He ain't much to look at, but he can pull a plow, hear better than a coon and outrun any horse'n these parts."

"Ha-ha-ha," Roseborough laughed and shook his head in disbelief. "Why that bag of bones looks like he might drop dead any minute."

"He can outrun that nag you're rid'n any day of the week," Robert replied with a twinkle in his eye.

"Not by a long shot," replied Rosenborough.

They were on a long, straight stretch of dirt road when Roseborough kicked his mare's flanks and yelled: "Git up!" The horse bolted forward, Roseborough grabbing the brim of his hat. Robert kicked the bay – "Go Johnnie!" – and gave him rein. The horses thundered down the road, Johnnie a dozen links behind, creating a cloud of dust. Roseborough's mare was fast, but soon began to tire. "Run Johnnie run," Robert said. The long ears perked up momentarily, then swung backward as the horse ran faster. Soon he was neck and neck with the mare.

"Laugh now," Robert hollered as he inched ahead and took the lead.

"Enough!" Roseborough yelled.

They reined and both horses were lathered and breathing hard.

Roseborough couldn't believe what had just happened. "That's bay may be ugly but he sure can run," he admitted. "I hope I haven't ruined my mare."

The Confederate Secretary of War had authorized Captain Lemuel G. Mead, a

417

lawyer from Paint Rock in Jackson County, Alabama, to raise troops with the view of forming a battalion or regiment from within enemy lines, north of the Tennessee River. He began recruiting in the summer of 1862 with limited success. However, when Union forces reoccupied North Alabama in the fall of 1863 volunteers flocked to his ranks.

Promoted to Colonel, Mead named Captain Milus E. Johnston commander of Company E of Mead's Cavalry Battalion in January, 1864.

When Robert Barksdale learned of the cavalry battalion, he and James Ragsdale, also of the New Market community, immediately requested to be transferred to it. They made a good argument. Both were familiar with practically every pig trail and stream in the area of operation. Not only that, they would be committed fighters to protect their homes and neighbors from marauding Yankees. Their prime motive, of course was to be near their homes and family. The transfer was forthcoming. They were ordered to report to Johnston, now a Major, who was temporarily encamped south of the Tennessee River near Vienna.

It was late November and biting cold when they rode south out of Tennessee toward New Market, in no hurry to report to Major Johnston. First, they wanted to stop and check on their families. Robert ached to hold Lucy and Mollie in his arms. He hadn't seen nor received a letter from them since departing home on October 1st. All along his route, he witnessed burned houses and barns. He was sick with worry about Lucy and Mollie. If they had suffered because he had joined the Confederate Army, he could never forgive himself.

Moonlight bathed the countryside with a soft glow and off to the east, silhouetted against the sky, was a gray mountain undulating toward Huntsville. Hayes Store and home wasn't too far away.

When they reached the outskirts of New Market, Ragsdale reined his horse. "Well, this is where I part," he said. "I'll see you day after tomorrow on the way out."

"I'll see you then," replied Robert.

Robert rode on, the cold cutting his skin like a knife. The only sound was the "clump – clump" of hooves and occasional snorting of his mount. He topped a rise in the road and where he expected to see a glowing light in the window, he saw nothing. The modest, single-story dwelling was silhouetted in the moonlight and the chimney was clearly visible. Thin streams of smoke should have been curling from it. Nothing. He was beside himself with anticipation. He kicked his mount and galloped forward. Where were the hounds? They should have already been alerted, barking and howling. He rode up to the porch, slid out of the saddle and rushed to the front door.

"Lucy! Mollie!"

Inside the house was pitch dark. But he knew every square inch blindfolded. He dashed from room to room, hollering. "Lucy... Mollie where are you?"

Furniture was still in place. He rushed back to the bedroom, felt under the bed for a small trunk. It wasn't there. No doubt Lucy had packed a few items of clothes and fled with Mollie to live with relatives or neighbors. His fear dissipated.

If they weren't with his neighbor, Thomas Pitts, he would surely know their whereabouts. He mounted and sped off. When he rode into the yard, dogs ran out, barking and snarling. It was risky to ride up at night in these dangerous times. People were afraid. And they were also armed. He called out. "Hallooo, Mr. Pitts!"

Shortly, a door opened and Thomas Pitts stepped out holding a lamp. "Who is it?"

"Robert Barksdale."

"You out mighty late," said Pitts and called off the dogs. "Get down come inside and warm up."

"I appreciate it, but I'm looking for Lucy and Mollie," said Robert.

"I heard they went down to John's. Yankees come through here several days ago, stealing and cussing women folks and generally scaring people, so Lucy left."

"Much obliged," Robert said and galloped off.

It was near midnight when he rode into his brother-in-law's yard, near Maysville, alerting a half dozen dogs to active duty. No lights glowed from inside the house.

"Johnnn!" he waited and a moment. "Johnnn!"

The latch clicked and the front door squeaked open.

"Who is it?" a man's voice asked.

"It's me Robert. Is Lucy and Mollie here?"

"Whew, you scared the dickens outta me," John said. "I thought it was Yankees. Yeah, they're here. What are you doing out this time of night?"

"Passing through on the way to join Bushwhacker Johnston."

"Come inside and thaw out," said John. "I'll put up your horse."

The disturbance woke Lucy, who was holding a lamp when he entered the house. She set down the lamp and rushed toward him with open arms. "Ohhh, Robert! Are you okay? You're so cold you've turned blue."

"I'm okay," he said, embracing her. "How about you?"

"Making do. I got scared and left home after Yankees came through cussing and threatening to burn us out. They wanted to know where my husband was. I lied and told them that I was a widow."

"How's Mollie?"

"Fit as a fiddle and asleep, with John's girls."

"I want to see her," Robert said, grabbing the lamp and tiptoeing into the room where several children were piled in one bed, snuggled together and fast asleep. He bent down and gently kissed her forehead, careful not to wake her. He stood and looked at her for a long time, his heart bursting with joy. He wanted to pull her into his arms and squeeze her and never let go.

Later, Robert cuddled close to Lucy in a featherbed, feeling her warmth and smelling her unique sweetness.

"You are nearly frozen, I'll warm you," she whispered and scooted against him until his coldness had been replaced with hot desire. Both were hungry for each other and after they were filled, they collapsed into a deep and satisfying sleep.

---

Crossing the Tennessee River into Dixie in the middle of winter with Yankee gunboats plying the waters and patrols on the north bank proved to be a challenge. Robert and James Ragsdale made contact with a Confederate sentry across the river by whistling a verse of *Dixie*, which was answered with another verse.

"Where y'all head'n?" the sentry asked in a hushed tone.

"Looking for Preacher Johnston," Robert replied in a loud whisper.

"Hide and we'll send a boat after dark," the sentry said.

Barksdale and Ragsdale hid in a canebrake on high ground. The greatest danger

419

was the horses neighing if Federal cavalry rode near. They saw a Yankee gunboat steam up river looking for targets of opportunity. Near sundown, the two horses suddenly turned their heads and looked in the same direction, ears pointing.

"Someone's coming," whispered Robert. They placed their palms over the horses' muzzles and gentry stroked them. One neigh and their position would be revealed. Voices. Robert's heart beat so loudly he was sure it could be heard by the approaching men. The voices grew louder. He caught a glimpse of several blue coats and heard them more clearly. They were well out of range of Confederate sharpshooters across the river and were discussing getting back to camp and a warm fire.

Ragsdale exhaled. "That was close."

"Yeah, I was so scared, I forgot about being cold," Robert whispered.

"I'm freez'n to death," Ragsdale said. "I can't feel my nose. Is it still there?"

"It's mighty blue, but it's there," replied Robert, massaging his fingers that felt like wood.

After darkness fell, someone across the river whistled a verse of *Dixie*. Robert answered.

"Y'all boys gett'n cold?" asked the sentry.

"Freez'n," replied Robert.

A paddle slapped the water and then a clunking noise as a boat bumped against the near bank.

"Y'all need to hurry," a voice said in the darkness. "Never can tell when Yankees'll show up."

The crossing was uneventful except that the horses were reluctant to enter the cold water. Once in, they swam to the opposite bank, climbed out and shook, flinging cold water in all directions. The sentry pointed south. "Y'all can find Major Johnston about a mile thataway."

Robert and Ragsdale rode into an encampment where men hovered around numerous fires. "We're looking for Major Johnston," said Robert.

"That's him yonder," a trooper said, pointing to a tall, slender man with a full beard. They reined and slid from their saddles.

"We looking for Preacher Johnston," said Robert.

"I'm Johnston," the man said, offering his hand. "Some of my parishoners called me Reverend, others Preacher. Yankees call me Bushwhacker, but you can call me Major."

"Yes sir Major," said Robert and Ragsdale in unison.

"You boys look like you're nearly frozen," said Johnston. "Gather round the fire and warm yourselves." He noticed that both men were eyeing a coffee pot resting on warm coals. "Pour yourselves a cup of Dixie Rio. It's parched wheat and rye, but it'll warm your insides."

They poured a cupful of the black liquid and took a sip. "Ahhh," said Ragsdale smacking his lips. "It ain't coffee, but it ain't bad."

Robert learned that he and Major Johnston shared something in common – both had once lived in Lincoln County, Tennessee. In 1862, Reverend Johnston was in charge of the Fayetteville Circuit of the Methodist-Episcopal Church, South when General Ormsby Mitchell's Army invaded.

"I was born in Fayetteville in 1833," said Robert. "Ma's folks are McElroys."

"Oh yes, I've met many of them. Good people," Johnston replied.

"Thank you sir."

"I was minding my own business, which is the Lord's business, when the Yankees arrested me without cause, preventing me from tending my flock. They even took my horse," snorted Johnston. "Finally, I moved my family to Vienna, near my wife's folks. They burned us out three times. That's when I decided to put preaching aside for a while and pick up a gun."

"I understand," Robert said nodding. "I had hoped to remain out of the conflict, but it was nigh impossible. Yankees came stealing, murdering and burning out innocent people. After they murdered the Davis boy, I knew I couldn't sit on the fence any longer."

Johnston grew steely-eyed. "'Vengeance belongeth to me, saith the Lord,' Hebrews 10, verse 30. However, someone has to wield the Lord's sword," he said. "I'm glad to serve him in that capacity."

Johnston was a preacher, but Robert also saw something else. He was a tough, determined man – and he had God on his side. He decided he liked his new battalion commander.

He and Ragsdale were assigned to Company G commanded by Colonel W. M. Campbell.

The partisan band operated inside Union lines in Madison and Jackson counties and like all guerilla units their mission was to raid, create havoc and generally disrupt Union military operations. They would strike, then escape south across the Tennessee River into "Dixie" for sanctuary.

# 41 | FORREST CAPTURES ATHENS

Athens, Alabama.

Friday, September 23, 1864.

It was near 4 p.m. with clouds gathering in the west when Daniel Barksdale and Thomas walked out the back door of their home and strolled over to the vegetable garden where turnip greens had been sown the previous week. The young sprouts should be peeping through the earth any day now. Two geese waddled through the patch, pausing frequently to scratch and peck. Pa bent over and picked up a small stone and threw it at the geese. "Shoo- shoo outta there."

"It's sure dry," Thomas.

"Yeah, we need a good rain."

"BOOOOOM!"

"Is that thunder?" asked Pa, straightening and looking west.

Tom squinted toward Athens. "It ain't thunder."

"BOOOOM..... BOOOOM."

"It sounds like cannon fire," Pa said.

"BOOOOM... BOOOOOM."

"It is!" exclaimed Tom.

"Is it us or them?"

"I'd say it's com'n from the Yankee fort," Thomas replied.

The unmistakable rattle of musketry commenced. It sounded like a big fight was shaping up.

Pa seldom went to Athens. He didn't have any money to spend, but mostly he didn't enjoy being harassed by Yankee soldiers. They strutted about like they owned the town. He had seen the fort located west of town near the Daniel Coleman mansion several weeks earlier when he had hitched up the buggy and driven Ma to town to visit her sister, Sallie David. After dropping her off at the Davids' house, he sallied down the Browns Ferry Road and drove past Fort Henderson.

The Federals had constructed an earthen work measuring about 180 by 450 feet on the crest of the hill. The dirt walls were at least four feet high and festooned with spikes and brush. Outside the wall was a ditch about twelve feet wide. The fort was garrisoned with approximately 1,000 troops of which folks estimated at least 600 were Negroes.

Pa and Thomas went back inside the house where the women had also heard the firing. "Everybody stay inside," Pa said.

The cannon and musket firing continued off and on all day. As night fell Cal stood peering out the west window toward Athens. "Look!" she exclaimed.

Everyone rushed over. A large red glow lit up the night sky.

"It looks like they're burn'n Athens!" exclaimed Thomas.

Moments later, George Edward burst through the back door with news.

"Our boys are giving the Yankees some of their own medicine," he said smiling.

"Who is it – General Wheeler or General Roddy?" Pa asked.

"Don't know for sure," replied George Edward, "but they cut the railroad tracks and wires south of town. The Yankees are in an uproar, firing at everything that moves. They set Roswell Hine's store on fire so they could see movement. It spread to William Hine's. Then they burned Press Tanner's store."

Thomas sat on guard all night in a chair near the window. No telling what the Yankees might do. Finally, a thunderstorm moved through and the large drops of rain splattering against the window lulled him to sleep.

---

Earlier in Athens, Postmaster Robert C. David stood inside his darkened house and looked out his living room window toward downtown where flames leapt high into the air, illuminating the square. Cannon fire thundered, rattling his windows, as Federals at Fort Henderson shelled the woods south of town. Musket fire sounded like corn popping, and at the jail, muzzle flashes spurted from windows. It appeared that most of the Federal firing was directed toward the depot where the fight had begun near 4 p.m. when Confederates had blocked the train north of town that was coming from Nashville.

Sallie clung to her husband's arm. "Why do they have to burn?" she asked.

"In order to see," he replied. "They don't care who they hurt."

"Please get away from the window," she begged and tugged at his arm. David felt his way to his favorite chair where he sank down in the dark, eyes closed, and listened as shells screamed through the night sky and bullets cracked through foliage and tree limbs. Finally, around 11 p.m., the firing ceased and he went to bed. Sometimes during the night he heard thunder followed by rain splattering against the window panes.

Saturday morning came early for David. When the clock struck five, he rose and dressed, anxious to see what damage had been inflicted on Athens. Skipping his usual coffee, at first light he pulled on his hat and quietly exited his residence. He had never seen a quieter nor more peaceful morning. The troops of the 110th and 111th U.S. Colored Infantry had returned to Fort Henderson. Fall was in the air and the tops of the big oaks that lined Jefferson Street were beginning to turn rusty orange. Limbs and leaves lay scattered beneath them, sheared off by minie balls.

On the square, damp coals smoldered, sending up plumes of smoke in the still air from the rubble that had once housed fine mercantile stores. Except for smoke and ashes, smashed windows and broken fences, Athens appeared to be a peaceful community.

David was headed to the post office when the early morning quietness was shattered by the clatter of hoofbeats, creaking saddles and the clanging of equipment. Riding slowly down Jefferson Street toward the courthouse and churning up mud was a column of 25 to 30 Confederate cavalry. An officer asked a passerby if there were any Yankees in town.

"Over yonder at the fort," the man pointed. The column continued south.

Following some distance behind was a much longer column. Riding in front was a tall, slender man wearing a gray uniform and broad brim hat turned up on one side, giving him an air of importance. A shock of gray hair protruded from beneath his hat, quite a contrast to his short black beard and mustache. David immediately recognized the rider – General Nathan Bedford Forrest.

---

At 7 a.m. Forrest's battery of eight guns opened fire on Fort Henderson and pounded it for two hours. One cannon was positioned in the Negro graveyard north of the fort and the first shot demolished a house outside the fort and ripped off a Negro woman's head.

423

Fearing that it would be costly to overrun the fort, Forrest hatched up a plan to hoodoo the commander, Colonel Wallace Campbell. At about 9 a.m., Forrest sent forth his Adjutant, Major John P. Strange, under a flag of truce demanding surrender. Campbell agreed to meet with Forrest down the hill near where Town Creek crossed Browns Ferry Road.

Forrest sat tall in the saddle, a grim look on his weathered face.

"Colonel, Suh, I intend to take the fort," he said. "And have it I will. I have sufficient force to do it. If I am forced to storm the works, it will result in a massacre of the entire garrison."

Colonel Campbell swallowed hard, knowing that Forrest had stormed Ft. Pillow in Tennessee and killed 350 Negro troops after they refused to surrender.

"General, how many men do you have in your command?"

"Ten thousand," replied Forrest without hesitation. "If you doubt that, you and one officer may review my force."

Campbell returned to the fort and discussed the offer with his officers. If Forrest did have 8,000 to 10,000 men, it would be suicide to attempt to hold the works.

Meanwhile, Forrest prepared to activate the second prong of his plan of deception, one that had worked successfully against Col. Abel Streight. He ordered his soldiers march and countermarch through the streets of Athens, making it appear that it was a much larger force than it was. Colonel Campbell needed time. Hopefully re-enforcements from Decatur would soon arrive.

He and Forrest rode around town. Rebels were seemingly swarming around everywhere. Campbell managed to stretch out the negotiations for three hours, hoping that troops from Decatur would appear any minute.

"General, I need more time," he said.

"No suh, your time is up," replied Forrest.

"General, I must confer with my officers," said Campbell. "I'll let you know my decision directly." He went back to the fort and told his staff that the "jig is up."

Hoisting a flag of truce, Colonel Campbell and his escort rode down the hill on Browns Ferry Road. Townspeople, seeing the flag and thinking that surrender was imminent, sent up a great roar of shouts and cheering which continued for several minutes. They had suffered much under the heels of the Yankees who finally had their comeuppance.

Forrest met Colonel Campbell and his men in the middle of the road near the corner of Samuel H. Crenshaw's residence just before 1 p.m. and walked over to his yard.

Colonel Wheeler rode up. Forrest, ever the wily one, saluted and said, "General Wheeler, suh."

Colonel Wheeler, quickly catching onto the ruse, returned the salute. Campbell thought it was General Joseph Wheeler, the famed Confederate cavalry leader.

"How many men do you have?" asked Forrest.

"Seven thousand."

"Where are they?"

"Right down the road," replied Colonel Wheeler, pointing west. "They're about a mile away."

Colonel Campbell had seen and heard enough. "I surrender, General Forrest," he said quietly.

Union officers passed around cigars to the Confederate brass and they all lit up and smoked. Campbell surrendered approximately 900 men, all of his arms and supplies.

Although Forrest had 4500 men under his command, a much smaller number were available to assault Fort Henderson. The rest were thrown out in all directions guarding his main force in Athens.

Shortly, a brigade of approximately 700 bluecoats marching from Decatur were attacked by Forrest's men from the rear and driven toward Athens where Forrest attacked them. They surrendered along with two block houses guarding the railroad north and south of Athens. Forrest burned the wooden building inside Fort Henderson. In all, Forrest bagged 1,300 Yankees, 38 wagons, 300 horses, much supplies, two cannons and a large quantity of fire arms.

---

Early Sunday morning, September 25th.

General Forrest's cavalry rode north out of Athens, tearing up tracks, burning cross ties and bending rails around trees, arriving at Sulphur Creek Trestle before daybreak. The wooden trestle was approximately 100 feet long and rose about 75 feet above Sulphur Creek and guarding it was a large block house located on high ground, south of the creek. Garrisoned by 400 colored infantry and 500 cavalry troops, it was an imposing redoubt. Its only weakness was the surrounding hills that were higher in elevation. Forrest positioned his battery of eight guns on the four surrounding hills and sent in his usual demand of surrender. It was refused. The eight cannons opened up near daybreak, firing 800 rounds in two hours. The Union troops made no real resistance. Their commander had been killed. When Forrest made a second demand for surrender, it was forthcoming.

Anne Grigsby, a young slave girl, was holed up in the two-story brick Grigsby house nearby and watched spurts of fire as the attack was started and heard spent bullets fall on the roof like rain.

"De nex' day, after de sojers was gone, my masoter tuk me over here," she later related. "Ev' thin wuz upside down. Trees was cut off near de ground. Dey wuz trenches filled wid dead men, wid hogs in dere a-rootin's dem up."

The death toll was staggering. More than 200 soldiers were dead, some blown apart with shells. Forrest captured two guns, twenty wagons and teams, 350 cavalry horses and ammunition and supplies. After burning the block house and trestle Forrest headed north toward Pulaski, Tennessee.

---

On Monday morning, Daniel Barksdale hitched up his buggy and drove to town. He would go by the post office and see his brother-in-law, Robert C. David. There might be a letter from one of his boys. But mostly, he was anxious to learn what had happened in Athens.

Ol' Maude strained against the harness as the buggy creaked and wobbled down the Fayetteville Pike. She was the only horse remaining that Yankees hadn't taken. Though her teeth were worn to the gum, she could still pull a plow. They sloshed into Swan Creek where the nag stopped in mid-stream and sucked up cold water. Pa never pushed her hard. When she had drunk all the water she wanted, she lifted her head, blew and walked forward, grunting as she climbed the slightly inclined creek bank.

They wobbled past the Golighty mansion just across the creek on the left, then went by "The Cedars," Captain Jim Henry Malone's two-story mansion that sat on a rise in a grove of cedar trees.

In the distance, he saw the large columned building that housed the Athens Female Institute. It was a darn wonder the Yankees hadn't burned it. Farther on, when he neared the railroad tracks, something caught his attention. There were no tracks! Up and down the railroad bed, there was nothing but rocks and cinder gravel. All of the rails and cross ties had been ripped out and what appeared to be the end of cross ties smoldered in gray ashes. Rails had been heated by the burning cross ties and then bent around trees. As far north as he could see, there were piles of smoldering crossties and bent rails.

He hitched the mare to the fence that surrounded the courthouse and walked to the post office. Many people were milling about the square, mostly Confederate soldiers. The one thing he didn't see were Yankee guards and pickets that constantly harassed folks. The only Yankees remaining in Athens appeared to be prisoners and the wounded.

There was an unmistakable spring in the steps of citizens. Maybe the Yankees were gone forever.

David was standing at a tall desk, sorting the few letters that came through and poking them into cubby holes, when Pa walked into the post office.

"Morn'n," he said.

David looked up and smiled at his brother-in-law.

"And a good morning it is," he said. "How is Nancy and the children?"

"Oh, she's tolerably well except for bouts of rheumatism. Mostly, I think she's worry'n herself to death about our boys off fight'n. The girls are fine. Thomas is sickly with fever."

David nodded knowingly.

"Sallie and I don't have children to worry about," he said, "but I can imagine what a state of anxiety parents live in during these trying times. Every day brings news that some of our local boys have been killed or wounded."

"Praise God, all of our boys are alive – or at least they were when we last heard from 'em," Pa said. "I just got word that Coleman is home on sick leave; Dudley's with Hood's Army somewhere in Georgia and Robert Beasley is riding with ol' 'Preacher' Johnston over in Madison County. Course, James Greer and James Newby are up north yonder in a Yankee prison."

David leaned over and whispered. "I wouldn't mention Coleman being home. There are a lot of ears listening."

A man that Pa didn't recognize walked in the post office to mail a letter. He was full of news about the battle of Athens. He didn't know how many Yankee soldiers had been killed – but a bunch – but only about 30 of Forrest's men were dead. Haywood Jones's mansion on South Clinton Street had been taken over for use as a hospital as well as the William Richardson mansion one block north. Both houses were filled with wounded Yankees and Rebels. "They say that the blood of the dead and dying has turned them beautiful floors plum red," said the man. "Dr. Stith Malone is doctoring both Yankees and Confederates at his place. They say his house is running over with the wounded."

After the fellow had departed, David lowered his voice almost to a whisper. He walked a tight rope as postmaster and tried not to offend anyone. "Did you hear what General Forrest did to that block house where Town Creek flows underneath the tracks?"

"Can't say that I did," said Pa.

"One of the block houses surrendered its 85 men following Colonel Campbell's surrender," said David. "However, the other one refused. It was commanded by a Dutchman. He said, 'tell Shernal Forrest dat I vill not surrender. Git away from here damn quickly or I'll have my guns shot your damn head from your shoulders off.'

"Forrest didn't care for the reply and instructed his artillery to open up. Soon a white cloth appeared. Forrest pretended he didn't see it. After a few more shots, the Dutchman surrendered."

Pa chuckled. "I wish I could've seen it."

"Me too," replied David, grinning.

---

Later September, 1864.

Dog days had arrived at Johnson Branch. It was hot and dry and the brown wilted grass crunched beneath Coleman's bare feet. He bent over a row of cotton stalks, his nimble fingers plucking locks of cotton and dropping them into a hickory basket he pulled along. He straightened and looked back at his children who were also picking, but talking and falling behind.

"Catch up! We gotta get this cotton picked before I leave," he said.

He looked toward the house where Eliza was busy making hominy when he heard a horse whinny. He cocked his head and listened. Hoof beats! The hounds lazing in the shade of the cotton stalks stood, their ears perked, looking down the dirt road. Coleman wasn't taking any chances. He left his basket of cotton and loped toward the woods. The dogs ran barking down the road.

"IT'S GRANDPA!" exclaimed Bob. Coleman turned and saw a buggy coming fast up the dirt road. Thomas was at the reins. Ma and Pa were bouncing on the back seat, Ma holding her bonnet down with one hand and clutching the seat with the other.

"Slow down, Thomas!" she shouted. "You're gonna bounce me out."

Coleman chuckled. Thomas heard only what he wanted to hear and right now he chose not to hear Ma. They pulled up in a cloud of dust.

"Whooooaa."

Ol' Maude was lathered and breathing heavily. Ma was mumbling to herself.

"Y'all get out and stay a spell," said Coleman, going to assist his mother down from the buggy.

"I declare that boy is gonna rattle my teeth out one day," she said, straightening her bonnet. She grabbed both of Coleman's hands and looked him over. Tears welled in her eyes. "Mercy, you're nothin' but skin'n bones."

He wrapped his arms around her slim frame and pulled her to him, feeling her heave against his chest. "Ma, I'm fine," he said patting her back. "How 'bout you?"

She backed away and wiped her eyes. "Other than worrying myself to death, I'm doing fine for an old woman."

Pa walked over, slapping dust off his pants with his old black hat, while Thomas tied ol' Maude to a tree and then lifted something from the buggy.

"How are ya Coleman?" his father asked.

"Pa, I'm fine," he said and hugged his father. Thomas walked over smiling, hugged Coleman and handed him a jug of sweet milk. The barefoot children had abandoned the cotton patch and were pouring into the yard squealing, Eliza on their heels.

"Lordie Mercie!" exclaimed Ma. "Would you look how much these young'uns have grown?"

After hugging them and giving each one a tea cake, she turned to Coleman. "Have you seen Dudley?"

"Not since the Army fell back from Dalton. As far as I know he's fight'n somewhere around Atlanta."

After the children returned to picking cotton, Ma assisted Eliza with making hominy. The men sat beneath the shade of a large oak tree overlooking Johnson Branch, enjoying a nice breeze rattling the dry leaves as they talked.

"How are things in the county?" asked Coleman.

"Bad," replied Pa. "We all rejoiced and thanked the Lord after Forrest captured Athens last week, but the Yankees have returned and they're mean'rn ever and seek'n revenge. Folks are livin' in fear. With four of my boys in the Army –"

"– four?" interrupted Coleman.

"Hadn't you heard? Robert Beasley enlisted in ol' Preacher Johnston's Partisans over in Madison County," said Pa.

"Well, I'll be doggone."

"Anyway," continued Pa, "I'm surprised the Yankees hadn't burned us out. When a soldier comes home, it ain't long 'til the Yankees know about it and come call'n." He told Coleman about them showing up at night looking for Dudley six months earlier and mistakenly dragged Thomas out of bed.

"They scared me plum to death," said Thomas loudly.

"Thomas, you don't need to talk so loud, we can hear you," said Pa.

"Sorry Pa."

"Who's tell'n the Yankees?"

"Folks say it's the Isoms and Doc Coman just to name two," replied Pa. "I voted for Doc Coman when he run for delegate to the secession convention. He was opposed to secession and so was I. But after that scoundrel Turchin sacked Athens most people with good sense joined the cause in order to protect their families. But not Doc Coman. He's a homemade Yankee through and through."

"It's a thousand wonders that somebody hadn't killed him," said Coleman.

"The soldiers protect 'im," said Pa. "All of 'em are feeling cocky now that the troops are back. Sheriff McKinney has threatened to hang Emanuel Isom. If they learn that you're home, they'll turn you in, so lay low."

"I will," said Coleman thoughtfully. "Changing the subject, how have y'all been doing?"

"Thomas has planted a small patch of cotton –"

"What?" asked Thomas, hearing his name. Pa ignored him and continued.

"–and has a pretty good stand, but hasn't sold any. It takes a wagonload of Confederate money to buy a plug of tobacco. Folks are afraid to sell their cotton because of inflation. Salt is nigh impossible to find so we can't cure meat and what horses and mules the Yankees hadn't stolen, the Confederates have taken. I don't know how much longer we can last."

"And George Edward, how's he doing?" asked Coleman.

"Still driving the stage to Fayetteville," said Pa.

"I'd love to see Cal and Cornelia," said Coleman.

428

"Well, we couldn't all get in the buggy, but they send their love."

"Have y'all heard from James Greer and Jim?" asked Coleman.

"We don't hear much, but they're still in Rock Island Prison."

It was late afternoon when Ma said, "I guess we need to get home and milk the cow."

"Not before y'all eat supper," replied Eliza. "I wouldn't think of letting y'all leave without eating. Anyway Cal and Cornelia can milk the cow."

"This is dangerous country and I don't want to be out past dark," said Ma.

They suppered on boiled potatoes mixed with green beans and onions, vine-ripe tomatoes, fried okra and squash and washed down with sweet milk, the first Coleman had drank in nearly a year.

Coleman assisted his parents into the buggy. Pa was misty-eyed and Ma wiped away tears. "When will we see you again?" she asked.

"When the war's over."

"It's hard for a mother to see her sons go off to war. I pray for all of y'all without ceasing. Be careful and may God bless you."

Coleman nodded and slapped Thomas on the back.

"Bye, Thomas, you take good care of Ma and Pa."

Thomas smiled. "I will," he said and slapped the reins. "Gitty up."

Coleman watched and choked back tears as the buggy wobbled down the dusty road and finally disappeared from sight.

That night when he was readying for bed he noticed a pair of shoes at the foot of the iron bedstead.

"Where did these come from?" he asked Eliza, picking them up.

"Why they're Thomas's!" she exclaimed. "Darlin' he left 'em for you."

---

Early November, 1864.

It was late night when Eliza shook Coleman's shoulder and whispered, "Wake up, I hear something!"

Coleman heard the dogs scramble from beneath the cabin and run down the road barking. "Someone's coming," she said.

Fear gripped Coleman. Regular folks don't come visiting at midnight. He jumped out of bed, pulled on his pants and ran to the window and peered out. Pale moonlight cast light on a lone rider.

"Is it Yankees?" Eliza asked.

"I don't think so."

The rider came up at a gallop, halted in the front yard and slid from the saddle.

"Why, it's Uncle Robert!" exclaimed Coleman.

Robert C. David walked briskly toward the door as Coleman opened it.

"Uncle Robert, it's good to see you –"

"–Coleman, we don't have much time," he said. "You need to leave immediately –"

"–Why?"

"Late this afternoon Dr. Coman came by the post office and casually mentioned that he had heard that you were home and inquired about your welfare – like he was concerned. He was pumping me for information. I'd bet my life you'll be visited by

Union troops before sunrise."

"It's all so sudden," replied Coleman. "I hadn't planned on this happening. I don't even know where the Army is located."

"They passed through Decatur a few days ago, headed to Tuscumbia. Union troops in Athens are watching every ferry on Elk River. The safest way for you to reach Tuscumbia is to swim the Tennessee near Mooresville and ride west toward Tuscumbia. Go now and may God ride with you."

Coleman swallowed hard. "Thanks Uncle Robert."

Eliza filled a sack with food while Coleman saddled the gelding and poked ears of corn into the saddle bags. He led the horse to the front of the house and hugged Eliza briefly, finally having to break her away from his arms.

"Tell the children that I love 'em," he said and swung into the saddle. Eliza laid her head against his thigh. "I love you Coleman. Darlin' please come back safe."

"I will." He kicked the horse and departed in a cloud of dust. He was fording Johnson's Branch where it crosses Nick Davis Road when he noticed the gelding's ears. They were pointing sharply ahead. He whinnied. Horses were coming! Coleman had no sooner left the road for a sweet gum thicket when horsemen appeared over the crest of a hill. They thundered past, clearly visible in the moonlight. Yankee soldiers! A few hundred yards away, they took the road to his house. A strong urge told him to follow them and protect his family, but logic intervened. He had no gun and no powder. He kicked the gelding in the flanks hard and rode toward the Tennessee River.

---

Wednesday, November 16th dawned cold, miserable and depressing – just like the preceding several days. Pa sat in front of the fireplace silently staring at the leaping flames, his mind heavy with worry. Ordinarily, he would have been thinking about killing hogs the following week and rewarding himself with a delicious slab of tenderloin eaten with hot biscuits, scrambled eggs and gravy. It wouldn't happen this year. Yankees had shot his hogs and caught all of his chickens except an old rooster and one laying hen that happened to be scratching in the woods when they appeared several days earlier, thieving. Fortunately, they didn't find the cow in the woods nor a side of bacon he had hidden in the loft or they would have surely stolen it. Thank the Lord, Thomas was a good squirrel hunter. Several of the Yankees were Dutchmen. "Ve fight to bring the South back in the Union," one said. *Killing, burning and thieving and cursing women folks all because they want us back in the Union family?* Pa thought, at least they didn't harm any of the family and that was something to be thankful for.

He had hoped that peace would come, but with Lincoln's reelection on November 8th, all hope was dashed. General Lee was still holding on at Petersburg, south of Richmond, and Hood's Army of Tennessee was at Tuscumbia waiting to cross the Tennessee River and march on Nashville, where, it was said, vast amounts of food and supplies were stored. If Nashville fell, North Alabama and Tennessee would be rid of Yankees. The way Pa figured it, if Hood failed, the jig was up – the cause lost.

Thomas brought in a hickory back log and laid it on the fireplace. Shortly, the wood was popping and hissing and emitting a sweet aroma. After Ma and the women folks had completed their chores, they and the grandchildren gathered in the room. Young Worley Martin Newby, who was almost 8 years old, climbed onto his grandpa's lap and rested against his chest. Pa laid his pipe aside and handed the large leather Bible

430

to Thomas.

"Read the 23$^{rd}$ Psalm," he said.

Thomas read haltingly and loud.

"Don't read so loud," Ma said, interrupting him.

"You'd think he learned to whisper in a sawmill," Pa muttered.

"Huh?" asked Thomas, looking up.

Ma shot Pa a hard look.

"You're doing fine Thomas. Keep reading," she said. "But not so loud."

After the reading, young Worley looked up at his grandfather and asked, "Is it Sunday, Grandpa?"

"No, it's Wednesday, child. According to the newspaper, President Davis has asked everybody to worship and pray for our country today. It's too cold to go to the church house and the way I figure we can talk to God right here in front of the warm fire. Y'all bow your head."

Pa prayed earnestly that God would bring his sons back home alive and give the soldiers victory and save the Confederacy. "And Lord, I pray that you will rid our land of Yankees, who are like the locust plague, they have overrun our land, killing, burning and stealing and lastly, Lord, we pray for peace. Amen."

Young Worley added: "And we pray for Papa and Uncle Jim in that Yankee prison."

"Amen," everyone chimed.

Tears ran down Pa's cheek and disappeared in his grizzled whiskers.

"What's wrong, Grandpa?" asked Worley.

"This reminds me of an earlier time and another little boy who sat in my lap on a day of prayer and we fasted many years ago," he said, his voice breaking.

"Who was the little boy?" the child asked.

"Achilles. He was about your age when he died."

431

# 42 | BUSHWHACKER SMITES THE ENEMY

Near Meridianville, Alabama.

Late November, 1864.

Company G was strung out in a long column riding south on the Meridian Road, looking for marauding Yankees who, it had been reported, were stealing horses, mules, chickens, corn, fodder and smokehouse meat, in addition to cursing and frightening women and general terrorizing folks in the area. It was Robert Beasley Barksdale's first mission against the enemy. He had never struck any man in anger, much less shot at anyone. Captain Campbell was at the head of the column and Ol' Bushwhacker was bringing up the rear. It was late afternoon and cold and the sky was clear as glass. A good day to be alive, thought Barksdale. It didn't seem real that violence and death could be lurking around the next bend in the road. He didn't like to think about it. He shivered, not so much because he was cold – he was – but as if to shake away the thought from his mind.

It was pretty country where the soil was rich and fine plantations bumped up against a gray mountain in the east. From his home near Hayes Store, the mountain was a familiar sight. It made him think of Lucy and Mollie, but mostly of Lucy. Only a few nights ago, he was cuddled against her warm body, now he was bouncing in a saddle, cold and scared.

Ragsdale, who rode beside him, nervously twisted his neck in every direction, searching the horizon.

"You're gonna wear out your neck," said Robert.

"I don't wanna be surprised."

"Have you ever shot at a Yankee?" Barksdale asked.

"Naw, but kill'n one would be as easy as kill'n a gopher."

"I'm not too worried about killing one myself," said Barksdale. "I'm more worried about them killing me."

They rode through the village of Meridianville and as they neared a mountain just north of Huntsville, the column abruptly halted. Word was passed back that Negro union soldiers had been seen at the front. No one knew how many were present. Barksdale felt fear creep up his throat. He cleared it and turning to James Ragsdale and asked haltingly, "Reckon... there'll be... a fight?"

"If they don't run off there will be. Ol' Bushwhacker will fight Ol' Scratch himself."

Confronting untrained and badly armed "home-made" Yankees was one thing. Fighting regulars armed with repeating rifles was quite another. Barksdale's instinct told him that he was about to "see the elephant" in a major way.

The men were checking their revolvers and rifles when Bushwhacker rode past, headed to the front of the column to reconnoiter. Word was passed back that the Negro troops were mounted, heavily armed and behind the cover of trees. While Barkdsale stood in his stirrups to get a better view he saw Bushwhacker at the front of the column raise his arm in the air and point toward the black soldiers.

"FORWAAARD!" he shouted.

The Confederates kicked their mounts and charged forward, greeted by a volley of blazing rifles and flying lead. A bullet passed near Barksdale's head, making a snapping sound. He braced for the next one to knock him from the saddle. Apparently, the Yankees were as scared as he was, he thought, or perhaps they were bad marksmen. Before he could decide which one it was, they were riding pell mell through their ranks, firing as they went. Barksdale had never killed a man, but at the moment he wasn't thinking about whether it was morally right or wrong. Kill or be killed was the only question. And he wanted to live. He fired his big revolver at anything that wore blue; heard their screams while some begged until a bullet silenced them. The savage melee ended as abruptly as it had started.

Barksdale looked down on the ground and counted seven dead Yankees and nearly gagged. He had seen dead men before but they were laid out nicely in a casket, hands folded and looking peaceful – nothing like what he was witnessing on the ground. The Negroes were sprawled in ignominious positions, blood oozing from numerous bullet holes, a look of terror frozen on their faces. He turned his head and rode away. Death came so quickly. He could have been one of them.

One of the black troopers escaped to Huntsville. Later, Barksdale learned that the soldiers were on their way to torch southern homes. They had been robbing smokehouses, cursing women and stealing wagons and horses.

———————

Eastern Madison County.
Several days later, 1864.

It was midday and cold as Barksdale sat around a crackling campfire with the other gray backs, smoking, passing the time and shooting the bull. Ever since a large number of Federal troops had been shifted west to defend against General Hood's invasion of North Alabama and middle Tennessee, the guerillas had been leading a more leisurely existence.

"Look yonder," Barksdale said to Ragsdale and pointed toward a sentry who was escorting several men into camp. That wasn't unusual as locals often came in bringing food and information. But this was different. They were elderly, stumbling, ill-clothed and shivering, and all were armed.

"Where y'all head'n grandpa?" Ragsdale called out when they neared the fire.

"To see Preacher Johnston," replied one.

"Better thaw out first," Barksdale said. "Gather 'round the fire and warm a mite."

The old men, skinny as rails and half frozen, gathered around the flames, shivering and massaging their bony fingers and dirty hands.

"When did y'all last eat?" asked Barksdale.

"Yesdidy," replied one.

Barksdale produced hard tacks that he had taken from a Yankee's knapsack and passed them around. Most of the old men didn't have good teeth and couldn't chew the hard crackers. Someone poured each of them a cup of Dixie Rio. "Soak the hard tacks in the coffee to soften it up," offered Robert. They did and gnawed on the crackers in silence, savoring every crumb.

"Where y'all from?" asked Ragsdale.

"Over yonder in Jackson County," said one. "Home-made Yankees showed up in our neighborhood night before last and burned us out. We've come to join Preacher Johnston and fight."

"They was some of our own neighbors," added another old fellow. "They've

433

been mighty plucky and daring with Union troops to back 'em up."

All of the old men said they had sons in the Confederate Army.

Later, Bushwhacker assembled his men. "Boys, home-made Yankees are weeding a wide path over in High Jackson, burning out good southern folks and mistreating them because their sons are in the Confederate Army. While most of their blue belly protectors are out chasing General Hood, I think we need to walk up and pay 'em a visit and mete out some justice."

The men were chomping at the bits for action and responded with an enthusiastic cheer.

On a cold morning after cooking rations and hiding their horses in the mountains, Bushwhacker guided his men by foot up Paint Rock Valley, staying in the woods and avoiding houses. Barksdale blew hot breath on fingers that ached from the cold and thought he couldn't get more miserable, that is, until they waded across the Paint Rock River and his toes almost froze, losing feeling in them. They had a scare when a young woman unexpectedly appeared at the river and dipped out a bucket of water. However, some of the men knew her to be reliable and instructed her not to speak of what she had witnessed.

Late afternoon, the guerillas halted in a thick forest east of Woodville and rested. Bushwhacker sent out scouts, including three of the elderly men who were familiar with the neighborhood, to reconnoiter and report back. After dark the graybacks moved back to another location where they rested and waited fireless in the cold night. Near 10 p.m. the scouts returned and reported that there were three groups of Federals nearby.

"There is a squad down here," a scout said and placed a rock on the ground, "and a large number right here," he said and placed another rock nearby. "A whole company is stockaded in a hewn-log barn on the Belle Fonte Road. The logs are heavily chinked with portholes for firing."

In appeared to be a formidable redoubt.

"Are there any dry straw or shucks near the barn?" Bushwhacker asked.

"Yes sir," replied a scout.

The men set about making turpentine balls and searching for matches.

The barn ran east-west with one side facing the road, and behind the barn was a ditch that angled off westward. Lieutenant Miller took ten men and captured the small camp of Federals and returned with prisoners. A larger group up the road was not molested. Bushwhacker divided his men into three groups. The sharpshooters were posted west of the barn in some willow trees and ordered to remain quiet. Millyard's squad was to move along the Belle Fonte Road until they were opposite the barn. Bushwhacker would select two men to sneak up to the barn with the turpentine balls and wait. The third group, which included Barkdale and Ragsdale, would cover the south side of the barn. Their objective was to crawl to a ditch near the barn and hide there until daylight when the attack was to begin. The men crawled on their bellies across the cold ground, inching through dead weeds, being careful not to bang their rifles and equipment against rocks. When they were halfway to the ditch, someone in the barn exclaimed: "I hear somebody out there!"

Barksdale and the men froze in position. "Shhh," someone whispered. Some of the men were rotten with colds. He hoped and prayed to God that no one coughed.

"Somebody is down yonder!" said another voice from the barn.

"You didn't hear anything," argued another.

The gray backs lay still until the Yankees settled down, and then inched forward, finally reaching the ditch before daylight.

BANG! A gun fired inside the stable.

"HERE THEY ARE!" yelled a Yankee. The gray backs hunkered quiet as mice. Word was whispered down the ditch. "Shhh, a sentry shot 'Doc Russell.'"

BANG! The second shot was fired from the ditch. One of the graybacks saw a horse in the stable door swinging his head and thought it was a Yankee.

"They know we're here," Barksdale whispered to Ragsdale.

"Yeah, they'll be waiting for us when we rise out of the ditch."

Barksdale's fingers and toes were numb from cold, but his insides churned up with heat. The thought of a ball hitting him in the head when he raised up sent terror raging through his mind. He had seen what a lead ball does to a man's head; the entrance hole being the size of a little finger and the exit hole big as a fist.

Two men carrying turpentine balls crept to the barn and lay down, waiting for the order to attack.

At dawn, Bushwhacker rose slightly in the ditch and called out: "SURRENDER THE BARN!"

"NO!" someone yelled from the barn, followed by loud cursing.

"CHARGE THEIR FRONT! FIRE!" he commanded.

Barksdale sighted his rifle at chinks between the logs and squeezed the trigger. The rifle bucked and a red flame lit up the early light, joining the other two squads, sending a storm of lead from all directions toward the barn and blowing out hardened chinks.

"LET'S GO," someone shouted and the men jumped from the ditch and charged the barn, firing and blowing out more chinks. On reaching the barn, they poked their rifle barrels through openings and port holes and blazed away where the Yankees were trapped. Barksdale and several men knocked open the door and rushed inside, stepping over the wounded and dead. Several soldiers were down on their knees begging for their lives and others were praying.

"WE SURRENDER – WE SURRENDER!" they cried out.

Bushwhacker and his men took the prisoners, made a litter for "Doc" Russell and quickly headed to Dixie, but they were too late to save Doc. The larger company of Yankees encamped up the road, apparently hearing the firing skeedaddled for a stockade on the nearby railroad.

"Boys, you did a fine job," Bushwhacker said to his men. "I don't believe the homemade Yankees of High Jackson will be as apt to mistreat their neighbors in the future, but if they do, we'll pay 'em another visit."

435

# 43 | FIVE BLOODY HOURS

Florence, Alabama.

Monday, November 21, 1864.

It was his cold feet that woke him. He wiggled his toes and realized they were protruding from beneath the blanket. He turned on his side and pulled up his knees and was almost asleep when something cold splattered on his cheek. Rain. Dudley Barksdale tugged his hat down over his face and tried to sleep, but couldn't; he was too damn cold and wet. Now he wished he had one of those rubber slickers that the Yankees carried. He wished he had shoes... and a tent to sleep in... and a plate of fried eggs, ham, hot biscuits covered in gravy and hot coffee. And while he was wishing, he wished he was home. It was hog killing day in Athens. About now, Pa, Thomas and George Edward would be building a fire and filling the vat with hot water preparatory to slaughtering hogs. Christmas and birthdays were special, but he loved hog killing day best of all. It meant fried tenderloin, scrambled eggs and hot biscuits for supper. The thought caused his stomach to contract and growl. Then it occurred to him that the Yankees had driven off the hogs and there would be none to slaughter. He had to get food off his mind.

Reveille sounded. It was dark and drizzling rain when the regiment fell in formation and was informed that they were moving out.

"Every man should have three days rations on hand," announced Sgt. Patterson.

"That means corn, corn and corn," groused Junior Bill.

The encampment was soon a beehive of activity as stubborn mules were harnessed and hitched to supply wagons and horses were hooked to caisons and limbers. The feet of hundreds of men, many of them barefoot, churned the wet earth into a sucking mud as rain continued to fall.

Two days earlier General Forrest and 5,000 cavalry had arrived from Tennessee to act as the eyes and ears of the Army ranging out in front of it, much like bird dogs scouting for quail. Forrest's command crossed the 1,000-foot expanse of the Tennessee River on pontoons in a cold rain, divided into three columns and rode north. One column rode to Waynesboro; another to Pulaski and Forrest and his Escorts Company headed to Lawrenceburg, confronting and pushing Yankee cavalry before them. The main Army of 35,000 men consisting of three corps crossed on pontoons and marched north toward Nashville some 100 miles away. Dudley was in General A.P. Stewart's Corps; his brother Coleman, whom he had visited after his return from home, was in General Stephen D. Lee's Corps. The long gray line of many barefoot and ill-clothed men struggled through mud and cold rain as it turned to sleet and ice, culminating in a hard freeze that night.

Dudley and his messmates were huddled around a fire beneath an oak tree near Lawrenceburg, Tennessee, attempting to roast strips of beef on the end of their ramrods, when Sergeant Patterson joined them. He shivered and leaned over the fire, warming his hands.

"Sarge, I'd offer you beef, but this is all we got," said Dudley. "Would you like a handful of corn?"

"Much obliged, but I've already got plenty of that," said Sergeant Patterson. "I dropped by to lift ya spirits. We'll be in Nashville 'n three days livin' off the fat of the land. They say Federal warehouses are bulging with food 'n blankets and shoes and warm clothes."

"I suppose them Yankees are gonna share it with us," quipped Junior Bill.

"Boys, all we gotta do is take it," said Sergeant Patterson, "then we eat 'til we're poppin.'"

On Sunday evening, November 29th, bitter cold and snow falling, Hood's Army reached the outskirts of Columbia occupied by approximately 25,000 Yankees under the command of General Schofield. Snow lazily falling and collecting in the branches of numerous cedar trees presented a peaceful scene, but Dudley was focused on his freezing toes and fingers. First priority was starting a fire. He and Junior Bill searched for wood and found a rail fence and hauled back as many rails as they could carry on their shoulders. They were stealing someone else's property, but at the moment it seemed insignificant. They conserved the wood, knowing that it must last all night. With wooden fingers, Dudley hung a strip of rancid beef on the end of his ramrod and held it over the fire to roast. The mess mates were unusually quiet as they roasted their beef.

"Pa always said that behind every dark cloud is sunshine," said Junior Bill.

"No sunshine tonight," replied Jackson.

"I ain't talkin' 'bout that. I's thankin' more deeply," said Junior Bill. "I'se thank'n 'bout the good things that cold weather has brought us."

"Good things!" exclaimed Dudley. "Junior Bill, you've got to be going loco."

"We don't have no more chiggers, ticks, mosquitoes and poison oak," he said.

"Huh," harrumphed Thornton. "I'd rather be scratch'n than freez'n any day of the week, but I gotta say Junior Bill, you are the level-headest fellow I ever know."

"Level headed!" exclaimed Jackson.

"Yeah, level headed," Thornton said. "Tobacco juice runs out both sides of his mouth at the same time."

Junior Bill grinned and said, "Waalll we've got plenty of wood and I've got an idea."

"What?"

"I'll show you later."

After the fire burned down Junior Bill scattered the hot coals and ashes on the ground and built another fire nearby. The men slept on the warm ground where the first fire had burned.

Dudley woke Monday morning cold, stiff and hungry. Company G fell in formation and after the morning report, Sgt. Patterson gave "at rest."

"Men, I've got good news. The Yankees have made a big mistake," he said. "Last night some 25,000 in Columbia moved across the Duck River burn'n the bridges behind 'em. Cavalry scouts have reported that their Army is now split: 5,000 troops are a few miles up the road at Spring Hill. We're gonna march around the 25,000 and whip the 5,000 at Spring Hill. This will open the way to Nashville and all the food we can eat."

Cheers went up. Not only were they hungry, they wanted to whip the Yankees for bringing suffering down on their heads.

Soon the Confederate Army was in motion. The main force consisting of Cheatham and Stewart's Corps swung around General Schofield's Union troops, crossed the Duck River on pontoons and marched toward Spring Hill. Two divisions of General Stephen D. Lee's Corps remained behind to demonstrate against Schofield. Hood, riding at the front of his army, reached Spring Hill on Tuesday afternoon around 3 p.m. Orders were issued for the men to cook rations and rest. Dudley and the 35th Regiment bivouacked that night south of Spring Hill near the Columbia-Franklin Turnpike. The men were in high spirits as they warmed around the fire and roasted beef. The weather had changed and Indian summer had arrived. They had successfully sneaked around Schofield's 25,000 blue coats and were in position to attack the 5,000 in Spring Hill the next morning at daylight. Maybe there was sunshine behind every dark cloud.

"Ol' Hood has pulled a fast one on the Yanks this time," said Jackson.

"If I's runn'n this heah Army," said Thornton. "I wouldn't be sitt'n around here warm'n and cook'n. I'd be up there on them Yankees in Spring Hill like a duck on a June bug."

"We need a rest after that long march," said Dudley.

"Yeah, but how ya know them Yankees are gonna sit still while we're rest'n?" asked Thornton.

"I'm tired of eat'n roasted beef," said Jackson. "If Junior Bill hadn't lost our skillet we could be eat'n some good ol' coosh."

"Doggoneit, where is Junior Bill anyway?" asked Thornton.

"Look'n for firewood," said Dudley.

It was twilight and a good fire was burning when a tall, lanky kid with a shock of red hair rode up bareback on a skinny gray mule.

"Anybody seen Junior Bill Pendergrass?" he asked.

"Who wants to know?" asked Thornton.

"Lifus, his brother."

"Get down and warm yourself," said Dudley. The boy slid off the mule and lifted a burlap bag that rested across the mule's protruding withers. Dudley poked out his hand. "I'm Dudley Barksdale. Remember me? I'm the fellow that was in ya bed."

"Yeah, 'bout scared me to death."

"Whatcha doing here?" asked Thornton.

"Ma and Pa heard the Army was pass'n through and sent me with some vittles – and a letter."

Junior Bill walked up carrying several fence rails on his shoulder. He dropped them to the ground. "Lifus! Boy whatcha doin' here? You ain't enlisted have ya?"

"Naw, I brung you some vittles 'n such," he said and handed Junior Bill the burlap sack.

"How's Ma and Pa and the family?" asked Junior Bill.

"We're all tolerable."

"Have you seen Earline lately?"

Lifus dropped his head and handed the letter to Junior Bill.

"Lookee heah, I got me a letter!" exclaimed Junior Bill waving it in the air like a prize. "Hee...hee... heee." He unfolded the letter and moved into the circle of firelight.

"I can't see good. Here Dudley, read it for me," he said and handed him the letter.

"Out loud?" asked Dudley.

"Shore."

The writing was barely legible. Dudley cleared his throat and began reading.

"Dear Junior Bill – I shore hope you are healthy and safe. Ma and me are in good health... and your brothers and sisters are okay too. Your coon hound had a batch of pups–"

"–Does it say how many?" interrupted Junior Bill.

"Naw." Dudley read on. "I sent you a sack of food... and a skillet to cook in –"

"–Doggoneit that's good news!" interjected Thornton.

"–Lot of folks around here have been sick with fever... and some have died. Earline McLemore come down with fever last month –" Dudley lowered the letter to his side.

"And what!" demanded Junior Bill. "What happened to 'er?"

Dudley read on. "And they buried her two weeks ago."

"Aw no," moaned Junior Bill. His chin dropped and his body trembled. Without saying a word, he walked off into the surrounding darkness.

It was past midnight when Dudley was awakened by someone throwing a stick of wood on the low burning fire. He cracked an eye and saw Junior Bill rolling up in his blanket.

"Are you okay?" Dudley asked.

"Shore."

"I's worried about ya."

"I's out walkin'."

"Junior Bill, I'm awful sorry..., about ya loss."

"I shore did love that gal. Now that she's gone I don't have nothin' to live for. If them damn Yankees weren't down here I'd be home and I could've took good care of Earline. Now she's dead. It's the Yankees' fault and if I could kill every damn one of 'em I would."

"We'll get our chance in a few hours," replied Dudley.

"I think part of the Army is mov'n out now," said Junior Bill. "When I's out walk'n miles 'n miles of soldiers were head'n north."

"Which brigades?"

"Don't know – too dark to see, but it was a bunch of 'em," Junior Bill said.

---

Wednesday, November 30th.

The bugler had barely sounded reveille when the snare drums rolled. Dudley knuckled sleep from his eyes and hurried to formation. Officers were scurrying about on horseback shouting orders.

"What 'n tarnation is going on?" asked Jackson as they fell in formation. The answer was forthcoming.

"Last night while we slept," said Sgt. Patterson, "the 25,000 Yankees we left behind in Columbia marched right up the Columbia-Franklin Turnpike and joined the 5,000 in Spring Hill. Both are now up the road at Franklin, no doubt digging in."

Dudley and Junior Bill's eyes met.

"Them weren't our men I seen last night. They were Yankees!" exclaimed Junior Bill.

"I told ya," said Thornton. "We ought'n been cook'n 'n rest'n. We oughta been whipping the Yankees at Spring Hill."

Soon the gray backs were marching north toward Franklin, winding around cedar-covered hills and across grassy valleys. General Hood rode at the front of Stewart's Corps that spearheaded the Army and close behind was Dea's Brigade and the 35th Regiment. Cheatham's Corps followed. The rutted turnpike was littered with castaway equipment, and in the ditches lay dead mules, horses and wrecked supply

439

wagons burned by the Yankees.

---

Columbia, Tennessee.

Wednesday, November 30, 1864.

Coleman Barksdale figured he was the luckiest flat footer in Hood's Army. His health had improved, he was gaining weight and he was wearing a new set of clothes. And he owned a pair of shoes! Not only that, Indian summer had come as quickly as the snow, sleet and ice had disappeared. Life could change at the drop of a hat. Three months ago he was ill, barefoot and wearing rags. Granted, the march from Tuscumbia to Columbia through rain and sleet, culminating in freezing nights had been difficult but now… ahh, Indian summer.

He looked across the low-burning fire where Peavine sat ragged and dirty, sopping up the last morsels of breakfast coosh with a piece of hoecake, when the bugler sounded assembly and snare drums rolled. The men looked up nervously.

"Reckon the Yankees done crossed the river and com'n for us?" asked Tom Butler.

"Naw, it's probably just a drill," replied Coleman.

The regiment, part of Deas' Brigade fell in formation. The officers appeared nervous. "We're moving out immediately," said the First Sergeant. "Scouts have reported that the Yankees slipped away last night and marched to Franklin."

Franklin, a village of some 750 souls, was 22 miles south of Nashville and straddled the north-south Columbia-Nashville Pike. East of the pike were the tracks of the Nashville and Decatur Railroad.

Soon, General Stephen D. Lee's Corps, consisting of several thousand men and most of Hood's artillery, was tramping and rumbling north up the turnpike toward Franklin, 24 miles away. Regimental colors fluttered in the cool breeze beneath a clear Indian summer sun as the band played *Dixie*. Peavine was limping, his feet having been cut and bruised by the icy roads on the march from Tuscumbia. Each time his foot hit the ground, he winced. Coleman wished that he could do something to relieve his friend's pain. After all, when he was ill with flux and barely able to march, Peavine had carried his rifle.

"Peavine, you're limping real bad."

"I got a gravel in my shoe."

Coleman chuckled. You ain't wearing shoes."

"Dadgumit, I hadn't noticed."

"I gotta idea," said Coleman.

"What?"

"My feet are in good shape," said Coleman. "You wear my shoes for a spell."

"Naw, the first dead Yankee I see I'll get me a good pair. But thanks just the same."

They walked on and Coleman noticed that Peavine favored his left foot. "I got a better idea," he said. "Step outta formation with me a minute."

"What for?"

"I'm gonna let you wear my left shoe," said Coleman.

"Naw, I'm not gonna take my best friend's shoes."

"You carried my rifle when I's sick, now, by golly, I'm gonna help you. Now

440

step out!"

They sat on the side of the road and Peavine carefully pulled Coleman's left shoe onto his swollen foot, laced it and wiggled his toes.

"Fits real good."

They hobbled down the road enjoying the fine weather. "Peavine, we've been friends for over a year and a half and I don't even know your real name," said Coleman.

"They call me Peavine 'cause I'm skinny."

"Friends need to know about one another," said Coleman. "If I got killed, you'd know to write Eliza 'n tell 'er. On the other hand, if something happened to you, I wouldn't even know how to address the letter except 'Peavine, at Mt. Rozell, Alabama.'"

"I ain't too proud of my name," said Peavine.

"Whisper it to me."

Peavine thought it over. "Promise you won't laugh and you won't tell nobody?"

"Promise."

Peavine leaned over and whispered into Coleman's ear, "Delbert Fostian Romine."

Coleman chuckled. "Well no darn wonder you wouldn't tell us!"

"Now there you go, you said you wouldn't laugh."

Coleman's left foot ached, but he never let on lest Peavine return the shoe. He felt honored to endure pain so that his friend might not suffer.

The sides of the turnpike were littered with knapsacks, haversacks, dead horses and charred wagons, discarded by Yankees hurrying toward Franklin.

---

Afternoon, November 30th.

From where he stood in formation with the 35th Alabama, Dudley could see the wide and gray plain all the way to the village of Franklin, slightly elevated, tree-lined and peaceful-looking. Blue smoke gently curled from chimneys into an Indian summer blue sky. But Dudley wasn't deceived. He knew that behind earthen entrenchments were thousands of nervous blue bellies with sweaty fingers on the trigger of repeating rifles – waiting.

Stewart's Corps was positioned east of the Nashville and Decatur Railroad tracks near the Lewisburg Pike. Slightly east of the pike was the Big Harpeth River that wound lazily southeastward. To the front where Dudley waited was a large, two-story Federal-style red brick house with double fireplaces at each end.

"I ain't never seen a house that big," Junior Bill said. "It's bigger 'n the courthouse in Athens."

"That's Carnton," Thornton said.

"Now how'd you know that?" Junior Bill asked.

"Cause I heard somebody say it was."

"Waall, I've heard of naming your young'uns, your cat, your dog and your cow, but I ain't never heard of naming a house," Junior Bill drawled.

"Rich folks do such things," Dudley said.

Positioned west of the railroad tracks was Cheatham's Corps. As far as Dudley could see to the west there were graybacks by the thousands, their bayonets glistening in the afternoon sun. In fact, they stretched for three miles. Regiments were drawn up in battle line and tattered flags fluttered in the breeze like a parade was about to begin.

441

To reach the entrenched Yankees they would have to angle across the railroad tracks and fight through a thicket of thorny osage orange hedge. The men grumbled.

"Shorely, we ain't gonna attack head on," said Junior Bill. "It'd be plain suicide."

"It's the shortest route to the Yankees," said Thornton.

Dudley looked toward Franklin and felt his heart pounding against his chest. A trickle of sweat ran down his back. The men had grown quiet, sensing that this battle was going to be difficult. Maybe, they wouldn't attack, just demonstrate and keep the Yankees off balance. Junior Bill was right, thought Dudley. It would be next to suicide to make a frontal assault.

Jackson broke the silence. "What time is it?"

"Why, ya gonna be late for supper?" asked Junior Bill.

"Naw, he thinks he might be late for his death," quipped Thornton.

"It's four o'clock," someone said.

"Is that a.m. or p.m.?" Jackson asked.

It was nervous talk and Dudley chuckled, releasing some of the nervous tension from his body.

"Check your cartridges and fix bayonets!" commanded Sgt. Patterson.

Metal clicked metal against metal as bayonets were fitted. In the rear, the brass band struck up the *Bonnie Blue Flag.*

"Company, FORWAARRD!" The preparatory command was repeated down the line.

"MARCH!"

Dudley and 300 men of the 35th Alabama stepped forward, walking shoulder to shoulder. Two corps consisting of some 18 brigades moved across the plain like a giant gray wave. The attack was on. Behind the troops, the band played *The Bonnie Blue Flag.* He knew the verse – "Hoorah, hoorah, hoorah for the Bonnie Blue Flag…"

They swept through the yard of Carnton and Dudley noticed the two back porches that extended across both floors. How nice it would be to sit there in a rocker looking out at the peaceful river, he thought. The feet of thousands marching men shook the earth and sent rabbits scurrying from their holes – in front, he saw a cotton field. It had already been picked over, but many late bolls had popped open, revealing their billowing white contents. Ah, so peaceful looking.

Then it happened. Union artillery thundered, sending shards of iron ripping through the brigade, tearing bodies to pieces and propelling arms, legs and entrails through the air and souls to Kingdom Come.

Without command, and with bayonets glistening in the afternoon sun, the men swept forward like a giant tidal wave toward the Yankee outer entrenchment, giving the Rebel yell, a high, keening, whooping cry that sounded like a thousand hyenas screaming at the same time. They were greeted by a torrent of lead that thinned their ranks. Miraculously, Dudley and Junior Bill were still standing. Not slowing, they swept over the Yankees, and those not bayonetted and shot threw down their weapons and fled for refuge to the main rear works.

"THEY'RE RUNNING LIKE RABBITS," hollered Junior Bill over the din of the Rebel yell.

The charging Rebels were within a hundred paces of the Yankee mainworks when hell's gates flew open. A sheet of lead erupted from repeating rifles and shot and

442

canister roared from cannons tearing bodies apart and spraying a shower of blood. Over the din of shouting and musketry, Dudley heard the sickening thud of minie balls as they impacted flesh and bone and heard men screaming out for God's help. Dudley's eyes darted over at Junior Bill, who was on his left where he had been in every battle and skirmish. Junior Bill opened his snaggle-toothed mouth to speak, when a hole suddenly appeared over his left shirt pocket. The impact of the ball sent tiny particles of thread and dust flying into the air. For those few milliseconds, it was like a dream. Junior Bill's eyes locked on Dudley; his jaw sagged and he pitched backward on the ground.

"NOO-NOO! Not you, Junior Bill!" Dudley screamed, falling to his knees and cradling his friend's head in his arms as blood spurted from a gaping chest wound. Junior Bill tried to speak.

"What?" Dudley asked, lowering his ear to his mouth.

"Good frieeend."

"Yes, good friend – best friend."

Junior Bill barely nodded and grinned.

"Don't leave me, don't leave me. Hold on. I'll be back," Dudley said as someone grabbed his arm and snatched him to his feet. It was Sergeant Patterson.

"Dammit. Move forward!" Patterson screamed. "Don't you know you could be executed on the spot for stopping?"

Dudley jumped to his feet and stumbled over the dead and dying. *I'd rather be shot while caring for my friend than killed by a damn Yankee bullet,* he thought.

They encountered the prickly osage orange hedge which fenced them inside a slaughtering pen. Artillery raked them. Nearby, he saw Thornton and Jackson go down. Colonel Ives, Commander of the 35th, was wounded, shot four or five times, along with all of the regimental officers. Some of the gray backs made it to the Yankee entrenchment where they clung beneath it, dodging sheets of lead that poured over their heads. The fighting was fierce for two hours. By 5 p.m. it was evident that the attack had failed. The entire brigade began falling back. General Loring, Division Commander, rode out to the front of his men in a hail of heavy rifle fire. Miraculously, none hit him.

"STAND FAST – STAND FAST!" Loring yelled. Dressed in full gray uniform with a sword strapped to his waist and wearing a hat with a large ostrich plume that hung to the side, he sat on his horse for a full minute, bullets splitting the air around him.

"GREAT GOD! DO I COMMAND COWARDS?" he cried out. They weren't cowards, they were being massacred.

---

It was near 4 p.m. when the 50th Alabama reached Winstead Hill a mile and a half south of Franklin. At the front, artillery thundered and thousands of rifles rattled. A hot battle had erupted. Coleman Barksdale's guts tightened.

"Reckon we'll be sent in?" he asked Peavine.

"Yeah, and I got a bad feeling about it."

From his vantage point north of Winstead Hill, Coleman witnessed the attack. Approximately 18,000 Confederates in a mile-wide formation with regimental colors snapping in the late November breeze and bands playing moved forward toward the outer Federal entrenchment. Cannon fire raked their ranks and sheets of bullets from the entrenched Federals slowed but didn't halt the Confederates. Smoke from exploded gun powder rose in a cloud, obscuring the sinking sun, and its acrid odor burned his nostrils.

Thundering cannons shook the earth and the rattle of thousands of muskets was deafening. Men fell by the scores. Coleman felt he was going to die, never to see Eliza and his precious children again, and be buried in a common grave. Peavine noticed Coleman's trembling hands and offered encouragement, "Don't worry, it'll be dark pretty soon and common sense says the fighting'll stop 'til morning."

"Common sense!" exclaimed Coleman. "What common sense?"

He pulled a folded sheet of paper from his pocket and stored it in his hat. "If I don't make it and you do, would you see that Eliza gets this letter?"

"Yeah, I promise," replied Peavine.

Coleman bent over to unlace his shoes. "I want you to have my shoes."

"Thank ya but I'm gonna get me a good pair of Yankee shoes."

They watched as Confederates charged forward toward the outer works, giving the Rebel yell and jumping into the trenches with the Yankees, firing, thrusting and slashing with bayonets. Federals that weren't killed and wounded fled back to the main works a half a mile to the rear. Yelling Confederates were in hot pursuit. When the graybacks neared the main entrenchments, there was no protection from the massive fire power of the Federals, who were lodged safely behind an embankment of earth and logs. The attack slowed and the carnage began.

It was dark and cold when Coleman and the 50th Alabama were finally sent in to reinforce a position west of the Franklin-Columbia Turnpike and east of the Carter Creek Pike. Not familiar with the terrain, they fumbled through the darkness, stumbling over dead bodies, until they reached the Federal entrenchments. Red blazes spurting from Yankee rifles pointed the way. The Confederates attacked the stronghold, firing point blank and running the enemy through with bayonets. The din of gunfire and the screaming and cursing of desperate men filled the night; smoke burned Coleman's eyes and the caustic odor of spent gun powder seared his nose. It was hellish. The Confederates were repulsed. They regrouped and attacked again.

Lt. Adams was yelling, "FALL BACK – FALL BACK!" when a minie ball cut him down. Coleman looked around for Peavine. Had he been hit? He was about to panic when he saw him on his knees, bent over a dead Yankee removing his shoes. Coleman ran toward him and yelled, "COME ON PEAVINE, FALL BACK!"

Peavine looked up and his head flew backward. When Coleman reached him he saw a hole the size of a thimble where a minie ball had entered and on the opposite side was a ragged hole as large as a man's fist where the ball had exited. Coleman dropped his rifle and knelt down and cradled Peavine's head. "Why didn't you... take my... shoes?" he asked, choking back hot tears. He felt something sticky like molasses on his fingers and realized it was blood.

Meanwhile the regiment had regrouped and was attacking. Someone was screaming at Coleman to move forward. He gently lowered Peavine's head to the ground, grabbed his rifle and joined the attack.

The 50th finally overran the Federal position, jumping into the trenches where there was bloody hand-to-hand fighting. Confederates prevailed. General Hood finally called a halt to the slaughter and after the guns fell silent only the cries of the wounded could be heard during the night.

Afterwards, when the panic that gripped his mind and body had faded, Coleman realized that he was freezing. Indian summer had abruptly ended. His fingers and toes were numb. He located Peavine's corpse and, after retrieving his shoe, he curled up in

444

his blanket beside his friend's corpse and slept.

---

It was dark and near freezing on another part of the battlefield when Dudley pulled a thin blanket around his shoulder and, stumbling over corpses and wounded men begging for water, searched for Junior Bill. Maybe he was alive? He found him lying on his back, arms outstretched and legs sprawled apart. He knelt down beside him and lifted his arm to feel his pulse. Rigor mortis had set in. After closing his eyelids he bent his stiff arms and positioned them across his chest. A flood of emotions welled up inside Dudley and his chest ached.

"I love you.... Junior Bill..." he choked. "I've never said that to any man. I'll.... always remember... you." The emotional dam broke and hot tears flowed down his grizzled whiskers. After he had emptied himself of tears, he lay down beside Junior Bill and listened to the cries of the wounded begging for water, praying and calling out for their mothers. Exhausted, he finally fell asleep next to his friend.

---

Bright sunlight in his face woke Dudley. He sat up and looked around at the carnage around him. Hundreds of men wearing both blue and gray lay dead amid equipment and dead horses. There was eerie silence except for the groans of men writhing on the ground.

The Federal entrenchments were empty. During the night the Yankees had stolen away to Nashville to join the main army under the command of General George Thomas.

Dudley had no intention of leaving Junior Bill's corpse unburied. He looked around for a shovel, and, not seeing one, began digging at the earth with his bayonet and scratching it out with his fingers. The grave was shallow, but deep enough to be respectable. He rolled Junior Bill's corpse inside a blanket and gently placed his body into the hole. He scratched his name on a scrap of wood with the point of his bayonet and stuck it in the soft dirt.

Later, he was told that Carnton was being used as a hospital and he walked there hoping to find his friends, Thornton and Jackson, alive. The old mansion was packed with hundreds of wounded Confederates and, after every nook and cranny was filled, they were laid out on the ground. On the back porch were the stiff bodies of Confederate Generals John Adams, Patrick Cleburne, Otho Strahl and Hiram Granbury. And outside an opened window was a large pile of bloody amputated legs and arms.

Dudley walked through hundreds of dead and dying lying on the ground but didn't find Thornton and Jackson. Perhaps their bodies had already been thrown in the deep trench that was still being lengthened.

---

Thursday morning, December 1, 1864.

Somewhere in the distance a bugle sounded. The notes were pure and snappy. It was like a dream. Dudley balled his knees to his chest and reached for the tattered blanket and pulled it over his head. His body shivered uncontrollably. Someone nudged his foot and said, "It's reveille."

Dudley sat up and looked around and was about to tell Junior Bill to cook up a batch of coosh for breakfast when he realized that Junior Bill was dead, along with Spotwood, Thornton and Jackson. An oppressive cloud of despair enveloped him. It felt like an anvil on each shoulder. He stared off blankly into empty space, unable to move. He became aware that his feets and hands were aching with pain. He looked down at his hands first. They were black with dirt and grime, and they throbbed with pain. He tried to clench his fists, but the joints were too stiff. Maybe frozen. His bare feet and toes were the same. Indian summer had abruptly ended and the temperature had plummeted. He had never seen a winter this cold. Everyone agreed it was a record breaker.

Someone threw a fence rail in the fire and a blaze shot up. Dudley huddled close to the flame together with the other men, and they held their hands over it. The heat on his frozen fingers caused more pain and he cried out, "Oh God!"

One of the men said, "The word is we're moving out this morning."

"Where?" asked another.

Later that morning an Officer read a message from General Hood telling the troops that victory was within their grasp. "Be of good cheer... all is well."

"Shucks, who's he fooling?" grumbled a Reb.

Soon, what remained of Hood's Army was in pursuit of the Federals. Dudley had miraculously survived while 150 of his colleagues were casualties. The 150 or more survivors of the 35$^{th}$ Alabama, which had once numbered over 750, picked themselves up and plodded forward. Dudley felt that God had spared him and he also knew that many men had died at Franklin, but it was a long time afterwards before the truth surfaced. In the five bloody hours, 6 Confederate Generals had been killed; also 54 Regimental Commanders had been killed or wounded together with 6,200 men, not to mention 702 captured. The once-vaunted Army of Tennessee was shattered.

The Confederates camped on frozen ground near ice-covered trees. In front, Dudley could see the stars and stripes flying over the State Capital in Nashville. They waited in the bruising cold, hungry and disappointed, as a cold, sharp wind pierced their tattered clothes and bit at their skin. Because they were within range of Yankee artillery, for several nights, fires were not allowed. The penetrating cold occupied every moment of Dudley's thoughts. Later, the men each dug a grave-like trench, stretched a blanket across the top and built a small fire at one end. It kept out most of the rain and snow, but the smoke nearly suffocated them.

When his mind wasn't focused on the cold, it was on food. He dreamed of being home, sitting in front of a warm fire and eating Ma's squirrel dumplings.

He climbed out of the hole and walked back toward where he had seen the officer's horses tethered and fed. Frozen snow crunched beneath his feet and great clouds of vapor streamed from his nostrils when he exhaled. "Oh God! When will this madness end?" His wooden finger scratched on the ground for a few kernels of corn that had fallen from the horse's mouth. He found a few and carefully placed them in his pocket. Parched in grease, they would not only taste good, but quell his gnawing stomach.

On Friday, December 16, Hood threw his bedraggled army of 16,697 against 55,000 well-fed and warmly clothed Federals. The results were not unexpected. The long gray line that had bested the Yankees at Chickamauga and on scores of other battlegrounds buckled, then routed. Many threw down their muskets and ran like rabbits.

What remained of Hood's once-feared Army of Tennessee retreated south toward Florence, Alabama.

446

As they dragged themselves through the snow and ice someone began singing a ditty to the tune of the Yellow Rose of Texas; others joined in until the long gray column was singing:

"And now I'm going southward
For my heart is full of woe.
I'm going back to Georgia
To find my Uncle Joe.

You may talk about Beauregard
And sing of General Lee
But the gallant Hood of Texas
Played hell in Tennessee."

# 44 | HOME FOR CHRISTMAS

Near Lexington, Alabama.

December 23, 1864.

Dudley winced with pain as he limped barefoot down the frozen rutted road. Except for the groans of men whose feet were bruised and bloody, there was no sound other than the rustle of marching men. The 15,000 infantry that remained of Hood's Army was strung out for miles on the Pulaski-Florence Pike headed toward Bainbridge Ferry, east of Florence. Their path of retreat was clearly marked by bloody tracks on the road. That night they biouvacked near Lexington. Dudley sat near a damp fire, wrapped in a thin blanket, shivering, coughing and nursing a rotten cold. Many of the men were sick – and all were hungry. Surely, God hadn't spared him from Yankee bullets so that he could freeze and starve to death. If he had been a boulder when he enlisted, fear, lack of food, inclement weather, illness, loss of friends and just plain misery had ground him down to pebble size. His heart ached when he thought of Junior Bill. So many good men had died – Spotwood, Thornton, Jackson and others. Even little Jesse Holt, who had encouraged him to enlist, was gone – discharged in October, 1862, because of his disability. He realized he barely knew the men who sat shivering around the fire with him. He had willingly shared hardship with his old compatriots and would have taken a minie ball for any one of them, but not these people. He hadn't fought for the cause: he had fought for his friends. He had enlisted to find adventure and seek glory and it had all come down to this – cold, hungry and homesick.

He removed the New Testament from his shirt pocket where Ma had placed it the day he departed home, admonishing him, "Carry it over your heart and read it daily." He had promised her that he would, but he hadn't. At the time he had Junior Bill, Thornton and Jackson to fill up his life. Now, he had no one. He opened the book to the 23rd Psalm and read in silence.

"….Yea, though I walk through the valley of the shadow of death, I will fear no evil: for thou art with me; thy rod and thy staff they comfort me…"

He closed the Bible, dropped his head and prayed in silence. *Dear God, I've been filled with pride and arrogance. Now, I have nothing. I've lost my friends and I'm cold and hungry. I surrender to you. Show me the way. Please, show me the way. Amen.*

It was near midnight when he quietly arose and pulled the blanket around his shoulders. The men in his mess were scrunched against each other and snoring. The night was cold and clear. He carefully made his way out of camp. If stopped by a guard he would tell him he had flux – nearly all had it – and that he was headed to the bushes. When he reached a safe place outside the camp, he stopped, wrapped his frozen feet and hands with rags, then turned east. The dirt road ran from Lexington, through Anderson and straight to Athens. He guessed it was about thirty miles, but he wouldn't think of distance, only placing one foot in front of the other.

The greatest danger was running into Yankees foraging the countryside. He must be careful. Just before daylight he saw what remained of a burned-out log barn. Nearby was a pile of gray ashes and blackened chimney. Yankees! He napped a couple of hours inside the barn, and then struck out walking, keeping in the edge of the tree line and away from houses. He stopped at a spring in the woods where he lay down on his stomach to drink, first gently blowing away the trash. That's when he saw his reflection in the water. His skin was stretched tightly against protruding facial bones and his blue eyes were set in deep dark sockets. He sucked in the fresh water, rose to his feet, threw several kernels of parched corn in his mouth and continued walking.

He had seen devastation, but none worse than what he now saw in North Alabama. Only blackened chimneys remained where once fine homes had stood. Rail fences had been broken down and burned. There were no horses, no livestock and no fowl to be seen. Barns lay in ashes. Once-fertile fields were now covered with briers and brambles. Folks were suffering. How would they survive the winter? He wondered about Ma and Pa.

When the sun set the temperature dropped like a falling rock. He had never been colder. All feeling in his feet was gone. His fingers were numb and when he touched his nose, he couldn't feel it. Diarrhea had wrung every drop of fluid from his bony body. All that remained in his stomach was pain. He stumbled several times. If he fell he might not get up and he would surely freeze to death.

He had been thinking for some time about the problem of crossing the Elk River. When he came home the previous time he and the mare swam across. Not this time. He would be frozen before he climbed the opposite bank. There was only one thing to do – borrow a boat. And that's what he did near Buck Island. After rowing to the opposite bank, he carefully tied the boat to a tree so that it would be secure.

"One foot in front of the other," he said to himself, more to stay awake than to give himself encouragement. Then he hit upon a better, more rhythmic chant. "I can do it – I can do it – I can do it," he whispered each time his left foot hit the ground.

The Limestone County Courthouse would be his beacon of hope. When he saw the tall spire rising in the night sky he knew he would be only three miles from home. If necessary, he could crawl that far. He had to be careful since Yankees would have pickets and guards posted in every direction. He kept off the main road, away from the houses and barking dogs, and walked through fields and pastures.

It was past midnight when he neared Athens and looked for the courthouse spire. It wasn't there! He walked on, squinted and rubbed his tired eyes and looked again. It still wasn't there! Where the courthouse once stood were blackened brick walls.

He stumbled across the foot log over icy Swan Creek. Only a few more hundred yards to go – then home! He summoned the last ounce of energy and picked up his pace. When he saw the old log house in the moonlight his chest ached with emotion. Hot tears streamed down his cheeks onto his grizzled whiskers. He wept with joy and broke into an unsteady jog. He ran beneath the big oak trees in the back yard and called out. "MA – PA – I'M HOME!"

Ol' Luther came out barking and growling. Dudley noticed that he was dragging a rear leg. He staggered over to his hound, but Luther would have none of it. "It's me Luther – it's me." More growling and snarling. It was obvious Luther didn't recognize him.

Thomas stepped out the back door holding a candle aloft. "Who is it?"

"Dudley Richard!" Thomas walked cautiously over close enough so that he could see the figure inside the small circle of light. He looked with puzzlement at the man standing before him.

"Thomas, it's me, Dudley."

Thomas recognized his voice and smiled. "Dudley, you're home!" he exclaimed and grabbed him with a one-arm bear hug.

"What happened to ol' Luther?" asked Dudley.

"Yankees shot him," Thomas replied, putting one arm around Dudley's waist and assisting him into the living room. There were only a few hot coals in the fireplace but Dudley thought it was the warmest place he had ever been. Thomas lit another candle.

"Who is it, Thomas?" Pa asked, entering the room sleepy-eyed and looking directly at Dudley. "Who's this man?"

"It's me Pa – Dudley Richard."

Pa cocked his head and stared at the miserable-looking creature in front of him. Surely, it wasn't Dudley. Then he recognized the blue eyes and began to heave with emotion. They rushed toward each other arms open and hugged until Ma entered the room. She looked much older than when he last saw her. Her once-raven-black hair had turned white.

"Dudley, my son – my son!" She bounded toward him, hugging and kissing his cheeks. "What have they done to you?" Tears streamed down her wrinkled cheeks.

Cal and Cornelia stood in the doorway staring at the ragged figure in front of them, hands at their mouths, as if to express their disbelief. They bolted toward Dudley. "Brother!" they exclaimed in unison.

"Get some food," Ma commanded the girls, "and a quilt!"

Thomas stoked the fire and Cal and Cornelia soon produced a plate of hoecakes, slathered with butter and molasses on the side. Dudley tore into the food like a hungry dog, wolfing it down in silence and enjoying every morsel. With the last bit of bread he wiped the plate clean.

"I've never tasted anything so good in my life," he said, then drank a glass of milk in one long gulp.

The rest of the family was awake, including his young nephews. The children sat around the warm fire staring at Dudley. Finally, "Are you home on furlough, Uncle Dudley?" asked 11-year-old Luke Pryor Newby.

Dudley wiped dribbles of milk from his beard and nodded, "Yeah, you might say that."

"How many Yankees did you kill?" asked Luke Pryor.

Dudley looked up. "Plenty I guess, but not nearly enough."

Ma drilled the child with a cold stare. "Hush young'un, I've heard enough about war 'n killing."

"Yes ma'am."

After scrubbing himself with warm water and lye soap Dudley piled into a feather bed with Thomas.

"I'm finally home," he mumbled.

"What'd ye say?" asked Thomas.

Before he could reply he was asleep.

---

Dudley woke to the rattle of pots and pans and the aroma of fried pork. He closed his eyes and thanked God that he was alive and finally at home with his family. Tears of joy rolled down his cheeks, then he went back to sleep.

Later, he was awakened by something tickling his nose. He slapped at it and rolled over. Then something tickled his ear. When he slapped again he heard giggling. The next time he felt something on his ear, he reached around and grabbed the hand of the perpetrator. It was young Luke Pryor Newby.

"I caught me a prowl'n Yankee," Dudley said.

"I'm no Yankee!" said Luke Pryor. "When I'm sixteen, I'm going to join the Army and shoot Yankees."

"You'll do no such thing," Dudley said. "You'll follow a team of mules and plow the land, if I have a say 'bout it."

"Get up Uncle Dudley and tell us about whipping Yankees."

It was late afternoon when Dudley finally got up and slipped on clean clothes that Ma had laid out for him.

He entered the living room where a warm fire burned in the fireplace. Pa set the big brown leather-bound Bible he had been reading onto a side table. Thomas was smoking his pipe. George had just loaded his pipe and was trying to light it when Dudley walked in. Children were running everywhere, filling the house with shrieks and laughter. The women were in the adjoining room, talking and setting food on the table. It sounded like heaven.

"Welcome home, brother," said George Edward and gave him a warm hug.

Dudley sat down in a ladder back chair near the fire, noticing for the first time a Christmas tree standing in the corner, with several wrapped presents beneath it.

There were numerous questions. Had he seen William Coleman? "No, but the 50th fought at Franklin and went on up to Nashville with us," he said.

They wanted to know how bad a licking Hood had taken.

"We lost a lot of boys at Franklin," said Dudley. "We marched straight at those Yankees head on. I hope I never see anything like it again. So many of our boys were killed at one time, they had no place to fall. They were dead and still standing."

"Ol' Jeff Davis shouldn't have replaced Joe Johnston with Hood," Pa said.

"The Army is shattered," said Dudley. "Most of the men are shoeless, wearing rags, sick and starving to death. It's all over. We've lost."

There was an unspoken question that no one dared ask Dudley, but he answered it for them.

"I'll take the oath if I have to, but when spring comes, I'm gonna make a crop. I wanna smell fresh earth, not gunpowder; walk barefoot in plowed ground and hear trace chains rattle on a plow, not the roar of cannon."

"We got land, such as it is," said Pa. "Most of it's grown over with briers and bushes, but I'm thankful the Yankees didn't burn us out. At least we have a roof over our heads. They took Thomas's team, most of our chickens and hogs and just about cleaned out our smokehouse, but we're still alive."

"When they pulled out of Athens several weeks ago," added George, "the courthouse burned. Some claim it was by accident, I don't know. Of course they had already burned the fairground and several buildings downtown when Forrest liberated us back in September."

"Confederate money is worthless," said Pa. "You could find hen teeth easier than you could find a Yankee dollar. Everybody is living on pure grit."

When Ma called suppertime, the table wasn't nearly large enough to seat all the family. The kids grabbed plates and began looking for an empty spot on the floor. There was a crowd: George Edward and his wife, Mary who lived next door with their five children were there. James Rufus "Rufe" was 13 and growing like a weed. James Edward was 10; Micajah was 8; and Georgiana and John were 5 and 3 years old

451

respectively. Together with the three Newby children and James Greer Barksdale's two young'uns there were 10 kids, all talking and laughing.

Pa took his seat at the head of the table and Ma at the opposite end near the back door leading to the log kitchen. Dudley, Thomas, George Edward, Mary and Sarah Newby, Cal, Cornelia and Susan squeezed in. Pa cleared his throat.

"Shhhh, you young'uns be quiet," said Ma. "And bow your heads."

"Thank ya Lord for this day of life you have given us," Pa prayed, "and for the food prepared by loving hands; for delivering our son Dudley Richard back home to us, safe and sound. Lord, we pray that our beloved son, William Coleman, is safe and well and that Eliza and the children are safe too. Protect our son Robert Beasley and Lucy and little Mollie. We especially pray for James Greer and James Newby in that Yankee prison. Provide them food and warmth and bring them home safely to us. Lastly, we pray that the evil Yankees will soon be gone from our midst. Amen."

"Amen," everyone chimed.

Ma spoke up. "Pa, always calls out the full names when he prays, like the Lord don't know who he's talking about."

"The Lord has a lot on his mind these days," Pa replied. "I'll just wanna make sure he don't get confused."

The adults chuckled.

Dudley spooned out stewed potatoes onto his plate, poured on bacon grease, got a strip of fried fatback and a hoe cake. Just before he dug in, Ma handed him a fried egg on a plate.

"The old hen laid it this morning just for you," she said.

"It's the best Christmas dinner I ever had," Dudley said.

Afterwards, the children opened their presents that were under the tree. Each of the boys received a whistle that Pa had whittled from a hickory tree branch and the girls got corncob and shuck dolls. That night, buried deep in a featherbed and beneath a pile of Ma's quilts and listening to the wind whistle through the chinks in the old log house, Dudley knew he had made the right decision.

# 45 | BUSHWHACKER STRIKES AGAIN

Paint Rock Valley, Jackson County, Alabama.
Saturday, December 31, 1864.

The night was bitter cold. Three inches of snow lay on the ground and hung like blankets in the numerous cedar trees that covered the steep, rocky ridge, giving them the appearance of ghosts. A few miles distance the ridge jutted above the railroad bridge that crossed Paint Rock River. The men tethered their horses while the officers assigned sentries to guard them and made last-minute inspections as each man checked to see that his rifle and pistols were loaded.

"Leave everything behind that jingles or jangles," Bushwhacker commanded in a low voice, "and watch where you step. Loose rocks are everywhere and if you step on one and it rolls down the mountain, the Yankees will know that we're here."

Robert Beasley Barksdale gazed up the ridge, white and peaceful-looking beneath the starlight. "Let's move out," Bushwhacker said in a hushed tone. The 35 men slowly made their way upward, their feet crunching in the snow. By the time they reached the summit, Robert was breathing hard but otherwise warm except for his hands and feet. When the column paused for a breather, he massaged his hands in an effort to warm them. The column moved westward toward the objective, a company of home-made Yankees hopefully asleep in a house located at the south end of the bridge and a company of regulars in a house on the north end of the bridge. Following Hood's retreat at Franklin and Nashville, Union soldiers had returned to North Alabama by the thousands. Securing the Memphis and Charleston Railroad tracks and bridges was a top priority with them.

Going was slow as the men picked their way around the boulders, rocks and trees. They crept down the ridge for several hours and when they got close to the bridge as they dared, they halted and waited quietly in the darkness. They would attack at first light.

Robert blew warm breath on his numb fingers and wiggled his toes. The cold was excruciating. The more he focused on his own misery, the more miserable he became. *Think of something pleasant.* Several miles north of the valley, Lucy and little Mollie would be sound asleep and cozy warm buried deep in a feather bed. Ahhh, to be there with them, cuddled against the two people who meant the most to him. Then his mind took on a more unpleasant subject. Shortly, when the fight began, he might catch a ball and be dead. The thought terrified him, but at least it kept his mind off his cold fingers and toes for a moment.

When the first streak of pink appeared on the eastern horizon, someone whispered, "Move out. Pass it on."

The men inched down the mountain, the crunch of snow beneath their feet and heavy breathing being the only sound. The fear that welled up inside Robert combined with physical exertion soon thawed his toes and fingers. When they neared the bridge, they halted and sat in silence. The pink streak on the eastern horizon grew wider.

"Move down the mountain," whispered Bushwhacker to the man next to him, who passed it on. The men crept down the mountain and over to the house at the north end of the bridge where the regular blue coats were asleep. When the men had surrounded the house, Bushwhacker gave the command:

"LET 'EM HAVE IT BOYS!"

453

Robert and a handful of men giving the Rebel yell burst through the door of one house with rifles and pistols drawn. "SURRENDER, SURRENDER!"

Dazed and groggy after being suddenly awakened, most of the soldiers threw up their hands and surrendered. A few foolish ones didn't and were shot.

The company of homemade Yankees at the south end of the bridge, having been awakened by gunfire and loud noise, sprang from their beds and fled. Most didn't pause to put on shoes, pants, coats or hats. They ran for their lives through the snow, clad only in their underwear.

Robert and the guerillas horse laughed. Witnessing the sight of half-naked Yankees skedaddling made spending the night in insufferable cold worth it. The victory was complete. Forty-five Federals were taken prisoner and a captured cannon was spiked and rolled into the river. They torched the bridge and with prisoners in tow returned to their horses and headed toward the Tennessee River.

---

Near Athens.

Monday morning, January 16, 1865.

The Daniel Barksdale house was quiet except for cold wind moaning around the eaves, the crackle of wood in the fireplace, and the "thump – thump – thump" of the treadle on the spinning wheel. Pa sat in his rocking chair near the warm fire, eyes closed and chin on his chest, the large brown Bible resting in his lap. Cal was carding cotton lint, handing it over to Cornelia who rolled it between her palms, creating a rope that Ma spun into thread. Dudley and Thomas were slouched down in their chairs, staring sleepy-eyed into the leaping flames.

Dudley thought about General Hood's skeleton army, now camped at Tupelo. It was reported that fewer than one-half of the men had blankets and shoes. They were hungry and many were ill. Rain, snow and freezing weather compounded their misery. Dudley couldn't clear his mind of the awful slaughter he had witnessed at Franklin; the misery the men had endured on the retreat south to Florence; the lack of proper food, clothing, shoes and blankets. His brother, Coleman was still with the Army and no doubt suffering this minute. *Why don't he come home like I did? The cause is lost. What will Coleman and my other brothers think when they return home and learn that I've deserted? Desertion. Oh, what a foul word. No matter how I dress it up by calling it a self-furlough, I gave up. Quit. But, I'm not sorry that I did.*

The Fourth Corps, USA, that pursued Hood had halted at Florence and come through Athens on the way to Huntsville. A division of cavalry had also passed through on January 2nd. Yankee soldiers were thicker than locusts, entering homes and taking what they wanted, cleaning out smokehouses, killing chickens, ducks and geese and leading off milk cows. One bunch had appeared at the back door the previous week, entered the smokehouse and took all their meat, then stripped the barn of corn and fodder. Thank Heaven that he and Thomas had taken the precaution of hiding some corn, fodder and bacon sides in the woods near Swan Creek, otherwise they would be destitute. Ol' Maude was so broken down they didn't want her. The story was the same all over the county. He had walked to Johnson Branch and checked on Eliza and the children – they still had meat and corn and their milk cow – and Eliza was pregnant again. He smiled. Every time Coleman came home he got her in a family way.

"BAM – BAM – BAM!" Someone knocking on the back door brought Dudley

454

erect in his chair. His pulse quickened. Yankees? Ma stopped the spinning wheel. Pa woke abruptly. Everyone's eyes met, but no one muttered a word. Yankees usually didn't knock, they just took what they wanted. Ma got up and quietly went to the side window and pulled back the curtain and peeked out.

"I don't see horses or blue uniforms," she said and breathed a sigh of relief.

"I'll see who it is Ma," said Dudley.

"No! Not you," said Ma. "You go in the other room until we know who it is."

"I'll see," said Thomas and went to the door and opened it, letting in a cold draft.

"Why Miss Mary!" he exclaimed. "Come in outta the cold."

Mary Fielding entered the living room, topcoat buttoned to her chin, bonnet tight around her head, red face and runny nose.

"Whew, I've never seen a colder day," she said.

Mary, the 32-year-old spinster daughter of William and Sarah Fielding, lived approximately two miles northeast of the Barksdale home. Her father had died ten years earlier and she lived with her widowed mother and siblings when not residing in Athens taking care of Mrs. Anna Eliza Maclin, a semi-invalid. Four of her brothers were serving in the Confederate Army: William Eppa "Eppie", Henry Rhodes, John Everett "Jack" and James Madison "Jimmy".

"What'n the world are you doing out on day like this?" asked Ma.

Pa stood. "Take my chair and warm yourself."

"Thank you Mr. Barksdale, but I'll stand a minute in front of the fire," she said. "I've come to ask to borrow your buggy to go to town."

"Why certainly," said Pa then looked at Thomas and spoke loudly.

"Hitch up ol' Maude to the buggy?"

"Yes sir Pa," Thomas said and slipped on his coat and hat. "Scuse me, Miss Mary," he said and departed.

"How y'all been gett'n by?" asked Pa.

"As well as most folks," Mary said, rubbing her cold hands over the fire. "Yankees appeared at Mr. John Fraser's place a couple of weeks ago and without so much as a hello, cut his beautiful grove to make crossties."

"All those big chestnuts, oaks and poplar!" exclaimed Pa with disbelief.

"Certainly did."

"By crackies, they oughta be shot!"

"The cavalry that stopped in Athens just about scoured the county clean," said Mary. "Some of them came to our house and took nearly all of our corn, quilts and most of our meat, clothes and so forth. They searched our house three or four times a day. I'm surprised they didn't stop here."

"Oh, they did," Ma said. "They just about cleaned us out too."

"Ma went to town Thursday with receipts that had been given to her hoping to be paid," continued Mary, "but they sent her from here to there, said they didn't have blanks and couldn't give her the vouchers–"

"They didn't bother to give us a receipt," interjected Pa. "They just took what they wanted."

"They completely cleaned out some families, leaving nothing for them to eat," Mary said. "That's what happened at Dr. Stith Malone's residence. The children are crying with hunger. And just think, back in December, Dr. Malone took in wounded

Confederates and Yankees alike and treated them equally."

"Pa, we need to share some of our corn with the Malone family," said Ma.

"I'll see to it," he replied. 'We have a dab kept in hiding."

"I never considered that I'd starve," said Mary. "But I don't know where I'll get the next bite of bread."

"Now, don't you worry Mary, we'll share a little cornmeal with you," said Ma.

"There is one bit of good news," said Mary flashing a wicked smile at Pa.

"Well, don't keep us in the dark," he said.

"The Yankees completely cleaned out Mr. Isom," she said smiling, "Took all of his meat and corn and –"

"-By crackies!" exclaimed Pa and slapped his leg. "It couldn'ta happened to a more deserving fellow. Maybe Emanuel will change his tune now."

"Pa!" exclaimed Ma. "Watch your tongue. The Lord will judge the righteous and the unrighteous."

"I know my Bible," replied Pa. "It also says that a man reaps what he sows."

"I guess his Union sympathies didn't help him," said Mary, a twinkle in her eye.

Dudley entered the room. "Hello Miss Mary. How you?"

Mary looked up, surprised. "I didn't know you were home!"

Dudley averted her eyes. "Come home Christmas," he said flatly.

"I see," she said disapprovingly.

"You may as well hear it from me," said Dudley. "I came home; got my sights set on plant'n cotton 'n corn come spring."

There was a moment of awkward silence. Mary looked around at her hosts and said, "Well, I guess I better be on my way to Athens. Thank you for sharing the warm fire and thank you, Mr. Barksdale, for the use of the buggy."

"Any time. That's what neighbors are for," said Pa as Mary buttoned her coat and retied her bonnet and departed.

---

Near Hazel Green, Alabama.
January 18, 1865.

Approximately 25 miles east of Daniel Barksdale's warm log house, his son, Robert Beasley, and a handful of guerillas led by Bushwhacker Johnson rode northwest toward Hazel Green. It was biting cold and, so far, a peaceful Wednesday morning.

New Year's had come and gone and brought with it more Yankees and harder times. Whenever the guerillas struck, Federals retaliated by burning out those suspected of aiding them, including torching clothing and bedding, turning people out in to the cold with no food, with no shelter and only the clothes on their backs.

Hood's defeat at Franklin and Nashville had sounded the death-knell for the Army of Tennessee. Although the Army had fought on under General Joe Johnston, any reasonable person could see that it wouldn't last much longer. But defeat wasn't a subject openly discussed.

"Have you ever thought about quitt'n and going home?" Robert asked Ragsdale, who rode next to him, his head scrunched between his shoulders to ward off the cold.

Ragsdale, whose thoughts were elsewhere, didn't answer immediately. Finally he said, "I've thought about it once or twice. What about you?"

"Yeah," Robert replied.

456

Ragsdale looked at Robert with surprise.

"But it didn't take long for me to reach a decision," Robert continued. "I didn't enlist to defend State's Rights or Slavery. I enlisted to defend my home and family and all I have left is my family, my friends and my honor. As long as the Lord gives me strength and good health, I'll keep on fighting."

"Same here," replied Ragsdale. "We're both fit as a fiddle, so I guess we'll fight on till we're killed or the war ends."

The conversation was interrupted when Bushwhacker Johnston signaled a halt after a scout rode up and reported that Regimental Commander Colonel Lemuel Mead and a squad of men were nearby. The two groups combined forces with Mead in command. Shortly, scouts brought fresh news that a large wagon train of Federals were nearby, scouring the area and taking what they wanted. Robert temporarily forgot about the biting cold on his face and fingers. Here was an opportunity to strike the devils who had visited so much misery on the community. The men were chomping at the bits to get at them.

Colonel Mead gave a hand signal and in a low tone said, "Advance slowly." They rode quietly through a wooded area in the direction of the wagon train. When they neared the main road, Mead spied the wagons parked at a residence. He ordered a halt and observed them for several minutes. Robert counted at least twenty wagons and saw dozens of troops loading them with provisions taken from the house and out buildings.

"Move forward," Colonel Mead said quietly and they rode forward and halted again. After formulating a plan of attack, he selected a squad of men and told them: "Boys, I want you to charge them fast and hard. Now do it!"

Eager to punish the Yankees who had been terrorizing the countryside, the men kicked their mounts and bolted out of the saplings, the horses thundering forward dirt flying from their hooves and the riders giving the Rebel yell.

Robert watched with apprehension as the Yankees hastily drew their wagons in a line to form a barricade from which they fired behind. Some of the Federals fled into the residence and others into nearby cabins. Obviously, they had spotted the Rebels before the charge was launched and now greeted them with lead. The Rebels fell back. Colonel Mead stood in the stirrups observing the action, jaws rigid, consternation on his face. He turned to Bushwhacker Johnston and barked: "Major Johnston, take your men and give support."

"Yes sir," said Bushwhacker. He turned and spoke to his men: "Boys, let's give 'em the sword of the Lord. Follow me!"

They sprang forward at a gallop toward the wagons, then wheeled to the right and swept down a lane that lead from the north directly to the house where many of the Yankees had taken refuge and were firing. Robert's fine bay horse loved to race and he had to rein him back to keep from running ahead of the charging horsemen. Just as they charged from the north giving the Rebel yell, the first squad recharged from the east, catching the Yankees in a pincer movement. Resistance melted. Yankees fled from the house and cabins and from behind the wagons, running pell mell, trying to escape. The Rebels rode through the fleeing troops, slashing and cutting them with swords and firing their pistols. The fight ended abruptly when the Yankees threw down their weapons and surrendered.

Captain James L. Baxter of Company H that had been organized in Lincoln County, Tennessee, was the only casualty. After capturing a surrendered soldier, he had

457

turned his back and the man shot him. Dr. David Shelly, a local physician, was summoned, but there was little he could do, other than give comfort.

The wagons loaded with forage were captured, along with their teams. The wagons were burned but the horses and mules were kept. The tally of prisoners exceeded the number of Rebels. That night they camped at "the barrens" north of Hazel Green, where the captors and the captives engaged in a singing competition. The Rebels gave a rousing rendition of *Dixie* which was answered with a Yankee war song; tit-for-tat continuing into the night. The next day they rode southeast toward Jackson County where they crossed the Tennessee River at Laws Landing and delivered the prisoner into "Dixie".

---

Rock Island Barracks.
Rock Island, Illinois.
February 18, 1865.
James Greer Barksdale and James M. Newby, together with other prisoners, were crowded around the pot-bellied stove that huffed and labored to push back the cold, but when the thermometer dropped to zero it became a losing battle. Outside, the wind swept across the icy Mississippi River and howled between the barracks before whistling through the board walls and filling the room with a cold that penetrated to the bone marrow.

The front door opened, sending an icy draft into the room.

"Close the door!" shouted one of the men.

Barksdale looked up and saw a tall, ruddy-faced man walking toward them.

"Can I wedge in?" asked the man, rubbing his cold hands near the stove. The voice sounds familiar, thought Barksdale. He moved over and eyed the man closely – hazel eyes, auburn hair and about his own age. He poked out his hand. "Jim Barksdale, welcome to hell," he said.

The man seemed stunned, his eyes teared and lips trembled. "Jim – Jim–" his voice quivered. "Don't you recognize me?" he asked, grabbing Barksdale's hand and pumping it.

Barksdale shook his head, "No..."

"I'm Mike – Micajah McElroy, your first cousin."

Barksdale stared at the man for a moment, unable to speak, as emotions welled inside him. "Well, break my leg if it isn't," he said wiping his eyes. The two men hugged and slapped each other in the back. "When did you arrive?" asked Barksdale.

"Today after the longest and coldest journey I ever took."

"Where were you captured?"

"In Shelbyville on January 7th," replied McElroy. "They shipped me to Louisville, where I arrived on February 8th, then sent me here."

Barksdale introduced Newby and the other men, all clambering for news.

"There's no good news," said McElroy. "Lincoln was re-elected, Hood was defeated at Franklin and what's left of his Army crossed the Tennessee River and is wintering at Tupelo. If the rest of the Confederate states look anything like Tennessee the whole Confederacy is in shambles. General Lee is still holding on near Petersburg, Virginia, but there isn't much hope."

"What about Rufus Cooley and Jack?" asked Barksdale.

458

"Rufus Cooley is with McLemore's Fourth Tennessee Cavalry and .... Well, Jack furloughed himself and took the oath."

"Deserted?" asked Barksdale.

"Yeah, if you want to put it that way."

Barksdale gave his cousin all the news he had about the family back in Athens, but it was sparse. "I've been here since Missionary Ridge."

Barksdale and McElroy sat around the stove talking about family and growing up in Fayetteville and fishing and swimming on Cane Creek, coon hunting and squirrel hunting.

"It's sure good to see family," said McElroy. ""It makes life a heap easier here."

"Yeah, you're right."

"Maybe, we'll all go home before too long," said McElroy.

"Home... That's the sweetest word in the English language," said Barksdale.

---

The mountains of Jackson County, Alabama.

March, 1865.

Robert Beasley Barksdale woke before daylight, sweaty and clammy, which was odd since he was sleeping on the cold ground. He threw back the wool blanket that he had taken from a blue coat and pondered the oddity. The morning air was crisp and around him men were asleep, rolled up in blankets. He had eaten little the day before – he just wasn't hungry – and he had gone to sleep with a dull headache which was now worse. He was sick! Many of the men were ill, dysentery being the most common. A few had flu and many were hacking, sneezing and coughing with common colds. Chilled, he pulled the blanket around him, shaking one minute and burning up the next. His jaw throbbed with pain. He felt behind his ear and there was swelling.

Ragsdale sat up and yawned and eyed Robert in the early light.

"You moaned half the night," he said.

"I'm coming down with something," Robert muttered.

Ragsdale bent over, inspecting Robert, and then jerked back. "Probably the flu," he said.

During the day Robert's symptoms grew worse. Fever climbed and the gland on the left side of his neck continued to swell and ache, making it difficult for him to swallow. First Sergeant Council, accompanied by a local physician who was present checking on the sick, strolled over to where Robert was lying and asked how he felt.

"Awful," he replied weakly.

The doctor bent over and felt Robert's forehead. "Ummm, burning up with fever," he said to no one in particular, then palpitated both sides of his neck, one of which was swollen.

"Mumps. No doubt about it," the doctor declared. He stood and spoke to Sergeant Council. "Mumps are highly contagious. This man not only needs to be cared for, he needs to be removed from camp immediately. There is no telling how many other men have already been infected, but the symptoms haven't appeared yet."

The doctor addressed Robert. "Your duty is over, soldier – at least for a while. I'm going to request that you be sent home as soon as possible. You need to be careful lest orchitis develops."

459

"What's that?" Robert mumbled.

"Mumps can fall and inflame your testicles," the doctor replied. "It's very painful and, if bad enough, can cause sterility."

That afternoon Ragsdale assisted Robert into a wagon, tied his horse to the back and hauled him to a nearby log house where a widow and her young teenage son resided. She agreed to put Robert up in a separate room for a few days. Throwing a blanket on the board floor, she said: "put 'im there, it's the best I have to offer."

Ragsdale assisted Robert onto his new bed, covered him with a blanket and handed him some Yankee hardtacks. "Good luck," he said and departed.

"Keep up the fight," Robert said weakly.

Widow Puckett, thin and sickly-looking, had lost her husband a year earlier to disease; one son had been killed at Chickamauga and another son was currently serving with General Johnston in the Carolinas.

Having had mumps at an early age, she checked on Robert frequently and provided him with drinking water. He shared hardtack with her and the boy.

Every outside noise sent the poor woman scurrying to the window to see if Yankees had returned. "They took just about everything we had – food, furniture and most of our clothes," she said. "I live in constant fear they'll be back. I ain't afraid for myself, but I'm afraid for my boy, Zeke."

Robert knew if Yankees found him present, they would most likely shoot him and the boy and burn the house, but the likelihood of Yankees prowling around "Bushwhacker" country was minimal. But Widow Puckett didn't know that.

"I'll be leaving tomorrow morning," he said with as much enthusiasm as he could muster.

"You still have fever."

"It ain't as bad as it was. Anyway I'm dying to see my wife and daughter."

Early next morning Zeke brought Johnny from the hiding place in the woods and with assistance, Robert climbed in the saddle. "Much obliged for everything," he said.

"Wrap this blanket around you real good," Widow Puckett said, handing him his Yankee wool blanket. He pulled it tightly around his shoulders and the warmth it offered was welcomed.

"Keep a sharp eye out for Yankees, they're everywhere," she offered.

"I will and again, I thank both of you." He clucked to Johnny and nudged him forward.

"God bless you!" Widow Puckett yelled and waved as he rode out of the yard.

He rode west across the rugged mountains and toward New Market. As the crow flies, it wasn't over twenty miles, but the going was slow as he picked his way up and down ridges and through timber and rocks. Once he reached Paint Rock River valley, traveling would be easier. But, the valley also offered the greatest danger for Yankee patrols. If he was caught armed and riding a good horse they would accuse him of being a Bushwhacker and shoot him on spot, but there was no turning around. He would take his chances.

Later afternoon, he halted on the brow of a wooded ridge and studied the valley below where the Paint Rock River flowed generally south. Seeing no movement, he slowly picked his way down the mountain and forded the river, getting his feet wet in the cold water. When he climbed the opposite bank and came out on level ground, Johnny's

460

ears stopped moving rhythmically back and forth and suddenly pointed to the front. Before he had a chance to react, he was face-to-face with three blue coats standing beside their horses and urinating. They were as surprised as he was and scrambled to draw their pistols.

"HALT!"

Robert didn't think – he didn't have time. Instinct took over. He kicked the bay's flanks hard and yelled "Go Johnny!" Giving the rebel yell and keeping low in the saddle, he rode straight at the surprised soldiers as they bolted to get out of his way.

"SHOOT HIM!" A pistol fired, then another, but with no effect. He came to a dirt road that led north up the valley and swung the bay onto it and gave him plenty of rein. He glanced back and saw the Yankees coming fast. They were riding well-nourished mounts and firing revolvers. Robert knew that his life depended on his horse. "Run Johnny run!" The horses ears perked up, and flew backward as he bolted forward, neck stretched and nostrils flared. Gradually the blue coats faded in the distance. When they finally disappeared in a cloud of dust, Robert reined back and rode into the woods and let his horse rest. He was lathered and sucking air. Robert stroked his neck. "Good boy Johnny, good boy."

He decided to wait until darkness before proceeding. With luck he ought to be at his brother-in-law's place around midnight. Then he became aware that he was cold and had fever, but he was alive.

He was burning up with fever and slumped in the saddle when he turned off the road and rode toward his brother-in-law's darkened house. Barking hounds came out led by Brownie. "Quiet Brownie!" Robert hollered, "HELLOOO Johnnn."

John Giddens came out on the porch. "Who's there?"

"Robert," replied Barksdale, weakly.

"Well, come on in."

"I'm sick with mumps."

"I've had 'em," John said and came off the porch and assisted Robert from the saddle. "The first thing we've gotta do is thaw you out." He helped Robert inside and stoked the fire.

"Take care of my horse, will ya John?" Robert asked. "He's in worse shape than me."

John nodded. "Okay."

"And give him an extra helping of corn if you have it," Robert added. The adults were awake and had come to inquire about the disturbance.

"Robbbeeerrrt," Lucy exclaimed and bolted toward her husband, who was slumped in a chair in front of the fire.

"No Lucy," Robert said holding up his hand. "I've got mumps."

"I don't care," she replied and ran to him. "Thank God you're home and I can take care of you."

Later, Robert related his narrow escape from the Yankees in Paint Rock Valley. "They'll be combing the countryside looking for me," he said. "If they find me here John, they'll burn you out for sure."

"Did they get a good look at you?"

"I don't think so. They were about as surprised to see me as I was to see them. But, they won't ever forget Johnny. He gave 'em a run for their money."

"You'll remain here where we can care for you and I'll hide your horse in the

461

mountains," said John.

Lucy made a pallet on the floor in front of the fireplace and Robert slept fitfully, waking several times in the night when Lucy placed a cold, water soaked rag on his forehead. Once, he awoke when she was kissing his cheek and stroking his face. He smiled and went back to sleep. The worst part was waking up the next morning and seeing Mollie standing in the doorway, looking scared with tears streaming down her cheeks, and not being able to hold her.

"I'll be okay," he said, reassuring her.

"Papa, I love you."

"And I love you darling."

When Mollie had departed, Robert closed his eyes and thanked God that he was alive and finally home with his family.

The following day Lucy made a pallet in the attic where Robert recuperated. It was cold there at nights, but Lucy kept him warm with plenty of quilts.

---

Barking hounds woke Robert. He lay motionless in the pitch-dark attic and listened. It was the manner the dogs barked and snarled that disturbed him. He heard horses. Riders were present. Yankees! He heard the front door slam and then his brother-in-law ask, "What do you want?"

"You John Giddins?"

"Yeah."

"We're looking for your bushwhacker brother-in-law," a voice said.

"Well, you won't find him here," John replied.

Maybe they will ride off, Robert told himself. Why would they suspect that he was present? He had arrived at night and hadn't been out of the house. They were merely guessing that he was present. No worry.

"Then you won't mind if we look around," he heard the voice say.

Robert's heart jumped to his throat; his mind raced. If they came up to the attic he was a dead man. He heard the thud of boots downstairs as the soldiers searched through the house from room to room. Children shrieked. The devils were scaring the kids. He rolled over on his belly and through the slits in the board floor saw light that glowed from a lamp that his brother-in-law carried. And he also saw armed soldiers.

His heart pounded so loudly that he couldn't hear the conversation, but he did hear a soldier ask John, "What's up there?"

"The attic."

"Is anyone up there?" the soldier asked.

"One of the children."

"I'll see for myself."

Robert heard boards creaking as someone climbed the steps. He pulled his knees to his chest and made himself look as small as possible then jerked the quilts over his head.

"He has mumps," John said casually. The footsteps stopped.

"Mumps?" the voice asked.

"Yeah, he's real sick."

"Pass me the lamp," the Yankee ordered and continued to climb the stairs.

Suddenly, light glowed dimly in the attic. Robert lay still, holding his breath

462

pretending to be asleep. He could feel the man's eyes on him. An eternity passed. Then he heard boards creaking and darkness returned as the soldier backed down the steps. Robert breathed deeply and exhaled slowly. Fear and tension had sapped his strength — his hands trembled and his heart raced as he heard the soldiers mount up and ride off. Someone was coming up the stairs.

"Are you okay?" asked John.

"Yeah, but I'm so weak I can't move."

# 46 | A LOST CAUSE

Hillsboro, North Carolina.
Monday, April 17, 1865.
Coleman Barksdale and the bedraggled men of the 50th Alabama watched in silence as the retinue of horsemen trotted past them headed south toward Union lines hoisting a flag of truce. General Johnston, appearing tired and worried but still nattily attired in a full gray uniform, rode at the head of the small column of officers. Birds chirped. Maybe it was a good omen.

Well, ain't nuth'n we can do but wait," Tom Barker said. "We might as well play some cards."

"I don't feel up to it," Coleman said and walked off to be alone. He felt antsy. His guts roiled but he knew it wasn't flux this time, or the fact that he was hungry. Nor was it fear. He decided it was uncertainty. If terms of surrender were worked out, he would soon be going home to see Eliza and his children. If terms weren't reached, he could be going into battle by the end of the week greatly outnumbered against a well-fed and well-equipped enemy. And he could be dead within days. One day his luck would run out. So many men had fallen around him at Franklin that there wasn't enough room for them to hit the ground. Some stood erect but dead beneath the earthen works. Yet, he was unscathed. Following that horrible slaughter and the battle of Nashville, they had retreated south across the Tennessee River and camped at Tupelo where they were shipped by a patchwork of rails to the Carolinas to fight Sherman. General Lee had surrendered a week ago and now Sherman was at their back door.

He had fought at Kingston on March 7-10, where they captured a stand of colors and 300 men of the 15th Connecticut, and battled again at Bentonville a week later and emerged unscathed. What was the Lord saving him for? How long would his luck hold? How much longer would his fragile body endure?

His maternal ancestors had bloodied this land previously. Grandfather Micajah McElroy had fought Tories at nearby Lindley's Mill 85 years ago and his mother had been born less than 40 miles away in Wake County. Had he returned to his roots to die?

That evening around the campfire rumors ran rampant. "It's a Yankee trick to lull us into a trap," said one gray back.

"I heard we'll be leaving for home tomorrow," Tom Barker said.

The next week was agony. There was nothing to do but wait. Rations were cut again. Men were hungry. They learned that President Lincoln had been shot through the head and had died on April 15th. If a surrender agreement wasn't reached every gray back knew the Yankees would be seeking revenge. There would be a slaughter. The uncertainty increased. Finally, on Wednesday, April 26th the bugler blew assembly and the men fell in formation.

"General Johnston has surrendered," Captain Richardson said flatly. Murmuring swept through the ranks. Groans. But mostly, the men said nothing. Four years of fighting and privation and it came down to this – quitting! There was no celebration.

Coleman felt neither jubilation nor disappointment. He was empty inside. For the first time, he heard the birds flutter and chirp noticed crocuses peeking through the ground and the blooming redbuds that dotted the edge of the fields.

On Sunday morning, April 30th, Coleman stacked his Enfield rifle, signed an

Oath of Allegiance to the United States Government and drew ten days rations and departed by railcar for home. Gradually, his emotions returned. The nightmare was finally over and yes, he was going home to Eliza and his precious children. The thought brought a wide smile to his face.

"Tom, can you believe it? We're going home."

"The first thing I'm gonna do when I reach Elkmont is eat fried chicken and fluffy biscuits, cream potatoes with thick'n gravy poured over 'em and –"

"Hush Tom! You're making me hungry."

"Then I'm gonna drink a gallon of coffee. Just pick up the pot and pour it out the sides into my mouth –"

"Hum, what I'd give for a cup of coffee and a good smoke," said Coleman.

"Then I'm gonna sit on the front porch with Ma and Pa and smoke 'til just before I pass out."

"Then, what are ye gonna do?" asked Coleman.

"Take a long bath in Sulphur Creek til I squeak, that I'm gonna sleep on a real bed."

"When you wake, what are you gonna do?" asked Coleman.

"Go hunt'n."

"For what?"

"Squirrel, rabbits, coon, possum," Tom laughed. "Then females!"

All along the route, Coleman saw the aftermath of war; blackened chimneys standing in heaps of ashes, burned out barns, grown-over fields, broken-down rail fences and practically no livestock or fowls. He was in the same condition as the countryside – all broken down and used up. He was barefoot again, ragged and his ribs showed.

The cars made the Memphis and Charleston iron rails sing as they chuffed through Chattanooga, Bridgeport and Huntsville before finally screeching to a halt in Decatur, where he and Tom got off, shook hands and parted company. Coleman thought about stopping to see Ma and Pa and the family on the way home, but that would have to wait for another time. He ached to hold Eliza and his children. Tom headed north on the Athens-Decatur Pike and Coleman walked east to Mooresville, and then hobbled north up the dirt road to where it intersected with Nick Davis. Almost being home set him to whistling. To be alive on a beautiful spring day was a great gift; something to be happy about, especially since hundreds of thousands of lives had been lost. And, he was going home to his wife and children. He raised his face toward heaven and shouted. "Hallelujah! Thank you Lord!"

The sun was setting behind his back and he followed a long shadow when he came to Johnson Branch, waded across it, then cut through the woods. The house was no more than a mile away. When he exited the woods onto a dirt road, he would be able to see the home place. Would it still be standing or would it be a pile of ashes? He quickened his pace. He stepped onto the dirt road and saw the house and separate log kitchen. "Thank the Lord," he mumbled. Ophelia was at the well in the front yard drawing water. He threw his arm in the air, waving.

"OPHEEELIA!"

She looked up and, seeing him, dropped the bucket.

"PAAA!"

The children scrambled from the cabin and ran down the road to meet him. Samson and the other dogs ran toward him, barking and yelping. Eliza waddled slowly toward him as the children jumped with glee. "Papa... Papa! You're home!" they screamed and assaulted him with hugs.

Finally, Eliza waddled up. He looked at her and knew why she had been so slow in coming. She was very pregnant.

"When?" he asked.

"Any day now."

The pickings were slim at supper, but Ophelia, almost thirteen years old, managed to scrape together a tasty meal of fried potatoes and black-eyed peas, cornbread and thick molasses.

"I know you're sick 'n tired of eat'n cornbread," she said and placed a large pone on the table, "but it's awfully good with potatoes and peas."

"Daughter, I'm so hungry I could eat skillet and all," Coleman replied.

"Papa's gonna eat the skillet too!" exclaimed four-year-old Emmit.

They all laughed.

Coleman said grace, thanking the Lord that he was home, his family safe and the war finally over.

"Any milk?" he asked.

"Not a drop," replied Eliza. "Ol' Bossy has gone dry."

"Oh, what I'd give for a glass of sweet milk and a big hunk of butter on my cornbread."

"Maybe she'll be in before long," Eliza said.

"Did the Yankees steal all our chickens?" he asked.

"We have three hens and they're all sitt'n. We'll have baby chicks soon."

Coleman sopped up molasses with crusty cornbread and declared it was the best supper he'd ever eaten.

That night in bed Eliza placed Coleman's hand on her bulging stomach.

"I feel it kicking," he said.

"This represents the future," she said. "Today, our lives begin anew. Welcome home darling."

Coleman scooted closer and kissed her gently on the cheek. "There's no other place I'd rather be."

After sleeping late the following morning, he breakfasted on leftovers, and then walked over his small farm to take account. Jim Dan and the children old enough to work had kept a small plot of land cleared where they had grown a patch of corn and sorghum and a vegetable garden, but the rest of the farm was grown over with sassafras bushes, blackberry briers and weeds. Much work needed to be done. He would borrow a team of oxen from his father-in-law, Hansel Harvey, begin cleaning and readying the ground for planting. The children had already planted potatoes, onions and early corn. Blackberries would be coming in soon; there were wild muscadines in the woods and fish in the branch. And the sow was about to pig and Ol' Bossy would soon be calving. They wouldn't starve. The rail fence around the pasture was practically non-existent. Chestnut rail would have to be cut and split. Whew, a lot of work lay ahead. Just thinking about it made him tired.

Federal troops occupied the county, scalawags ran the Government and freed Negroes were jobless and roaming the countryside. He had no money. Times were hard, but shucks, hard times were his stock and trade. And after four long years of war, his future looked nothing but bright.

466

Rock Island Prison
Rock Island, Illinois
Saturday morning, May 27, 1865

Post Adjutant Lt. Hayes stood near a table bearing pen and paper that had been set out beneath a blue spring sky. A warm breeze wafted across the lazy Mississippi River, bringing with it the scent of fish.

"Rebel prisoners, give me your attention," barked Lieutenant Hayes. "I have good news for you."

The ragged formation of grizzled and disheveled gray backs made no visible response, merely continuing to slouch while some yawned as if to show disrespect. All looked at him grim-faced and vacant-eyed. It should have been a moment of great joy and jubilation, but the men wouldn't give their captor the satisfaction of knowing that they were happy. In truth, James Greer "Jim" Barksdale's heart was about to burst with joy. Men had been departing for home almost daily from this hellhole where he and others had nearly starved and frozen to death. Now, he was about to leave. Evidence would later reveal that out of 12,409 men confined during its 19 months existence, 1,945 prisoners and guards had died, some killed by sentries, but most by disease.

"You will depart Rock Island Barracks tomorrow," the Lieutenant said, pausing to let the message sink in. No response from the gray backs. "But first, you must sign the oath of loyalty to the United States." Still no response. "Very well," said Lieutenant Hayes. "Que up to the table and let's begin."

"I've said I'd never take the oath," groused James Newby.

"I'd rather be wormed with my Ma's tar elixir than take the oath, but I'll hold my nose and do it," said McElroy. "The way I see it, I've always been a citizen of the United States. I didn't shoot at them 'til they come down home shooting at me. If they want me to sign a damned old piece of paper so that I can go home and be with my family, I'll do it. I'd just about share a pipe with ol' Scratch himself if it got me outta this place."

"Yeah, it's just a piece of paper, James," added Barksdale, glancing at Newby.

"I guess I have no choice if I want to go home," said Newby. "But I'll sign with mental reservations."

They fell in line. Lieutenant Hayes lifted a sheet of paper from the stack and asked McElroy for name, city, county and state; filled in his physical characteristics, dated it and pushed it before him to sign. Without reading it, McElroy leaned over, inked the pen and signed his name with a flourish. Barksdale and Newby did the same. There, it was done!

The men spent part of the day outside enjoying the sunshine until they were ordered to clean the barracks. That evening Newby casually said: "Since we're now fellow citizens with the Yankees, I think we should serenade them."

"Doing what?" asked Barksdale.

"With song."

"Taking the oath has made James plum crazy," said McElroy.

Newby smiled and began singing softly:

"Oh, I wish I was in the land of cotton..." Barksdale and McElroy grinned and joined in. "... old times there are not forgotten, Look away, look away, look away

467

Dixieland."

Other prisoners joined in until the rafters shook.

"In Dixieland, where I was born early on one frosty mornin'; Look away, look away, look away Dixieland.

"I wish I was in Dixie, hooray! Hooray!

"In Dixieland I'll take my stand to live and die in Dixie..." Barksdale looked around at the men, as tears flowed freely down their cheeks.

"...Away, away, away down south in Dixie."

A guard burst through the front door and hollered menacingly: "SHUT UP, YOU DAMN REBELS!"

Initially, the prisoners were to get home by whatever means available to them, primarily walking, but General Grant subsequently ordered they be evacuated by boat and train.

On Sunday morning scores of Confederates, Barksdale, Newby and McElroy among them, were crowded into railway box cars. Two shrill whistles were sounded and the cars lurched forward and slowly chuffed away, heading toward the sunny southland.

Unfriendly faces stared as the train rumbled through Chicago. The men slept on the hard floor and ate hard tacks, but unlike the journey to Rock Island, there were no guards. Barksdale's thoughts were of home. Were Susan and the children healthy? What would be the first words out of his mouth when he saw his wife? What about Ma and Pa? He was filled with anticipation and excitement and found it difficult to sleep. They passed Indianapolis; later slowly crossed the Ohio River into Louisville and proceeded to Nashville. Along the route, Barksdale peeked between the board slats at the rolling green hills dotted with blooming dogwoods and redbuds. "Ahhh," he said, inhaling warm air deep into his lungs. "I smell the sweet aroma of the sunny South."

Newby and McElroy crowded beside him and peered out at the green countryside flying past.

"The trip home is a sight more pleasant than the one we took to Rock Island," Newby remarked.

At Nashville the cars were switched, the door slid back and a Yankee Sergeant stepped forward and ordered: "All Rebels going to Fayetteville, Chattanooga and southward, get off now!"

"I guess this is where we part company," said McElroy, poking out a hand to Barksdale and Newby.

"Goodbye and good luck," said Newby.

"Y'all come to visit us," added Barksdale.

Soon, the brothers-in-law were rumbling down the iron rails toward Athens on the Nashville & Decatur Railroad, the car swaying back and forth. A black cloud of smoke boiled from the locomotive's smoke stack, burning their eyes and coating their faces with soot as they pressed their faces against the slats peering out at the rolling green hills. Both were excited as children on Christmas morning when they passed through Pulaski. Only thirty more miles to Athens. Newby looked at Barksdale, who was skinny as a rail, barefoot, ragged, his face black as tar, and he laughed.

"What's so darn funny?" Barksdale asked.

"Jim, you're the ugliest sight I've ever seen."

"You look worse than forty miles of bad road yourself," Barksdale replied. They both burst out laughing – the first time in a long time.

468

"What's the first thing you gonna do when you get home?" asked Newby.

"Squeeze Susan and the kids half to death, then drink a whole dishpan of coffee and afterwards... well... I'm not telling you." He grinned. "What about you?"

"I'm gonna hug and kiss Sarah and the children until they're blue in the face, and then eat till I'm sick."

Barksdale was tingling with excitement. "James, can you believe that we're alive and almost home?"

Newby laid a hand on Barkdale's shoulder. "Jim, if it hadn't been for you, I wouldn't a made it."

"Same here."

The train slowed to a crawl as it crossed Elk River, then chuffed through Veto without stopping.

"BOYS, WE'RE IN LIMESTONE COUNTY!" someone shouted over the roar of the locomotive. A loud cheer went up. The train slowed at Elkmont, but didn't stop, and crept across the wooden trestle high above Sulphur Creek where the evidence of a battle was still fresh. Only a few more miles to go. The train sped up then began slowing. They peered through the wooden slats at the passing countryside. Where fields should have been green with rows of young cotton and corn stalks were bushes, brambles and weeds. Lone chimneys, burned-out houses and barns, and broken-down rail fences dotted the landscape. They saw few livestock. It was late afternoon when the whistle sounded long and shrill several times and the train began braking, causing the men in the car to lurch forward, nearly falling.

"ATHENS!" someone shouted. Barksdale's heart was pounding like a snare drum. The rail car jerked to a stop and the door screeched open. He and Newby stood frozen, stunned by what they saw.

"You damn Rebels getting off or staying aboard?" asked an armed Union soldier. They and a handful of men climbed down.

"It's hardly recognizable," Newby said. Barksdale nodded sadly. Davidson's Hotel, near the southeast corner of the square and once the town's finest, was a pile of ashes. Soldiers on horseback churned the dusty street; military wagons rattled past and Negro soldiers crowded the board sidewalks.

"It don't look like Athens," Barksdale said.

They walked toward the square. Where the two-story red brick courthouse once stood proudly in the center of town were only blackened walls. The east side of the square had been burned to the ground, and Roswell Hine's, William Hine's and Press Tanner's stores were gone.

Barksdale tugged his old brown slouch hat down with determination and said, "Let's go home James."

They walked east on the Athens-Fayetteville Pike, crossed Swan Creek by footlog and came up a slight rise. A quarter mile in the distance was Daniel Barksdale's log house nestled peacefully in a grove of large oak trees, green with foliage. Newby dropped to his knees and scooped up a handful of fresh-plowed dirt and passed it beneath his nose and kissed it. "Except for Sarah and the kids, this is the sweetest smell on earth."

"Com'on James, let's go!" Barksdale exclaimed, grabbing his brother-in-law's hand and pulling him to his feet.

---

Sisters-in-law Susan Newby Barksdale and Sarah Barksdale Newby were crossing Fayetteville Pike, each carrying a bucket of water they had dipped from Cove Spring, when Susan saw someone coming toward them. She shaded her eyes against a sinking sun with her hand and studied the two gangly men who were trotting toward her.

"Sarah," she said quietly.

"What?"

"Look yonder," said Susan, pointing. "That looks like... It is! Lordy mercy it's Jim and James!" She dropped the bucket of water, wetting her feet and skirt hem, and bolted toward the approaching men.

Sarah screamed, "James!" dropped the bucket, lifted her skirt and ran toward her husband, arms outstretched.

Barksdale stubbed his big toe on a rock, cried out with pain; grabbed his foot and hopped on one leg toward Susan until they crashed into each other's open arms.

Newby, who was several paces in front, was running so fast that when he reached Sarah he almost knocked her down.

"Thank the Lord, you're home!" exclaimed Susan as Jim lifted her small frame off the ground into his arms and swung her in a circle while she clung to his neck. He kissed her a dozen times on the cheek then stood still and gently kissed her on the lips.

"Jim! What will folks think?"

"I don't care," he replied. "I'll kiss you again." And he did.

Newby was squeezing Sarah with both arms as she wept and screamed with joy.

Barksdale placed his hands on Susan's shoulders and pushed her back arm's length. "Let me look at you," he said. Tears welled in his eyes and ran down his cheek into his grizzled whiskers. "Not a day – an hour – a minute – passed during the last year and a half that I haven't thought of you and the children and wondered what I would say when this moment arrived..." his voice quavered. She looked deep in his eyes and gently wiped away his tears with her hand. "... And the same thing kept coming back to me," he said, choking up.

"What, darling?"

"Susan... I love you with all... my heart and all my soul..."

"Ohh, Jim," she moaned and grabbed his neck and kissed him long and hard on the lips.

He came up for air. "Susan, what will folks think?" They both laughed until they were breathless.

"What's so darn funny?" asked Newby. Then all four erupted into laughter.

"Come on," said Susan. "Let's go home and doctor that big toe and see your Ma and Pa."

---

Pa, who loved to piddle in the garden in the cool of the evening, was chopping grass from around potato plants when he straightened and rubbed his low back. Ma was nearby, hoeing weeds from the peas.

"My lumbago gets worse every year," Pa said, squinting at four people entering the yard.

"By crackies, my eyes ain't that good anymore, but that sure looks like Jim and James."

470

Ma stopped chopping and looked up. "Ma – Pa!" yelled one of the men.

Shocked, Ma's jaw dropped, unable to speak or move as her eldest son and son-in-law approached the garden. The hoe fell from her hand, clanging on a rock, bringing her to full attention. "Jim – Jim. Thank the Lord! It's Jim and James. Glory be." She tore across the garden toward her son, stepping on tender plants.

"Don't step on the peas!" Pa shouted, dropping his hoe and running behind her as fast as his sixty-one-year-old legs would carry him. Cal and Cornelia had heard the commotion from inside the house and ran out the back door, trailed by Dudley, Thomas and a passel of grandchildren.

Jim grabbed his mother around the waist and lifted her small frame into the air.

"Oh... Jim, you're home!" she exclaimed, tears streaming down her cheeks.

"Yes Ma, I am. Thank God, I'm home at last."

"Put me down and let me see you," she said. He set her down and she looked at him, sobbing. "You're thin as a rail. They've starved you half to death. But you're alive – all of my children are back home and alive and that's what counts."

Pa hobbled up, wet-eyed and embraced his son. "Welcome home Jim. How are you, son?"

"I'm fine, Pa."

"You need some flesh put on those bones," interjected Ma. "I'll see to that right away."

Cal and Cornelia, Dudley, Thomas and the grandchildren ran up, the children bouncing and clapping their hands with excitement. Jim lifted Waddie, age 5, in the crook of one arm and Benjamin Dudley, age 6, in the other and kissed and nudged them with his scratchy beard until they begged to be put down.

Newby's three children, Luke Pryor, Worley Martin and Oscar Brook, made a dash for him. "Papa! Papa!"

In the midst of the pandemonium, Thomas was slapping Jim on the back and welcoming him in a loud voice when Dudley walked up with a broad smile and extended his hand. "Welcome home big brother."

Jim took his hand and pumped it vigorously. "When did you get home little brother?"

Dudley lowered his eyes and dropped his head. The merriment ceased.

Jim looked around and asked. "Did I say something wrong?"

All eyes focused on Dudley. "No, you didn't," he replied.

"Then what?" demanded Jim.

"I came home early," Dudley said quietly. "After Franklin and Nashville I furloughed myself." He couldn't bring himself to say that he had deserted.

"I can't say that you made the wrong decision," said Jim. "I wasn't there and I won't judge you."

"Yeah," interjected Newby. "While Jim and I were laid up in a Yankee prison living on the fat of the land, you were fighting and dodging Yankee bullets."

Dudley cracked a grin at Newby's attempt to lighten a difficult moment for him.

"Well," Dudley said. "I guess I hold the family record for the first to go to war and the first to come home."

Newby grabbed Dudley's hand and shook it. "I was proud to join this family when I married Sarah and I'm still proud."

The moment Dudley had dreaded had passed. Tension drained from his body and tears welled in his eyes. "I'm glad to be a member of this family too," he said, choking up.

"If I had a fatted calf, I'd slay it here and now – like they use to in biblical days," said Pa, changing the subject.

"We don't have much, but we'll make a feast with what little we do have," said Ma and called out for Thomas.

"Yes Ma."

"Catch those two young pullets and wring their necks," Ma said. "Cal, you and Cornelia fry it up and pick a mess of greens and get 'em boiling. We have cornmeal for cornbread. You young'uns go look for some fresh eggs."

"Ma, that sounds like a feast in the making to me," said Jim.

The two skinny pullets, including neck, back and gizzards, barely made a meal for one person, much less eight adults and the grandchildren, but Ma intended this to be a memorable dinner for Jim and her son-in-law. She forked each a breast onto their plates, together with fried eggs and said, "you young'uns share the rest of the chicken. The rest of us will eat turnip greens and cornbread."

After the last morsel of food had been devoured, including the pot liquor in the bowl of greens, Ma pushed back from the table, and without explanation went to the kitchen.

Soon the house was filled with the rich aroma of brewing coffee. Ma returned with a pot so fresh that steam was still puffing out the spout. She poured Jim and Newby a cup full of the black gold and said, "Your Aunt Sallie David gave me this and I've been hoarding it for a special occasion."

Jim turned up the cup, took a sip and savored its richness. "It's the best cup of coffee I've ever had," he pronounced. "A little bit strong, but mighty good. I may not sleep for a week."

"There won't be any sleeping around here 'til tomorrow," Pa said and reached for his fiddle. "Y'all push back the furniture. We're gonna celebrate." He sawed on the fiddle, beginning with *Oh Susanna.*

They danced until the log house shook. "Pa you're gonna shake the chinks from between the logs," exclaimed Ma.

"Let 'em fall out," said Pa. "Grab your partner Ma," then he struck up *Turkey in the Straw.*

On the front porch, a dog howled. "Ol' Luther has treed a coon," exclaimed young Worley Martin Newby.

"That's no coon," replied his brother, Luke Pryor. "He's howling at Grandpa's fiddle playing."

"By crackies, that dog never did have an ear for good music," Pa said and everyone laughed.

---

Next morning at breakfast Ma announced her decision. "Our family is gonna get together and I mean it!"

"We are together," Pa said.

"I mean the entire family – all of us at one time," she said. "I'm wanting to see 'em so bad it hurts inside. I don't know if Eliza had her baby and I hadn't seen Robert Beasley, Lucy and little Mollie in over two years. Why that young'un is almost 7 years

472

old now. All I know is that Robert Beasley was sent home from the Army sick. He may be dead for all I know."

"I'm for it," said Pa. "When do you want to get everybody together?"

"The Fourth of July."

# 47 | HOMECOMING

Near Athens.

Early morning, Tuesday, July 4, 1865.

Pa gazed east at the rosy band of clouds that were slowly turning red. Nearby, mourning doves cooed. Early morning was his favorite time of the day. Peaceful and quiet. Ordinarily, he would have been alone somewhere pondering and watching the sunrise. But today was different. And, not because it was already extraordinarily hot and no breeze stirred, or that the earth was so dry that when ol' Luther thumped his tail on the ground where he rested beneath the tree, dust rose. Nor was it because of the Nation's 89th birthday.

"By crackies, it's gonna be a scorcher," he said, mopping his brow and watching as Dudley placed hickory wood in a fire pit. "We need a real gully washer to cool things down. But not today – maybe tomorrow," he quickly added.

When the wood turned to red charcoals, Dudley shoveled and spread them evenly beneath a spit, then lay on a feral shoat that had, until the previous night, been roaming wild and eating acorns along Swan Creek. Shortly, fat dribbled down over hot coals, sending up plumes of hickory smoke that permeated and flavored the meat and made Dudley's mouth water.

"It oughta be done by two o'clock," Pa said. "Don't let it cook too fast."

Ol' Luther rose from his resting place, wagged his tail and ambled toward Thomas, who was approaching from the direction of Swan Creek, holding a musket in one hand and squirrels in the other.

"How many did you get?" Pa asked.

"Four," Tom replied, holding them up by their furry tails.

After dressing the squirrels and throwing their innards and skin to the dogs, he took them into the kitchen.

Ma was scurrying about the dingy, dark log room like a waterbug, issuing orders to Cal and Cornelia who were sleepy-eyed and moving slowly. A black iron pot hung over the fireplace half full of bubbling water.

"Cal, get the squirrels to cook'n," Ma commanded, then turned to Cornelia. "Go to the garden and pick a big mess of butterbeans and okra and tomatoes and don't forget to pull some fresh onions too. I know the vegetables are about burned up, but do the best you can."

"You want me to make the dumplings?" asked Cal.

"You know I don't trust anybody with my dumplings. Trot out to the spring and fetch the butter and milk and when the squirrel meat is good 'n done pick out the bones, then you can start churning. The old cow is so poor she can hardly stand, but with the Lord's help she keeps on giving milk."

"Yes ma'am," Cal replied dutifully and headed out the door to Cove Spring across the road.

When the squirrel meat was done and bones separated. Ma sifted flour into a bowl, spooned in a dollop of lard and butter and added just the right amount of buttermilk, then whipped the mixture into dough. Using her whiskey bottle rolling pin she rolled the dough thin, cut it into strips one inch wide and about three inches long, dropped them into the bubbling brew and sprinkled in pepper and a dash of salt that she had been hoarding for this occasion.

"Mercy, it's hot!" she exclaimed, wiping her face with her apron hem. "Has Thomas started building the tables?" she asked Pa. "Somebody get to shelling butterbeans. Has Coleman and Eliza arrived? Somebody look up the road and see if Robert and Lucy are coming."

During 38 years of marriage Pa had never seen his wife this excited – nor happier. Outside while Dudley tended the meat, Thomas placed saw horses beneath the large oak trees and laid wide yellow poplar boards on top to form a table. The boards came from Pa's supply hidden in the barn loft that he kept to construct coffins for family members, neighbors or anyone else who couldn't afford to purchase one – which was just about everyone these days.

First to arrive by foot from their home nearby was George Edward, his pregnant wife Mary, and their five children. James Newby and Sarah and their children, Luke Pryor and Worley Oscar, continued to live in the ell addition built to house drovers. Shortly, James Greer and Susan Barksdale and their two children, Waddie, age 5, and Benjamin Dudley, age 3, ambled up, hot and sweaty, having walked from their place on Piney Creek.

The kitchen was crowded with adults and grandchildren begging to sop the bowl and lick the spoons, but mostly getting in Ma's way. "You young'uns go outside and play," she commanded. "Better still, watch down the road and let me know when you see Coleman and Eliza coming. Now git! Mercy, I sure hope Robert and Lucy got my letter. I'm dying to see 'em."

The children, led by Micajah, George Edward's 8-year-old, ran out the door, racing to see who could reach the road first.

They sat on the edge of the pike and looked east. "I see somebody coming," yelled Micajah. "I bet it's Uncle Robert."

"If Grandma hears you say 'bet' she'll wear you out," said Luke Pryor Newby. "That's gambling talk."

"No it ain't."

"Yes it is."

A wagon came in sight. "It's Uncle Coleman!" exclaimed Micajah and tore out to the house and burst into the kitchen. "Grandma, Uncle Coleman is coming!"

"I gotta see that new baby," Ma said, wiping her hands on her apron and hurrying outside. The wagon, pulled by a bony horse, rattled into the backyard and squeaked to a halt. Eliza was holding a baby to her breast, rocking it gently in her arms. The boys – Bob, age 11; Jim Dan, 7; and little Emmitt, age 4 – jumped from the wagon and ran to join the other boys who were romping in the yard. Ophelia, a skinny 13-year-old, was holding baby William Matthew, and LouElla, age 9 and growing like a weed, was standing quietly. Ma hurried over and reached out her arms. "Let me hold that baby," she said, taking the infant into her arms. "Ohhh, isn't he precious? Just look at those tiny feet. Sooo... precious. What's his name?"

"Edgar Eugene," replied Eliza. "He was born on May 30th."

After greeting and hugging his mother, Coleman joined the men, who were sitting and talking beneath the shade of the large oak.

---

The buggy bumped and rattled west on Limestone Road with an urgency. When they reached Limestone Creek, west of Madison Crossroads, Robert Beasley Barksdale reined the bay and let him drink and blow. He sat in silence, looking in all directions, and then pointed. "Right over there is where we camped when we moved to Limestone County in '39. I was six at the time, but it seems like it was only yesterday. In my mind's eye, I can still see Ma sitt'n in the wagon seat nursing Dudley, and Pa is perched next to her clucking to the horses."

"How long did the trip take, Papa?" Mollie asked.

"Three days," replied Robert. "I guess it was awfully hard on Ma and Pa but we young'uns were having the time of our lives – seeing new country, swimming in creeks and throwing rocks at rabbits and birds.

"George Edward, who was about 11 at the time, threw Coleman in the creek – clothes 'n all – to teach 'im to swim. He was floundering about slapping the water and hollering 'help, help, I can't swim.' Then Jim yelled 'snake' And Coleman – like the Lord – walked on water, gett'n outta there." Robert laughed and fell silent again. "Lordy mercy, time flies," he finally declared. "Now we've grown up, married had children, and fought a war. I admire my brothers for the fight they made; you know Dudley was the first to go. I can't wait to see 'em."

The buggy splashed through the water and rolled up on the opposite bank. "We're in good ole Limestone County now," Robert said.

When they reached the Athens-Fayetteville Pike," he said, "We're not far now."

"Faster Papa, faster!" exclaimed Mollie from the back seat of the buggy.

Robert slapped the reins on the bay's back and clucked. "Com'on Johnny." The horse broke into a trot, causing the buggy to sway back and forth in the dusty ruts. Lucy, eight months pregnant, grabbed her protuberant belly with both hands and exclaimed. "Robert, if you don't slow down, I'm liable to have this baby here and now."

Robert reined back and slowed. "When do you figure it's gonna be?"

Mollie leaned forward to listen. Her mother swiveled around and gave her a piercing stare. "Young lady, sit back, you're not old enough to listen to such things."

"Yes ma'am."

Lucy leaned close to Robert and whispered, "I got pregnant when you stopped on your way to join Preacher Johnston. That was early December so I expect to deliver sometime next month when the moon is full."

Robert smiled. "What's it gonna be?"

"It kicks like a mule."

Robert smiled again, but broader. "I need a man on the farm to help me raise cotton 'n corn. We gotta lot of work ahead of us."

"It's not a good time to bring children into the world," Lucy said.

"Any time is a good time to be alive and to have kids," he replied. "The war is behind us. We're gonna start a new life just like we did when we married. All we had then was each other. Now, we have experience at living; we have Mollie and a boy is on the way; we have Johnny to pull a plow and God to give us rain and sunshine to make our crops grow. And do you know our greatest blessing?"

Lucy hoped she knew the answer. "What?"

"Each other."

Lucy rested her head against her husband's shoulder. "Ahhh, I love to hear you say that."

They had departed home the previous day after receiving a letter from Ma several days earlier and spent the night at a drover's stand near Madison Crossroads, where they were fed and then fed upon by bed bugs. Robert and Mollie had scratched and rolled and twisted all night, and all that poor Lucy could do was lie flat on her back and scratch.

The red land between Hazel Green and Madison Crossroads where rows of cotton and corn used to stretch as far as the eye could see was now mostly grown over with brambles and bushes. Blackened chimneys rose out of ashes, barns had been burned, rail fences had been used for firewood and the once-productive country was now desolate.

When they reached Piney Creek the bay picked his way down into the cool current and sucked water until his belly swelled. They sat in the middle of the creek for a spell, enjoying its coolness while Johnny rested.

"How far, Papa?" Mollie asked anxiously.

"About two miles."

"Oh, I can't wait. Let's go!"

"When Johnny's ready, he'll let us know."

"You'll get to see family you've never met," her mother said.

"Are there any girls?" asked Mollie.

Lucy laughed. "Several."

Refreshed, the bay strained against the harness, sensing the excitement. A few minutes later, Robert said, "Look, Mollie!" He pointed to a log house down the road. "That's where I was raised."

"Oh, hurry Papa!"

"Hold your belly Lucy," said Robert and clucked to the bay. "Let's go Johnny!" The horse broke into a trot and the buggy creaked and swayed up the dusty road.

---

Young Luke Pryor Newby rushed into the house and yelled: "Grandma, a buggy's coming up the road fast. I think it's Uncle Robert."

"Glory be!" Ma had barely exited the house when a buggy bounced into the yard, pulled by the ugliest bay horse she had ever seen. "Whoa... Johnny," commanded Robert.

Mollie, tall and beautiful, jumped down from the buggy and ran to her grandmother, who embraced her. "Oh Mollie, Mollie, you are grown up and so pretty. Just let me look at you."

"I'm eight years old, Grandma," she bragged.

"I know," replied Ma, tearing up. "I'm so happy that my family is here. Now I can die in peace." She turned her attention to Lucy, whom Robert was assisting down from the buggy.

"Glory be! Y'all are alive and safe – and here with us." She hugged Lucy and then grabbed Robert. "I's afraid y'all wouldn't make it. This is the happiest day of my life," she said and broke down and sobbed.

The strain of the war had taken its toll on her, Robert thought. She looked much older than her 62 years.

"Now, if Sallie and Robert come, we'll all be together," she added.

Robert turned around and standing before him was his father, five brothers and his brother-in-law, James Newby. The old man's hands shook and tears streamed down his grizzled cheeks. He was trying to speak, but his trembling lips couldn't form the

477

words.

"Pa!" exclaimed Robert, embracing his father who heaved with emotions. It was comforting to hold his father and smell his peculiar odor, one of honest labor. *He's 65 years old, his hair is nearly white and he's unsteady on his feet,* Robert thought.

"I didn't... know... if ... I'd ever... see you again," Pa finally uttered.

Robert patted him on the back. "Thank God I'm here – we're all here, Pa," he said, tears forming in his eyes. He didn't want to cry like a little baby in front of his family and he changed the subject.

"Let me see my brothers," he said and grabbed George Edwards' hand and passed a few words, and then he did the same with James Greer and James Newby. "I heard that you boys have been on Rock Island. How'd the Yankees treat y'all?"

"As well as any other Southern," replied Jim.

"Which was like a dog," interjected Newby.

Then Coleman stepped forward, much thinner than he had remembered him.

"I was thinking about you this morning," said Robert. "Remember the time George Edward threw you in Limestone Creek and Jim hollered snake?"

Coleman laughed. "That's the day I learned to swim."

Thomas, whiskered and bedraggled, came forward, poked out his hand and in a loud voice said, "Howdy Robert. My hear'ns worse so speak up."

Robert gave his younger brother a firm hand shake and slap on the back and said, "Thanks for taking care of Ma and Pa."

Dudley was lingering back and looked far older than his 26 years.

*I wonder what's going on with him?* Robert thought, and walked over and poked out his hand.

"It seems like yesterday you were only a boy going fishing," he said. "I heard that you tramped all over the south with the Army of Tennessee. I respect you for what you did."

Dudley dropped his head. The other men lowered their eyes. "Did I say something wrong?" asked Robert.

"You haven't heard?" said Dudley.

"Heard what?"

"I quit," Dudley said, flatly.

Robert was at a loss for words momentarily, and then he embraced his younger brother. "You served longer than any of us and I'm proud of you," he said. "Every man has a breaking point. Heck, they sent me home and all I had was a little ol' case of mumps."

Dudley grinned. "You don't say?"

"It's the truth." Robert slapped him affectionately on the shoulder. "The war's over and what happened is behind us. We have to look to the future."

Micajah and Luke Pryor ran into the backyard, breathless. "Aunt Sallie's com'n!" exclaimed Micajah.

"I saw her first," interjected Luke Pryor.

"No you didn't."

"Yes I did," retorted Luke Pryor.

Ma raised her hand. "Y'all stop fussing young'ns, both of you saw 'er."

A black surrey pulled by two horses lumbered in the yard. "Whooooaaaa," said Robert C. David, pulling back on the leather lines. When the carriage stopped rolling, the

478

children rushed to help the woman down.

All loved Aunt Sallie. Sallie, mumbling something about the dratted Yankees, straightened her dress and bonnet, and then spoke to her husband, who was tethering the horses. "Robert, will you get the packages from the carriage?"

Children were bouncing up and down with joy because they knew their Aunt Sallie never visited without bringing gifts.

"Now calm down," she said. "The longer y'all wait the more exciting it will be. Now let me look at all of y'all fine children." She hugged each one.

Ma was ecstatic. "I'm so glad that y'all could come," she said and embraced her older sister.

"I didn't know if we would make it," Sallie said. "That dratted Yankee Provost tries to keep track of who's going and coming. I'll be glad when they are gone for good. The soldiers laugh at us and try to provoke us. It isn't safe for a woman to be on the streets of Athens these days."

"This pig's done," announced Pa, then directed Micajah and Luke Pryor to go down the road and cut several sassafras branches while he and Dudley sliced off tender slabs of pork. The women ferried food from the kitchen and placed it on the crude table. In the center was a large pot of squirrel dumplings, surrounded by bowls of butter beans, cornbread, stewed okra, tomatoes and onions and large slabs of cornbread.

"Ma can scratch out a feast from nothing," Pa bragged.

The older children brought chairs from the house and placed them beneath the shade trees. Louella and Mollie fanned flies away from the food with the sassafras branches while someone rounded up the other children who were running and playing in the yard.

"Dinner's ready!" announced Ma. When everyone had gathered around the table she nodded at Pa, who stepped forward. Children giggled happily.

"Hush young'uns!" Ma said sternly. "Mind your manners!"

They grew silent and all eyes turned to the patriarchy of the family.

"I'm gonna say my piece. When your Ma and me moved here twenty-six years ago," Pa said haltingly, "we brought with us all of our earthly possessions on two wagons – which wasn't much. We had seven children and each other and a heap of faith. Jesus said that if we have the faith of a grain of mustard seed, we can move a mountain; that nothing is impossible. The Lord blessed us with more fine children, fertile land and good crops. All of our children are alive and well except for little Achilles. Now, we have..." He paused and looked up as if searching the sky for the number of grandchildren.

"Seventeen!" interjected Ma. Laughter.

"And from the appearance of some of my daughter-in-laws, more on the way!" More laughter.

Pa continued. "We have survived a terrible war and our former enemies occupy our county. The future will be difficult and times hard, but we'll keep the faith of a grain of mustard seed. We must never forget who we are. We carry the blood of our ancestors who declared our Independence 89 years ago and fought to gain it against the most powerful Army in the world. War has divided us, but we're still Americans. I charge you – now, grandchildren hear this – always speak the truth, be honest and let your word be your bond. One day our offspring will be many and my legacy to you and them is a good name. As the Good Book says, 'A good name is rather to be chosen than great riches.'

479

"This Nation will eventually heal and I want us to be a part of that process. As far as the Yankee boot that's on our necks, I say, we may be defeated but our heads are unbowed." He paused and his lips trembled. "You will never – never conquer our spirit." He paused again as if searching for something else to say. "I believe I've said my piece." He turned to James Newby. "James, will you return thanks?"

Plates were loaded with barbecued pork, squirrel dumplings and vegetables, and everyone found a shady spot beneath the trees where they ate and laughed.

"It sure feels good to have my family here," Ma said, looking around at her brood.

Jim wiped his mouth and said, "Thinking that someday I would again eat your squirrel dumplings kept me going while I was at Rock Island." Everyone agreed that her dumplings were the best she had ever made.

After everyone ate, Aunt Sallie broke open the packages. For the girls she had bought print material for dresses and for the boys, coarse cloth for shirts.

"The material was hard to come by and expensive," she said. "Now you have decent clothes to wear to church." She looked at the younger children, who were eagerly anticipating her next move. She took her time picking up a sack, drawing out the drama. The children knew what the sack contained and couldn't stand still.

"Line up," she said and the children rushed to get in line. "And don't push," she added.

When the children were in a line that was satisfactory to her they passed by and each was handed a piece of stick candy for which they dutifully thanked her.

Meanwhile the women drifted off to themselves and talked about the children while the men gathered in the shade of a large oak and discussed the future. As far as the Barksdale family was concerned they all agreed that it would be the following year or maybe the next before they could plant cotton; that is if they could borrow the money to make a crop.

The cotton land was grown over with bushes and would have to be cleared. "All we can do right now," Pa said, "is begin clearing land, plant a little corn and a big garden and try to keep from starving. It'll be tough to hang on."

"It will get worse," said Robert C. David. All eyes turned toward him. "Living in town and operating the Post Office I see and hear a lot. Carpetbaggers are arriving daily. Along with the scalawags, they will run our government, and whoever controls the government has the power to regulate taxes. They will raise taxes that we can't pay. Homesteads and farms will be lost. But, the most immediate threat is the lawlessness that exists in the county. Citizens ain't safe."

Luke Pryor and Micajah, previously sent across the road to fetch cold water from Cove Spring, came charging back with empty buckets.

"Grandpa – Grandpa!" exclaimed Luke Pryor, gasping for breath. "There's Yankees at the spring!"

"Maybe if we don't bother 'em, they won't bother us," Pa said.

Pa got out his fiddle, positioned his chair in the shade and played *Oh Susanna*. Feet were tapping, hands clapping and faces beaming. Children giggled when Ol' Luther began thumping his tail on the ground, seemingly keeping time with the music. Suddenly, the clapping stopped. Pa looked up and saw six mounted Yankees in the yard – a white Corporal and five Negroes.

Ol' Luther, still limping from a Yankee bullet, was on his feet making a low guttural sound. The children huddled near their stone-faced parents. Pa lowered his fiddle and asked: "Can I help y'all?"

"You secesh having yourselves a mighty big time," said the Corporal, a Dutchman who spoke with a heavy accent. Daniel didn't respond. Ol' Luther continued to growl. The Corporal looked over at his laughing men and asked: "Vould you like to hear a tune?"

"Yasssuh," they replied.

Pa positioned his fiddle under his chin. "What about this one?" And he played *Yankee Doodle* until the Corporal stopped him and said, "Ve want to hear patriotic music."

"That number was mighty popular during the Revolution," responded Pa.

"Ahhh, I know nothing about dat," said the Corporal and waved his hand in disgust. "Ve vant to hear *John Brown's Body*."

Pa stared at the Dutchman for a brief moment then said in a measured tone, "I don't know that piece and if I did, my fiddle wouldn't play it."

The Corporal's face grew red and the men ceased laughing.

"I do know a patriotic number that was one of Mister Lincoln's favorites," Pa said. "I've read that he requested it be played following General Lee's surrender; said it was one of the best tunes he ever heard. For once I'll have to agree with Mister Lincoln."

The Yankees were all smiles again.

"This is especially in honor of my boys and son-in-law," Pa said and struck up *Dixie*. Dudley, Jim, Coleman, Robert and James Newby stood. The women, some with babies on their hips and young children clinging to their skirt, rose to their feet. Robert C. David continued to sit, but not Aunt Sallie. She stood like the Rock of Gibraltar and glared steely-eyed at the soldiers; then grabbed her husband by the hand and pulled him to his feet. "Stand up, Robert."

The soldiers sat grim-faced, staring at the crowd for a moment, and then the Corporal jerked the rein on his horse and wheeled around and trotted away, followed by the blue-coated men. Ma jumped to her feet and shook her fist.

"We ain't bothering y'all so don't you come back bothering us!" she yelled.

"Mmmm, I guess they didn't agree with Mister Lincoln's choice of music," Pa quipped. Everyone relaxed.

Late afternoon, when all the dumplings and barbeque had been devoured and Robert and Aunt Sallie had departed, Pa noticed a breeze rattling the leaves on the large oaks. A black cloud formed in the west and before the men could get the crude table dismantled and the poplar boards stored in the barn, a storm crashed, sending everyone scurrying into the house. Wind rattled the windows, logs shook and rain poured down. Each clap of thunder caused Dudley to jump, but he knew it was only thunder and not cannon fire. After the storm had passed everyone walked outside. Pa looked around at the freshly washed earth and sucked up the clean air and declared, "By crackies, it's been a mighty fine day, family, food and now a good rain. The Lord has truly blessed us."

"Glory be," Ma added. "This has been the best Fourth of July ever."

Pa placed his arm around her shoulder and squeezed firmly, then stroked her long hair. "Remember that afternoon twenty-six years ago when we pulled in here, tired to the bone, after traveling from Fayetteville?"

"How could I forget?"

"And I said, this is where we are gonna plant our roots."

"It seems like it was only yesterday," Ma said.

"In spite of bad crops, Mister Lincoln, marauding Yankees and staring at starvation, we're still here and we're still standing," Pa said.

"All we have to worry about now is the future," Ma said.

"We'll put our future in God's hands," Pa said. "The Good Book says that ravens neither sow nor reap; they don't have storehouses nor barns and God feeds them." Pa gently turned her around and looked deeply into her blue eyes. "All we have to do is keep the faith... and never, never give up."

Ma straightened and nodded. "We'll rise from these ashes, so help us God."

Pa embraced her. "I love you, Nancy McElroy."

"That's Nancy Barksdale, if you please."

# | AFTERMATH

Following the war, the Barksdale brothers and James M. Newby returned home to a devastated land. According to Robert H. Walker's *History of Limestone County, Alabama*, when General Hood marched through North Alabama in October, 1864, his men found "most of the fields they passed were covered by briers and weeds, the fences were burned or broken down. The chimneys in every direction stood like quiet sentinels and marked the site of once prosperous and happy homes, long since reduced to heaps of ashes. No cattle, hogs, horses, mules or domestic fowl were in sight. Only birds seemed unconscious of the ruin and desolation which reigned supreme."

Many of the returning Confederate soldiers were ill. They were forced to take an oath of loyalty to the Federal Government before they could start their life anew. Starvation lurked just around the corner. Confederate money was worthless and U.S. currency was scarce.

At Pulaski, Tennessee, several young former Confederates organized the Ku Klux Klan in early 1866. Originally, it was just to have some fun. Later, it became deadly serious as a means of controlling the carpetbaggers, scalawags and lawless elements. According to Susan Lawrence Davis in *Authentic History of Ku Klux Klan*, the second Klavern was organized at Cove Spring, three miles from Athens, which is believed to be the spring across the road from Daniel Barksdale's house on the Fayetteville Pike. "The cove, the chosen spot for the meeting of the Ku Klux Klan," according to Davis, "was a natural amphitheater then studded with thick pines and hid from the highway, in the center of which is a deep, ice cold spring."

Colonel Lawrence Ripley "Rip" Davis (son of Nick Davis) organized the Klan, and its officers were prominent men of Limestone County.

"A week later," wrote Davis, "the Athens KKK held another meeting at the "Cove" and initiated hundreds of members."

The Klan was rallied to action by ringing of dinner bells. "Dr. Richardson rang the bell and each plantation took up the signal until the county had been notified," wrote Davis.

The Barksdale family struggled to keep body and soul together and survive financially. Life was hard. They borrowed crop money in early spring from individuals and businessmen who "furnished" cash-strapped farmers, usually pledging everything they owned to secure the loan.

The first evidence of crop planting was on March 1, 1867, when Dudley Richard Barksdale borrowed $400 from S & P Tanner and mortgaged "2 mule's ages 4 years, black mule age two years. 2 bay mares, age four." The money was used most likely to purchase the mules and horses and make a cotton and corn crop. The crop was successful. Dudley Richard paid off the mortgage on March 5, 1868.

On March 16, 1867, George Edward Barksdale borrowed "$100.00 "in bacon, corn, oats, salt, etc." from S & P Tanner "obtained to enable me to make a crop." He mortgaged "two horse wagon and two horses, one bay mare and 1 black horse."

Three weeks later, Dudley again borrowed from S & P Tanner. He and his father, Daniel also borrowed $175.00 from James L. Coman and gave him a mortgage on the West one-half of the Southwest one-quarter of Section 2, Township 3 South, Range 4 West; also Southwest Quarter of Northwest Quarter of Section 2, Township 3 South,

Range 4 West; also Southwest Quarter of Section 10, Township 3 South, Range 4 West; also twenty acres, containing in all 300 acres. Dudley was single and was farming his father's land on shares. The debt was paid in full.

In 1874, Democrats nominated George S. Houston of Athens for Governor. Republicans nominated David P. Lewis. Federal troops were held in readiness to deal with the "atrocities" in Alabama. Federal soldiers dragged citizens from political meetings in their homes. In November, Houston and a Democratic Legislature were elected, sweeping the Carpetbaggers, Scalawags and Republicans from power. Reconstruction ended, but hardship had not.

The local newspaper wrote: "Let Hell mutter in groans that the victory is lost, that heaven and virtue have overcome vice and corruption that the day of sniggling Scalawags is over in Limestone County, never to return again." After the 1876 election, United States troops were withdrawn from the state, but the effects of Reconstruction remained for many years to come.

NANCY MCELROY "MA" BARKSDALE, (daughter of Micajah McElroy) died at the home where she had lived for 42 years on "Monday at 8 o'clock, July 12, 1881, age 77," according to the *Athens Post News*. She was buried "Tuesday afternoon" and laid to rest next to 8-year-old Achilles, Lot 12 in the Athens City Cemetery. Her sister, Sallie David, erected a monument over her grave.

JAMES DANIEL "PA" BARKSDALE, continued to live in the log house on the Athens-Fayetteville Pike (Ala. 251) with Thomas and Cal. A large goiter had grown on his neck caused by iodine deficiency in his diet. On June 3, 1896, he bent over and picked up a rock to throw at geese in his garden. The goiter burst and he bled to death. *The Limestone Democrat* observed that he was the oldest citizen of Limestone County at the time. Daniel was buried next to Nancy, Achilles and Dudley Richard, Lot 12 in the Athens City Cemetery.

DUDLEY RICAHRD BARKSDALE (son of Daniel Barksdale) the first to enlist in the Confederate Army, returned home following the war and resumed farming He borrowed $400 from S & P Tanner on March 1, 1867 to make a cotton and corn crop and mortgaged: "2 mules, ages 4 years, 1 black mule age two years, 2 bay mares, age four."
Three weeks later he and his father, Daniel borrowed $175.00 from James L. Coman and gave a mortgage on 300 acres that Daniel owned.
On February 10, 1869, Dudley Richard received from his Uncle Robert C. David, 2 brown mares, 1 mare about 7 years old and a horse about 4 years old besides bacon and money "which has been furnished to me to enable me to make a crop this year on the Poplar Place." The consideration was $1,200.00.
In 1870, James Hanks and Thomas Brice, farm laborers, resided with him.
He was doing well enough financially that in 1869, he advanced $226.00 to Richard Harris to make a crop in 1870 on the Thomas Place.
Dudley continued farming and borrowing money up through March 13, 1873, when he and his brother, James Greer, borrowed $108.00 from A. C. Legg and mortgages: "One brown mule, one bay horse mule about 6 years old."
Dudley Richard never married. He died March 14, 1888, at age 49 and was buried on Lot 12, Athens City Cemetery, next to his parents. A Confederate tombstone marks the site.

THOMAS MICAJAH BARKSDALE, (son of Daniel Barksdale) never married and lived with his parents and farmed.

Following the war, Thomas filed a claim against the Federal Government for $475.00 for horses that Yankee soldiers took but, the claim was denied. Following his sister Caledonia's death, Thomas went to live with his nephew, William Matthew Barksdale, on present-day Barksdale Road, where he died on August 30, 1922, at age 86. He is buried in the Robert C. David plot next to Aunt Sallie David and his sister, Cal.

JAMES GREER "JIM" BARKSDALE, (son of Daniel Barksdale) returned home from Rock Island prison and according to a descendant "drank a whole dishpan of coffee." He owned 200 acres on the east side of present-day Hall Road, near Piney Creek, before the war. The 1870 census showed that he was 38 years old and a "farm laborer," probably farming with his brother Dudley Richard. On March 13, 1873 he and Dudley Richard borrowed $108.00 from A. C. Legg and mortgaged two mules to secure the debt. He farmed the Polly Malone place in 1873-74. James Greer taught school at Bethel on the Mooresville Road near French's Mill and by 1900 all of the children had moved out of the house except Stonewall Jackson (S.J. or Jack) and Benjamin Dudley, both single and farming. Thomas M., his 63-year-old unmarried brother, was also living in the household.

In 1899, James Greer applied for a Confederate pension. The medical examiner wrote: "applicant is 70 years of age and is not able to work but little on account of age and infirmities. I know the old man well and he gets along very slowly. I don't think he could make money at all by labor." The pension was granted.

James Greer and Susan (Newby) Barksdale had six children:
1. Waddie Tate (b. 1860) married Prudence Maria Johnston on January 29, 1887.
    a. Clint Larmore married Mary Hall.
        i. Clifton (Bud) married Annie Ruth Kennemer
            - Danny Clifton married Ruth Ann Douthit
            - Donald Anthony married Judy Bowen
            - Jennifer Denise married Dave Wood
            - Sherry Diane married Jackie Rogers
        ii. Cali P.
        iii. Mary
        iv. Dick
    b. Gussee married Walter Sandlin
    c. Mack Richard married Addie Menefee
        i. Prudie Marie
        ii. Lura Will
        iii. Loretta Maxine
        iv. Gordon Richard
        v. Jim Guy
        vi. Henry Kenneth (Crick)
        vii. Alice Jeanette
        viii. Russell Dwight
    d. Susie married Lawrence Meadows
2. Benjamin Dudley

485

3.  Texamiria (b. 1865 d. 1-19-1888) married Charles A. Strong
4.  Idella (b. 1868) married William T. Strong
5.  Stonewall Jackson (Jack or S.J.) (b. 9-27-1867 d. 7-8-1935) married Mattie E. Clem on 10-30-1901
    a.  Ann Idell Barksdale married Roy Malone (Buck) Johnson, Jr.
        i.  John William Johnson married Peggy Elliott
            - Anne Elizabeth Johnson
            - Laurie Clayton Johnson
            - John William Johnson, Jr.
            - Emily Elliott Johnson
        ii.  James Ned Johnson married Faye Partain
            - Melody
            - Timothy
        iii.  Martha Jackson "Jackie" Johnson married Fred Bickley, Jr.
            - Fred P. Bickley, III
            - Anne Lamar Bickley
            - Molly Johnson Bickley
        iv.  Morris Malone Johnson married Helen Neeley
            - Leisha Dale
            - Morris Malone, Jr.
    b.  Alvis, never married.
    c.  Marvin A. (b. 6-27-1908 d. 9-22-1956) married Martha Leopard. No children.
6.  Nancy Jane (b. 9-9-1870 d. 9-11-1965) married Wiley Clem.

ROBERT BEASLEY BARKSDALE, (son of Daniel Barksdale) and wife Lucy were living in the Brownsboro community east of Huntsville in 1870 where they farmed. Two years later he and his brother-in-law, James M. Newby sold their 40 acres near Johnson's Branch to William Coleman Barksdale. The purchase price was two bales of cotton. Robert Beasley and Lucy had 5 children:
1.  Mary Beasley "Mollie" (b. 8-26-1857) married V. Styles.
    a.  Robert S. Styles
    b.  Claude Styles
2.  Robert Walter (b. 8-31-1865 d. 12-03-1904) married Adie B.
    a.  Marion E.
    b.  Grace
3.  Lucy Kate (b. 6-23-1871 d. 1988) married Richard Barley
    a.  Grace
4.  Thomas Arthur (b. 1-7-1884 d. 3-24-1945) married Addie Ragsdale
    a.  Willis
    b.  Arthur O.
    c.  Alfred Fletcher
    d.  Unknown
    e.  John Robert
    f.  Mamie
    g.  Homer

h. Roy
i. Joe Wheeler
5. Daniel Gidden "Gid" (b. 10-20-1877 d. 9-6-1955) married Fannie Lou Dunlap
   a. Paul
   b. Emma Lucille
   c. Hilda

Robert Beasley applied for a Confederate pension on July 30, 1902, and listed no real estate and the following personal property: 2 horses, $100, 2 head of cattle, $20, 4 hogs, $20, 1 watch, $4 and $30 worth of household and kitchen furniture and $10 worth of farming tools. The pension was finally granted in 1914. He died Dec. 30, 1919 and is buried next to Lucy, who died April 6, 1904. Both are buried in Locust Grove Cemetery in New Market, Alabama.

GEORGE EDWARD BARKSDALE, (Son of Daniel Barksdale) borrowed $100 on March 16, 1867 "in bacon, corn, oats, salt, etc." from S & P Tanner "obtained to enable me to make a crop." He mortgaged two horse wagon and two horses, one bay mare and 1 black horse."
On March 16, 1868, he borrowed $300 from S &P Tanner and mortgaged his crops.
On March 25, 1869, he gave a mortgage to S & P Tanner "in consideration of two hundred dollars and necessary provisions such as bacon, corn, oats which said provisions have been advanced to me by S & P Tanner." He mortgaged his "entire crop --- and 2 bay mares aged about seven or eight and a two-horse wagon."
In 1870, he farmed "Cotton Hill" Plantation owned by Luke Matthew, located at the intersection of Cambridge Lane and Huntsville-Brownsferry Road (presently owned by Cecil Armstrong). He gave mortgage to S & P Tanner "in consideration of two hundred dollars in supplies – to make and secure a crop for the year 1870." The mortgage was secured by his crops and "one bay mare, ten years, one sorrel horse, age twelve years, one wagon – 2 horses."
On January 24, 1872, George Edward borrowed $384.22 from S & P Tanner and mortgaged: "1 two horse wagon, one bay mare 8 years old, 1 colt one year old, one stud horse 9 years old, 8 head of cattle, 60 barrels of corn, his interest in the crop of 1870, also my entire crop of cotton and corn grown on the Cain Place in the year 1871."
Afterwards, George Edward and wife Mary (French) Barksdale and family moved to Giles County, Tennessee. However, James Rufus (his child by Mary Hicks) and wife, Nancy "Nannie" Rebecca (Stewart) Barksdale remained in Limestone County with their two children, Mary and William.
George Edward died of "dropsy" after a long illness and is buried at Poplar Hill Church Cemetery in Giles County along with several of his children.
George Edward and Mary E. (Hicks) Barksdale had one child:
1. James Rufus Barksdale (b. 10-9-1851) who married Nancy "Nannie" Stewart (b. 8-10-1856).
   a. Mary "Mollie" (b. 8-18-1878)
   b. William Thomas (b. 1-25-1880 d. 10-15-1916)
   c. Katie (b. 3-7-1881 d. 10-8-1949)
   d. Lillie "Lillian" b. 4-12-1883- d. 8-6-1967)

487

e.   George Rufus (b. 5-26-1887 d. 12-18-1965)

George Edward and second wife, Mary (French) Barksdale had six children;
1. Micajah (Mike)
2. Georgiana (Georgia)
3. Euzarah
4. Zeno
5. James Edward
6. John (married Susie Toomb)
   a. Lacy
   b. Mildred
   c. Roy
   d. Dallie
   e. Homer
   f. Hobert


SARAH ANN (BARKSDALE) NEWBY, (daughter of Daniel Barksdale) and husband James Martin Newby borrowed $600 to make a crop in 1869. Newby was furnished "merchandise such as bacon, flour, land to enable me to make a crop this year on the Lane place." He mortgages "3 black and 1 sorrel mule and 1 black mare as well as entire crop of cotton grown." The Lane plantation was located east of Tanner Crossing to the Huntsville-Brownsferry Road in the Dogwood Flats area. Newby continued to borrow money and farm the Lane plantation for a couple of years and gave mortgages to make crops for years afterward. Sometime prior to 1877, he purchased 320 acres located southeast of French's Mill on Newby Road where he built a "dog-trot" log house. He continued to farm and buy and sell land. Newby's health deteriorated and he spent his final year confined to a wheelchair. He died April 2, 1908 at age 85 and is buried in Newby Cemetery on Ridgelawn Drive, Athens. Sarah died on pneumonia on April 19, 1910, at 5 a.m. at age 75. She is buried next to her husband.
Sarah Ann (Barksdale) and James Martin Newby had 3 children:
1. Luke Pryor married Mary Eliza Johnson
   a. Sidney
   b. Minma
   c. Kate married Oscar Thomas
   d. Rowe (Unmarried)
   e. Herbert Jackson married Oma Sanderson
2. Oscar Brook married Sarah Ann Thomas
   a. George Douglas
   b. William L. married Memory Clem
   c. Eva married J.B. Cleghorn
   d. Dell married Larkin Sanderson
   e. Exum married C. Garner
   f. Sewell (unmarried)
   g. Sarah married Frank Pepper
   h. Nick
   i. Effie
   j. Ila Mae married Unknown McConnell

3. Worley Martin married Mollie P. Allison
   a. Bruce Martin
   b. Cloyd Pryor married Irene Thomas
   c. Mary P.
   d. James Horton married Cora Vessels
      1. James M. Newby married Martha Allen
         - Jimmy
         - Jerry
         - Susan married Bill Ming

FRANCES CALEDONIA (CAL) BARKSDALE, (daughter of Daniel Barksdale) never married and remained home with her parents, Daniel and Nancy. After Nancy died in 1881, Daniel deeded his 300 acres of land to Cal and Thomas, provided that they take care of him. In 1900, Cal, age 54, was residing with her sister and brother-in-law, Sarah and James M. Newby. She died at the family home on Athens-Fayetteville Pike, September 1917, of pneumonia.

> "Miss Caledonia Barksdale, another good woman of the county passes away Sunday at the residence of her brother, 4 miles east of Athens.
> Miss Barksdale died of pneumonia, and she was 72 years of age, and she and her brother, Thomas M., lived together for many years. The funeral services were in Charge of Drs. John D. Simpson and Riddle, and the interment took place in the Athens Cemetery."

She was buried in the Robert C. David plot, Athens Cemetery, next to her Aunt Sallie McElroy David.

CORNELIA ANTONETT BARKSDALE, (daughter of Daniel Barksdale) married Zebulon Pike Johnston on February 6, 1868 at the residence of Mrs. Mary A. Clem in Limestone County, W. Eniry, Esq, officiating. She was age 26 and Zebulon was 20. Sometime prior to 1890 they moved to Travis County, Texas, near Austin.
   Cornelia Antonett (Barksdale) and Zebulon Pike had 4 children:
   1. Josie B. Johnston
   2. Thomas Luther Johnston (b. 2-15-1874 d., 4-26-1939)
   3. Rufus Johnston
   4. Ossie Armealis Johnston (b. 5-10-1885 d. 1-13-1943)

Cornelia was the last surviving child of Daniel and Nancy Barksdale. She was 80 when her brother, Thomas died in 1922. She most likely died in Rule, Texas.

WILLIAM COLEMAN BARKSDALE, (son of Daniel Barksdale) continued to reside in his log house on Johnson Branch (presently Ed Ray Road) for many years. Before his death he acquired approximately 240 acres of land nearby which he deeded to his children. Mr. George Wells later purchased the land where the log house stood and tore the house down. The outside log kitchen stood for many years. The only remaining evidence of the home site today is a well that is mostly filled with trash.
William Coleman and Eliza (Harvey) Barksdale had 10 children:
   1. Robert Coleman (Bob) married Leona V. Clem.

489

2. James Daniel (Jim Dan) married Josephine "Polly" French.
3. William Matthew (Willie) married Mary Louise Hollingsworth.
4. Henry Emmit married Allie Jene Willis.
5. Ophelia married Rheubin G. Isom.
6. Lou Ella married William H. Patterson.
7. Edgar Eugene (Ed) married Ada Isom.
8. Sarah L. (Sallie) married Nathaniel (Fate) Inman.
9. Mary Elizabeth (Eliza) married Joe Davis Clem.
10. Fletcher married Florence Cary.

William Coleman died August 22, 1905 at age 75 and is buried in Johnson Cemetery on Mooresville Road.
Eliza died of "old age and bronchitis" on December 3, 1909, at age 76, 9 months and 19 days and is buried next to her husband.

OPEHLIA BARKSDALE, (daughter of William Coleman Barksdale) married Rheubin G. Isom (son of Matthew and Mary Gray Isom) on October 7, 1878, at her father's log house on Johnson Branch. Patrick Henry Dickerson "PHD" Newby (brother of James Martin Newby) performed the ceremony. Ophelia was age 26 and Rheubin was 22. Ophelia died childless two years later and was buried near her parents in Johnson Cemetery on Mooresville Road. Later, Rhuebin married Sarah Sanderson.

EMMIT BARKSDALE, (son of William Coleman Barksdale) departed Limestone County sometime in the late 1880's and went to Travis County, Texas, most likely attracted there by his Aunt Cornelia (Barksdale) Johnston (daughter of James Daniel) and her husband, Zebulon Pike Johnston who moved there prior to 1890. Emit remained in Texas and is reputedly buried at Buda. It is thought that he married Allie Jene Willis.

JAMES DANIEL "JIM DAN" BARKSDALE, (son of William Coleman Barksdale) married Mary Josephine "Polly" French (daughter of Jerry M French) in 1887 and set up housekeeping in a log house not too far from where he was born on Johnson Branch.
James Daniel "Jim Dan" and Mary Josephine "Polly" (French) Barksdale had 9 children:
1. Bertha married Ernest Ruf.
2. Thomas V. married Ida Locke.
3. Ruth Ella married Theo Pepper.
4. Cora Lee married Logan Pepper
5. Clayton E. married Cora Prentiss
6. Wade married Algie Butner
7. Hassie married Argil Leopard
8. Hazel married William Arnett.
9. French died at age 4.

James Daniel died on April 11, 1950 at age 92 and Polly died 9 days later at age 84. Both are buried at Johnson Cemetery on Mooresville Road.

LOU ELLA BARKSDALE, (daughter of William Coleman Barksdale) was a child when her father volunteered for the Confederate Army. On May 18, 1876, at age 20, she married William H. Patterson, age 23 at her father's home on Johnson Branch. Prior to 1900, she and William moved to Madison County, Alabama.

Lou Ella (Barksdale) and William H. Patterson had 7 children:
1. Henry.
2. Carlisle married Thelma.
    a. Carlisle Patterson, Jr.
3. Jessie married Charles Crute.
    a. Charles Crute, Jr.
    b. Martha married Walton Fleming.
4. William Emmitt "Brewer" married Nora Bell Osborne.
    a. Richard Washington, Sr.
        1. Richard W. Patterson, Jr.
            a. Joe Patterson
            b. Dot Patterson Whitt
5. Grady married (1) Unknown (2) Marie
6. Wheeler never married.
7. Virginia married Charles Stewart
    a. Russell Stewart
    b. Milton Stewart
    c. Glen Stewart

WILLIAM MATTHEW "WILLIE" BARKSDALE, (son of William Coleman Barksdale) was 2 years old when the war ended. He grew to manhood on Johnson Branch farming cotton and corn. On December 6, 1886, he married Mary Louise (Lula) Hollingsworth and they had 10 children:

William Matthew "Willie" Barksdale and Mary Louise (Hollingsworth) had 10 children:
1. James Edward died at age 1.
2. Myrtle Gertrude (b. May, 1889) married Lester Carpenter
3. Elton Lawrence (b. May, 1801 married (1) Ollie Parks from England (2) Emogene Moore.
4. Frances "Fannie" Brown (b. Oct. 1893 married Willie Eiseman.
5. William Greer (b. Dec. 1885) married Essie Menefee
6. Clarice Marie (b. Jan. 1897) married Walter Vinson.
7. Thelma Louise "Baby" married (1) Russell Hall (2) Vernon Castle
8. Gladys Constance married Hassie F. Williams
9. Ronald Winston married Elizabeth Mills.
10. Dorothy Lorna married George Winston.

William Matthew died at home on Barksdale Road on June 26, 1930, and his wife Mary Louise died Jan. 14, 1939.

ROBERT COLEMAN (BOB) BARKSDALE, (son of William Coleman Barksdale) born on March 16, 1854, married Leona V. Clem on March 11, 1884. He was kicked to death by a mule on May 28, 1900, and buried at New Garden Cemetery. Leona died the following year of pneumonia.

Robert Coleman "Bob" Barksdale and Leona V. (Clem) Barksdale had 7 children:
1. Wallace married Beatrice Ashby
    a. Reba

        b.  Mildred
        c.  Billie
        d.  Robert M.
    2.  Joe Davis
    3.  Lena Ann married Luther Meadows
        a.  Marvin
        b.  William
        c.  Joe
        d.  Robert
        e.  Mahlon
    4.  Rachel married Turner Clem.
    5.  Maud married Will Black
        a.  Mary Lou
        b.  Aileen
        c.  Ruby
    6.  Burrell married Minnie Lindsay
        a.  Wesley
        b.  Virginia
    7.  Robert Coleman married Ethel Limley
        a.  Howard
        b.  Odell

SARAH L. (SALLIE) BARKSDALE (Daughter of William Coleman Barksdale) married Nathaniel (Fate) Inman, a carpenter and painter.
    Sarah L. "Sallie" Barksdale and Nathaniel Inman had 2 children:
    1.  June (a male)
    2.  Mary Ella

FLETCHER BARKSDALE (Son of William Coleman Barksdale) born 1868, married Florence Cary. Fletcher was a prominent Athens merchant and a champion fiddler. He died in January 17, 1942, and is buried in the Athens City Cemetery. They had 5 children:
    1.  Elizabeth Loucille
    2.  Louise
    3.  William Ryan
    4.  Mary Frances
    5.  Marilyn

MARY ELIZABETH BARKSDALE (Daughter of William Coleman Barksdale) married Joe Clem.

EDGAR EUGENE (ED) BARKSDALE (son of William Coleman Barksdale) on reaching age 21, sold his horse to finance several months of formal education at a boarding school north of Athens. Later he traveled to Texas to visit his brother Emmit. Tired of driving cattle, he swapped his wages to Emmit for a fiddle and returned to Limestone County, where he married Ada Isom (granddaughter of Emanuel) on January 16, 1896. Ed spent his life farming 120 acres where he grew up on Johnson's Branch (present day Ed Ray Road). He was a skilled carpenter and loved to fox hunt and play the fiddle.

Ada died at age 66 on January 1, 1943 and Ed died at age 86 on November 13, 1952. Both are buried in Athens City Cemetery.

Edgar Eugene "Ed" and Ada (Isom) Barksdale had 9 children:

1. Lee Edgar married Annie Richardson
   a. Richard David
   b. Nelson Reubin
   c. Ira Mae
   d. Annie Lee
   e. Harold K.
   f. William Eugene
   g. Benjamin Franklin
   h. Douglas M.
2. Joshua Inman married Cathleen Butner.
   a. No children.
3. Velma married George Stovall
   a. Margaret
   b. Jean
   c. Wilma
   d. Sarah
   e. Ann
   f. Clifton "Buck"
   g. Hubert "Buddy"
   h. Billy Joe
   i. Dwight
4. Laura Mae married Russell Menefee
   a. Joyce
   b. Jane Ola
   c. Peggy Nell
5. Edna Levenia married Ed Ray
   a. Nella Ruth
   b. Mary Jo
6. Robert Eugene married Linnie Peace.
   a. David Lee
   b. Faye
   c. Kathy
   d. Robert Wayne
   e. Sylvia
7. Rufus Daniel married Edna Florene Burch
   a. Jerry Rufus
8. Martha Rebecca married LeRoy Turner
   a. Larry
   b. Don
   c. Daryl
9. Lottie Irene, died of tetanus at age 7-9

AUNT SALLIE (MCELROY) DAVID, (daughter of Micajah McElroy- outlived her husband Robert by 15 years. She was considered the "leader of fashion" and no one would think of buying a fine dress, new bonnet or other nice articles without first consulting Aunt Sallie. She always had plenty of cash on hand and according to the local newspaper she was a "woman of great industry and economy and in this way secured a handsome fortune."
Following the death of her husband she became enfeebled in health. She died on May 3, 1888, at age 88 and was buried next to her husband. "During the burial services all the business houses were closed and the schools suspended in respect to the honored dead."

ROBERT C. DAVID, died on May 4, 1873, at age 74 years and 10 months, leaving a widow, Sallie McElroy David. The couple was childless. He was buried with full Masonic honors on Lot 159, Athens City Cemetery and according to *The Athens Post* "the stores and all places of business were closed and an immense concourse followed the remains to the grave, the Sabbath School going in a buggy. David, a founding member of Athens Masonic Lodge No. 16, served as town trustee and Postmaster.
The Masonic Lodge and the Methodist Church both passed resolutions of respects which were published in full in *The Athens Post*.
He left a sizable estate of 1364 acres of land in Limestone County, several town lots, land in Arkansas and Texas, railroad stock, bonds, etc.

HANSEL HARVEY, (father-in-law of William Coleman Barksdale) died in 1866 at age 75. William Coleman purchased 80 acres that lay south of his cabin at an estate auction for the sum of $50.00.
    Hansel and Patsie Harvey had four children:
1.    Jane Harvey married Alfred Clem
2.    Martin Harvey married Mary C. Clem
3.    Eliza P. Harvey married William Coleman Barksdale
4.    Elizabeth Harvey married John R. Evans.

EMANUEL ISOM stuck to his Union views and Methodist religion. In 1865, he owned nearly 500 acres of land on Mooresville Road and nearby.
    Emanuel and Rebecca Gray Isom had 11 children:
1.    Susan Agnes, never married.
2.    James Franklin married Ann Inman
    a.    Cordelia married J. D. Meadows
    b.    Mary Ann married Morgan Meadows
    c.    Monroe married Aza Blanton
    d.    Martha married Alf Craft
    e.    Ida married Robert M. Holland
    f.    Ada married Edgar Eugene Barksdale
    g.    Nina married Connie King
    h.    Benjamin married Madeline Thomas
    i.    Rebecca married Asa Holland
3.    Sarah Jane married Reuben Clem
4.    Parthania married Tom Allen
5.    William Robert married Gertrude, last name unknown

6. Angeline Amelia married John W. Johnson
7. John Stinnett married Mattie Craft
8. Manerva died as an infant
9. Thomas Benton married Etta C. Thomas
10. Elbert Wickham married Hester J. Blanton
11. Mary Elizabeth married Walter Starling

Emanuel died on Oct. 7, 1900, and is buried at Isom's Chapel Cemetery. He lived long enough to see his granddaughter, Ada Isom marry Daniel Barksdale's grandson, Edgar Eugene Barksdale thereby ending the rift caused by the war, at least in that family. The latter are the author's paternal grandparents.

SARAH JANE ISOM, (daughter of Emanuel Isom) married Reuben Clem.
Sarah Jane (Isom) and Reuben Clem had 8 children:
1. Robert Clem married Sarah T. Johnston.
2. Mary Sue Clem married John Freeman.
3. Lucy Clem married Vernon Smith.
4. LaFayette Clem (Fate) married Julia Keyes.
5. Mattie Clem married Stonewall Jackson (Jack) Barksdale.
    a. Alvis Barksdale
    b. Marvin Barksdale
    c. Idell Barksdale married Roy Malone (Buck) Johnson
        i. Malone Johnson married Helen Neely
        ii. Jackie Johnson married Fred Bickley, Jr.
        iii. John Johnson married Peggy Elliott
        iv. Ned Johnson married Fay Parton
6. John Clem married Martha Hanks
7. Emanuel Clem (1) married Lota Puryear
    a. James Clem
    b. Hobert Clem

    (2) married Clara Hine
    a. Marvin Clem
    b. Elizabeth Clem married Harvey (Buddy) Gilbert
    c. Clara Hine Clem married William (Bill) Totten
        1. Michael Totten
        2. Dan Totten
8. Wiley Clem married Nancy J. Barksdale

WILLIAM EPPA FIELDING, younger brother of Mary, moved to Harrison, Arkansas following the war where he and his brother, Henry were attorneys and publishers of the *Boone County Banner*. William Eppa died in Arkansas November 15, 1917. His diary, "To Lochaber Na Mair" is available at Pablo's on the Square. Source: *The Lure and Love of Limestone County* by Chris Edwards and Faye Axford.

MISS MARY FRANCES FIELDING, a spinster, taught school in Pettusville following the war and later moved to Ft. Worth, Texas, where she lived with her niece, Mrs. Sallie Love Peele, daughter of Louisa Fielding Love, where she died in 1914. Miss Fielding's diary kept during the war can be purchased at Pablo's on the Square. Sources: *The Lure and Lore of Limestone County,* by Chris Edwards and Faye Axford.

JAMES GILLILAND DEMENT, was released from Rock Island Prison at the end of the war and returned to his home near Elk River on present day Dement Road in Northwest Limestone County. He died on December 28, 1915, at age 92 and is buried in Dement Cemetery.

JOHN A. (JACK) MCELROY, (grandson of Micajah McElroy) deserted the Confederate Army and took the oath on Nov. 23, 1863. He returned to Lincoln County; was never married and lived in a small house owned by his brother, Rufus Cooley McElroy, where he died on Dec 21, 1911. His obituary is as follows:

> "Mr. Jack McElroy, aged 73 years. Was found about 1 o'clock Tuesday afternoon lying with his head and arm in the fireplace and badly burned. He was never married and occupied alone a small house on the farm of his brother, R.C McElroy, 3 miles N.W. of Fayetteville. The unfortunate man had been in declining health for a year or more & had become weak & feeble. It is not known why he fell, but it is supposed to have resulted from heart failure."

Following the Civil War, true to his word, Jack went to Texas in a covered wagon to visit an uncle. According to his grandniece, Miss Eula McElroy, his old dog John accompanied him on the trip. They remained in Texas about a year and when the visit ended the uncle begged to keep old John.

A year later after Jack returned to Fayetteville, he got up one morning and found old John in the front yard his feet bleeding and in a pitiful condition. "I'll never let him go away from here again," Jack said. And he didn't.

MICAJAH L. (MIKE) MCELROY, (grandson of Micajah McElroy) returned to Lincoln County, Tennessee, following release from Rock Island Prison.
He and Mattie Whittaker had six children:
1. Edgar
2. Thomas
3. Susan B.
4. Fannie F.
5. James
6. Arthur.

RUFUS COOLEY (R.C.) MCELROY, (grandson of Micajah McElroy) returned to farming in Lincoln County, Tennessee following the war where he died on May 17, 1912. His obituary was published in the local newspaper:

> "Mr. Rufus C. McElroy, aged 82 years, died at his home 3 ½ miles NE of Fayetteville at 4 o'clock Tues. afternoon May 7, 1912. He had been failing in health for some time which announced to his friends that the end was near & when the summons came it was as one who pulled the drapery of his couch about him & laid down to pleasant dreams. Mr. McElroy spent his life in this county & everyone knew of his splendid worth. During the war he was with Forrest's Invincibles &' was one of

the most intrepid followers of the "wizard of the saddle." He was a member of the Primitive Baptist Church & was prepared when the summons came. Funeral service by Elders E.T. Hampton & T.C. Little. He is survived by 3 sons: T. T. McElroy of Lampsas, Texas, Con & Clyde McElroy, Burial at McElroy graveyard by the Masons."
He was buried in the Buchanan-McElroy Cemetery located on the Micajah McElroy plantation in Fayetteville. His wife, Amanda died of "flux" on July 24, 1895.

Rufus Cooley McElroy and Amanda had 3 children:
1. Thomas T. McElroy
2. Constant "Con" McElroy (b. 1857 D. 1933)
3. Clyde McElroy

JOSHUA P. COMAN, a delegate from Limestone County to the Secession Convention practiced medicine in Athens. He served in the State Legislature, State Senate and was Probate Judge of Limestone County. He died December 2, 1885, and is buried in the Athens Cemetery.

LUKE PRYOR and THOMAS H. HOBBS, while serving in the Alabama Legislature, secured funding for constructing the Tennessee and Alabama Central Railroad that ran through Athens. The first locomotive to run on the line was the "Luke Pryor." Pryor practiced law with George S. Houston and was later elected to the U.S. Senate. He died August 5, 1900 and is buried in the Athens City Cemetery. Source, *The Lure and Lore of Limestone County,* by Edwards and Axford.

THOMAS JOYCE MCCLELLAN, a delegate from Limestone County to the Alabama Secession Convention moved from Lincoln County, Tennessee, in 1844 and settled on Limestone Creek near Nicholas Davis Sr.'s, plantation home "Walnut Grove."
He and his wife, Martha had 7 children:
1. William Cowan, who enlisted in Co. F, 9th Alabama Infantry Regiment commanded by Captain Thomas H. Hobbs which departed Athens in June, 1861 and headed for war in Virginia.
2. Sarah Ann married Lawrence Ripley "Rip" Davis, son of Nicholas Davis.
3. Matilda never married.
4. Martha Catherine married Felix Grundy Buchanan of Fayetteville, Tennessee who was Major of the 1st Tennessee Provisional Regiment during the Civil War.
5. John B. served with the 26th – 50th Alabama Regiment and became Captain of Company H; lost his arm at the Battle of Murfreesboro and served as Probate Judge of Limestone County 1864-1866. Later, he served as State Representative.
6. Robert Anderson "Bob" served in Company C, 7th Alabama Cavalry and following the war, practiced law in Athens; served in the Alabama Senate and was Mayor of Athens. He married Aurora Pryor. Their son became an Associate Justice of the Alabama Supreme Court.
7. Thomas Nicholas was Chief Justice of the Alabama Supreme Court.

Thomas Joyce died October 14, 1887, and he and wife, Martha McClellan are buried in the family cemetery located on Limestone Creek behind Creekside School just south of the Limestone Prison. Source: *Welcome the Hour of Conflict,* an excellent book by John C. Carter.

DANIEL ROBINSON HUNDLEY graduated from Harvard Law School, practiced law in Chicago until Alabama seceded from the Union, then returned to Hundley Hill, the family plantation in Southeast Limestone County. He organized the $31^{st}$ Alabama Infantry, which he commanded until his capture at Big Shanty, Ga. Source: *The Lure and Lore of Limestone County* by Chris Edwards and Faye Axford.

COL. JOHN B TURCHIN, following his court martial conviction for sacking Athens, was promoted to Brigadier General and saw action in Chickamauga and Missionary Ridge. He resigned from the Army, after suffering a stroke and returned to work for the Illinois Central Railroad. He was an accomplished musician and gave violin concerts. He died at a hospital for the insane on June 18, 1901. Source: *Historic Limestone County* by Robert Dunnavant, Jr.